SPRING *Brides*

Cathy Gillen Thacker
Judy Christenberry
Debbi Rawlins

MILLS & BOON®

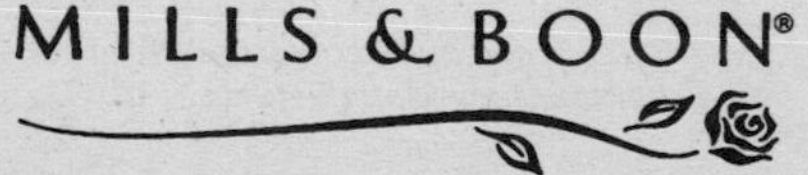

First published in Great Britain 1999 by Harlequin Mills & Boon Limited, Eton House, 18-24 Paradise Road, Richmond, Surrey, TW9 1SR

ISBN 0 263 80809 2

98-9901

Printed and bound in Great Britain by Caledonian Book Manufacturing Ltd, Glasgow

Dear Reader,

It's Spring at last, and everything has burst into life again. It's a time of new beginnings and the perfect time for a wedding. In *Spring Brides*, there are *three* fabulous stories where couples marry first—and fall in love later!

Firstly, meet sexy Zach Grainger—with his trousers down!—in *A Shotgun Wedding* from favourite author Cathy Gillen Thacker. Then in *Daddy on Demand*, Judy Christenberry has created a wonderful, heart-warming story where an adorable five-year-old rents a daddy for a day, and ends up with a daddy for ever! And in *Marriage Incorporated* by Debbi Rawlins, a marriage that's supposed to be a temporary business merger goes all wrong because the bride and groom fall in love!

We're sure you'll adore all three stories, so happy reading!

The Editors

Cathy Gillen Thacker

is a full-time novelist who once taught piano to children. Born and raised in Ohio, she attended Miami University. After moving across the United States several times, she settled in Texas with her husband and three children.

Judy Christenberry

lives in Plano, Texas, with her two daughters, where she still teaches French. A baseball fanatic, Judy follows the Texas Rangers whenever she finds time. Her advice to aspiring writers: 'Don't wait around for it to happen—make it happen!'

Debbi Rawlins

Debbi is originally from Kailua, Hawaii, but has lived in Cincinnati, Chicago, Detroit, Tulsa and Houston during the past fifteen years. She currently makes her home in Michigan with her husband, Peter, and their dog, Brandy. She's had a passion for books ever since she learned how to read her first one and quickly figured out that torches worked well for reading past curfew.

Cathy Gillen Thacker

A SHOTGUN WEDDING

Prologue

Here Comes Temptation

She was a vision, with her angel's face and her glorious mane of curly hair streaming down her back and gleaming red-gold in the sunshine. Her slender curves were encased in knee-length khaki hiking shorts, a powder blue-tan-and-white plaid shirt and powder blue vest. Thick white knee socks came halfway up her long, spectacular legs. Serious hiking boots were on her incredibly dainty-looking feet.

Not ready to leave his unexpected find just yet, Zach braked his truck and paused for a second leisurely look.

A backpack slung over one shoulder, the angel in the meadow resembled a classy ad for ultraexpensive camping gear. The only exception in the picture of beautiful woman and nature at its alluring best was the clipboard and pen in her hands. She appeared to be writing something down as she went from tender sapling to sapling, moving among the wildflower-strung Tennessee property with unexpected grace.

Unfortunately, Zach thought with a frown as he took in the rest of her surroundings, he wasn't the only one who had noticed the pretty lady, and he was quite sure she had no idea she was being followed. Since he was the only other person within miles of the rural mountain property, he figured it was up to him to warn her. Scowling at the potentially risky nature of his mission, he steered his pickup to the side of the narrow country road, parked and got out. He shut the door quietly, then moved around the front of the truck.

The angel had her back to him. She was busy checking out leaves and scribbling on the clipboard in front of her.

For safety's sake, Zach decided to head north of her. He hopped the fence stealthily, giving the pending disaster wide berth, then moved to the north. He wished he could just shout, tell her not to move, but a call from him was liable to startle her, and given what was at stake—for both of them now—he didn't want to chance it.

His strides long and easy, he closed the distance between the woman and him. Behind her, to Zach's growing chagrin, disaster closed in, too. He was already beginning to regret his gallant actions. Doing his best to blend in with the environment, he whistled "Bob-white, Bob-white."

To his frustration, the angel didn't look up.

So much for ye olde Mother Nature approach. Zach reached into his pocket. He withdrew a dime. Aiming carefully, he tossed it at her shoulder. It hit her, bounced off and fell to the ground. She frowned and rubbed her arm without even looking up from the tree she was examining.

Zach swore softly. The woman was right in the middle of disaster and she was too absorbed in whatever she was doing even to realize it.

Knowing speed was of the essence now, he withdrew a quarter and aimed this coin at her clipboard. It bounced off the paper. She glanced up in alarm, stepped back quickly, saw Zach and let out a piercing yelp of surprise.

''Don't move!' he mouthed silently, letting his eyes convey the immediate physical danger she was in. But it was too late; her assailant was already zipping into action. Heart pounding, Zach knew there was only one thing to do. He called upon his years of high-school football, dashed in and grabbed the angel about the middle. To his chagrin, they were both hit with gargantuan force, even as he knocked her aside. Teeth clenched, Zach swore like a longshoreman. His first job in Carlisle was more than he bargained for.

Chapter One

You Done Me Wrong (And That Ain't Right)

"Arrggh!' Sunny Carlisle screamed as the horrible skunk spray assaulted her with hurricane force. Choking on the tear-gaslike fumes, she extricated herself from the big stupid oaf who had tackled her and stumbled to her feet. Dimly aware that he was yelling, coughing and choking, too, she grabbed her backpack and clipboard and headed for the ice-cold mountain stream at a run. She had to get this stuff off of her!

She reached the stream first. Without a glance at the hopelessly inept good Samaritan behind her, she dumped her gear on the bank, waded blindly in up to her waist and then knelt to submerge herself to her shoulders.

He came in right after. "Sorry about that," he apologized, right before he went under. He came up, his ash blond hair slicked back, his face all red from the fumes. After several more dunkings, he introduced himself. "I'm Zach Grainger."

"I'm Sunny Carlisle," she sputtered grimly, barely able to believe she was in such a predicament. "And if I didn't know better, I'd think you were yet another decoy sent to distract me," she muttered. After all, she huffed angrily to herself, the other interlude had started out almost exactly like this—minus the misguided attempt at heroism, of course.

"What are you talking about?" Zach demanded, flinging the water from his face.

"My parents. Do they know you're here?" It was possible they'd found out Zach was coming and had bought him off, too. She knew they hadn't given up getting her out of Carlisle altogether.

To his credit, though, Zach looked thoroughly confused.

"Who are your parents?"

"Elanore and Eli Carlisle."

"Sorry, I haven't met them. Yet, anyway." He paused. "Should I have?"

"No!" Sunny said. She studied Zach Grainger a moment longer. He seemed to be telling the truth. And given that he'd been born and raised in Tennessee, unlike her, there was little chance he'd ever met her parents, never mind agreed to one of their well-meant schemes. She was just overreacting, she assured herself boldly, because of what had happened before. Deliberately Sunny pushed her past romance and the humiliation she'd suffered at the hands of her ex-fiancé from her mind.

Still a little befuddled, Zach watched as she washed herself vigorously through her clothes, then followed suit, scrubbing uselessly at his own shirt and jeans. To Sunny's chagrin, they both smelled to high heaven and looked even worse. Realizing they were both using up tremendous energy with little result, she stopped what she was doing and glared at him. "I can't believe this," she muttered to no one in particular. "My life has turned into an episode of 'I Love Lucy'!"

He reacted defensively. "Well, so has mine, and don't stare at me like that," he counseled sternly. "I was trying to do you a favor by alerting you to the danger you were in!"

Well, that made all the difference. "Some favor. You got us both sprayed," Sunny grumbled, trying hard not to notice how devastatingly handsome Zach Grainger was in person. The black-and-white photo he'd sent in with his application did not convey the windblown appeal of his straight ash blond hair, long-lashed blue eyes, athletic build and all-American face. He was sexy in a very clean-cut, outdoorsy way.

"How long is it going to take for the skunk smell to go away?" Zach asked.

Sunny sighed pragmatically and tried to compose herself. "It won't. It's on our clothes. We'll have to burn them."

"What about us?" he inquired dryly. "We can't exactly set fire to ourselves, can we?"

Actually, Sunny thought, he had already done that to her senses, first with the tackle and then when he'd given her the once-over, but he didn't need to know she had personally reviewed and approved his application for employment. "No, I guess we can't," she said sagely. She gave him a brisk, purposeful smile.

"So what are we going to do next?" he asked.

Good question. "We're in luck. I have a can of vegetable juice in my backpack."

"What good will that do?"

"Boy, you are a greenhorn, aren't you?"

"Give me a break. I'm a complete novice when it comes to skunks."

"How well I know that."

"I'm also the new physician for the area."

"I know that, too," Sunny retorted, and then wished she hadn't.

Zach edged closer, his brawny shoulder temptingly near.

"How do you know that?"

Sunny paused uncomfortably as she tore her eyes from the broad, muscular planes of his chest, beginning to feel a little guilty, although there was no reason she should, she told herself stubbornly. Her part in bringing Zach to Carlisle had been completely aboveboard. "Carlisle is a small town, with a population of just 317."

Deciding they were standing much too close, Sunny stepped back. "Although they'll be changing the sign to 318 if you plan on staying."

Zach shrugged and kept his eyes on hers. "I don't really have much choice, since this is where the state assigned me to go," he said. He regarded her curiously. "Are there many people our age in Carlisle?" he asked.

Again Sunny had a tinge of regret. This was something she felt Zach should have been told up front. The other people on the selection committee had disagreed with her, and the majority vote had won out.

"Actually, there are very few people our age in the area," Sunny admitted. "Almost none of them single. So it can be hell trying to find someone to date."

That was one of the few serious drawbacks to living in the small Tennessee mountain town. But to Sunny, it was a manageable situation, at least for the time being. Since her failed engagement six months earlier, she hadn't wanted to date.

"I assume you live in Carlisle, also."

"Yes, I work there, too."

Zach tilted his head and studied her silently. "You any relation to the Carlisle Furniture Factory?"

Sunny nodded, unable to prevent her pride from bubbling forth. "I run it—for my grandfather."

Zach nodded, impressed. "So what do you do for entertainment on Saturday nights?" he asked, after glancing at her left hand and seeing no wedding ring.

"Usually I work."

"Oh." Zach felt a little disappointed.

Deciding they'd chatted long enough, Sunny began to unbutton her shirtsleeves. Zach turned his back to her. "I suppose you've got a spare set of clothes in that backpack," he said hopefully.

"Unfortunately," Sunny said tightly, "no." She was just going to have to make do. Determined to get on with this and do what absolutely had to be done, she tore off her clothes and hurled them into the bushes one by one. Then she popped open the can of vegetable juice. Using the hem of her bandanna, she saturated it with the juice and began rubbing it all over her body.

"Are you sure you should be doing this here and now?" Zach asked, glancing over his shoulder in the opposite direction, toward the road. "I mean, what if someone comes by?"

Sunny blew out a breath. "We've already established who you are and that you're a gentleman, if a novice at living in the country and knowing how to properly handle skunks. Besides, one false move and I'll hit you with the pepper spray I've got in my backpack."

Zach sighed. "If only you had used that on the mother skunk first," he lamented.

"I might've, had you given me a proper signal so that I'd known she was there."

"I tried. I whistled."

"Well, I didn't—wait a minute." Sunny paused and did a double take. "You did the Bob-white thing?"

"Yes."

"That was pretty good," Sunny admitted reluctantly. "So good, in fact, that I paid no attention to it. You should have tried some other kind of whistle."

"Such as?"

"I don't know." Sunny noticed the back of Zach was every bit as sexy and enticing as his front. "You could have whistled a country song."

Zach swept his hands through his hair, the muscles in his back rippling as he moved. "I'm not that good a whistler. I can only manage a couple of notes."

Sunny watched as he began to slowly unbutton his drenched cotton shirt. "I bet you could have fired off a wolf whistle, though," Sunny countered.

Zach did not deny experience in that regard. "Good point."

Sunny became unaccountably aggravated again. "Yeah, well, remember it next time," she muttered, just loud enough for him to hear.

"Believe me, I will," Zach muttered back, mocking her cantankerous tone.

Silence fell between them. Sunny finished scrubbing herself from head to toe. She'd need to soak in a tub of vegetable juice before the skunk smell dissipated. But at least it was to the point where her eyes were no longer burning and she was able to breathe without coughing and choking.

She set the half can of precious juice aside and ripped a red-and-white checkered tablecloth from her backpack, then began to dress. Already the sun was beginning to set. Thank goodness. They could head back to town under the cover of darkness. And then this whole sorry episode would be over. "Okay," she said, "your turn."

ZACH SWIVELED AROUND. Sunny Carlisle was up on the bank above him. She had a red-and-white checkered tablecloth wrapped around her, toga-style, and secured in a knot behind her neck. She still had her hiking boots on. Her glorious hair was streaming over her shoulders in a mass of thick curls that, when wet, looked dark red.

"Strip down and use the vegetable juice all over you," Sunny instructed calmly. "The tomato juice in it will help neutralize the smell. Then we'll head back to town."

Zach had no qualms about stripping in front of a woman, but he decided to have a little fun with Sunny. He grinned at her, glad he was not in the market for romance. "Turn your back first."

Sunny shot a droll look at him, then turned around. Zach kept his eyes on her as he hurled his clothes into the bushes on the opposite bank, just as she had done. Damn, but she was beautiful. Feisty, too. But she appeared awfully young and somehow *innocent* beneath her sage country ways. "How old are you anyway?" Zach asked, as he climbed down from the bank and kicked off his soggy tennis shoes. Naked, he began rubbing the juice all over him, savoring every drop.

"Twenty-four. How old are you?"

They weren't so far apart in age after all. "Twenty-nine."

Sunny peered at him from beneath a fringe of red-gold lashes. "Why did you want to know how old I am?" she asked.

"I just wondered." Zach shrugged. "You seem a little young to be running a factory."

"I'm old enough," she said. "Are you done yet? I want to get back to town."

Zach emptied the can. "Unless you've forgotten," he deadpanned, "I'm still buck naked. What have you got in that backpack of yours that I can wear?"

"Nothing," Sunny said. "Surely you have something in your pickup truck," she insisted blithely.

"A chamois." A used one, Zach thought grimly.

She made a sweeping gesture in the direction of his pickup. "Have at it, then."

"Sunny, you *want* me to run buck naked through that field over to my truck," Zach drawled.

"Want to borrow my clipboard?"

"What if someone drives by and sees us together?"

Sunny shrugged, unconcerned. "No one has yet."

Nothing seemed to bother Miss Carlisle, Zach thought.

"What were you doing out here today anyway?" Sunny asked.

"I got here a few hours ago. I dumped my gear at the clinic and decided to go for a drive to see the countryside." And that decision had led to his introduction to the angel with the feisty spirit. Zach grinned. Life in Carlisle was definitely looking up.

"WHAT DO YOU MEAN we can't ride in your pickup?" Sunny asked ten minutes later, as she and Zach rejoined each other and squared off next to his shiny new truck.

In hiking boots and a tablecloth, she knew she looked ridiculous. He didn't look much better in that soft clinging chamois. She had expected him to put in on diaper-style or something. Instead he had ripped it in two, torn off a strip and secured it like a loincloth around his waist. It dipped just low enough to allow him some modesty, but not much, and made him look like one of the warriors in *Last of the Mohicans.* All tanned, muscular and so very male. Just seeing him made her pulse jump.

"Zach, we have to take your truck," Sunny continued. It was beginning to get dark.

"We still smell pretty bad." Hands on his hips, he leaned down so he and Sunny were nose to nose. "Or hadn't you noticed?"

"I know how we smell," Sunny said, exasperated. She stepped back and waved her arms at him. "That's why I want to go home. So I can soak in a tub of pure tomato juice."

Zach regarded her with all the sensitivity of a rock.

"Well, we're not getting into my truck smelling this way," he said firmly, carefully extracting a flashlight from the glove compartment and then locking his vehicle up tight as a drum. "This truck is brand-new and I'll be damned if I'm going to see it ruined with the aroma of skunk."

Sunny folded her arms in front of her. "You're being ridiculous," she fumed.

Zach gave her a complacent smile. "I may be a greenhorn, but I know how long the smell of skunk lingers wherever it's sprayed. Besides, I don't see you offering your vehicle," Zach continued irascibly.

"That's because my Land Rover is parked another two miles from here on an old logging road," Sunny said hotly.

Zach shrugged his broad shoulders uncaringly. "So let's start walking," he suggested.

It did not appear Sunny had any choice. Her mood souring even more, she fell into step beside him and hoped for the best.

"Isn't there a house near here?" Zach said after a while, as they kept to the other side of the ditch and followed the road.

"Nope. We're on company land."

His brow furrowed. He turned toward her slightly. "I thought Carlisle Furniture Factory was on the other side of town."

"It is. We grow the trees for the furniture here."

"Is that what you were doing today? Checking out trees?"

Sunny nodded. "We replant at three times the rate we harvest, but we're thinking of upping that to maybe five times if the land will support it."

"You really know your business," Zach said, looking a bit surprised.

"It's my job to know about reforestation," Sunny said as they approached her vehicle. Like his truck, her Land Rover was brand-new and sported four-wheel drive. She unlocked the door and climbed in. Tossed her gear in back.

Zach studied the pristine interior. He was feeling a little guilty about not using his truck. "You're sure about this?" he said. "You know, we could just keep walking. It's only another five or six miles to town."

Sunny shook her head. "The later it gets, the more likely we'll run into traffic on this road. The kids come from miles around to park out here. The sheriff drives by on a regular basis to catch them."

Zach groaned. That was all he needed. Because they had no choice, they both got in. Zach arranged his loincloth to give him maximum coverage and folded his arms in front of him. He felt ridiculous.

Sunny drove toward town. "What time is it?" she asked after a while.

Zach looked at his watch. "Nine o'clock."

She scowled. "Damn, that's awfully early."

"Drive by the clinic. I'll see if I can sneak in."

Sunny tightened her hands on the steering wheel. "The clinic is on Main Street!"

"So drive around the back," Zach suggested affably, his gaze discreetly following the movement of one sensationally curved leg from accelerator, to brake and then back again.

"No." Sunny blushed at just the thought of being seen like this. "No way. Not with streetlights. I'm not going to be seen driving you around town like this.

We'll just have to go to my house, over on Maple Street, sneak in the back and wait until later to drop you at the clinic."

"Fine, whatever." Zach was really at his breaking point. Every time she moved, he could see the fluidness of her breasts beneath the thin cotton cloth, a more revealing slip of thigh.

"Do you think it's hot in here?" He rolled down his window a little more.

"I think it's freezing."

Zach glanced at her. He could see that, too. She had goose bumps everywhere.

They hit the edge of town. "Oh, damn, here comes another car. Get down!" Sunny said. As Zach bent out of sight, she turned off on a side street.

Finally the Land Rover stopped. Zach stayed where he was. His face just inches from the soft skin of Sunny's knee, he wondered what kind of perfume she wore. The prospect of finding out conjured up many exciting thoughts.

"We're here," Sunny whispered, relief quavering in her voice.

Reluctantly Zach straightened and moved away from her soft knee. He looked at the small, neat, two-story red brick house with the ornate white gingerbread trim and glossy pine green shutters. Leafy trees and neatly kept flower beds inundated the yard. A stand-alone garage in matching red brick was behind the house, at the end of a long drive.

"We're going in the back," Sunny said. "And don't slam your door," she commanded.

They crept out of her Land Rover. In the distance, a dog barked. The sounds of a television floated out from an open window across the street. Sunny moved stealthily from the cover of a shade tree, to a lilac bush, to the back door. Zach followed. She was fumbling with the lock, when another car hit the drive.

Sunny swore and dropped her keys. "Duck!" she ordered. "Maybe whoever it is won't see us!" Too late. They were caught in the headlights of a sedan. She swore and slowly straightened as the motor died and a car door opened.

Grimacing his displeasure, Zach straightened, too. He wasn't pleased to be in this situation, but he figured he might as well face it like a man.

"What in tarnation is going on here?" a raspy voice demanded.

The voice belonged to a tall, fit man in his early sixties. He had short red-gold hair that was laced with gray, piercing whiskey-colored eyes and a familial resemblance to Sunny Carlisle that was unmistakable. He carried a shotgun in his hand.

Sunny blanched. "What are you doing here, Gramps?"

"You were supposed to meet me for dinner tonight, remember? When you didn't show up or call, I knew something must be wrong. I called the police station to let them know there might be trouble and came out looking for you." He eyed Sunny sternly. "I can see it's a good thing I did, too."

"Now, Gramps, I can explain all this!" Sunny admonished with a nervous little laugh. "It's all quite amusin—oh, no!" She moaned as a second car pulled in her drive.

Two patrolmen jumped out, their guns drawn, and ran toward Sunny and Zach. "We got here as fast as we could, Mr. Carlisle!'' one of them yelled. ''What the heck—''

The other cop stopped short as he got a good look at Sunny and her tablecloth.

''We got hit by skunk spray,'' Sunny said to one and all.

''I can smell that,'' Gramps admitted grimly. ''The question is,'' he continued, glaring at Zach, his distrust evident, ''what were *you* doing when the two of you got hit?''

Zach had learned in medical school that there were some people you just didn't mess with, particularly when they were upset. Augustus Carlisle was apparently one of them. He was not only the town mayor and the owner of the largest business in town, but his company was paying half Zach's salary, with the state and the community picking up the other portion. Keeping his hands high in a gesture of surrender, Zach said calmly, ''I was trying to warn Miss Carlisle that she was about to get sprayed.''

''As you can smell, we got sprayed anyway,'' Sunny said. ''We had to ditch our clothes, since they bore the heaviest concentration.''

''You sure you're okay, Miss Carlisle?'' the patrolman asked. When she nodded, he and his partner holstered their guns.

Zach could see Sunny's grandfather was still very upset. He looked at the patrolmen. ''Perhaps you guys could give me a ride back to my clinic?''

''Sure thing,'' one of them said.

Gramps held up a hand to stop him. ''I'll admit the young fella needs some clothes. As for the rest...''

Gramps looked at Sunny deliberately, then continued in a stern, determined tone as he picked up the shotgun and pointed it at Zach, "There's only one way to handle this!"

Chapter Two

Stand By Your Man

"I have this friend who's been having some chest pains every now and again," Augustus Carlisle began the moment he walked into the clinic.

Dressed in fishing gear, the scent of lakewater clinging to his clothes, Gramps made it appear as if his were a casual visit. Zach knew it was anything but.

"My question is, Doc, how would this friend of mine know the difference between ordinary chest pains that come from getting older versus those generated by something serious like a heart attack about to happen?"

"It depends." Zach sat down in a waiting-room chair. "Is your friend having any numbness or tingling with these chest pains of his? Any loss of consciousness?"

"No, not so far," Gramps said carefully, fingering one of the intricate fishing lures he had pinned to his vest. His eyes glowed with relief. "Does this mean my friend is off the hook as far as his heart goes?"

"Not necessarily. Those chest pains could be early warning signs of heart trouble. Then again, they could just as easily be something else, too. If I were you I'd advise your friend to get a physical. And speaking of physicals, when was the last time you had one, Augustus?"

"Never you mind." He shook a finger at Zach. "You worry about my granddaughter. I'll see to my health." Gramps took off in a huff.

No sooner had he driven off than Sunny walked in. The warm spring wind had tossed her red-gold hair into sexy disarray. Sunshine added color to her cheeks. But she was dressed for business, in a trim navy suit that clung to her slender curves.

"What was that all about?" she asked a little breathlessly, flattening one hand over the jewel neckline of her white silk blouse.

"I'm not sure," Zach frowned. He eyed Sunny. "What's up with you?" She sure looked pretty today, sexy in an unconscious way.

"The same." Sunny dropped her handbag into a chair. "Everyone thinks I should marry you."

"Only one problem," Zach said dryly, ignoring the mysteriously determined sparkle in her whiskey-colored eyes. "I haven't asked."

Sunny leveled a gaze at him as she dropped into a chair with a sigh. "Under the circumstances, Zach, maybe you should."

LONG MOMENTS LATER, Zach was still regarding Sunny incredulously. "This is nuts," he said as he paced the empty waiting room restlessly.

"My parents would agree with you, I'm sure," Sunny murmured. "Fortunately, I am not planning to tell them about our marriage until it's legal, so we don't have to worry about them interfering."

Zach pushed the edges of his starched white lab coat back, revealing a pin-striped blue-and-white dress shirt, matching tie and jeans. "Listen, Sunny, I think you're a great gal, but I won't marry you! I don't care how we were undressed or dressed the night we met."

Sunny glared at Zach. "You think I want to go through with this?" She plastered a hand across her chest, aware she only had thirty-three minutes of her lunch hour left. "You think I want my reputation besmirched?"

Zach couldn't believe the town was making such a big deal out of an innocent situation. He sank down on the vinyl sofa beside her. "People have actually been giving you a hard time?"

Silence fell in the room as they measured each other. "Everyone feels sorry for me...but wants to kill you."

"I know." Zach swept a hand through his hair. "For some crazy reason they think I took advantage of you."

Sunny rolled her eyes. What an understatement that was. She smiled at him consolingly. "I know you were only trying to help me." Unfortunately, that didn't change things.

"So now what?" Zach asked wearily.

Remembering she had brought them both lunch, Sunny opened the brown paper bag by her side and pulled out two containers of frozen strawberry yogurt. She handed Zach a container and plastic spoon, then popped hers open.

"I can't go on like this. I thought—hoped it would get better if we just stayed away from each other, but it's been two weeks now." She had neither seen nor spoken to Zach, yet he had never been very far from her mind. There was just something about him that made her heart race. "And nothing has changed."

"I know." Zach considered her a moment.

"And I understand it's been worse for you," Sunny sympathized.

He nodded grimly. "Not a single patient has come to see me. I've been open two weeks, and they're still driving sixty-five miles to see another doctor."

"That really upsets you, doesn't it?"

"The success of my first assignment means everything to my future."

"Has anyone even made an appointment?"

"Your grandfather stopped by to inquire about a friend who might need medical attention. And I advised his friend to get a checkup," Zach replied. If indeed Gramps had been talking about a friend.

"I guess everyone else must still be driving sixty-five miles to see another doctor," Sunny said dispiritedly, feeling all the more responsible for the predicament Zach was in.

"And all because I refused to marry you, even at the end of the gun."

"I admit Gramps can be a little dramatic," Sunny conceded dryly.

"A little?" Zach echoed, the first hint of humor curling his lips. He studied Sunny with great care. "I thought he was going to shoot me right on the spot."

The scene on her porch that night had been right out of a Li'l Abner comic strip, Sunny thought. But the dramatic effect it and the resulting community concern had worked on her life was all too real. "I hate to suggest it, but maybe we really should get married," Sunny said reasonably, adding, "just for a little while." It would quiet gossip and get Zach off the hook. And it would teach her parents a lesson and perhaps head off any further matchmaking schemes on their part. She kept expecting them to turn up with another prospective beau.

Zach's expression grew stony with resolve. His amiable mood vanishing, he set down his frozen yogurt with a thud and vaulted off the couch. He stared out the window at the sparse traffic on Main Street, his expression unaccountably dark and brooding. "No one backs me into a corner or tells me what to do, Sunny. I am in control of my destiny, not the other way around."

"Look, I am not enjoying this, either," Sunny yelled. "But it's interfering with both our professional lives. People are giving me so much sympathy at the factory I can't get any work done. Like it or not, we have to do something to control the damage. Proclaiming our innocence hasn't helped. The only solution is marriage." And wouldn't her parents just faint if they found out she had married a small-town doctor, instead of a big corporate giant. It might be worth it, just to see the stunned looks on their faces. She would no longer have to worry that every eligible male she met had been sent by them.

"Then—" she took a deep breath, determined to make Zach see reason as she continued with her plan "—when we've been together a month or so and people see for themselves that it's not working—and I for one plan to vividly demonstrate that concept for all to see—we'll have our marriage annulled. You can leave and go practice medicine somewhere else—" Sunny said.

"Not for two years I can't," Zach interrupted. "I have a contract with the state government. They paid my last two years of medical school. In turn, I agreed to practice for two years in whatever rural Tennessee community they could find to cosponsor me." That community, of course, had turned out to be Carlisle.

Sunny was aware the town was paying half of Zach's current salary. Her grandfather's company underwrote the living allowance that had bought, among other things, Zach's new truck. And it foot the bill for the day-to-day operating expenses of the clinic. Without Carlisle Furniture Factory, Zach would not have a job. And that made this situation very sticky indeed. Sunny thought it best to keep the information to herself. Apparently he did not know all the specifics behind the monthly check he received from the state.

"So put in for a transfer," Sunny advised. "As soon as you get it, we'll proceed with the annulment. My reputation will be saved. You'll be free and, more importantly, out of Carlisle. No one will ever have to know our marriage was a sham."

Zach did not want to see Sunny hurt, but he also didn't want to marry. "How's your Land Rover?" he asked casually to change the subject.

Sunny strode back and forth, her high heels moving soundlessly on the carpeted floor.

Her lips curved ruefully. "I still can't drive it and I've tried darn near everything. I don't think that skunk smell is ever going to go away. But that's my problem, and not something you have to worry about, Zach. Our getting caught in flagrante on my back stoop, however, is a worry we share.'' Sunny whirled abruptly to face him. She pointed a lecturing finger his way.

''Look, we're young, healthy, vital. No one would believe we could strip down naked in proximity to each other and not even be tempted to kiss.''

That wasn't exactly true, Zach thought. He had been tempted. He just hadn't acted.

Her solution made sense. And he had already put in for a transfer out of Carlisle. The problem was, it wouldn't come through for several months, if it came about at all. Meanwhile, he didn't want anyone in Carlisle finding out about it—not even Sunny. ''I am going nuts not being able to use my medical training,'' Zach admitted.

''I'm really tired of this situation interfering with my work over at the furniture factory,'' Sunny said.

Maybe her solution was worth a shot, Zach thought. ''A marriage in name only,'' he stipulated firmly.

Sunny nodded. ''That's the only way I'll have it.''

Zach paused. ''What happens if we change our minds?''

''We won't,'' she said quickly, drawing an unsteady breath.

Zach studied her. ''If we do... is there a possibility the relationship could become intimate?''

Sunny flushed, beginning to feel as though she were in an ''I Love Lucy'' episode again. She trembled as he neared her. "Boy, you don't pull any punches, do you?"

"I like to know what my options are. And you didn't answer my question."

Sunny had the feeling a lot was riding on her answer. "Only if it was what we both wanted. But I have to warn you, Zach, the chances of that happening... are next to nil."

SUNNY WAS FOOLING herself if she believed their marriage was going to be simple and uncomplicated, Zach thought as he dressed for the bachelor party cum poker game. Even if they were married three or four weeks, there were bound to be problems, the least of which was the mutual attraction simmering between them. Sunny might want to pretend it didn't exist, but he saw it every time he looked deep into her whiskey-colored eyes. He hadn't even kissed her yet, and he had an idea how she would taste. Sweet as sugar, hot as fire. Putting them under one roof was not a good idea, but as she'd said, what choice did they have?

When Zach arrived at Slim's grocery store everyone was ready to play poker.

One of the men, George, set out the subs and beer, dill pickles and chips. "Hope you brought your wallet with you, Doc," he teased. "We take our games serious here."

His wallet was not the problem, Zach thought. It was Gramps. Unless Zach was mistaken, he was in obvious discomfort. The glass of bicarb and water in his hand was the first clue. Zach said hello to the rest of the guys and moved over to Augustus Carlisle's side. A fine sheen of perspiration dotted his upper lip. "You're in pain," Zach said in his ear.

"So I am," Gramps admitted, taking another sip of bicarb.

"What'd you do today, Augustus?" George asked, as he pulled the chairs up around the table.

"I moved some files from my office into Sunny's," he replied.

Zach moved around so his back was to the guys. "Where does it hurt?" he asked, very quietly. Augustus looked scared.

"Here." Augustus placed his hand on the center of his chest, then over his heart, toward his left shoulder.

"Any numbness? Tingling?" Zach asked. Augustus shook his head. "I want to run an EKG on you," Zach continued.

"You can't do that now!" Gramps shot back.

"You guys about ready?" a man named Fergus asked, snapping the cards.

Zach turned around and gave the men a sheepish grin. "I left my wallet over at the clinic. Gramps doesn't believe me, so he's going with me to retrieve it." Zach wrapped an arm around Augustus's shoulder. "Back in a minute." He winked at the guys. "Don't start without us."

"YOU SEE, I told you my EKG would be normal," Gramps said, buttoning his shirt, then his fishing vest over that.

Zach folded the readout from the machine and slipped it into a file jacket bearing Augustus's name. He was relieved it was not a heart attack, too. "There's a reason for the pain you were having a few minutes ago,'' he said. ''You need more tests, ones I'm not equipped to do here.'' Zach wanted to determine the cause, then treat the problem, whatever it was.

To Zach's frustration, Augustus waved off the suggestion. ''More tests would be a waste of time and money.''

''Sunny wouldn't think so.'' If Augustus wouldn't do it for himself, maybe he'd do it for his granddaughter.

Augustus's face turned dark. ''I forbid you to mention it to her—or anyone else, for that matter. I'm fine. I'm just getting older, that's all. Now, let's get back to the game!''

Zach recognized denial when he saw it. He stopped Augustus at the door. ''It's not good to keep secrets. Sunny has a right to know if you're ill.''

''Let's get something straight, young man,'' Augustus lectured, his normal feistiness returning as the last of his mysterious chest pain faded. ''I am not going to ruin Sunny's wedding tomorrow with any worries about me. And neither are you! One way or another, you are walking up that aisle to the altar tomorrow to say your 'I do'!''

''NOW, SWEETHEART, stop looking so nervous. You're doing the right thing,'' Gramps soothed Sunny in the anteroom behind the altar in the community church. He was dressed in his best suit and tie, and seeing his contented expression, she couldn't help but think maybe he wasn't so much angry as delighted to see her in this mess. He had wanted a great-grandchild for a long time. Sunny was his only grandchild, and therefore his only hope for one.

"Then why don't I feel more relaxed?" Sunny asked. She didn't know how she'd let her aunt Gertrude and Gertie's friend Matilda talk her into wearing her grandmother's wedding gown, but she had. Standing before the mirror in ivory lace, a veil on her head, she was aware what a hoax she was perpetrating on the people of Carlisle.

"All brides are nervous." Gertie tucked a new blue-and-white hankie in the long sleeve of Sunny's gown. She fastened a borrowed antique locket around her neck. "That's just the way you're supposed to feel."

All brides were not marrying a complete stranger, Sunny thought. Of course, her marriage to Zach was not going to be real. It was only a temporary arrangement. Once it was over, she would use her "broken heart" to fend off any further attempts at matchmaking on her behalf.

The organist began the "Wedding March." "Guess this is it." Gramps took Sunny's elbow and led her around to the back of the church.

Zach was waiting at the altar, beside the minister. He looked resplendent in a dark suit and tie. Gazing up into his face, Sunny could find no visible evidence that he was being forced into this.

He was a better sport than she had figured he would be. Unless, she thought uncomfortably, he planned to get more out of this than she had promised him. Pushing the unwelcome thought aside, she stood next to Zach and faced the minister. Her hands were shaking as she held the bouquet in front of her. All too soon, the minister had finished his introductory remarks about the seriousness of marriage. Sunny was handing her bouquet to Aunt Gertie and turning to face Zach.

"Do you, Sunny, promise to love, honor and cherish Zach for as long as you both shall live?"

As long as it lasts, she amended silently. "I do," Sunny said. She looked deep into Zach's eyes. He looked into hers. A thrill went through her. She knew they were only doing this for everyone else, but dressed in wedding clothes and standing before a church full of people, she found it hard to remember that this was all just pretend.

"Do you, Zach, promise to love, honor and cherish Sunny for as long as you both shall live?"

Zach took her hand in his, held it warmly. As he gazed at her his eyes glinted with a subdued humor, as if he could hardly believe he was going through with this, too. "I do."

Under the minister's direction, Sunny and Zach exchanged rings. The minister grinned at Zach. "You may kiss the bride, son."

Sunny's breath stalled in her lungs as Zach took her masterfully into his arms. He lowered his mouth to hers. Electricity sizzled through Sunny at the brief, but sensual, contact.

Appearing quite pleased with himself, Zach stepped back. The organist resumed playing. To Sunny's relief—or was it disappointment?—it was over.

"I DIDN'T KNOW it was possible for anyone to blush for three hours straight," Zach remarked in Sunny's ear after he swept her up into his arms and carried her across the threshold, into her home.

Arms still hooked around his neck, Sunny gave him an adoring look that, she assured herself, was strictly for the benefit of the crowd of onlookers who had accompanied them on the short walk from the church to her home. Smiling up at him, she whispered, "When I agreed to marry you, I didn't know a wedding was included." Then, turning to those still watching them, she lifted her hand in a merry wave. The crowd waved back.

Zach gently set her down and wrapped an arm around her waist. Tugging her close, he leaned down and whispered in her ear, "Seems like everyone in town is rooting for us." Zach glanced at Augustus in the crowd. Sunny's grandfather seemed fine this morning, but Zach was still worried. He'd have to do his best to keep an eye on Gramps from afar until he could get him into the hospital for a complete series of tests.

Sunny allowed herself to lean into Zach's side only because she was tired from all the festivities. "They want you to do right by me," she admitted. With one last wave at the crowd, they stepped back, inside the foyer, and shut the door.

Exhausted, she leaned against it. Zach propped a hand next to her head and looked down at her. For one insane second, she thought he was going to kiss her again, really kiss her. A sizzle of desire swept through her.

Zach's gaze swept her upturned face in leisurely fashion. "That's quite an old-fashioned notion, even for southern and proper Tennessee, don't you think?"

"Quite. But that's the town of Carlisle for you," Sunny said lightly. "In fact, the sense of family, community, caring and warmth is one of the things I like best about the town.''

''You don't find the intrusion of others into our private life annoying?'' Zach asked. He did.

Sunny apparently knew what he was referring to. ''I sidestepped the invitation for the honeymoon cabin, didn't I?''

''Yes, although I don't think anyone was pleased about it.''

''We can't help it. We both have to work,'' Sunny said stubbornly. She folded her arms in front of her, still radiantly beautiful in her veil and wedding dress.

''I don't tonight,'' Zach said, ''unless someone gets sick.''

''Well, unfortunately, I do have to work. All the brouhaha of late has left me behind.''

Zach was surprised at his own unwillingness to have the festivities end. ''You're not going into the office!'' He had an idea what chaos an action like that would cause.

''No, of course not, silly,'' Sunny said, slipping off her veil. ''I brought all the work home with me.''

Zach didn't find that much more reassuring. ''Don't you think we should get to know each other a little better if we're going to be sharing space?''

''Eventually,'' Sunny said with a cool smile that arrowed straight to his heart. ''Not tonight.'' She slipped from beneath his outstretched arm. ''I made up the guest room for you. Shall I show you where you'll be bunking?''

Zach nodded. He moved his arm in gallant fashion. ''After you.''

Zach followed her up the stairs. They creaked beneath her weight, and a little more beneath his. At the top of the stairs was the master bedroom. A large brass bed dominated the room. It was covered with a patchwork quilt and numerous pillows. Sunny moved on down the hall, past the linen closet and the bath. "We're going to have to share the bathroom while you're here," she informed him with a sigh. "This is an old house, and there's only the one."

"I think I can rough it," Zach said. But that was before he'd seen his bed.

SUNNY SPENT her wedding night in a buttercup yellow sweatsuit and white cotton socks. She curled up on her bed, writing and rewriting letters on behalf of Carlisle Furniture, soliciting more business for the company on her laptop computer. She could hear Zach roaming around downstairs. She felt a little guilty for sticking him in the tiny guest room, where the rollaway bed was half the size needed to accommodate his tall, rangy frame, but that couldn't be helped on such short notice. Besides, she reassured herself, he wouldn't be here long.

Around 10:00 p.m., Zach knocked. Sunny kept typing. "Come in," she said, without looking up from her keyboard.

Zach carried a tray in. It had a pot of tea, a sandwich and some wedding cake. "I could hear you typing. I thought you might like something to eat," he said.

"Thanks for the tray. I'm sorry if I disturbed you." A tingle of awareness rushing through her, Sunny kept typing.

Zach lingered in the doorway. "What are you working on?"

"Business letters."

"Oh."

For a second, Zach appeared so lonely Sunny's heart went out to him. She thought about how it must be for him. Newly married to a woman he didn't even know. And Carlisle wasn't exactly a hot spot. TV reception was spotty at best, and cable was not available. A few people in town had satellite dishes. Sunny wasn't one of them.

"Can I do anything to help? Address envelopes or something?"

Sunny shook her head.

"Can I get you something else to eat or drink?"

He wants company. Sunny had grown up feeling the loneliest child in the world. Seeing it in Zach made her heart ache. Finished with the letter she was working on, she put her laptop aside. "This is fine. Did you get something for yourself?"

Zach nodded. "I also did a hundred sit-ups and push-ups, put all my clothes away and read the last four issues of the *Journal of the American Medical Association.*"

"Bored out of your mind, right?"

Zach nodded. "How do you stand it here?"

"I've got plenty to keep me busy."

"That isn't what I meant."

"I know, but I'm not interested in discussing my romantic life prior to you." It was just too embarrassing. Besides, she didn't want Zach to know how she'd been duped.

"Too late," he said smugly. "There were some hints dropped at the bachelor party last night."

Sunny froze. "Exactly what did you hear?" She was going to kill those men!

"That you were engaged to one Andrew Singleton III shortly after arriving in Carlisle to take over your grandfather's company."

Sunny felt the blood rush to her face. "Yes, well, that was a mistake."

"No one really knows what happened to break the two of you up," Zach continued.

And no one was going to know, not if she had anything to do about it, Sunny thought stubbornly. She forced a smile. "We weren't suited to each other, all right?"

"Still carrying a torch for him?"

"Heavens, no!"

Zach raised a brow skeptically, seeming to know there was much she wasn't saying. Even more disturbing was the awareness that he wouldn't rest until he did know it all.

"If you don't mind, I'd like to change the subject," Sunny said prudently.

"No problem." Zach grinned. "So how's the factory doing?"

"Okay. It could be better, though. That's why I'm writing letters to solicit new business. In the past, the company has only sold furniture to other independently owned stores in the state. I think we could do a lot better if we expanded our markets."

"Hence the letters." He nodded at the stack of neatly typed envelopes beside her.

Sunny nodded. "That's not the only change I'm making, however. I've arranged for a computer-run order-entry system that will be on-line twenty-four hours a day, and I'm also putting together a catalog of mail-order items."

"That is a lot."

"Which is why I'm so busy." Sunny took the time to show him glossy color photos of their new rustically designed Tennessee Cabin line of furniture. "I've even been thinking of purchasing a few pieces at employee discount for my house. You may have noticed my guest room needs a little work."

"I noticed."

Zach leaned against the bureau, radiating all the pure male power and casual sexiness of a big screen hero. Unbidden, all sorts of romantic thoughts and fantasies came to mind. Sunny pushed them away.

She finished her sandwich and tea. "Well, thanks for the supper, but I've got to get back to work now."

Zach moved toward her gallantly. "Let me get that for you."

Sunny caught a whiff of his brisk, sexy scent and backed away. She hoped he had no idea how much having him in her bedroom this way was affecting her. "I can handle it."

"No. Really. Let me."

"Zach," Sunny insisted, as heat began to center in her chest, then moved outward in radiating waves, "you don't have to wait on me."

They both tugged at once... and let go. The tray went crashing to the floor. And so did Sunny's china. She grabbed a wastebasket and knelt to pick up the pieces. Zach knelt beside her.

"I'm sorry," he said.

"It's okay," Sunny said, unable to keep the irritation completely from her voice. Having him in such proximity seemed to make her all thumbs. Unless she got ahold of herself, who knew what else might happen?

"Where do you keep your vacuum cleaner?" he asked.

"In the hall closet downstairs."

He retrieved it. While he started sweeping the immediate area, in an effort to pick up all remaining tiny shards of glass, Sunny carried the wastebasket of broken dishes out to the trash. As she was carefully transferring the contents, the neighbor's dog ran into her yard, barking.

Matilda followed. Quickly she took in Sunny's jogging suit, sweat socks and bunny slippers. "Sunny, for heaven's sake! What are you doing taking out the trash on your wedding night?"

Sunny felt herself turning red as she offered an airy wave. "Oh, we broke some dishes. Nothing to worry about."

Briefly Matilda looked worried. Composing herself hurriedly, she advised, "Well, have fun, darlin'. Einstein, come here! We have to finish our evening walk!"

Sunny walked back inside. She carried the wastebasket back to her bedroom.

Zach straightened as she tried to sidle past him unnoticed and caught hold of her. The next thing she knew, she was anchored against him, hip to breast. He was grinning down at her, evidently enjoying the perfect way their bodies meshed, and in no hurry at all to let her go.

"Nervous, aren't you?" he said softly.

"I don't—"

"It's okay. I am, too. And I know why. Sometimes in medicine the cure is worse than the disease. And sometimes in romance the anticipation of a situation is more unnerving than the actual event. So maybe we should just get this over with," he said, and then his mouth came down to cover hers.

Caught off guard, she felt her mouth soften beneath his. Not again, she thought, alarmed. But even as her mind was telling her no, her body was already saying yes....

The kiss in the church had been properly restrained. This kiss was claiming her as his woman, Sunny noted, as Zach began a deep, achingly sweet exploration of her mouth.

And claim her he did, his mouth moving possessively over hers, his tongue coaxing her lips apart, drawing her deeper and deeper into the sensual battle, until she was no longer sure of anything but his strong arms and body, and the wonder of his mouth, and his sizzling, yet tender kiss.

Excitement pouring through her, Sunny wreathed her arms about Zach's neck. Surrendering to his will, she surged against him and felt her knees turn to butter. Murmuring his encouragement, he gathered her closer, enveloping her masterfully in his warmth and strength. He kissed her again, long and deeply, the hunger inside him matching hers. And though it warmed her, it left her feeling hollow, too. Wanting more...needing...Sunny thought dizzily—she wasn't quite sure what.

Reveling in the sheer intensity and wonder of their embrace, she sighed her pleasure softly. Zach's hand slid down her back, guiding her nearer. Sunny's breasts were crushed against the hardness of his chest. Lower still, she felt the unmistakable proof of his desire, the rock-hard brace of his thighs. With a start, she realized where things were headed if she didn't halt this forward pass of his right now.

It didn't matter how accomplished a lover Zach Grainger was. She had no intention of making this a real honeymoon.

Hand to his chest, she broke off the sizzling embrace. "What was that for?" she gasped.

"Because you look so good in those yellow sweats," he murmured, ducking his head once again.

Sunny sucked in another quick breath and wrested herself from his embrace. Heart pounding, she smoothed her tousled hair from her face. "You can't...I never said I'd—damn it, Zach, what do you think you're doing?"

He gently traced her cheekbone with his thumb, then bent to kiss her temple. "I'm making life more interesting."

"I don't want my life to be more interesting," Sunny insisted.

"That's not what your lips said when you were kissing me just now," he teased, his clear blue eyes glinting with humor. "It's not what your lips said when you kissed me back after the ceremony."

"That was all for show," Sunny huffed.

"Keep putting on a show like that and no one will believe our claims of annulment later on." Arms folded in front of him, he leaned close, his eyes twinkling. "And besides, if you didn't want me to notice you, how come you're wearing a different perfume tonight than you were this afternoon?"

"I'm notoriously absentminded when I have a lot of work to do," Sunny fibbed.

"Funny," Zach drawled, giving her the slow, sensual once-over. "You strike me as a woman who'd be in perfect control of her faculties all the time."

That had been true, Sunny thought. Until Zach had charged into her life. "Well, I am. Absentminded. Sometimes. I mean."

"Hmm." He rubbed his jaw contemplatively. "I guess I'll have to take your word for that."

"Not to worry, Zach," Sunny assured him, feeling yet again as if she were in an "I Love Lucy" episode. "It won't happen anymore!"

His expression was one of comically exaggerated misunderstanding. "No more perfume?" he asked sadly.

Sunny flushed, aware he had gotten under her skin in a way no man ever had. "No more anything!" she said firmly.

"Now, Sunny," he teased, his gaze sliding over her, "don't make any promises you can't keep. Especially since we have the rest of our honeymoon weekend ahead of us."

Sunny tossed her hair. "I've never made any promises I couldn't keep," she vowed hotly. "Furthermore, you're the one who is in for a surprise! Now, out!" Her pulse pounding as she half anticipated another kiss, she pushed him out of her bedroom and slammed the door.

From the other side of the door, Zach chuckled softly, victoriously, then sauntered away. Sunny waited for his footsteps to recede all the way down the hall, then let go of the breath she had been holding. Her knees were so weak and trembly she nearly collapsed against the door. Leaning against it, she knotted her damp hands in front of her and briefly closed her eyes.

Zach could call this whatever he liked, but now that she'd had a moment to contemplate it, she knew darn well what this newfound behavior of his was all about. It wasn't so much desire as his payback to her for having been forced by her family and friends into marrying her. Obviously he blamed her for their predicament. Hence, he intended to extract his own style of vengeance by torturing her with kisses and treating her like a real wife and potential lover every chance he got.

Well, Sunny surmised grimly, her usual confidence returning, Zach was fooling himself if he thought he was going to get the best of her. She could torture him, too...simply by turning herself into the kind of wife he *wouldn't* want.

Chapter Three

Take Me as I Am

If he didn't know better, Zach thought, as he awoke to the delicious smells of blueberry muffins and hot coffee, he'd think he'd fallen into a velvet-lined trap. Here he was, in Carlisle less than three weeks, and he had a beautiful wife who even cooked him breakfast.

Not that he had ever expected to find himself in this position. He had figured that the scandal would die down if he just imposed an iron will and stayed away from her. And, Zach admitted honestly, it had taken all his strength to stay clear of the local angel with the red-gold hair.

But the uproar over Sunny's compromising hadn't died down. And that was her fault, too. After all, he might have been a virtual newcomer, but she resided in town. She should never have stripped down out there in the country or induced him to do the same no matter how skunky their clothes had been. She should have known the odds were they'd get caught sneaking back into town. Particularly since her grandfather had worried when she hadn't shown up for dinner and had been out looking for her.

Which brought him to the marriage. He had agreed to it, but that didn't mean he'd had to like it. He hated losing control of his life. But he had tried to make the best of this mutually bad situation they found themselves in by taking the supper to her the evening before. He hadn't anticipated kissing her; that had just happened. And though he had no plans of staying in Carlisle, he did want to make love to her. And if their lovemaking was even one-tenth as sweet as their kisses had been, well, who knew what would happen after that? Zach mused happily as he rolled out of bed and grabbed a robe.

Her fixing breakfast for them *had* to be a good sign. It meant she was willing to meet him halfway on this. Zach's smile faded as soon as he walked into the kitchen.

Sunny sat at the kitchen table. Her gorgeous hair was wrapped in curlers. She had something that looked like whipped cream smeared all over her face. She was wearing an oversize man's shirt that was stained with paint. Her jeans were old and ripped at the knees. The kitchen was a huge mess. The muffin tin stood empty.

Trying hard not to laugh—for Sunny could not be anything but beautiful to him, no matter how she outfitted herself—Zach strolled over to pour himself some coffee. He wasn't surprised to find the carafe was bone-dry.

"There aren't any more muffins," she said.

Zach's glance roved her slender figure in a sensual way designed to annoy her. "You ate a dozen muffins all by yourself?" he asked mildly.

"I only made two." Wielding a pair of scissors, she continued cutting out big patches of the morning paper.

Zach noted with chagrin she had done particular damage to the sports page. He could get another newspaper. He could also easily make another pot of coffee. The muffins were another matter. "I didn't know you could make just two muffins," he said casually.

"I cut the recipe down to size."

If she could do it, he could, too. He began to look around for a recipe and ingredients.

"I also used up the last of the blueberries." She hid her grin behind her full coffee cup.

Zach knew she was giving him hell. Whether it was to punish him for kissing her the night before or discourage him from doing it again didn't really matter. He could handle her. In fact, as she would soon find out, he could dish it out, as well. Sunny, the darling princess of Carlisle, might be used to having her own way all the time, but that was going to change.

"I think I'll go back upstairs and get dressed," Zach announced laconically.

"You do that," Sunny murmured in an unconcerned voice as she buried her nose in the morning paper.

"You just wait, honey," he whispered, a smile of anticipation on his lips. "I'll best you yet."

SUNNY WANTED to leave the face mask on all day, just to irritate Zack, but she was afraid of what would happen to her skin, so she rinsed it off in the kitchen sink and replaced it with a thick coating of winter-strength moisturizer. Satisfied her face had a disgusting oily gleam to it that would be bound to discourage any further kisses from her new husband, she went back to cutting more holes in the morning paper.

Seconds later, loud footsteps sounded on the stairs. Zach walked into the kitchen. Sunny never would have believed it, but the rascal had outdone her.

He was dressed in a white undershirt that was ripped down the center, white socks, black shoes and high-water pants. She wasn't sure what he had put on his hair, but he had fixed it with numerous cowlicks spiked up in the back. He hadn't shaved and the morning beard gave him a piratical look.

Zach cleared a place on the counter with a swipe of his arm that sent even more flour flying. "Think I'll fix me a little breakfast," he said.

Taking that to be her cue to leave, Sunny slipped out of the kitchen and back up the stairs. Now what? she wondered as she barricaded herself in her bedroom. She had wanted him to know this marriage, temporary or not, was going to be no picnic with free sex. She hadn't counted on him trying to outdo her.

If she backed off now—by acting and dressing normally—he would think he had won. Therefore, Sunny decided, she would just have to tough out the rest of the weekend. She only had twenty hours and forty-three minutes left before she could go to work again.

The rest of the morning passed quickly. She had a few bad moments when she smelled the hash brown potatoes cooking. That was, after all, her favorite dish. But she forced herself to stay in her bedroom and get some more Carlisle-company work done. It was the sound of the baseball game on the radio that eventually drew her out. It was loud enough to be heard in every room of the house, and worse, it was a doubleheader, which meant it would be on for hours.

Wanting something to eat, she ambled on back downstairs.

Squelching the urge to ask him to turn the radio down, she headed for the kitchen. It was in an even bigger mess than she had left it. Zach walked in behind her. His closeness made her senses spin.

"Where do you keep your spittoon?" he asked in an innocent voice.

Hanging on to her temper with effort, Sunny whirled to face him. Like her, he had done nothing to improve his appearance. They looked like characters in a comedy show.

Ignoring the sudden heavy jump in her pulse, she smiled at him firmly. "I don't have a spittoon," she replied calmly.

Zach slowly ripped open a pouch of chewing tobacco. "Then where am I going to put my spit?"

Sunny had put up with a lot, but there were limits, even if she had to sacrifice a little pride to enforce them. "You are not doing that in my house," she announced firmly.

"It's our house now, sugar," he corrected, patting her rollers condescendingly with the flat of his hand. "And don't worry about not having a spittoon for me right off the bat. I forgive you."

"You are so—" As Sunny sputtered for words that would be precise yet ladylike, Zach edged closer. As he neared her, the room seemed to do a half spin.

"What?" Zach's eyes took on a predatory gleam.

"Thoughtful," Sunny said.

"Aren't I?" He turned away from her and opened the cupboard. "I suppose I could put a teacup in every room and use that in lieu of a spittoon."

Sunny slipped between Zach and her teacups and crossed her arms in front of her. "Over my dead body."

"Is that a challenge?"

Sunny's temper began to flame. "Babe," she drawled, "it's an ultimatum."

Zach grinned at her and plucked a big wad of tobacco from the pouch. "Don't you dare," she said. "Zach, I swear—"

He kept going anyway. She grabbed for the pouch with one hand and knocked the pinch from his fingers with the other. Loose tobacco sprayed the floor at the exact moment he stepped forward, trapping her against the counter. "Give me my tobacco back," he ordered mildly, one hand braced on either side of her.

Sunny's heart pounded at his proximity. Even in the outrageous getup he was enormously attractive. But she was *not* giving in. "If you want to do something that disgusting, you can do it outside," she said, clutching the pouch and trying not to think about the intimate way his muscled thighs were now pressing against hers.

Zach's dimples deepened. "What if I want to do something even more disgusting inside?" he whispered.

The way he dipped his head toward her mouth caused a distinct melting sensation in her knees.

Oh, no. He was going to kiss her again. Sunny sucked in a breath, determined not to let him make her feel all weak and hot and compliant again, and turned her head to the side. Her eyes widened as she saw Aunt Gertie, Matilda and a very pregnant Rhonda-Faye Pearson on the other side of the screen door. Sunny exchanged mortified glances with Rhonda-Faye, knowing that if anyone could understand even an inkling of what was going on here, it would be her best friend. And even that, Sunny thought, studying Rhonda-Faye's stunned expression, would be a stretch.

"Oh, dear," Gertie said, shifting the foil-wrapped casserole dish in her hand.

The sole proprietor of the town's only department store, Gertie felt it her duty to dress with perfect panache and style all the time. Her polished appearance only made Sunny feel all the more comically disheveled.

"It appears we've come at an inopportune time," Gertie said.

The forty-five-year-old Matilda was not only Sunny's friend and nearest neighbor, but also a key employee over at the furniture factory. "We rang the bell, dear," she said, putting a plump hand to her cheek.

"I guess you all didn't hear since the radio was on so loud," Rhonda-Faye added, looking resplendent in a white maternity outfit.

"So we came around to the back," Gertie continued, flattening one white-gloved hand over the signature pearl necklace around her neck. "We brought you some dinner so you wouldn't have to cook while you were on your honeymoon. But I can see that you two already have been cooking."

Sunny was so embarrassed she wanted to sink right through the floor. She never had a messy kitchen!

And as for their appearances, she recollected in silent misery, this was going to be all over town in no time.

"Thank you so much. Zach and I were just goofing around, weren't we, honey?" Sunny elbowed him in the ribs.

"It's been a barrel of laughs so far," he said.

Sunny turned to Zach and gave him a glare only he could see. *Help me out here,* she ordered with her eyes.

"Well, we'll be going, dear. If you're sure that everything is okay?" Gertie said, taking in their mutually comical state.

Rhonda-Faye giggled and backed out the door. "I think we ought to leave, ladies, and let these two get back to whatever it was they were doing."

"Thanks for the food. If Sunny doesn't eat it all herself, I'll be in seventh heaven," Zach said.

Sunny gave him another elbow as the ladies laughed. When they were alone again, she faced Zach. Unlike him, she wasn't laughing. "We are in so deep now," she moaned miserably. "You have no idea."

ZACH OPENED the clinic at 9:00 a.m. Monday. Sunny's grandfather marched in at 9:02. Zach eyed her protector with courtesy and respect, hoping this was a professional visit. "What can I do for you, Mr. Carlisle?" he asked politely.

"You can call me 'Augustus', now that we're related," he said, fastening his piercing eyes on Zach. "And there's nothing wrong with me—today anyway—so you can put that darn stethoscope away. I just came in to talk."

Zach had been afraid of that. "About what?"

"Sunny, what else. I heard what went on over at your home yesterday."

Zach had had a feeling it would get all over town. He had not expected to have to endure any lectures on his behavior.

"If you sincerely want to make a go of your marriage to my granddaughter, son, you are going to have to work a little harder."

Had the marriage to Sunny been a real one, Zach would have worked hard.

"You do want to make a go of this marriage, don't you?" Augustus persisted.

It was funny. The day he had agreed to marry Sunny, making a go of the ill-advised union had been the last thing on his mind. Seeing her in a wedding dress, holding her in his arms, kissing her, had softened his resistance somewhat. To his surprise, her orneriness had appealed to him even more. Zach liked the idea of a little mischief in his wife.

"Of course I want what's best for Sunny," Zach said honestly, aware Augustus was still waiting for an answer.

"Yes, well, Sunny is more fragile than she appears," Augustus warned.

"She seems inordinately strong willed to me," Zach disagreed.

"About business, yes. But her personal life hasn't always been easy."

"Are you taking about her broken engagement again?" he asked.

Augustus frowned and held up a warning hand. "I've said too much as it is. If Sunny wants you to know about her life before she came to Carlisle, she'll tell you. In the meantime, if you plan to stay married to my granddaughter, you need to shave, even on weekends."

"Yes, sir."

Augustus looked Zach up and down. "You be good to my granddaughter, you hear? I expect you to treat her with the love and respect she deserves."

Again Zach nodded. He didn't mind the lecture nearly as much as he expected. Maybe because he saw the love Augustus felt for Sunny. As for the marriage, he knew he should have minded that more than he did, even if it was only a temporary social fix for a local scandal. He needed to be careful not to get too involved here. He had his own life to live.

"SUNNY, I AM SORRY, but I will never get the hang of this new computer," Matilda said late Monday afternoon.

"Yes, you will. Just give it time."

"I have. But I just can't remember anything that Chuck Conway told me to do," Matilda said with a sigh.

"Then maybe he needs to come back and show you how to work this new order-entry system again," Sunny said. "I'll call him right now and set up a time."

No sooner was Sunny off the phone than Aunt Gertie appeared in the doorway to Sunny's office. "May I have a word with you, sugarplum?"

"Sure." Sunny knew it had to be important. Otherwise Gertie never would have left Carlisle Department Store during business hours.

She came in, shut the door behind her and inched off her gloves. "Sugarplum, I am gonna be frank with you. I don't know what your mama and daddy told you about marriage—"

"Gertie, this isn't a sex talk, is it?"

"Well. Sort of. I mean I—I expect you know about the birds and bees."

"Yes, ma'am, I do."

"But there's a lot more to sex and marriage than just the birds and the bees," Gertie continued seriously.

Sunny tried, but could not contain a flush of embarrassment. "Aunt Gertie, I love you for trying to help me out on this, but we couldn't save this talk for another time?"

Gertie patted Sunny's shoulder fondly. "Sugarplum, after what I saw at your home yesterday morning, I think we need to have this talk now, before any more damage is done to this sweet new union of yours."

Sunny could see there was going to be no getting out of this lecture. When Aunt Gertie had something on her mind, she did not rest until she had said it. Sunny sat down. Gertie took her hand in hers.

"First of all, technically speaking, you are still on your honeymoon. And it's important for you to act like a newlywed. And not wear curlers in your hair and goo on your face and old clothes. Even on weekend mornings.''

Her embarrassment fading, Sunny folded her arms in front of her. ''I'm not going to pretend to be something I'm not,'' she told her aunt stubbornly.

''Good. Because you're not the kind of woman who goes around with curlers in your hair. Unless, of course, you're trying to send that new husband of yours a message that you aren't interested in him sexually.''

''Aunt Gertie!'' Her face flaming, Sunny bolted up off the sofa.

Gertie patted her own perfect bob of red-gold curls. ''We may as well speak frankly, sugarplum. I know this marriage of yours was more or less arranged.''

''Against my will and better judgment, I might add,'' Sunny interjected, as she paced back and forth.

''But that young man of yours is quite a catch. He's a doctor, he's kind and good-looking and your age and he's from Tennessee.''

''But he's not going to stay in Carlisle,'' Sunny said, deciding now was as good a time as any to lay the groundwork for her and Zach's eventual annulment. Sunny planted her feet firmly on the carpet and regarded her great-aunt willfully. ''I am.''

''He'll be here for two years. Who knows what can happen in that time? You might have a baby. He might change his mind about leaving.''

''It's still an arranged marriage,'' Sunny persisted, trying not to let herself get sidetracked with idyllic images of Zach and a baby.

''Oh, I know arranged marriages aren't really an 'in' thing these days, but they do work. My own marriage to your uncle Fergus was arranged, and we've been married for nearly forty years now."

"I know, and I'm glad you're happy, but—"

A knock sounded on the door. Matilda poked her head in. She was beaming. Sunny frowned, instantly knowing from the excitement crackling in the air that something was up.

"We're ready," Matilda sang out.

A group of women burst through the doors to Sunny's office. They were all carrying gaily wrapped gifts. Matilda came last, wheeling in a pink-and-white cake in the shape of a wedding bell and a crystal bowl of pink-lemonade punch.

"Surprise!" everyone shouted.

"We're giving you a wedding shower," Rhonda-Faye said.

"Rhonda-Faye made the cake over at the diner."

Sunny smiled at her friends. This was what she liked about living in Carlisle. The closeness and camaraderie. The way everyone watched out for everyone else. She had never had that growing up and she had missed it dearly.

"This is wonderful! Thank you!" She hugged everyone in turn and then settled in to enjoy the party.

It was only after the gifts had been opened, the games played and the cake eaten that Gertie stood to make an announcement. "We have one last present for you, Sunny."

"I can't imagine what," Sunny joked. "You've already given me everything but the kitchen sink. Cookbooks, nightgowns, several bottles of blackberry wine."

"But this is something really special," Gertie said.

"Yes," Matilda added. "We all know how you love to learn, Sunny."

"So we pitched in and hired an instructor for you," Gertie said.

"An instructor on what?" Sunny asked, visions of Masters and Johnson textbooks dancing in her head.

"On how to be happily married, of course," Gertie explained.

Matilda leaned forward excitedly. "The course tells you everything you need to know about being a good, loving wife in five easy lessons that are spaced out over a period of two weeks."

Oh, my gosh. "This is so sweet, really—" Sunny began.

"Honey, you don't have to be embarrassed," Aunt Gertie soothed. "We know the newlywed phase isn't easy."

The very pregnant Rhonda-Faye nodded. "We've all been there. And we all feel we have something to learn, too." She leaned forward earnestly. "I mean, what marriage couldn't be made better?"

"What are you saying?" Sunny asked with trepidation.

"We all signed up to take the course with you," Rhonda-Faye replied, her excitement about the endeavor evident.

"So what do you say?" Matilda asked enthusiastically. "Are you ready for your first lesson?"

Chapter Four

That Kind of Girl

"Getting pretty busy here, aren't you, Doc," Fergus Walker said when he came in to have his blood pressure checked the next day.

That was a matter of opinion. Zach wasn't doing nearly as much for the community as he could, given half a chance. "I've seen four patients here today," Zach said dryly, noting it was nearly 6:00 p.m., closing time for the clinic. "I think I'm setting a record."

"Now, now, don't you fret none," Fergus said as he pushed up the light blue sleeve of his post-office uniform. Fergus watched as Zach fitted the blood-pressure cuff around his upper arm. "As word filters out around the mountain that you done right by Sunny, folks will be lining up to see you, 'cause it's either that or a sixty-mile trip to the nearest doctor."

"Sixty-five," Zach corrected absently, already pumping air into the cuff.

Fergus was silent as Zach read his blood pressure. "So how am I doing, Doc?"

Not as good as he would have liked, considering Sunny's uncle was only fifty-five. "How long have you been on your current medication?" Zach asked, pulling the stethoscope from his ears.

Fergus stroked the handlebars of his thick black mustache. "About two years now, I reckon."

"And the dosage is—?"

Fergus told him. "Why do you ask?"

Zach went to the cupboard and pulled out a sample packet of pills. "Your blood pressure is a little high. I think you might do better on this."

Fergus shrugged uninterestedly. "Whatever you think, Doc, will be fine. Now, back to that new bride of yours—"

"I wasn't aware we were discussing Sunny," Zach said, already writing out a prescription.

Fergus stroked the ends of his mustache. "C'mon, Doc, don't mess with me. I know what happened over the weekend. Hell, everybody in town knows."

"Well, that makes me feel better," Zach drawled. Not that he was surprised about this. Fergus was married to Gertie—one of the eyewitnesses.

Fergus stabbed a finger at Zach. "And I know you're probably wondering what you've done, marrying a beautiful gal like that. But I am here to reassure you that damn near anyone can be a good husband. All it takes is a little work."

Zach ripped the prescription off his pad and handed it to Fergus. "Is that so?" he asked blandly.

He knew he should have minded this advice from Fergus more than he did, even if his marriage to Sunny was only temporary. And that puzzled Zach, too.

Sunny Carlisle was still a virtual stranger to him. Why should he have cared whether she was happy or not?

"Yes, sirree. Nevertheless, you're going to have to work a little harder if you want to make a go of this marriage. You do want to, don't you, Doc?"

Zach wouldn't mind making love with Sunny, but as for the rest... the idea of being married to anyone at this point made him feel as though he were suffocating. "To tell you the truth, Mr.—"

"Call me 'Fergus.'"

"I'm not all that sure I'm the marrying kind," Zach confessed.

Fergus's affable grin widened. He clapped Zach on the shoulder. "Then it's high time we changed all that. Now, do you want to do something that will make Sunny sweet on you? 'Cause, if so, I've got just the thing."

ZACH WAS STILL mulling over Fergus's suggestion as he locked up the clinic and drove home. Fergus had had a good idea, although a little corny, but Zach didn't know if he wanted to follow through on it. He didn't really need to get more involved with Sunny than he already was, or make their relationship any more intimate or romantic. Besides, Zach mused as he parked his truck in front of her house, got out and started up the walk, did he want her to think he was the kind of guy who could be pushed, coerced and generally led around by the nose?

Zach heard the temperamental banging of kitchen-cupboard doors from halfway up the walk. He found Sunny in the kitchen, scowling as she slid a plate of food into the microwave. "What's got you in a lather?" he asked.

"I don't want to talk about it!"

But she needed to, he thought. When no other information was forthcoming, he shrugged. "Fine. I'll just call the town grapevine and ask for details there." He pivoted toward the phone on the wall, knowing just about anyone would do, since everyone knew everyone else's business in Carlisle.

Sunny caught up with him as he lifted the receiver from the cradle. Her hand tightened on his wrist, forcing the phone back down.

"Don't."

Zach sucked in a silent breath and tolerated the sizzling warmth of her touch. "Then start speaking," he said gruffly.

Sunny's lower lip pushed out petulantly as she dropped first her gaze, then her hand. "I suppose you'll hear about it anyway."

Briefly she told him about the belated bridal shower the ladies had held for her and their mutual gift. Zach tried to hold in his amusement, but the look of righteous indignation on her face sent him over the edge. He laughed until tears streamed from his eyes and he was doubled over at the waist.

"You, in a class on how to be a loving wife?"

"It's not funny! I am not looking forward to this."

"Oh, but I am," he teased.

"Don't think I am going to turn into some mousy little thing who lives and breathes to do your bidding," Sunny warned.

Zach clapped his palm to his chest in a parody of hopefulness. "I can dream, can't I?"

Sunny removed his hand from his chest and forced it back down to his side. "I'm serious, Zach," she stormed. "I am not looking forward to this."

He appreciated the rosy color in her cheeks and the indignant sparkle in her whiskey-colored eyes more than he knew he should. "So don't go through with it," he advised. "Tell them thanks, but no thanks."

Sunny paced away from him, her hips swaying sexily beneath her trim black skirt.

"I can't do that, either."

"Why not?"

Sunny whirled to face him in a drift of flowery perfume. She pushed the red-gold curls from her face with the heel of her hand.

"Because I'd hurt their feelings. They put a lot of thought into that gift."

"The wrong kind of thought." Zach got a plate out and dipped a generous heap of Gertie's mostaccioli casserole on it. "You're setting a dangerous precedent, allowing them to meddle in our lives this way. Furthermore, I don't know how you tolerate the intrusive behavior of our neighbors."

Sunny watched as he added tossed green salad to a bowl, then Italian dressing. "If you are referring to the other morning, you're lucky it wasn't Gramps who walked in on us."

Zach shrugged. Deciding Sunny needed a salad to round out her meal, he dipped some for her, too. "We have a right to behave any way we want in our own home."

"My home," Sunny corrected, taking the salad he handed her. She carried it to the table. "And maybe we do. . . but they also had a point. If you and I are going to stay married, even for a little while, we need to do better, Zach. The other morning we both behaved ridiculously."

"Oh, I don't know." Unable to resist teasing her just a little, he sauntered nearer and gave her the once-over. "I kind of like dressing up—or down, as the case may be—every once in a while."

Sunny's chin set stubbornly as she added a pitcher of freshly brewed iced tea to the center of the table. "Well, I don't like being embarrassed." She waved her arms at him, agitatedly punctuating each and every word she spoke. "And I felt like a fool, being caught in that getup, with my kitchen a mess."

Zach shook his head at her and gave her a censuring glance. "You care too much about what the neighbors think."

"And you don't care enough."

Her words were casually—maybe even gently—spoken, but they hit a nerve. It bothered him, too, but he was not able to change the way he felt. Right now he wanted a wall around his heart. Which was yet another reason he never should have let himself be talked into this temporary marriage.

Silence fell between them as Sunny removed her dinner from the microwave and carried her plate to the table. Zach popped his dinner in and pushed buttons. As he waited for it to heat, he regarded her curiously, realizing she was as much a mystery to him as he was to her. "Why doesn't all this bother you?"

Sunny sat down at the table, spread her napkin on her lap, then waited for him to join her. "Maybe because I know what it's like to have the shoe on the other foot."

Zach stared at her. "You mean you were ostracized for something else?"

"No, silly," she said as the microwave buzzer sounded. "I mean I didn't always live here."

Zach carried his plate over and joined her at the table. "Where did you live?"

"Various European countries. My parents are both international-law attorneys. They specialize in helping U.S. companies expand their operations overseas and are generally involved in the setup and so on. It's difficult, demanding work."

"So you moved around a lot as a kid."

"At least once a year. Sometimes more."

"That sounds exciting."

Sunny stared down at her half-eaten casserole. "I suppose it had its advantages," she said carefully.

Zach read between the lines. "But you didn't see what those advantages were at the time, did you?" he said softly.

Again she was silent. Zach could tell he was probing too fast and hard. He would have to back off. At least a little. He tried again. "Aren't you bored living in a small mountain community?"

Sunny shook her head, her love of her surroundings shining through. "I love the warmth and the sense of community here in Carlisle."

"Is that the only reason you stay? For family?"

"My grandfather needs me to help run his business," she said.

"Surely he could hire a plant manager."

"He doesn't have to, not when he has family." Sunny got up and retrieved the peach cobbler Matilda had baked for them. "Do you want ice cream with this?" she asked.

Zach knew exactly what his new bride was doing. "Waiting on me, or just trying to change the subject?" he drawled.

Sunny flushed. She stacked two desert plates on top of the ice cream, picked up the cobbler with her other hand and carried it all to the table. "I don't see you volunteering much about yourself," she asserted as she sat down again.

"That's because your life sounds like more fun," Zach said as he finished his dinner and helped himself to dessert. "So, tell me more about this class. What are you going to learn?"

Sunny toyed with the cobbler on her plate. "I don't know yet."

Leaning close, Zach noticed the faint blush of freckles across her nose. "Why would they think you need it?"

Sunny rolled her eyes and dropped her fork. "You have to ask after those getups they caught us in?"

Zach grinned at the exasperation in her tone. He knew how much the locals loved Sunny. This gift was something special. Obviously they had given it to her for a reason. "You haven't answered my question," he teased.

"They know I love to learn."

"And how do they know that?"

She drew a deep breath and looked him straight in the eye. "Because I delayed taking over my grandfather's company for two years, until I had gone back to school and earned an M.B.A."

"You didn't feel comfortable taking it over with just him to guide you?"

"No. I'm the kind of person who likes to be well versed in whatever subject I tackle before I dive into it."

"Hmm...I'm just the opposite. I tackle something first, then read the directions only if I can't figure it out on my own."

"I figured as much."

"So how long is this class going to take?" Zach didn't want it to take up too much of her time, since she already seemed quite busy at the factory. Besides, the house was lonely without her.

"I have five lessons and a graduation party, spread out over the next couple of weeks. Each class is supposed to be an hour or so in length."

"You're going alone?" If it was down the mountain somewhere, maybe he could drive her.

"No. Five other women have signed up to take it, too."

"Don't they already know how to be loving wives?"

"They hope to learn something. And so do I," she said firmly.

"To use on me?" Zach asked hopefully.

"No way." Sunny rose gracefully and carried her dishes to the sink. "I signed up to learn something that will help me when I really give my heart to someone and get married."

That wasn't the welcome prospect it should have been, Zach thought as he began to take care of his own dinner dishes. Instead of feeling relieved to know that she one day intended to end this farce of a marriage to him, as promised, he felt a flash of jealousy. Determinedly he pushed the feeling away. What she did was no business of his. He'd been hurt to the quick when Lori had died; his pain had intensified when he'd become involved with Melody; he wasn't going to open himself up to that kind of pain again. Not for Sunny, not for anyone.

"IS EVERYONE ready for lesson number one?" the instructor asked.

As ready as I'll ever be, Sunny thought, settling into a folding chair in the community church basement. Booklets stamped *How to be a Loving Wife* were passed out. Sunny stared at the cover, taking in the photo of a bride being scooped up in her husband's arms. If only married life were that simple, she thought wistfully. She sighed. Life with Zach was much more complicated than she had anticipated.

"Sunny, what did you and your husband have for dinner tonight?"

Sunny offered a mortified smile. "Casserole that was brought to us over the weekend."

"Describe how the table was set, what your centerpiece was and any special touches you added, like sprigs of mint."

Sunny shrugged. "I didn't set the table. We took what we needed to the table with us. And each did our own dishes afterward."

A gasp of dismay was uttered by the entire group. Sunny looked at them. "I am not waiting on him hand and foot."

"Then how do you expect him to ever want to wait on you?" the instructor asked gently.

"I don't!" Sunny said, flushing all the more as she recalled Zach bringing her the supper tray up to her room the first night they were married. She had yet to pay him back for his thoughtfulness. And that made her feel guilty.

"One kindness begets another, Sunny," the instructor said sternly. "Now, please, try to keep an open mind...."

ZACH AWOKE the next morning to the delicious smells of bacon and hot coffee. He shifted onto his stomach, his arms and legs hanging off the rollaway bed, and buried his face in the pillow. No doubt Sunny had made just enough for herself again. "She sure knows how to torture a man," he grumbled to himself.

"I beg your pardon?"

Zach rolled over with a start. Sunny was standing in the doorway with a tray in her hands. He shook his head to clear it, sure he must be dreaming. "Breakfast in bed?"

"Well, I'm in a hurry. I have to get to the office, and you weren't up yet," Sunny explained. She marched in as crisply as her fuzzy bunny slippers would allow.

Zach caught a drift of her perfume—it was lemony this morning—as she bent to help him put a pillow behind his head and settle the tray on his lap. She looked very sexy in a business suit. "Did something happen I'm not aware of?" he asked.

"If you think this is payment for staying out half the night, you're wrong," she said.

Was that a tinge of jealousy in her voice? "I was over at the clinic, reading files. Now that people are coming to see me, I figured I should be more up on patient history."

"Sure you just didn't want to avoid seeing me?"

Zach shrugged, aware she was looking at his bare chest and the sheet that came *almost* to his waist. He knew what she was thinking: he wasn't wearing much. Considering the way his body was reacting to her nearness, Zach shared her wish that he had on more than his glen-plaid boxer shorts. He yanked the sheet up to cover his navel and ran his hands through his hair. "I wasn't sure what kind of mood you'd be in after you took that class, so I thought I'd make myself scarce."

"As you can see, Zach, my mood is fine."

That was a question open for debate. She was serving him breakfast in bed, but she didn't look happy about it. "So why are you waiting on me hand and foot all of a sudden?" And why did she look so damn cuddly and kissable, even in her ultraconservative business attire?

"Can't you guess?" Sunny took a small notepad from the pocket of the frilly gingham apron she had tied around her waist. "It's an *assignment.*"

"Oh." Zach's spirits took a nosedive. He had hoped that she had done this out of the goodness of her heart. In retrospect, he could see how irrational that hope was. Sunny didn't believe they were really married any more than he did. She wasn't interested in playing house, either. Never mind having the kind of hot, passionate fling with him that he wanted to have with her.

"So?" Sunny stood poised with her pencil over the pad. She eyed him expectantly.

Zach nudged his sheet a little higher, so it rested against his ribs. He leaned back against the pillow and the wall casually. "So what?"

Color stealing into her cheeks, Sunny blew out an exasperated breath. "Make some inane comment about what I've just served you, Zach."

He looked down at the tray and couldn't help but be pleased by what he saw. The French toast was golden brown, perfectly prepared and dusted with confectioner's sugar. The bacon was crisp, the orange juice chilled, the coffee black, strong and steaming. She had even put a flower from her garden out back in a vase. "Breakfast looks wonderful, Sunny," he said softly, meaning it.

"'Breakfast...looks...wonderful...Sunny,'" she murmured as she wrote. Finished, she gazed at him and offered an officious smile.

"Now what are you doing?" he asked dryly.

"Making notes, of course, for my report back to the class. I found out last night that every lesson has a homework assignment. We all have to do them and report back to the class on the results of our assignment."

Now, this, Zach thought, sounded like trouble. "What other kind of assignments are you going to be asked to do?"

Sunny looked bewildered. "I don't know."

"Give me a hint." Zach cut into his French toast.

"I wish I could, but I truly don't have a clue. Our instructor wants to surprise us. Now, do you have any other comments to make about breakfast?"

"For you to write down?" he asked, feeling a wave of orneriness coming on.

"Yes," she said primly, her pen at the ready.

"Well, the food is delicious."

"'The . . . food . . . is . . . delicious. . . .'"

"But it doesn't look—"

"'Doesn't look—'" Sunny was so busy writing she didn't see him get out of bed.

"Nearly as delicious as you," Zach said, taking her into his arms, so that her hands and the notepad were trapped between them. She smelled and felt as delicious as she appeared.

"Zach—" Sunny's soft voice carried a warning, as did her stiff, unrelenting posture.

"Hmm?" he asked. Taking advantage of her inability to move, he feathered light kisses down her nape.

"Don't." She shifted against him restlessly, her breath hitching in her chest.

Zach's heart started a slow, heavy beat as he studied her upturned face. "Why? Going to put this in your report, too, Sunny?" he asked, hoping he could make her understand how foolish and invasive of their privacy this class was.

Sunny drew an indignant breath and stomped on his bare foot with her bunny slipper. He let her go. Grinning, he got back into bed. Sunny in a temper was something to see.

"You think I won't write this down, don't you?" she said sweetly.

"Which part? Where I kissed your neck or you stomped on my foot?"

"I'm writing them *both* down."

Oh, no. Zach could feel another lecture from a well-meaning patient coming on. "Both?" he croaked unhappily.

"Of course my stomping on your foot was done accidentally—" Sunny continued blithely.

Like hell it was, Zach thought. Not about to let her know she was getting to him, he kept his face expressionless. "Accidentally on purpose, you mean," he corrected.

"But—" Sunny ignored him and kept writing furiously "—it was enough to spoil the mood." Finished, she grinned victoriously. "There. I completed my assignment. It didn't work, despite my very best efforts, which you, Zach, can attest to if asked. And our marriage is still doomed! Perfect!"

Zach shook his head. "You want to fail?"

"Of course," Sunny said smugly, closing her notebook with a snap. "Don't you?"

ZACH WAS STILL asking himself that question as he let himself into the clinic. He knew he should want to fail at this marriage business. Failing at it would give him and Sunny both an easy out. But failing—at anything—went against his grain. He didn't like playing games. Whereas like a chameleon, Sunny excelled at them. He wondered why she would put up with this, then determined he would find out.

In the meantime, it wouldn't hurt to keep her off her guard, Zach thought. She'd caught him by surprise, serving him breakfast in bed. He could do the same, too. Put her in a position where she didn't know what to think, either. Besides, if she could tell everyone he had sent her flowers, maybe the nosy townsfolk would get the idea that things between Sunny and him were fine and they would stop pushing them to become the perfect newlywed couple. It was worth a try anyway, Zach thought.

He reached for the phone book on his desk and thumbed through the Yellow Pages. There were three florists in the vicinity. He was trying to decide which one to use, when the door to his office banged open. Sunny's grandfather stood in the portal. As usual, he was dressed in his fishing apparel.

"I ought to shoot you on sight," Augustus Carlisle said.

"What for this time?" Zach asked.

"Breaking my granddaughter's heart—that's what!"

Zach frowned. "What are you talking about?"

Augustus shook his finger at Zach. "She's over at the factory right now, locked in her office, and she won't come out, and all on account of you."

"Did she say what I'd done?" Zach asked curiously as he folded his hands behind his head. No doubt about it. Sunny was a woman who was full of surprises.

"No. But it was clear to the women who work with her that it had something to do with that class on marriage they're all taking down at the church." Augustus peered at him suspiciously. "One of them said she mighta been trying out some sort of lesson on you. Did she?"

"I think that's a private matter, best left between Sunny and me," Zach said calmly.

Augustus sent a fulminating glance at Zach, then just as abruptly became more reasonable. "I understand that Fergus was over here yesterday, offering you some advice.''

Zach took his feet off the edge of his desk and put them back on the floor. ''He told me to send her flowers.''

''And did you do it?'' Gramps pressed.

''No.'' Not then, Zach added, but right now he had been about to order some. And not because Fergus had told him to do so.

''So what stopped you?''

Zach shrugged. ''Unlike Sunny, I don't like to be told what to do,'' he said emphatically. ''*Especially* in my private life.''

Augustus's eyes narrowed to slits. ''You know, I should have taken my shotgun to you while I had the chance. But for whatever reason my granddaughter has taken a shine to you, and the two of you are married, so I won't.''

''Gee, thanks,'' Zach said sarcastically.

''I will, however, insist you do something to cheer her up. We can't run a business if she is locked in her office.''

Then maybe you should take that up with Sunny, Zach thought as the outer door to the reception area opened. Zach saw a mother with twin babies troop in. Deciding the only way to get rid of Augustus Carlisle was to agree with him, he said impatiently, ''Look, I'll order flowers and give them to her this evening.''

Augustus assessed Zach with a frown. ''You'd better do it right, son,'' he warned.

Zach gave Augustus a flip look. ''Is there any other way?''

Augustus scowled. "In the meantime, I have something to discuss with you. Do you still want to give me a physical?"

"Yes."

"Then let's get down to it."

Augustus was already unzipping his fishing vest. Zach led the way to an examining room. The next twenty minutes were spent obtaining a complete medical history, the fifteen after that doing an exam.

"So how am I?" Augustus asked when Zach had finished listening to his heart and lungs.

"On the surface, everything's fine, but something has to be causing these chest pains you've been having."

"How do you know I'm still having pains?"

"I know because you're here, asking me to examine you. If you weren't, you'd likely put it off another month or two." Augustus said nothing to disagree. "So when were the last ones?" Zach asked.

"Last night, when I got back from the stream. I was cleaning some fish for dinner and the pain went from here—" Augustus pointed to his chest "—all the way down my left arm into my hand."

"Sounds scary," Zach said.

"It was. *Is.*"

"How long did the pains last?"

"Only about five or ten minutes. They quit after I went over and sat down."

"What about the fish?"

"I put it away, to finish up later. I figured maybe I'd overdone things, so I went to bed early. I felt a lot better when I got up this morning."

"But you're scared the pains will come back."

Augustus nodded grimly. "That's why I'm here. What do you think it could be? Angina?"

"It's possible. To say for sure, we'd need to admit you to a hospital and do a complete series of tests."

Augustus vetoed that. "I don't want Sunny upset."

"We can do this without her knowing," Zach said calmly.

Augustus hesitated. "You promise you won't breathe a word of this to my granddaughter?" Zach nodded. "Okay, then do it," Augustus said.

Zack picked up the phone and began to make arrangements. Half an hour later, it was all set. Augustus would have the necessary tests done at a hospital in Knoxville, the following week. A physician friend of Zach's would personally oversee Augustus's care. Sunny would never know anything, at least while the tests were being done. Afterward, when a diagnosis was made, Zach would use every means at his disposal to persuade Augustus to tell Sunny what was going on.

Zach spent the day seeing a steady stream of patients. By the time five o'clock rolled around, he was pleasantly tired. He hadn't felt such a sense of satisfaction since arriving in Carlisle, he thought, as he took off his lab coat and loosened his tie. The only thing he hadn't done was call the florist. But he figured they had to have something in stock. When he reached the door to the florist, he swore softly in frustration. A big Closed sign hung on the door. Zach peered inside. The lights were off. The building appeared empty. Now what? he wondered.

It was too late in the day to order from the two other florists on the mountain, and they were probably closed up, too.

Augustus drove up in his big black Cadillac sedan. He rolled down a window on the passenger side. "I figured you'd forget," he said.

"I didn't realize the florist closed so early." Even as Zach said it, he knew it was a lame excuse. He should've taken care of this earlier.

"Yeah, well, I owe you a favor anyway." Augustus thrust a large ribbon-wrapped box at Zach. "Sunny's favorite—yellow roses." He rolled up his window and roared off.

Zach went back to his brand-new pickup truck and drove home. Sunny was dropped off right after him. She got out of Matilda's car, briefcase in hand, then waved as Matilda drove off. She looked tired and frazzled after a day at the office. She saw the florist's box and instantly became wary. Zach suddenly felt as tongue-tied as any kid. Wordlessly he handed the box to her.

"Where did this come from?" she asked, in a voice that sounded oddly rusty.

You don't want to know, he thought guiltily, and wished like hell he had followed through on his initial instincts and done this himself early that morning. But he hadn't, so he would just have to make the best of it. "Open it and see," he said.

Sunny put down her briefcase and struggled with the ribbon. She gasped as she pried off the lid and saw the two-dozen roses inside. "Oh, Zach," she said, her voice choking up even more. She looked up at him, eyes glistening. "Yellow roses are my absolute favorite! How did you know?"

Zach shrugged, feeling even guiltier. "Your grandfather." And that was true, he reassured himself. There was no way he wanted Sunny to know how she had really happened to get this beautiful bouquet tonight.

"I'll take them inside and put them in water," she said.

"Want to go out to the diner to eat?"

Again she looked surprised. "Well...I guess we could. Zach, are you sure? Eating out is going to be like being on public display again."

"We don't have anything to hide," he said gruffly. "Besides, maybe it's time people got used to seeing us together." Maybe it was time he and Sunny got used to being together.

"Well, all right, but I want to change into something more comfortable first." Sunny flushed the moment the words were out.

For once Zach passed up the opportunity to put a sexy twist on her utterance. He nodded. "I'll go out and get your mail for you."

He was surprised to find his own mail in the box, as well. He hadn't changed any of his addresses. Leave it to Fergus to go ahead and do it anyway, Zach thought.

Minutes later, Sunny bounded down the stairs in jeans, sneakers and a white long-sleeve T-shirt. She had a pretty blue sweater tied around her neck, to ward off the chill of the spring evening. She had taken her hair down, and it fell over her shoulders in a riot of glorious red-gold curls. Irritated to find his heart slamming against his ribs, Zach stood and offered her a casual smile. "Ready to go?"

"Yep. I just want to run the casserole dish over to Matilda before we go, okay? You can wait for me in your truck. And grab up my mail, will you? I want to read it on the way to the diner."

"Pretty good at giving orders, aren't you?"

"You could say that!" Sunny bounded out the kitchen. The back door slammed.

Zach locked up and went out the front. He slid behind the wheel and waited. To his relief, she wasn't long in returning. To his dismay, she no longer looked the least bit happy. In fact, he thought as she neared, there was a decidedly militant edge to her posture. "What happened?" he asked as she climbed in stiffly beside him.

Sunny swiveled to face him. "What do you think happened?" she shot back, so angry she was trembling. "I know the truth about the flowers, Zach!"

Chapter Five

Roses in the Fire

"Zach, how could you?" Sunny stormed.

He braced one hand on the steering wheel and cautioned her with the other. "Whoa, now. Just hold on. It wasn't my idea."

Sunny lifted a brow skeptically, recalling, Zach supposed, just how difficult it was to get him to do anything against his will. "Well, it was and it wasn't," he amended hastily. "I was going to send you flowers—"

"Because Fergus told you to send them," Sunny declared sagely.

Zach paused. "You know about that, too?"

"Aunt Gertie can't keep her mouth shut—never could. And what do you mean do I know about that, too? What else should I know?"

Zach swore and said nothing. He was in up to his neck now.

"Zach, you better tell me. If I find out any other way—" Sunny warned, eyes flashing.

Zach knew there would be hell to pay. "I got the flowers from your grandfather to give to you."

"So they weren't from you after all." Sunny's expression saddened even more.

"No."

"So why did you pretend they were?" she asked, visibly upset.

"Because sometimes honesty isn't the best policy."

"Oh, really." Sunny surveyed him with glacial cool.

Zach regarded her in exasperation. "Haven't you ever kept something—some bit of information—to yourself because you knew it would hurt the other person?"

His words struck a nerve. She had done just that the day she'd met Zach, in not admitting up-front that she knew who he was, which made her as guilty as he was.

"Besides, I didn't want to hurt your feelings, and you had already assumed that the flowers were from me before I got a word in edgewise, so I went along with it."

Just when Zach thought he was getting through to Sunny, she abruptly got angrier.

She shook her head at him and studied him grimly. "I can't believe it. I can't believe my past is repeating itself this way!" She slammed out of the truck.

Zach vaulted out after her and followed her halfway up the drive. "What are you talking about?"

Sunny stopped so suddenly their bodies nearly collided. She pivoted to face him. "My parents did the same thing to me." New color swept into her cheeks. "They had my nanny or their secretaries buy presents for me because they could never remember, or make the time, to go shopping themselves."

"They *told* you this?" Zach was shocked.

"No, of course not," she said, her eyes gleaming with suppressed hurt. "But I caught on eventually. Kids have a way of sensing things."

Zach couldn't imagine growing up like that. His parents had always taken special care choosing gifts and he had learned to do the same. Which made what he had done to Sunny even worse. There was only one remedy for this. He would have to find some way of doing something special for her... all on his own.

Zach took her hand and led her over to the front porch. "What happened when they realized you knew what was going on?"

"They stopped pretending and gave me money, instead, to spend as I chose." Sunny sat down on the steps.

Zach followed suit and took her into the curve of his arm. "Did that make it easier? Or worse?"

"A little of both, I suppose." She rested her head on his shoulder. "It was a relief knowing I didn't have to pretend they'd put any thought into anything. But it hurt knowing they couldn't spare the time."

"I'm sorry," Zach said. Sorry he'd taken the easy way out with the flowers.

Sunny straightened and shook off his sympathy, her expression determined. "I shouldn't complain. My parents are good people and they work very hard. If they'd had less-demanding jobs, maybe it would have been different for me."

And maybe it wouldn't have, Zach thought. Maybe this was the key to Sunny's heart and soul, the reason she not only tolerated, but seemed to relish, the community's interference in their lives. "Tell me how it was," he encouraged softly, lifting her chin to his, wanting to know more about what had caused the glimmer of hurt in her eyes.

She looked deep into his eyes. "What do you want to know?"

"Were you an only child?"

Sunny nodded, still holding his gaze.

"You said you had a nanny," Zach continued softly, covering both her hands with one of his.

"A succession of them, actually, from the time I was born." She tightly enmeshed her fingers with his, then went back to resting her head on his shoulder.

"Why more than one?" Zach used his free hand to stroke her hair. It felt like silk beneath his fingertips.

Sunny snuggled closer. "We moved around a lot. You name it, I've lived there. They could never find a governess willing to travel around with us for more than a year or so at a time, so when one left, another came in to replace her."

"How long did that continue?" he asked quietly.

"Until I was twelve. Then I went to boarding school in Switzerland."

"Where did you go to college?" Zach asked, liking the way she felt in the curve of his arm.

"Where my mother went for undergrad, Smith. Wharton School of Business, for my M.B.A."

"Prestigious schools," he commented, impressed. "Your parents must be very proud of you."

Sunny shrugged. Lifting her head, she drew back again. "I really don't want to talk about this any longer."

He could see the walls around her heart going up again. It surprised him how much he wanted to tear them down. Usually he took his cues from other people. If they didn't want to talk, he didn't push it. But with Sunny, he couldn't help it; he had to be closer. "Why not?" he asked.

His question was met with silence. With every second that passed, Zach could feel her drifting further away from him. He wanted desperately to keep her near, so he tried once more. "What's your relationship with your parents like these days?"

"I'm not close to them, okay? Now, can we just leave it at that?" she asked impatiently, aware she was trembling with unresolved emotion.

Zach's expression was concerned. "On one condition," he drawled, as the two of them squared off.

Sunny lifted her chin contentiously. "What condition?"

He smiled and took her hand in his. Time to enact part two of figuring out what made his new wife tick. "That you have dinner with me tonight, just as we planned."

"THIS ISN'T going to work!" Sunny said outside the diner. She didn't even know why she had agreed to come here with him, after the flower fiasco, except that dining out would be much less intimate than eating at home.

"Sure it'll work. All we have to do is pretend to be cooing lovebirds and word will get out that we don't need any more help in the romance department. Everyone will back off. Then we won't have any more problems like the one we had today with the flowers," Zach said.

He was doing it again, Sunny thought. Realizing intuitively where she was vulnerable, then attempting to somehow attend to all her hurts, past and present. Because he was a healer by profession? Or because there was something special between them? She only knew for sure that the more he learned, the closer she felt to him. If they kept on this path she was going to have a hard time resisting him when he did make his move for her. And she felt sure that it would be very soon. Sunny backed up slightly on the sidewalk. "I'm no good at acting."

"So don't act," Zach said with a shrug. "Just be nice and remember the way you looked and felt when I kissed you the other night."

That was the problem, Sunny thought. She couldn't get those kisses out of her mind!

"Okay, so wing it," Zach advised cheerfully under his breath.

"Better." That matter settled, she breezed through the diner doors.

Rhonda-Faye looked up from behind the counter. Sunny knew, from the flushed, yet pale, color in her friend's face that something was wrong. She slipped onto a stool in front of Rhonda-Faye. "You feeling okay?"

Rhonda-Faye nodded. "Just a little backache—that's all."

Zach sat down beside Sunny in a drift of wintry cologne. Suddenly he was all physician. "Any contractions?" he asked.

"No. Besides, I'm not due for another week, Doc."

Zach quirked a brow. "Babies have been known to come early."

Rhonda-Faye rubbed at her lower back. "Truth to tell, I wouldn't mind having the birth over with, but I'm not in labor, not yet anyway."

"Think George is going to do any better this time?" Sunny asked, recalling how excited Rhonda-Faye's husband tended to be at times like this.

Rhonda-Faye shook her head. "Heaven only knows. Though he's promised me this time he is going to stay calm."

Zach frowned. "Isn't this your fourth child?"

"Yes, and you'd think George would be used to the whole birth process by now," Rhonda-Faye drawled affectionately. "But you never know."

Sunny grinned. If Zach was around for the birthing of the baby, he was in for a real surprise. "You seem to need to get off your feet anyway," Sunny said. "Why don't you go on home and let me take over tonight?"

"What do you know about running a diner?" Zach interrupted.

Sunny gave him an incensed look. "I've helped out before. Haven't I, Rhonda-Faye?"

"You saved my life last Labor Day weekend, when two of my high schoolers came down with chicken pox at the same time. But really—the two of you being newlyweds and all—I couldn't impose."

"Sure you can," Zach said genially. "You go home and rest and Sunny and I will take over here. I'm sure we can handle it."

Rhonda-Faye squeezed Zach's arm and leaned over and gave Sunny a hug. "I'll pay you back," she promised. With a grateful nod at them both, she grabbed her sweater and slipped out the back door.

"Mighty sweet of you," Zach said, stepping behind the diner counter.

Sunny tied on an apron as two families with young children walked in. "You ain't seen nothing yet." She met Zach's eyes, stunned at the easy way she and he had slipped into couple mode. "You want to take the orders, while I fill the plates?"

Zach grinned. "Only if you promise not to break any over my head."

"Very funny. The booster chairs are in the back."

The next few minutes were a flurry of activity. Sunny was surprised to see that Zach was no novice when it came to waiting tables. He got the two families situated and took their orders in a jiff.

Circling back around to the grill, he said, "Two burger platters, cremated, extra grass. Both kids want short stacks and Grade A and their mom insists on side dishes of whatever fruit we've got to go with it."

Sunny poured silver dollar-size puddles of pancake batter onto one end of the griddle, then added two hamburgers to the other. "Applesauce and milk are in the fridge."

He whisked over to give the family their drinks, the kids their dishes of fruit, then swaggered back to Sunny's side, looking as at home in an apron as he did in a white lab coat.

"We're running a little low on draw one," Zach reported softly. "Harlan down at the end is going to be wanting more." His breath brushed her hair as he watched her slide perfectly made pancakes onto two kid-size platters, then reach over and flip the sizzling burgers.

"Harlan always wants more coffee," Sunny said. "He works the night shift at the factory." She handed the kiddie platters over to Zach, unable to help but be both pleased and surprised at the eager way he had pitched in. She never would've expected it of him. But then, maybe she just hadn't given him a chance. She had to admit the skunk incident had gotten them off on the wrong foot. And that in turn made her wonder what their relationship would have been like if they had met some other way.

The bell over the door tinkled as another group of customers walked in, pulling Sunny from her trance. Telling herself sternly that this was no time to start getting warm, fuzzy feelings about her new husband, she forced herself to snap out of it and said, "The coffee is down below the coffeemaker."

"No problem," Zach said.

He chucked her under the chin, then bent to press a light, fleeting kiss on her lips. Her mouth was still tingling as he drew back.

Eyes still holding hers, he said softly, "I'll get the fire going under it right away."

The coffee wasn't the only thing with a fire under it, Sunny thought with a rueful grin, as she continued to run the grill while Zach waited tables.

When closing time rolled around, she was pleasantly exhausted. Zach pulled the shades, switched off the outside lights and locked the door, as Sunny dished up the last of the day's chili, two generous salads and warmed a slab of Rhonda-Faye's homemade sourdough bread. She settled in a booth in the back, while Zach dimmed the lights and fed quarters into the jukebox. Seconds later, the lively sound of Robben

Ford and The Blue Line singing "Start It Up" filled the room.

The music Zach had played made her want to get up and dance. She was tapping her foot to the jazzy rhythm as he brought two frosty mugs of root beer to the table and set them down.

Before she knew what he was doing, he had pulled her up out of the booth, and they were jitterbugging to the bluesy beat. Eyes locked, bodies moving in synch, they spun their way through the song.

Breathlessly they returned to the booth.

"Thanks for helping out," Sunny said, as she slid in opposite him. "I'm sure Rhonda-Faye appreciated it."

Zach nudged her foot with his. "What about you?"

"Fishing for a compliment?" she teased.

"More like trying to find out if you're still mad at me over the flower business."

"Ah, yes, the yellow roses." She squeezed his hand. "What do you say we go home and throw them in the trash and start over, as friends this time?"

Sunny knew she wanted to give him a second chance. "But if we're going back to square one, we don't know very much about each other," she said cautiously, aware her heart was thundering against her ribs.

He focused on the turbulence in her eyes. "What do you want to know?"

Everything, she thought. Sunny smiled. "Have you ever been tied to a community before?"

He pinned her with a look. "I have a fondness for Murfreesboro, where I grew up, and Nashville—because I went to med school and did my residency there—but I don't particularly need to live in either place to be happy, if that's what you're asking," he said.

It was. Sunny suppressed her relief. "What about your romantic past? Have you ever been deeply involved?"

He nodded grimly. "Like you, I was engaged once."

Compassion welled up inside her. "What happened?"

"I knew from the beginning that Melody was close to her family. In fact, her abiding love for them was one of the things that attracted me to her. What I didn't realize until after we became engaged was how totally dependent she was on them. Everything that happened in our life together was somehow dictated by her family. She couldn't buy groceries without consulting her mother first. Needless to say, planning the wedding was a nightmare, finding a place to live even worse. I realized I couldn't live that way. I needed a wife who would put our relationship first, a woman who would make our marriage a priority and not just a convenience. With Melody, it was never going to be like that, so we broke it off."

Sunny knew firsthand how devastating it was to end an engagement, even when you were sure you had no choice. "That must have been a difficult time for you," she said sympathetically.

Zach nodded. "My own parents understood, of course. Hers didn't."

Sunny grinned. "Another sign you weren't meant to be together, I guess." She lifted the mug of root beer to her lips. "I think I'm going to like being friends," she said softly. She certainly understood him a lot better.

"Me, too," Zach said quietly. He leaned back against the booth and studied her.

Sunny knew he was thinking about kissing her again. Unbidden, the image of Zach as he had been that morning came to mind. Wearing nothing but his glen-plaid boxer shorts, his long, strong body stretched out sexily on his uncomfortably small bed. Just looking at him had made her heart pound and her mouth go dry. When he'd kissed her, her senses had gone into an uproar. They were still topsy-turvy every time she was near him.

As for her fantasies, Sunny knew she didn't need to be asleep to dream of what it would be like to be led down that forbidden path and be made love to by Zach.

Sunny drew a tranquilizing breath. With effort, she forced herself to put her daydreams aside and concentrate on the reality of the situation, which was that he didn't love her. And without love, any passion they shared would be meaningless.

She had waited too long to indulge in meaningless sex—with anyone, even her husband. She cleared her throat, determined to keep them on the right track. "Zach—"

"I know."

He touched her face with the palm of his hand, and it was all she could do not to lean into the incredible warmth and gentleness of his caress.

"Friends," he said, keeping his eyes locked on hers. "For now."

The way things were going, Sunny wondered how long they would stay that way. Because despite their efforts to keep theirs a marriage in name only, they were getting closer to making love every moment they were together.

EXHAUSTED FROM her impromptu stint at the diner, Sunny was sound asleep when the telephone rang. Groggily she pulled the receiver into bed with her and mumbled a sleepy hello. "Sunny? It's George! Get Zach on the line! Quick!"

"Hold on." Recognizing the panic in George's voice, she put the receiver down and stumbled into Zach's room across the hall.

Hand clamped to the smooth, warm skin of his muscular shoulder, she shook him out of what appeared to be a sound sleep. "Zach, wake up! Rhonda-Faye's husband is on the phone."

"Thanks, Sunny." Clad only in his boxer shorts, he shot out of bed and moved across the hall. "George, what is it?" He listened intently, then said, "Calm down. Everything is going to be fine. Just get Rhonda-Faye in the car...no, don't bother to get her dressed...and meet me at the clinic as soon as you can. I'll be there in five minutes. Bye."

"Rhonda-Faye is in labor?"

Zach nodded, already striding back across the hall to retrieve his pants. "Apparently her water broke about fifteen minutes ago. The contractions have been going on ever since. George says they are about a minute and a half apart."

"A minute and a half!"

"Yeah, I know. At that rate, they'll never make it down the mountain to the hospital. Looks like I may have to deliver her baby in the clinic." Zach tugged his zipper up, slid his feet into his Topsiders and pulled on a shirt.

Sunny grabbed the clothes she'd worn earlier and slipped on her shoes. "You'll need help." Her clothing bundled in her arm, she raced down the stairs after him. "I'm going with you."

SUNNY DRESSED in the pickup on the way over. They had just opened up the clinic when George pulled up in his Suburban. "Where's Rhonda-Faye?" Sunny asked, since George appeared to be alone.

"Maybe lying down in back?" Zach suggested with a shrug, already circling around to help.

George grabbed a suitcase and hopped out. He was red in the face and completely out of breath. "I got here as soon as I could!" he yelled.

"You did fine," Zach said. He peered into the middle seat. It was also empty. "Where's Rhonda-Faye?"

George looked inside the vehicle, then back at Zach. His expression was panicked. "Oh, my God—"

"You forgot to bring her?" Zach guessed.

George nodded. "I was in such a hurry to get here—"

"Calm down, George," Sunny said.

"It's going to be fine," Zach reassured him. "You drive back and get her and Sunny and I will go into the clinic and call Rhonda-Faye to let her know you're on your way."

George nodded, still looking completely in a dither. "Right." He put the suitcase back in the car, climbed behind the wheel and took off.

"The way George is acting, you'd think he was a first-time father," Zach mused, swiftly unlocking the clinic door.

Sunny grinned. "Rhonda-Faye says she gets more worried about him than delivering the baby."

Zach chuckled and shook his head as he headed for the phone. "Rhonda-Faye? Doc Grainger here. George is on his way back to get you. How are you doing? Every minute and fifteen seconds now, hmm? How long are the contractions lasting? Three minutes. Yeah, I agree—it'd be ridiculous to try to make the trip to the hospital at this point. No problem. Sunny's here with me, so she can help handle George. I'll see you in a few minutes." Zach hung up. "Looks like we're going to deliver a baby."

While Sunny kept an eye out for George and Rhonda-Faye, Zach spread out the sterile sheets and brought out the emergency incubator. Sunny gasped as the Suburban pulled up. "Zach, Rhonda-Faye is driving!"

Zach rushed out with her. George was sitting in the passenger seat beside his wife, a bloody cloth pressed to his head.

"He fell!" Rhonda-Faye said.

"I was running up the front steps to get her," George explained through gritted teeth.

Zach helped Rhonda-Faye step down from behind the wheel. Perspiration matted the hair on her forehead. She was pale and trembling. "Ohhhhhh," she moaned, doubling over as another contraction hit her.

"Rhonda-Faye, honey?" George said, sounding even more panicked as he stepped down, too.

"Zach's got her," Sunny said. She wrapped a steadying arm about his burly waist. "Let's just get you both inside."

NO SOONER were they both inside than Rhonda-Faye let out a yelp. "The baby's coming!"

"Now?" George said, looking as if he were going to faint.

Sunny pushed him into one examining room, while Zach helped Rhonda-Faye into the other. There was another scream from Rhonda-Faye. George went even paler. Sunny guided him to the examining table. "Lie down before you fall down, George."

He groaned, even as he complied. "Rhonda-Faye—"

"Zach's got her. I'm sure they're doing fine." Struggling to recall what first aid she could, Sunny removed the bloody cloth from George's temple. The bleeding had stopped, but it was clear from the depth of the cut that he was going to need stitches.

She reached for a packet of sterile gauze and ripped it open. "I'm going to put a bandage on your head and then I'm going to go in and see if Zach needs any help. Okay?"

"Okay."

"You just stay here until Zach can get to you."

Hurriedly Sunny covered the gash on George's forehead. She patted his arm reassuringly, then dashed into the other examining room just as Rhonda-Faye let out another strangled sound. A sterile surgical gown tossed on over his clothes, Zach was sitting on a stool in front of Rhonda-Faye.

"Now," Zach said calmly, "one more push. C'mon, Rhonda-Faye. You're doing fine. Help me out here. Push...."

Rhonda-Faye bore down with all her might. The next thing Sunny knew Zach was holding a new baby in his hands. Sunny's eyes filled with tears as the baby let out a healthy squall of outrage.

"It's a girl, Rhonda-Faye," Zach said, laying the feisty newborn on the sterile cloth draped across her mother's stomach.

"Oh, she's beautiful," Rhonda-Faye gasped, gathering her close.

"That she is," Sunny agreed emotionally, as Zach swiftly cut the cord. Sunny grabbed a sterile gown to wrap the baby in, while Zach tended to his patient. "And she'll be even prettier once we get her cleaned up."

"One bath and a set of soft, warm clothes coming up," Zach promised.

"Oh, take her in to let George see first," Rhonda-Faye asked.

Zach smiled at Sunny and nodded his approval.

"Time to go see your daddy," Sunny said. Gently she lifted the baby in her arms. She carried the bundle in to George. He took one look at his beautiful new daughter, then fainted dead away.

"YOU SURE you're doing okay now, George?" Zach asked as he and Sunny escorted the trio out to the Suburban, where a neighbor was waiting to drive the happy family home.

"You mean except for the splitting headache and the six stitches in my temple?" George asked, tongue in cheek. Now that all the excitement was over, he had calmed down swiftly.

"I don't know why he fainted," Rhonda-Faye said. "It's not as if we haven't been through all this before."

"I think it was the way the baby looked," George said. "All that goo she had on her—"

"That was the vernix caseosa," Zach explained. "It covers the skin and protects the baby in the womb." Zach paused. "You were never in the delivery room before?"

"He was afraid he would faint," Rhonda-Faye said, and they all laughed.

"You call me if you have any problems today, and I'll stop by your housc this cvcning to chcck on you all," Zach said.

"Thanks, Doc," Rhonda-Faye said.

"Thank God you were here tonight," George said. "We sure are lucky to have you here."

"I'm glad I was here, too," Zach said.

Zach and Sunny waved as the couple drove off. Together they walked back into the clinic and began to clean up and tidy everything. When they were finished, Zach put a pot of coffee on. They each filled a mug and went outside to sit on the back steps. Five in the morning, the stars and the moon were still visible. Sunny was as charged up as he could ever remember seeing her. Zach was wired, too.

It wasn't supposed to be like this. They weren't supposed to act like two members of a well-rehearsed team. They had signed on for a marriage of convenience with little or no exchange of feelings, yet almost from the moment he'd met her, his emotions had soared out of control. The medical emergency tonight had shown him yet another side of her.

She would, Zach decided, someday make some man a very good marriage partner. The only problem was, he realized uncomfortably, that he didn't want to think of her married to anyone but him.

His feelings puzzled him. After his engagement to Melody had ended, he had sworn never to get involved with a woman who put friends and family ahead of her relationship with him. Yet there he was, getting more and more tied to Sunny with every second that passed, knowing all the while that she cared every bit as much about the opinions, needs and wants of her family and friends as Melody had. Knowing that, he should have been running as fast and as far away as he could, but he didn't want to lose or halt what had begun between them.

"Is that the first time you've ever seen a baby born?" he asked. She was sitting so close to him he could feel her body heat.

"Yes. It was amazing, wasn't it?" As Sunny turned partway to face him, she nudged his muscular thigh with her knee. Her eyes were bright with wonder. "I mean, you always hear about the miracle of birth and all that, but to actually see it, be a part of it..." Aware she was rambling, Sunny stopped. Aware her knee was touching him, she pulled back.

Zach didn't want them to stop touching. He smiled at her and linked hands so that their fingers were intertwined. It was all he could do not to pull her into his arms and make love with her then and there. "I feel the same way," he admitted huskily. "Life is very precious." Drawing a breath, he gazed at the ever-lightening sky overhead. "I don't think any of us ever realize how much so except for times like this, when we're witness to a new life or—" Zach blinked and his voice thickened revealingly as pain exploded deep inside him "—we see one taken away."

"It must be hard for you when a patient dies," she said softly.

Zach nodded. He pushed the difficult memories away. "Losing someone close to you is hard on everyone," he said huskily. But he didn't want to talk about that, he thought as he wrapped an arm affectionately about her shoulders, squeezed and pressed a kiss into the fragrant softness of her red-gold hair. "Thanks for helping me out tonight. I don't know what I would have done without you."

"All a part of being a doctor's wife, I guess," Sunny said. "At least, a doctor's wife in a small town," she amended hastily, then paused.

Leaning her head on his shoulder, she noticed that Zach was still looking extraordinarily thoughtful, almost moody, tonight. She wondered if he was thinking about another patient of his, one he perhaps hadn't been able to help.

Straightening, Sunny took another sip of the hot coffee. Cupping both hands around the stoneware mug for warmth, she asked, "Did you mean what you said to George and Rhonda-Faye earlier—about being glad you were here?" *With them and with me?*

Zach turned to her. He knew a lot was riding on his answer. The first pearly-gray lights of dawn filtered over the horizon, illuminating his handsome face. The brooding look of moments before vanishing, he cupped her face in his hand. "Yes," he said, brushing her lips with a brief, all-too-fleeting kiss. "I did."

Chapter Six

Better Your Heart than Mine

"No, I understand, Gramps. Of course I can ask Zach." *I just don't want to,* Sunny thought. This morning, in front of the clinic, Zach had almost kissed her. If he had, she was sure they would have succumbed to the passion simmering between them and made love. He'd known it, too. He'd also probably known the reckless, highly romantic nature of their moods had come not from the joy they were finding in being with each other or their pretend marriage, but from the romance and excitement of delivering a baby into this world. And that excitement would fade, Sunny told herself severely. And when it did they would still have to live in the same house every day. And they would still be married.

"Yes. I'll see you in your office around ten. And I'll have the sample pages for the new mail-order catalog with me."

Sunny hung up the phone. She turned, to find Zach lounging in the doorway of the kitchen. He was dressed for work in shirt, tie and jeans.

"Ask me what?" he said.

"Nothing."

"C'mon, Sunny," he demanded impatiently.

"Gramps can't give me a ride into work, and it's so late that Matilda has already left."

"And you still can't drive your Land Rover because the skunk smell is still in it."

"Right."

Exasperation glimmered in his eyes. "If you need a ride, why didn't you say so?"

Because I'm beginning to feel too close to you, Sunny thought, a little desperately. "I didn't want to impose."

"You wouldn't be imposing."

The look in his eyes almost had her believing it. Sunny tapped a high-heeled foot against the parquet floor. "I need to fix that skunk smell."

Zach's expression softened sympathetically. "You've already tried damn near everything, haven't you?"

Sunny nodded, embarrassed. Zach had been right about that; they shouldn't have gotten into her vehicle until they had rid themselves of the smell. She shrugged and held the sample pages of the catalog to her chest. "Everyone says to just give it time."

"Time can work wonders in lots of areas," Zach agreed with a teasing grin, as his gaze roved her slender form.

He was thinking about kissing her again. Sunny could tell by the gleam of anticipation in his eyes. Her heart racing, she sidestepped the sensual embrace she sensed was coming if they dallied any longer. She was *not* going to be foolish enough to fall in love with him, not when she knew he couldn't wait for this farce of a marriage to end. Keeping her back to him, she gathered up her belongings. "I'm in a hurry, Zach," she said impatiently.

When she looked around at him again, he grinned, not the least bit put off by the edginess in her tone.

"And testy, too."

"I can't help it." Picking up where she'd left off when the phone had rung, Sunny swept a brush through her hair with long, practiced strokes. "It's aggravating me to no end not having a car to drive. I'm used to being completely self-sufficient."

Zach watched as she clipped her hair at the nape with a gold-filigreed barrette. "I know what you mean. I'm a pick-up-and-go type of person myself. In med school, my ability to leave town for a weekend now and then was the only thing that saved my sanity. I still like to get away for a weekend when I can."

"Where's your favorite place to go?" Sunny asked curiously, applying lipstick to her lips.

"I like water. Lakes and streams over beaches, generally. They're less crowded and I prefer the country to the city any day when looking for a little R and R." Zach watched as if mesmerized as she pressed her lips together to set the lipstick. "What about you?" His eyes trekked slowly back to hers.

"I don't know." His face was inches from hers as she recapped her lipstick and put it back in her purse. "I never really take vacations per se." Although Zach was making her regret that, too.

"How come?" He stepped behind her. Placing his palms on her shoulders, he kneaded the tenseness from her shoulders.

Sunny leaned into his soothing touch and briefly closed her eyes as his stroking, massaging fingers worked their magic. "Habit, I guess. As a kid, I saw plenty of the world, since my parents worked all over Europe, but every trip was always combined with work somehow. They'd go off to meetings. I'd either tag along and read a book while they labored and negotiated, or go tour a museum with my nanny. Either way, it seemed more like an extension of my education than a vacation." Relaxed now, she leaned against him.

Zach's hands stilled and he pressed a kiss in her hair. "Maybe that's why you're so crazy about those old 'I Love Lucy' reruns, like the ones you were watching last night before bed. If there was any fun to be had within a hundred miles, Lucy would find it," he said as he wrapped an arm around her waist and held her near.

Sunny grinned, enjoying the warmth and gentleness he exuded. "You're right about that."

His arm still hooked around her waist, Zach turned her to face him. "A little zaniness is good for the soul," he said, looking down at her affectionately.

Sunny felt her resistance to their marriage fading, inch by precious inch, even as they strayed into uncharted territory. Zach was becoming genuinely fond of her, as she was of him; that was not her imagination. "And you're the expert on zaniness, I suppose?" she teased back, thinking that if ever she had longed for her Ricky Ricardo, she had found him in Zach.

"Damn straight I am. Furthermore, one of these days I'll show you how to take a long, lazy weekend where nothing at all productive gets done."

"Sounds fun."

"In the meantime, I'll drop you at work," he said, handing her her purse and briefcase and tucking her arm in his.

Sunny looked up at him and saw something—a feeling, an emotion—that she couldn't analyze. "Don't you have to be at the clinic?"

Zach's eyes glinted with good humor. "I think I can be fifteen minutes late arriving one morning. I'll just put a note on the clinic door telling people when to expect me."

He was still going way out of his way. Sunny dug in her heels, afraid that if he evidenced much more kindness she really would be head over heels in love with him. "You don't have to do this for me, Zach."

"Yes, I do, Sunny," he replied, tightening his hold on her possessively. "You're my wife."

"WHAT'S GOING ON?" Zach asked as he pulled his pickup into the Carlisle Furniture Factory parking lot.

Sunny groaned as she looked at the fifty or so employees scattered in front of the building, now interestedly gazing their way. "I completely forgot. It's Earth Day and the local chapter of the Sierra Club always comes out and celebrates by planting a tree."

Zach didn't mind the two of them being seen together. In fact, he was beginning to kind of like it. But it was apparent Sunny did mind. He brought the truck to a halt. Leaving the engine running, he put the vehicle in park, then turned to her. "Looks like we have quite an audience,'' Zach murmured mischievously, unable to resist teasing her. Maybe it was time he stopped fighting it and played his husband act to the hilt. As long as they were together, they might as well have a little fun, he thought.

''Well, not to worry. There's not going to be anything for them to see,'' Sunny announced.

''On the contrary, Sunny,'' Zach drawled as he gave in to the temptation that had been plaguing him all morning and took her by the shoulders and kissed her soundly. Finished, he lifted his lips from hers and sifted a hand through her hair, knowing even as he did that he would never get enough to satisfy him, not even if he kissed her a thousand times. ''I think there should be quite a lot for them to see. We are newlyweds, after all.''

Sunny regarded him with a steamed glance, resenting, Zach supposed, the easy way she surrendered to him whenever he took her into his arms. What she didn't realize was that the feeling—of surrendering beyond their will—was mutual and just as difficult for him to fight. ''I should have known you'd take advantage,'' she huffed.

Zach raised his brow, his desire to possess her, heart and soul, growing all the stronger. ''Sunny, honey, that wasn't taking advantage,'' he murmured playfully. ''This is.''

Before Sunny had a chance to draw a breath, he had pulled her back into his arms and slanted his mouth over hers. Their kiss was hot and sweet and completely overwhelming in its intensity. Apparently forgetting her decision not to give an inch where he was concerned, she wreathed her arms around his neck and met him halfway. Engulfed by a wave of passion and need long held at bay, she let him pull her closer, deepen the kiss to tempestuous heights. Time lost all meaning as emotions swirled, and still it wasn't enough, Zach thought, amazed and shaken. It would never be.

He hadn't meant for this to happen. But now that it had, he was having a difficult time stopping himself. Only the thought that they had an audience kept him walking the straight and narrow. With difficulty, he ended the kiss, and lifted his lips from the tantalizing softness and warmth of hers.

She released a shaky breath. "You're not playing fair," she accused, her eyes shooting indignant sparks while she gave him an otherwise adoring look that was strictly for the benefit of their audience.

She wanted to talk about fair? Zach thought, still caught up in the moment and the essence that was her. There was nothing fair about this situation they found themselves in. Nothing easy about the circumstances that were compelling him to fall in love with her.

He cupped a hand under her chin, enjoying the slightly bedazzled state she was now in as much as he had loved leading her there. He tweaked her on the nose. "I never play fair, Sunny."

"WELL, LADIES, ready for lesson number two?" the instructor asked.

"If you ask me, Sunny's lessons are already working," Matilda said. "You should have seen that kiss Zach gave her in front of the factory this morning. Whoo-eee! It nearly knocked my socks off!"

"Thank you, Matilda," Sunny said dryly. She felt herself flushing bright red.

"Now, Sunny, don't you go getting embarrassed on us," Aunt Gertie counseled. "What you and Zach have is something to be proud of, to savor!"

"I agree," the instructor said, "and that is the basis for your next lesson. There is nothing sexier or more compelling to a man than the feeling of being the lord and master of his own castle. I am telling you, ladies, let your man take charge on the home front, and he will reward you with kisses galore."

"That's ridiculous," Sunny said.

"I don't like the sound of that, either," Matilda said.

"Let's put it to the test and then see," the instructor said. "Here is your assignment. I want all of you to give your husband free reign over his home for a period of six hours, starting tomorrow evening after work. His every wish is to be your command. You are to anticipate his every need. And most important of all, you are *not* to tell him or anyone else what you are doing or why. Not even a hint."

"Why?"

"Because if we tell them, they'll take advantage of us," Rhonda-Faye grumbled.

"Close, but no cigar," the instructor said. "Quite simply, if your husband thinks this is a game, he will treat it as a game. And this is serious, ladies. I am teaching you a whole new way of life."

"I don't know about the rest of you, but I did not sign on to learn how to become slave labor," Sunny said.

"I don't want you to be a slave," the instructor corrected. "I want you to treat your husband like a king. And when you do, you will find out that he will of his own volition treat you like his queen. Naturally, I'll expect you to keep a diary of your efforts and the results. During the next lesson we will share them with the class."

Sunny groaned, anticipating Zach's reaction. Could it get any worse?

SUNNY EMERGED from the kitchen just as Zach walked in the front door. His glance slid over the navy silk lounging outfit she had just put on, then moved to the yellow roses prominently displayed on the pedestal table in the front hall.

"Are those my flowers?"

"Yes. Thcy are."

He narrowed his eyes at her. "I thought you were going to throw them out."

"I decided it's the thought that counts," Sunny said cryptically. In this case, she wanted everyone to think she cherished the flowers. Whereas in truth, she was using them for a little visual on-site reality check. No more getting caught up in the idea of playing husband and wife the way she had in front of the factory this morning. No more steamy kisses. No more pent-up desire. No more falling in love with Zach! She was going to forget what they were teaching her in that class and live in the real world. And the reality was, no matter how tantalizing the idea of being really married to Zach or making wild, reckless, passionate love with him, neither thing was going to happen. Therefore, the only way to protect her heart was to keep her emotional distance.

Zach set down his medical bag with a thud. "What's going on here, Sunny?"

She regarded Zach innocently. "I'm trying to be nice," she said breezily. "So play along with me. Now, what would you like for dinner?"

"You're offering to cook for me?" He regarded her skeptically.

Sunny felt ridiculous, like a character out of some fifties sitcom trying to please her man. She wet her lips. "If you like." She was hoping desperately he had other plans.

"Uh-huh. What are my choices?"

Sunny shrugged, the irony of the situation not lost on her. She was married to the man and she had no idea what he liked. "Fried chicken. Steak on the grill."

Zach's lips compressed into a thoughtful line. "Fried chicken takes a while, doesn't it?" he prodded.

"Yes."

He faced her, an eyebrow raised in question. "Aren't you tired?"

Never too tired to make you happy, dear—at least, for the next six hours. "It'd be my pleasure," Sunny said, sidestepping his question altogether.

"To serve me?" Zach countered with a penetrating look. "I don't think so," he said drolly. "What's going on, Sunny?" He closed the distance between them and pointed to the yellow roses. "Are you trying to pay me back for the flowers mistake?"

"No, of course not." Sunny flushed.

"Then why the sudden eagerness to please me?" Zach towered over her. "Gramps going to pop in or something?"

"Not to my knowledge," she said truthfully, then pivoted. "I'll go start dinner."

Hand on her shoulder, he tugged her back to his side and gently spun her around. "I haven't decided what I want yet."

"Oh." Sunny folded her hands primly in front of her and took a deep, calming breath. "Right."

His eyes gleamed with mischief. "You know what? I think I'd like prime rib."

Leave it to Zach to make things more difficult, she thought. "I don't have any, but I think I can get to the market before closing. Unfortunately," she murmured, "it's not the sort of thing our butcher usually carries."

"I guess fried chicken will have to do, then," Zach drawled.

Sunny smiled and didn't comment. Every time she commented she got herself into trouble. Deciding this assignment would be a lot easier if they spent a few minutes apart, she said, "The newspaper is in the living room, dear."

Zach gave her a testing glance. "My slippers, too?" he asked innocently.

Sunny paused. As far as she knew, he did not wear slippers. But she supposed, for the sake of the class, she could give the idea some play. "I haven't seen your slippers."

"If you had, would you go get them?"

This assignment was a killer. "If you needed me to get them," Sunny specified sweetly. She couldn't think of a single reason where that would be the case.

Aware he was still ruminating over the sudden change in her behavior, Sunny slipped into the kitchen.

To her chagrin, he joined her there.

While he removed his tie and unfastened the first two buttons on his blue-and-white striped cotton dress shirt, Sunny got out the chicken.

He watched as she rinsed and patted it dry, pulled out the seasoned flour, then beat an egg and milk into a frothy mixture.

Zach poured himself a glass of iced tea as she prepared the chicken.

"You've done this before, I presume?" he said finally.

Sunny nodded, not shy about admitting, "Many times."

"Who taught you?" he asked softly, drawing closer.

"I taught myself by reading cookbooks."

His eyebrows lifted. "Julia Child?"

Sunny's mouth curved wryly as she added oil to the skillet and waited for it to heat. "Try Betty Crocker, Fannie Farmer, Pillsbury and anyone else who specializes in home-style cuisine. Since my parents preferred nouvelle cuisine and continental fare, I wanted pizza, hog dogs, fried chicken, grits and so on."

"Naturally." Zach grinned.

"What did you grow up eating?"

"Home-style American cuisine."

Sunny dropped pieces of chicken into a black cast-iron skillet. "What did you want?"

Zach stood looking over her shoulder. "Home-style American cuisine."

Satisfied the chicken was cooking nicely, Sunny went over to the pantry. She contemplated various side-dish possibilities. "Mashed potatoes okay with you?"

"As long as you make gravy. I can't eat mashed potatoes without gravy."

Sunny chuckled at the absurdity of that. Finally a character flaw she could identify with, she thought. She had begun to think Zach hadn't a whimsical bone in his body.

"Want me to make a salad to go with it?" He started for the refrigerator.

Sunny intercepted him midway. Zach's helpfulness was not in her lesson plan. "No. I have to do it," she said quickly, before she could think.

Some of the pleasure left his eyes. It was replaced swiftly by hurt. Sunny could have shot herself for the slip.

Zach folded his arms in front of him calmly. He quirked a brow. "What do you mean you have to do it?" he echoed.

Sunny flushed. Now that he was alerted to her deceptiveness where the evening was concerned, he would never just let it go. Nevertheless she tried to bluff her way out of trouble. "You know what I mean."

"I'm starting to." He trapped her against the refrigerator door. An arm on either side of her, caging her in, he murmured silkily, "If I didn't know better, I'd think you'd do just about anything to please me tonight."

Sunny inhaled jerkily. Unable to move without bringing them into closer contact, she remained motionless and held her ground.

"That's it. Isn't it?" Zach asked.

Their earlier camaraderie vanished. Hurt shimmered in his eyes, turning them an even darker blue.

"This is some sort of lesson...an experiment for your class."

"Now, Zach, I'm just trying to be cordial," Sunny said breathlessly.

He studied her. "Suppose I told you I'd changed my mind about the chicken and now I wanted steak."

Sunny kept her eyes on his. "Then I'd finish the chicken, save it for tomorrow and heat up the grill in the meantime."

"Hmm." Zach strode away from her and retrieved his glass of iced tea. "I think I will read that paper."

Sunny couldn't believe he was just going to walk away from her, now that he knew what her task was, but he did. Heart pounding, she waited for him to come back, to deliver the next zinger. He did neither, and she spent the next hour in the kitchen alone, preparing dinner, while he watched the television news and read the paper.

This proves he is definitely not husband material. No, she corrected herself wearily, her innate sense of fairness coming to the fore. It just proves he doesn't like to be a lab rat for some how-to-be-happily-married class. And for that, Sunny couldn't blame him.

"YOU REALLY OUTDID yourself with dinner," Zach said, after they had finished their strawberry shortcake and coffee. And that was a surprise. He had half expected her to ruin it on purpose, after he'd caught on to the reason behind her sudden change of heart.

Fool that he was, he had thought it was due to the passionate kisses they'd shared, the fact that they were getting to know each other and more often than not now liking what they found. He should have known that the idea of Sunny meeting him halfway to try to make this temporary marriage of theirs work was too good to be true. She had been forced into it, too. She also had to deal with that class. But that didn't excuse what she'd done this evening, raising his hopes unfairly by dressing in that silky navy blue outfit that made the most of her slender curves.

"Thank you," Sunny said politely. "I'm glad you enjoyed dinner."

Not as much as I'm going to enjoy this, Zach thought. Deliberately he let his eyes drop to her breasts before returning to her face. "You know what I really feel like doing?"

Sunny flushed. "The dishes?"

"No, Sunny," he drawled, sitting back in his chair. He folded his arms in front of him. "I think the dishes can wait indefinitely, don't you?"

Her tongue snaked out to wet her lower lip. "What did you have in mind, then?" She kept her eyes on his.

"I want to play a little game," Zach said, testing her reaction, and finding it every bit as uncertain and off kilter as he'd hoped.

"I've got Scrabble upstairs," Sunny said, already jumping up to get it.

Zach caught her wrist as she passed by. "I want to play Simon Says," Zach announced. He tugged her down onto his lap. "And I want to be Simon."

"That's a child's game."

"Not the way I intend to play it."

Muttering something indecipherable, Sunny attempted to vault off his lap but was held in place by his arms. "Darn you." She tried to release his arms from her waist. Failing at that, as well, she wiggled around to free herself, then stopped seconds later, apparently realizing what her subtle shifting was doing to his already much-aroused lower half. She drew a deep breath, the silk shifting beneath her thighs, and began in a much more reasonable tone, "Zach. I don't think—"

He touched a gentle hand to her lips, silencing her. He was aching all over and was sure he would pay for this hours later in terms of pent-up need, but he was not willing to stop until he had given Sunny a taste of her own medicine. "So you're refusing to do what I say—is that it?" he asked mildly. He knew how she liked to succeed at whatever she did, even the meddlesome class. In fact, he was counting on that trait in her to get them back to a level playing field, where honesty of feelings and not silly games prevailed.

Sunny flushed guiltily. She drew another bolstering breath, glanced down at her watch, as if contemplating how much time she had left on this particular assignment. "I thought you might want to rent a movie," she said finally.

Zach shook his head. Watching a video would do nothing to get Sunny to drop the compliant-wife act. "I think I'd prefer the game."

She bit her lip and looked up at him. He knew what she was thinking—that Simon Says, in the hands of a lascivious male, could be dangerous. "Shall we give it a try?" he asked softly, in a tone meant to incense her. "Or are you afraid to play games with me?"

Her temper visibly igniting, Sunny glared at him. "I am not afraid," she announced loftily.

"Good, then let's give it a try," he said, ready to get down to business. "Simon says put your arms around Zach's neck."

Sunny's eyes darkened angrily, as they always did when she was forced to do something she did not want to do, but she followed his instructions.

Zach smiled. Lucky for her, he had scruples. "Simon says close your eyes."

Rebellious color flooded her pretty cheeks, but she reluctantly lowered her thick red-gold lashes anyway, closing them almost all the way.

Zach frowned. "Are you cheating?"

"What?"

"Sunny, c'mon. Close those eyelashes all the way, now," he commanded sternly. "If you're going to play this game with me you have to play it right."

Murmuring a protest, she frowned nervously and started to shut her eyes completely. "Aha," Zach announced victoriously, "caught you!"

"Caught me!" Sunny echoed, incensed, as her eyelids flew open.

Zach shook his head at her in mocking report. "Simon never said you could open your eyes, either," he teased.

Her cheeks burning as she realized she'd been duped, Sunny pummeled his chest with her fist in aggravation. "This isn't fair!"

"No, Sunny, it's the way the game is played." Zach put his hands around her waist and started to shift her off his lap before any real damage could be done, any real temptation succumbed to. "You lose." *In fact, because of your playacting tonight, we both do.*

To his surprise, she refused to move in the direction he wanted her to go. Instead she remained squarely on his lap. Her lower lip was thrust out in a seductive pout. Her breasts were rising and falling seductively with each breath she took.

"I want another turn," she demanded stubbornly.

As Zack felt the warm, silk-clad weight of her settle in more comfortably on his lap, it was all he could do not to groan aloud in frustration. He had known all along how she hated to lose. He had even suspected she might purposely lose the game quickly, just as a way of getting out of having to play. He hadn't figured she would get genuinely flustered so soon, lose and then insist on playing another round.

"Sure now?" Zach taunted, no more willing to lose face than she was. "I could confuse you even worse this time," he warned.

"Just start playing!" she ordered bad-temperedly. "Now!"

"Okay." He grinned, keeping his hands around her slender waist, as he orchestrated a quick end to the game. "Simon says touch your lips to mine." His whole body throbbing, he waited for her to leap off his lap.

But this time, to his dismay, Sunny kept her cool. She quirked a brow. "You think I won't do it, don't you?"

Zach ignored the urgent demands of his body and gave her a look. "Babe, I know you won't do it."

"Ha! Just goes to show what you know!" Sunny muttered. Anger sparking in her eyes, she leaned forward and lightly touched her lips to his.

Zach knew what she was expecting. She was expecting him to play around a little more.

In truth, he had initially intended to do just that. But there was something about the softness of her lips against his, the cozy feeling of having her on his lap, that sent the rules of the game—and caution—to the wind.

He knew he shouldn't do it. He no longer gave a damn. Wrapping a hand around the back of her neck, he tilted her head beneath his. Their lips fused. He felt the need pouring out of her, mingling with the desire and the temper. And beneath that, he felt the tenderness that was so much a part of her, too. His need to be close to her was as overwhelming as it was magical. He threaded his fingers through her red-gold hair, tipped her head up to allow himself greater access, and claimed her as his.

As her mouth opened to his, he kissed her long and hard and deep. He kissed her until she moaned softly and melted in his arms. Until it felt as if they were both on a long magic-carpet ride. Realizing it was either stop now or take her to bed—and she wasn't ready to be made love to, at least not yet—Zach slowly, reluctantly, drew the kiss to an end.

His mouth tingling, his whole body trembling, he moved back slightly. He expected to see fury in her face. And he saw it, but only after the wonder and the stars in her eyes faded. "Guess I got a little carried away," he drawled.

"I guess you did," Sunny said, almost too sweetly.

And once again, to Zach's acute disappointment, she reined her feelings in.

"But then," she continued, gazing up at him with all-too-innocent eyes, "that kiss you gave me is nothing that can't be remedied."

"Remedied?" He did not like the sound of that.

"Sure," Sunny said, as she slid gracefully off his lap. "Because now it's my turn to play Simon."

Zach shrugged. "Give it your best shot."

"Simon says stand on one foot."

Zach rolled to his feet and stood on one foot.

"Put both feet on the floor."

His expression benign, he remained on one foot.

She looked him up and down, like a farmer examining a prize bull at market. Zach's feelings of unease increased. He sensed she was about to order him to take a long walk off a short pier.

"Simon says... turn toward the back door."

Keeping his shoulders loose and relaxed with effort, Zach turned casually toward the back door. No need to let her see she was getting to him, he thought.

Her smile widening, Sunny dropped her voice a seductive notch. "Simon says turn toward the sink."

He turned toward the sink.

"Simon says wash the dishes!"

It was all he could do not to groan. There were a lot of dishes.

"And Simon says don't stop until you're done!"

Sunny threw a napkin at him and stomped out of the room.

His body still humming with unslaked desire, Zach watched the provocative sway of her retreating backside. Maybe he had overdone it, but it sure had been fun while it lasted.

Chapter Seven

Ain't Misbehavin'

Zach awoke at dawn to the sound of water hitting metal. He looked outside to see Sunny in cutoffs and an old Smith College sweatshirt, hosing down the *inside* of her Land Rover. Finished, she tugged a red bandanna bandit-style over her mouth and nose, picked up a bucket of soapy water and a scrub brush and leaned into the Land Rover.

Pulling on a pair of running shorts, T-shirt and shoes, he headed downstairs. He heard Sunny swearing her displeasure as he neared. The top half of her was inside the truck; her bottom half extended out of it. As Zach neared her, he couldn't help but notice what spectacular legs she had. Or how much he liked seeing her in those Daisy Mae short-shorts she was wearing.

Sunny let out another litany of swear words as she continued to scrub her vehicle's interior carpet.

"Need any help?" he asked.

She started, and would have bumped her head if Zach hadn't caught her in time. She pivoted toward him, her bare legs rubbing up against the length of his. ''Must you always sneak up on me like that?'' she demanded.

''Do you have any idea what time it is?'' Zach countered, his nose wrinkling at the pungent smell.

''Six-fifteen.'' Sunny shot him a look that told him she still hadn't forgiven him for kissing her so thoroughly during their Simon Says game.

Aware he wasn't due over at the clinic until nine, he stuck his hands in his pockets and lounged against the side of the truck. ''Don't you have to go to work today?''

''Don't you?'' she retorted, without bothering to answer his question.

So she wasn't going to make it easy on him. Zach rubbed at the stubble on his unshaven jaw. He felt just a little contrite, even though he didn't really believe he had anything to apologize for. Sunny had only gotten what she'd had coming to her for trying to put one over on him. But, as always, she didn't see it that way.

Aware the silence between them was growing, he drawled, ''So what are you doing out here?''

''Trying to get the skunk smell out of my Land Rover. What are you doing out here?'' she asked in a muffled voice.

Enjoying the view, Zach thought. Trying to make peace. ''Checking up on you.''

''Well, as you can see,'' she said temperamentally, letting go of the bandanna, so that it fell around her neck, ''I'm fine!''

Zach didn't think so. He pushed away from the rear of the vehicle and ambled closer. ''Need a hand?''

Sunny shrugged. ''Be my guest and scrub away.''

"What are you using this time?" he asked. She had done this at least every other day since they'd imbued her Land Rover with the fragrance of skunk. She had also air-dried it in the sun repeatedly, also to no avail.

"I think a more apropos question is what haven't I used. Today it is a solution of detergent and water."

Zach wrinkled his nose. "I hate to say this, but so far it doesn't seem to be working."

Sunny scowled and dipped her brush back in the bucket. "You got any better ideas?"

"Actually...yes."

She straightened, hands on her hips, and gave him an expectant look. "I'm all ears, husband dear."

"What do you say we hand wash the whole interior in tomato juice?"

"Because the tomato juice would also stain the carpet."

"So rip out the carpet and forget about it. The seats are leather, so the tomato juice will rinse right off."

Sunny studied the sudsy carpet on the floor of her truck. "I don't know, Zach. It seems like a waste."

Zach understood her reluctance to spend money unnecessarily. He also knew, in this case, that it was going to be inevitable. "Have you tried your insurance?" he asked.

Sunny nodded unhappily. "My policy only covers theft, wrecks and natural disasters involving fire or flood."

"A skunk isn't a natural disaster?"

Sunny made a face. "Only to you and me."

Zach regarded her Land Rover. "Thought about driving it off a cliff? Then you could collect."

"Very funny and the answer is yes, numerous times." Sunny kicked at a tire. "Dammit Zach, I want a vehicle to drive!"

"You could borrow mine," he suggested gently.

Sunny shook off the offer. "You need it for house calls."

Zach sighed. "True."

She gave him another droll look. Moving several feet away from her vehicle, she fingered the bandanna she still had looped around her neck. "I think now is the point where you're supposed to say something soothing," she remarked, tongue in cheek.

Zach searched his mind for a comforting bromide to fit the bill. He couldn't come up with much. "Well, look at it this way, Sunny," he said sagely at last. "No good smell stays forever, so no bad smell can stay forever, either."

Sunny tilted her chin and kept her eyes on his. "Meaning what, exactly?"

Zach shrugged. "In a year it should smell better?"

Sunny closed her eyes and silently counted to ten. Finally she opened them again. "That's not helping," she said flatly.

Zach grinned down at her. "Then maybe this will."

He swung her up into his arms and carried her, protesting loudly all the way, over to her front porch. He set her down on the narrow steps.

"What do you think you are doing?" she demanded.

Zach touched the tip of her nose with his index finger, amazed at how much she had come to mean to him in so short a time and how dull his life was going to seem if he was ever without her again. "I'll continue scrubbing—it will be my good deed for the day. Now, sit here and be quiet for all of five minutes, okay?"

"I SAW Zach carrying you around this morning. My, the two of you certainly have a lot of energy," Matilda said, as she drove Sunny to work an hour and a half later.

Sunny knew she shouldn't have been laboring over her truck again before work, but she'd had to do something to use up the excess adrenaline pouring through her veins. She had barely slept at all last night, just thinking about Zach's kisses. Which were getting more and more frequent and potent all the time. She was beginning to seriously contemplate making love with him . . . to live dangerously for a change. She and Zach would never really be man and wife. They were just too different. But they could have a wild, reckless, passionate love affair. . . .

A love affair she'd remember and cherish the rest of her life. More important, she knew by the way he was kissing her, that he wanted to make love to her, too. So what was stopping her?

"Sunny?" Matilda said loudly, breaking into her thoughts. "You haven't heard a word I've said, have you?"

Sunny blinked. "Hmm?"

"Whatever are you thinking about?"

Zach, and how much I am beginning to care for him, Sunny thought.

"And why do you have that silly besotted look on your face?" Matilda continued, as she turned off

Main Street and onto the two-lane highway that led to the factory.

"I—" Sunny brought herself up short. "I don't know." She frowned. "I'm just worried about so many things." *Like getting out of this marriage with my heart and soul intact.*

Needing to change the subject, Sunny sniffed the inside of her wrist. "Do I smell like skunk?"

Matilda shook her head. "Apricot bath soap."

Now, there was a possibility she hadn't yet considered. "Hmm. Maybe I should try that on the interior of my car," Sunny mused.

"Maybe. Although I'm with Zach that nothing will get rid of a skunk odor when it gets on cloth or anything," Matilda said.

"We'll see," Sunny said.

Matilda gave Sunny a bluntly assessing look. "So how did your assignment go last night?" she asked casually.

Recalling how it had felt to sit on Zach's lap, her arms wreathed around his neck, and kiss him like there was no tomorrow, Sunny flushed. "We're not supposed to talk about it until class, remember?"

Matilda grinned. "He liked being king of his own castle, hmm?"

Heavens, yes! Sunny thought.

She turned toward Matilda, wondering if everyone else had gotten the same results from the experiment. "Did Slim?"

"He didn't notice anything different. That newlywed husband of yours apparently did," Matilda said with a sly look.

"That's because Zach notices everything." Even more telling, Sunny thought, was the fact that she noticed everything about him, as well. Including the fact that he was much too big for that rollaway bed he was sleeping on in the guest room.

Knowing he was uncomfortable every night made her feel so guilty she'd begun to consider solutions. And she knew what Zach wanted, of course—to move into her bedroom.

ZACH REALIZED something was going on the moment he walked in that evening and saw the disassembled cardboard furniture boxes littering the front hall. He took the stairs two at a time, strode past the folded-up rollaway bed he had been sleeping on and skittered to a halt in the guest bedroom doorway.

Sunny was home and still dressed in the tailored green tunic and black skirt she'd worn to work. Oblivious to his presence, she was standing next to a maple bedstead that dominated the entire guest room, calmly unfolding a white cotton mattress pad.

Looking at the bed, Zach couldn't help smiling. "What's going on?" he asked laconically as he went to give her a hand.

"I know how uncomfortable you've been sleeping on the rollaway bed. And I've been meaning to do something about it," she explained, avoiding his eyes as she smoothed the mattress pad onto the bed, covering the gathered elastic corners on her side, while Zach wordlessly covered the corners on his side.

"So I brought home a new bed for you," Sunny said. "It's a double bed, which should be large enough for you to sleep comfortably on, I think. If you're sleeping alone, that is."

Enjoying the easy way they were able to work together, Zach helped her cover the mattress pad with a set of sage green cotton sheets. "How about if I'm not sleeping alone?"

Sunny gave him a droll look and tossed him a pillow. "Then it might be a little crowded," she said dryly.

She was determined, Zach thought, not to be anything more than politely friendly to him this evening. No matter what they had been through together bringing Rhonda-Faye and George's baby into the world, or the closeness they had shared afterward, or the way they had teased each other the night before. She was backing away again. Zach was not going to let her do that, even if he had to tease her mercilessly to draw her out of the cocoon she had woven for herself.

Anyone could know Sunny the public person. No one knew the private one. At least not the way Zach wanted and intended to know her.

He watched as she covered one pillow with a sage green case, then followed suit.

"Oh, I don't know. I think we could cuddle up on it quite nicely," Zach drawled. In fact, he could easily imagine making love to her on the thick new mattress.

Sunny sent him a sassy glance. "Dream on."

"Trust me. I intend to."

He dropped his pillow onto the left side of the bed. She dropped hers on the right.

"Okay if I try it out?" he asked casually, watching the way the late-afternoon sunlight drifted in through the windows, setting fire to her red-gold hair.

"Sure. I guess so. In fact, it's probably a good idea."

Zach kicked off his shoes and stretched out on the crisp, fresh-smelling sheets. Aware Sunny was watching his reaction to the bed closely, he frowned and asked, "Is this bed from the factory?"

"Yes."

Her expression became sober. Her teeth sliced into her soft, bare lower lip. For the first time since he had walked into the house tonight, she looked uncertain. He wondered if she was reevaluating the boundaries they had set out for their relationship, just as he was. He wondered, too, if she was beginning to feel as married as he was beginning to feel.

"It's one of the floor models for a discontinued Hearthside line," Sunny continued.

"Hmm." Zach closed his eyes and concentrated on the enormously comfortable feel of the bed beneath him. There was only one thing he needed to make this bed complete now.

He folded his hands behind his head and continued to study her. "What about the mattress and box springs?"

"They're from the factory, too. I bought the whole set at an employee discount." She leaned toward him to remove a tag that was still looped around the knobs on the headboard. As she moved, he was inundated with the fresh floral scent of her perfume. It was all he could do not to groan.

Tag in hand, Sunny straightened. She looked down at him, her eyes all at once businesslike and solicitous. Once again, he was struck by her innocence, and the lack of it in himself. It was impossible to go through what he had, not to mention what he had seen in the emergency rooms, and still retain any semblance of culpability. There was no fate or grand plan. Life was random. People did and said foolish things. And it was true, the worst things happened to the best people. Which was all the more reason he should have fun now, while he could, Zach thought, his playful mood returning full force.

"Why do you ask where the bed came from?" she inquired quietly.

"I don't know." Zach hesitated. Watching her, he could see she was determined to prove she could be in his presence and not react. Just as he was determined to prove that when in each other's presence, they couldn't help but react.

"I hate to say anything," he continued in a way he knew would provoke her curiosity and keep her there with him a little longer.

Sunny frowned. A tiny pleat formed between her eyes. "If there's something wrong with the bed you need to tell me, Zach."

He worked to suppress a wicked grin. He doubted she would like his analysis of what his new bed needed.

"Maybe you should just try it and see what you think," he said. Maybe then she would come to the same conclusion he had.

Ever the devoted businesswoman, Sunny assumed a worried look. She kicked off her shoes hurriedly and sat down on the edge of the bed, then, apparently unable to tell anything from that, rested her head on the pillow and stretched out. She wiggled her shoulders and hips slightly, testing the mattress beneath her for flaws. Finally she said briskly, "My side of the bed feels fine."

"Good."

"How about yours?"

"I don't know. I think there's something wrong."

"Where?"

Zach turned toward her a bit and patted the space next to him solemnly. "Here. Right in the middle."

"Are you serious?" Sunny sat up with a jolt. The idea that there might be something wrong with a product her furniture company manufactured was very alarming.

Zach shrugged in a way that allowed he was no expert when it came to furniture. "Maybe it's just me," he said. "You try it." He patted the mattress center. "Tell me what you think."

With a frown, Sunny scooted toward him a little more. Shoulders stiff, she lay back down. Again she wiggled her hips and shoulders, getting settled.

Watching her, Zach felt his mouth go dry. The loneliness he'd been feeling for months now intensified in a solid ache around his heart. He had never wanted to reach out to a woman more than he did at that moment.

"You know you're right, Zach." Oblivious to the swirl of feelings in his heart, Sunny stared up at the ceiling. "It is a little stiff," she decreed finally.

She wasn't kidding, he thought, as the ache in his lower half intensified by leaps and bounds.

A contemplative grin tugging at the corners of her soft lips, Sunny propped her head on her bent elbow and rolled toward Zach a little, so they were lying face-to-face. "But with any new bed there's always that breaking-in stage," she continued with the soothing zeal of a good furniture salesperson. Her eyes danced as she related, "Did you know that it can take up to three months to get to feeling really comfortable in a new bed?"

Zach grinned and Sunny blushed as they both became aware of the double meaning of her words.

"Oh, I don't know. I think I'm comfortable now," he drawled. "I think," he said as he gave in to temptation, pulled her into his arms and bent his head toward her softly parted lips, "all I needed—all I ever needed—was this."

Zach bent his head for a kiss. The feel of her lips beneath his was sweet, soft and all too intoxicating.

All too soon, Sunny broke off the kiss, her hand to his chest.

"Now, just hold on there a moment, lover boy," she drawled, gasping for breath. "This was not part of the deal."

But she liked it just the same. "I know." Zach grinned. "But maybe it's time we rethink our situation," he said.

Sunny regarded him suspiciously. "Rethink it how?"

Zach lay back on the pillow. He folded his hands beneath his head. "Maybe we should stop fighting what we're feeling."

For a second, Sunny looked tempted. She braced a forearm on his chest and rolled so that she was lying across him. "And what are we feeling, Zach?" she asked very, very softly.

He knew much depended on his answer. "For starters, a very strong, very undeniable attraction to each other." Unable to resist touching her again, he wound a curl of her silky red-gold hair around his fingertip.

Sunny leaned into his touch instead of away from it.

"I admit there's some chemistry," she said, surprising him with her honesty.

She looked down at his chest and tightened her fingers on the ends of his striped necktie. "But that doesn't mean we have to act on it."

Zach considered the way his lower body felt, the way she had responded to his kiss, trembling at just the mere touch of his lips to hers. They were fooling themselves if they thought they were going to keep this marriage of theirs platonic. It was time Sunny dealt with that fact, too.

He slid his hand beneath the veil of her hair and gently caressed her nape with his thumb. "We may not be able to help it, Sunny."

She bit into her lower lip tremulously, then gave him a smug look. "Oh, I think we will."

Zach felt another battle coming on, one he anticipated greatly.

"I don't know." He shook his head in exaggerated confusion, then teased, "We're living in extreme proximity, Sunny. We're married. Heck, who knows? Some night we might even find ourselves doing some lesson for one of your classes that involves us sharing the same bed."

The notion of them sharing the covers was apparently as disturbing to her as it was to him. Pink color climbing from her neck into her face, Sunny sat up. Swinging her legs over the edge of the bed, she turned her back on him. The fabric of her skirt pulled against her trim hips as she bent to retrieve her heels.

"I think I could get around any such lesson my instructor might cook up. Besides, I only have a few left."

Not ready to let her go just yet, Zach pried the suede shoes from her hand and shifted her so she was prone again and they were touching in one long, tensile line. "All the more reason we need to take things a step or two further and begin to explore some of what we've both been feeling," Zach said. "Because there's so much I want to learn about you, Sunny. So very, very much."

She was prepared to be drawn into his arms and kissed once more, but what she wasn't ready for was how fast she went from simply being kissed to kissing in return. She didn't even know how he did it. All she knew was that her world was taken over by the taste and touch and smell of him, that she'd never been so excited and that she felt wild and free and womanly for the first time in her life.

Giving in to the subtle pressure and gentle wooing of his lips, Sunny opened her mouth to the rapaciousness of his tongue and returned every touch and pressure tenfold. Before she knew it, one kiss had turned into many. It no longer mattered, she thought dizzily, as the yearning inside her, the sensation of being cherished, intensified into a fierce, unquenchable ache. All that mattered was that this touching, this tenderness, this gentle loving, never stop.

Zach groaned as she kissed him deeply.

Feeling the hypnotic stroke of his hands as they swept over her, Sunny started to succumb to whatever it was that came next. Then realized, as Zach began to unbutton her tunic, that no matter what he wanted, no matter how much she ached to be one with him, she couldn't give her body without also giving her heart.

For Zach, she feared, it was *not* the same. All too aware of the thundering of his heart and the rigid tension in his thighs, she tore her mouth from his and put a staying hand on his. "Zach, no. I—" The right time might come, but it wasn't here yet.

He sighed and released his hold on the button he'd been about to undo. "I was afraid you were going to say that," he murmured as he let her go.

Sunny studied him. Even though she'd said no to lovemaking, it was clear he was not giving up.

Zach touched a finger to her lips and gently wiped away the dewy residue of their kiss. He surveyed her tenderly. "You expect me to be angry with you for putting on the brakes, don't you?"

That was usually the drill, she thought. Say no to a man and he flew into a rage.

"Aren't you?" she asked curiously, still testing his reaction to her denial.

"No." Zach shook his head, his eyes glowing with pleasure. "I see this as a very necessary first step."

Sunny took a deep, hitching breath. A very necessary first step. To making their marriage a real one? "That sounds ominous," she quipped, aware her hands were trembling.

"Pleasurable," he corrected huskily with an unabashed grin. "And it will be, I promise."

Sunny was afraid of that, too.

She was irritated by the way she kept melting in his arms, despite all her intentions to the contrary. "I know you think so," she said tartly. She had yet to see. Yet to be brave enough . . . to go all the way. But Zach didn't know any of that. And she wasn't about to tell him. Her lips still tingling from his kisses, Sunny slipped away from him.

He relaxed against the pillows, making no move to follow her. "One of these days I'm going to get you back in this bed and we're going to find out what we've been missing," he teased. They were going to be together. It was only a question of when.

Chapter Eight

A Little Less Talk and a Lot More Action

"Yes, sir. Absolutely. We'll have it to you within the month!" Sunny promised with a smile, then hung up the phone.

Matilda set a neatly typed list of new orders on Sunny's desk. "Good news?" she asked as she popped the lid on a can of diet cola.

"The best. Where's Gramps?"

Matilda picked up her steno pad. "Last I saw he was in his office, preparing for the sales meeting in the showroom this afternoon. After that, he's going fishing. You ready to dictate those letters yet?"

"Not quite. I want to tell Gramps my news first."

"Okay. I'll go back to figuring that new computer out. Now, that's a chore that should last me the rest of my life."

Sunny patted her assistant on the shoulder. Chuck Conway had been out three times to work with Matilda in the past two weeks, but she was still struggling to make the transition from one order-entry system to another. "Just keep at it. You'll get the hang of it yet."

"That I don't know about," Matilda murmured. " 'Course, it might help if I actually read the instruction manual from cover to cover."

Sunny lifted a brow. "Any particular reason you haven't?"

"Yes. It's written in technogibberish. I don't understand a word of it."

Sunny grinned. "Think it'd be better if we hired Chuck to come in for a solid week, work with you and make up an emergency manual for you in language you do understand?"

"Maybe." Matilda tapped her pen against her steno pad. "I mean, I always get it when he's here. It's only when I try to work it on my own that I seem to get confused about what I'm doing and muck things up."

"I'll call Chuck again today," Sunny promised.

Sunny finished up her business with Matilda, then dashed off in search of her grandfather. Though she was now officially running the company, he still came in for a few hours every morning to lend a hand and answer any questions she might have. And the truth was, she liked having him around. He lent her plenty of moral support, and he believed in her gut instincts when it came to business, and her ability to manage the company. He also felt she was doing work she should be proud of. Sunny sighed, wishing everyone in her family felt the same way.

Her grandfather's door was slightly ajar. He had his back to her, but Sunny could see he was on the phone. Not wanting to interrupt, she lingered in the hallway.

While she waited patiently for him to finish, his voice floated out to Sunny. "That boy has a responsibility to this community, never mind my granddaughter! I don't want another doctor in Carlisle!"

Another doctor! she thought, straightening abruptly. Was Zach going somewhere? She could not recall ever seeing her grandfather look so angry.

Gramps glared up as Sunny slipped inside his office. He frowned. "I'm going to have to hang up. Yes, later." He put the receiver in its cradle. "What is it, darlin'?"

Sunny shut the door behind her. She stepped around the fishing gear that seemed to go everywhere with Gramps since his semiretirement. Hands shoved in the pockets of her trousers, she approached her grandfather's desk. "We won the bid. Carlisle Furniture is going to supply the beds, bureaus, tables and chairs for all the rooms of the new Southern Hospitality Inn in Nashville."

Gramps beamed and leaned over to give her a hug. "Congratulations, honey. I knew you could do it."

So had Sunny. If only her parents had the same confidence in her ability, she thought wistfully. "What was that all about—on the phone just now?"

"Nothing."

Sunny sent her grandfather a brief, dissenting glance. "It's not nothing if it's about my husband," she remarked sagely.

Gramps studied her. Without warning, his expression grew exceedingly grim. "You don't know what that rascal's up to now, do you?"

Sunny lifted her shoulder in an eloquent shrug. "How could I unless you tell me?"

"He asked for a transfer out of Carlisle."

The news hit her like a sharp blow to her chest, but she kept her demeanor impassive. "When?" Sunny asked quietly.

"A day after the two of you got caught draped in nothing but a chamois and a checkered tablecloth."

That fast, Zach had wanted the hell out of Carlisle. She had realized he had been unhappy about their predicament even before the two of them had been forced to marry. She hadn't realized he had put in for a transfer.

"And?" Sunny pressed for more details.

"And the person in charge of the physician recruitment program for rural areas called me to say they're still working on finding one."

"Why call you?"

"Because Carlisle Furniture chipped in on the moving costs for the new doc, remember? We'd have to pay moving and living for the new doctor. Not to mention recall the selection committee to review another round of appointments."

"Oh. Right."

Gramps stepped forward. "Everything okay?"

"Everything's fine," Sunny said, though she felt as though her whole world were coming apart.

"I take it Zach didn't mention this to you."

"No," she admitted tightly, doing her best to hide her inner misery. "He didn't."

"Yet another reason to wring his fool neck," Gramps muttered.

"Don't you dare," Sunny warned hot-temperedly. "I'll handle my new husband."

"Sure?" Gramps picked up the fishing lure he'd been working on while he was on the phone. He bent his head over it again. "I could talk some sense into him," Gramps offered slyly.

Sunny was hoping that wouldn't be necessary. "It may be he has already changed his mind about staying," she said optimistically.

Gramps's hands stilled and he looked up. "And if he hasn't?" he prodded with a frown, pausing absently to massage his left shoulder and the center of his chest.

Sunny drew a deep breath. "Then that's his decision." She wasn't about to force Zach into anything. Her parents had imposed their will on her; she was still reeling from the pressure. She wouldn't do the same to Zach.

Gramps surveyed her distressed expression. He set the lure in his left hand on his desk. "This is ridiculous. I'm going to call and tell them to cancel his transfer request."

Sunny lifted a staying hand. "No. I don't want you to interfere."

Gramps frowned unhappily. He looked around his desk until he found a roll of antacid tablets. "Why the devil not?" he demanded as he popped one into his mouth.

"Because you've done quite enough already in forcing Zach to marry me."

Gramps chased the antacid tablet with a gulp of water. "No one held a gun to his head."

"Close enough," Sunny said ruefully. "Besides, this is his decision."

"You mean that, don't you?" Gramps said.

Sunny nodded. She took a closer look at her grandfather. He seemed a little pale. "Say, are you feeling okay?"

He waved off her concern. "Too much spicy food for lunch. It was Mexican Day over at the diner. Listen, I forgot to mention it, but I'd like to go off on a fishing trip for a few days. That okay with you?"

Sunny nodded. "Of course."

"Are you sure?" Without warning, he looked a little anxious. "'Cause I could cancel it if you need me here."

"Don't be silly. You just go off and have fun. I'll hold the fort down." And wait for Zach to make a decision and retract the transfer. Sunny could only hope he would make the right decision for both of them. Their marriage had started out for all the wrong reasons, but now that they were married, they were growing closer day by day, maybe even falling in love. She wanted a chance to see their relationship through. She didn't want to look back later and think they might have had something really special if only they'd given themselves the chance.

"YOUR MAMA IS just going to kill me," Gertie told four-year-old Toby as she ushered him into the Carlisle Clinic.

Toby looked at Zach, then Gertie. "Did you swallow a marble, too?" Toby asked Gertie.

"Toby swallowed a marble?" Zach interrupted.

Gertie wrung her hands. "That's what he said. I didn't even know he had any marbles with him."

"I always keep them in my pocket, right here," Toby said importantly. He patted the front right pocket on his child-size jeans, then reached inside and pulled out a white-and-green marble. "See?" He held it up for both adults. "It was just like this one and I put it in my mouth—"

"No!" Gertie and Zach said in unison when Toby started to demonstrate how he had swallowed the first marble.

"Here, honey, let me hold that for you," Gertie said as perspiration broke out on her brow. She placed the marble in her purse.

"When did you realize he had swallowed a marble?" Zach asked, perplexed because Toby was showing none of the expected signs of respiratory distress or physical discomfort.

"When he told me, about ten minutes ago," Gertie said, looking as if she might burst into tears at any second.

"Where's Rhonda-Faye?"

"At home with the new baby, asleep. She was up all night and I told her that I would take Toby this morning while the others went to school, since it's my day off."

"That was nice of you," Zach said.

"Rhonda-Faye will not think so when she finds out what happened," Gertie said, nervously fingering the strand of pearls around her neck. "She will think I am a complete novice with kids."

"She doesn't know what happened?"

"After all she's been through with George and the baby coming early, I thought I'd better find out how bad it was, first. How bad is it?"

Zach touched Gertie's shoulder reassuringly as Toby gravitated to the box of toys and books in the far corner of the room. "There's one way to find out."

"So you'll take a quick look at him before we call Rhonda-Faye or George and tell them?" Gertie said.

Zach paused, watching as Toby tried out a child-size chair and seemed to like it. What Gertie was asking of him was highly unusual. "Normally, I need a parent's verbal or written permission to treat a child."

"What about on an emergency basis?" Gertie pressed.

"Then treatment can be rendered after getting express permission from the adult caring for the child," Zach said.

"Which is me," Gertie interrupted.

"Right."

"So what do you say?" she asked anxiously.

Zach smiled. "Under the circumstances, I think it would be permissible to find out what kind of shape Toby's in before we call his folks. There's no use upsetting them unnecessarily."

"And you know how excited George gets in any medical emergency," Gertie murmured.

Zach nodded. "We don't want him having another accident trying to make it to the clinic." One set of stitches had been enough.

Zach stepped closer to his young patient, who, unlike Gertie, was remarkably calm. "Toby, how about coming into an examining room so I can listen to your lungs?" Zach said.

Toby moved away from the box of toys in the corner of the waiting room. He had a storybook in his hand. "Can I bring this with me, Dr. Zach?"

"Sure." Zach grinned. "So how do you like your new sister?"

Toby made a face. "She cries a lot and she goes to the bathroom in her pants."

"Diapers," Zach corrected.

"Whatever," Toby said, climbing up onto the pediatric table with Zach's help. "It's disgusting. All my brothers think so."

"I bet."

"Sounds like sibling rivalry," Gertie said.

Zach nodded. He helped Toby pull off his shirt, then looked into his young patient's throat. "Say 'ahhh.'"

"Ahh."

Zach listened to Toby's chest. "Are you sure you swallowed that marble? That it didn't just fall out of your mouth—maybe on the floor somewhere?"

"I swallowed it all right. It hurt a little when it went down, too," Toby declared.

"Does it hurt now?" Zach asked.

"No. But it did then," Toby said.

Zach took another long careful look at the boy's throat. He could find no evidence that the four-year-old had swallowed anything. "If he did swallow a marble, it appears to have gone into his stomach," Zach told Gertie.

Gertie looked as if she were going to burst into tears any second. "Can't you find it?"

"Not so far, but to be on the safe side, we'll do an X ray and see if we can locate it that way," Zach told her.

"It's not there," he said, fifteen minutes later as the three of them studied the X rays.

"But how is that possible?" Gertie cried, looking all the more upset.

Zach wondered the same thing. He turned to Toby, who was looking sideways at the pictures of his insides. "Toby, when did you swallow the marble? Was it before or after Gertie picked you up?"

"Before."

"How long before?"

"I dunno." Toby shrugged his small shoulders.

"This morning?" Zach pressed.

Toby shook his head. "Last Christmas."

"Last Christmas," Zach echoed as he and Gertie shared a relieved laugh.

"Yeah." Toby appeared confused. He did not get what they were chuckling about.

"Did you tell your mom and dad you swallowed this marble?" Zach asked.

"Nope."

"Why not?"

"I dunno. I forgot, I guess. Christmas is a pretty busy time. Can I have a sticker now?" Toby asked hopefully.

"Sure." Zach got out a whole box of them from the cabinet. "You were such a good patient, you may have two."

"Okay, but can I look through all of them first before I have to pick?" he asked.

"Take your time," Zach said.

Gertie turned to Zach. "I suppose it's safe to assume the marble went the way of everything else Toby ingests but doesn't need?"

Zach nodded.

"I'm so embarrassed," Gertie said, covering her eyes with her white lace hankie.

"Been there," Zach said.

Gertie grinned at him. "I suppose you have. So, how are you enjoying married life?"

Zach hesitated. What could he say to that? He liked being with Sunny. But marriage... what kind of marriage was it when the vows were not taken seriously and the couple didn't even share the same bed?

"Just what I thought," Gertie said. "The two of you still have the honeymoon blues."

"Honeymoon blues?" Zach asked.

"You know. The getting-adjusted-to-everything blues. But take it from me, Zach—" Gertie patted his arm reassuringly "—I know just what the two of you need."

"NEED A RIDE?"

The low, familiar voice sent shudders of awareness down her spine. "Zach." Sunny flushed as she clasped her clipboard to her chest and turned to face him. He was wearing a blue chambray dress shirt, red tie and jeans. His hair was wind tossed and sexy, his jaw freshly shaven and scented with the after-shave she liked. "What are you doing here?"

"Enjoying the scenery." Looking relaxed and at ease, he stepped away from the entrance to the factory display room and closed the short distance between them.

Her shoulder nudging his, Sunny said, "There is no scenery in here."

He chucked her on the chin and grinned down at her. "Gotta differ with you there, babe. There's plenty of scenery in this room."

The compliment was as heartfelt as it was teasing. Response trembled along her skin. "The new display rooms are nice, aren't they?" Sunny said, being deliberately obtuse.

Zach nodded and cast an admiring glance around. The room they were standing in featured living room furniture, done in a timeless traditional style.

"Yes, it's very nice. I noticed, coming in, that the rooms are really put together down to the last detail. Having the right accessories makes the furniture look even classier."

Sunny nodded. "I know. I've been thinking the same thing. That's why I'm trying to get my grandfather to enlarge our operation here and sell accessories—like quilts and pictures and lamps. Maybe even a line of coordinating, custom-made draperies."

"Going to turn Carlisle's into the next Sears Roebuck?"

"More like an L. L. Bean Furniture store and catalog. Our look will stay pure Tennessee."

He took her hand in his and tugged her over to the red-and-green plaid sofa. "None of that eclectic post-modern stuff for you, hmm?"

Sunny made a face. "No way."

"How come?" He sat down next to her.

Sunny sat back against the cushions. "Because I love what warm, cozy furniture can do to a room—transform it from a utilitarian space to a place to regroup, and replenish the soul."

"Old-fashioned furniture for an old-fashioned girl."

"Absolutely. Does that bother you?"

"Just makes me curious. You seem so open-minded about everything else. Why not with modern furniture, too?" Zach's eyes locked on hers.

Sunny shrugged. He was seeing too much again. Zeroing in on her vulnerable side without half trying. "That's all we ever had in our home, growing up. There's something very cold about it, at least for me. And I just don't like it, so I'm not going to make it, and I'm not going to sell it."

Zach wondered if she was talking about furniture now or her parents. "Sorry. I didn't mean to upset you."

"No." Sunny shook her head and ran a hand through her hair. "I'm sorry for snapping at you. It's just been a long day."

Gertie had been right. Sunny did need some tender, loving care. Fortunately, he was just the man to give it to her, Zach thought, as he walked her out to his pickup.

Sunny stopped short when they reached the door and she looked inside. "What's all this?" she asked, pointing to the wicker picnic baskets, blankets and thermos.

"Supper. I thought maybe you'd take me up to the top of the mountain so we could enjoy the view."

"You haven't been there yet?" As she gazed up at him, her breath was uneven, shivers raced along her spine.

"No. And I've been told it's the greatest place to watch the sunset."

"It is." It was also highly romantic. For that reason alone, Sunny told herself she should not go there with him. She turned and stepped up into the truck. Aware she felt happy and sad simultaneously, she asked, "Why are you doing this?"

Zach leaned in to assist her with her seat belt. He smiled at her, his blue eyes dazzling in their intensity.

"You pampered me," he said softly, pausing to kiss her temple. "I thought it was high time I did the same for you."

One kindness begets another...wasn't that what they'd taught in her marriage class? Was it possible the theory worked, even in their case? Sunny wondered, amazed as Zach drove the short distance to their picnic site and parked the truck at the end of the old gravel logging road.

"You're awfully quiet," he said. He got out, grabbed the picnic gear and circled around to her side.

Sunny was wishing she were not nearly so susceptible to him. She was also wishing she had her tennis shoes instead of her flats. She was lucky, though, that she had on trousers instead of a dress. "I was thinking about the bid we won today," Sunny fibbed. As they spread out the blankets, she told him about it.

"The Southern Hospitality Inn is part of a big hotel chain, isn't it?" Zach asked as he brought out beef-brisket sandwiches, potato salad.

Sunny nodded. "They've got four-star hotels in practically every major city of the country."

"So this could lead to other jobs and really put Carlisle Furniture on the map," Zach said as he added zesty vinegar slaw, homemade dill pickles and an assortment of black and green olives to their plates.

Sunny poured them each generous glasses of iced tea. "We hope it leads to more work." Famished, she bit into her sandwich.

"If that happens, would you move the factory elsewhere, open a second one or expand here?"

"I think I'd try to expand here," she said cautiously. She settled in beside him, appreciating the quiet beauty of their surroundings and the intimacy of being with him. Zach had put a lot of thought into the evening, and she had needed to get away from it all, more than she had realized.

"Bringing a lot of people in would change the community."

"I know, and that worries me." Sunny set her plate aside. She brought her knees up to her chest and wrapped her arms around them. "I like living in a small town."

Zach looked out at the countryside below. Carlisle was visible in the distance, rooftops popping up between the trees on peaceful shady streets. Old-fashioned but neatly kept, the town resembled something out of a Norman Rockwell painting. And though it was beautiful, it was also dull. "You don't think you'll get bored here eventually? Carlisle is awfully small."

Sunny's jaw set stubbornly. "I need more than an intellectual challenge to keep me happy. I need the feeling of belonging and closeness, of community, that living here gives me."

"Your parents didn't feel the same way, I guess."

"No, they didn't. For all their lawyerly brilliance, they are never going to understand why I care so much about the people in this town, or why I want to take care of the business and keep it growing and thriving so the town can still exist. The employees aren't numbers to me. They're people, with faces and names and personalities and families to support. I like knowing everyone here. I like knowing that what I do is making a tremendous difference in their lives and in the overall soundness of Gramps's company."

"Taking care of people is very satisfying."

Sunny gazed into his eyes, saw the compassion there, and knew he really did understand. More so than she had expected that he would. "You're speaking as a physician."

Zach shrugged. For an instant he was moodily silent, pulling away from her. "And a member of my own family."

His brooding look gone almost as soon as it appeared, Zach lifted a forkful of potato salad to her lips. "Recognize the recipe?"

Sunny smiled. "Gertie's."

"Right." Zach fed her another forkful of potato salad. "She cooked the whole meal for us."

"That was sweet of her. I'll have to thank her."

He smiled at her warmly as she took another bite of her sandwich. "I already did, for both of us."

He was acting as if they were a real couple, she thought. Or maybe he was just getting into the swing of pretending, for as long as he was there.

The sandwich suddenly turning to sawdust in her throat, Sunny swallowed. She felt angry and hurt, and she had no right to feel either, she told herself sternly. He wasn't breaking any promises to her, because he'd never made any commitment.

Around them, the sunlight faded to a dusky romantic glow. Zach paused to light an outdoor candle in a mason jar.

"You don't mind that I agreed to let her cook for us, do you?" he said, his expression concerned.

"No, of course not," Sunny said, sitting Indian-style again. *I mind that you are trying to leave here, and you haven't even bothered to tell me. Despite the fact that I am your wife!* Then again, she thought, he wasn't acting like a man with one foot out the door tonight. And Gramps had succeeded in blocking his transfer, at least temporarily. Thinking of Gramps, she wondered if he still had his indigestion tonight. He had left the factory early to pack for his trip, which was slated to begin that evening.

"Sunny?" Zach touched her hand. "You look... upset. Is everything okay?"

She slipped her hand in his, glad she had him to confide in. "It's Gramps," she said, swallowing around the lump in her throat. "I don't think he was feeling all that well today."

Zach grew very still. "What seemed to be the matter?"

"He was rubbing his shoulder and guzzling antacids."

Zach's eyes darkened. "Did he say he was in pain?"

"No." She lifted her face to his. Without warning, her heart was pounding. "Why would you ask that?"

"Because I'm a doctor." Zach regarded her patiently. "Those are the kinds of questions I'm supposed to ask."

"Oh." Sunny forced herself to calm down. "No, he just seemed . . . I don't know . . . generally uncomfortable, a little anxious and upset."

Zach looked down at his plate. "He's taking a few days off to go fishing, isn't he?" he said casually.

Sunny nodded, not sure why but she felt something was amiss here. "How did you know that?"

"He mentioned it to me last week."

"So you don't think I should worry?"

Zach shifted restlessly on the blanket beside her. "I don't think Augustus would go off on a three-day fishing trip if he were ill, do you?"

"No." Sunny forced herself to relax. "You're right. He wouldn't. I guess I'm just overreacting—that's all. Gramps means so much to me." Her voice caught. "He's the only one who's ever believed in me." Tears stung her eyes. "I don't know what I'd do without him."

Zach reached over to squeeze her hand. "Luck willing, he'll be with us a long time to come, but if it will make you feel any better, I'll check up on him, too."

"Thanks, Zach. I appreciate it."

"Is everything okay with you?" he continued. "You look a little stressed out tonight, too."

Sunny shook off her confusion. It was going to be dark soon, and with the stars and the moon overhead, oh, so romantic. "I'm just tired—that's all," she said. And that was true. She didn't want to talk about his transfer request or what Gramps had done to block it. She smiled at Zach encouragingly. "How was your day?"

At the mention of his work, Zach broke into a wide grin. "I saw one of Rhonda-Faye and George's little boys." He recounted the marble incident in great detail. By the time he had finished, Sunny was laughing right along with him.

"Toby is something else," she murmured sympathetically, pleased that Zach had such a sense of humor about the whole incident and that he was quickly warming to the people in the community.

Zach shook his head. "I should have asked the little tyke *when* he swallowed the marble right off."

Sunny shrugged. "Live and learn." And that could be said about everything.

They both smiled. He leaned over in the picnic basket and brought out another container. "And now for the pièce de résistance," he said with a flourish. "Double-chocolate walnut brownies."

Sunny groaned in feigned ecstasy. "My favorite."

"I can think of something I like better," Zach murmured as he started to take her in his arms.

Her heart racing, Sunny flattened a palm against his chest to keep him from coming any closer. She wanted him, and she didn't. "No, Zach. No kissing," she said breathlessly.

He fastened his eyes on hers as he teased, "Not even just one?"

She shook her head firmly, ignoring his obvious disappointment—and hers. "Not even one."

SUNNY'S LOW melodious voice floated out into the backyard as Zach headed toward the door, sack of groceries in his arms.

"Matilda's really having trouble." Sunny laughed softly, then continued speaking into the phone. "Easy for you and me, but we grew up using computers. She didn't. I think it would be a good idea if you came back and stayed until she has the hang of the entire order-entry system." She paused, head bent, listening intently. "I know it'll be expensive, but it'll be worth it." Sunny paused again, then laughed softly. "I really appreciate it, Chuck. I consider it a personal favor. Right. See you then. Looking forward to it."

Sunny hung up the phone and turned around to see Zach lounging in the kitchen doorway. From the expression on her face, he guessed she had been wondering how much he had overheard of her telephone conversation. Enough to make him damn jealous, Zach thought. Never mind that the emotion was completely irrational; it was there.

"Back already?" she asked lightly.

He nodded, trying hard not to notice how much she wanted to get rid of him this evening, or how much it stung to realize she felt that way. He carried the single bag of groceries into the kitchen and set it down on the counter, next to the fridge. "Milk, cereal and a fresh loaf of bread, just like you asked." He began putting them away. "And I also checked on Gramps—" who was now in the Knoxville hospital, undergoing tests "—and he's fine."

"Thank you," Sunny said gratefully.

Zach nodded. He just wished he could tell her everything about her grandfather.

Noting the coffee had stopped brewing, Sunny poured herself a mug. She had work papers scattered over the kitchen table. "And thanks for getting the groceries, too. Normally I wouldn't ask you to run an errand, but I have so much to do tonight. And I didn't want you to wake up to an empty refrigerator and no breakfast."

"Sounds like those how-to-be-a-loving-wife lessons are really sinking in," he teased.

Sunny's jaw set rebelliously even as she studiously avoided his eyes. Zach stepped closer and took her into his arms. She splayed a hand across his chest to prevent him from coming any nearer. Hurt and wariness glimmered in her eyes.

Suddenly Zach knew he had to ask. "What's wrong, Sunny?" Acquiescing to her obvious wishes, he dropped his hands from her shoulders. "You've been acting funny all evening."

She stepped back and tossed her head. "I'm a regular laugh riot, aren't I?" she retorted sadly.

Zach struggled against the urge to bury his hands in the shimmering softness of her red-gold hair. He lounged against the counter, instead, bracing a hand on either side of him. "Have I done or said something to make you uncomfortable?"

She regarded him indifferently. "What would make you think that?"

"The fact that you wouldn't stay and watch the sunset with me at the top of Carlisle Mountain."

Sunny shrugged. She picked up her coffee mug again and took a sip. "The roads get dangerous after dark."

Zach knew an excuse when he heard one. It infuriated him to see her putting up barriers between them, just when he'd begun to tear them down. "Ten to one it never bothered you before."

She flushed guiltily, confirming his suspicions that she was trying hard to keep them from getting any closer. ‘‘And then there is the quick way you sent me off to the store, the determined way you are immersing yourself in your work.’’

Sunny tightened her hands around her mug. ‘‘I have things to do tonight, Zach.’’

He sensed her work was nothing that couldn't wait until morning. ‘‘You're hiding something from me, Sunny.’’

‘‘Because I didn't want to kiss you tonight?’’ she said coolly.

‘‘That's part of it,’’ he said slowly, knowing in his gut there was more to the sudden distrust in her eyes. If he'd done something to annoy her, he wanted to know about it.

Sunny released a troubled sigh. Confusion colored her low voice. ‘‘I don't want to play house with you, Zach.’’

‘‘Is that what you think we've been doing?’’ *He* thought they'd been building something important here, growing closer.

Sunny raked her teeth across her lip. ‘‘I don't know what we've been doing. Or even how or why I allowed myself to get sucked into this. All I know is that our marriage is only a temporary arrangement, Zach, one we both entered into for all the wrong reasons.’’

He couldn't dispute that. But he thought that they'd been making progress by the way she kissed him and melted in his arms at the slightest touch, that she wanted to make love as much as he did. Apparently he'd been wrong. ‘‘Meaning what?’’ Zach returned, unable to keep his disappointment in check. "That our marriage is going to remain one in name only?"

"Of course." Sunny planted her hands on her hips and regarded him exasperatedly. "Why would you ever have expected anything else?"

Chapter Nine

Woman, Walk the Line

"I'm glad you're back," Zach told Gramps several days later, when he stopped by the clinic upon his return.

Augustus handed over copies of his files, sent by the Knoxville Hospital. "So am I. If I'd had to pretend to be on a fishing trip much longer, Sunny would've gotten suspicious."

Zach had already been informed of the test results by phone, but he welcomed the chance to look at the lab reports himself. "How are you feeling?"

Augustus sank into a chair. "Better than I have in weeks, though why that should be after three days of lying around in a hospital bed is a mystery, to be sure."

"The rest in between tests probably did you good."

"Made me antsy is more like it. When will I know what's causing my chest pains?" he asked, frowning anxiously.

"I'm not sure," Zach said honestly, wishing he had better news to relate. Augustus's symptoms still had them all baffled. "So far all we've managed to do is rule things out. Your heart and lungs are fine. The dentist says there's no sign you've been grinding your teeth, which is something that can also cause chest pain. And your GI series was fine. Of course, the pain you've been experiencing could still be indigestion and linked to something you're eating, a particular spice or food. It just didn't show up as inflammation or anything serious in the tests.'' And Zach was relieved about that. Whatever was going on, Augustus was not dying.

"So what next?'' Augustus asked with a relieved sigh.

Zach picked up a pencil and turned it end over end. "There's got to be a pattern to these episodes. It's up to us to play medical detective and track it down. So the moment you have chest pain,'' Zach admonished seriously, "I want you to drop everything and come and see me. I don't care what time of day or night it is. We will figure this out.''

Augustus nodded. "In the meantime, is it all right if I go fishing—for real this time? I've missed my rod and reel.''

"Sure. As long as you don't overdo.''

"I won't. Sunny doesn't suspect a thing, does she?''

"No,'' Zach said. And he felt bad about keeping it from her. He'd wanted to confide in her the other night so much. These days, he didn't want anything between them holding them apart, not even her grandfather's secret.

"SO WHAT DO you think, Doc?'' Matilda said, showing Zach her red, blistered hands.

"I think you've got one of the worst cases of contact dermatitis I've ever seen. What have you been doing?"

"I've been washing dishes over at the diner and filling in for Rhonda-Faye, who's still out with her new baby."

"Well, you need to wear gloves when you put your hands in water, and apply this cream to your hands four times a day in the meantime."

"Will do. And Doc?"

"Yes, Matilda?"

"About those classes Sunny has been taking. She's really been putting her heart into them."

This was news to Zach.

"The only thing is, and I don't know quite how to say this and still be tactful."

"Just spit it out, Matilda."

"Well, judging by the reports Sunny has been giving back to the group, the other ladies and I feel that you may not be doing your part in return."

"Let me get this straight." Zach tamped down his anger with effort. "Sunny has been telling your group that I'm a bad husband?"

"Oh, no. Sunny would never say that, Doc. It's just sometimes when she's making her reports I get the feeling she's kind of disappointed in the way things have worked out. Don't get me wrong. She puts on a brave front and speaks in a cheerful tone, but underneath...well, I think in her heart she was wishing you all had had a more conventional or romantic start."

She wasn't the only one, Zach thought.

"But I think she really is trying. I think she wants this marriage of yours to work." Matilda pressed a hand to her ample bosom. "Oh, dear, I can see I've offended you with all my frank talk, haven't I?"

"It does seem like a violation of privacy, knowing what's going on in our marriage is being reported back to that class," Zach said.

"Slim doesn't like it, either," Matilda freely admitted. "And some of the lessons have given us rather confounding results. But overall he likes the changes the class is bringing to our marriage. And the same goes for all the other husbands. Why, we haven't paid this much attention to each other in years!" Matilda said. "If you would just give the class—and Sunny—a chance, Zach, I know the two of you could be happy," she said kindly.

Could they? he wondered, a little guiltily. He knew he hadn't given the relationship or Sunny a chance initially, but lately they had become a lot closer anyway. Was it possible that she was more serious than he'd been led to believe? Was it possible she wanted to make their marriage a real one, too? And that her testy behavior was due to her disappointment in him rather than her chafing at the increasingly intimate situation in which they found themselves? If that was the case, if Sunny was really trying to make this marriage of theirs work in her own convoluted way, Zach saw he owed her an apology.

"Furthermore, I know how you can make it up to her. Slim and the boys have all offered to help," Matilda continued exuberantly.

Making up with Sunny seemed like a good idea. Having the whole community in on the plan did not. "Help me how?" Zach asked warily.

"Why, help make Sunny feel better," Matilda said. "All you have to do is show up at our house, say around 9:00 p.m.?"

"YOU'RE WHERE?" Sunny gasped into the telephone. She had expected her parents to be angry with her, not rush to her side.

"About ten minutes away from your house," her mother replied. "You had to know that as soon as we received your letter we'd want to see you."

Suddenly her desire to get even with her parents for trying to dupe her into marrying Andrew did not seem like such a good idea. "You're planning to stay with Gramps, aren't you?" Sunny asked nervously.

"Honey, we want to stay with you. We want to get to know your husband and well...help you straighten things out. Oh, your father's waving at me. Gotta run."

Sunny stared at the phone. Her parents there in ten minutes? Heart pounding, she raced for the stairs. Grabbing a stack of Zach's clothes and medical journals, she tossed them about the master bedroom, then raced back to the guest room to get the rest of his stuff. Her parents mustn't guess this was a marriage in name only or she'd never hear the end of her foolhardiness. And considering the way things were turning out, Sunny thought, as she wiped a stream of perspiration from her brow, she knew they would be right.

Finished moving most of his stuff, she put a set of clean sheets on the bed in the master bedroom, hung fresh towels in the bathroom, tidied the sink and then raced for the linen closet again. She had just picked out a set of fresh sheets for the guest-room bed, when she heard it. The unmistakable sound of Slim's fiddle, Fergus's guitar, George's banjo and Gramps's harmonica! And a familiar voice singing…"Love Me Tender"?

She swore again. She didn't know what Zach was up to now, but his timing couldn't be worse.

ZACH FELT LIKE a fool standing in front of Sunny's stoop, a bunch of daisies in hand, singing love songs off-key. Worse, the racket he and the band were making was causing quite a commotion. Doors and windows were opening all over the neighborhood. Including Sunny's.

A come-hither smile on her face, she sauntered out to greet him. "Welcome home, sweetheart," she purred, lacing her arms about his neck. Standing on tiptoe, she kissed him soundly on the lips.

Telling himself the best way to end the impromptu concert was to act as if he and Sunny had much better things to do than stand out there singing all night, Zach wrapped both arms about her waist and shifted her close. Ignoring the way she stiffened in surprise, he gave the kiss all he had and then some.

Male laughter sounded behind him. Then applause.

"See, Zach?" Slim said. "Told you that serenading her with love songs would work."

"Always does," George agreed.

"I think you fellas better let me take my husband inside," Sunny crooned. "Before we really put on a show."

Zach inclined his head in Sunny's direction. "You heard the woman, fellas." He was glad he didn't have to do any more singing.

"We'll let y'all cook while the griddle's hot," Fergus said with a naughty wink. "But if you need us to come back, so Zach can do some more singing, y'all just holler."

"Will do," Sunny promised, wrapping her slender arm about Zach's waist. She rested her head against his chest.

Zach liked the feel of having her so close. They waited on the sidewalk and waved goodbye as the fellas all drove off. "Thanks for rescuing me," Zach said with a sigh of relief.

Sunny stayed where she was as yet another car drove up. "We're not rescued yet," she murmured. "Far from it. So play along with me. Mom, Dad!" she said as an elegantly dressed couple in their fifties emerged from the rented Lincoln. "I'm so glad you could come!"

"YOU DIDN'T TELL ME we were having company," Zach whispered in Sunny's ear.

"That's because I didn't know myself until ten minutes ago," she whispered back.

"So this is your husband," Sunny's dad said, giving Zach the once-over as Sunny moved out of Zach's arm and into his.

Zach immediately snapped to attention, while Sunny hugged her folks.

"Sir." He shook hands with her father. Somehow meeting Sunny's folks made their marriage all the more real. He nodded at her mother, not sure what was expected of him, only knowing he wanted things to go smoothly for Sunny's sake. "Mrs. Carlisle."

"Please, Zach. Call us Elanore and Eli."

"You should have let us know you were coming," Sunny said as they started up the steps.

Zach had never seen Sunny's cheeks so pink, her eyes so vulnerable. He wanted to wrap her in his arms and hold her close, reassure her everything was going to be all right.

"How about some coffee?" Sunny said the minute they got in the door.

"Actually, sweetheart, we'd like to talk with you alone, if you don't mind," Eli said.

Zach excused himself. Sunny sat down on the living room sofa. "What is it?"

"You married him to get even with us, didn't you?" her father said.

"It would serve you right if I had," Sunny retorted, folding her arms in front of her. "I still can't believe you actually sent Andrew Singleton here!"

"Andrew's a nice man," Elanore said.

"Oh, please! He wanted a merger, not a marriage!" Sunny shouted back. "And to think I almost fell for it."

"What happened?" Zach appeared in the doorway, a grim look on his face. Sunny could tell he'd heard everything.

"Zach, this is none of your concern," Elanore said.

"He's my husband. Of course it's his concern," Sunny interrupted, motioning Zach into the living room. "My parents set me up with the son of a fellow attorney shortly after I moved here. He pretended to be vacationing. He was really sent here on a mission to sweep me off my feet and get me out of Carlisle permanently. It would have worked if I hadn't figured out the connection as we started to make our wedding plans."

"Sunny confronted Andrew about the situation," Elanore continued. "And the wedding was off. She's still angry with us, which is why, no doubt, she did not let us know about your wedding in time for us to attend."

Sunny thrust out her chin stubbornly. "I didn't want you to try to stop it."

"You're saying it should have been stopped?" Eli retorted.

"Eli, dear, we did not come here to fight with Sunny. We came here to make up with her and lend whatever assistance she needs." Elanore cast a glance at Zach, who was hovering protectively at Sunny's side. "Perhaps she doesn't need as much help as we thought. At any rate, this is probably something best talked out in the morning."

Eli sighed. "I guess you're right. We have been on our feet for twenty-two hours straight now."

They did look exhausted, Sunny noted. Maybe they cared about her more than she'd thought. "I've already made up your room. You can have ours," she said.

Her parents said good-night and went quietly up the stairs. Zach waited until he heard the bedroom door shut, then took her by the hand and led her out onto the front porch. "Did you marry me to get back at them?" he asked grimly.

"It started out that way." Sunny swallowed, knowing she owed him honesty and a lot more. "But now it's turned into so much more than that, Zach. And furthermore," she said, her heart beating wildly, "I don't care what my parents think about my marrying you the way I did. They are not going to interfere in my relationship with you and that's final!"

Zach realized Sunny was offering him what he had always wanted in a relationship. "I'm glad to hear that," he said with a grin, "because those are my sentiments exactly."

"YOU DIDN'T TELL them the truth about our marriage, did you?" Zach asked as he and Sunny made up the bed in the guest room.

Sunny paused to look at Zach. For a person who hated familial interference, he was taking this all remarkably well. "They already think my moving to Tennessee was a mistake."

"How come?"

Sunny poured her heart out to him. "Because in their opinion, there's nothing for me here." She plumped a pillow almost violently. "They saw I had the very best education. Now they want me to put it to better use," she confided bitterly, as she plopped down on the edge of the half-made bed.

Zach sat down beside her. He wrapped a comforting arm around her shoulders and pulled her close. "They don't know you at all, do they?" he commiserated softly.

Sunny rested her face on his shoulder. She loved the way he felt, so warm and solid and strong. "They never have," she admitted sadly. "I used to think it was my fault, but now I know that's not true. They love me in their own way. But it's in a detached way one moment, a smothering way the next. There's never any happy medium with them."

He held her closer. "I'm sorry." He rubbed her arm consolingly and turned toward her.

"Why?" Loving their intimacy, Sunny buried her face in the curve of his neck.

"Because living that way has obviously been very tough on you."

Sunny luxuriated in the brisk wintry scent that was him, then drew back to look at him seriously. "Are you close to your folks?" she asked quietly at length, wondering if he'd had a happier childhood than she had.

Zach nodded, all too willing to admit it as he squeezed her hand in his. "I can tell them just about everything."

The edges of her lips began to curl. "Except that we're married," she said, taking a guess.

Zach nodded. He looked deep into her eyes. "But only because they'd worry about me if they knew it wasn't a real marriage, and they'd want to celebrate with me if they thought it was. I felt we already had enough interference in our lives as it was."

Sunny breathed a shaky sigh of relief. "I'll second that," she said with a light laugh. She didn't know what she would do if they had another set of parents on their doorstep.

Turning slightly toward him, so their knees were touching, Sunny rested the palm of her hand just above his knee. "Do you have any brothers and sisters?"

"It's just me, my mom and dad now," Zach said, a brooding look appearing suddenly on his face. "I had a sister who died," he said quietly after a moment.

But to Sunny's increasing disappointment, he didn't continue. He climbed in on his side of the bed, turned his back to her and shut his eyes. Seconds later, he was asleep.

Sunny lay staring at the ceiling, thinking of all the kisses they'd shared, and the ones they hadn't. So much for her worrying about her virtue, she thought. Even in the same bed, married to the man, she couldn't have been safer. It was turning out to be exactly what she wanted, a night that was affable enough to fool her parents into thinking everything was fine between her and Zach. So why was she feeling so disappointed?

ZACK AWOKE at the first light of dawn to find a stack of pillows and a rolled-up blanket between Sunny and him. He eased from the bed, grabbed a robe and headed downstairs. He wouldn't be able to dress for work until he could get to his clothes, which Sunny had stuffed in her closet. And he wouldn't be able to do that until her parents were awake.

To his surprise, Eli and Elanore were already in the kitchen. They had made a pot of coffee and were working on a thick stack of legal papers.

"We're still on European time," Elanore explained.

Zach nodded. "I saw the packed suitcases in the front hall," he said. He wondered how Sunny would react to that.

"We've got a meeting in New York late this afternoon," Eli explained. "We're flying out of Memphis-Nashville at 1:00 p.m."

Which meant they would have to leave in a few hours, Zach thought. Sunny was going to be so disappointed.

"So where did you go to med school, Zach?" Eli asked.

"Vanderbilt," he said, knowing the third degree had a purpose. They wanted to know if he was good enough for their daughter.

Eli and Elanore beamed their approval at his alma mater.

"Good school. Very prestigious," Eli said.

"So how did you end up here?" Elanore asked.

Zach resented the implication that Carlisle was somehow less important because it was a rural location. "I had a contract with the state. They paid my tuition. In turn, I promised two years of service in a rural area."

"Of your choice?"

"Actually, it was a little more complicated than that. I applied to a number of places and then was assigned," Zach said. Which reminded him, he should check and see how his transfer request was going. Not that he was so inclined to leave now that he was beginning to get settled in at the clinic and he and Sunny had declared a truce. In fact, were things to progress to the point where he and Sunny became lovers he wasn't sure he would want to leave at all. Until his two-year assignment in Carlisle was up, of course.

"Well, Sunny had an excellent education, too," Elanore said.

"Her mother and I really think she is going through a phase and that she'll live up to her potential as soon as she gets this sojourn here out of her system," Eli said. "It probably had something to do with all those sociology classes she took at Smith."

"My being here has nothing to do with all the classes I took at college," Sunny said angrily. She stormed into the kitchen, hair in disarray, her terry-cloth robe wrapped tightly around her waist. "Furthermore, I resent your telling Zach that is the case."

"Now, Sunny," Elanore said with a beleaguered sigh. "It's not that we want to fight with you."

Sunny spread her hands. Her eyes sparkled with tears. "Then why did you come here? Why are you saying all these things?"

"Because we feel you're wasting your potential here," Eli explained gently. "With your education and credentials, you could be working for a top Fortune 500 company."

"I'm a CEO here," Sunny stressed.

"Of a regional furniture company, honey!" Eli shot back.

To Zach's surprise, Sunny kept quiet about her plans to expand Carlisle Furniture with a mail-order catalog business.

She folded her arms in front of her. "Why don't you just say it?" she retorted thickly. "The fact that I've come back here to live and work is embarrassing you in front of all your colleagues and friends."

"It's just that you're capable of so much more," Elanore said gently.

Eli nodded in affirmation. "We've got friends in influential places. We could call in a few markers and get you a job on the fast track, in Europe or here in the States."

Sunny swept a hand through her hair. Her mouth tightened. She stared at her parents in exasperation, then looked at Zach.

He knew she needed him. "I think Sunny is happy right where she is," he said firmly, moving to stand beside his wife and lace an arm about her shoulders. "And as far as I'm concerned, that's all that matters."

"THANKS FOR helping out like that," Sunny said after her parents had left, and they were both upstairs getting ready to go to work. "Though given the way you feel about living in Carlisle yourself, I'm not sure why you did."

"You've got to make your own decisions, Sunny. Although their remarks did leave me with a few questions of my own."

"Such as?"

She plugged in her curling iron and sat down at the vanity table next to the bathroom sink. She was dressed in a mint green shirtdress with a cinched-in waist and a long swirling skirt. She looked beautiful in a hands-off sort of way...and was also highly emotional. So much so, in fact, that Zach wished he could take the day off work and spend it just being with her, offering her what comfort he could.

"Have you ever had any second thoughts about settling here permanently?" he asked as he smoothed shaving cream on his face.

"Let me guess," Sunny said grimly as she began to brush her hair. "You think I'm wasting my time, too."

Zach began to shave with long, smooth strokes. He hadn't agreed with Elanore and Eli's approach, but he knew they did have some valid points that should be considered. "You are well educated, with a lot of business savvy. Your parents are right. There probably are a lot of other opportunities out there for you."

Sunny leaned toward the mirror as she curled her bangs. "Living in Carlisle is like being part of one big family, and I adore it." Finished, she set her curling iron down and swiveled toward him. "Maybe if I hadn't already lived in Europe I'd want to see more of the world. But thanks to my parents, I've already seen and done so much. Right now what I want is a home, pure and simple, and I've got that here."

Zach rinsed and towel-dried his face. "Carlisle is a friendly town—I'll give you that. Everyone cares about everyone else."

"But—?"

Zach shrugged as he reached for his dress shirt and slipped it on. "I don't like having to fight for control of my own life."

Sunny raised a lecturing finger his way. "If your life is out of control, it is not because you're living in Carlisle, Zach."

He reached for his tie and put it around his neck. "Then what is it?"

Sunny brushed past him in a drift of cinnamon-scented perfume.

"Maybe the close quarters and intense public scrutiny have just forced you to really examine your life for the first time. Maybe you're uncomfortable because you don't like what you find."

Zach followed her into her bedroom. He watched as she tossed shoes out of her closet, finally settling on a pair of ivory flats. "Hey, I've got nothing to feel ashamed about. I'm working in a noble profession. I've devoted my life to caring for other people."

"But what about your private life, Zach?" Sunny asked as she slipped on her shoes. "Take it from me, there's got to be more than meaningful work to make you happy. You've got to have a personal life, too."

Zach steadied her with a hand on her waist. "That's kind of hard to do when I'm married to a woman who barely gives me the time of day." He touched a gentle hand to the side of her face. "Unless, of course, that is going to change, and we're going to have some sort of private life together?"

Sunny extricated herself from his light, possessive hold and stepped aside. Her shoulders were stiff as she turned away from him. "You knew what the terms of this arrangement were going to be when we got together, Zach."

Yes, he had. He just hadn't realized it was going to be so hard living with her and not loving her. He wondered if she was feeling as deprived of intimacy and affection as he was. "Unless you're prepared to renegotiate our agreement—" he countered hopefully.

Her eyes lit up like firecrackers. "If you're talking about sex—" Sunny warned.

Zach grabbed his billfold off the bureau and slid it in his back pocket. He figured, as long as they were laying everything on the line, they might as well be honest and up-front about this, too. "What else?"

Love, Sunny thought. *I want love. I won't settle for anything else.* "Well," she said with an arch expression, "there's cooking and cleaning—"

"Forget that," Zach grumbled. That sounded like another have-to lesson from her class on marriage.

Sunny gave him a chastising look. He wanted to make her his, all right, she mused, but only in a physical sense. "That's what I thought," she stated grimly.

"What?" Zach followed her out the bedroom and down the stairs.

She picked up a pair of gold earrings on a downstairs hall table and clipped them on her ears. "You're not interested in an equal-opportunity marriage." Her jaw set in silent censure.

Zach lounged against the banister, watching Sunny. He wasn't pleased to be sparring with her this morning. He'd much rather spend his time loving her. But at least their latest battle of the sexes had gotten her mind off her parents.

It had also brought excited color to her cheeks and a sparkle to her eyes. "Of course, I might be interested in a more chore-equitable arrangement," he teased, unable to help himself from provoking her a little more. "Providing the price was right."

Sunny shot him a look meant to cool his jets. "For instance?"

"I can see us doing the dishes together if we cozied up afterward."

Sunny knew he could. Worse, she thought, she could imagine cuddling with Zach, too. But the easy, vivid images that came to mind would not keep her heart from being broken. Only she could do that. Slowing her pulse with effort, she looked at her watch.

"I've got to get going. Matilda's waiting to give me a lift to work."

"What time do you think you'll be home tonight?" he asked. Maybe the two of them could drive down the mountain, go out to dinner...

"I don't know." Sunny frowned. "I've got a full day ahead of me, plus a supper-hour meeting with the catalog photographer and a marriage class after that. And I want to stop by and see Gramps this evening and catch him up on what's been happening at the factory since he got back from his fishing trip."

Zach shifted uncomfortably. Sunny was going to be furious when she found out where Augustus had really been.

"Don't look so upset," she scolded, misinterpreting the reason behind his dismay. "I really do have a lot to do."

Zach didn't doubt that. He also knew it wasn't his imagination. She was avoiding him like the plague. "You'll be home late, then?" he said grimly. And wondered what the men in the community would advise him to do about that. Put his foot down or weather the storm?

Sunny nodded, her expression brisk and businesslike as she picked up her briefcase. "Don't wait dinner for me."

ZACH SLID his TV dinner in the oven as the front door slammed with hurricane force. Seconds later, Sunny was framed in the kitchen doorway.

"How could you not have told me my grandfather was just hospitalized!" she stormed.

Zach swore. "How'd you find out?"

"The hospital. They called Personnel because there was a question about his insurance."

"Have you talked to him?"

"He's out fishing!"

Zach steered her resisting body into a chair. "Sit down and I'll explain." Minutes later, when he'd finished, she stared at him, looking even more upset.

"And there's still no diagnosis?" she asked, her lower lip trembling.

"No. There isn't. But we're working on it and I'm sure—" Zach's eyes tracked the sound of a car in the driveway. He looked out the window, to see a black Cadillac in the drive. Augustus got out of the car, winced as he moved toward the house. Sunny and Zach were outside in a flash. Together they helped him into the house.

"When did it start?" Zach asked. It was obvious Augustus was in pain.

"While I was fishing."

"Tell me exactly what you were doing," Zach ordered.

"Nothing to tell." He demonstrated with his left hand. "I was casting my line in the stream—" Augustus winced as he moved his arm above his head. "Damn, there it goes again."

And suddenly Zach knew what it was.

"Bursitis!" Augustus said minutes later when Zach had finished his exam and had injected steroid medication and local anesthetic into the painful joint. Together he and Sunny packed Augustus's shoulder in ice.

"All that fly-fishing you've been doing since you semiretired has aggravated your shoulder joint. The pain you felt originated there, then spread out into your chest and down your arm, mimicking heart pains or angina,'' Zach said. ''We didn't pinpoint the source because up until now there's been no swelling or inflammation in the joint.''

''But it's there now,'' Augustus said.

''Yes. Very visible, too. Which means you are going to have to lay off the fishing for a couple of weeks, until you heal.''

''Okay,'' Augustus said. He blew out a weary breath. ''Thanks, Zach.''

''You're welcome,'' Zach said with a smile. He felt as relieved as Augustus looked. Sunny was not nearly as happy. She let him have it after they saw her grandfather home.

''I can't believe you kept that from me,'' she said tersely, marching back to Zach's truck, her hands balled into fists at her side.

''I had no choice.'' He walked along beside her, his shoes crunching on the gravel drive. ''Augustus was my patient. And he did not want you to know.''

''But what if something had happened? What if he'd been in the hospital and—'' Sunny whirled to face him at the truck door. ''You still should have told me. Dropped a hint. Something! I'm your wife!'' Her voice was choked as she regarded him tearfully. ''I thought we were close,'' she whispered.

''We are,'' Zach insisted, aware that she looked more hurt and confused than he had ever seen her.

But she only shook her head at him in a way that let him know she was comparing his machinations with Augustus to those of her parents. They had deliberately conspired to keep her in the dark.

"Not close enough, apparently," she said grimly.

His own frustration and disappointment boiling over, Zach studied her upturned face. As he had feared, Augustus's secret had driven a wedge between them. It was going to be a while before Sunny forgave him. If she did at all.

"YOU RENTED a what for us?" Zach asked Friday afternoon, when he arrived home to find Sunny lugging a suitcase down from the attic.

"I rented a houseboat for the weekend," she explained patiently, avoiding his eyes all the while.

Had she done this because she wanted to be close to him, Zach would've been exultant. But it was all too clear from the determined expression on her face that this was not the case. She was still as confused as ever, wanting to trust him, not quite sure she should. But that was something, Zach assured himself firmly, that could be overcome.

"Let me guess what prompted this," he said dryly, giving her a hand with the suitcase. "Your class, right?"

Sunny popped the case open and began filling it with clothing. "My assignment was to plan something special for just the two of us," she admitted sheepishly, pausing to look up into his face. He could tell, even if she wasn't quite ready to admit it yet, that she wanted to make up with him, too.

She wet her lips and continued softly, still holding his eyes, "I remembered what you said once about going away for the weekend being your salvation in med school and thought it might be nice to try it. That is. . .if you don't mind."

"I don't mind," Zach said, already anticipating their time alone, away from the prying eyes of the community. This was his chance to make amends with her.

As he pictured Sunny in a bikini, sunbathing on the deck of the boat, it was all he could do not to groan. The close quarters were going to be murder, just as not making love to her was going to be sheer torture. But he was looking forward to spending time with her alone, he realized, as he began to pack, also. And he could no longer deny that he did not want this marriage of theirs to end.

Chapter Ten

This Can't Be Love

"Maybe we should turn back," Sunny suggested, peering at the gray sky overhead.

"After we drove two hours to get here?" Zach said, striding down the dock. He tossed their suitcases onto the deck of their rented houseboat, then returned for the cooler full of ice and soft drinks. "Not on your life, Sunny."

She grabbed a sack of groceries from the front seat of his pickup. "What if it rains?" She didn't know why, but suddenly she was very nervous about spending the entire weekend alone with Zach. Maybe because he looked so incredibly sexy and at home on the shores of the Tennessee lake.

Zach swaggered back to her side, happier than he had been in weeks. He grabbed the last two sacks of groceries, a portable stereo and a first-aid kit. "Then we'll throw out our fishing lines and stay inside the boat."

"I don't know." Sunny continued to drag her feet. What if she found herself succumbing to the heat and passion of his kisses? A lot could happen in forty-eight hours.

Zach dumped the rest of the stuff on the deck, then turned and put his hands on her shoulders. He gazed down at her warmly. "Sunny, trust me. Everything is going to be fine. A little rain never hurt anything. Besides, the forecast calls for bright and sunny skies tonight and tomorrow. We're going to be fine."

He was right. She was being silly. "If it rains I'll just work on the catalog."

Zach lifted his brow, suddenly a lot less happy. "You brought work with you?"

"In my suitcase," Sunny confirmed. Her work had sustained her on more than one occasion. This would be no exception, she told herself firmly.

"Gonna tell your class that when you get back?" Zach teased as he gave her a hand onto the deck of the houseboat.

Sunny blushed. She could imagine the lectures she would get if she did. "That'll have to be our little secret, Zach."

"I don't know, Sunny," he drawled, rubbing his jaw.

He gave her a temptation-laced glance that set her heart to pounding.

"I'm not very good at keeping secrets."

Nor was he any good at hiding his growing desire for her, Sunny thought. "Well, try," she advised airily, aggravated to find she was blushing all the harder. Zach was acting as if this trip were going to be the honeymoon they'd never had. And damned if his feelings weren't just a bit contagious.

She had to stop thinking like this. Had to get busy.

"I'll put the galley in order," Sunny said with an outward calm she couldn't begin to feel. Aware of Zach's eyes on her, lovingly tracing every inch of her, she grabbed the groceries and slipped inside the houseboat.

Out on deck, Zach leaned over the bow of the thirty-two-foot boat and brought up anchor. Seconds later, they were on their way.

By the time they had reached the middle of the lake, the clouds had rolled in. Thirty minutes later, it began to sprinkle. Two hours later, fat raindrops thudded on the deck and roof of the houseboat.

Sunny groaned. She should have known the weather would work against them. She should have listened to the regional forecast before she'd left. Now it was too late. They were here and would just have to muddle through as best they could.

That, too, became more of a test than she'd expected as visibility soon dropped to ten feet. Swearing at the treacherous conditions, Zach steered the boat over to a secluded cove surrounded by a thick forest of trees and a steep, rocky shore. He cut the motor, then turned to face her.

"Don't suppose you located a rain slicker or umbrella anywhere in the cabin?" he asked languidly.

Sunny shook her head, aware he was going to have to leave the cabin and go out on deck to secure the boat. "Sorry."

"No problem," he said.

Sunny watched him stride out into the pouring rain. He moved around the rear of the boat. By the time he had dropped anchor and come back inside the cabin, his shirt and shorts were soaked clear through to the skin.

Sunny handed him a towel.

"Thanks," he said.

Mouth dry, she watched as he stripped off his shirt and headed into the bedroom to change. He came back out in shorts and a polo shirt, his hair slicked back from his face.

Rain pounded overhead, so loudly they had to shout to be heard. "The storm'll pass soon," Zach promised, as Sunny handed him a cup of coffee.

But the rain didn't stop. And that was when the real trouble began.

LIGHTNING SHIMMERED above, followed by a nearly simultaneous crack of thunder. Four o'clock in the afternoon, and the sky was nearly pitch-black. It was getting very scary, Sunny thought nervously as she peered out the windows for the thousandth time. In fact, it looked like tornado weather.

She paced back and forth in the small interior of the cabin, the galley on one side of her, the booth where Zach lounged on the other. Great gusts of wind rocked the boat, while rain still pounded on the roof overhead.

"You're not supposed to be in water during a thunderstorm," Sunny said shakily.

"We're not in the water. We're in a boat."

"A boat that's on water," Sunny said pointedly, wringing her hands in front of her.

"Please relax, will you?" Zach said as another jagged fork of lightning exploded in the sky. He stood impatiently. "It's just a storm. It'll be over soon."

"Just a storm," she muttered, covering her ears as another crack of tremendous thunder sounded overhead and another gust of wind shook the boat. Up above them on the bluff, lightning sliced into a towering walnut tree. A flash of fire followed, then the branch went tumbling down into the water ten feet from the bow of the houseboat. Above them, the trunk continued to smoke. The only thing that saved it from leaping into flames was the continuous downpour of rain.

Sunny shook her head, trembling over the close call. "Okay, that does it. I'm getting us out of here." She went to the captain's wheel and reached for the key in the boat ignition.

Zach was by her side in an instant. "What the hell do you think you're doing?"

"Getting us out of here." She started the boat with a roar.

He covered her hand with his and just as decisively turned the motor off. "I dropped anchor, remember?"

Fuming, Sunny whirled on him. "Then pull it up," she ordered anxiously. They were going to die out there and it was going to be all his fault.

"We're safe here in this cove," Zach said.

His implacable certainty infuriated her even more. "The only way we'll be safe is if we're back on land. Now, are you going to pull up that anchor or not?" she asked, frustrated beyond belief.

"Not." Zach took the key from the ignition, pocketed it and sat down grimly.

"Fine." Sunny leapt off the captain's seat. Her mind made up, she headed for the sliding-glass door at the front of the boat, which led out to the covered deck. He might be fool enough to want to die on this stupid boat, but that did not mean she had to join him.

Zach vaulted after her. "Come back here!" he shouted.

Sunny was already struggling around the side of the boat. The wind blew her back. She landed in Zach's arms. He clamped his arms around her decisively. "Come back inside, Sunny!" he ordered.

Bristling at the cool decisiveness in his voice, she pushed against his chest. "No!"

"You're hysterical," he shouted in her ear, holding her all the firmer.

"No, I am not, but I will be screaming if you don't let me get us out of here!" she shouted back.

Again he refused to let her go, merely turned her around so she was facing him. Arms locked around her middle like a vise, he commanded, "Stop fighting me and come back into the cabin!"

It wasn't only Zach she was fighting. It was the idea of them being alone, the thought that something terrible might happen now, this very afternoon, and her life would be all over, and she would never have known. She had to get out of there. Pulse pounding, she twisted in his arms. Swearing at her lack of cooperativeness, Zach held her all the tighter and dragged her toward the door, regardless of her feelings. The next thing she knew, she and Zach landed in a heap on the wet deck.

Still, rain pounded them, the wind roared. In the distance, Sunny saw what she had feared. The tail end of a funnel cloud touching down on the opposite side of the lake. "Oh, God, Zach!" Shaking, she pointed in the opposite direction.

His arms tightened protectively around her as he saw the tornado, too. In terrified silence, they watched it head across the lake, in a path parallel to them.

"Let's go into the cabin now," Zach said. He helped her up from the deck. They scrambled inside, both of them soaked to the skin.

The tornado continued on across the lake, touching down occasionally, sending debris flying in its wake. Finally it passed out of sight. The storm quieted somewhat. Sunny stared at the horizon for long minutes afterward, still shaking badly. "Now can we get out of here?" she said, distressed tears filling her eyes.

Zach looked at the storm around them. "I know it's bad, Sunny. I'm sorry. But we're still safer where we are," he said.

Sunny pushed the damp hair off her face. "What if another tornado comes?"

"We're still better off here than out on the lake," Zach said. He narrowed his eyes at her. "I don't suppose you brought any liquor with you?"

She shook her head mutely.

"Then we'll just have to use what we've got to calm you down," Zach said. Before she had time to resist, he scooped her up in his arms and carried her back to the bedroom...and the queen-size pull-down bed. He set her down next to it. "You're still shaking," he said, already rummaging through the clothes she'd hung up in the tiny closet. "You need to get out of those wet clothes."

"So do you." Sunny winced as lightning illuminated the curtained windows and thunder flashed overhead. But she noted the rain pounding against the windows was finally abating, the wind dying down, just a little.

He tossed her a robe and slipped out of the bedroom with his in hand. When he returned seconds later, her shorts and top were draped over the closet door to dry and she was wrapped in white terry cloth from neck to ankle. Zach was wearing a brown velour monk's robe.

"I wish the storm would end," she said miserably, glancing anxiously out the window one more time.

"So do I." Zach took her hand and led her toward the bed, while lightning flashed outside. "But since we have no control over that, we'll just have to talk until it ends."

His manner resolute, Zach guided her down and stretched out beside her. Lying back on the pillows, he dragged her wordlessly into his arms and held her close.

Sunny figured if she was going to die, she might as well go happy.

"Now, tell me," he said as he stroked his hand through her hair, "why are you so afraid of storms?"

Sunny buried her head in his chest. She felt safer with his arms around her, as though nothing could hurt her, not as long as he was there. "It goes back to the summer I was five," she said in a muffled voice, clinging to his warmth and strength. She closed her eyes, trying to relax. "We were living in Greece."

"Sounds exciting," Zach said, now stroking her hair with the flat of his hand.

"Not really," she murmured, recalling that for her the time had been anything but that. "My parents were working on an important international merger, and we were living in a villa along the coast."

"Big or little?"

"Huge. Old. Scary. Anyway, they hired this governness to take care of me. She seemed ancient at the time, but looking back, I think maybe she was only middle-aged."

"Not very nice, I guess?"

"She could put on the charm for my parents."

"But not for you?" Zach asked sympathetically.

Sunny nodded. Getting caught up in the past, she paid less and less attention to the storm outside. "Mrs. Miniver didn't believe in coddling children, and I was a kid who needed a lot of attention."

"Because you spent so much time away from your parents?" Zach said, taking a guess.

"Yes. So one night when a really bad storm blew in off the sea, Mrs. Miniver decided I needed to learn to handle my fear of thunder and lightning. So she put me in my bedroom upstairs, turned out all the lights on the floor and went back downstairs." Sunny shook her head in abject misery, remembering. "The storm went on forever, and I cried and cried. When my parents got home around two in the morning, they found me under the bed. She got fired, of course. But my fear of storms has remained. I know it's irrational, but I really hate them." Sunny shuddered, clinging to Zach all the harder as he wrapped his arms around her tightly. "I can't stand feeling as if my life might be blown apart at any minute. I can't stand not feeling safe."

"I know what you mean," he said, stroking her hair. "Safety is important to me, too," he said softly. There was a heartbeat of silence. "There's nothing worse than seeing someone you love hurting and not being able to do anything to change it," he said softly.

"You talk as if you've been in a similar situation," she said.

Zach nodded, his expression grave. "When we found out my sister, Lori, was terminal, I tried to be there for her as much as I could. It was still one of the worst times in my entire life," he said thickly. "When she died, I made a vow to myself that I would never feel that helpless again. And as you can see," he remarked with dark humor, exerting incredible self-control over his emotions, as another rumble of thunder sounded overhead, "I haven't made much, if any, progress on that score. But what the hell," he concluded with a rueful shrug and a bittersweet smile, "I'm trying my best to control the universe."

"I've noticed," she said dryly.

"Yep, I bet you have," he drawled back.

Silence fell between them once more. He grinned at her. Sunny met his smile with one of her own. It was important to her that he had confided in her. It meant a lot to be able to confide in him.

His gaze turned gentle. He traced the curve of her mouth with his fingertip, the fragile caress heating her blood.

"Feeling better?" he asked softly.

Yes and no, Sunny thought. She wanted to make love with him so badly she ached. The edges of reality and fantasy were blurring. She was beginning to feel really married to Zach, committed to him, even though she knew that was not the case. And until it was, maybe it would be better if she put some distance between them.

"You don't seem as frightened as you were," Zach continued.

The truth was, when she was in his arms, she wasn't scared at all, Sunny realized. The problem came in how she would feel when he was gone. If he left. She was still working on somehow inducing him to say.

"You know, I am feeling better, now that the worst of the storm seems to be past us," she admitted on a ragged breath, aware that wise or not, it wouldn't take much convincing at all to get her to surrender everything to him. "In fact, I think I can get up now," she said briskly, deciding the inevitable could be postponed for just a little while longer.

"Not yet," he murmured gently, rolling so she was beneath him, framing her face with his hands. He looked down at her, his eyes glowing with love. "Not until I tell you how I feel." His voice caught. "If something had happened just now, Sunny. If that tornado had hit us. If I'd lost you—"

"I know, Zach, I know. I felt the same." She held on to the edge of his robe, the raw vulnerability in his face giving her the courage to say what was in her heart, had been there all along. "But we are here. And we're together and safe."

In that instant, the world fell away, and it was just the two of them. She knew, more than anything, what she wanted. The love and closeness that had always eluded her, the desire only Zach could give.

Eyes darkening, he lowered his mouth to hers. His tongue parted her lips and swept inside her mouth. With a moan, she wreathed her arms around his neck and clasped him to her and felt his body and hers heat instantly in response.

In a haze, she let him open her robe. His hands skimmed her breasts, sensitizing the curves, until she thought she might die from the pleasure of it. Needing, wanting, more intimate contact, Sunny arched into his touch. She trembled beneath his questing fingertips, caught up in the intensity of what she was feeling, all they had become to each other and all they could be, if only they took that giant leap of faith and made their marriage a real one.

"Oh, Sunny, I want so much to make you mine." He caressed the side of her face with his thumb. "I want so much to stop thinking and just feel . . . to stop planning so damn much and take a chance."

She knew exactly what he meant. "So do I, Zach." Her arms about his neck, she fitted her mouth to his and kissed him deeply, tenderly. She didn't know what the rest of her life held. And right now, selfish or not, she didn't care. She knew only that she had the chance to have a wild, reckless, incredibly passionate love affair. The chance to be with Zach like this might never come again. If she didn't take advantage of it, she would regret not making love with him the rest of her life. And she didn't want any regrets where he was concerned. She wanted only love and sweet, wonderful memories.

"Sunny, are you sure?" Zach asked, as his hands skimmed lower, slipping between her thighs. He touched her intimately, the heat of his caress sending her arching up into his questing hand.

"Yes, Zach, I'm sure," she said huskily, knowing if they weren't together now she would die.

Zach looked down into her eyes. He caressed her face lovingly, first with his eyes, then his fingertips and finally his lips. "Then I'm going to show you what love really is," he said softly, already working the robe from her shoulders, shrugging off his.

The light in the cabin was dim, but Sunny could see the beauty of his masculine shape. He was hard all over and lower still, below the waist, aroused beyond belief. Her heart pounding, the need in her an incessant ache, she closed her eyes, afraid she would lose her nerve if she thought about the enormity of the situation too much. She gripped his shoulders and took a deep breath. "All right if I let you lead the way?" she asked tremulously, never needing or wanting him more than she did at that moment, knowing what was at stake.

Zach sifted his fingers through her hair, his expression fierce with longing and the primal need to possess. Cupping her head in his hands, he angled her chin up to his. "I wouldn't have it any other way," he whispered, lowering his mouth to hers again.

His kisses melted one into another. She returned them passionately, her body feeling as if it were on fire from the inside out. She arched against his hands, yearning fervently. Sensations hammered at her. She strained against him, her body moving in undulations. "Now," she said softly, clutching at his shoulders. She was only sure she couldn't bear any more of this. She had to find a way to reach fulfillment. She had to find a way to be closer to him.

"Sunny—" He spoke as if in a haze, the hot, heavy fullness of him straining against her closed thighs.

"I want you, Zach." She slipped her hands around his hips and guided him lower still, so he was positioned precisely where he should be. She was trembling with a fierce, unquenchable ache. "I want you so much." More than she could ever have imagined. "Please. Now."

"I want you, too." He turned the words against her lips. Then he was pushing her thighs apart with his knees, stroking her gently. Sunny arched again, his name tumbling from her lips as he surged against her, penetrating the final barrier. Eyes full of wonder and fierce possessiveness, he stared down at her...and knew what she hadn't told him. "Oh, God. Sunny—" he breathed.

"Just love me, Zach," she whispered, bringing his mouth back to hers for another slow, searing, sensual kiss. "Just love me," she said again. And love her he did. His hands touched every inch of her, until she was weak with longing, overwhelmed with sensation. She surged up against him, every inch of her wanting every part of him.

ZACH LAY on his back, Sunny sprawled against his chest, her head on his shoulder. Outside, the storm had abated. Inside, as he wrapped his arms around Sunny and held her close, the storm was just beginning. In retrospect, he could see the signs had been there all along. He just hadn't wanted to deal with them because he had wanted her so much. Not just as a lover. But as his wife. "Why didn't you tell me?" he asked, stroking his hand over her slender shoulders.

Sunny snuggled against him contentedly. "Because it wasn't important." Her voice was muffled against his chest.

Like hell it wasn't. Zach was surprised by the fierce possessiveness welling inside him. He wanted only the best for Sunny. What had just happened did not fall into that category.

"Besides, I know how gallant you are at heart. You've demonstrated it many times. If I had, you would've—" She stopped, as if abruptly deciding she'd revealed too much.

Needing to see her face, he rolled so that she was beneath him. He cupped her shoulders warmly as his gaze roved her flushed features and kiss-swollen lips. "You're right, Sunny. I never would have made love to you if I'd guessed—"

She traced idle patterns on his chest. "That I was a virgin?"

Zach nodded, feeling even worse now that she had said it. "Yes." He had handled this situation all wrong, let his feelings for her carry him away. He wasn't used to being out of control; the knowledge that he could be, under any circumstances, was hard to handle.

Sunny shrugged, as if it were no big deal. "Well, now I'm experienced," she said cavalierly.

Zach released a frustrated breath. "That's not funny, Sunny," he said, chastising bluntly, as guilt flooded him again. He had taken something precious from her, something that couldn't just be given back. And that in turn made their relationship even more complicated than it already had been. And dammit all, she had known that.

"Look, Zach, it had to happen sometime," she reassured him gently, her fingertips stroking his chest, making him want her all over again.

Zach scowled. Once again, Sunny was too naive for her own good. She should have had a real marriage, and until he'd come along she'd held out for just that, he admitted grimly to himself. But maybe it wasn't too late. "I'll make it up to you," he said softly, realizing he was more of an old-fashioned guy than he'd thought. "I promise."

Sunny's face flamed, as she mistakenly took his concern for her as rejection. Before he could correct her misimpression, she pushed away from him and sat up, dragging the sheet over her breasts. Her eyes flared with a temper she was working very hard to subdue.

"Listen, Zach," she lectured. "I never asked you to hold the key to my chastity belt. In fact, if you want to get technical about it, the way things were going...you had every right to expect we'd eventually make love."

No, Zach thought, he hadn't. He'd only hoped.

"This doesn't have to change anything," she persisted willfully.

He shook his head at her, amazed at her innocence once again. "You're wrong, Sunny," he said gently. "What happened between us just now changes everything." Because she had given her heart to him—body and soul—and now their marriage was a real one in every respect.

SUNNY VAULTED from the bed, the sheet draped about her like a long white toga. She couldn't believe he was filled with ambivalence about the most wonderful thing that had ever happened in her life. Now reality was sinking in. "Why does it have to change everything, Zach?" she asked coolly, slipping out of the bedroom and into the galley. She bent to extract a can of icy lemonade from the cooler and settled into the booth. Outside, the storm had passed. Only a gentle rain remained.

"Because it does," he insisted.

Sunny watched as Zach wrapped himself in his robe. His straight ash blond hair all tousled, his face shadowed with just a hint of evening beard, he had never looked sexier. "You don't have to feel guilty," Sunny said quietly. *You don't have to feel trapped.*

"How do you expect me to feel?" He got himself a cold soda and joined her in the tiny vinyl booth. Maybe if he got her talking, he'd find out how she was feeling about all this, too.

How about pleased, instead of horrified, Sunny thought, taking a long sip of her lemonade. But seeing that wasn't about to happen, at least not today, she shrugged. "Sexually satisfied, I guess." She turned to look at him and said slyly, "You were satisfied, weren't you?"

Zach swore, the heat of his embarrassment and chagrin moving from his neck into his face. He looked heavenward for his answers. "Why me?"

Sunny grinned, enjoying his discomfiture. It wasn't often the tables were turned. "That's no answer, Zach," she answered with an inner steeliness she couldn't begin to feel.

He leveled his glance back at her. "You know I...was," he said thickly.

"How would I know?" she shrugged. "It's not like I've had a lot of experience in the area, you know," she said dryly.

"Yes, I know," Zach drawled.

His blue eyes glimmered as if he had every intention of making her his again. But not before they'd talked, Sunny surmised.

"And now that we're on the subject—" he captured her bare legs beneath the table and shifted them onto his lap "—why haven't you had a lot of experience?"

She closed her eyes and didn't answer. Zach stroked her legs, from ankle to knees. "You wanted the first time to be with your husband, didn't you?" Not just someone who was pretending to be your husband, he thought, then swore inwardly again. Maybe if they'd agreed to stay married and make their union a lasting one, it would have been different. But they hadn't. So he'd have to convince her...to make their marriage last, not just for a short time, but forever.

Sunny ignored the tingles starting beneath his caressing fingertips. She stared at the tabletop, beginning to get embarrassed now despite herself. "I waited because I wanted it to be special," she admitted reluctantly, not meeting his eyes.

"And it wasn't," Zach interrupted, with a self-effacing sigh.

She glanced up. He was so hard on himself sometimes. "What makes you think that?" she asked curiously. For her, it had been very special.

"Because it just wasn't—that's all." At least not special enough to make her want to stay married to him, Zach thought, his determination growing. "But it could be," he said as he took her hand and pulled her out of the booth.

"Zach—"

He wrapped her in his arms and pressed his lips into the fragrant softness of her hair. "Sunny, we can't leave it like this."

Sunny shook her head. Through the opening of his robe, she could see the suntanned column of his throat, muscled chest and crisp golden brown hair. She pressed the flat of her palm on his skin. Confusion clouded her eyes. "I haven't the slightest idea what you're talking about."

Zach's heart thudded heavily beneath her hand.

"Precisely my point," he said dryly.

Sunny sighed and ran her hand up to his shoulder. "I think what happened was wonderful." She couldn't ever remember feeling as loved as she had when he'd made her his for the very first time.

Zach traced the swell of her breasts, above the tucked-in sheet. "You're right—it was great—but it could have been a lot better."

Sunny tilted her head back to better see his face. Zach was half teasing, half serious. "What do you mean?" she said softly, wondering all the while if he was falling in love with her as hard and fast as she was with him. Had it not been for the crazy way they'd gotten together, would he have been this open with her?

Zach raked his fingers through her thick red-gold hair. "If I'd known you were a virgin, I would have gone about it very differently," he said gently. "You'll just have to trust me on the fact that your introduction to lovemaking could have been a lot more ... um ... enticing. Fortunately," he teased, sifting his hands through her hair and giving her a decidedly sensual glance, "it's not too late for me to make amends."

But did he love her? she wondered. Or was he just trying, once again, to right another wrong? Until she knew for sure... "Zach, I—I'm tired," Sunny fibbed.

Just as he'd suspected, Zach thought, she already had one foot out the door again. He quirked a brow. "Too tired to see what else you've been missing all this time?"

Sunny hesitated. He would have to point that out. She had always been curious about what it would be like to have a lover. She studied his face, liking the rapt adoration she saw there beneath his overriding concern, loving even more the idea of making love with him all night. Though she couldn't imagine it being any more enticing . . .

The temptation to find out what else she'd been missing was great, but so was her anxiety, and right now, she felt she and Zach were poised on the brink of either total happiness or disaster. "If I'd known this was what we were going to be doing on this boat, I would have brought some champagne with us," Sunny groaned. "Anything to help me relax."

He massaged her shoulders. "You are a little tense."

"Now that I'm thinking about what's going to happen, Zach, I'm getting nervous about it again."

Zach paused. He dropped his hands. "Then maybe we should put it off a little while," he suggested.

Sunny wavered between relief and disappointment. It seemed he was full of surprises today. One minute possessive, the next willing to let her go her own way.

"The rain's stopped," he continued affably. "We could take a break, go on deck and enjoy the sunset. After all, we've got all weekend to perfect our love-making skills."

Sunny sighed. She had her reprieve. She just wasn't sure she wanted it.

"TRUST ME, Sunny. There's nothing like sleeping under the stars."

Sunny stood motionless beside Zach. She'd waited for him to make his move, and he hadn't. Not during dinner. Not after. Not at all.

She looked at the foot-high solid white Plexiglas railing on top of the houseboat. "At least we don't have to worry about falling off in our sleep. But if it rains, we're in trouble."

"It's not going to rain," he said firmly.

"If my memory serves me correctly, that's exactly what you said before," Sunny remarked sagely.

"Yeah, well, this time it wouldn't dare," Zach said as he dragged the mattress up on top of the sun deck, atop the houseboat cabin. Together he and Sunny spread out blankets, sheets and pillows. He took her hand and tugged her down beside him. They were both clad in menswear pajamas, thick cotton socks and deck shoes. "Trust me, Sunny, this will be a great place to spend the evening."

"I admit it's cozy up here," she said, looking up at the stars and the moon overhead. "Kind of like camping out, only better."

"It seems we're the only two on the lake tonight, doesn't it?" Zach said.

"Probably the only two people fool enough to be out here after that storm we had this afternoon," she joked, settling back on the pillows, her hands folded beneath her head.

"Yeah, well, there's something to be said for storms," Zach said softly, drawing an imaginary line down her middle.

"Oh, yeah?" Sunny teased, as the warm rain-scented air blew over them.

"The storms in your eyes are magnificent to see." He reached over and began to undo her pajama top.

She inhaled a shaky breath. "Zach—"

"Relax, Sunny."

He turned her on her side; she was nestled against his warmth, so she could see the gentle, serious light in his eyes.

"We've got all night." He cupped a hand behind her head and kissed her slowly, deliberately. "And I intend to take my time."

Where before there had been passion and urgency, there was only tenderness and care. He undressed her one button, one snap at a time.

He lingered over her breasts and her thighs and every sweet inch between. He kissed her repeatedly, languid kisses that were as intimate as his caresses. He kissed her in ways that revealed his soul. And she loved him back, starting shyly, growing more and more bold. Spearing her hands through his hair, across his shoulders, down his torso to his thighs, she offered him whatever he wanted from her, whatever he needed. And this time, she took, too.

She was lost in him. She was in love with him. And she needed him. Oh, Sunny thought, surging toward the outer limits of her control, how she needed him...needed this...wanted to feel loved...and so incredibly cherished.

ZACH PARKED in the driveway and cut the motor. Wordlessly he snapped off his seat belt and hers, dragged Sunny across the bench seat of his pickup into his arms and settled her on his lap.

"What are you thinking?"

She sighed wistfully, not sure when she had ever felt so content or so loved. "That what happened this weekend changes everything."

"For the better," Zach agreed as she laid her head on his shoulder. He chuckled softly. "Living with you and not loving you was getting to be damn hard."

Sunny stroked his chest with long, soothing strokes. She sensed he was delaying going back inside for the same reason she was. "Now that we're home again, Zach—" she began.

Reading her mind, he touched a fingertip to her lips. "I want to share your bed every night. Or you can come to mine. It doesn't matter, as long as we're together."

Sunny drew a deep breath. She could feel the thundering of his heart beneath her palm. "So this wasn't a fling?"

Zach shook his head. "We're married partners involved in a full-fledged love affair." He paused, studying her face in the moonlight. "How does that set with you?"

It frightened and thrilled her all at once. "I think I can live with it," she said cautiously, curling her fingers in the fabric of his shirt. As long as it doesn't ever end.

Zach smiled, his happiness as potent as hers. "So it's settled," he said, running a possessive hand down her spine. "From now on, we'll be together every night."

"Yes," Sunny said softly. They would make love endlessly and sleep wrapped in each other's arms. And for once, she wouldn't worry so much about the future.

Zach's eyes darkened passionately. He cupped the back of her head and kissed her gently. Within seconds, they were both trembling.

"If we stay out here much longer, we're going to end up giving the neighbors a show," he teased.

Sunny grinned, unable to imagine a time when she wouldn't want to make love with him over and over again. "You always did look cute wrapped in nothing but a chamois loincloth," she murmured.

"Not to mention what you do for a red-and-white checkered tablecloth," Zach quipped back, as they drew apart reluctantly and she slid off his lap. "But if we're going to play Nature Walk dress-up, we'll have to do it inside the house this time."

He hopped down and circled around the truck to help Sunny down. She paused as her feet hit the ground, frowning as she caught sight of her Land Rover. She was sure she'd left it parked out back. It was now next to the house and sporting a huge red ribbon across the top. Sunny glanced at Zach. He was grinning complacently. "Do you know anything about that?"

Zach gave her an aw-shucks look. "I just might." He set down their bags and took her hand. "Let's go see."

"It smells like . . . pine!" Sunny said in unmitigated delight, once they'd opened the door and the interior light had come on. "And is that new carpet on the floor?" Her vehicle looked brand-new again inside.

"Yep."

"Zach, how did you manage this?"

"I enlisted a chemist friend of mine from Vanderbilt. He was able to treat the leather seats, but he feared the carpet would be a lost cause, just as I did, so I had the local garage rip it out and replace it with new."

"I can't believe it!" Sunny stuck her head inside the truck. "No skunk smell! I can drive my Land Rover again!"

Zach pulled her against him, so they were both still facing her vehicle and touching front to back in one long, tensile line. "No more bad memories?" he said, clasping his hands in front of her.

Sunny grinned up at him. "From now on, Zach, the only memories we have of skunk are the funny ones."

"Good. Now there's only one thing left to do," he said, scooping her up into his arms. Holding her against his chest, he strode toward the front door of her house.

"And what is that?" she asked, her heart thudding heavily against her ribs.

Zach winked at her. Pausing on the steps, he bent his head to give her a slow, leisurely kiss that sent fire sizzling through her in waves. "Make some new memories," he said.

Chapter Eleven

Hearts in Armor

"That must have been some vacation you and Zach took," Gramps said slyly. "You haven't stopped glowing all morning!"

Sunny flushed. She had been afraid it would show. But she couldn't help it. She had never felt more loved in her life, even if Zach hadn't yet said the words.

"He even carried her up the steps and through the front door upon their return, honeymoon-style," Matilda added, as she joined the conversation around the coffeemaker.

Sunny's eyes widened in surprise.

"Sorry, honey," Matilda continued, "but the two of you are the talk of the town. It does all our old hearts good to see you two young-uns looking so happy."

"Especially mine," Gramps said. "I knew Zach was the man for you all along."

Sunny had known it, too; she just hadn't wanted to admit it to herself. And she wasn't going to confide it to Gramps, either, at least not yet. "I'm glad you all are so happy,'' she said dryly, ''but now it's time to get back to business. Has Chuck Conway arrived yet?''

''He's supposed to be here any minute to work with me on the new computer system,'' Matilda said.

''Please ask him to stop by my office and see me when he's through,'' Sunny said. ''I've got a few questions of my own to ask him.''

''Will do,'' Matilda said.

''Well, I'm going to check out the new designs and then go fly-fishing,'' Gramps said.

Sunny kissed his tanned cheek. ''Enjoy yourself. You've earned it.''

Gramps grinned back at her. He patted her shoulder affectionately. ''Thanks, I will.''

Sunny spent the rest of the morning in her office. Around noon, Chuck Conway appeared in her door. The thirty-year-old software engineer was wearing a gray herringbone suit that looked brand-new. An overabundance of after-shave clung to his jaw. ''Hey, Sunny,'' he said as he breezed in. ''Heard you wanted to see me.''

''Yes, I did, Chuck. Come on in.''

He shut the door behind him and strolled closer, running a hand through his slicked-back brown hair.

Sunny noted he appeared more self-conscious than usual.

''So what's up?'' Chuck asked, his eyes glued to her face.

Sunny got up from her desk and motioned him closer. Chuck's voice carried and she didn't want anyone overhearing what she was about to say. ''Do you think Matilda can handle that new system you installed for us?'' she asked.

Shoving both hands in his trousers, Chuck shrugged. "I think so."

Sunny bit her lip. "You're sure we don't need something simpler?" she insisted worriedly.

He shook his head. "Something simpler wouldn't meet your needs, Sunny. Therefore it'd be a bad business decision."

She sighed and looked into Chuck's eyes. She wanted him to understand. "Making Matilda feel incompetent because she can't understand the complicated system you installed is bad business, too."

"You could always hire someone else to help you out with it," he said. "Someone younger. And assign Matilda to something else."

"No, I don't think so."

"Well, then." Chuck grinned as if she'd given him an unexpected Christmas gift. "I guess I'll just have to come up here every day and see you all until we get things squared away," he said, stepping even closer.

Again he looked at her funny.

"Is everything okay?" Sunny asked, puzzled by the way he was peering at her.

"It will be," he said. "Once I get this over with."

Before Sunny could guess what he was going to do, he had bear-hugged her around the middle. Knowing he was about to kiss her, she shoved her elbows into his ribs. His legs got tangled up with hers.

He tripped and they both went sprawling, with Sunny crashing sideways into the display of untreated wood samples. She gasped as the soft pine splintered beneath her weight, ripping her panty hose and embedding in her skin.

"What the hell's going on in here?" George came crashing into the office. "Sunny, are you all right?"

George stepped over Chuck to get to Sunny. He helped her to her feet.

She looked down at her burning thigh and groaned. "Oh, no."

"YOU WANT to tell me how you got this injury?" Zach said.

"Not particularly," Sunny replied breezily. She kicked off her shoes, rolled down her panty hose. Hiking up her skirt, she carefully climbed up on the examining table and rolled onto her side. "However, if you must know, I crashed into a display and fell on some wood."

Zach narrowed his eyes at her, his proprietary male side coming to the fore. "It's not like you to be clumsy."

How well Sunny knew that. But she hadn't expected Chuck Conway's five-year crush to suddenly manifest itself in a pass today. In retrospect, she could see she never should have called him at home after-hours, asked him to meet with her alone. All had been "clues" he had added up the wrong way.

Both irritated and embarrassed to find herself in this situation, she propped her head on her hand and grumbled, "Can't you hurry it up with the medical treatment? I need to get back to the office."

Zach treated the area with antiseptic. "I'd love to oblige you, but these splinters are going to take time to get out."

Sunny groaned. She couldn't think of a more ridiculous and humiliating position to be in, though Zach didn't seem to mind the work, or the fact that she'd had to take off her panty hose and hike her skirt nearly to her waist.

"So. How has your day been?" she asked, in an effort to keep her mind off what he was doing.

"Busy. I saw fifteen patients this morning, and I have a nearly full appointment book this afternoon, too."

Sunny winced as he removed a splinter and put it in the basin beside him. "Word's spreading."

"You can say that again," Zach agreed. "And not just about my skills as a physician." He paused to take out two more splinters, then gave her an interested glance. "Do you know people saw me carry you across the threshold last night?"

Sunny blushed, even as she noticed how good he looked in a white lab coat. "It was mentioned to me, too."

Zach's face split into a grin. "Everyone thinks we're on a honeymoon," he reported, his voice dropping to a sexy whisper.

"It feels that way to me, too," she said. Which was another reason she didn't want to spoil the current romantic mood with stories about Chuck and his hopelessly misguided attempt to kiss her. In this instance, what Zach didn't know wouldn't hurt him, she decided.

"I'm glad to hear that you feel that way," he said. Finished taking out the splinters, he treated the area with antiseptic cream.

"Why?" Sunny asked, watching as he expertly bandaged her thigh, then ripped off his surgical gloves.

Zach leaned over her, caging her against the examining table. "'Cause this honeymoon of ours is not over yet," he warned in a voice that made her heart pound all the harder. "Not by a long shot," he promised as he pressed his lips to hers and delivered a long, leisurely kiss.

Sunny was trembling when he finally lifted his head. She knew if they hadn't been in the clinic, he would have made love to her then and there. With effort, she marshaled her thundering pulse.

"I've got a class tonight after work, but I'll try to be home as soon as I can after that. Maybe by around seven-thirty," she promised.

"I'll be home as soon as I can, too," he told her, looking as if he were anticipating their reunion after a day spent apart every bit as much as she was. "Unfortunately, tonight is my night to make house calls on the shut-ins in the area, so you'll probably beat me home. But not by much if I have anything to do with it," he vowed softly.

"WHAT A beautiful baby," Zach said, as he finished examining Heidi Pearson later that same day. He had stopped by their house at the end of his house calls to save Rhonda-Faye and George a trip to the clinic. Now, inside their warm cozy home, which was brimming with kids, he was glad he had.

"I didn't think physicians were supposed to be partial to their patients," Rhonda-Faye said, bundling her newborn daughter back up in swaddling clothes.

Zach winked at Rhonda-Faye and stepped over one of Toby's toys. "I won't tell if you won't."

"Are you going to have babies with Sunny anytime soon?"

Good question, Zach thought. Maybe it was time to start a family.

"Hi, Doc." George came into the room.

"Ready to get those stitches on your forehead out?" Zach asked.

"Sure thing." George sat down in the chair Zach indicated as Rhonda-Faye slipped from the room, Heidi in her arms. "Sorry about the way I acted when Rhonda-Faye went into labor," George said. "I get a little crazy whenever our kids are born."

"So I heard." Zach grinned.

"Think you'll do the same?" George asked.

That, Zach didn't know. "I consider myself to be pretty calm during medical emergencies," he said finally.

"You're pretty calm about what happened to Sunny today, too," George remarked casually, surprised.

"You mean about the splinters?" Finished taking out the stitches, Zach cleaned his scissors and tweezers thoroughly with alcohol.

"Yeah, the way it happened and all," George said matter-of-factly.

Once again, Zach had the feeling Sunny was deliberately shutting him out. Ever so casually, he replaced his scissors and tweezers back in his medical bag. Time to go on a fishing expedition. "What did you think about what happened?" Zach asked, folding his arms in front of him.

"Well, I know Sunny didn't see it coming, but I knew he'd make a pass at her eventually."

Zach froze. "What was the guy's name again?"

"Conway. Chuck Conway."

The same guy she had talked to on the phone. "I've never met him," Zach said benignly. "What's he like?"

George ran a hand over his hair. "Harmless. Nerdy. Kind of clueless, if you know what I mean."

I'm beginning to. "So he's had a crush on Sunny for a long time?" Zach asked.

"Yeah. I don't think she was even aware of it. You know how Sunny is. She doesn't see stuff like that, but me and the other guys did."

Then how come you didn't stop it? Zach tamped down his anger deliberately. "How was she at the time it happened?" Zach asked, then explained, "She was calm when she got here. She had kind of shrugged it off."

George rubbed at his jaw thoughtfully. "I think she was shocked, but she didn't take offense. She just figured it was a misunderstanding, that Conway read her wrong, which isn't surprising, 'cause like I said, the nerd's clueless."

Sunny should have told me this! Zach thought.

"Ticks you off, doesn't it, Doc?" George stared with a provoking grin.

"Well..." Zach shrugged. "She is my wife."

"So naturally you feel protective of her," George continued affably.

"Naturally."

"Want my advice?"

Zach knew he was going to get it anyway. Maybe George knew how to handle a situation like this. "Sure," Zach said.

"A woman likes a man to take charge. This Chuck Conway incident, for instance. Sunny would probably never admit it in a million years, but she probably secretly wanted you to go all jealous on her and get upset and so forth."

Zach didn't have to pretend to feel that way. He was upset. And Sunny was going to know it!

"I CAN'T DO THAT!" Sunny told her marriage class.

"Honey, with a body like yours, you've got nothing to hide," Gertie said.

"Right. It's the rest of us that ought to be worried about greeting our husbands at the door covered in nothing but plastic wrap!" Matilda said.

"Particularly me, since I just had a baby," Rhonda-Faye said, patting her ever-flattening tummy. "And can't participate in the...um...follow-through yet."

"Rhonda-Faye, you have permission to delay this particular exercise until your physician gives you the okay to resume relations," the instructor said.

"Seems fair," Matilda commented.

"Speaking of fairness," Sunny interrupted. "Can't we amend the lesson a bit?" she asked. "Forget the plastic wrap and just dress in a suggestive manner and greet our husbands at the door? For instance, I have a beautiful negligee I got as a wedding gift that I haven't even worn—"

"Sunny Carlisle, why ever on earth not?" Gertie demanded.

Sunny blushed. "I was waiting for the right occasion."

"That was for your wedding night!" Gertie said.

"Well, I uh—"

"What she's trying to say is she didn't need it on her wedding night," Matilda broke in, in an attempt to save the day. "And even if she had put it on, that cute young husband of hers probably would've taken it right off...so why not save it for later, when the love life got a little dull? But so far there hasn't been time for it to get boring, right, Sunny?"

Sunny knew she was blushing to the roots of her hair. She sank down in her chair, covering her red face with her hand.

All the women laughed. "I think you hit the nail right on the head," Rhonda-Faye drawled. "Not that it's surprising. Sunny and Zach are both young and gorgeous, and at that age where their hormones are in full bloom. They'd have to be monks not to appreciate each other, especially in this newlywed phase."

"Back to my question," Sunny said as she doodled aimlessly on the notepad in front of her. "Couldn't I just greet Zach at the door in that negligee? Maybe with some champagne?"

Maybe if she did, he would forget to ask more questions about how she'd gotten those splinters in her thigh earlier today, Sunny thought.

"All right, Sunny, if you'd be more comfortable, you can wear a negligee instead of plastic wrap. But the rest of the assignment still stands. And we want a full report during the next and last class!"

SUNNY LOOKED at herself in the mirror and shook her head. The negligee she was wearing was made of pale peach silk. The bodice was low-cut and clinging, the fabric blissfully opaque.

She wore matching peach silk mules and a matching peignoir. Had it not been for the weekend they'd spent together on the boat, she would have felt ridiculous. But now that they were lovers, she felt nothing but anticipation. Last night, making love to Zach in their bed, in their own home, had been wonderful. Tonight, Sunny decided as she poured two brimming glasses of champagne, would be beautiful, too.

A car engine sounded in the driveway. That had to be Zach, and he was right on time.

Picking up the glasses of champagne, Sunny switched on the stereo and floated to the front door. Looking through the front screen, she did not see Zach. Instead she saw two people she had never met. She hadn't a clue who they were, but from the looks on their faces they apparently knew just who she was.

"You must be Sunny Carlisle," the woman said.

Sunny set down the champagne. She drew the edges of her peignoir together, a little embarrassed to be caught in a nightgown during the dinner hour. "And you are?" she asked, already afraid she knew.

"Nate and Maxine Grainger, Zach's parents." Zach's father held out his hand.

Sunny shook it warmly.

"He didn't tell me you were coming," she said nervously, glancing at the wood-paneled station wagon in her driveway.

Zach's mother smiled. Petite, blond, she was dressed in a long-sleeved knit blouse, denim wrap-around skirt and sneakers. She had the same Nordic good looks and blue eyes Zach did. "That's because he didn't know," she said kindly.

His dad, who was as tall and fit as Zach was, added, "We wanted to surprise him."

"Well, you've certainly done that." Sunny opened the screen door to let them inside.

"But why did you come here looking for him?" she asked. Zach had not told his parents he was married as far as she knew. "I mean, I—we—"

Zach's father held up a hand. "No need to pretend, Sunny. Maxine and I don't want to pry, but we might as well tell you the secret is out of the bag. We found out on Saturday, when we called the clinic looking for him. The answering service operator told us he was out of town with *his new wife.*"

"Naturally—" Maxine picked up the story where Nate had left off "—we were shocked to find out he had married without even telling us. So we decided to drive on up here today, after we finished teaching school, and find out for ourselves what was going on."

Sunny blushed. She wished Zach were there to take the heat right along with her. "I don't know what to say," she murmured. This was *so embarrassing.*

Fortunately she was saved the trouble as Zach turned his pickup into the drive. She pointed behind the Graingers and smiled cheerfully, unable to completely disguise her relief. "There's Zach now."

"He has a lot to answer for," Nate said, pulling a pair of glasses out of the pocket of his seersucker shirt.

Zach bounded out of the truck, his medical bag in hand. He grinned wickedly as he caught a glimpse of Sunny's outfit, then bounded across the yard and up onto the porch, where he hugged his mother and father warmly. "I guess you know," he said finally.

"I guess we do," Maxine said.

The trio looked at one another with so much affection it made Sunny tingle.

"I was going to tell you," Zach said eventually.

"Why didn't you?" Maxine said.

Sunny held her breath. She didn't know why exactly, but she hoped he would not tell his parents their marriage was a fake and that they were forced into it by the well-meaning members of the close-knit, but old-fashioned, community.

Zach shrugged and wrapped a possessive arm around Sunny's shoulders. "Isn't it obvious? I wanted to keep my beautiful wife to myself. Besides," he continued in a more serious tone, "I thought you might object to my hasty wedding."

Maxine leveled an admonishing finger at her son. "The only thing I object to is you not inviting us to the wedding."

Zach shrugged and said with a careful honesty Sunny applauded, "It was one of those affairs that was thrown together at the last minute."

"I see." Nate regarded his son with a combination of sternness and love.

Sunny felt a lecture coming on. "I think I'll go upstairs and change," she said, eager to take off the negligee.

"I REALLY AM sorry that you got the news about my marriage to Zach the way you did," Sunny told Maxine as the two of them whipped up a salad for dinner.

"No need to apologize, dear," Maxine said as she rinsed the lettuce leaves and then placed them in a colander to drain. "I think I know why Zach didn't tell us. He probably thought we'd make a fuss, which we would have. And he probably felt he couldn't handle the emotional aspects of it."

"I don't understand," Sunny said slowly.

Maxine drew a breath. "Because of Lori. He took her death very hard. We all did, and since then big family gatherings and holidays have been hard on the three of us. Zach's wedding would have been bittersweet. He probably thought—erroneously, I might add—that he was protecting us by not including us."

Sunny didn't know about that, but it did explain Zach's distance from other people and the walls he had put up between himself and the community.

"He loved Lori a lot, didn't he?" Sunny said, wishing Zach would talk about his kid sister's death with her as freely as his mother did.

Maxine nodded. "The two of them were extremely close. I don't think they had any secrets from each other." Maxine teared up, and she had to pause to wipe her eyes, as she confessed thickly, "Zach sacrificed so much of his own life, just to be with her. And then he took her death very hard. I don't think he has really let anyone close to him since. Oh, he has plenty of friends, both male and female, but I think there's been a fence around his heart ever since then. Until you, of course. You must have really thrown him for a loop."

"I think that goes both ways," Sunny said. He had certainly thrown her feelings into turmoil. She had never been so simultaneously happy and sad as she was right now.

"Perhaps we should talk about something else," Maxine said.

Sunny nodded. She and Zach would work this out. It would just take a little more time for him to get his life back on track. When he did, he would see there was no reason for him to keep from getting close to those around him.

Sunny sliced carrots with a vengeance, aware she wanted Zach as she had never wanted anyone or anything else. How she wished theirs were a normal marriage.

"YOU AND MY MOM were in the kitchen a long time tonight," Zach said as he and Sunny got ready for bed.

Sunny slipped a long white nightgown over her head and sat down on the bed. As she brushed her hair, she lifted her eyes to his. "She told me about Lori, Zach."

Somehow, he had figured that was the case.

He kept his glance level. "She did."

"She thinks Lori is the reason you never married until now."

Zach tensed. "She's probably right," he said in a matter-of-fact tone. Clad only in pajama bottoms, he eased down beside her. "Lori's death took everything out of me that I had to give. I had enough left over for patients, but that was all."

Sunny clasped his hand tightly in both of hers. "Tell me about her."

Zach stared down at their entwined hands. Talking about what happened to Lori made his gut twist, but he knew it was past time he started talking about his loss. There was no one he wanted to confide in more than Sunny.

Marshaling his inner strength, Zach looked into Sunny's eyes. The compassion and understanding he saw there gave him the courage to continue. "Lori was two years younger than me. From as far back as I can remember, it was always my job to protect her. And I did until she was thirteen, and she got leukemia. She was sick off and on for the next twelve years. She suffered through three all-too-brief remissions before finally dying of the disease two years ago. I was her cheerleader, her patient advocate. I did everything I could think of to help her get better, including a lot of research on my own." He sighed wearily. "I was so sure we could beat the cancer if we went after it together."

"I suppose she had all the newest treatments?"

Zach nodded, recalling with difficulty how hard it had been on his sister. And through it all, she'd been such a trooper, never complaining, never giving up, even at the bitter end. His eyes welled with tears; determinedly he blinked them back. "I even gave her a bone-marrow transplant," he said thickly. "It didn't help." He gripped his hands in front of him until the skin around his knuckles turned white. "Nothing did."

"Is that why you became a doctor?" Sunny asked gently, covering his hands with the warmth of hers. "Because of what happened to your sister?"

He nodded slowly. "I went to the hospital with her every time she needed chemo. Thc more I learned about her disease and what they could and couldn't do for her in terms of treatment, the more I wanted to know."

Sunny put her hairbrush aside. "Your mom said you sacrificed much of your own life to be with her."

"I don't think it was such a big deal. Although—" Zach grinned, recalling what a stir that had caused "—I think Mom's still mad at me for skipping out on my senior prom."

"You didn't go?"

"Lori was sick and was in St. Jude's hospital. How could I have had a good time, knowing what kind of shape she was in? So I canceled and spent the night at her bedside."

Sunny released an unsteady breath. She was looking at him as if he were some sort of a saint, Zach thought uncomfortably.

When in truth, all he could focus on was the fact that he had failed his sister.

"I wish I had known her," Sunny said finally.

Funny, Zach could imagine the two of them together. It was a poignant vision. "I do, too," Zach said softly. "I think she would've liked you.

"And she would've especially liked," Zach added, simultaneously blinking back tears and laughing lightly, "the way you don't hesitate to give me hell when you think I need it."

Sunny's lips curved in a teasing grin. "Let me guess," she deadpanned. "Lori gave you hell, too?"

Zach nodded, the good memories crowding out the bad once again. "You bet she did. Lori read me the riot act all the time, as any good kid sister would. She wanted to bring me up right she always said. And in her opinion, Mom and Dad were both too soft on me."

Sunny smiled. "You really have a loving family."

Zach nodded, shifting his grip so that he held both of Sunny's hands in his. He knew how lucky he was, never more so than now. "I'm glad you like them," he said. "They've taken to you, too." Just as he had known they would. "My mom said she really enjoyed talking with you tonight. And speaking of talking to someone," Zach said, reminded of what he had been waiting all evening to find out. "What's this I hear about Chuck Conway putting the moves on you today?" He was still surprised by the amount of jealousy that information had evoked in him.

Sunny flushed. "How did you hear about that?" she moaned, looking as though she wanted to die of embarrassment.

"Never mind how I found out," Zach said sternly, for once glad the efficient grapevine in Carlisle existed. ''Why didn't you tell me Chuck was the reason for your splinters?''

''Because I was afraid you'd react like a jealous husband,'' Sunny said, rolling her eyes.

He felt like a jealous husband. It didn't bother him as much as he would've expected. ''I don't want him putting the moves on you,'' Zach said firmly, meaning it. The next time he wouldn't let it go by without incident.

''It won't happen again,'' Sunny told him confidently as she slid beneath the covers and lay back against the pillows.

Zach slid in beside her, but delayed turning off the light. ''How do you know it won't happen again?'' he said, studying her upturned face.

Sunny shifted onto her side and regarded him smugly. ''Because I told him what no one else had bothered to report to him—that I am married now.''

Zach shifted onto his side, too. ''How could he not have known?''

''Chuck doesn't reside in Carlisle, Zach.''

''Even so—'' he began.

''I don't know.'' Sunny waggled her eyebrows at him teasingly. ''Maybe he isn't as into gossip as everyone else, including you, in this town is.''

''Very funny.''

Sunny lifted a hand in warning. ''Just don't go getting any ideas about fistfights on my behalf.''

Zach grinned and began to unbutton her chaste white nightgown. ''Only if you put that peach negligee on again.''

''Zach!'' She swatted at his hands.

He pushed her hands away and kept unbuttoning. "I mean it. My blood has been boiling ever since I caught a glimpse of you in it."

She nudged his thigh with her knee and whispered hoarsely, "Your parents are just across the hall."

Zach grinned, not the least bit upset. "They think we're newlyweds." And these days, he felt like one. "They won't mind."

Zach bent to kiss her. Her lips parted for him and she uttered a soft little groan in the back of her throat.

"What if they hear us?" Sunny said, worrying out loud.

Zach slid a hand inside her gown to cup her breast, and felt her nipple bud against his palm. "Then you had better be quiet, hadn't you?" he whispered back, dropping his palm lower, exalting in the way her soft curves heated beneath his touch.

"Mmmmm." Sunny moaned again, arching up against his questing fingers, even while she initiated a few clever moves of her own. "Gramps was right," she teased. "You *are* bad news...."

"You ain't seen nothing yet," he promised, and then set about divesting her of her nightgown and making her his all over again.

"If I'm going to be naked, you're going to be, too," Sunny declared, unsnapping his pajama bottoms.

"Sounds good to me." Fierce desire already swirling through him, Zach covered her with his body. Dipping his head, he kissed her thoroughly until she was feeling the same way and her lips were hot and wanting beneath his.

"Oh, Zach, you make me feel so good," Sunny murmured. She nestled against him, softness to hardness, their caresses flowing one into the next, until there was no ending, no beginning, only a sweet continuum of unrelenting pleasure that drove him on and on.

Slowly he filled her, and she received him, arching at the pleasure, taking him deeper and deeper inside.

Feeling as if he were drowning in her softness, the sweet solace her lips offered, he moved with her, molding the length of his body to hers.

They came together, the power and the emotion of the moment stunning him, leaving him lost and free all at once.

He had not ever imagined it could be like this. Sunny drew a passion and tenderness from him that he never would have dreamed possible. And she did it without half trying, Zach thought, holding her close and drinking in the soap and perfume scent that was uniquely her.

He knew this was love. But was it marriage? He sensed they would both find out soon enough. Whatever happened, he was not letting her go, not giving up. Life was too short, too precious, for them not to be together, he decided fiercely. The only question was, how was he going to convince Sunny of that? How was he going to make her believe that they needed to live their lives free of gossip and community pressure?

As strange as it was, she actually liked the interference.

"Zach?" Sunny said sleepily, cuddling close.

"Yeah?" He brought the covers up around them, his heartbeat settling down to a contented purr.

"I'm glad you told me about Lori."

"I'm glad, too." He stroked a hand through her hair, a wave of tenderness washing over him. "It felt good to talk about it. Maybe because I never do."

And it had brought them closer, Zach thought with a satisfied grin as he curled an arm possessively around her.

If everything continued to go right, the two of them might get past their shaky beginning and make a real marriage of this yet.

Chapter Twelve

I Don't Fall in Love So Easy

"How's the poison ivy, Slim?" Zach asked at the graduation party for Sunny's how-to-be-happily-married class.

"Lots better, thanks to the medicine you gave me," Slim said with a wink. "Though I gotta admit it's the first time I've ever had poison ivy where the sun don't shine."

Zach laughed softly. Slim was nothing if not honest. "Guess you appreciated the side benefits of having your wife take this class, hmm?"

"Didn't you?" Fergus asked, coming up to join the group. "It certainly brought a lot of zip to my marriage with Gertie, and that was something...well, let's just say after thirty-one years of marriage, I didn't expect it."

"What about you, Doc?" George asked, joining the men at the punch bowl. "Did this class lend any zip to your marriage or were you so deep in the honeymoon phase that you didn't even notice?"

It would have been hard not to notice Sunny in that peach silk negligee, Zach thought, the memory of the night they had spent in each other's arms after his parents had left still vivid in his mind. "Since I've never been married, that'd be kind of hard to know," he said.

"Got a point there, Zach," George agreed. He cast a fond look at his wife, who was cradling their new baby in her arms. "All I know is that I wouldn't trade Rhonda-Faye for any woman in this world, I love her and the kids so."

Zach knew how George felt. He didn't want to trade Sunny, either. And that had given him second thoughts about leaving Carlisle.

"WHAT DO YOU MEAN my transfer request was put on hold a long time ago?" Zach asked the clerk in charge of the outreach program incredulously.

"We had a call from the governor several weeks ago, right after your request came in. He said he had talked to your local sponsor, Augustus Carlisle, and that you had changed your mind. Something about you marrying his granddaughter Sunny and settling in there right fine."

"So you're telling me he canceled my request *for* me?" Zach asked.

"Well, yes." The clerk paused. "Does this mean you want to reinstate it?"

"Yes! No! I don't know," he said. "I'll have to get back to you." He hung up and charged out the door of the clinic. He and Augustus were going to have it out once and for all.

Unfortunately Augustus wasn't home, and he wasn't fishing, according to his housekeeper. He was at the factory with Sunny.

Zach thought about waiting, then decided this confrontation couldn't wait. Augustus had crossed the line for the very last time.

Zach stormed into the factory. Sunny and her grandfather were in the showroom with a group of prospective buyers. Sunny left her group and crossed to his side.

"Is everything okay, Zach?"

He didn't want to upset Sunny. This wasn't her fault. Like him, she knew nothing about it. "I just need to talk to your grandfather. Clinic business." Which was true, as far as it went.

Sunny turned. "Gramps, Zach needs to talk to you." With a dazzling smile, she rejoined her group. "Now, where were we?"

"What's so all-fired important?" Augustus said.

"This conversation needs to happen in private," Zach said grimly.

Gramps took a good look at his grandson-in-law's face. "No problem," he said smoothly. "We'll use my office."

They strode in silence to his office, a cubbyhole next to Sunny's executive-sized haven. Gramps shut the door behind him. He immediately faced off with Zach. "Let's have it, greenhorn."

"I just talked to the outreach office in charge of rural physician assignments."

"Oh." Augustus had the grace to look chagrined.

"Yes, 'oh'," Zach said heavily. "I notice you're not denying you called the governor?"

"I talk to him regularly. We're old friends."

"You put a halt on my request."

"What did you expect me to do? You had just married my granddaughter."

"I don't care," Zach said evenly. "That wasn't your call to make."

"I don't know what you're so all-fired upset about." Gramps was incensed. "It worked out in the end, didn't it? You and Sunny are as happy as can be."

"That's not the point," Zach roared, exasperated beyond belief. "You trapped me into marrying Sunny and then you manipulated me into staying well past what was necessary under the circumstances."

"Now you're talking nonsense," Augustus growled.

No, Zach thought, he wasn't. In fact, judging by the increasingly guilty look on Gramps's face, there might be even more to it than he'd originally realized.

"Who exactly was on the selection committee that brought me here?" Zach asked cordially.

Gramps blanched and didn't answer.

"Sunny was on the selection committee, wasn't she?" Zach pressed.

"So what if she was? A lot of other people were on it, too."

"Did she get to choose me, or was it more a group effort?" he asked.

"I don't know what you're talking about," Augustus returned hotly as he picked up a fishing lure from his desk. But he wouldn't meet Zach's eyes.

Barely able to believe how stupid and gullible he'd been, Zach stalked nearer. He planted his hands on Gramps's desk and leaned across it. "Are you denying that Sunny went through the files that were sent here, picking and choosing among the candidates?"

Gramps shrugged and looked all the guiltier as he tied a piece of line to a feather. "I admit she helped us try to find a good match by reading through the résumés right along with the rest of us. But that was all she did, Zach."

It was more than enough. His jaw clenched.

"The idea of us choosing you for some evil purpose is just ludicrous," Gramps continued.

Was it? "So why didn't you choose a woman physician?"

"Because we live so far out in the country, it made more sense to choose a man!"

"And I was the one Sunny was most interested in!" he said, guessing slyly.

"You had a fine résumé," Gramps retorted, exasperated. "A fine education."

Zach recalled how impressed Sunny's parents had been by his education background; he wondered if that had factored into the decision, too.

As he realized how well and easily he'd been duped, it was all Zach could do not to slam his fist into the wall. "So you admit you all lured me to the community with the idea of me marrying your granddaughter in mind!" he shouted back triumphantly.

"I wouldn't say we had the idea of marrying you two right off," Gramps said hotly.

Zach read between the lines, his experience with the wily old man telling him there was a lot more to this than what appeared at first glance. "But you did expect me to keep company with her!" he asserted baldly.

"Well, why not? The two of you were both well educated and among the few young unmarried people in this town. Sure, I hoped she might date you when she finally got to know you!!"

"Let's be honest," Zach said grimly. "This was all a plot from the beginning, wasn't it? You lured me to Carlisle so that your granddaughter would have a husband. You used me to keep Sunny here in Carlisle, make her happy and give you a grandson." Zach didn't know why he hadn't put it all together sooner. Now that he had, he felt like such a damn fool. "Well, the game's up!" he said furiously. "I'm through being caught in a snare!"

SUNNY STOOD outside Gramps's office, her face going alternately white and red. Reminded of how she and Zach had really gotten together, she wanted to die. There was no love involved here, only passion. She had been fooling herself into thinking there was.

Bracing herself for the battle to come, she opened the door and stepped inside.

Zach looked at her. "I heard everything," she told both men, her expression stony with resolve. "Including the fact that Zach thinks he's been had."

"Can you blame me for feeling I walked into a trap?" he asked.

Hell, yes, Sunny thought. But not about to let herself sink to the shouting level of the men, she shook her head and shut the door quietly behind her. "You're right, Zach," she said sweetly, moving closer to join them. She looked at him innocently. "It's all been a nefarious plot. I paid those skunks to trail me and made sure you were driving on that particular country road, on that day, at the precise time I was checking out the reforestation of that select slice of company-owned land. Then—and this was the truly difficult part—I somehow convinced those skunks to follow me, knowing all the while that you were bound to see me in danger and pull your pickup to the side of the road, leap over the fence in a single, soundless bound, creep up from behind and scare the life out of me and get us both sprayed with skunk. Then, not content with that, devious woman that I am, I made sure you were driving a brand-new truck that you would of course refuse to let us ride in. I had nothing in my knapsack but a tablecloth, and you nothing but a chamois—"

Zach silenced her with a look. "All right, all right. So maybe the skunks were an accident, but they played right into your grand plan," he asserted.

Sunny looked heavenward. "Right, Zach. I wanted to get caught by my grandfather and two policemen with me in nothing but a tablecloth and you in a chamois. I wanted to be humiliated beyond belief."

Zach's mouth tightened. Sunny knew she had finally gotten through to him; he knew how ridiculous he sounded, even if he wasn't about to forgive her or Gramps.

"You didn't object to marrying me!" Zach thundered.

"No," Sunny said very quietly as tears of frustration sparkled in her eyes. "But I should have. It was a bad idea."

"You two were happy the past few days," Gramps interrupted. "And you can't deny you were!"

No, Sunny couldn't deny that the past few days had been among the best of her life. But that was apparently where it stopped. "We were deluding ourselves!" she said miserably, blinking back her tears. "We got caught up in the honeymoon aspect of things, but we weren't dealing in reality. The reality is we got married for all the wrong reasons. It took us a while, but we have finally woken up. Now that we have, I want out, and so apparently does Zach. So you have your wish. I'll start divorce proceedings tomorrow. Gramps will call the governor back and ask him to expedite your transfer request. *Won't you, Gramps?*"

"Of course, Sunny."

"And in the meantime, Zach, you can sleep at the clinic! Now, is everybody happy and satisfied?" she asked with icy control. She knew she wasn't! Not waiting for an answer, she turned on her heel and stormed from Gramps's office.

"Sunny—" Zach started after her. He caught up with her in the central bull pen. Disregarding the company employees gaping at them, she shrugged off the grip he had on her arm. "Leave me alone, Zach. We have nothing further to discuss."

"The hell we don't!" He clamped a hand on her wrist and directed her into her office.

There was a murmur of approval and excitement behind them. Sunny ignored it. She waited until Zach had shut the door behind them and released her. "I don't know what this is going to prove," she said, moving away from him defiantly.

He rounded on her. "I want to know why you married me."

She regarded him stonily, feeling as if her heart were encased in a block of ice. She let out a long breath and looked away.

Hands braced on his waist, he eyed her implacably. "You regret it, don't you?"

"Yes. Because what's happened here today has made me realize that the marriage was a mistake. It was unnecessary. And I knew it in my heart all along." Sunny's lower lip trembled as she forced herself to admit. "But I wanted to be with you, so I let them bully and talk me into it. Just as you did," she conceded miserably.

Zach nodded his understanding grimly. He pushed impatient fingers through his hair. "So what now?"

Sunny knew they were at a turning point. This time she was determined to make the right decision, to behave as an adult rather than a lovestruck teen.

She moved to the window and stood looking out at the Tennessee mountains she'd come to love. "I knew when I moved here that I was not going to put my energy into lost causes anymore. For years, I did everything positive to win my parents love and affection, and as you saw for yourself, they still barely know I'm alive. That isn't going to change. I'm not going to beat my head against the wall anymore, trying. And I'm not going to torture myself like that again. Especially when I know through my easy but newfound relationship with Gramps and everyone else in Carlisle that unconditional love does exist."

"Unconditional love, my shoe. He pressured you into marrying me, Sunny." And he could not forgive her grandfather for that.

Sunny raised her chin. "Yes, he did, because he was old-fashioned and hopeful enough to think that was the best thing for both of us to do under the circumstances. But had I stood up for myself and said no and meant it, he would have stopped pressuring me. He would not have stopped loving me then any more than he did just now when I read him the riot act."

Zach shook his head in silent censure of all that had happened. He felt as miserable as she did. "I can't live here anymore."

Sunny sighed. She was not surprised. Zach had wanted out of Carlisle almost from the moment he'd arrived. "I figured as much," she said tightly.

He gave her a long look, his expression stony. "So what about us?" he asked grimly.

If he had shown her the least sign, indicated he was in love with her or wanted to try again, Sunny would've moved heaven and earth to be with him. But he didn't. Instead he acted as though this were a business agreement in need of resolution, and nothing more. Well, she thought wearily, perhaps that was all it had ever been to him. A business deal, with passion thrown in. Initially that was all it had been with her, too. She'd just had the bad sense to fall in love with him.

"What about us?" Sunny echoed dispassionately. *Tell me it's not too late, Zach,* she pleaded silently.

He stared at the floor for a long moment. A muscle worked in his cheek. Finally he looked back at her, the expression in his eyes bleak and unforgiving. "You said you wanted to file for divorce?" he stated, very low.

She saw the guilt in his eyes, the regret. And suddenly she knew that he had only stayed as long as he had, tried as hard as he had, because he'd wanted to make a success of his career in Carlisle and thereby guarantee his future as a physician. "Yes, I'll handle the expense and paperwork involved in a divorce,"

Sunny said, knowing she couldn't bear this heartbreak for one more second. "You won't have to do a thing, Zach. You're free to go. Your life is your own again."

Chapter Thirteen

Life Is Too Short to Love like That

"I can tell from the heartbroken looks on your faces that you've heard the news, too," Sunny told her marriage class, as they gathered in Rhonda-Faye's diner after hours.

"It's true, then?" Rhonda-Faye said as she served strawberry sodas to everyone. "You and Zach are calling it quits?" She was incredulous.

Sunny put on her bravest face. "He thinks I brought him to Carlisle to trap and coerce him into marrying me, so I cut him loose."

"Oh, surely he knows that isn't true!" Matilda said, appearing as upset as Sunny and the rest of the group.

Sunny stirred her soda disconsolately. "The circumstantial evidence is running against me. He knows I went through the profiles of the various physician candidates with Gramps and said Zach's was interesting."

The ladies grinned as if that were proof Sunny had been head over heels in lust with Zach even then. "You can't fall in love with a picture," she said dryly.

"But you can fall in love with the flesh-and-blood reality of an intriguing picture," Matilda said slyly.

Sunny sipped her soda. It was delicious, but she could take no pleasure in it. "Whether I'm attracted to Zach isn't the issue here. He is through being used and wants out of Carlisle. Like it or not, my marriage is over," she reported dejectedly.

The ladies exchanged concerned looks.

Rhonda-Faye eyed Sunny seriously. "All I know is that a marriage takes work, even for the most in-love couple on earth."

"Rhonda-Faye's right. The two of you gotta break each other in," Aunt Gertie said. "And have a few tiffs as you settle into matrimony. That's all that's been going on between the two of you. You had a tiff. You told him to take a hike, more or less, exactly as you should have, under the circumstances. Now it's time to tell him that you forgive him for his stupidity—and that it's okay to come back to you. We've all done the same thing with our men, haven't we, ladies?"

The group nodded unanimously.

Her expression both serious and helpful, Matilda elaborated on Gertie's advice. "Sacrifice is the key here, Sunny," she said. "For you and for Zach."

"And let's not forget compromise," Gertie added. "You can't have a marriage without both those ingredients."

"You can't have a marriage without love, either," Sunny said morosely, staring into her strawberry soda. If Zach had really loved her, he would've known that she had never meant to trap him into marriage, and he never would have left.

"Oh, now, honey. Zach loves you!" Gertie said.

Rhonda-Faye nodded vigorously in agreement. "I've never seen a man so silly with it. He's head over heels in love with you."

He's head over heels in lust with me, you mean, Sunny thought. And they were not the same thing. "Then how come he never said so?" she asked the group belligerently.

"Maybe because of the way your marriage started—at the end of a shotgun," Rhonda-Faye said softly.

Sunny didn't want to admit it, but Rhonda-Faye had a point. Zach had been forced into this more or less against his will. The only way he'd been able to salvage his fierce pride and self-respect was to tell her repeatedly that he refused to give in to the social pressures being exerted on him. Admitting he loved her probably was tantamount to failure, at least in his view. At the very least, it was proof he'd lost his independence and done what everyone else had predicted would happen all along.

"Try reading his face instead of his lips," Matilda advised.

"Oh, I don't know," Aunt Gertie teased, "you can tell a lot from the way a man kisses, too. Tell me true, Sunny. Does Zach kiss you like he means it?"

And then some, Sunny thought wistfully.

"If there's love in his kiss, there's love in his heart."

No matter how much she tried to forget them, Aunt Gertie's words stayed with her the rest of the impromptu meeting. Zach did kiss her as though he loved her, she thought. And there had been other signs he cared about her, too. The way he'd fixed up her car, for instance, helping to get rid of the skunk smell. Then there was his jealous reaction to Chuck Conway's pass at her. The way he had comforted her after her parents' visit and protected her during the storm.

So what if he hadn't come right out and said the words? Neither had she. Yet she had felt his love. And would still be feeling it if she hadn't overheard his conversation with Gramps.

Was it too late for a second chance? She hoped not. All she had to do was swallow her pride, find Zach and try one more time to work things out. She knew that if she didn't, she would always regret it.

She left the diner and went straight to the clinic.

To her disappointment, the front door was locked. A Closed sign was in the window. Beneath that was a printed notice announcing that another doctor would be arriving to take Zach's place at the clinic just as soon as the state agency and the local selection committee could arrange it. Zach's truck was nowhere in sight.

Sunny blanched. Was it possible he had already left? Moved out and on?

Despondently she returned to her house. Her hopes rose as she saw his shiny new pickup sitting in her drive, then fell again as she noted the bed of the truck was filled with his belongings. Either he'd come home to her—which seemed damn unlikely, considering how they had left things between them—or he had just stopped in to talk legalities with her before he left town.

Aware her legs were shaking, Sunny stepped out of her Land Rover. She moved toward the house, the first few steps taking all the willpower she had. And that was when she saw him, slouched on the steps of her front porch. In jeans, dress shirt and tie, he had never looked more handsome. Or more unapproachable. She eyed him cautiously, unsure of his mood.

Zach unfolded himself and stood with a determined, lazy grace that quickened her heartbeat.

"About time you got home, woman," he said softly, curling his thumbs through the belt loops of his jeans.

Sunny stared at him, not sure whether to laugh or burst into tears. She knew only that she had never felt more tense or uncertain or full of bittersweet anticipation in her life. And Zach, damn him, was to blame.

Pride stiffened her shoulders. "Since when did you turn into John Wayne?" she returned, regarding him with a coolness she couldn't begin to feel deep inside.

"Since I was cornered by Slim, Fergus, Gramps and George." He swaggered laconically down the porch steps like the hero in a Western movie, not stopping until he towered over her and they stood toe-to-toe. His blue eyes were shrewdly direct as they locked on hers.

"*They* think I handled you all wrong."

Sunny's lips curved sardonically. Whether he wanted to admit it or not, they had formed their own marriage-counseling service for men, although it was a little less organized. She folded her arms in front of her and adopted a contentious stance. "Well, it'll warm your heart to know that the women in the community think I've handled you all wrong, too."

Zach braced his hands on his waist. "Is that a fact," he drawled.

Sunny nodded, her temper soaring as all the things they had said to each other at their last meeting came rushing back to hit her square in the heart. Honestly, how could Zach ever have thought she had set him up for a shotgun wedding? Shouldn't he have known instinctively she was not to blame? And where did he get off acting all macho now? As if she were the one to blame!

"Furthermore," Sunny continued loftily, drawing her own line in the sand, "I think they're right," she fibbed, twisting things around for the sake of her own argument. "I think I should have kicked you out weeks ago!"

"Okay," Zach said, "that's it. I've heard quite enough for one evening." He scooped her up in his arms, carried her across the porch.

"Creating yet another scene for the neighbors to see?" she asked sweetly.

He shrugged as he entered the house. "It's not my fault there's nothing this entertaining on TV."

"Zach, I'm warning you. I am in no mood for games."

He paused just inside the threshold. Still holding her in his arms, he cradled her against his chest, the passion he'd always felt for her gleaming in his eyes.

"I don't want to play games, either, Sunny. I want to make things right."

Sunny's heart pounded at his proximity, but she refused to sacrifice her pride, when she'd already sacrificed so much. "By divorcing me?" she asked coolly.

"By loving you," Zach corrected as he slowly set her down so her feet touched the floor.

Sunny saw the intent look in his eyes. It kindled her own fires. Needing to clarify things for her sake, to make sure he was there because he loved her, she stepped back, announced defiantly, "Zach, I can't go back to having an affair with you, even if we are legally married."

Framing her face with his hands, he tilted it beneath his. "How about being my wife, then, in every sense?"

Unable to move without risking closer contact, Sunny held her ground. She wanted so much for them—a happy marriage, children and everlasting love. She wanted him to want them, too. "And how long is this offer good for, Zach—as long as you stay in Carlisle?"

"No, Sunny, as the vows said," he told her, blocking her in place, when she would have tried to march past him once again, "for as long as we both shall live."

Sunny swallowed. She stared at his tie, her pulse racing; she was unwilling to admit how much just the thought of letting him go disturbed her. It appeared it was about to happen. "So you're still planning to leave Carlisle, then?" she asked, a little sadly, aware her mouth was dry and her palms were damp and that she'd never had so much at stake in her entire life.

"I received my official transfer." He gestured toward his truck matter-of-factly. "As you can see, I even packed up and got ready to leave town."

Unable to help herself, Sunny moved another half step closer, so they were standing just inches apart. "What stopped you?" She knew the answer she wanted to hear.

"You." Eyes darkening seriously, he dove his hands into her hair. "I realized I not only didn't want to leave, Carlisle, I couldn't." His voice caught. After a moment in which he stared long and hard at the horizon, he forced himself to go on. "The thought of a life without you is unbearable, Sunny."

Her heart leapt at what he had just admitted. She tipped her head up to his. "Because of the passion between us?" she asked slowly, knowing that if they were going to be together again, their relationship had to be real, and it had to be right.

"I admit I love the way we make love, Sunny, but that's not what is keeping me here," he said hoarsely. "I'm here because you hold the key to my happiness. I gave you my heart without ever knowing it. Just as you gave yours to me. I love you, Sunny," he said huskily. "And I always will."

Nothing he could have said would have pleased her more. "Oh, Zach." She wrapped her arms about his neck and kissed him sweetly. "I love you, too," she whispered emotionally. "So very, very much." They kissed again, putting everything they felt into the caress. "But I want you to be sure this is what you want," Sunny said tremulously at last.

"It is. Although I regret to admit it's taken almost losing you to make me realize it. I know I've been unfair to you, to everyone." He paused and shook his head in silent admonishment. "Lori's death took so much out of me that I wasn't sure I had any love to give. And for a very long time I didn't want to find out if, or even when, that would change. And I sure as heck didn't want to fail anyone I cared about again," he finished fiercely.

Sunny hugged him hard as the rest of her doubts melted away. "Oh, Zach, you didn't fail Lori," she reassured him gently. She leaned back against the warm cradle of his arms to gaze into his face. "You did everything you could for her."

Zach's fingers tensed, then relaxed again as he talked openly about his pain. "Only it wasn't enough, and it damn near killed me. I didn't want to fail you, too." His eyes sobered. "But I realize now the only way I could fail you is by walking away."

Sunny swallowed. They had one more bridge to cross. "What about feeling trapped?"

Zach gave her a long, steady look and admitted on a rueful sigh, "The only trap I fell into was putting a fence around my heart. Coming to Carlisle, meeting you, set me free again."

Euphoric relief surged through her. Against all the odds, despite all the meddling, she and Zach had a future together. She had never felt more complete. "Big talk there, fella," Sunny teased, laying a hand over his heart. Beneath her fingers, she felt its strong, steady beat, and knew her world had righted once again.

"Yeah, but it's from the bottom of my heart," Zach said in a rusty, trembling voice. "All these how-to-be-a-proper-husband hints from the guys must've sunk in," he offered with a teasing wink.

"Must have. They're working on me, at any rate." Sunny wrapped her arms around his waist and leaned in close, savoring his warmth and his strength and the essence that was him.

Zach lifted the veil of her hair and kissed her exposed throat. "Does this mean you forgive me?"

"Guess so," Sunny quipped as her heart soared. Her eyes danced as they met his. "You're a hard man to stay mad at."

"Now, why is that, I wonder," Zach drawled, looking incredibly happy and content, too. He kissed her full on the mouth, a long, slow kiss that made her tremble.

"Maybe because I love you, too," she confessed. Surging into his embrace, she guided him back to her for another soulful touch. Finally they drew apart. "Zach?" Sunny said, her knees so weak and trembly she could barely stand. She knew where she wanted all this to lead.

"Hmm?" Once again sweeping her up into his arms, he carried her up the staircase.

"About our marriage—" she began.

"It's a real one, in every sense," he confirmed, striding unhurriedly down the upstairs hall. "Truth to tell, I think it has been for a long time." He put her down gently, then followed her down on the bed, kissing her long and slow and deep, drawing on all the power and the wonder of their love. Sunny had never been happier, or more replete.

"Zach?" she said breathlessly after a while, as she began to work off his tie and he undid her buttons.

"Hmm?" He slid a warm palm against her skin.

"About that baby we've both talked about in the hypothetical, the one we both want someday but have been afraid to plan on." Sunny caught her breath at what he was doing and looked into his clear blue eyes. She saw the promise of the future. "How about making it a real possibility?"

Zach paused, his face aglow with delight. For the first time, they really did have it all. "Sunny, love, you read my mind."

Judy Christenberry

DADDY ON DEMAND

Chapter One

"I got money."

John Crewes looked up in surprise. He was stretched out on a lounger on his carefully-maintained patio, looking forward to a relaxing afternoon. His plans had not included children. Specifically, the child hanging over the fence.

"Who are you? And what are you doing invading my peace and quiet?" he demanded.

"I want to have a business discussion," she pronounced with all the poise of a bank president.

He turned back to the *Wall Street Journal*. It made no difference to him if she discussed the downfall of capitalism. As long as she didn't bother him. "Fine. Just go away."

"No, with you," she protested. "I got money."

"Why do you keep saying that?"

"'Cause I want to hire you."

That got his attention. He was a financial expert; some said, a genius. This child wanted investment advice? Suddenly he remembered where he'd seen her. She lived next door. She and her mother had moved in at the beginning of the school year.

"Where's your mother?"

"Shh!" she warned, panic on her face. "Don't tell her."

"I don't think I should help you do something your mother doesn't approve of."

"It's my money. She says I can spend it however I want, as long as it's not bad."

Her determination amused him. "Do you want to come over?" He didn't know what she was standing on, but her little snub nose just topped the fence.

"Yes."

Her face immediately disappeared from view. He heard a rustling noise as she ran from his fence to the gate, then the creak of the latch. He needed to oil it. Nothing squeaked or was out of place on his property.

She came into view—a little girl dressed in shorts and a T-shirt, with grubby knees and a streak of dirt on her cheek. Her dark brown hair was in a scraggly ponytail. Coming to a halt beside his chair, she suddenly showed signs of bashfulness.

He rested the newspaper in his lap and crossed his arms over his chest. "Well, now, what kind of advice do you want?"

She frowned, putting one slightly smudged finger to her rosebud lips. "No. Not that. I don't want you to talk to me. I want to hire you. I got money."

Amused by her persistence, he replied, "I don't do lawns anymore. Maybe you'd better get your mom to help you."

"No. She can't. She's a girl."

Tears would have irritated him. But the sadness in her eyes touched something inside him. "Has to be a guy, huh? Okay, what do you need?"

"A daddy."

She watched him as if he were a prized specimen under a microscope. She was lucky he hadn't choked.

"Sorry, honey, but you're out of luck. I'm not interested in marriage." Understatement of the year. He'd tried that celebrated institution once and hadn't fared so well. He kept his social commitments to the strictly temporary kind now.

"Me, neither."

He was beginning to think a friend was playing a practical joke on him. "That's good. You're a little young to consider tying yourself down."

"But I need a daddy."

"I think you need to discuss this with your mommy."

The little girl licked her lips before saying, "Nope. Mommy says we don't need no men. We're just two girls on our own."

"Ah. Well, then, I guess you don't need a daddy."

"Yes, I do. I'm tired of being the only one."

"The only one what?"

As if she thought he really cared, she settled on the edge of his recliner. "All the other kids have daddies."

"I'm sure that's not true. As many people as get divorced these days, there have to be other kids in your class without daddies."

"Lisbeth's mommy found her a daddy. That only leaves Earl and me, and he doesn't count."

"Why?"

"'Cause he doesn't care."

"Look—" He broke off. "What is your name?"

"Jacey."

"Okay, Jacey, this problem is between you and your mother. If Lisbeth's mommy can find a daddy, I'm sure your mommy can, too." In fact, from what he'd seen of her mommy—from a distance, of course—he suspected she could find any number of daddies. She had long dark hair, a curvaceous figure and full, pouty lips that begged to be kissed. Not that he'd noticed.

"'Course she could," Jacey agreed. "But she don't want one."

Why did he feel like he was spinning his wheels? This conversation didn't seem to be going anywhere and he still hadn't even read the headlines of the paper.

"Well, I need to read my paper now, Jacey. So why don't you go back to your yard and play."

She stood and John breathed a sigh of relief. He hadn't thought it would be that easy to get her to go away. Instead of leaving, however, she slid her hand into a pocket and pulled out a small cloth bag. Even as he watched, she struggled to untie the string that held the bag closed.

"What are you doing?"

"I'm showing you my money. I told you I got money."

"Yes, you did, but I don't understand—"

"I want to hire you. To be my daddy."

That stubborn tilt to her little chin found a spot of warmth in his soul. She'd go a long way in life. But not with him. "That's not a job you can hire someone for."

"Why not? It'd just be once in a while."

"What are you talking about?"

She sat back down on the edge of the recliner and patted his blue jeans-clad leg. "It wouldn't be very hard."

"What wouldn't be very hard?"

"Telling the other kids about your job. You could tell'm about capturing the bad guys and shooting guns and—"

"Whoa! Wait just a minute. I'm not a policeman."

The disappointment on her face struck hard.

"Oh. I thought maybe— Do you fight fires and ride a fire engine?" Her voice rose on a hopeful note.

"Sorry, sweetheart. I'm in finance."

"What's that?"

"I invest people's money and make it grow for them."

He could tell she wasn't impressed. Suddenly she leaned forward and patted his cheek with her soft, pudgy little hand. "That's okay. They'll like you anyway."

An unexpected grin forced his lips to curve up. What a kid. "Thanks for the reassurance, but I can't—"

"But it wouldn't take long. The daddies don't stay all day. And besides," she said, her face taking on a hangdog air, "I told'm you'd come."

Ah. Now they'd come to the crux of the matter. "Jacey, I'm afraid you'll just have to tell your teacher you weren't honest."

"I got three dollars and sixty-seven cents," she hurriedly said and began struggling with the opening of her bag again.

"Jacey—"

"Isn't that enough?" The anxious look on her face bothered him.

"Look, sweetheart, your mom would find out about it, and you'd get in trouble."

"No, she won't. She's not at my school. See, I could hire you for—for the rest of school. Then, next year, I'd just say you left, like Earl's daddy did."

He had to admit she had everything figured out. There was only about a month left of school. Even though he told himself he shouldn't, he asked, "Just when are the daddies supposed to speak at your school?"

"Monday morning."

He got his second wind. "Jacey, I don't think—"

"I'll get my allowance next Friday. I'll have a whole 'nother dollar. I'll give that to you, too." The desperation in her voice reminded him how much things mattered when you were a kid.

"How about if I discuss this with your mother?"

"No! It would make her sad. She says we don't need no boys." Big blue eyes stared at him. "But I *do.* Just every once in a while, so's I can be like the other kids."

He remembered how important it was to fit in. When he was eight and on his first baseball team, he'd died of embarrassment when it was his turn to provide refreshments. His mother had arrived in heels and pearls with a bakery box of petits fours. The other boys had goggled at her as she'd passed out dainty napkins. How he'd longed for homemade cookies and a blue jeans-clad mom like the other kids.

Hell, what could it hurt if he went along with Jacey's plan? She was a cute little urchin and he didn't have a full calendar Monday. "Okay. But only this once, okay?"

"No," she immediately responded, that stubborn chin in evidence again. "You have to do it 'til school's finished. Not all the time, just when I need you." She held out her bag of money. "It's a lot of money."

He guessed it was a lot of money to Jacey. Reaching out for the cloth bag, he said, "Okay, just when you need me."

"Thank you," she said, beaming at him. Then she launched herself on his chest, smacked his cheek and ran away.

Only when he was alone again did he realize he didn't know the name of her school or the time he was to appear.

He'd wait until tomorrow to see if she returned to give him the information he needed. If not, he guessed he'd have to pay his beautiful, independent, "We don't need no boys" neighbor a visit.

RACHEL CASON SCRUBBED the sink with a vengeance. A navy blue stain encircled the white porcelain. *That's what you get for trying to save money, Rachel,* she said to herself. She'd dyed a pale blue dress with stains to a navy blue, hoping to stretch another year's wear out of it.

Now she had extra work, trying to remove the dye stains from the sink.

The back door slammed. "Jacey?"

"Yes, Mommy. I'm here."

She looked over her shoulder at the bundle of energy that was the center of her universe and grinned. "Hi, sweetheart. Ooh, I can see you've been having fun, but you're quite a mess. I think you'd better have a bath before dinner tonight. Go get clean pajamas and—" The phone rang. "Oh, answer that first, sweetheart."

Jacey climbed up on the stool by the wallphone and lifted the receiver. "Cason residence."

Rachel smiled. Her daughter was so self-possessed it scared her sometimes.

"It's for you, Mommy."

Rachel took the receiver automatically, but her gaze registered the look of alarm on Jacey's face. "Hello?"

"Mrs. Cason? Of course, that's not your name now, but I don't have time to visit tonight. I'm already late as it is. This is Mrs. Wilson. I just wanted you to tell your husband to be at school at nine-thirty Monday. He's going to be the second daddy. Thanks so much. Bye."

Rachel stood there with the receiver in her hand until the beeping alerted her to hang it up. Then she turned to her small daughter, who was still staring up at her, her eyes abnormally large with fear.

"Maybe you can explain that phone call, young lady."

"Who was it?"

"I think you know. It was Mrs. Wilson, your kindergarten teacher."

"I did good on my work, Mommy."

"You always do, sweetheart. But this wasn't about your work. It was about your daddy."

If anything, those eyes grew even bigger. "I don't *have* a daddy, Mommy. Don't you remember?"

Rachel studied her child, wondering exactly what was going on. "I remember, and I believe you remember. Why doesn't Mrs. Wilson remember?"

"She probably mixed me up with Lisbeth. Did I tell you Lisbeth got a daddy?"

For the first time, Rachel noticed a touch of forlornness in her daughter's expression. She knelt down to put her arms around Jacey. "Yes, you told me. Does it make you want a daddy?"

"No!" Jacey squeezed her neck tightly. "It's just you and me, Mommy."

"That's right. Just you and me, kid, and we're doing fine."

Jacey pulled back from their hug. "I'll go take my bath now, Mommy. I don't want to go to bed late."

Jacey might be smart—brilliant, in fact, as her teacher had told Rachel at Christmas—but thankfully she was woefully inadequate at lying.

"That's very good of you, Jacey, but first I think you ought to explain why Mrs. Wilson thinks you have a daddy."

"Oh." Jacey stared at her toes, one little forefinger between her teeth. When Rachel said nothing, she finally looked at her mother. "I said I had a daddy."

"Why did you do that?"

"'Cause I was tired of all the others daddies coming and telling us about their work. Now, even Lisbeth's daddy is coming."

Rachel nodded. "I understand why you might be disappointed, but you shouldn't lie. Would you like me to come tell the kids about *my* job?"

Jacey's solemn little face broke into a gentle smile. "Thank you, Mommy, but you're a teacher. We know all about teachers."

"Ah. And what were you going to do Monday morning when your new daddy didn't show up?"

"Oh, he would be— Uh, I don't know."

"He would what?" Rachel demanded. She knew her daughter very well. A more practical five-year-old didn't exist. "Jacey, what have you done?"

"I used my own money."

"Money? What are you talking about?"

"I hired me a daddy. Just 'til summer, Mommy."

"Your savings? You used your money to hire a daddy?" She couldn't believe what she was hearing. "Just how much money have you saved?"

"Three dollars and sixty-seven cents."

Great. What kind of a sleaze would take money from a child and promise such a ridiculous thing? "And who did you hire?"

"Him." Jacey accompanied her one-word answer with a gesture toward the house next door. The house in which, according to neighborhood gossip, a financial genius lived. A single financial genius.

Several times Polly, her neighbor across the street, had offered to set Rachel up with the man. She couldn't remember what Polly had called him, and it didn't matter. Each time she'd refused.

The divorcée next door to Polly had pursued the man for a while, but she had conceded defeat, telling her neighbors that he was a cold fish. Mr. Donaldson, the head of the neighborhood group, had agreed, reporting the man had no interest in attending their meetings, or helping them in their efforts to fight crime and littering.

This was the warmhearted soul who'd taken her baby's savings and offered to pretend to be Jacey's daddy?

"You hired our neighbor to be your daddy? He actually agreed to such an insane proposal?" She regretted her words as soon as they were out. She never made fun of Jacey.

Jacey took her words literally. "No, Mommy, he said he didn't want to marry you."

Hysterical laughter bubbled up in Rachel and she bit her bottom lip. "Well, I'm grateful for that, at least.

I think you would've paid too much if marriage was included."

"Me, too," Jacey agreed, nodding sagely. "He should pay *us* to marry us."

Leave it to Jacey to carry the concept too far. Rachel needed to do some backtracking. "Sweetie, you don't use money for—for marrying and things. You're only supposed to do those things because of love."

"Oh. Then I'm glad he didn't want to marry you."

Rachel wished Jacey would quit repeating that fact.

She stood and held out her hand. "Come on, Jacey. We've got to go clear things up with that man. I'm afraid he can't pretend to be your father Monday morning."

Jacey put her small hand in her mother's but she didn't try to hide her unhappiness. "But, Mommy, I *paid* him!"

"Too bad, sweetie. You just lost your savings."

JOHN WAS WATCHING the last holes of a golf championship on television, enjoying the first free day he'd taken in a long time. He'd become a workaholic after his divorce, and it had paid handsomely. But lately, he wasn't finding the frenetic pace as satisfying.

In fact, Jacey's visit this afternoon was the most interesting thing, other than making money, that had happened to him in a long time. He began mentally preparing his speech to the children. After all, he didn't want to let Jacey down. It was bad enough that he wasn't a policeman or a fireman.

Inspiration suddenly struck him and he hurried to the storage closet. With every box neatly stacked and labeled, it took only seconds to find the one he was looking for.

The doorbell rang as he carried the box back to the den. Setting it down, he impatiently strode to the door. It could only be a salesman. He'd already bought several boxes of Girl Scout cookies, and he avoided his neighbors, especially the neighborhood kingpin, Donaldson. The man persisted in trying to get John to attend those meetings. The thought of spending several hours discussing lawn beautification over lemonade and cookies drove him crazy.

The one neighbor he hadn't avoided that day, Jacey, stood at his door with the beautiful woman he'd seen only from a distance. Up close, she was a knockout.

At least, she would be if she smiled, he was sure. She wasn't smiling now.

"Hello, Jacey," he said and looked pointedly at the woman.

"I'm afraid I don't know your name, but I'm Rachel Cason," she said, her nose in the air. "I understand you and my daughter made an agreement today."

"John Crewes," he said, extending his hand, which she pointedly ignored. "Won't you come in?"

"That won't be necessary. I apologize for Jacey interrupting your day. And, of course, the agreement is null and void."

Jacey pulled on her mother's arm. "What's null and void, Mommy?"

"It means that Mr. Crewes won't be pretending to be your daddy Monday morning."

He noticed her voice warmed considerably as she talked to her daughter, even though she sounded very strict. Good. He wanted Jacey to have someone who loved her. Although it was none of his business, of course.

"Well, Mrs. Cason," he began, waiting until her gaze returned to him before he continued, "I promised Jacey, and I don't like to go back on my word." He smiled at her, determined to see if he could thaw her out just a little. After all, he'd been told his smile was attractive.

Nada. Zip. Nothing.

"I appreciate your feelings, Mr. Crewes, but, as Jacey's mother, I can't condone lying."

He looked down at Jacey, her hand held by her mother. She was staring up at him, not crying, just looking, accepting, wishing.

Clearing his throat, he said, "Can't we find a compromise?" What was the matter with him? he wondered. Here he was being offered a way out of a ridiculous situation and he wasn't taking it.

"I really don't see—"

"If you'd come inside, we could at least explore the options. After all, I've already been paid. It hardly seems fair to make me return such an enormous windfall."

His attempt at levity was almost ignored. The corners of her tempting lips quivered just slightly. He was mesmerized even though she quickly flattened them out into a stern line.

"There's no need to return Jacey's money. It will teach her not to make such poor decisions in the future."

"Man, you are one tough bird. How do you stand living with her, Jacey?"

Jacey gave him a shy smile and leaned against her mother's leg. "She's my mommy," she explained.

The woman looked down at her child and then at him. "Why do I get the feeling I'm being ganged up on?"

"Why, Mrs. Cason, I have no idea," he said in tones of mock amazement. The lightheartedness that filled him was a surprise. Usually, he played the heavy, whether it was with his employees or clients importuning him. That was something else he was tiring of.

"What big eyes you have, Grandma," she returned, narrowing her gaze in speculation.

"The better to see you with when you accept my invitation and come inside." He watched exasperation, and maybe something else if he was very optimistic, fill her gaze before he added, "Come on. What can it hurt if we discuss this a little, explore our options?"

"Please, Mommy?" Jacey whispered, sending imploring glances to her mother.

"Definitely ganged up on," her mother muttered before giving a nod. "Very well. But nothing you do or say will get me to agree to your telling Mrs. Wilson that you are Jacey's father."

Chapter Two

Jacey watched the clock as she nibbled on her finger. Lisbeth's father was speaking to the class, but Jacey wasn't interested. No, she was waiting for John.

Her pretend daddy.

She swallowed the bad feelings that filled her tummy. She and John had convinced her mommy to let John come to school today. But she was supposed to tell her teacher that John was just a friend, not her daddy.

Supposed to.

"I was going to," she muttered under her breath and received a frown from Mrs. Wilson. But she wanted to wait until John got here. Somehow, with him beside her, telling the truth wouldn't seem so difficult. But he hadn't come.

"He promised," she whispered to herself, fighting back the tears. Daddies were supposed to keep their promises.

When the students around her began clapping, Jacey did, too, but the applause made her feel even worse. It was time for her father to talk. Not only did she not have a father, she didn't even have a pretend father.

"That was lovely, Mr. Wester. I admire your work tremendously," Mrs. Wilson said, smiling at Lisbeth's daddy. There was a pause in the room, like everyone was waiting for the show to continue, Jacey thought to herself.

She raised troubled eyes to look at her teacher. Mrs. Wilson was staring at her, a question in her gaze.

Before Jacey could come up with an excuse, the door to the classroom swung open. There he was!

Jacey grinned from ear to ear. Without conscious thought, she leaped from her desk and raced to the back of the room, throwing her arms around his legs and hugging as hard as she could.

"Sorry, baby," he murmured. "I got held up on a phone call."

Baby. She was a big girl, as she told her mommy all the time, but she decided she didn't mind *him* calling her a baby. It felt . . . nice. "That's okay."

"Mr. Crewes," Mrs. Wilson said, having walked to the back of the room to meet him and extending her hand. "If you'll come forward, I'm afraid you'll have to start at once. We have reading circles in a few minutes, and we wouldn't want to get off schedule, now, would we?"

John looked at Jacey, and she knew what he wanted to know. Had she told her teacher he was a friend, not a daddy? Her finger went back to her mouth and she barely shook her head no. She knew he understood because he looked unhappy, like *his* tummy didn't feel too good, either.

She returned to her desk and screwed her eyes tightly shut. *Please, please, please . . .*

"Class, I want you to welcome John Crewes, Jacey's new daddy."

The class applauded, as Mrs. Wilson had told them to, but Jacey just stared at the tall man standing beside her teacher.

HELL! WHAT WAS HE supposed to do now? Rachel had told Jacey to explain to her teacher before John got there. Which seemed pretty tough to him. But Rachel had made them both promise that they'd be honest with the teacher.

But being honest with the teacher in private and being honest with the teacher in front of sixteen kindergartners were two different things. Especially when one of them was pleading with big blue eyes.

Eyes just like her mother's.

"Now, don't be nervous, Mr. Crewes," Mrs. Wilson prompted, gesturing to his audience.

Nervous? No, he wasn't nervous about his presentation. He'd rehearsed it in front of his mirror yesterday afternoon. The only thing that made him nervous was facing Rachel if she found out he hadn't explained.

He cleared his throat. He would come clean after his talk.

"Good morning. Jacey asked me to tell you about my job."

He smiled at the little girl, reassuring her, and her face lit up. Man, he was a sucker for her smile.

"I deal in money, but I'm not a banker. I take other people's money." He paused, leaning forward to touch the ear of the little boy nearest him, and held up a coin. "Like this boy's money. This is your money, isn't it?" he asked.

"No! I don't have no money!" the child protested.

"Then this isn't your money, either?" he asked, pulling a coin from the boy's other ear.

"Where's that comin' from?" the boy asked, covering his ears with his hands, and the class roared with laughter.

"Oh. Well, just pretend it's your money. You see, kids, if you have money, you want to save it for the future. But it would be good if, while you were saving it, your money made more money. So, my job is to take your money—" he held out the two coins and then put his hands behind his back "—and make it grow."

He extended his hands to show four coins. "And grow," he added, returning his hands behind his back and extending them again to show eight coins, to great applause from his small audience, and then repeated the process until there were sixteen quarters.

After he passed out a quarter to each of the children, he did a few more tricks, tying them in with money management, although he doubted the kids cared about his job.

"Where's your rabbit?" one little boy called out. Even Jacey's eyes lit up at that idea, but John shook his head. "Sorry. My rabbit is out of town. Any other questions?"

There were no questions but a lot of applause. The best reward he received, though, was the approval shining in Jacey's eyes.

"That was marvelous, Mr. Crewes," Mrs. Wilson said, walking forward. "We didn't know we'd get a magic show as well as an informative talk. Thank you so much for coming." She shook his hand.

Just as he was going to ask to speak to her alone, she looked over his shoulder and said, "And you, too, Mr. Wester. I'm so impressed with your career."

John turned around, a sinking feeling in his stomach. Yep, he was right. Mr. Wester was David Wester, a well-known psychologist who, for the past ten years, had been raking in money hand over fist, first with his books on relationships and then his videos showing how to make a marriage stronger.

The man, at least ten years older than John, with gray hair mixing with blond, extended his hand. "I enjoyed your talk as much as the children, Mr. Crewes. Which little girl is yours?"

"Uh, Jacey," John replied, just as a small hand slid into his. "Hi, sweetheart. Was it okay?"

He bent down and scooped Jacey up into his arms. She hugged his neck. "It was perfect, John."

Returning the kiss she'd given him on Saturday, he almost forgot the powerful man standing beside him. Almost.

"Hello, Jacey," David Wester said, as he was joined by Lisbeth. "I believe you and Lisbeth are best friends."

The two little girls nodded.

"Well, I'm especially glad to meet you, John, if I may call you that," the man continued. "I believe it's important to know the families of your child's playmates."

"Uh, yeah, that's a good idea."

"Well, thank you both for coming, but it's reading-circle time. We mustn't get off schedule, you know," Mrs. Wilson said. "Back to your desks, girls."

Jacey hugged his neck again, taking the opportunity to whisper, "I didn't tell her."

"I know," John whispered back. He set Jacey down and she scampered to her desk under Mrs. Wilson's stern eye. "Uh, Mrs. Wilson, could I talk to you for a minute?" he asked, hoping David Wester would leave before he made his confession.

"I'd love to have a visit with you and your wife, Mr. Crewes, but I can't stop right now. You understand, don't you? Even schoolteachers have busy schedules. Call me for an appointment. Thank you again for coming."

The woman walked back to the head of the class and began instructing her pupils.

With a sigh, John turned toward the door, only to find David Wester waiting for him.

"You know, I could buy and sell this entire school without the blink of an eye. But a schoolteacher can reduce me to a tongue-tied student in no time. Mothers and teachers must have some kind of special magic," he finished with a smile.

John couldn't agree more. And he knew one mother and teacher who seemed to have incredible power over him. "Yeah, they must."

Outside the building, David Wester shook his hand again and repeated how much he'd enjoyed John's talk and then each got in his own car and drove away.

On the way back to his office, John had a lot to think about. First of all, there was the satisfaction he'd gotten from pleasing Jacey. She was a sweetheart. He hadn't spent much time around kids. He'd been afraid he'd be even more out of place than his mother with her pearls and petits fours. That was when he'd hit on the magic he'd practiced religiously as a teenager to get over his shyness.

He was glad it had worked for Jacey.

Meeting David Wester was food for thought, too. He'd approached Wester's company once as a potential client, but Wester's assistant had assured him they were happy with their financial adviser. He didn't even know who represented Wester, but whoever it was, he was making a fortune.

What a surprise that Lisbeth's new daddy was David Wester. He was glad the man wasn't his client. That made one less person to whom he would have to explain his lie.

At least that had worked out okay.

Rachel wasn't going to be happy with him. That thought was almost as disturbing as Jacey's approval was pleasing. He had promised to straighten out the lie Jacey had told. Well, he and Jacey had promised. Rachel wasn't going to let Jacey off easy, either.

But she wouldn't refuse to speak to Jacey.

He suspected she might never speak to him again.

The hollowness such a thought brought disturbed him. He didn't need any woman. And had promised himself he never would again. His first wife had almost bankrupted him and ruined his business. He was through with women.

Except Jacey.

Rachel was another matter. He'd found himself wanting to touch her; had wanted to from the moment he'd opened his door to find her standing there. The half hour they'd spent negotiating his appearance this morning had only intensified that odd, compelling longing.

The way she handled Jacey, lovingly but firmly, had impressed him. The way she'd shifted in her chair when she was thinking drove him crazy. She'd worn jeans and a T-shirt that had clung to her curves. Generous curves . . . Well, generous in some places—the places that counted.

He licked his lips, finding them suddenly dry. Without question, he needed to avoid Rachel Cason.

Somehow, he didn't think that would be a problem when she found out what had happened.

RACHEL PULLED INTO the driveway of the child-care center where Jacey stayed after her morning kindergarten. She was a few minutes early, but she was anxious to see if Jacey had been hurt by her revelation that morning. She didn't want her child to suffer, but she also didn't want her to get away with a lie. There was an important lesson to be learned here.

She reached the door of Jacey's room and searched with her eyes for her daughter.

Obviously Jacey hadn't suffered too much. She was playing house with several little girls, pretending to cook something on the toy stove, giggling with the others.

"Oh, Mrs. Cason, you're here," the worker said, noticing Rachel for the first time.

Jacey heard her mother's name and dropped everything to come running. "You're here early, Mommy!"

Rachel hugged her, reveling in the little-girl smell, a combination of juice, cookies and pure sweetness. "Just a little, Jacey. Are you ready?"

"I have to put away my toys," Jacey explained and hurried back to her friends.

"Your little girl is so good. She's never a bit of trouble," the worker said, beaming at Jacey.

"Thank you," Rachel murmured, thinking about the mess Jacey had created this past weekend with her hiring of John Crewes. He was the kind of man Rachel avoided. Attractive, powerful, self-centered. At least, according to the divorcée and Mr. Donaldson.

"Ready, Mommy," Jacey announced, interrupting Rachel's thoughts.

Once the two of them were in the car, driving home, Rachel asked the question that had been on her mind all day. "So, how did Mr. Crewes do this morning? He did come, didn't he?"

"Oh, yes. He did magic tricks. And look," Jacey said, digging beneath the seat belt into the pocket in her shorts. She held her hand out to her mother and Rachel glanced down briefly before returning her gaze to the road.

"He gave you money?"

"He gave all of us a quarter! After he pulled it from behind Bobby's ear! Then he put it behind his back and made more money! Isn't that neat? I didn't know anyone could make money like that. If you learned how to do his trick, then you could stop working and stay home with me!"

Oh, great! Thanks to John Crewes she was learning that her daughter wanted a daddy and didn't want her mother to work. She owed the man a big thank-you! Maybe she could repay him by running over him. She didn't need this!

"Sweetie, you know I have to work in the summers to pay off my school loan. This is the last time, and then I won't have to teach summer school. We'll be able to be lazy together."

Jacey leaned over to pat her mother's arm, reassuringly. "I know, Mommy. I just thought it would be fun."

"Of course it would, angel. But what Mr. Crewes did was a magic trick. He didn't really make all those quarters."

"He didn't?"

Rachel sighed. "No, he didn't." Okay, so now she was bursting another of Jacey's bubbles. Chalk up something else she owed dear John. Maybe running over him was too nice.

"Oh." Jacey's little face reflected the same emotions she'd shown when she'd asked about Santa Claus. Rachel had hated to tell her this past Christmas that Santa was make-believe. But she'd always been honest with her child.

And Jacey had gotten over her disappointment. At least, it hadn't stopped her from enjoying her presents. She'd get over this disappointment, also. Especially if she didn't see John Crewes again.

"How about if you watch some cartoons for an hour, and then we go to McDonald's for dinner." She tried to save Jacey's favorite fast food for a special treat. Tonight, Jacey needed something to make up for her disappointment.

"Okay," the child agreed, a smile returning to her face.

And that hour of cartoons would give Rachel time to unwind, from both her teaching and the worry she'd had all day about Jacey and John Crewes.

As Rachel slipped into jeans and a knit shirt, she realized she hadn't asked Jacey what Mrs. Wilson's reaction had been. Oh, well, she'd get the nitty-gritty over dinner, when Jacey had her favorite food to distract her.

In the meantime, Rachel would fantasize about the punishment she'd wish on John Crewes's head for encouraging Jacey to believe in a fantasy even more far-fetched than Santa Claus.

JOHN LEFT WORK EARLY, shocking his staff. Normally, he was the last out of the office, usually finishing up at around eight or nine. He'd stop at a favorite restaurant and eat dinner on the way home. Then he'd work out with weights in his basement, read some financial reports, and go to bed at eleven.

Not an exciting life. But productive.

Today, he was anxious to be there for Jacey when the child told her mother she hadn't corrected her lie. After all, he was just as guilty. He would shoulder the blame for the little girl, shield her from her mother's disapproval. It was the honorable thing to do.

He whipped into his driveway, loosening his tie and unbuttoning the top button with one hand. He couldn't see any sign of life in the house next door, but an old Chevrolet compact car was in the driveway. He'd seen it before.

Grabbing his briefcase, he rushed into his house and up the stairs. In two minutes he'd discarded his suit and slipped on jeans, a shirt and tennis shoes.

In one minute flat he was down the stairs, out of the house and standing over on Rachel's front porch, pressing her doorbell. He was in a hurry because he wanted to protect Jacey. Not because he was anxious to see Rachel.

Not at all.

Almost at once the door opened and both ladies were standing in front of him.

Jacey beamed at him but said nothing. Rachel blinked several times, as if in surprise, then said, "Yes?"

She didn't look happy with him, but she also didn't appear ready to kill him. He glanced down at Jacey and received the merest hint of a headshake.

"Uh—" He stalled, wondering if it was possible that Jacey hadn't explained what had happened.

"Yes?" Rachel repeated.

For the first time, he noticed that she had her purse with her. "Were you on your way out?"

"We're going to McDonald's," Jacey announced, still beaming. "You want to come, too?"

"Jacey!" Rachel exploded, frowning at her child.

"Hey, I'd like that, Jacey, if your mom doesn't mind?" He looked at Rachel, waiting for her approval. His earlier idea of being there for Jacey made dinner a good idea. The way his heart thumped in overtime just looking at Rachel should have had him thinking the opposite, but it didn't.

Of course, he wasn't going to force his way in where he wasn't wanted, but...he put as much begging in his gaze as Jacey was putting in hers.

"You're ganging up on me again!" Rachel protested, looking at first one of them and then the other, fighting a smile.

"It'll be fun, Mommy," Jacey assured her.

"My treat," John offered as an inducement.

He realized he'd made a mistake almost at once. Rachel stiffened and her gaze froze him. "Jacey and I pay our own way. Bribery is not acceptable."

"Bribery? Hell, I— I mean, heck," he quickly amended when Rachel's gaze dropped another fifty degrees in temperature. "I wasn't trying to bribe you."

She gave him one of those teacher looks.

"Well, maybe I was, a little, but what's the big deal? A trip to McDonald's isn't like moving in together."

If her expression was anything to judge by, he'd gone from bad to worse.

Jacey tugged on her mother's hand. "Please, Mommy? John was really good today. We could say thank-you and pay for his hamburger. You always say we have to say thank-you when someone does something nice for us."

Once again, he was reminded of what a terrific mother Rachel was. When she turned to her daughter, all the anger and coldness had left her face. "You're right, Jacey. I forgot. We'll buy Mr. Crewes a hamburger to say thank-you."

John wondered if he'd only imagined that she'd added that they'd never see him again after his hamburger. It certainly seemed clear when she turned back to look at him.

"We'll worry about who pays when we get there. Step this way, ladies. My carriage awaits." He swept his arm toward his Porsche in a grand gesture.

"What's a carriage?" Jacey immediately asked, pushing past her mother and out the door.

"It's what Cinderella rode in to the ball," Rachel murmured and then added, "we'll take our car and meet you there."

"Don't be silly, Rachel." Another mistake, he realized as she turned to stare at him, one eyebrow rising in warning. He hurriedly added, "There's no reason to take two cars."

"You're right. You can ride with us."

He looked at the ancient car in her driveway and then the gleaming black Porsche he drove and swallowed. But he wasn't going to let her keep him from going with them. "Okay."

Jacey clapped her hands and ran to her mother's car. She slipped into the back seat and fastened her seat belt at once. John walked around the car and took the passenger seat, even though every instinct told him to offer to drive. He wasn't used to a woman driving him somewhere.

"Good girl, Jacey," he praised as he fastened his own seat belt.

"What did I do?" the child asked, her eyes wide.

"You fastened your seat belt."

"Mommy won't start the car until I do."

Rachel was settling in behind the wheel and ignoring them.

"Ah. Good mommy."

Jacey giggled and Rachel smiled at her daughter, but she didn't extend that warmth to him. So far, everything was normal.

When they reached McDonald's, all three stood in line together. Rachel pointedly gave the order for her and Jacey and pulled out her billfold to pay.

John looked at the teenage boy behind the cash register. "We're together." He added his order and handed over a twenty-dollar bill before Rachel realized what he was doing.

"No! We—"

"Don't be difficult, Rachel," he said and grinned at the boy. "Women!" he murmured and Rachel glared at him again. "You and Jacey go find us a place to sit."

Frustration flattened out her wonderfully full lips and she whirled around and walked away. He hoped she wouldn't keep walking until she reached her car.

He picked up the quickly loaded tray and scanned the restaurant. He'd gotten lucky. She and Jacey were sitting on one side of a booth for four people over by a window. He carried the tray over and slid in across from them.

"Okay, Jacey, my girl. Here's your Happy Meal."

He offered Rachel her choices also, before taking his own food off the tray.

Rachel didn't start eating, like Jacey did. Instead, she fixed a steady look on John. "Jacey said your speech went well this morning. But how did Mrs. Wilson react to your explanation about not being Jacey's daddy?"

He'd been right. Jacey hadn't explained.

He didn't want to, either.

Chapter Three

Rachel stared at the man across from her, waiting for an answer. When he looked at her daughter, she turned to Jacey also.

"Jacey?" she asked, noting her daughter's fearful expression.

"It really wasn't her fault," John hurriedly said. "I was late, so..." He trailed off, shrugging his shoulders.

"What wasn't Jacey's fault? Did you tell your teacher that Mr. Crewes was not your new daddy?" Rachel asked her child.

Jacey picked up a French Fry and slowly swirled it through a puddle of thick catsup. "Not 'zactly."

"Janet Cecilia Cason!" Rachel exclaimed.

"Mommy!" Jacey protested. She hated it when Rachel used all her names. It meant she was upset.

"I think you have some explaining to do, young lady."

"Now, wait a minute," John began, trying, she supposed, to save her daughter from a scolding. She glared at him, halting his interruption. She feared he could charm her into a lot of things, but her role as a parent was too important to give in to any persuading from him.

"I was going to, Mommy, but I waited for John to arrive, 'cause, well, 'cause he's so big, I wouldn't be afraid if he was with me, like a real daddy."

Soulful eyes looked first at John and then at Rachel. It didn't take a rocket scientist to see that John was completely taken in by Jacey's statement.

"Aw, Jacey, I'm sorry I was late," he said and extended his hand across the table to hold hers.

Rachel worked to keep a frown on her face as the pair of them turned their pleading eyes her way. "Oh, no. I'm not that gullible, Jacey. I told you to explain to Mrs. Wilson as soon as you got to school."

"She was busy, Mommy."

"And why didn't you explain when you got there, John Crewes, since you seem so willing to excuse Jacey for not setting the record straight?"

"Mrs. Wilson shoved me in front of the kids at once because I was late. Lisbeth's father had already finished. If I was going to confess, everyone in the room would've heard me. I didn't want to embarrass Jacey like that."

Rachel almost groaned aloud. It was hard enough to be strict with Jacey, even though she knew it was in Jacey's best interests, without someone else siding with her little girl. Squaring her jaw, she asked, "And afterward?"

"Reading circle," he explained gravely, then added, in a fairly close rendition of Mrs. Wilson's precise tones, "We wouldn't want to get off schedule, now, would we?"

She ignored Jacey's giggly appreciation of his talent. "It is not polite to mock Mrs. Wilson. She is a fine teacher."

He ducked his head and mumbled an apology in the manner of some of the senior boys she taught. With an exasperated sigh, she turned back to her daughter.

"Jacey, why didn't you explain afterward?"

"'Cause the van came for child care, Mommy. I was afraid they'd leave me behind."

Since Jacey had been left behind once because she dawdled over putting away her supplies, her mother had lectured her about being on time for the van.

"Come on, Rachel, it's not that big a deal," John assured her when she covered her eyes with one hand.

She quickly glared at him again. "Maybe not to you. But now my child's teacher thinks I'm married to a total stranger!"

"How often do you talk to the woman?"

Rachel drew a deep breath. Maybe John Crewes was right. She'd write a note tomorrow, explaining how the silly misunderstanding had occurred. And that would be that.

"Okay, I'll straighten it out tomorrow."

"Do we have to tell Mrs. Wilson?" Jacey asked in a small voice.

Rachel noted that Jacey, who loved a Happy Meal, had scarcely eaten anything. She hadn't meant to ruin her daughter's treat. "Yes, we do, sweetheart, but I'll do the explaining this time. Everything will be all right." She peered into Jacey's box. "Did you find your surprise in the Happy Meal?"

"No."

Jacey leaned against the back of the booth, a sorrowful look on her face.

"If you don't want it, I saw a little boy over there who didn't get a Happy Meal. Why don't you offer it to him so it won't go to waste."

Her ploy distracted Jacey from her thoughts as she scanned the restaurant searching for the little boy who might take her prize. "I think I'd like to keep it, Mommy."

"If you want." Rachel picked up her hamburger and took a bite, as if everything was A-okay. If she ignored the handsome man sitting across from her, maybe it was.

"What are you going to use to distract *me?*" he murmured to Rachel as Jacey turned her attention to the toy in the plastic bag.

"Why would I want to distract you?"

"I don't know. So I'll eat my hamburger?"

The twinkle in his hazel eyes invited her smile, but she put the brakes on even as the corners of her mouth began to turn up. "Frankly, Mr. Crewes, I don't care whether you ever eat again. You and your ridiculous response to Jacey have caused me all kinds of problems. Watching you starve to death might be quite enjoyable."

"I've said it before but I'll say it again. You are one tough lady, Rachel Cason."

"Yes, I am," she agreed, hoping her smile didn't reveal how much his teasing affected her; how tempting it was to relax and invite him to come closer. Instead, she vowed to avoid her neighbor from now on.

Life seemed so easy for John Crewes. A smile, a wink, and the world was his. Money didn't hurt either. According to her neighbors, he was loaded. Quite a difference from her own life, with its constant struggle to provide for herself and Jacey.

Yes, she should definitely avoid this man, if for no other reason than that his all-American good looks—from his sandy hair casually brushed back to his hazel eyes that could twinkle with such mischief—were too tempting. His broad shoulders and strong physique were the icing on the cake.

Ignoring John Crewes might take more strength than she had.

JOHN RAN A HAND through his hair in frustration. What was the matter with him? He couldn't concentrate this morning. Annual reports held no interest in comparison to Rachel. Her blue eyes, her full lips that she tried to keep firmly set, her enticing curves, all lured him away from business.

He might as well forget her, though. She'd made it clear last night that she wanted nothing more to do with him.

And shc was right. What did they have in common? He was a businessman, dedicated to making money, for himself and others. She was a schoolteacher, sacrificing to bring knowledge to a bunch of unappreciative teenagers.

Besides, she was a mother.

Jacey. The name alone brought a smile to John's face. What a kid! She'd finally brightened up last evening and finished her Happy Meal. Then she'd invited John to join her on the playground. It was the best offer he got, so the two of them went off, hand in hand, leaving her mother at the table.

They'd had a great time, even though he'd kept an eye on Rachel, too. Just in case she needed him. There could be some bad guys lurking at McDonald's, just looking to hit on a beautiful woman all alone.

Yeah, sure.

He'd tried to make up with Rachel when they reached their respective houses. She'd listened to his apology and thanked him for his concern for Jacey.

Then she'd told him to get lost. Only in nicer words.

"Mr. Crewes?" His secretary's voice intruded into his thoughts through the intercom. "David Wester is on line two."

"Thanks," he calmly acknowledged, but surprise mixed with a mild panic filled him. What could the man want? Did he already know that John had lied yesterday?

"David, this is John. How can I help you?"

First David complimented him again on his magic show of the day before. Obviously he didn't know *yet* just how much magic John's appearance had involved.

"The real reason I'm calling, John, is because I'm in the market for a new financial adviser. After meeting you yesterday, I checked into your reputation, and I must say, I am very impressed."

John took a deep breath. His small company had grown over the past few years, with the occasional hiccup, or maybe a choke, like during his divorce. He certainly was earning a large sum of money each year. But David Wester's account would at least double his company's size.

"Thank you, David. We're doing all right."

"Better than all right. But I wouldn't consider your company based solely on the numbers. I was impressed with you yesterday because of your ability to relate to the children, in particular Jacey. You're the kind of man I want to work with. A family man, one who puts people above money."

John thanked David again, feeling guilty about the misrepresentation, but unsure exactly how to explain. "I'd certainly be willing to look at your investments and give you my opinion of what I could do for you."

"No," David replied and John was surprised at how much relief was mixed with the disappointment. "No, I've already made up my mind. I want you to take over my commodities investments at once."

"But, David, shouldn't we talk first? Let me tell you what I might have in mind?"

"No, John, that's not necessary. I make my decisions based on the person, not his performance record, though yours is excellent. I'm a psychologist, remember?"

"But—"

"Now, I want you to get together with Bud Cassidy, my vice president. He's putting together all the information you'll need and can answer any questions. I work more on the creative end of our business and I've got a new project going that I think you'll be interested in. But more about that later."

"But—"

"You *can* meet with Bud right away, can't you?"

"Of course, but—"

"Great. Now, Friday night, I want you to come to dinner at seven. And bring Jacey and your wife. Lisbeth and her mother are looking forward to visiting with them. Casual, of course. Okay?"

"David, I—"

"I have to go now, John. See you Friday."

Before John could say anything else, the line went dead.

Stunned, he hung up the phone and sat staring at the far wall. David Wester was turning some of his investments over to him. John had no fears about being able to do the job; he was good at what he did.

His only fear was that David had based his decision on a falsehood. What would happen when he found out the truth? And he was sure to find out. After all, Rachel had said she would straighten out the misunderstanding today.

After ten minutes of debating his options, John decided that honesty was essential. He called David Wester's office.

"Mr. Wester, please, John Crewes calling."

"I'm sorry, Mr. Crewes, but Mr. Wester is out of the office. May I take a message?"

"But I just talked to him a few minutes ago."

"Oh, he probably called you from his car phone. He was on his way to the airport."

"When will he be back?" He certainly couldn't make the explanation to a secretary.

"He'll be back in the office next Monday, but I believe he'll be back in town Friday afternoon, late. May I take a message, or could someone else help you?"

"Is Bud Cassidy in?"

"Mr. Cassidy is in a meeting. I'll ask him to return your call when he's available."

Frustrated, John hung up the phone. Great. Just great. The biggest challenge of his career, and he was going to lose it. Even worse, he was losing it because he'd broken one of his own rules. He believed in honesty. In fact, it was his constant honesty that had saved him when his wife had tried to destroy him. He and Jacey, between them, had broken that rule. Only she was just a little girl. *He* should have known better.

Maybe if he had a chance to explain to David before he heard the truth from Lisbeth, John might be able to convince him that his motives were pure, even if he had lied. But that wouldn't happen. David would hear it from Lisbeth if from no one else, when—

What if Lisbeth, or Mrs. Wilson, didn't find out about the lie until Monday? What if he could convince Rachel to put off her explanation?

Memory of her attitude last evening made such a possibility doubtful. Normally he would approve of a woman who believed in honesty above all else. It made a rare but pleasant change from his ex-wife. *Great, Crewes. You find a woman who insists on honesty just when you need a good lie.*

He grinned as he remembered Rachel's stubborn little chin. But she had a weakness. One that was swiftly becoming a weakness for him, too. Jacey. She might agree to help him because of Jacey. It was worth a try. If he could just have a little breathing room, until he could talk to David face-to-face, maybe—

He reached for the phone and then realized he didn't even know where Rachel taught, much less the number. The one person in his neighborhood he knew was Polly Meadows, an elderly widow. He seized the telephone directory to look for her number.

"Polly, this is John Crewes from across the street. I'm trying to get hold of Rachel Cason."

"Why, John, I didn't even know you knew each other. Every time I've offered to introduce Rachel to you, she always refused."

That was an irritating thought that he put away for another day. A less hectic day.

"Uh, Polly, I'm kind of in a hurry. Do you know where Rachel teaches school?"

"Why, yes, of course. She's at Daniel Webster High School. She teaches history."

"Thank you, Polly," he hurriedly said, before she could launch into a description of Rachel's day. The woman was kind but long-winded. He searched through the telephone directory again and dialed a second number.

"Webster High School."

"Rachel Cason, please," he said authoritatively.

"I'll be happy to take a message. Mrs. Cason is in class right now."

"When will she be out of class?"

"I'm not sure. I'll put a message in her box and she'll return your call at her convenience."

"But I need to talk to her right away."

"I'm sorry, but—"

"But it's an emergency! Surely you have a way of reaching your teachers in an emergency?" Frustration was building in him.

"Well, if it's really an emergency..." The stern voice paused, as if waiting for him to confess to a practical joke.

"Yes, it is!" Well, it was for him. And what could it hurt to interrupt a class for a few minutes?

"I'll send a student to her class with a message. What shall I say?"

"Ask her to call John Crewes at 555-8714 at once."

"And shall I say it's an emergency?"

The lady still doubted him.

"Yes!"

He slammed down the phone and waited. He'd had no idea teachers were so incommunicado. How did Rachel stand it? He felt lost if he didn't have a telephone beside him.

Fifteen minutes later, he was still waiting, frustration building in him. When his secretary finally announced Rachel's call, John clenched the receiver as if it were a lifeline.

"John? This is Rachel. What's the matter?"

"Why did it take you so long? I said it was an emergency!"

"John, I had twenty-six seniors in class. I couldn't just walk out and leave them to their own devices."

"What if Jacey had been sick? Does she have to wait until it's convenient?" he demanded, outrage filling him.

"Jacey? Is this call about Jacey?" The rising panic in her voice filled him with guilt.

"No. At least, not exactly."

"Hurry up, then, John. My next class starts in two minutes."

"Have you talked to Mrs. Wilson?" he demanded, although he wanted to protest at being limited to such a short call. But he couldn't afford to waste the time.

"I sent a note with Jacey this morning."

"Oh."

"What's the matter?"

"I was going to ask you to postpone telling her."

"What difference does it make when I tell her? I think it's better to do disagreeable tasks at once."

"You would," John muttered, the tension flowing out of him like air escaping from a punctured balloon.

"What? I couldn't hear you."

"Never mind. I'm sorry I disturbed you."

"John? What's wrong?"

He could hear a bell ring in the background and Rachel gasped. Afraid she would hang up, he hurriedly said, "I'll explain later. When we both have more time."

Before Rachel could ask again, he hung up the phone and sagged against the back of his chair.

"Mr. Crewes, Mr. Cassidy is on line one," his secretary announced.

John sighed and picked up the phone again, punching the appropriate button.

After a brief introduction, Bud Cassidy wanted to set up a meeting time for the next day.

"Look, Mr. Cassidy, I—"

"Make it Bud. We'll be working together a lot."

"Okay, Bud, I don't think— I mean, I can meet with you tomorrow, but I'm not sure David is going to want me to handle his account."

"He's already decided. David's that way, John. He makes fast decisions and is seldom wrong."

"I think in this instance—"

"Look, he's out of town for a few days. Why don't we hold some preliminary meetings and we'll go from there."

John gave up. It was like he was caught in the undertow in the ocean, powerless to change his direction. "Okay. How about tomorrow at ten? Shall I come to your office…? No, I'll be happy to have you come here. All right. I'll see you then."

John hung up the phone and swiveled around in his chair to stare out the window of his office. What a mess! All because he couldn't resist a pair of big blue eyes. Make that two pairs of big blue eyes.

JACEY FINGERED THE piece of folded paper in her shirt pocket as she waited for class to begin. Her mother had told her exactly what she was supposed to do with it.

She had intended to follow her mother's directions.

She really had.

But Lisbeth had run up to her as soon as she arrived and started talking about the summer and the vacation her new daddy was going to give her—the three of them—at Walt Disney World. Then another little girl started talking about the family vacation she was going to take. Soon Mrs. Wilson was letting everyone tell of their plans.

Then she asked Jacey where her new daddy and her mommy were going to take her, and she said Disney World, too, because she wanted everyone to think that her new daddy was just as wonderful as Lisbeth's.

"Let's go together!" Lisbeth squealed. "It would be just like we're sisters!"

"Yeah, sisters!" Jacey exclaimed eagerly, but already she was discovering the truth of her mother's warning. Lies always got you in trouble. She might be able to pretend that John was her daddy, but she knew he wasn't going to take her to Disney World just because she wanted him to.

That was why she was fingering the note in her pocket. She should give it to Mrs. Wilson at once. Like her mommy had told her to. But Mrs. Wilson would make her apologize to the class, like she did Peter last week when he said a bad word. On the playground afterward, everyone had laughed at him.

"All right, class, it's time to practice our counting."

Too late. Mrs. Wilson was starting class.

Jacey would give it to her later. Maybe at the end of school, before the van came. Maybe.

Jacey watched for the right moment, not wanting to fail her mother, but not wanting to be laughed at and teased by the other students. Finally, when the bell rang, she took her courage in her hands and approached Mrs. Wilson's desk.

"Come along, child. You don't want to miss the van again," Mrs. Wilson encouraged as the last of the others went through the door.

Jacey opened her mouth to explain why she'd waited, but the appearance of the principal at the door with another child and two adults halted her.

"Jacey, run along, child," Mrs. Wilson insisted as she greeted the new student and her parents.

With a shrug of her shoulders, Jacey ran along.

But she wasn't sure how she was going to explain to her mother that, once again, she had failed to keep her promise.

Chapter Four

Rachel picked Jacey up from child care without her usual smile. Nor did she ask any questions about Mrs. Wilson's reaction to the note.

"Are you okay, Mommy?" Jacey asked after riding in silence almost all the way home.

"What?" Rachel looked at Jacey as if she was surprised to see her there. "Oh, sorry, honey, what did you say?"

"Are you okay? You're not talking."

"I'm fine. I—I just had a hard day at school, baby. One of my students was upset."

Uh-oh, Jacey thought. If her mommy was already unhappy, the fact that she hadn't given the note to Mrs. Wilson wasn't going to cheer her up. Jacey slid down as far as the seat belt would allow and closed her eyes, as if she, too, had had a bad day.

The two rode in silence until Rachel turned into the driveway. Jacey opened her eyes and looked at John's house. She saw his car in the driveway and then noticed him standing inside by the big window at the front of his house. Funny, before she'd asked him to be her daddy when she needed one, she never remembered seeing his car at home.

"Look, Mommy, there's John," she said as she opened the car door and scooted out, waving.

"Come inside, Jacey," her mother said, and her tone wasn't friendly.

"Don't you like John, Mommy?"

"Jacey—"

"Hello!"

Both Jacey and her mother turned to see John striding across his yard and driveway to greet them.

"Hello," Rachel said in return, but she didn't smile.

"I thought I'd explain about the phone call," John said.

"What phone call?" Jacey asked. She smiled as John's hand came to rest on her head, just like a real daddy's.

He squatted down beside her and grinned. "I called your mom at school today. How did your day go? Was it rough?"

She knew what he was asking, and that was the one question she didn't want to answer. "Uh, not as bad as Mommy's."

His eyebrows almost came together and he looked all worried like the daddies on television when something was the matter with their family. She liked it.

"Rachel, my phone call wasn't what made your day so bad, was it?" John asked.

"No, of course not. Just forget it," she said and abruptly turned away to walk toward the house.

Jacey and John exchanged looks before they both followed Rachel. When they got to the door, Rachel had already entered the house.

"May I come in?" John called as he paused at the door.

"Yes, if you must," Rachel answered.

John knelt down beside Jacey again. "Maybe you'd better let me talk to your mom alone, Jacey."

"Okay," she agreed and hugged his neck. Sometimes, when her mommy was sad, like today, she wanted to make her happy, but she didn't know how. It was nice to have someone else to take care of her mommy.

And besides, it meant she didn't have to tell her mommy she hadn't given Mrs. Wilson the note—just yet.

"I'll go upstairs," she whispered and ran to her room.

"WHAT WENT WRONG today?"

Rachel spun around, her hand at her throat. An inquisition by John Crewes was the last thing she needed. It had been one of those days when everything went wrong. She'd ruined her nylons on the rough wood of her old desk and been run over by one of the football players making a mad dash to practice. Then she'd found out about Diane. "Look, John, what do you want? I don't have time—"

"I was just concerned, Rachel. Can't I be concerned? You look like you lost your best friend."

There was a warmth in his voice that was incredibly tempting. Rachel had stood alone for so many years without the luxury of a shoulder to cry on, figuratively or otherwise. She looked at him, trying to imagine resting against his lean body.

Then she didn't have to imagine anymore. He took a step closer and pulled her into his arms, offering her his shoulder. She was too stunned, too tempted, to say no. He felt so heavenly, so strong, so...so male.

Contrary to her earlier thoughts, crying wasn't what came to mind as she rested against him. Feelings she'd thought buried long ago were tunneling through her, seeking life. No! she silently protested. She didn't need a man—any man.

With more strength than she realized, she pushed him away and turned her back on him.

"I'm fine. What did you need?"

He circled around her. "Why are you blushing?"

"Don't be silly. It's just the afternoon heat." And the nearness of John Crewes. He'd changed out of his business suit and into cutoffs and a polo shirt. Except for his broad shoulders and a few laugh wrinkles at the corners of his eyes, he looked more like a college kid than a businessman.

He sighed and she peeped at him from under her lashes. She wished he'd quit staring at her.

"Okay, I just wondered how things went with Mrs. Wilson. You know, if Jacey had a hard time when you explained to the woman."

"Oh, dear," Rachel muttered. "I forgot all about it."

"You mean you didn't tell her?"

There was an eagerness in his voice that reminded her of his phone call. "Wait a minute. That's the reason you called, isn't it? You wanted me to wait. Why?"

He shrugged his shoulders and his face had that sheepish look that Jacey wore when she'd been caught doing something she shouldn't.

"I got a call from David Wester today," he said, as if that would explain everything.

Rachel vaguely recognized the name but it didn't mean anything to her. Probably someone big in the business world. She shrugged. "So?"

"You don't know who he is?"

"No, sorry."

"He's Lisbeth's new daddy."

Ah. Now she caught the significance. "The other daddy who came to show-and-tell?"

"That's right. He spoke to the class before I arrived." John ran his hand through his thick, sandy hair and Rachel looked away hurriedly. She was far too tempted to do the same thing.

To put some distance between the two of them, she walked around the couch and sat down in the rocking chair she'd had since Jacey was born.

"Rachel, are you paying attention?" John asked, following her.

She pressed against the back of the rocker as he leaned toward her. Her breathing speeded up as she fought the urge to feel his arm around her again. "Of course, I am. What's the point to the story?"

"Do you know what David Wester does?"

"John, why should I care what he does?" she asked in frustration. "It's been a long day. I'm tired and hungry, I have a five-year-old to feed, and a stack of papers to grade." *And you're too hard on my nervous system.*

Silence reigned and Rachel finally opened her eyes to find John staring at her. "Look, I'm sorry. I know that was impolite, but—"

"But you need a little space."

She was surprised to discover that he understood how she was feeling, and even more surprised to discover how desperately she needed some time to herself. "Yes," she agreed with a big sigh.

"Okay. I'll take Jacey to get some dinner for us. Chinese okay? We won't hurry. You put your feet up and relax."

"No! You can't do that. You bought dinner last night." She wasn't turning her life over to this man. She'd just met him Saturday.

John ignored her protest and walked over to the foot of the stairs. "Jacey!" he called.

Getting up from the rocker, Rachel followed him, prepared to protest again. Her daughter appeared at the head of the stairs.

"Let's go get some Chinese food for dinner while your mom rests, okay?"

"Oh, boy, can I have sweet-and-sour chicken?" Jacey asked as she rushed down the stairs. "I love that, and baby corn, and fortune cookies!"

"You can have all of it, sweetheart."

"And can we stop off at the park and feed the ducks?" Jacey added.

"Sounds good to me," John agreed.

Rachel protested, but the two of them were ignoring her and making plans faster than she could even think. "John, don't—" she tried again.

"We'll be back in about an hour, Rachel," John calmly said, taking Jacey's hand. Then he startled Rachel by leaning over and kissing her cheek, casually, as if it were a common thing.

Before she could pull herself together, the two of them were out the door, smiles on their faces.

Rachel stared after them, her mouth hanging open. He'd acted just like a husband. A real husband, who understood that his wife needed his care as much as his child did, sometimes. A husband of her dreams.

Get real, Cason! She mustn't let this temporary intrusion into her life upset her. Or mislead her into thinking anything was going to be different.

He wasn't her husband. He wasn't Jacey's daddy. And he wasn't going to remain in their lives.

JOHN AND JACEY STOPPED at a drive-in grocery and bought a loaf of bread and some canned sodas before they went to the park. The big white ducks were bold when they discovered the little girl had food.

Jacey shrieked and giggled, chasing and being chased, for more than half an hour. John hovered in the background, anxious to protect her but not wanting to spoil her fun.

Finally, he called her over to a picnic bench and offered her a cold soda. "You should be about ready for this," he said with a grin.

"Do we have some for the ducks?"

"Jacey, you can't give ducks soda. They drink water from the pond."

"Ooh, but it smells. And Mommy says I can't drink the water in the swimming pool."

He gently tweaked her button nose. "That's because you're not a duck."

"Okay. I'm having fun. Thank you."

"You're welcome. You have very nice manners."

"My mommy taught me."

"You have a very nice mommy, too."

"I know," Jacey agreed with a giggle.

"Does she come home upset often?"

"No. Only when a kid at school makes her sad," Jacey said, her gaze on the ducks.

"How do they make her sad? Do they do bad things?"

"No, Mommy makes them behave. But sometimes they don't have anyone to love them, and that makes her sad."

"I see," John said. And he did. Rachel Cason had a big heart. He knew her child never doubted for a minute that her mother loved her. He'd seen it in the way she dealt with Jacey. Even when Jacey had misbehaved, Rachel showed her love.

John's father had been busy with his job. His mother had had her charity work. And he had been left alone, with rules to follow and chores to do. He hadn't suffered. Affluent parents were an asset he didn't discount. But the idea of having a mother like Rachel, giving her child a hug, a smile, her time—ah, that would have been heaven.

Of course, a hug from Rachel now might be even better. He chuckled, thinking about her reaction to his thoughts.

"What's so funny?" Jacey asked, tugging on his shirt.

"I was just thinking about how nice your mom is."

"Yeah," Jacey replied in a satisfied voice.

"Where's your daddy?" The question slipped out before John thought about the implications for Jacey. He wished he could take it back, but he discovered the child was quite at ease.

"He left before I was borned. Mommy says he didn't know I was going to be this good, or he wouldn't have left."

He hugged her to him. "I'm sure your mommy is right, 'cause you're one special kid, Jacey."

"You're a good daddy, too," Jacey said, smiling up at him. "I picked a good daddy to hire."

"I don't have any experience."

"Mommy didn't have no experience to be a mommy, neither. She said she was scared. But she learned real fast."

"She certainly did. Let's go get some Chinese food and go back home. Maybe she's feeling better by now."

He hoped so. When she looked at him with those forlorn blue eyes, all he wanted to do was to take her into his arms and comfort her. He didn't think Rachel would react well to such an offer. But he couldn't help thinking about what Jacey had said. Her daddy had left before she was born.

Who had stood by Rachel? Her parents? Jacey hadn't mentioned grandparents. It seemed to him, if she had a grandfather, she would have asked *him* to do show-and-tell.

Did that mean Rachel had been all alone, pregnant? How old was she when Jacey was born?

His mind occupied with all the questions he wanted to ask Rachel, John didn't think of his original question until they'd gone through the drive-through at the Chinese restaurant and were almost back home.

"Say, Jacey, what did Mrs. Wilson say when she found out I'm not really your dad?"

The smile that had been on Jacey's face the entire trip abruptly disappeared.

"Was it bad, sweetheart?" John asked, his heart going out to Jacey. "I'm sorry."

Jacey's chin dropped down to her chest and she muttered something. John frowned, but he couldn't take his eyes off the road long enough to comfort her. That teacher must have been brutal.

He pulled into the driveway and killed the motor, then turned to Jacey. "Come on, sweetheart, tell me what she said."

"I can't," Jacey whispered.

"She can't have been that mean, Jacey. Did she make you tell the class?"

She shook her head no.

A thought struck him and he looked at Jacey in horror. "She didn't spank you, did she?"

"No."

"Jacey, talk to me. Did she chew you out?"

The child shook her head again.

Frustration built in him. As cute as he thought Jacey was, John wanted an answer. He was beginning to understand why parents lost their tempers with children.

"Jacey?"

"I didn't give her the note." Jacey kept her gaze focused on her toes.

Prepared to comfort her for the horrible punishment she'd received, John needed a moment to understand what she'd said.

"What? She doesn't know?"

Jacey shook her head.

"Did you tell Lisbeth?" he asked, checking all his bases.

Jacey shook her head a second time. Then, looking at John briefly before turning her gaze down again, she added, in a rush, "Lisbeth's going to Disney World with her new daddy."

John had no interest in Lisbeth's activities. He was busy thinking about the significance of Jacey's answer. "Okay," he said absently.

"I said we were, too."

"Fine. Sweetheart, have you told your mother that you didn't give her note to Mrs. Wilson?"

"No." They sat in silence. Then Jacey asked in a small voice, "You aren't mad?"

John laughed out loud. "Mad? No, I'm pleased." Then he thought about the message that might give a small child. "But I'm not your mother. She's not going to be happy that you didn't obey her, you know."

"I know."

"When are you going to tell her?"

"I could just give Mrs. Wilson the note tomorrow."

"No!" John hadn't meant to snap his reply. "No, I mean, I don't think that's a good idea."

"Why not?"

"Because—because I think you should tell your mommy tonight."

"But then she'll be upset, and she's already sad."

Jacey was right. And if he didn't need to discuss with Rachel the idea of not telling Mrs. Wilson until Monday, it would have been a perfect answer. Jacey wouldn't get in trouble and Rachel wouldn't be unhappy.

He felt like a rat.

Because of his needs, Jacey was going to have to confess to her mother that she hadn't given the note to Mrs. Wilson.

"Sweetheart, I—"

Tapping on his car window scared both of them.

He discovered Rachel bending over, looking in at them. The view of her blouse gaping just a little, revealing shadowy mounds of flesh that would figure in future dreams, was almost worth the interruption. As he brought his gaze back to her face, she grabbed her blouse and straightened, her cheeks red.

Jacey opened her car door.

"We had fun, Mommy. We fed the ducks lots of bread."

"Good. You were gone a long time."

John got out of the car, juggling the cartons of Chinese food and the extra sodas in a grocery sack.

"Hungry?" he asked, his gaze searching her face.

"Yes, starving, but I feel bad about your going to so much trouble."

"No trouble. We had fun, like Jacey said."

Which was more than they were going to have now, John thought to himself as he followed Jacey and her mother into the house.

Maybe he'd wait to bring up the subject of Mrs. Wilson and the note until after dinner. No point in ruining everyone's meal.

Chapter Five

Rachel studied John out of the corner of her eye as he talked to Jacey. What a surprise the evening had been.

First, he'd understood her need for solitude. Not only understood, but also done something about providing it. Then, he'd brought home a delicious dinner and proceeded to share it with them.

And entertained them.

He'd told funny stories that even she couldn't resist. Jacey had giggled all evening long. Now she was curled up in John's lap, helping him read his fortune from the broken fortune cookie on his plate.

"'You will have health, wealth and happiness,'" John read, pointing to each word for Jacey's benefit.

"Is that good?" the little girl asked, hoping, Rachel decided, that John would only get good news.

"The best," he assured her and kissed the top of her head.

Rachel wanted to protest. Her child was growing too fond of this man. And they'd only known him less than a week. Jacey would be terribly upset when John bowed out of their lives.

"What does mine say?" Jacey asked, pulling the thin strip of paper from her fortune cookie.

John took the paper from her and then laughed as he silently read it.

"What does it say? What does it say?" Jacey asked anxiously.

"It says, 'It is wise to listen to your elders.'" His gaze lifted from the paper to meet Rachel's, inviting her to laugh with him.

The best she could muster was a smile.

"What's an elder?" Jacey wanted to know.

"Your mom and me," he said.

"An elder is someone who is older than you, Jacey. Usually much older," Rachel added.

Jacey didn't seem as amused as John. She looked up at him and then at her mother. "Okay," she said with a sigh and began to slide down from John's lap.

"Jacey? Where are you going?" he asked.

Rather than answer him, Jacey came around the table and stood in front of her mother. "I have to tell you something, Mommy. John said I should."

Rachel glanced at John and then Jacey. Before either she or Jacey could speak, however, John stood.

"No, Jacey. I was wrong. Do it your way."

Jacey's finger stole to her mouth, as it always did when she was worried or scared. Rachel cupped her stubborn little chin in one hand.

"What is it, Jacey?"

Her daughter looked back at John. "No, you were right, John. Mommy, I didn't give the note to Mrs. Wilson today."

Rachel closed her eyes briefly and then looked at Jacey. "Why not, sweetie?"

"Because I was afraid she would make me apologize to the class, like she did Peter. Everybody laughed at him." Tears welled up in her big blue eyes. "I'm sorry, Mommy. Are you mad at me?"

Rachel wrapped her arms around her daughter and held her. "No, I'm not mad. I'm a little disappointed that you didn't do what I asked, but maybe I expected too much."

"I'll give it to her tomorrow, Mommy, I promise!" Jacey exclaimed, her little arms encircling her mother's neck and hugging tightly.

"We'll see, Jacey. I'll think about what I want to do." Rachel hugged her again. "Now, thank Mr. Crewes for our dinner and go get ready for bed."

Jacey did more than thank John. She threw herself into his arms.

"May I give her a ride up the stairs?" he asked as he picked Jacey up, swinging her to his shoulders.

The move had surprised a chuckle from Jacey and she grabbed his ears to hold on. How could Rachel say no when in one move he'd brought a smile back to Jacey's face?

"Yes, of course." Rachel stood back for him to pass in front of her and then followed the two of them up the stairs.

John deposited Jacey on her bed and told her goodnight. Rachel tried to thank him for their dinner, in case he wanted to leave while she was helping Jacey into bed, but he assured her he'd wait downstairs for her.

She didn't want him to wait. She didn't want to be alone with him, without Jacey's distracting presence. She didn't want to be tempted by his sexy body, his warmth, the sense of caring he'd dispensed that evening. She knew better than to believe such things would last.

He ignored her protests and went down the stairs.

"I love John," Jacey announced, as Rachel pulled her pajama top over her head.

"Jacey, John is very nice, but—but he's not a daddy, you know. Yours or anyone else's. He won't be coming here after tonight."

"Why not? He lives next door, Mommy. It's not a long way."

"I know it's not, sweetie, but men who aren't married, who don't have children, have lots of other things to do. They're too busy to play with little children." *Or single mothers.*

"Oh."

"Thank you for being honest about the note."

"I'm sorry I didn't give it to her."

"That's all right. Let's say your prayers now."

She listened as Jacey recited the prayer she used each evening. After the memorized words, Jacey always added her own special prayers, and Rachel cringed as her child talked.

"Thank you, God, for John. Let him come back to play with us. I'm sorry I didn't mind my mommy. Love, Jacey."

Rachel thought it was time to tuck her in, but Jacey had one more plea.

"And P.S., please make John be my daddy for real. Amen."

"Jacey!"

"What, Mommy? You said I could ask God for whatever I wanted."

"Yes, but—but he may not give you what you ask for. Remember?"

"I remember. But I thought I should ask."

"Good night, Jacey," Rachel whispered, kissing her daughter. She didn't want to discuss Jacey's request.

He might be the answer to her daughter's prayers, but John Crewes was a temptation she intended to avoid.

JOHN PACED THE FLOOR as he waited for Rachel in the comfortable living room. Earlier, he'd distracted himself by silently admiring Rachel's skill at taking old worn-out furniture and making it look comfortable and welcoming. Clearly, she and Jacey didn't have a lot, but she'd made a nice home for the two of them. Those thoughts didn't distract him now, however.

What mattered was convincing Rachel to wait until Monday before she told the truth to Mrs. Wilson.

"Thank you for telling Jacey to confess," Rachel said as she entered the room.

John's head snapped up and he stared at the beautiful woman before him.

"I can't take credit for that."

"Why not? She said she told me because you said it was the thing to do."

Her blue eyes were as large as Jacey's and even more delicious... along with the rest of her. He took a step closer and then stopped.

"When I said she should tell you, I was thinking about myself. After I thought about it, I decided it would be wrong to get Jacey into trouble just to help me."

Rachel's eyebrows rose as the warmth in her eyes faded. John knew exactly how a student might feel if he was guilty of breaking one of her rules.

"How would getting Jacey into trouble help you?"

"I needed to talk to you about telling Mrs. Wilson the truth. I couldn't do that if you thought Mrs. Wilson already knew."

She continued to pin him in his place with her stare as she crossed her arms. "This has to do with the phone call you made to me, doesn't it?"

He nodded.

"John, Mrs. Wilson must be informed of the truth. Otherwise, she'll change all Jacey's records, everything. I can't let this lie continue."

"I'm not suggesting you do," he assured her, taking another step closer. He wanted to run his hands up her arms, warm them into relaxation, cuddle her against him. He wanted to, but he wouldn't. At least not yet.

"Then just what are you suggesting?"

He gestured toward the couch. "Come sit down and let me explain. It might get a little complicated and there's no need to be uncomfortable."

Even though she moved toward the couch, she cast a suspicious eye on him. "The last man who wanted me to sit down and get comfortable was trying to sell me a set of encyclopedias. What are you trying to sell, John?"

"Nothing so expensive, I promise you." He was amused, however. He could think of a lot of things he'd want her to relax for. None of them involved encyclopedias.

Once seated a discreet distance from her on the couch, John tried to decide how best to explain his dilemma.

"Well?"

He gave her a sideways smile and plunged in. "David Wester called today to offer me his business because I'm such a family-oriented man."

"What? But that's not true!"

"I know."

"You did tell him, didn't you?" She was giving him her teacher look again.

"I tried, Rachel, but he was in a hurry, and he surprised me."

"John, I won't be a part of any lie, no matter how much money it would bring you."

"I'm not asking you to," he hastily assured her.

"It sounds like you are."

"That's because you haven't let me explain." He reached out and took her hand, surprised at how much he yearned just to touch her. The electric spark that flashed between them must have been obvious to her, too, because she pulled her hand away at once.

"I'm waiting," she assured him, but she wouldn't look at him. Her gaze was fixed on her hands, clasped in her lap, out of his reach.

"After David hung up, I thought about it for a few minutes. I'll admit," he said in response to her derisive look, "I thought about keeping quiet. But that's not how I do business. So I called him back to tell him the truth."

"Good."

"But he wasn't there. He'd called me on the way to the airport. He'll be out of town until Friday evening."

"Then it doesn't matter if I tell Mrs. Wilson tomorrow. He won't hear the news until he returns." Rachel gave a satisfied nod, as if she thought the matter had been settled.

"That's not true, Rachel. If Mrs. Wilson tells the class, Lisbeth will tell her mother and Mrs. Wester will tell her husband when she talks to him."

"But if you're going to tell him the truth anyway—"

"I am, I promise," he assured her, since he heard some doubt in her words. "But *I'd* like to be the one to tell him—not a five-year-old, or her mother."

"I don't see why—"

"Rachel, I was married once."

She stared at him blankly, not understanding his change of subject. He wished he didn't have to make this explanation, but Rachel needed to understand his situation.

"My wife was not happy with our marriage. She decided to divorce me, and she wanted to be sure she didn't have to work, so she tried to take me for everything I was worth. She lied and cheated and spread rumors that almost destroyed me. My good name is my most important asset. I almost lost it."

Rachel stared at him, her eyes round with astonishment.

"It is important to me that I be honest with David Wester. Whether he gives me his business or not, I must maintain my reputation for honesty and trustworthiness."

Her clasped hands tightened and she stared straight ahead, but she didn't say anything. He hadn't convinced her yet. Time for the heavy guns.

"I'm not asking you to lie to anyone. I'm just asking for a little time so I can explain everything to David myself, face-to-face. Then, if he doesn't want to give me his business, I won't complain."

Still no response.

"Is that so much to ask? After all, I was just trying to help out your little girl," he reminded, his eyes rounded in innocence. He hated to use Jacey, but it was the truth.

"John Crewes! I was against the idea in the first place, and Jacey is just a little girl! How dare you blame it on us!" She jumped to her feet and glared at him, her hands on her hips.

He rose to stand beside her, grinning. He loved to see Rachel all agitated, her bosom rising and falling in enticing rhythm. Besides, when she was upset, she forgot to keep him at a distance. "I'm not blaming Jacey. It's not her fault she doesn't have a daddy."

The heat faded from her, was replaced by a glacial look. "Please leave, Mr. Crewes." She turned her back, crossing her arms over her chest.

"Rachel," he said, "I helped Jacey. I'm only asking for a little help in return."

She whirled around, her eyes shooting darts of anger. "So far you have used my child against me, and then you had the gall to blame me for not hanging on to a man who wanted nothing to do with me or his baby. And you think *I* owe *you?*" She advanced toward him, pointing her finger at him.

John backed away, hoping to avoid an out-and-out fight. "Now, Rachel, let's be rational."

When his back hit the paneled wall, he decided it was time to take the offensive. Overwrought, Rachel didn't seem to realize he'd run out of territory. She was practically stomping on his toes when he grabbed her shoulders and pulled her into his arms. His lips seized her full, soft ones, halting her words.

He'd dreamed of tasting her lips, of mingling their breaths, of feeling her against him. He'd had no idea how glorious it would be, better than his dreams. Rachel didn't fight him. At first, he could feel the shock run through her body. Then there was a lightning flash of recognition, as there had been when he'd held her earlier. She sank against him, her lips opening to him, her arms stealing up around his neck.

Heaven.

What he'd started as a way of controlling Rachel was quickly turning into an uncontrollable riot for John. While his lips caressed hers, his hands slid to her waist, tugging at her blouse. *Forget David Wester. Forget Mrs. Wilson. Forget the world.* As his fingers caressed warm skin, he was lost to everything but Rachel.

As quickly as she'd given in, Rachel suddenly jerked away from his hold. "What do you think you're doing?" she demanded, her voice high with tension.

"The same thing you were doing," he assured her. "We were kissing, Rachel, and it felt damn good."

She crossed to the other side of the room. "Go away!"

"That's your response to everything that's happened? Go away?"

"Yes!"

"That doesn't sound very mature," he said, drawling his words with sarcasm. He'd really blown it. He feared Rachel wouldn't even talk to him after that kiss.

Something he'd said affected her. She drew several deep breaths before she spoke again. "You're right. I'm overreacting." Much to his surprise, she moved around the room, always keeping her distance from him, but didn't repeat her order for him to leave.

Finally she turned to face him, although her gaze went somewhere over his shoulder. "I will promise to wait until Monday to straighten out the—the situation with Mrs. Wilson, if you will promise to stay away from Jacey."

Her request electrified him, as if he'd burned himself. "What do you mean? Why can't I see Jacey?"

She looked him in the eye this time. "Because she's already beginning to care for you. I don't want her hurt."

"I care for her, too."

Rachel rolled her eyes and turned away.

"What's that supposed to mean?" He hurried around the end of the sofa to cut off her escape.

"I didn't say anything," she retorted, her chin in the air.

"You said something, all right. With your eyes, like you didn't believe me. Jacey is a sweetheart. I'd have to be made of stone not to care about her."

He reached for her shoulders, wanting to make his point physically, and also wanting to touch her again. Just for a minute. Or longer, if she didn't protest.

She backed away.

"You may think you care about her, but something else will come along to distract you. You'll pursue it, and Jacey will be left crying because you didn't keep your promise." Her words were laced with bitterness, and he remembered Jacey's words about her father.

"I'm not Jacey's father."

"Exactly my point," she agreed vehemently.

"No, Rachel. I'm saying I'm not like Jacey's real father."

Her eyes widened and there was a vulnerability there that grabbed his heart. Before he could reach for her, however, she recovered.

"This is a pointless discussion, John Crewes. I'll keep the secret until Monday, but I don't want to see you over here again." Suddenly she was the poised teacher, staring down a difficult child.

John took a deep breath. Clearly, she wasn't going to continue their discussion. He should be grateful that step one was accomplished. But now, it was time for step two.

"Uh, thanks, Rachel. There's just one little problem."

"Only one? Are you sure? You seem to be full of problems." She was glaring at him again.

"Yeah. Only one. David invited the three of us to his house Friday night, and I was kind of counting on you and Jacey going with me."

He ducked as she picked up a big book and drew it back over her head.

Chapter Six

Rachel gasped as she saw John duck. His action brought home to her what she'd been about to do. Feeling decidedly silly, she lowered the book from over her head and carefully placed it back on the table.

"Rachel? I know that was a bit unexpected, but if you'll let me explain—"

"That's what you said about keeping the truth a secret for a few more days." The man was dangerous, no question about it. Dangerous because he appeared to be able to talk her into anything. Dangerous because he evoked an out-of-control reaction that frightened her. Dangerous because she was attracted to him.

"Just give me a couple of minutes."

She nodded, unwilling to trust herself to say anything. How did he do it? She'd been around attractive men before. She'd even tried dating a little after Jacey became a toddler. That was when she'd discovered that single men didn't want anything to do with a single mother.

She hadn't been heartbroken. No, she'd accepted the fact that having Jacey in her life eliminated certain things. And considered her child well worth the sacrifice.

Now her heart, her body, were sending messages to her brain that she'd thought didn't exist anymore. They'd picked an inconvenient time to emerge from a deep sleep.

"Rachel?"

"Very well. Explain."

"I don't suppose you'd consider getting comfortable again?" he suggested with a smile that would charm the birds from the trees, as he gestured toward the couch.

"I think not," she murmured and looked away. She didn't intend to get within touching distance of him ever again. She had to root these feelings out of herself.

"Look, Rachel, David extended the invitation with all the authority of a general ordering his troops. Now his wife is planning on having the three of us to dinner. If I'm the only one who shows up Friday night, we'll be starting the evening off on a bad note."

She gave him an exasperated look, hoping he'd understand how little that argument accomplished, although she admitted to herself that he was right.

"If the three of us go, you and I can explain to David and his wife about the mistake. If the two of us can laugh about it, I think it will minimize the damage. Then I can tell David that he's still free to make a choice about hiring me. And Jacey can spend the evening with Lisbeth."

"You don't honestly expect me to believe that you made these plans to provide Jacey an evening with Lisbeth, do you?" she asked, shaking her head.

"Of course not. *I* didn't plan any of this. All I wanted to do was help Jacey feel good about herself," he reminded her with a little testiness.

He was right, of course. His intentions had been good, even if the result was turning into an unending nightmare. And he'd done it for Jacey.

Rachel had promised herself long ago that she would be independent, relying on no one, owing no one. But she owed John Crewes for doing something special for her child.

Abruptly she asked, "What time Friday night?"

John stared, then moved toward her, a warm light in his eyes.

She put up a hand in defense and moved away from him. "Don't come near me."

"Why? I just wanted to say thank-you. At least, I assume your question meant you'll help me."

"Yes, I will, but I don't need you to thank me."

"But it would be so much fun, Rachel," he teased, seemingly lighthearted now that she'd agreed.

"John, I'm willing to go along with you because I don't think it will hurt anything and because you've been very kind to Jacey. But that's it. I'm not going to sleep with you."

Her words stopped him in his tracks. "Well, Rachel, I don't believe I asked for such a sacrifice."

With a grim smile, she said, "Yes, you did, John. Not in words, but with those hot looks you've been giving me. With your touching, with that kiss. I may not date right now, but I know men. How do you think I got Jacey?"

"From under a lettuce leaf?" he teased and took another step toward her.

"John!" she warned, moving away again.

He held up both hands in surrender, although, of course, she wasn't foolish enough to believe it.

"All right. I admit I'm attracted to you. You felt it, too, didn't you, Rachel? And I wouldn't complain if you stripped naked right this minute and lured me upstairs. No red-blooded male would, because you're a beautiful woman. But that's not what our agreement is about."

"No, it's not or I wouldn't have agreed," she assured him, keeping her voice cool even as her thoughts were turned to the word picture he'd created—only she thought about him stripping naked, not her. Ouch! Time to think of other things.

"Your cheeks are red again," he murmured, his gaze trained on her face.

And she knew why. His casual clothes couldn't hide the strength and breadth of his shoulders, his flat stomach, muscular legs. But even more tempting was the warmth in his eyes when he smiled at her child, the consideration he'd shown Rachel, and the silent offer to shield the two of them from the harshness of reality.

He was playing the role of knight in shining armor.

It was incredibly seductive.

And completely unbelievable.

After all, she'd been down that road once. It was a dead end. The only person she could trust was herself.

"It must be the heat," she said with a shrug.

"Yeah. I've felt the same heat. Are you sure you want to ignore it?"

"Absolutely." Before he could offer further arguments—and she could see he intended to—she repeated her earlier question: "You never said what time Friday night."

"Seven."

She nodded and began walking toward the door.

"We should probably leave here about a quarter 'til."

She nodded again, keeping her back to him.

"And this time I'll drive."

She turned to face him. "I could take my car, too. Then, after the explanation, Jacey and I could leave and you could have your business discussion."

"Rachel, we're not going to walk in the front door, spill our guts and turn around and walk out. We've been invited to dinner."

"Spilling their guts," as John had phrased it, seemed a lot easier than sitting down to dinner with people she'd lied to. "I don't think—" she began, only to discover she'd trapped herself against the front door, with John cutting off any hope of escape.

With a gentleness that was sexier than any bare chest she'd ever seen, he grasped her shoulders and smiled at her. "It will be all right, Rachel. Don't worry about it."

As if she could dismiss her worries—all one million of them. And most of them were centered on John Crewes.

"By the way," he suddenly said, "you never said what had upset you earlier."

She shrugged her shoulders. It was hard to switch gears so abruptly from the roles of mother and woman to that of teacher. Besides, she didn't want to confide in him. Did she?

"Jacey said you're sad sometimes because some of your students have problems."

She shrugged again, but this time his gaze caught hers. Finally, she muttered, "One of my students attempted suicide."

"Is he all right?"

"She's all right . . . for now."

"Do you know why?" His furrowed brow gave him the appearance of concern.

"Her boyfriend dumped her."

He stared at her for several seconds. Then he said, "Rachel, not all men are bastards. And she has to take responsibility for her decisions."

"Thank you, Doctor."

Much to her surprise, he grinned at her sarcastic response. "Okay, okay. I know it's not that simple. And I'm sorry, for her and for you."

"Why me?" she demanded, fearful that he'd read her mind, or knew of her past history.

"Because it upset you. Jacey and I don't like it when you're upset." That heart-stopping grin filled his face and her heart flipped over. Then it almost stopped beating as his gaze grew more serious and the grin changed to a startled look.

"Don't concern yourself with me," she hurriedly said, afraid of what he might say next. "You've got enough problems to deal with."

"You're right," he agreed with a sigh. "I'm going now. I just want you to know that the dinners I've shared with you and Jacey last night and tonight have been more fun than I've had in years. The two of you make me realize how lonely I've been. Thank you for spending some time with me."

Enthralled with his words, Rachel didn't realize his intent until it was too late. He brushed his lips against hers in a kiss as innocent as a young teenager's first experiment in romance. If she'd been prepared, Rachel was sure she would have protested. But she wasn't. So her lips clung to his, moved against them and then opened to his touch. He didn't refuse her invitation.

It was John who ended the kiss. That teasing grin of his reappeared and he murmured, "I can't wait for Friday night."

She slammed the door shut behind him and then sank against it, wanting to protest his inference. That there would be more kisses on Friday. But it was too late. He'd left.

She would have protested, she assured herself, even as she relived the feel of his lips, her fingers touching her own still-tingling ones.

Of course, she would have.

Of course.

BUD CASSIDY ROSE TO HIS feet and extended his hand.

As John grasped it, the man said, "You know, John, I'm used to David's genius in choosing the right people, but he certainly demonstrated it again when he selected you."

"That's very kind of you, Bud, but I'm not sure it's justified. Besides, as I told you Tuesday, nothing's settled, yet."

"It will be, as soon as David sees the suggestions and projections you've made. You'll have those on paper for me by Monday?"

John assured him he would, although, in truth, he planned to have them with him Friday night. In case he got a chance to show them to David.

He escorted Bud from his office, then checked his watch. Just a little after four. Last night he'd worked at the office until almost midnight. When he'd arrived home, he'd looked longingly at the house next to his, but it had been dark, both its occupants, he assumed, fast asleep.

Gathering up the papers pertaining to Wester Enterprises, he stuffed them into his briefcase, grabbed his suit coat and strode past his secretary.

"I'll see you in the morning, Beth. Go on home and spend a little extra time with your family."

He barely heard her surprised thanks as he ran for the elevator. All he could think about was getting home to see Rachel and Jacey. Telling them about his day. Hearing about theirs.

"This is crazy," he told himself as he slid behind the wheel of his Porsche. Rachel probably wouldn't even speak to him. Tuesday night, she'd warned him away.

Leaving her alone last night wouldn't be enough to convince her to change her mind. He pressed down on the accelerator. It was as if he was addicted. *Addicted to love,* he sang to himself.

The wail of a siren and flashing red lights in his rearview mirror drew him away from his startling thoughts. He immediately pulled to the side of the road.

"Good afternoon, sir. May I see your license and registration, please?" The cop standing beside his car was faultlessly polite.

"Here you are, officer."

"Could you tell me why you were going fifty miles per hour in a thirty-mile zone? Do you have an emergency?"

John couldn't read the policeman's expression because he wore mirrored sunglasses, but he didn't bother to come up with a lie. "No," he grinned ruefully. "I didn't even realize how fast I was going. I was in a hurry to get home and see—and see my family."

The officer looked from John to his license and back again. Finally, he handed the license back to John.

"I'm just giving you a warning this time, Mr. Crewes. You've got to keep it within the speed limit, or you might not make it home. Okay?"

"Thank you, officer. I'll remember."

He felt a little guilty about using Jacey and Rachel to manipulate the cop. Nor was he sure why the policeman had decided to be generous. Not that he was complaining, but he *had* been speeding.

In more ways than one.

He'd been speeding down an emotional highway with no thought to the consequences. What was he doing? Rushing home to a nonexistent family? Rachel wasn't going to welcome him with open arms. Jacey might, but not Rachel.

And did he want her to? Of course, he was attracted to her. She was a beautiful, intelligent woman. But he knew better than to expect love, commitment, "forever," from a woman.

Deliberately, he turned off into the shopping center where a deli was located. He was just having an early night. It had nothing to do with the two females next door. He purchased enough food for one, then drove home.

As a test of his will, he allowed his gaze to rove over the house next door, then turned away, feeling he was moving in slow motion. With dinner in one hand and his briefcase in the other, he slammed the car door shut with his hip and started up the short sidewalk to his door.

That's when he realized Jacey was sitting on his front porch.

So much for detachment and disinterest.

"Jacey? What are you doing over here?"

Her blue eyes were big, rounded with questions. "You didn't come home last night," she said quietly, in a hushed voice, her little chin supported by two fists as she leaned on her scrunched legs.

"Of course I did, sweetheart. I just worked late and then left this morning before you were awake. You didn't worry about me, did you?"

She nodded her head solemnly.

"I'll bet your mommy told you I was working late," John teased as he put the food and briefcase down on the porch and joined Jacey on the step.

She nodded again.

"Then what's the problem?"

"Earl said that's when he knew his daddy was gone. He didn't come home at night anymore."

He remembered from their first encounter that Earl was the one who didn't count, 'cause he didn't care about his daddy leaving. He wished Earl had kept his knowledge to himself.

"Sweetheart," he assured her as he lifted her into his lap, "I work late a lot, but I always come home."

"Always?"

"Always."

"Jacey?" Rachel's voice surprised them both and they looked across the driveway to Jacey's front porch where Rachel stood, looking up and down the street.

"Uh-oh," Jacey muttered under her breath.

"What's wrong?"

"I wasn't supposed to bother you."

"Jacey?" Rachel called again.

"We'd better answer or she'll get mad," Jacey said and then called out to her mother. "Here I am!"

John could see first the relief and then the withdrawal in Rachel. She released the door behind her and slowly came down her steps and across to his sidewalk.

"Jacey, you need to come inside." Rachel stood there, looking at her child, not him, her hand extended.

In denim shorts and a blue T-shirt, her long dark hair pulled back from her face, Rachel looked as beautiful as he'd ever seen her.

Jacey started to move, but he tightened his hold on her. "Aren't you even going to speak to me, Rachel?"

"Good evening, John. Jacey?"

John kept hold of Jacey, thus keeping Rachel only a few feet from him. "Have another bad day at school?"

"No. Jacey, come home."

He loved the sound of her voice. It was low, musical, full, as if her heart was in every word. "I don't think I'll turn her loose. I'll hold her hostage until the two of you agree to dine with me." He was teasing, of course, but Rachel glared at him.

"Release her at once, John, or I'll call the police."

"Hey, I was only teasing." He hugged Jacey and then released her. "But I can't afford another encounter with the police today."

Rachel had grabbed Jacey's hand and turned around to rush away from him, but she hesitated and said, "Another?"

"I didn't rob a bank or murder anyone, Rachel," he assured her dryly. He got the impression she was hoping he'd be thrown in jail and she wouldn't have to see him again. "I just drove a little too fast."

"Did you get a ticket?" Jacey asked, all concern.

"No, sweetheart. The officer just warned me to be more careful."

Rachel gave an elegant little snort that expressed her opinion of the officer's generosity.

"Sorry to disappoint you, Rachel."

She shot him a disdainful look, as if she had no idea what he meant. Then she tugged on Jacey's hand. "Come on, sweetie. We need to go home."

"I'd be glad to buy dinner, if you and Jacey would join me," he said, determined to give it the old college try. He stood and moved over to block her view of the deli containers on the porch behind them.

"I think you've fed us enough, Mr. Crewes. Thank you, anyway."

"John could come to our house and eat with us, Mommy. I haven't told him about Mr. Sam."

"Sorry, sweetie, but there's only enough for the two of us."

"Who's Mr. Sam?" John asked as Rachel managed to move Jacey a couple of feet along the sidewalk. He came down the steps to follow them.

Jacey's face lit up at his interest. "He's our turtle at school. Today, he got lost!"

"Got lost, did he? Must be an adventuresome creature."

Jacey screwed up her little face and said, "What's adven—what you said?"

John squatted down to her level. "I meant he must like to explore."

"That's what Mrs. Wilson said, but Earl said he ran away and wouldn't come back—like his daddy."

Ah. Now he knew why Earl had decided to share his knowledge of family dynamics. With one finger he tilted up Jacey's chin. "But Earl was wrong, wasn't he? You found Mr. Sam, didn't you?"

"Yes, he was under Mrs. Wilson's desk," Jacey told him with a giggle that brought a smile to his lips. Jacey's giggles reminded him of the fizz in soda. Irresistible. Life without hearing that giggle would be decidedly flat.

"Now you've told him about Mr. Sam, we have to go home, Jacey," Rachel said, reminding the other two of her stiff presence.

He really hadn't forgotten about her, of course—not with those long, tanned legs on view—but Jacey had claimed his attention for the moment.

"We're still on for tomorrow night?" he asked, holding his breath. The way she was acting today, he wasn't sure she'd even be speaking to him tomorrow, much less accompanying him to the Westers.

"We're going to Lisbeth's house tomorrow!" Jacey said, as if his words had reminded her of a treat.

"Yes," Rachel replied, ignoring Jacey's exclamation. Without another word, she pulled her daughter along behind her, leaving him standing on the sidewalk, watching them. At the last minute, Jacey turned to wave to him before Rachel swept her into the house.

DAMN! JOHN CRUNCHED the pages of the *Wall Street Journal* between his fingers the next morning. Who'd notified the paper that he was taking over some of Wester's accounts? It had to be Bud Cassidy. *He* certainly hadn't.

Now, if David decided he didn't want to do business with John anymore, it would look as if he'd found something disreputable or weak about John's company. No amount of reassurances or protestations to the business community would change that. David Wester's influence was too great. His withdrawal could cost John big time.

He chewed on his bottom lip, fighting the sinking feeling that filled him. He'd made a good recovery since his disastrous divorce, but he didn't know if he could survive another blow to his integrity, his reputation.

With the notice in the most important business paper in the country, there was no way he could keep David's withdrawal a secret.

Now it wasn't a question of making a lot of money.

It was a question of losing everything he had.

Chapter Seven

All day long, John contemplated his dilemma.

When the *Wall Street Journal* called for an interview, he'd stalled them. He hadn't yet decided what to do. It was a tough decision.

His company had been his life for the past five years. It was the major accomplishment of his lifetime. It was also the sole support of thirty-one employees, several of whom would have difficulty finding another job.

Finally, he decided he had to talk to Rachel, make her understand what his confession to David Wester was going to do. Surely she would see how the announcement had changed everything.

After driving home, he dressed for the evening in jeans, a knit shirt and a casual sport coat. Then, with his heart beating double time, he crossed over to Rachel's house.

He rang the doorbell and waited with impatience for her to answer it. When he finally heard footsteps, he stood at attention, preparing for the battle he knew he faced.

"You're early," Rachel said first of all, and she wasn't offering praise. She was dressed in a denim skirt and a raspberry knit shirt, its scoop neck inset with some kind of lace-like thing. John didn't know what it was called, but it drew his attention to a very distracting part of her anatomy.

He cleared his throat. "Uh, I know I'm early, but I need to talk to you."

"Hi, John!" Jacey exclaimed, racing to the door to poke her head around her mother's leg.

"Hi, sweetheart. Are you ready?"

"Yes. Mommy let me wear my new shirt." Jacey pushed past her mother to stick her little chest out with pride. "See? These are from the cartoons," she explained, tracing the picture on the front of her shirt.

"You look beautiful. But I need to talk to your mommy before we go. Could you go upstairs and play for just a little while?"

"Wait, Jacey," Rachel ordered as the child nodded and turned to follow his directions. Then she looked at John. "Jacey can stay down here with you while I finish getting ready. Then we'll switch places."

"Okay."

He spent the next few minutes entertaining and being entertained by Jacey. She told him all about her day at school and he even found himself chuckling a few times. But in the back of his mind, all he could think about was the loss of his life's work.

It wasn't the money. He had enough invested to survive, and he could probably get a job with another company. But this company was all he had to show for his life. He couldn't let it be dismissed as if it didn't matter.

Rachel came down the stairs and his breathing grew more shallow. The moment of decision was at hand.

She sent Jacey up the stairs, then sat down in the chair across from him.

"What is it?"

He sought for the right words, persuasive words, that would convince Rachel to let his company survive. He couldn't find any. Finally, he blurted out, "We can't tell David the truth."

Rachel's seemingly relaxed demeanor disappeared at once. She stiffened. "What did you say?"

"Rachel, someone leaked David's decision to the *Wall Street Journal*. It wasn't me. I told Bud Cassidy we could have preliminary talks but that nothing was decided."

"So they'll just print a retraction." There was no warmth in her beautiful voice. She spoke as if there was no alternative.

"Rachel, it wasn't printed as a rumor. It was an announcement. If David withdraws two days later, it's going to look like there's something wrong with my company."

"That's ridiculous. People change their minds all the time."

"Not when the topic is millions of dollars. Not unless there's a good reason." Rachel stared at him but didn't say anything. "Rachel, if he changes his mind that fast, people will assume all sorts of horrible things. It will destroy my company."

"Don't be silly. You may lose his business, but there will be lots of other people who—"

"Would you trust your money, your life savings, your company's future, to a man a famous psychologist dumps overnight with no logical explanation?" He paused but Rachel said nothing. "Even the smallest investor will look for advice from someone else."

"Mr. Wester's influence can't be that big," Rachel insisted.

"Financially, he's got more influence than he knows what to do with. And his popularity and fame have spread in the last few years. The videos he's marketing have brought him a lot of attention."

Rachel stood to pace across the room, her arms folded about her lithe body. "This is incredible, John. You can't ask me to continue with a lie just because—"

"Because my company's existence hangs in the balance? My employees' jobs could disappear overnight? My entire career would amount to nothing?" he finished, his voice heavy with concern.

"But you don't know that he'll fire you. You're just assuming the worst."

"With good reason. Last year, one of his associates had an affair. David kicked him out on his ear."

"But we're not— I mean, we're not doing anything immoral!"

"No, not at all. Lying is always good. Highly recommended."

"You don't have to be sarcastic!" Rachel snapped.

John covered his eyes with his hands to regroup. It helped not to be able to see her. Taking down his hands, he said, "Sorry, Rachel. But you're being naive. David Wester's reputation is the foundation of his success. Just as mine is. If there is any hint of a scandal, David could lose all he's built up. He's shown himself to be ruthless in protecting what is his."

"Well, I may not have millions of dollars, or financial success weighing in the balance, John Crewes, but Jacey is more important than either of those things. I have to protect her."

"And I wouldn't ask you to do anything less, but how is it going to hurt Jacey if David believes we're married?"

"It's going to teach her to lie. I can't do it! I'm sorry, John. I realize how important this is, but I can't lie about our relationship anymore!" She stood and walked to the bottom of the stairs. "Are we still going?"

"Yes," John said, standing, his heart heavy. "I've got to make the attempt to salvage the situation if I can."

"Jacey, come on," Rachel called up the stairs. "We're leaving."

RACHEL SAT BESIDE JOHN in his Porsche without saying a word. Over and over in her head, she replayed his remarks. Surely David Wester wouldn't get rid of John without giving him a chance to show what he could do.

She had to believe that. She didn't want to be responsible for the destruction of his company. John stared straight ahead, with a stillness about his features that told her he was suffering.

After several attempts to talk to the adults, Jacey seemed to understand that something was wrong. Rachel looked over her shoulder once or twice to smile encouragingly at her daughter, but Jacey's face was growing as solemn as John's.

When they pulled into the driveway of the Westers' large home, John got out of the car and then pulled his seat forward for Jacey to follow him.

"John?" Jacey asked as she got out of the car.

"What, Jacey?"

"Are you mad?"

Rachel, walking around the hood of the car to join them, didn't know what John would answer. He had reason to be angry, since he'd gotten trapped in this situation because he wanted to help Jacey. But if he upset her child, she would hate him.

Instead, he scooped Jacey up into his arms. "Mad? No, of course not. I just had something on my mind."

"Is it all gone?" she asked anxiously, putting her arms around his neck.

"No, sweetheart. Why?"

"'Cause I want you to have a good time. If you don't, you might not go with us again."

Jacey certainly reduced everything down to its basic level. Rachel was pretty sure John wouldn't be going anywhere with them again.

Hugging her against him, John said in a low voice Rachel had to strain to hear, "Nothing would make me not want to go someplace with you, Jacey Cason. We're friends, aren't we?"

She nodded, her ponytail bouncing up and down. "But Earl said—"

John groaned and grinned at the same time—an entrancing combination, Rachel decided.

"I don't think I want to hear Earl's explanation for what a daddy does, Jacey." With his free hand, he gently pulled Jacey's head down so that he could kiss her forehead. "You just remember that you're a special girl and I'll always want to go with you."

Jacey's one-hundred-megawatt grin flowed from John to her mother. "And tonight, I can call you Daddy if I want, can't I?"

"You bet, sweetheart. Call me anything you want."

Rachel stared at John's back. If what he'd said was true, the man was facing the destruction of the most important thing in his life, and he took the time to reassure her daughter. She was still staring when he turned around.

"Ready, Rachel?" He extended his hand to take hers, and she thought about the picture they must present. A man, a woman, and their child.

When they reached the front door, John nodded for Rachel to push the doorbell. He kept her other hand clasped warmly in his. She couldn't help thinking that if it had been her teaching career that was about to be destroyed, through no fault of her own, she might not be able to face it as courageously as John Crewes.

Carol Wester opened the door. Rachel had met her a few times, but she didn't know her well.

"Oh, welcome! You're early. Well, not really, it's just that few people ever arrive on time. Come on in." She held the door wide and smiled at them. "I'm glad you could come. And Rachel, I was surprised to hear you were married. These things happen so suddenly, don't they?"

Rachel could feel John's gaze on her, but she only murmured, "Yes, they certainly do."

"Where's David?" John asked.

"Oh, he called an hour ago. He was making a connection in Chicago and they were having terrible thunderstorms. He thinks he'll be here in about—" she paused to look at her watch "—about an hour and a half, I think."

Rachel and John looked at each other, but Rachel didn't know what to say. She'd promised John could be the one to tell David. That seemed the least she could do, in the circumstances, so she agreed that air travel was hectic and followed her hostess down the hall.

As Carol led them into a sprawling, beautiful den, she said, "We won't wait on him to eat, though. I don't believe in starving, even for David. And everyone else agrees."

Everyone else?

For the first time, Rachel realized they were not the only guests. Three other couples were seated on the leather couches and chairs in front of a huge fireplace, which was filled with a basket of flowers since it was almost summer.

"Let me introduce John and Rachel Crewes and their daughter, Jacey, Lisbeth's best friend. John also just became David's financial adviser. He's probably very good at what he does, but David was impressed with his magic tricks," she added with a laugh. "Maybe we can get him to perform for us later on."

She then named the couples. Rachel's mouth went dry as she recognized the president of the local school board. *Oh, dear.* John's arm went around her waist, drawing her attention. The last pair—an older man, baldheaded with glasses, and his gray-haired wife—rose and the man extended his hand to John.

"No need for an introduction here, Carol. John and I had several meetings this week. And I can tell you I was impressed."

He then turned to Rachel. "I'm Bud Cassidy, financial officer for Wester Enterprises, and this is my wife, Ethel. We'll see a lot of each other. David's real big on social events with his employees. We're just like a big family."

"We're expanding the family this evening with a few neighbors, too," Carol explained as the doorbell rang. "You two sit down and get comfortable. Jacey, Lisbeth is waiting for you upstairs." She swept out of the room before any of them could respond.

"You want to go upstairs, Jacey?" John asked quietly.

She nodded and wriggled in his arms. He set her down and watched as she checked with her mother before leaving the room.

"Such a charming child," Ethel Cassidy said, drawing Rachel's attention.

"Thank you."

"Come sit over here by me and tell me all about you and John. Bud's been raving about that man of yours for the past two days."

Rachel cast a panicked look at John and he stepped to her side, putting an arm around her.

"She can come if I can, too. I love to hear compliments about myself," he said to Ethel with a grin. Everyone laughed, but John stuck at Rachel's side.

Not that she was about to complain. She'd need some help if Ethel's questions grew too detailed. Like how old her husband was. How long he'd lived in Kansas City. Or anything other than his eye color and what kind of car he drove... and how his lips felt, pressed to hers.

The next two hours were tense ones for Rachel. She and John stayed together as much as they could. One lady guessed they must be newlyweds, and Carol hastened to assure her she was correct. Rachel could feel the heat in her cheeks as everyone beamed at the two of them.

The school-board president's wife pressed for details about their marriage. Rachel wondered if perhaps her career was in as much jeopardy as John's, now.

John, with his arm around her, leaned over to whisper in her ear. "I'm sorry. Do you want me to tell them now?"

She shook her head no and asked Carol if she'd taken Lisbeth to see the Disney movie that had just come out. That distraction worked until the sound of footsteps coming down the hallway signaled that their host had arrived.

Feeling John tense beside her, Rachel studied him under the cover of all the greetings David Wester received. The group had swollen to nine couples plus the host and hostess, so it took several minutes for David to reach them.

Those minutes seemed to last forever as Rachel thought about what was to happen. She'd just spent two hours pretending to be John's wife. She didn't like pretense, but she liked hurting other people less. She liked waste even less. And she liked rewarding a good man with a kick in the gut a lot less.

John was a good man. He'd done his best for Jacey. She couldn't repay him with an action that would destroy him. It was hard to think amid all the talk and tension, but she just couldn't tear down all he'd built up.

"John, glad you could make it. And you must be Rachel," David Wester said, smiling at her. Much to her surprise, she recognized the face of the man before her. She'd seen ads on television for his counseling tapes. He seemed a pleasant man with gray eyes that looked deep inside you, but he was older than she'd expected Carol's new husband to be.

She managed a wobbly smile.

"Where are the girls? Upstairs?"

"Yes, they're playing."

"I'll bet you've been up to check on them several times, though, haven't you?" He grinned as she nodded. "Just like Carol. We've got a couple of terrific mothers for our girls, don't we, John?"

"Yeah, we do. Uh, David, I know you just got in, but—"

She couldn't let him do it.

Taking his arm and leaning into his shoulder, she chided him in what she hoped were wifely tones, "Now, John, you should let David eat before you tell him how much you liked working with Bud. Even if he did make you promise to rave about him as soon as you saw David."

Since Bud was standing beside David, Rachel sent him a teasing grin that had him roaring with laughter. David joined in, and Rachel hoped neither of them noticed John's stunned expression.

Feeling he was moving in slow motion, John turned to stare at Rachel. What had she just done? She'd been adamant earlier that he must tell David the truth at once. Now she was stopping him, pretending they were husband and wife.

"You can tell those two haven't been married very long," Bud said as his laughter eased. "John, the proper answer is *Yes, dear.*"

"Yes, dear," John mumbled, offering a weak grin.

"That's a phrase all us old married men have memorized," Bud assured him. "It keeps us from sleeping on the couch a lot."

There was general laughter and several comments about John preferring sharing a bed with a beauty like Rachel. He couldn't even think, much less contribute to the conversation.

"I don't need dinner, since I ate on the plane, but I would like a cup of coffee and a chance to catch my breath. And, of course, I apologize for my tardiness," David said to the room in general.

"Of course. Actually, John's so excited about the work he's begun with Bud, he wanted to talk business tonight, but I told him it would be better to wait until Monday," Rachel murmured.

She was still leaning against him, holding on to his arm, as she spoke, and he scarcely took in her words.

"Good thinking, Rachel," David replied. "I know he loves his work, but I believe a man should keep work relegated to the office. I'm sure you'll help him do that."

"I certainly will. Though Jacey is even better at that than I. Before John could even get inside the house the other day, she was in his arms telling him about Mr. Sam. Did Lisbeth tell you about the pet turtle at school?"

David shook his head no.

Rachel's hand slid down to take John's and she pulled him back down on the couch beside her. "The pet turtle in their class escaped yesterday. Jacey just knew John would be as enthralled with Mr. Sam's escapade as she." She shot him a glance filled with teasing laughter before she added, "And he was."

"You know, that's exactly the reason I chose John. He is such a good father." David went on to describe John's kindergarten visit in exhausting detail.

"What are you doing?" John muttered to Rachel under his breath. His heart was thudding and his brain was fuzzy.

"I couldn't let you do it." She didn't have time to say anything else because David asked her a question.

The rest of the evening was a nightmare. All John could think about were the repercussions of their evening. Only his brain wasn't functioning clearly enough to work things out. As much as he didn't want to tell David the truth, he didn't think it was possible to continue the lie.

Rachel, however, seemed to have done an about-face. She clung to his hand all night, leaning against him, teasing him, smiling at him. He began to think he was dreaming the entire evening. But his body's response to her touch told him it wasn't a dream.

When he was almost at the point of exploding with all the questions inside him, Rachel told him they really needed to leave to get Jacey into bed.

"What is her usual bedtime?" David asked, looking straight at John.

"Uh, nine," he guessed, panic racing through him.

"Eight o'clock, actually," Rachel corrected. "Both she and John have been lobbying for nine, trying to convince me eight's too early."

"That's Lisbeth's bedtime, too," David said. "A good time. Leaves the two of you a little time for yourselves. That's important, isn't it?"

John could only nod his head. Oh, yeah, he really enjoyed those hours after Jacey was in bed. Especially since he spent them all alone at his house. And the hours before she went to bed, too.

"Now that I've met you, Rachel, I can go ahead with some plans I've made. I think you'll be as excited about them as I am," David said, smiling at her.

Rachel's eyebrows rose. "What are they?"

"Oh, I'm not going to say now. I think I'll be ready to show you in about a week. Do you two have plans for next weekend?"

"Uh, I don't think so, do we, dear?" John asked, staring at Rachel.

"Why, no, though, of course, it's getting close to the end of the school year. I don't plan too many things in May."

"Well, this will be special. Hold next weekend open for me, okay?" Then David told them goodbye and moved across the room to talk to some of the other guests.

"What did he mean, Bud?" John asked.

"Who knows? He's a genius, but he's a little demanding at times. The money's incredible, though. Ethel and I are going to have a great retirement." The older man grinned and winked at Rachel.

She smiled and then reminded John that they had to leave. She got no objection from him. He couldn't wait to get her alone and find out why she'd changed her mind. And if she realized what she'd done.

After bidding their hostess good-night, the two of them went upstairs and collected a sleepy-eyed Jacey. It was almost ten o'clock, and she wasn't used to such late hours.

John picked her up and her head flopped down against his shoulder. "I had fun," she whispered. "Did you?"

"Oh, yeah, baby, we had a barrel of laughs," he assured her, avoiding Rachel's gaze as he offered the baby-sitter, a teenager, some money for taking care of Jacey.

With Jacey still awake, although she was fading fast, the drive home was in silence. When they pulled into John's driveway, he lifted Jacey from the back seat and followed Rachel to her front door.

"I can take her now," she told John, reaching out her arms for her child.

"There's no need. I'll carry her up."

Did she think he was going to go tamely home, ignoring what had happened this evening?

She must have read the determination in his eyes, because she shrugged her shoulders and turned and unlocked the door. After putting Jacey down on her bed, John left the child to her mother's care and went down to the living room.

He didn't have long to think. Although he already knew what had to be said. Rachel came down the stairs and stopped at the door of the room, her eyes wide.

"Come on in, Rachel. We've got some talking to do."

"I'm really tired, John. Couldn't we—"

"Nope. I have to thank you for what you did tonight. But I wish— Never mind. I hope you realize what this means."

"Of course. It means your company is safe."

"True. And I really am grateful." He cleared his throat. "It also means we'll have to move in together."

Chapter Eight

Rachel stared at him. "You're out of your head."

"No, I'm not, Rachel. We both lied to David tonight. Now there's no chance he'll keep me if I tell him the truth. So, we're going to pretend to be married."

He kept his hands in his pockets, attempting a casual stance.

Rachel turned away. "I can't do that, John. I promised myself I'd never do such a stupid thing again."

Realization struck him like a bolt of lightning. "That's how you ended up pregnant with Jacey, isn't it?"

An abrupt nod was her only answer.

"So what are we going to do?"

She released a huge sigh before turning to face him. "I don't know, unless you're willing to really marry me." She gave a cynical laugh, as if she knew her remark was ridiculous.

But for John, much to his surprise, her words were an eye-opener. He'd thought he'd never marry again, would die before he reentered the state of matrimony, but the idea of marrying Rachel and Jacey had its appeal.

"Okay," he simply agreed.

She stared at him, disbelief on her expressive face. "What did you say?"

"I agreed with you. I think we should just go ahead and marry. For Jacey's sake if nothing else."

"Marry?" she repeated, as if she still couldn't believe what she'd heard.

"Just as a . . . a pretense," he hurriedly said, fearing he saw rejection on her face. He wondered if he'd made a mistake when anger clouded her eyes.

"And just how long do you think this pretense should continue? The rest of our lives?" Rachel crossed her arms in defiance. "Don't you think that's a little too much sacrifice, even for the sake of your company?"

One hand came out of his pocket to run through his hair. She realized he always did that when he was upset. "Hell, Rachel, I don't know. Six months, a year? How long would you consider?"

"You're serious?" she gasped, taking a step closer, "You're actually serious about our getting married? John, you can't be!"

"Why can't I? You decided tonight that my company was worth saving. And I appreciate it. But now we've got to find a way out of this mess. Marriage is the only answer."

"But—but we don't— That is, there's no—"

"Romance? Love? Feelings? Did you have those things with Jacey's father?"

She nodded, although she was reluctant to answer.

"I thought I did, too, with my wife. Instead, all she had feelings for was my bank account." He stood and paced several times about the room, talking as he moved.

"Look, Rachel, let's handle this like a business arrangement. We'll marry for a minimum of one year. I'll—I'll pay you a salary and—"

"No! I won't take money for..." She didn't know what to call his suggestion. But it wasn't something you did for pay.

He moved toward her and she took several steps back.

"Why not? You'll be putting a lot of money in my pocket with Wester's account."

"It doesn't matter. I can't do that."

"Okay." He turned away and began pacing again. "Okay," he repeated. "I'll support you for a year. It will save you living expenses. Your salary can go into savings. For a year, you'll appear in public as my wife. We'll live in the same house. To the world we'll appear married."

"And to ourselves?"

"What do you mean?"

He walked toward her again, and she fought to hold her ground. The attraction they'd both felt was a danger, but she didn't want to appear a coward.

"John, I'm a mature woman, not a teenybopper. We both know we're attracted to each other. But—much as I hate to confess it—I'm a romantic. I don't think sex should be an aerobic activity. It should be about feelings."

"I'm not interested in feelings," John replied crisply, stiffening.

"I know," she said, struggling to keep her voice even while her heart sank. "And that's why I don't think your plan would work."

"It could work for a year, Rachel. I'd let you decide where our relationship should go."

"But, John, you couldn't even have a relationship with anyone else or David would fire you. You'd be stuck with a monastic existence for a year." She looked him up and down. "Somehow I don't think that kind of life would be normal for you."

That sideways grin that was so alluring appeared. "Not by choice, but I'm not a swinging bachelor, Rachel. The only difficulty would be living with such temptation."

She blushed and looked away.

"You are, you know," he continued. "And you're right about the attraction between us. We've both felt it. And with an honest-to-goodness marriage license, I don't see why either of us should suffer. But that's your decision."

Sinking her teeth into her bottom lip, she shook her head. "It's too much, John. I need time to think—without you around."

"Okay. When? Tomorrow?"

"I don't know. I can't tell you when. Just give me a few days." A few days? She'd prefer weeks, years. There was too much to consider to make such a decision overnight.

He shrugged his shoulders. "Okay. I don't have much choice, do I? My company's life hangs in the balance. Don't forget that, Rachel."

"No, I won't forget."

"Can I offer any persuasion?" he asked, a twinkle in his eyes that told Rachel just what kind of persuasion he had in mind.

"No. Definitely not," she automatically replied, but there was a yearning inside her to feel his arms around her again. That traitorous yearning was what made a decision so difficult.

She escorted him from her house and closed the door behind him. Thank goodness he hadn't argued with her. If she gave in to what her body wanted, her life would become much more complicated. And when it all ended in a year, she'd be devastated.

RACHEL SPENT THE WEEKEND hiding. Every time she wanted to go somewhere with Jacey, she would peek out the window first to see if John's car was in the driveway.

"What are you doing, Mommy?" Jacey demanded.

"Just—just checking the weather to see if you need a raincoat," she improvised.

"The sun is shining."

"Oh, so it is." Not only was the sun shining, John was in evidence, doing some kind of work on his car, without a shirt. Her gaze concentrated on the muscles of his back as he bent over the motor, making it difficult to remember what she was saying. "So—so, I don't think we should go to the store right now. It's too hot."

Jacey stared at her in puzzlement, and Rachel couldn't blame her child. She wasn't making much sense. Her mind was too full of the questions John's suggestion had raised.

"Look! There's John. I'm going to go say hello," Jacey said and was out the door before Rachel could come up with a reason to keep her inside.

Through the window, she watched John hug Jacey and start showing her something under the hood. At least John wasn't lying about his feelings for Jacey. She'd never seen a man so patient. Especially one who had no children.

That was another unanswered question. Why didn't John have children? Did he not want them? Had his wife refused to have children? She wanted to know all about his failed marriage, but she didn't have the right to ask those questions.

If she refused his request that they marry, he wouldn't ever speak to her again, much less answer questions. But if she did accept? She rushed up the stairs and began cleaning out the hall closet, the most loathsome task she could think of. Anything to keep her mind off the relentless question she couldn't forget.

Monday afternoon, after picking up Jacey, Rachel pulled into the driveway, automatically noting that John's car wasn't in his. Thank goodness teaching allowed her to arrive home before him. By the time he pulled up, she would be well protected behind her four walls.

With the curtains pulled, she worked on dinner, having sent Jacey up to her room to play. Even so, she caught herself listening for his car. When she did hear it, she couldn't resist peeking out the window at him.

He looked directly at her, as if he could see her, after he got out of his car. She drew back with a gasp. Even if she decided to marry him, it would be a marriage of convenience only. She couldn't afford to let him think she had any personal interest in him. And of course, she didn't. Definitely not.

The phone rang and she answered it, still thinking about John.

"Rachel, this is David Wester. I'm sorry to bother you at home, but has John arrived yet? I just missed him at the office."

"Uh, missed him? Oh. Oh, yes, I just heard the car in the driveway. Just a minute and I'll go get him."

"There's no rush. We can just chat until he comes in," David said pleasantly. "I'm glad I reached the right number. I got it from the school directory. John's moved in with you?"

"Um, we're kind of living in both houses right now. We only just married, you know. It's h-hard to combine two households."

"Yes, I guess it is."

She had to get free of the phone. If she didn't run over to John's house and drag him back to hers, he'd never answer the phone.

"Sorry, David, I've got something in the oven and it's burning." Without waiting for him to answer, she laid down the phone and raced for the front door.

Thirty seconds later, she was pounding on John's front door. He swung it open as he loosened his tie and unbuttoned the top button of his shirt with one finger.

"Rachel. What a surprise."

He didn't act surprised, or particularly happy about her appearance. She didn't have time to think about that now.

"John, hurry. David is on the phone."

"My phone didn't ring," John assured her, a frown on his face.

"No! *My* phone. He thinks we live together, remember?"

"Damn!" John exclaimed and took off at a run.

"He thinks you've just pulled into the driveway," she shouted after him. Then she walked slowly after him. There was no need for her to hurry now.

By the time she reached her kitchen, John had hung up the phone, but his hand remained on the receiver and he was staring into space.

"Is everything all right?"

"Yeah, great. At least I didn't have a heart attack."

"What are you talking about?"

"My mad dash between our houses. Rachel, I've tried to give you time, but you've got to make up your mind. Either I go to him and tell him the truth and destroy my company, or the two of us get married."

"You said you'd give me time," she protested.

He shoved his fingers through his hair. "I did give you time. I gave you the entire weekend. Now it's time to fish or cut bait."

"Oh, that's romantic!" she retorted in disgust.

He froze and then grinned, his eyes lighting up. "You want romance?"

She recognized her mistake at once. "No! No, that's not what I meant. It was just—just an inelegant way to express yourself."

"I can be more elegant," he promised, as he started walking toward her.

"No. No, I don't want you to be more—more—Stop, John!"

"Hi, John!" Jacey exclaimed from the stairs just as John reached Rachel.

Rachel breathed a sigh of relief as John released her and went to hug Jacey.

"Hi, little one. How was your day?"

"It was fun. Did you know we're going to have a family picnic at the end of school? You can come, can't you? You said you'd be my daddy when I asked."

"Of course I can come, can't I, Mommy?" John asked, cocking one eyebrow at Rachel.

"Yes, but I'm not your mommy."

"I know," he replied, his gaze emphasizing that knowledge.

Desperate to change the subject, she asked, "What did David want?"

"He wants us to attend the Charity Ball, Friday night," John said, but he was tossing Jacey in the air at the same time, as if his request were perfectly natural.

"What?" Rachel moved closer to the other two. "Stop, John. Say that again."

"You're always telling me to stop," he complained.

Rachel closed her eyes to hide her irritation. Then she asked, "What charity ball?"

"The big one they hold every year. You've read about it, haven't you?"

"Well, yes, but—"

"David bought tickets for us. He likes the people associated with him to support the charities."

Rachel stared at him. He thought she could afford to go to the social event of the year? He thought she had a ball gown in her closet that would cost more than her annual food budget? And diamonds to go with it? The man was insane!

"I can't do that."

"Rachel, be reasonable. If you've made other plans, you'll just have to cancel them."

Almost hysterical, she said in exasperation, "You mean just cancel my date?"

John's happy-go-lucky smile disappeared. He set Jacey on the floor and grabbed Rachel's shoulders. "What date? Who are you dating?"

She pulled out of his grasp and crossed the room, folding her arms over her chest. "That's none of your business."

"It might be," he said gruffly as he followed her. "If you're dating someone, David might get word of it. You could ruin the whole plan."

"What plan?" Jacey demanded, yanking on the leg of John's trousers.

Momentarily distracted from Rachel, John knelt down to Jacey's level. "That's a secret, sweetheart. Can you keep a secret?"

"Yes. Real good." She nodded her head, too, to make sure he believed her.

"Well, Mommy and I have a plan where I'd be your daddy for a whole year."

Jacey frowned and cast an anxious look at her mother.

"What's wrong? Wouldn't you like that?" John questioned, and Rachel couldn't help but like the touch of uncertainty in his voice.

"Yes, but—but I don't got enough money. I gave you all the money I got."

John looked up at Rachel, but she wasn't sure what his expression meant. Then he scooped Jacey into his arms. "You don't understand, little one," he said after he hugged her. "Being your daddy is so special that *I'm* going to pay *you.*"

The radiance on Jacey's face almost brought tears to Rachel's eyes. She looked away.

"So, how much will you charge me?" John asked.

"John—" Rachel began in protest. She didn't want her child to believe that there was a monetary value on such a thing.

He held up his hand. "Let Jacey answer. I might not be able to afford her, you know."

Still beaming, Jacey, with both arms around his neck, said, "I don't want no money, John. If I can have you as my Daddy for longer, I'll be happy."

"Then we'll all be happy, sweetheart," he assured her and kissed her on the cheek. "Speaking of money, I have something for you, Jacey, if your mother doesn't mind, and this seems a good time to give it to you." He reached inside his coat pocket and brought out a small booklet.

"What's that?" Jacey asked, taking it from him, a puzzled look on her face.

"It's the money you paid me."

"No, John, this is a book," Jacey explained, frowning.

"Look inside. See that writing? It says three dollars and sixty-seven cents. The bank with its name on the cover is keeping your money, and it will make your money grow. And since you don't have to hire a daddy anymore, you can save more money."

"I give my money to you? And you put it in the bank?"

"Right. Okay?" Although he asked Jacey, he was looking at Rachel.

She nodded. His action was honorable and would teach Jacey about money at the same time. She couldn't object.

"Will you find money behind my ears so's I can put it in the bank?" Jacey asked, a speculative gleam in her eye.

"Jacey, I explained that John didn't really find that money there," Rachel protested, recognizing that Jacey was borrowing a page from John's book of manipulation.

John grinned. "You never know, Jacey." He set the little girl down. "Now, you run upstairs and play and Mommy and I will work out the details of our plan."

Rachel kept silent until she heard the door of her daughter's room close. "Thank you for the savings account, John. But please don't encourage her to accept money from you."

"An occasional quarter won't hurt, Rachel. And you have to keep her believing in magic, don't you? After all, it got her a daddy."

She was supposed to be thankful that her child's naïveté had gotten them into this mess? That thought brought her back to John's last words to Jacey. "What did you mean, telling Jacey we were going to work out the details? As if everything is settled?"

"It is. But first, let's talk about this date Friday night. Who is the guy?"

Rachel moved behind the couch. She didn't like the predatory look in John's eye. "There is no date."

He'd been stalking her, but her answer stopped him dead in his tracks. "What? You made that up?"

"Not—not on purpose. I was just responding to your ridiculous presumption."

"And what presumption was that?" he asked as he started moving toward her again.

She backed away. "That I could go to the Charity Ball Friday evening."

"But you'll have to, Rachel, if we're going to continue our little charade. And we are, aren't we? You're not going to destroy everything I've worked for over one little evening out, are you? Jacey approves," he told her, his manner confident again.

His last remark stopped her retreat. In a flash, she started toward him, fire in her eyes. "Thank you for reminding me! How dare you tell Jacey what your plans were before I agreed! How could you mislead her like that? Promising to be her daddy for a year. Do you think she has any concept of time? She doesn't know how long a year is!"

"Jacey? You've got to be kidding," John protested. He reached out and caught the finger she was shaking at him. "Come on, Rachel, Jacey understands a year."

In all honesty, she knew he was right. Jacey understood a year. What she wouldn't understand was John walking away from them when that year ended. And that was the part Rachel would have difficulty with, too. How did one put a time limit on the heart?

"That's not what's worrying you, is it?" John asked softly as he pulled her to him. Rachel leaned against his chest, her head bowed, unsure how much to reveal.

"I'm afraid she'll be hurt."

He tipped her chin up so he could see her face. "Rachel, I promise I'll try not to hurt her. And if we're honest with her, I don't think we will."

She read honesty in his eyes. And caring... for Jacey. She couldn't ask for anything else. Although her lips trembled, she nodded. "Okay."

Her sudden capitulation took him by surprise. But not her. She'd known since Friday night that she couldn't say no to him. She'd made her choice when she'd stopped him from revealing the truth. It had just taken her a while to admit it.

"Okay, what?" he demanded.

"Okay, we'll have a year's agreement."

"You mean you'll marry me." He made it a statement, not a question.

She nodded anyway.

"When?"

"I don't know. I guess as soon as possible." As if talking about the intimacy of marriage made her realize how close to each other they stood, she jerked away from his hold. "If we're going to—to do it, we should do so immediately."

"Right. I'll, um, I'll check on the requirements. Do you know anything about them?"

"No. You're the one who's been married," she reminded him.

"Oh, yeah. There was a waiting period, I believe. Uh, maybe we should consider Oklahoma."

"Oklahoma?" Rachel questioned, wondering if he'd lost his mind. What did Oklahoma have to do with anything?

"Yeah, we could get married tomorrow in Oklahoma. That's what we'll do."

"I have to teach tomorrow," she reminded him.

"Call in sick. I'll make arrangements for a private plane to fly us to the closest city, then fly us back. We could do it in two or three hours. I might only miss half a day at work, which is good, because I have a lot to do. Then, we'll—"

"Wait just a minute!"

He stopped in midsentence, seemingly surprised by her interruption. "What's wrong?"

"Just like that? I'm supposed to call in sick?"

"Well, you can't exactly tell them you're eloping since you're already supposed to be married."

"And what are you going to tell your office?"

He shrugged. "I'm the boss. I don't have to give excuses."

"What about Jacey?"

"You want her to come with us?"

"No! I can't leave her here while I go out of town, though."

"Why not? She'll be at school all day, as usual."

"What if she got sick? They wouldn't be able to find me." Somewhere, Rachel knew, there had to be a reasonable excuse not to elope tomorrow.

"She's perfectly healthy. But we'll tell her if she needs you to have them call my office, and they'll get in touch with us."

"And then they'd know I wasn't really sick," she declared triumphantly.

"Rachel, that's not going to happen. And if it does, they won't fire you for that. If they do, though, I'm supporting you, so what difference does it make?"

"That's my professional career, just as your company is your professional career, John. Are you willing to throw your career away? Seems to me we're going to great lengths because you aren't."

"You're right. I apologize. But I don't know what else to do. We can't afford to wait, Rachel."

With a sigh, she capitulated—again. "I know, I know."

He took hold of her shoulders, caressing her through her blouse. "Everything will be all right, Rachel. We'll get the marriage taken care of and then we can go Friday night with a clear conscience."

Friday night. Reminded of what had started their marathon argument, Rachel sighed again. "I can't go Friday night."

Chapter Nine

"Nervous?"

Rachel took a quick glance at John's face and then looked away. She didn't want to admit how much their plans, made the previous night, disturbed her. After all, she'd agreed to the marriage.

"We're almost there," he added when she said nothing in response to his question.

"Yes."

They had boarded a small plane just as soon as they'd dropped Jacey at kindergarten with a note in her pocket that gave John's office number, should she need her mother. For an emergency, of course.

The plane started its descent and Rachel thought the butterflies in her stomach had turned into bombers. She clenched her fists in her lap, then wished she hadn't when John reached over to hold them. She knew he was trying to reassure her, but she didn't need his touch. In fact, his touch was a complication she didn't even want to think about.

Once they were on the ground, she released her seat belt and stood. John guided her down the steps, after thanking the pilot and reminding him they would be returning in about an hour.

"This trip must be costing you a fortune," she muttered.

"That doesn't matter. You're doing me a big favor, and we both know it. Quit worrying about the money. And that goes for the clothes for Friday night, too. I don't intend to argue that issue again."

She sighed. They had had a rousing argument last night when she'd again said she couldn't go to the ball on Friday. John had worn her down, insisting that buying her outfit would be like giving an employee a uniform.

Well organized, John whisked them away in a rental car, a map in his hand showing the location of the justice of the peace where he'd made an appointment for their marriage.

Rachel sat beside him, feeling as if she were caught up in a bad dream.

"What happened to Jacey's father?"

John's sudden question immediately took her mind away from the marriage ceremony. "That's none of your business."

"I think it is. I'm going to be Jacey's stepfather in a few minutes. I ought to know what happened."

"You're not really going to be her stepfather. I mean, it's just a temporary thing."

"While we're married, I'm her stepfather." His tones were firm, allowing no disagreement.

"Fine. But that doesn't mean you should know all the dirty details of my past life. You haven't told me about your marriage."

"What do you want to know?"

"I don't want to know anything!" That wasn't true, but she wasn't about to let him think she had spent any time dwelling on the woman he used to love.

"Good. Now, tell me about Jacey's father. Does he send child support? And does Jacey ever see him?"

"No."

"No to what?"

"No, he doesn't send child support and no, she never sees him."

She watched him take his eyes off the road to stare at her before quickly returning his attention to his driving. "You haven't had any help from him at all?"

Looking out the window so she couldn't see his reaction, she briefly, unemotionally, outlined Jacey's past history. "When I told Dirk I was pregnant, he asked me to leave. He accused me of sleeping with someone else, said he would challenge his paternity if I tried to get anything out of him."

She expected him to ask if Dirk's accusations were true. Her parents had asked when she'd gone to them. But John surprised her.

"But that wasn't true, was it? So why didn't you take him to court and at least get some financial help?"

"How do you know it wasn't true?" she asked faintly.

He turned off the road into a driveway and parked by the sign advertising marriages before he answered. Then he turned in his seat and looked into her eyes. "Because you don't like lies, Rachel Cason. And because when you love someone, like Jacey, you do it with your entire heart."

Tears flooded her eyes and she ducked her head, hoping he wouldn't notice.

"So why didn't you take him to court?" he asked again.

"I was all alone, young, hurt. I didn't want to have anything to do with him ever again."

"Surely your parents advised you to do so? They must have realized what a financial burden raising a child on your own would be."

"My parents thought it was possible he'd told the truth, and they were concerned with the embarrassment it might cause them." She couldn't keep the bitterness out of her voice. Their betrayal had hurt more than Jacey's father's.

John muttered something under his breath and she flashed him a quick glance before looking away again.

"So you managed on your own? How old were you?"

"Almost nineteen."

"How did you do it?"

She shrugged her shoulders, as if those years had been easy. "I had some scholarships that helped pay the tuition and I took out student loans. I'll have them paid off after I teach school this summer."

"You teach in the summer, too? Doesn't Jacey need you to spend time with her?"

He'd touched a raw wound. She hated not spending the summers with Jacey. It was a time of renewal that she needed. But she also needed to relieve them of the debt her education had cost. "I don't have a choice!" she snapped. "I have to pay off the debt!"

He touched her shoulder. "You're right. That was a dumb question."

She kept her head turned from him. If he couldn't see her face, then he wouldn't know how much his words had disturbed her.

JOHN FELT LIKE A MONSTER, upsetting Rachel on her wedding day. Her first wedding day. When she'd said last night that he was the only one who'd been married, he realized she was an unmarried mother.

As he'd tossed and turned during the night, he kept trying to imagine the circumstances that would cause a man to walk away from Rachel when she was carrying his child. He couldn't picture it.

Now he had his answer.

"Come on, Rachel. Let's go get married."

Still without looking at him, she opened her car door. He reached into the back seat and picked up the box he'd ordered. Opening it, he took out a small bouquet. At least she'd have flowers for her wedding.

He rounded the car and held out the bouquet to her. Finally she looked at him, with a flash of surprise and gratitude that lit him up inside like a neon sign.

"Thank you."

"My pleasure. By the way, I don't think I've told you how beautiful you look today." Even if she hadn't, he would have said so, but Rachel made it easy. She was knock-down gorgeous in a champagne-colored silk suit. Her dark hair formed a glorious cloud of curls around her face.

With flushed cheeks, she gave him another quick glance before accepting his compliment. Then she started up the sidewalk, as if she wanted to get on with the procedure.

He followed her, but slowly. She was beautiful. And lovely inside as well as out. And he adored her child. Which didn't explain the clenching of his gut. But he knew the reason. Damn, he was unhappy about marrying again. Even to save his company.

His wife had taught him a tough lesson. He'd thought himself desperately in love when he'd waited for her at the altar in an elegant church wedding. But it had all been a lie. Six years later, she'd tried to destroy him.

How much power did this wedding give to Rachel? And would she ever use it against him? He didn't want to know the answer today. Otherwise he wouldn't be able to go through with it.

Feeling like a rank coward, he caught up with Rachel and they entered the house together.

The justice of the peace was an elderly man whose wife assisted with the ceremony, playing taped music at appropriate times and offering the use of a veil. Rachel refused, and the ceremony began.

"I now pronounce you man and wife," the man intoned after the vows were taken. "You may now kiss the bride."

Rachel looked at him, as if not sure he intended to take advantage of that custom. Hell, it was the best part. He wasn't about to pass up an opportunity to hold her.

He wrapped his arms around her and lowered his mouth to hers. She didn't resist. In fact, he wasn't sure but he thought she welcomed his caress. The magic he'd felt when he'd kissed her before seemed to have increased and he lost all awareness of the time or the place until the JP touched him on the arm.

"Ahem, excuse me, Mr. Crewes, but we have another couple ready to be married."

John felt like a teenager caught by his girlfriend's father. Rachel's cheeks were red, too, indicating she was embarrassed by their marathon kiss. John, with a quick payment, including a big tip, got them out of there promptly. The deed was done. That was the important thing.

RACHEL STUDIED THE slender gold band on her third finger. John had apologized after the ceremony, saying that was all he'd been able to manage before they left town, but he'd get her something nicer right away.

She didn't want anything else. Something plain and unpretentious suited her. Besides, diamonds for a business arrangement just didn't seem right.

"You've been quiet. Are you okay?" John asked just before they landed in Kansas City again.

"I'm fine."

"Good. We'll go have lunch now. One of my favorite restaurants is down on the Plaza. Is that okay with you?"

"I thought you needed to work."

"I changed my mind. A person doesn't get married every day."

He smiled at her, and Rachel looked away. She wished he'd be rude and curt. It would make it easier not to fall under his sway. She was determined not to let her hormones or whatever had betrayed her with Jacey's father do the same with John.

The meal was an agony. The restaurant was lovely, the food excellent, the waitress perfect. Her dinner companion was the most charming man alive. And she fought his every smile.

By the time the meal was finished, his smile had a terse edge to it. She regretted upsetting him. But she couldn't trust her heart to this man. After all, in a year, he'd be gone.

"Come on," he muttered as they left the restaurant. Since she was walking in step with him, she couldn't imagine what he meant. She had an inkling when he led her to the most exclusive store on the Plaza, Hall's.

"What are you doing?"

"We're going shopping for your dress for Friday night."

"We most certainly are not!" she snapped, trying to disengage her arm from his hold.

"Yes, we are. I can't take off the rest of the week, and I suspect it would be difficult for you, too. It only makes sense to shop now."

"I don't want—"

He pulled her to an abrupt stop and turned her to face him. "Rachel, we've already argued about this, and you agreed it was like a uniform. There's no point in doing this thing halfway. We're married. Husbands buy their wives clothes."

But they weren't really married. She knew it and he knew it. And that was why she didn't want him to buy her anything. She couldn't argue that point, however. He was right. If they were going to create this fabrication, they had to go all the way.

"Yes," she said with a sigh, her head down.

"Will it be so horrible, buying a new dress?" he teased, some of his good humor seemingly restored with her capitulation.

"No, of course not," she assured him, trying for a smile herself, but it didn't feel like a huge success.

Without another word, he led her into the department store. Within minutes, it seemed half the store employees were racing around to do his bidding. The gowns they presented to her were incredibly beautiful. But she knew her choice the moment they brought it out. A sapphire-blue silk, it had large puffed sleeves, an elongated, ribbed bodice that came to her hips and then flared into a full skirt. The neckline was cut straight across, low but not indiscreet. It was perfect.

John seemed to agree with her. "Try on that one, Rachel. I think it will look spectacular on you."

When she emerged from the dressing room, John was in deep consultation with one of the saleswomen. Rachel intended to wait patiently for his attention, although she was eager to see his reaction to the gown. However, the saleslady noticed her at once and motioned to John.

He came toward her with a gleam in his eyes that told her he approved. Taking her hands in his, he asked, "What do you think?"

"It—it's lovely."

"We'll take it," he told the saleslady over his shoulder.

"Just like that? John, did you look at the price?" she whispered urgently. She had. The gown amounted to almost two months' salary for her.

"They're bringing up some shoes for you to try on with it. And a few other things."

He added the last so casually, she didn't even think about his meaning until they began a long parade of casual and business clothes.

"John, what are you doing?" she whispered frantically, trying to avoid being overheard by the saleswomen.

"Just amplifying your wardrobe a little, Rachel. You're going to need more clothes for all the social occasions. It will be simpler to buy them now, instead of having to make extra trips every time something comes up."

His words were logical but the result was overwhelming. She felt like a doll being dressed and redressed over and over again.

"It's such a pleasure to work with you, Mrs. Crewes. Some of our ladies are difficult to fit, but you're a perfect size ten," the saleslady enthused.

"Thank you. But I don't think we're going to buy a lot. I shouldn't be taking up so much of your time," she said hurriedly.

"Oh, Mr. Crewes gave us specific instructions. Now, come along and show that pantsuit to him. What a wonderful husband you have."

Rachel was growing more agitated by the moment. Nothing she said seemed to have any effect on John. She felt like she was standing in the path of a large steamroller. When she came out of the dressing room, there was a shoe salesman waiting with about ten boxes of shoes. She'd already tried on the shoes to match her gown. Now what?

"Mr. Sanders thought some of these styles might go with the other outfits you've been trying on," John said with a smile—as if his behavior was perfectly normal.

Rachel looked at the beaming shoe salesman, the salesladies standing around with several hangers in each hand, at her new husband, who was assuming everything was wonderful, and she wanted to scream.

"May I speak to—to my husband privately for a moment?" she asked all the salespeople, a smile, albeit a small one, on her face.

"Yes, of course," they assured her and hustled ten feet away to stand in a circle, pretending not to watch.

"John, what are you doing?" she whispered, her back to their audience.

"I'm buying you some pretty things."

"John, this is totally unnecessary."

"We've discussed the clothing situation before, Rachel. You don't need this kind of wardrobe to teach school. You only need it as my wife. It's the right thing for me to provide it for you."

"I understand that, but a gown for Friday night is all that is necessary at the moment. You're buying me an entire wardrobe."

"It's more practical this way," he told her, but he didn't quite meet her gaze.

"I don't think that's your only reason. Are you ashamed of the way I look?"

His surprise reassured her. His touch did even more as he reached out with both hands to caress her shoulders. "Don't be absurd, Rachel. You know I think you're beautiful. It's not that big a deal. I have lots of money and you're doing me a favor. I'm trying to repay the debt."

What could she say? He'd managed to save her pride and use logic. Even if she wasn't sure she was getting the entire story. Licking her lips, she finally said, "Okay, but let's keep it to a minimum. This is costing a lot of money."

He readily agreed and then sent her off to the dressing room to try on more clothes. Somehow, she feared she'd lost total control of the situation with her agreement.

An hour later, she came out of the dressing room in her own clothes. "John, other than the ball gown, I think the ecru pantsuit and the turquoise dress would be nice. But the rest isn't necessary." She spoke firmly, determined not to let any interest in the other magnificent clothes creep into her voice.

"We're buying those," he assured her with a smile.

"Thank you," she said, surprised by his easy capitulation.

"Now, I think we should buy Jacey something new, too. After all, she's going to have to put up with me as much as you will."

"John, really, that's not necessary."

"Yes, it is. Come on."

"But where are our packages?" She looked around, suddenly noticing that the salespeople weren't hovering around them anymore.

"Oh, they're having everything delivered."

"There wasn't that much, just the three outfits and the pair of shoes for the ball gown."

"It will be easier than having to carry it. And we'll add something for Jacey to it."

John had so much fun in the children's department, Rachel could hardly bear to put restraints on him. But she did. He bought several outfits for Jacey, and a big stuffed lion that she knew her daughter would love.

Then, while the saleslady was writing up the ticket, he wandered over to the baby clothes. "Was Jacey ever this small?" he asked, fingering a newborn's sleeper.

"Yes. It's hard to believe, isn't it?"

He continued to admire the tiny clothing until they were ready to depart.

When they were out in the warm sunshine again, Rachel decided it was her turn to ask questions.

"Why didn't you and your wife have children? You're so good with them and you obviously enjoy them."

She could tell by the expression on his face that he didn't want to answer her question. But she'd answered his. Turnabout was fair play.

Chapter Ten

They reached the car before John answered Rachel's question. After fastening his seat belt, he looked at her. "Why do you say I'm good with kids?"

"Come on, John. You're wonderful with Jacey."

"Jacey's special."

"You're not going to get her mother to disagree with you," she told him with a laugh, "but it's more than that."

He shrugged, dismissing her compliment. "I've never been around children before. My wife didn't want children, at least not right away, and I agreed. Seems to me they complicate your life."

"Oh, yes," Rachel confirmed in heartfelt tones. "But I wouldn't trade anything for Jacey."

He gave her his sexy sideways grin. "Neither would I."

They drove to Jacey's school in silence and relative harmony. Rachel was still a little uncomfortable with the spending spree they'd had, although she knew John didn't consider three outfits in that category. But she was sure Jacey would love what John had bought her.

The lion was riding in the back seat, waiting for Jacey's arrival. Rachel dismissed the small nudge of envy she felt that John could buy something like that for her daughter when she couldn't. She wasn't going to ruin Jacey's fun with such selfish thoughts.

John remained in the car while she went inside the child-care center to get Jacey. Her daughter was full of questions about her day since she knew Rachel was spending it with John. They'd kept details to a minimum, not telling Jacey they were getting married. They would explain everything tonight. At least, she hoped they'd figure out how to explain everything.

"John came to pick me up, too?" Jacey asked, thrilled to have his company.

"Yes, sweetie. And we went shopping."

"What for?"

"Well, I needed a new dress for Friday night. And then, if you'll look in the back seat, you'll see something John thought you needed."

Jacey stood on tiptoe as they approached John's Porsche. The stuffed animal practically filled the small back seat. Jacey's eyes widened in surprise.

"It's a lion!" she squealed to John as he got out of the car.

"It is," he agreed solemnly, "and I think it needs a home. Do you have room for him?"

Jacey turned her little face toward her mother. "Do we, Mommy? I can keep him in my room."

"Well, if you think he won't eat too much," Rachel agreed.

"Mommy! He's not real!" Jacey replied, grinning from ear to ear.

"Okay, then, he can come home with us."

Jacey hugged first her mother and then John, throwing her arms around his neck as he knelt to receive his reward.

Once they were on their way home, John cleared his throat. "Um, there's something we haven't discussed."

Rachel lifted her eyebrows. "I would imagine there are a lot of things we haven't discussed."

"Yes, but this one is going to arise as soon as we get home."

"You mean telling Jacey about today?" She glanced over her shoulder to see her child was engrossed in the stuffed animal.

"No. I mean, moving."

It took her a minute to realize the significance of his remark. Everything had happened so fast that she hadn't thought through all the changes that were about to occur. "Oh. I don't suppose you'd consider moving into our house?"

That sideways grin again. "Rachel, my house is paid for, updated, has a pool. You're renting, the house is in disrepair and is smaller, too."

Everything he said was true, but she was reluctant to give up the home she and Jacey had made. Somehow, standing in front of the justice of the peace had seemed far less significant than moving.

"Yes, of course. But... but is it necessary for us to make such a drastic change today?"

"When would you suggest? Next Christmas?"

She almost agreed with him before she realized he was teasing her. With a grimace, she said, "No, I guess not."

"You can just move a few things tonight, whatever you'll need for tomorrow, because we've had a long day. Then we'll use the next few evenings and the weekend to get really settled."

His plan was sensible, but she looked over her shoulder again at her daughter. Explaining it to Jacey might not be as easy.

As if he read her mind—a disconcerting thought—he said, "Don't worry about telling Jacey. She'll like the idea."

When they pulled into the driveway and got out of the car, Jacey was concentrating on the stuffed animal. John helped her get it out of the car.

"Say, Jacey, let's take Mr. Lion to my house. He'll have more room there."

Rachel recognized at once the disappointment Jacey quickly hid. "Okay. He'd probably like to live with you."

John knelt down to Jacey's level. "I don't think he'd like it so much without you. How about if you come live with me, too?"

Jacey backed up to lean against Rachel's legs. "Thank you, but my mommy and me stick together."

"I know. I was planning on your mommy coming, too."

"You were?" Jacey asked in surprise. After a quick glance at her mother, Jacey moved over to John. "Have you asked her?" she whispered.

John nodded.

"What did she say?"

"She said yes."

Jacey erupted into a wild cheer.

John grinned at Rachel as he stood. Then he extended a hand to Jacey. "Let's go choose your bedroom."

Rachel was surprised when he grabbed her hand, as he and Jacey headed for his house.

"Come on, Rachel. You get to choose a bedroom, too."

"We each get our own room?" Jacey asked, skipping excitedly at his side.

"You bet."

"John," Jacey panted, pulling on his hand.

"What, sweetheart?"

"If I'm very good, can I swim in your pool? Just once?"

Rachel bit her bottom lip as John assured Jacey she was welcome to use his pool. Her child hadn't had all that many treats in her young life. The thought occurred to Rachel that at the end of their year, Jacey might have trouble adjusting to the austere life they would return to. True as that might be, she couldn't deny her daughter the opportunity to have some fun while it was offered.

They spent the next several hours carting belongings from Rachel's house to John's. A four-bedroom house, it had a guest room downstairs and the master and two additional bedrooms upstairs. John suggested Jacey and Rachel take the other two rooms near his. He even offered Rachel the master bedroom, but she refused. She and Jacey would share the hall bath while John used the bath attached to his bedroom.

Rachel was relieved. That would eliminate any embarrassing scenes. She hurried to unpack, hoping to dismiss the images in her head of John stepping out of a shower or shaving in front of the mirror.

"Mommy!" Jacey called, interrupting her mother's thoughts.

"Yes, dear?"

"You have a ring." Jacey pointed to the gold band on Rachel's left hand.

The moment of truth was at hand. Rachel sat down on the bed in her new room and took Jacey on her lap. "Yes. Since John is going to be your daddy for a year, we had to get married, you know. That's what people do before they live together."

Jacey nodded, as if she understood completely. Then she said, "Ellen's mommy lives with her boyfriend. They didn't get married."

"How do you know?"

"'Cause we asked her if he was her new daddy. She said he was just her mommy's boyfriend."

"Yes, well, sometimes people do that, but it's not a good idea." Rachel shuddered as she thought of her own past and her daughter's future.

"Everything okay?" John asked, having appeared in the doorway.

"John, you and Mommy got married!" Jacey exclaimed. She slid off Rachel's lap and ran to hug John's knees. "You really *are* my new daddy."

"That's right, Jacey."

"For a year!" Rachel reminded them both sharply.

"But we're not going to tell anyone that, are we, Jacey?" John said, casting a frown Rachel's way.

"No. I don't want this year to ever end," Jacey said.

The sound of a big truck stopping out front distracted all of them. Rachel stepped to the window.

"My heavens, that's a huge truck for our purchases."

"Yeah, well, I'm sure they're making other deliveries after us. Why don't you start dinner, if you're sure you want to cook? Jacey and I are getting hungry."

He had offered to take them out to dinner, but Rachel had refused. She had grocery-shopped over the weekend and needed to use her supplies before they went bad.

"Okay."

She went down to the kitchen as the doorbell rang, but left John and Jacey to let the deliveryman in. As she inspected the kitchen, she noticed the deliveryman's heavy tread leaving the house. Good. It was just the three of them again. She was still nervous around strangers.

She was still nervous around John, too, but that couldn't be helped.

Then she heard the deliveryman enter the house again. That was strange. Their purchases couldn't have needed two trips unless the man was frail. Her attention drawn from the cooking, she listened as the man went out again.

She moved into the hallway, looking out the front storm door, watching the deliveryman approach his truck. Subconsciously she heard Jacey giggling upstairs. She enjoyed being with John. Rachel hoped he wouldn't tire of a five-year-old's company.

Instead of entering the cab of the truck, the man picked up a load of boxes and set them on his cart. Rachel's eyes narrowed in thought, noting that those boxes looked quite similar to the shoe boxes of the ten pairs of shoes she'd tried on.

Suddenly she whirled and took the stairs two at a time, calling as she ran, "John Crewes!"

He and Jacey appeared at the top of the stairs just as she reached them. "Yes, Rachel?"

"What have you done?"

"What are you talking about?"

"Don't play innocent with me!" She pushed past him and ran to her bedroom door. There were boxes on her bed. She pulled open the closet door and discovered her closet full of plastic-bagged hangers holding all the beautiful clothes she'd tried on.

John and Jacey stood in the doorway, both of them grinning. "Surprise," John murmured just before he had to move out of the way of the deliveryman.

Stunned, she stared at him, finding it difficult to comprehend what he'd done. The presence of the stranger snapped her out of her trance.

"Please, return all this to your truck."

The man came to a halt, surprise on his face.

"Don't pay any attention to her," John said, stepping toward her.

The man look confused. "Sir, I—"

"It's all right. I paid for everything and I want it all delivered. This is my house." He was still smiling, which irritated Rachel all the more.

"Mommy, don't you like all the pretty things?" Jacey asked.

"No! No, I don't! And I won't keep them!"

"Does that mean I can't keep mine, too?" Jacey asked, her usual exuberance missing from her voice.

Feeling like a heel, Rachel sank to her knees and hugged Jacey to her. "No, of course not, sweetie. Yours were gifts from John. You can keep them."

"So why can't you accept a few gifts, too?"

John stood beside her, looking down at her. She didn't want to answer his question. But she had to.

"Because it's too much."

Before he could answer, the deliveryman stuck out a clipboard. "That's all of it, sir. If you'll just sign by the *X*."

Rachel looked at her bed, covered in boxes. Her closet was full of more clothing than she'd ever owned in her life. In one day, her life had been turned completely upside down. She was moving, she was married, and she was overwhelmed with "things"—"things" she'd never been able to afford.

FOR THE FIRST TIME SINCE John had known Rachel, she cried. Sinking down onto the floor, she stared at her bed and tears rolled down her cheeks.

John didn't know what to do. His ex-wife had cried frequently, using tears as a weapon. Rachel, however, had withstood every adversity proudly, with her head raised.

Until he bought her a new wardrobe.

Damn. He'd wanted to make her happy, to thank her for what she'd done for him. And maybe to justify what he was doing to her and her child. He hadn't wanted to make her cry.

"Jacey, why don't you go play with your lion and let me talk to your mom, okay?"

"But she's crying. Mommy never cries," Jacey insisted, her voice shaking.

Like a retired racehorse hearing the call to the gate, Rachel lifted her head and extended a hand to her daughter. "I'm okay, baby. Really, I am. Go—go play, and I'll get dinner ready."

Minding her mother, Jacey left the room, and John took Rachel's outstretched hand and pulled her to her feet.

"Look, Rachel, I was only trying to say thank-you. You've done a tremendous thing for me, and for the people who work for me. Didn't you think I'd be grateful?"

She was recovering quickly. "Grateful? If I'd saved the nation, maybe this would be justified. All I agreed to do was live in your house for a year."

"It's more than that and you know it, Rachel. Maybe I did overdo it a little, but I can guarantee you, Carol Wester has a much larger wardrobe."

"So you're competing with David Wester?"

"No! I'm not competing. But I didn't want you to feel out of place, or at a disadvantage." After hearing her tale of her treatment at Jacey's father's hands, he also wanted to pamper her, to take care of her. Temporarily, of course. But he wasn't about to tell her that.

"John, I appreciate it, really I do."

He didn't believe that. She was still glaring at him.

"But you've gone overboard. And what is in all those boxes, for heaven's sake?"

"I don't know. Once they had your size, I told the salesladies to send a complete wardrobe. Whatever they thought you'd like."

"Good heavens! You mean you don't know how much you spent?"

"Rachel," he protested, exasperated. "I told you I have a lot of money. I can afford it."

"Then why are you still living in this neighborhood? I mean, it's not a bad neighborhood, but it's not like the Westers'."

He shrugged his shoulders. "I like it here. I've fixed up the house the way I want it. Why would I move? To have rich neighbors?"

"John, I—"

"Rachel, just put it all away and use it if you need it. It's just a uniform for the role you're playing. At the end of the year, if you don't want it anymore, you can give everything back to me."

"What would you do with it?"

"How the hell do I know? I said that so you'd quit fighting me," he admitted with a grin.

"*You* are a manipulator," she said, but she smiled in return and his heart lifted.

"I try," he agreed modestly.

She shook her head in mock disgust. "Okay, John, I'll use these things to play my role. But no more purchases, okay?"

"Okay."

She looked around her and then back at him. "I'm going to cook dinner now. At least that's something I can do. I can't cope with all this right now."

"Okay. But you'd better reassure Jacey on your way to the kitchen. Those tears really shook her up."

Concern about Jacey was the one subject that always got Rachel's attention. She hurried to Jacey's bedroom, next to hers, and closed the door behind her.

John wandered into his bedroom. It had certainly been an exciting day. More than he'd thought it would be. Panic had filled him at the wedding. Maybe that had been partly the cause of his massive purchases. His first wife had wanted only what he could buy her. Had he been throwing material things at Rachel because he was afraid he might offer more?

He was being ridiculous!

Their marriage was only temporary. Necessary for his business survival. That's all it was.

He stretched out on the bed and relaxed, having reassured himself. Faint noises came to his ears—Jacey playing in her room; Rachel in the kitchen. In a few minutes, an inviting smell floated up the stairs.

Hell, this marriage business, even on a temporary basis, might be a pretty good deal. He'd never felt more at home.

THEIR FIRST MEAL together had gone well, Rachel decided, entering her bedroom after tucking Jacey in for the night. She was pleasantly tired, ready for a good night's sleep.

The sight of her bed piled high with boxes made her groan. How could she have forgotten all those purchases? She'd accepted John's arguments because she really didn't have a choice. And he was right. She would have to dress the part of his wife, or the Westers wouldn't believe her.

Although she tried to suppress it, there was also a rising excitement at the thought of opening all those boxes. It was like Christmas without the wrappings. A Christmas like she'd never had before.

Making sure her door was closed, she approached the bed, a huge grin on her face. Since she'd agreed to this outrageous deal, she might as well enjoy it.

Starting at one corner, she opened a dozen pairs of shoes, both dressy and casual. Then she discovered handbags to accompany them. Another box contained several pairs of designer jeans. Sweatshirts and sweaters in various colors were there, too.

She began putting the clothes into the numerous drawers of the dresser. The furniture John had in this bedroom was cherry, highly polished and elegant. Fortunately, it also offered a lot of storage space.

When all those things were put away, she turned back to the bed, wondering what the other boxes could hold. A dozen pairs of expensive panty hose pleased her, although she wouldn't wear them to school. Her desk had rough edges and she frequently ruined her nylons. She would continue to use the grocery-store brands for teaching.

A new swimsuit surprised her. Her old one could be thrown out. The elastic in it had died last year. She held the new one up before the mirror. The legs were high-cut, French-style, giving her pause. Oh, well, as long as she was using John's pool—without John present. The thought of his gaze on her while she was wearing the swimsuit sent chills all over her body. She was going to have to watch herself. She reacted too strongly to John's masculine presence.

After all, he had no interest in her other than as a partner to save his company. There was nothing physical between them. John thought of her as his coconspirator.

That settled, she drew a deep breath and turned her attention back to the rest of the boxes.

The shock she felt when she discovered the contents of the next box was quickly replaced by incredible anger. Grabbing the item on top, she charged across the hall and burst into John's bedroom without knocking.

Chapter Eleven

Stretched out in bed, the *Wall Street Journal* in hand, John was congratulating himself on how well everything had worked out when his door was flung open.

He sat up in surprise as a wild-eyed Rachel marched to his bed, her hand extended in front of her. To his surprise, he realized she was dangling a black lace bra.

"John Crewes, how dare you?" she demanded in outraged tones.

"How dare I what?" he asked, unable to make any sense of her question. His mind immediately connected Rachel's heaving bosom with the article of clothing. Was it the wrong size?

"How dare you purchase this—this garment for me!"

"I did?"

"Well, of course you did! It was in the boxes you had delivered. You said you bought all of that for show. Surely you don't think I'm going to show my—my undergarments to anyone!"

He reached out to take the bra from her, looking from it to her chest. "If you do, you'll certainly get their attention."

She snatched it away from him. "How dare you!"

"You're repeating yourself, Rachel." When she looked as if she wanted to hit him, he raised a hand in surrender, but he couldn't hide his grin.

"Rachel, calm down. I didn't know they were going to include underwear. I swear, I didn't."

"Are you sure?" Even though her voice still held anger, he noticed her eyes widening as if she suddenly realized how she had acted. She moved a step back from the bed.

"I'm sure. But it looks like they made a nice choice." He smiled again, waving his hand toward the bra she still held.

Like a child, she hid the offending garment behind her back.

"Did they just send the one?" he asked calmly.

"I—I didn't count. You shouldn't have—I'll send them back tomorrow."

"Why? Don't you like them?" He craned his neck, as if to look behind her back, just to tease her.

She backed away. "That has nothing to do with it. You shouldn't be buying me underwear, even if you knew nothing about it."

"Don't go away, Rachel. I can't come after you without embarrassing us both."

"Why?" she asked, her eyes growing even more wary.

"Because I don't wear pajamas. Wait, Rachel!" he called, but she was already out the door, closing it behind her.

With a sigh, he slid from the bed and found a pair of gym shorts in one of the drawers. After putting them on, he crossed the hall to Rachel's room. Unlike her, he knocked and waited for an answer.

"Go away."

"Rachel, I just want to talk to you. Open up."

She finally opened the door, her gaze on the floor. "I'm sorry I didn't knock. Thank you for being so polite."

"Come on, Rachel, it's no big deal. At least, it isn't if you'll ever look at me again." He waited for her gaze to meet his. When she finally looked up, he grinned and she smiled briefly in return.

"That's better. Now, why did the, um, underwear upset you so much? We've argued this wardrobe thing to death. Surely we don't have to go over it again."

"It's too personal. I can buy my own underwear."

"Well, of course you can. But there's no reason why you should. I know we haven't worked out the details, but for the next year, you and Jacey are my family, and I'll provide for you—underwear, steaks, jelly beans, whatever."

"We don't eat steak all that often," she protested.

"See, there. I'll have lots of money left over for underwear," he teased.

"John, I appreciate your trying to make it less embarrassing, but I just want everything to be understood."

"Ah. You mean you're not offering to warm my bed as well as cook my dinner?" He admired the picture she made as her eyes widened at his frankness and her cheeks flooded with color. She was definitely a beauty.

She also didn't back down. "Exactly. I shouldn't have lost control and burst into your room, but—but I panicked. What we've done today has scared me just a little."

"It's scared me a lot, sweetheart. But that doesn't mean I'm going to take advantage of the situation. We made an agreement, and unless you want to modify it, we'll stick to our plans.'' His gaze dropped to the lace bra she still held in her hands. He had to crack down on his imagination as pictures of her modeling the garment floated before his eyes.

''Thank you. I won't bother you again,'' she muttered, her gaze shifting away from his.

He nodded, his mouth dry, and turned to leave the room. Pausing at the door, he added, ''But I want you to know that I would be glad to have you warm my bed, should you change your mind.''

She raised her chin and stared him right in the eye. ''I won't.''

''Darn. See you in the morning.''

Although he closed the door behind him and returned to his empty bed and the *Wall Street Journal*, all he thought about until sleep claimed him was Rachel and a black lace bra. And then he dreamed about it.

JACEY AWOKE BEFORE HER mother called her for breakfast the next morning. She lay in the big bed, looking around her new room. The lion John had given her was standing guard at the end of her bed.

It was a nice room. It would look better when she brought more of her things from her house. But the nicest part about living in John's house was John. Now they were a real family. A mommy, a daddy, and a kid.

''Jacey, John, breakfast!'' her mommy called. Jacey shoved back the sheet and climbed out of the bed. Breakfast was her favorite time of the day. And today she got to share it with John.

An hour later, she reached kindergarten and couldn't wait to talk to Lisbeth. She couldn't tell her that they'd just moved into John's house. Mommy had said that was a secret. But she could tell her about the lion and her new clothes.

After she shared her news with her best friend, she said with a satisfied sigh, "New daddies are the best."

"Yeah. My daddy is neat, too. Hey! We're going camping this weekend."

"Really?" Jacey replied with envy. "With your new daddy?"

"Yeah. And you're coming, too."

"I am? Did my mommy say?" Jacey knew she'd have to have her mother's approval.

"I think so. My mommy said we were all going together."

"Wow! That'd be so neat."

"Yeah. It's my daddy's plan."

"Daddies are neat."

"Yeah."

Contentment filled the air until Lisbeth spoke again. "There's just one thing about my new daddy I don't like."

"What?" Jacey asked in alarm. She couldn't think of anything she didn't like about John.

"I don't get to sleep with Mommy anymore. Used to, when I was scared, I could go get in her bed. Now Daddy's always there."

Jacey's heart beat faster. "Do all new mommies and daddies do that?"

"Sure. Don't yours?"

"Of course," Jacey said quickly. "I just wondered if maybe some didn't." She hoped Lisbeth believed her. She didn't want her friend to think anything was wrong.

"I think they all do. And they always kiss each other even when I'm around. It's disgusting!"

"Yeah. Disgusting."

Mrs. Wilson called the class to order and Jacey slid into her seat. But she didn't pay as close attention as she usually did. She had a lot to think about.

"JOHN? DAVID WESTER. Bud showed me the suggestions and projections you made. They are superb. Let's move ahead with your plans."

"No questions, David?" John asked, grinning into the telephone receiver, glad that his client couldn't see his reaction.

"None at all. You've sold Bud, and I can trust both of you."

"Great. I'll get started right away."

"Okay. Do you remember me asking you to hold your weekend open?"

"Sure. We're planning on going to the Charity Ball. Rachel bought a gown yesterday."

David laughed. "Carol's been shopping, too. But that's not what I've been planning for the weekend. I'm organizing a family camp-out. I want you and Rachel and Jacey to join us."

John didn't know what to say. He hadn't been camping in years and had no idea how Rachel felt about outdoor activities.

"Uh, I don't think we have any camping equipment," he said, hoping to postpone any commitment.

"We're providing everything, including the food. Just dress appropriately and come willing to work. It will be great fun. We'll leave about ten o'clock Saturday morning and come back Sunday evening. Meet at my house, okay?''

''Okay, sounds great to me.'' What else could he say? ''Are you sure you don't want us to bring anything?''

''No, Carol's got it all arranged. We'll see you Friday evening.''

''Right, Friday evening.''

He hung up the phone and then stared at it. Could his life *get* any more complicated? His stomach had been tied in knots this morning facing Rachel over the breakfast table. After his interesting dreams of the night before, he could scarcely look her in the eye.

Now, he was facing a camping trip. And who knew how Rachel would react. With a sigh, he tried to rid his head of both David Wester's plans and Rachel. He found one easier to dismiss than the other. But work awaited. He had no choice.

''A CAMPING TRIP? Sweetie, I don't know anything about a camping trip,'' Rachel told Jacey as they drove home.

''Lisbeth said we were all going to go camping together this weekend. How long is it until the weekend?''

''Two more school days,'' Rachel said absentmindedly. She remembered David Wester asking them to hold their weekend open, but surely he would have said something to John by now, if he planned on them all camping together.

She sighed. That would be the last thing she needed. With only three weeks left of school, her students were turning in their term papers and she didn't have long to get them graded.

"Mommy?"

"Hmm?" Rachel answered distractedly.

"Does John kiss you?"

Rachel almost ran up on the curb. She straightened the car and quickly glanced down at Jacey's earnest face. "Let's wait just a minute until I stop the car, sweetie."

She pulled into her driveway and put the car into Park, then turned off the engine. "Now, what did you ask?"

"Does John kiss you?"

Rachel considered her answer. Clearly, this question was important to Jacey. Praying she was making the right choice, she said cautiously, "He has."

Jacey suddenly beamed at her. "Good." Then she undid her seat belt and opened the car door.

Rachel released the breath she'd been holding. Obviously she'd given the answer Jacey wanted. She hadn't added that she was going to be sure he never did again. But she was. She liked his kisses too much.

Rachel got out of the car, reaching into the back seat for her bag of term papers, then started up the sidewalk.

"Mommy!"

"Yes, sweetie?"

"You're going to the wrong house."

Screeching to a halt, Rachel looked longingly at her home before turning back to face her daughter. "Um, I think I forgot the key to John's house, Jacey."

"No, you didn't, Mommy. I watched John give you the key and you put it in your purse."

Her daughter was very good at remembering. "Oh, right. I'll have to look for it." Finding it just where

Jacey had said it would be, Rachel started walking over to John's house, reluctance filling her.

"Oh, Rachel!" a shrill voice called.

Recognizing Polly Meadows's voice, Rachel groaned. The woman was a dear, but the biggest gossip there was. "Hi, Polly," she said and kept walking.

"Are you visiting John? I don't think he's home."

Rachel was debating how much to tell the woman, when Jacey took the matter out of her hands.

"He's my new daddy. We live with him now."

Polly's reaction was shock. She dropped the hose she was using to water her roses, then screamed as cold water ran over the tops of her shoes.

"Lawsy me! Look what I've done." She snatched up the hose and then hurried over to turn off the water.

Rachel watched helplessly, knowing it would do her no good to run away. As soon as the water was turned off, Polly laid down the hose and came hurrying across the street. "What did that sweet child say?"

"John and I are married, Polly."

They hadn't discussed informing the neighbors, but Polly baby-sat for Rachel when she had to go out, and Rachel had planned on asking her to take care of Jacey Friday night. She had to know sometime.

"But he didn't even know where you were teaching just last week. When did the two of you meet?"

"A while back. We've kept things low-key because of—of Jacey, you know." She hoped Polly wouldn't question her deliberate vagueness.

"Of course, of course. Well, isn't that something? Does that mean you're moving out of your house?"

Reluctantly, Rachel nodded.

"'Cause a friend of mine has been looking for something on my street. It would be handy having her so close. I can't wait to tell her."

"I'm not sure yet when I'll be completely moved out. And I haven't notified the landlord yet. So I don't know when—"

"That's all right. She'll want to call them right away." Polly nodded her head and turned away. "My, my, my, what a surprise."

"Oh, Polly, I wondered if you could baby-sit for me Friday night? We have to go to the Charity Ball and—"

"The Charity Ball? That's a big social to-do. My, my, my, how quickly things change. Of course, I'll be happy to sit with little Jacey. Such a sweet child. Have you bought a dress, yet?"

"Yes, yesterday."

"I can't wait to see you all dressed up. You'll be as pretty as a picture! Now, I have to go call Beulah. She'll be so excited to hear about your house."

Rachel guessed she should be grateful for Beulah. Otherwise, Polly would have continued to ask questions for the next hour. But, somehow, she hadn't faced the fact that she wouldn't have her own house anymore. She'd even thought of continuing to pay the rent.

But that was absurd. She couldn't live next to John when their year was up. It would be too painful, for both her and Jacey. No, she might as well give up the house now and save all that rent money.

"Is Grandma Polly going to stay with me Friday night?" Jacey asked when Rachel reached John's front porch where the child had waited for her.

"Yes."

Since Rachel never saw her own parents, Polly Meadows had decided to adopt Jacey as her granddaughter. Both Jacey and Polly seemed happy with the arrangement and Rachel had no real objection. Every child should have at least one grandparent.

"Open the door, Mommy. I got to go," Jacey said urgently, and Rachel followed her orders. Time to remember she was a mother.

IT WAS ALMOST SEVEN before John got home, even though he'd hurried through his work. He'd called Rachel and warned her of his tardiness.

Opening the door, he immediately smelled something good. He couldn't remember the last time he'd come home to a cooked meal waiting for him.

"Rachel?" he called, and Jacey burst through the kitchen door, racing to greet him.

"Well, hello, Jacey," he said, putting his briefcase on the floor and swinging her into his arms. The warm hug she gave him was sweeter than the biggest deal he'd ever made.

"Hi, Daddy," she replied, smacking him on the cheek.

It gave him a jolt, having her call him Daddy, but he decided he liked it.

"Jacey, I told you to ask John first."

"Oops, I forgot."

Rachel shook her head at her child.

"I don't mind," John assured her, smiling, hoping to receive a smile in return.

"She should've asked. Are you hungry? I saved dinner for you."

"I'm starved, but you don't have to cook for me, Rachel," he hurriedly added, although he was salivating over the thought of dinner.

"It's no trouble. Jacey and I have to eat, too."

He shed his jacket and tie and followed Rachel and Jacey into the kitchen. The breakfast table had a yellow tablecloth on it that he hadn't seen before.

"Is this new?"

"No. It's mine." Without saying anything else, she set down a plate full of steaming meat loaf, mashed potatoes and green beans, accompanied by several hot rolls. "Ice tea?"

"Yes. This looks wonderful, Rachel."

"It's just meat loaf."

"I love meat loaf. It's even better than a steak."

She recognized his teasing because the corners of her mouth tried to turn up, but she said nothing.

Before he could start to eat, Jacey pulled on his arm. "You forgot something."

"Oh, sorry, Jacey." He bowed his head to say a blessing, assuming that was Jacey's complaint.

"No, not that."

He looked down at the little girl even as Rachel protested.

"Jacey, of course John should—"

"Before that!" Jacey insisted.

"What did I forget, Jacey?"

"I kissed you hello, and you kissed me hello."

Distracted by Rachel and the enticing smell of his dinner, John wasn't following Jacey's line of reasoning. "Yeah?"

"Well, nobody kissed Mommy."

"Jacey!" Rachel objected again, much more vehemently, her cheeks bright red.

John stared at the two of them.

"I saw it on television," Jacey insisted. "When the daddy comes home, he kisses everybody."

"Um, I think you're right. A definite oversight."

"John!" Rachel protested and stepped back from the table.

"Rachel, we have to do the right thing," he said, keeping his voice calm and rational. Inside, anticipation was revving up his heartbeat.

"And Lisbeth said her mommy and daddy kiss all the time," Jacey added, her gaze darting between the two adults.

"Ah. Well, we want to do things like Lisbeth's mommy and daddy, don't we, Rachel?" He hoped she got thc hint. If they were going to pull off this deal, they had to be thorough. And besides, he liked kissing her. A lot.

"Of—of course." Rachel didn't step away again, but she certainly wasn't rushing into his arms.

He rose from the table and went to her, taking her shoulders in his grasp. She raised one cheek toward him, but he wasn't about to settle for a peck. He covered her lips with his as Jacey clapped in the background.

Chapter Twelve

When John finally ended the kiss, leaving Rachel trembling, he didn't release her. In fact, he looked like he intended to repeat the gesture. In a panic, afraid she'd lose control completely if he did, Rachel pulled from his grasp.

"Your dinner will get cold."

"Dinner?" he repeated, as if in a fog.

"You were starving, remember?"

His gaze skimmed her body and that irresistible twinkle returned to his eyes. "Oh, yeah, I remember."

"John!" she chided, knowing he wasn't thinking of his meat loaf.

"Come on, Daddy. Mommy's meat loaf is good." Jacey tugged on his hand.

"I'm sure it is. Will you sit with me while I eat and tell me about your day?"

Jacey loved that idea and it gave Rachel some breathing room. She turned to the sink where she'd been rinsing their dinner dishes prior to putting them in the dishwasher.

"Camping? Oh, right, uh, Rachel," he called and she turned to look at him, a feeling of foreboding filling her.

"Yes?"

"David called today. He wants us to go camping with them this weekend."

"Yea!" Jacey cheered.

"Isn't this rather a surprise?"

"He did ask us to keep the weekend open."

"Yes, I know, but— Did you say yes?"

"What else could I say?" He shifted his gaze to Jacey and back again. "You understand?"

"Yes, of course," she agreed with a sigh. Everything they did seemed tied to the lie they were living. "We don't have a tent or anything. Do you?"

"David said not to worry. They'd provide everything, even food. We're just supposed to bring ourselves."

Rachel began mentally packing and making preparations. She'd bake oatmeal-raisin cookies. That would be a good snack for the kids. And she could buy some marshmallows for roasting. She could get most of her and Jacey's clothing in one bag.

"Maybe we'd better take my car. With bags and supplies, your car would be too crowded," she suggested.

John, his mouth full of his dinner, almost choked. Jacey leaned over and patted his back. He took a drink of tea and thanked her for her efforts.

"Um, Rachel, are you sure your car could make an out-of-town trip?"

She stiffened her spine. "My car may not be as luxurious as your Porsche, but it's in good running condition."

"Yeah, and only one window is stuck," Jacey chimed in.

John looked warily from her to Jacey and back again. "The air-conditioning does work, doesn't it?"

"We don't got none," Jacey said, smiling. "Mommy says we don't want to be all closed up when it's so pretty outside."

"Ah. I see. But on a long trip, it might be easier since we'll be going so fast. I think we could cram everything into my car."

"You want to take your car on a camping trip?" Rachel asked him, enjoying the look of dismay that filled him. "And let tree branches scrape the paint on it?"

"Hmm, I hadn't thought of that. How about I take your car in tomorrow for a thorough checkup before we drive it this weekend."

"My car is in good condition," she insisted huffily.

"Just to be sure, Rachel. Better safe than sorry," he added for good measure.

"I have to get to school. I can't do without a car."

"You can drive the Porsche."

She was amazed that he made the offer at all. After all, she knew how men were about their cars. But he said those words calmly, as if his offer was no big deal. She stared at him in surprise. "You've got to be kidding."

He looked at her and grinned. "Nope. Seems like the solution to me."

"But—but it's so expensive. What if I wrecked it, or one of my students damaged it?"

"Do they do that sort of thing?" he asked in surprise.

She turned her attention back to the sink. "It's been known to happen, if they get mad at you."

"Just don't make anyone mad tomorrow, okay?" he asked with another grin.

She rolled her eyes in exasperation. John turned his attention back to his dinner and her daughter. Rachel closed the dishwasher and then started making the cookies. It was a good thing she'd brought over the contents of her pantry last night, since John's had held only a few canned goods.

"What are you doing?" John asked, causing her to jump in surprise. He was standing right behind her, holding his empty plate.

"Making cookies. Did you want more dinner?"

"Nope. It was terrific. Need any help?"

She could tell he thought she'd refuse. "Thanks. If you'll just rinse your dishes and put them in the dishwasher, I'd appreciate it."

To his credit, he didn't blink an eye. "Yes, ma'am. My pleasure, ma'am."

"What's 'ma'am' mean?" Jacey asked, as usual standing next to John.

"You don't know what 'ma'am' means? Hasn't your mommy taken you to see any Westerns?" John asked in mock horror.

Jacey shook her head.

"What neglect! Your education has been sadly incomplete, my girl. Let's go in the den and discuss how we will rectify the matter."

Jacey stared at him, a puzzled frown on her face.

"He's teasing you, sweetie. Just humor him and take him out of the kitchen," Rachel ordered, smiling at her daughter.

RACHEL PULLED INTO John's driveway the next afternoon with a sigh of relief. She'd gotten the car home safely with no damage. In spite of John's casual attitude, she'd worried the entire day. Thank goodness she'd be back in her old, comfortable Chevrolet tomorrow.

Although her students would be disappointed. When one of her boys saw her pull into the teachers' parking lot in the Porsche, he'd raced over to examine the car. Then, of course, he'd immediately told all his friends, although she'd assured him it wasn't her car. She'd been the star attraction most of the day.

She and Jacey had just reached the porch, after carefully collecting any minute scrap of paper they might have dropped in the Porsche, when a brand-new green Volvo station wagon pulled into the driveway. As John got out of the driver's seat, Rachel walked toward him slowly, her mind examining the evidence.

"Where's my car?"

"Well, I got to thinking, Rachel. I didn't want you driving something that might break down at any moment, and a station wagon would give us all a lot more room."

When she didn't answer, and only continued to frown at him, he added, "It has air-conditioning."

"Where's my car?" she repeated.

"I traded it in," he finally admitted, that sideways grin on his face.

"How can you do that? The car is in my name."

"I told them you'd come down this evening and sign the title over to them." He held up his hands as she advanced toward him. "I know I shouldn't have done it without your approval, but I was sure you wouldn't agree. It's the only sensible thing to do, Rachel. Honest."

"Sensible? Sensible! How could you, John?" She glared at both him and the car as if they were monsters.

"Look, Rachel, we're putting it in your name. It's paid for. When the year—" He broke off, staring at Jacey before bringing his gaze back to Rachel. "It will be yours, no strings attached."

She stared at him in bewilderment and despair. It seemed impossible to stop him from making these expensive offerings. She didn't know what to do.

"John, you can't— This is totally unnecessary."

"That's not true, Rachel. It is necessary. You and Jacey could break down on the highway. That's dangerous. I can afford to provide you with a reliable car. It's not like I bought you a Cadillac or a Mercedes."

She gasped. Surely he wouldn't have— She saw in his gaze that he'd considered it. Closing her eyes, she prayed for guidance. This man was impossible.

"You mean it's ours?" Jacey suddenly asked, touching the car with one finger.

"That's right, sweetheart. Want to get inside?" He swung open the door and Jacey cautiously climbed in. After all the rules her mother had given her about riding in the Porsche, she knew how to treat an expensive vehicle.

"Mommy, it smells new," Jacey said reverently, as if she were experienced in such things.

"Rachel?" John asked, indicating the driver's seat.

"Mommy, aren't you going to say thank-you?" Jacey prompted, leaning out the back door to watch.

"Yes, of course," Rachel said stiffly, avoiding John's gaze. "Thank you."

"Don't you want to try it out?"

"Not now. I have to get the title from—from my house." She backed away from John's latest extravagance, as if afraid to get too close.

"Mommy, you didn't kiss John to say thank-you."

John must have read the panic in her eyes, or he wasn't interested in that kind of gratitude, either. He touched Jacey's shoulder and said, "Later, Jacey. Your mom wants to thank me later."

Much later. Maybe next year. Maybe never.

JOHN EASED THE COLLAR of his tuxedo shirt as he stood in the hallway, outside Rachel's door. Somehow, he didn't think she was going to appreciate his next move. His ex-wife had not only wanted gifts, she'd insisted he buy her anything she wanted. And he hadn't made a fortune then.

Rachel, on the other hand, made him feel like a villain because he bought her things. He looked down at the black velvet box in his hands. He was going to be truly evil this evening, in that case.

He raised his fist to tap on the door just as Rachel opened it. She jumped back, her beautiful lips shaped in a surprised *O* that made him yearn to touch them.

"You surprised me," she said, a hesitant smile on her face. "Are you ready to go?"

"Almost." He took a step back to take in Rachel in all her glory. She was magnificent. The blue of her eyes matched her gown. "Uh, before we go, I bought you something to go with the dress."

A wary look came into her eyes. "What?"

He'd automatically hidden the box behind his back when she'd opened the door. Before he showed her, he decided to do a little advance work. "Rachel, all the women tonight are going to be wearing jewels."

"I'm sure there will be many who won't have jewels, John. You're exaggerating. Besides, I don't have any." Her chin came up, as if he were impugning her honor.

John shrugged and grinned, bringing his hand forward. "Yes, you do."

She looked at velvet box and then up at him. As if he hadn't spoken, hadn't offered her the box, she swept up her long skirt and headed toward the stairs.

"Rachel! Where are you going?"

She ignored him.

He raced after her, grasping her arm just before she started downstairs. Although he pulled her to a halt, she refused to face him.

"Won't you even look at it?" he pleaded.

"No."

"Why not? You might like it."

Now she turned to him and pushed against his chest with both hands. "Of course, I might like it! Do you think I don't like new clothes, new cars, new everything? Do you really think I'm that odd?"

"Rachel—"

"You think I prefer beat-up old cars that have oil leaks and always break down? That I like to make my own clothes and teach summer school?" She continued to push him back, fire in her eyes.

"Rachel—"

"Maybe you think I like being alone, staying home, never going out. You probably think I'm an old fuddy-duddy who's no fun at all!"

John couldn't hold back a chuckle and his arms came around her slim curves. "Yeah. I think you're an old fuddy-duddy, the sexiest old fuddy-duddy I've ever seen." Before she could protest again, his lips covered hers. He loved the softness of her. The taste of her. Her.

He jerked back from her as he realized what had just passed through his head. No. No, he didn't love her. He was just turned on by a sexy lady.

"Here," he said, thrusting the box into her hand. "Put this on and wear it. If you don't want it after tonight, you can sell it, or give it back, or throw it away. But tonight, you have to look like your husband is successful, okay?"

He charged past her down the stairs, hoping to run away from his dangerous thoughts.

RACHEL HURRIED DOWN the stairs, belying her weariness. She wasn't used to such late nights. They'd gotten home about one-thirty in the morning.

While John had walked Polly across the street, Rachel had quickly removed the sapphire-and-diamond pendant he had given her earlier, put it back in its little velvet box and left it on the dresser in John's room.

If she hadn't given it back last night, she might have kept it forever. It was beautiful. But she couldn't keep it. Although John had given her a searching look this morning over breakfast, he'd said nothing.

"Ready, Rachel?" he called from the bottom of the stairs.

"Yes. What are you eating?" Her gaze traveled from him to Jacey, standing just behind him. "Jacey? Are you eating something, too?"

"I told you she'd catch us," Jacey said accusingly.

"Did you get into the cookies?"

"It's my fault, Rachel. They looked too good to pass up." John ducked his head as if he were ashamed.

"You can't fool me, mister. You're not sorry," she claimed in disgust. "It's nine-thirty. You just finished breakfast half an hour ago."

"We just had one, Mommy," Jacey chirped as she slipped her hand into John's.

Rachel couldn't hold back a grin any longer. "Okay, okay, since it was just one. But no more cookies at least until we get out of the driveway."

They both grinned at her leniency and headed for the door.

She sighed. John and Jacey were such friends already. Rachel worried about her child's disappointment when the year ended.

She joined them outside, where John was standing by the Volvo, although Jacey was already in the back seat.

"Do you want me to drive, or shall you?" he asked.

She appreciated the sensitivity of his question. After all, he'd made a point of putting the car in her name. She tossed him her keys. "You drive. I'm going to relax. I'm not used to late nights."

"But you had fun?"

"Yes, I did, which was a surprise."

"You thought everyone would be stuffy and no fun, didn't you? Maybe a bunch of fuddy-duddies?"

There was that blasted twinkle in his eyes again as he teased her. "Maybe that's why I enjoyed myself. I felt at home."

He burst out laughing and she stuck out her tongue, feeling like a kid again.

"What's so funny?" Jacey called from inside the station wagon. She already had her seat belt on, ready for their trip.

"Nothing, sweetie," Rachel assured her. How could she explain the pleasure she got from John's teasing? Or the relief she'd felt last night when she'd discovered she fit in with the people attending the Charity Ball. She didn't even want to try.

"Did you put the bag in the back?" she asked John.

"Uh, sort of."

They were each getting ready to slide into the car and she looked at him over its roof. "Now what?"

"I repacked everything into one bag."

She stared at him and then ducked down to look into the back of the station wagon. Instead of the beat-up duffel she'd packed, there was only a black leather bag, slightly larger. Popping back up, she demanded, "Why did you do that?"

"Because," he explained softly, "I thought it would look kind of strange for our things to be in different bags. Like we hadn't packed together."

Her cheeks reddened as she thought of the personal items he'd handled. "You should have let me repack everything."

"Not a chance. I didn't want you handling my underwear," he said primly, his nose in the air, but with that twinkle back in his eyes.

"John Crewes, I am definitely going to wring your neck as soon as I get you alone."

His grin spread. "I can't wait, Rachel Crewes. I just can't wait."

Chapter Thirteen

Other than Jacey's occasional comments or questions, they rode in silence until they were out of Kansas City. They were going to Perry Lake, only about an hour away. John watched Rachel out of the corner of his eye, enjoying her relaxed companionship.

"Oh, by the way," he said, suddenly remembering, "when I walked Polly home last night, she wanted to know how soon you'd be moved out of your house. She's got a friend who wants to rent it."

Rachel's body tensed, and she frowned. "I know. She mentioned it."

When she said nothing else, he prompted, "Well?"

"I don't know."

"I thought you were going to save your rent money for—well, for later?"

"I am."

"Then, the sooner you vacate, the better it will be for you," he reasoned.

"Thanks for that exercise in logic," she murmured, her face turned away.

"Rachel—"

"Just leave it, John. I'll take care of it."

Her attitude made him think more closely about how the move must be affecting her. She was probably having difficulty letting go of her home. If she wanted to keep it, he supposed he didn't mind, but it was senseless to pay rent when she didn't have to.

A sudden thought struck him. He glanced sideways at Rachel, as if to be sure she hadn't noticed anything, but she was still staring out the window. She'd refuse, of course, but he could do it without her approval. He'd just buy the house, put it in her name, and then lease it to Polly's friend. Not only would Rachel not have to pay rent, but she'd also get income from the house.

Then, when their year was over, she and Jacey would still be close enough for him to take care of them, watch over them. He already knew how lonesome he'd be when they moved out of his house. Four days, and he didn't want to go back to living alone.

It wasn't just the food Rachel cooked, although she was great in the kitchen. It wasn't just the companionship they shared, including Jacey. It wasn't even Jacey's smiles and hugs, which were warm enough to heat a house in winter. He couldn't even say it was the sexual tension that hummed between him and Rachel at certain moments. It was a combination of all those things.

After years of being alone, concentrating on work, he felt as if he'd broken out into the sunshine. His senses were heightened, his gaze sharpened, his body tightened to a new intensity that stimulated him to greater heights.

"Are we almost there?" Jacey asked from the back seat.

John automatically looked at Rachel as she turned, and their smiles met. He fought the sudden urge to pull over to the side of the road and kiss her senseless.

"Not yet, Jacey. It will only be about fifteen more minutes," Rachel answered.

"Can you tell time?" John asked, wondering why he hadn't thought of that question before.

"A'course," Jacey said indignantly. "I'm not a baby."

"But you don't have a watch."

"Mommy said maybe at Christmas," Jacey assured him.

"I could—"

"John!" Rachel snapped. "Don't even think about it."

"But, Rachel—"

"John, you can't keep buying us things."

Damn. He'd upset her again. And if she rejected the idea of his buying her daughter a cheap watch, how was she going to feel about his buying her a house? He already knew the answer to that question.

Squaring his jaw, he focused on the road ahead of him, but inside he was plotting. Rachel deserved the best. He owed her. And he was going to pay her for her sacrifice. One way or another.

When they pulled into the campground behind David Wester's minivan, Jacey was anxious to be released from the station wagon. Rachel gave her permission to find Lisbeth, and she and John stood beside their car to watch the happy reunion between the two little girls.

"You'd think they'd been apart for years," he murmured.

"It probably seemed like it to them."

John let his gaze leave the children to look at the people emerging from the other vehicles. "Six couples and a lot of kids. I wonder what David has in mind?"

"And one of them is very pregnant. I don't think she should be so far from a hospital," Rachel added, staring at a young woman just getting out of a sedan.

John noted the soon-to-be new mother and privately agreed with Rachel. He hoped there would be no emergencies. He knew nothing about childbirth.

"Were you ever that big with Jacey?" he asked, fascinated by the pregnant woman.

Rachel groaned. "I thought I was as big as a Volkswagen. Now, I'm not sure."

"And you were all alone?"

"Yes," was her clipped reply, and she pressed her lips tightly together.

He couldn't resist putting his arm around her shoulders. "I didn't mean to bring up bad times."

Much to his surprise, she relaxed in his embrace. "They weren't, really. At least, in the end they weren't. Jacey is the center of my universe."

"I can understand that," he replied, leaning over to kiss her forehead.

"That's what I like to see," David boomed behind them, jolting them both.

"What's that?" John asked, dropping his arm from Rachel's shoulders.

"Affection. Touching. All those good things. I firmly believe it's the little things that make a marriage work."

"Now, David, don't start lecturing," Carol Wester teased, coming up behind her husband. "You and John need to organize a tent-raising crew, while we women get started on lunch. Those kids are going to be hungry before you know it."

David led John away and Carol took Rachel over to introduce her to the other women. The children were sent to bring in firewood while the women got out the fixings for hamburgers.

Rachel watched the men set up the tents in a large circle around the campfire. With all the changes in her life the past week, somehow she hadn't considered the sleeping arrangements on this camping trip. She felt a little stunned by her obtuseness.

"How many tents will there be?" she asked, as casually as possible.

"I believe David planned on eight. One for each of the families, and then one for the older boys and one for the older girls," Carol told them. She turned to the other ladies. "Sarah, you have three kids, don't you, and Mary, you have four, and, of course, the one on the way."

"Yes," Mary said, pausing to rub her back. "And if this one doesn't come soon, I'm going to give up. I feel like I've been pregnant forever."

All the women nodded in understanding.

"The other two still have little children," Carol continued, "so we thought everyone could keep their little ones with them."

Rachel breathed a sigh of relief. "Good idea. Jacey wouldn't want to be with a group of strange kids." Even if she wanted to, Rachel wasn't about to permit it. She needed her daughter as a buffer between her and John.

"You'll also be glad to know we have air mattresses for everyone," Carol added with a chuckle. "David likes to go first-class."

Rachel certainly couldn't complain about the provisions the Westers had made for their convenience. Lunch was delicious and the cleanup relatively easy. David then asked the older children to escort the younger ones to the playground nearby while he talked with their parents.

Wondering what was coming next, Rachel shot a concerned look at John. He interpreted her worry as a mother's fear for her child's safety. "Jacey will be fine. We can see the playground from here," he assured her.

"Do you know what David wants to discuss?" she whispered.

"No, but it's probably nothing to worry about."

Easy for him to say, she thought, then wondered why it would be any easier for John. Jacey, of course. She was the added dimension that made it more difficult for Rachel. Except that John always considered Jacey. Rachel could give him credit for that.

"Everyone have a seat," David invited, gesturing to the camp chairs he'd provided.

John chose a flat rock near the campfire and pulled Rachel down beside him. When he draped his arm across her shoulders, she stared up at him, and he whispered in response to her unspoken question, "For show."

Since he added a kiss on her neck before turning his face back toward David, Rachel wasn't sure she believed him. He loved to tease her.

"The reason I asked you all to come camping with us this weekend is because I'm starting a new project, and I'd like your help." David paused to look at each couple. "I've seen all of you interact as a family, and I've been impressed with the love and happiness displayed there. What you may not know about each other, since most of you are strangers, is that every family here today is a blended family."

The couples all looked around at each other, smiling acknowledgment of their situations.

"As you know, I only recently joined your group, though I'm not the most recent newlywed. John and Rachel carry that honor. But I'm aware of how many couples in America are going or have gone through the adjustment period resulting from the mixing of two families. I want my next video to deal with that subject. And I want your help."

Rachel thought she was going to die.

JACEY AND LISBETH climbed the jungle gym on the playground.

"This is fun," Jacey said. "I'm glad you invited us."

"Me, too!" Lisbeth agreed with a giggle.

"Sleeping in a tent is going to be fun. I've never done that before."

"Yeah. But I'm glad I get to sleep with my mommy and daddy. It's a little scary."

"Do you all sleep in the same bed?" She remembered Lisbeth's earlier complaint.

"No. I get a sleeping bag by myself. Mommy and Daddy share the big one."

Jacey nibbled on her bottom lip. Was that what would happen in her tent? Would she see her mommy and John in the big sleeping bag? Somehow, she didn't think so. She thought her mommy would make John take the sleeping bag by himself. After all, they didn't share the same room at home.

She looked at her friend and then back toward the campfire where the parents were all sitting. "I wish we could spend the night together," she said, watching Lisbeth closely.

"Yeah! That'd be fun."

They swung down from the bars and then climbed them again. "We could tell each other stories to help us sleep," Jacey said wistfully.

"Yeah. And I've got my own flashlight," Lisbeth bragged.

"I don't have one."

"You need one at night. There's no bathroom in the tent," Lisbeth explained with a giggle. "But I could share with you if we were in the same tent."

"That'd be neat."

"I know!" Lisbeth squealed.

"What?"

"Let's ask my mommy if you can move your sleeping bag into my tent."

"Do you think she'd let me?"

"Sure. And we can ask your mommy, too."

"Let's ask your mommy first, and then she can ask my mommy. That would be best."

"Okay."

Yeah, that would be best. Because Jacey didn't think her mommy was going to like the idea. She didn't want to make her mommy or John angry. She just wanted them to be a family.

WHEN THEY TOOK A break from their discussions, Rachel carried the bag John had packed to the tent Carol had designated as theirs. She breathed a sigh of relief when she noted the double sleeping bag and the single laid out on the other side.

Close quarters might be a little difficult, but John was a gentleman. He would take the single and she and Jacey the double. With their tent flap zipped, no one would know the difference.

She pushed the bag to the back of the tent and sat down on the double sleeping bag. The air mattress was wonderful. She considered stretching out for a nap. Her late night and the tension of the day was catching up with her. David had asked that they have another discussion group before dinner.

She'd kept quiet most of the time this afternoon. After all, as the newest blended family, they weren't exactly the voice of experience. What an understatement. They weren't even a blended family. A marriage license didn't make them a family.

"Daddy!"

Jacey's voice sounded across the campground, and Rachel moaned. Jacey didn't need a marriage license to adopt John Crewes. She had been enthusiastic from the start.

"Rachel?"

John's voice sounded just outside the tent. "Yes, John, come on in."

"Everything okay?"

"Just fine," she assured him as he ducked into the tent. "I was just considering a nap."

"And I was just considering an oatmeal-raisin cookie. Got any left?" He looked around the small area.

"There were plenty left a few minutes ago. They're outside, on the picnic table."

"Damn. I'll bet those blasted kids have inhaled them."

"John! You're supposed to be a loving father, remember?" she protested, unable to resist teasing him.

"I love Jacey. I don't have to love those other kids. They're going to eat all my cookies."

"Daddy, Mommy!" Jacey called and then pulled back the tent flap. "Hi."

"Hi, sweetheart. Did you have fun?" John asked.

"Yeah, this is great!"

"Do you want to lie down on your bed and rest awhile?" Rachel asked, although she was sure she knew the answer. Jacey considered herself much too old for naps.

"No! Where are the cookies? Me and Lisbeth wanted a snack."

"They're on the picnic table. Mrs. Wester has something for you to drink, too."

Before Jacey could run off, John stopped her. "Jacey, bring me some cookies, okay? And a soda would be nice, too."

"Okay," she agreed and disappeared.

"I think she's having a good time," John said, satisfaction in his voice.

"Of course, she is."

"Are you?"

Rachel leaned back on the sleeping bag, propping her head up with one hand. "It's not bad."

"They seem like nice people."

"Yes, they do. Especially Mary."

"Yeah. She gets a lot done for someone as pregnant as she is." John moved to the edge of the sleeping bag, shifting Rachel's legs over as he sat down.

She pulled herself away from his touch, making sure there was plenty of room between them. "I thought you'd sleep on the single mattress and Jacey and I would take this one,'' she hurriedly explained.

''Yeah, I figured,'' he assured her, that twinkle in his eye.

Rachel was embarrassed and said nothing. John seemed content to sit silently. It was a pleasantly cool afternoon, but the shade of the tent was welcome.

''When you were pregnant with Jacey, did she kick a lot?''

''All the time,'' Rachel complained, although she smiled. ''I thought for sure I had a little boy, a future soccer star.''

''Girls can play soccer.''

''I know. I started to sign Jacey up for it this spring, but I thought we'd wait until next year.''

''Why?''

''It's difficult to get her to practice because of my job.''

''Oh. Does she take dance lessons, or piano lessons?''

''No.'' She didn't want to add that she couldn't afford lessons. After she taught school this summer and used the extra income to pay off her college loans, then she could provide her child with lessons.

''Would you want to stay home with Jacey instead of teaching?''

Rachel started to dismiss his question. She didn't want to get to know John better, or for him to know her. She was too attracted to him as it was. But the sincerity in his gaze wouldn't allow her to ignore his interest.

''No. Jacey's not home all day now. Next year, she'll be at school almost as long as I am. I wouldn't mind teaching part-time, maybe just the mornings.''

She shrugged. "That's a ridiculous thought, because teachers never get ahead financially. I'll always be teaching, until I'm old and gray and have to retire."

"This next year, you could—"

"No, John. Don't even start. This next year, we're going to continue as we always have. That's the best way."

"I'm not sure—"

"Rachel? Are you in there?"

"Yes, Carol. Come in." It sounded ridiculous to be so formal in a canvas tent.

The tent flap was pulled back and Carol ducked her head in. "You sure it's all right?"

"Of course. We were just talking," John assured her. "I can leave if you need to talk to Rachel alone."

Without thinking, Rachel grabbed the back belt-loop of his jeans. She wasn't about to be abandoned by that rat!

"No, that's not necessary. In fact, you'll probably both like what I have to say," Carol said with a smile that suggested naughty things.

John's eyebrows rose as he looked first at Carol and then at Rachel.

Blushing, Rachel sat up, letting go of John's jeans.

"Our two little darlings have come up with a plan," Carol explained. "They thought tonight would be a lot more fun if they got to sleep in the same tent."

Rachel worked to hide her dismay. Then she hurriedly tried to make the best of things. "Of course. We'll be happy to have Lisbeth stay with us."

"No, no, Jacey must come to our tent. You see, we have the largest tent. David said it's a perk he deserves because Lisbeth and I bring so much stuff," Carol explained with a chuckle. "There wouldn't be room to bring another sleeping bag and air mattress into your tent.''

Rachel looked at the space around her and knew Carol was right. But she didn't want to admit it. ''Couldn't the girls sleep in the same sleeping bag?''

''Oh, they'd never get to sleep that way. In separate bags, I'm hoping they'll drift off by midnight. And, in the meantime, that will give you and John a night without kids. I know she's in a different room at home, but you don't even have to worry about her tonight. I'll take good care of her.''

Assuming they were in agreement, Carol backed out of the tent. Just as she was lowering the tent flap, she added, ''And you two can do whatever you want.''

Dead silence followed Carol's departure.

''Does she think we're going to have an orgy in a canvas tent with neighbors five feet on either side of us?'' Rachel finally demanded, her voice tight with tension.

''I'm game if you are,'' John told her, a grin on his lips.

Chapter Fourteen

"John Crewes!" Rachel protested.

"Hey, I only offered to cooperate. You were the one grabbing hold of me, not the other way around."

"I didn't want you to abandon me to—"

"Knock, knock!" David called from outside the tent.

John rolled his eyes at Rachel even as he called out for David to come in.

"Shoot, John, if I'd known you were in here," David said as he lifted the tent flap, "I would've told Carol to make *you* move Jacey's bed."

Move Jacey's bed.

Rachel sat in frozen silence as the two men joked over the chore. Somehow, in the brief minutes since Carol's departure, Rachel hadn't realized exactly how much Jacey's arrangement would affect her and John. But when David, with John's help, rolled up the single sleeping bag and took it and the air mattress from the tent, the result was obvious.

She and John were supposed to sleep in the double sleeping bag—together.

Sharing a tent with John presented difficulties, but there was still enough space to avoid touching each other. Sharing a sleeping bag was a different matter.

She couldn't do it. She simply couldn't align her body with John's and go to sleep. A brief whimper escaped as she considered the torture of lying next to him in the darkness.

She'd been a naive girl when she'd met Dirk, Jacey's eventual father. He'd been experienced, sexy, determined to seduce her. And he'd done so with relative ease, much to her embarrassment afterward. But his kisses, his touch, weren't even on the same chart with John Crewes's.

Even understanding her sexual nature now, and taking all precautions to resist him, Rachel melted when John kissed her. Against all her self-admonitions, she simply melted.

And now she was going to spend the entire night in the same sleeping bag with him?

Maybe the relative closeness of their neighbors would save her. Or maybe John wouldn't kiss her. Or have any interest in touching her. Maybe.

John raised the tent flap and entered the tent again. Rachel looked away. She couldn't meet his gaze. He might realize how panic-stricken she was.

She felt the air mattress shift as he settled down beside her again, but still she didn't look at him.

"Want a cookie?"

Such a mundane offer was a ridiculous contrast to her steamy thoughts and she turned to stare at him. With a grin, he held out one of her oatmeal-raisin cookies. "I snagged a few on the way back."

He also offered one of the cans of soda he had tucked under his arm. "I thought a little sugar might lessen the shock of sleeping with me."

She glared at him even as she took both. "I suppose it won't bother you at all!"

"Oh, it'll bother me, Rachel," he drawled. "A lot."

"Then why didn't you say something? I didn't realize—"

"Neither did I, until David arrived. By then, it was too late. What reason would I have given for changing our minds? We didn't trust them to take care of Jacey?"

She knew he couldn't have said that. Truthfully, in all the time since his and David's departure, she hadn't been able to come up with an excuse. It was unfair of her to expect him to have done so in a lot less time. "I know. But what are we going to do?"

He took a long sip of his soda, tipping his head back, and she was tempted to stroke his exposed skin. With a gasp, she drew back even farther from him.

"I suspect we'll sleep on this air mattress."

"I have another solution," she said, hoping for a different outcome. "I'll give you the sleeping bag and you can sleep over there." She gestured to the empty side of the tent.

"Nope."

"John, we can't—we can't share this sleeping bag."

"That sounds better than waking up tomorrow morning a cripple. I'm too old to sleep on this hard, rocky ground."

It was hard. They hadn't worried about seeking out grassy knolls or rock-free areas because they had the air mattresses. But she would do what she had to do.

"Then I'll take the sleeping bag."

"Rachel, I can't let you do that. You wouldn't get any sleep and you'd be miserable the rest of the trip."

"No, I wouldn't."

"You remind me of Jacey. She gets that stubborn look just like you."

"I'm not being childish," she told him. "I'm just trying to prevent anything from happening."

"Rachel, as you so wisely pointed out, this is a canvas tent and we have neighbors on both sides. We're just going to sleep side by side, not have an orgy."

She didn't respond. How could she? Her mind was taken up with the mental picture of an orgy with only the two of them.

"Come on, let's go for a walk. We'll take Jacey and Lisbeth with us." He set aside his snack, stood, half bent-over, and offered a hand to Rachel.

She traded the soda and cookie for his hand without hesitation. She was all for getting out of the tent. By the time morning rolled around, she suspected she'd hate those four canvas walls.

THE REST OF THE DAY passed with relative pleasure—as long as Rachel didn't think about the night to come. They had hiked along the edge of the lake with the girls. John had shown infinite patience, pointing out things of interest and answering the millions of questions children ask.

Dinner preparation had given Rachel a respite from his continuous presence, but, perversely, she missed him, and her gaze kept straying to the game of horseshoes the men were playing. When their eyes met, she would quickly turn away, pretending some urgency in the task at hand.

After dinner, David asked them all, as a group, to discuss the difficulties they'd faced as they became families. John gathered Jacey into his lap and clasped Rachel's hand in his.

Rachel ignored the discussion going on around her. She watched her daughter and John. Jacey's ponytail bounced with her every move, brushing John's jaw. Occasionally he'd lean forward and place a kiss on her forehead, or she'd rest her head against his broad chest. Once, she leaned back and patted his cheek with her hand, whispering something Rachel couldn't hear.

"What did you want to say, Jacey?" David asked.

Concerned, Rachel leaned forward, but John squeezed her hand, telling her to trust Jacey.

"My daddy talks to me," Jacey announced, as if she'd said something of great import. "He asks me to sit with him while he eats his dinner and tell him about school and things."

"Like Mr. Sam?" David asked, smiling gently.

"Yeah, and he 'members."

"You're right, Jacey. That's very special." David nodded in approval at John.

David was right. It was special that John took the time to listen to Jacey. And he didn't do that to impress David. He hadn't known David would find out whether he took the time for Jacey. It was just something that came naturally to John.

It was a real shame that he wasn't a father to a dozen kids. Rachel thought he would be perfect. When their year was past, perhaps he would find a woman to love and have a family with. She wanted John to be happy. But her stomach hurt at the thought.

Too soon, in Rachel's opinion, the small children went to bed. She helped Jacey settle in the Westers' tent with Lisbeth, amid much giggling. When Rachel returned to the campfire, John had moved back to the big rock they'd sat on at lunch, and he pulled her down to sit between his legs, her back against his chest. His arms encircled her and she found herself gently cradled.

That was another amazing factor she hadn't expected in John Crewes. His gentleness. She'd expected a hardened man, bitter, thinking only of himself. Instead, John had been patient, teasing, kind. His love for Jacey seemed unending, and he was sensitive to Rachel's feelings before she even recognized them herself.

"Rachel, you haven't said much," David observed, looking at her over the campfire.

"We haven't been married all that long," she replied with a shrug, hoping no one guessed just how short their marriage really was. "I think we're still in the honeymoon phase."

"And loving it," John assured their audience. She looked up in time to see him wiggle his eyebrows suggestively.

Talk continued for another couple of hours, but Rachel said nothing else. How could she? Her senses were engaged in warfare. John's touch encouraged abandonment of all self-discipline. She fought giving in.

Close to eleven, John whispered, "Ready for bed?"

The low, seductive timbre of his voice sent shivers all over her, and Rachel shifted uneasily. "Uh, no, I'm not sleepy at all."

"Liar," John accused with a chuckle. "You've been yawning for the past half hour."

"Just nerves," she whispered tersely.

"Well," David said with a stretch, "I think Carol and I will turn in. After all, we have dual alarm clocks in our tent in the persons of Jacey and Lisbeth. John, we'll keep an eye on Jacey in the morning if you two want to sleep past dawn."

"Thanks, David. I'll owe you one."

John's arms disappeared from around her and his rock-hard chest no longer supported her. Before she could adjust to the change, he was in front of her, offering a hand to help her stand.

"Come on, Sleeping Beauty. Time for bed."

Since there was a general exodus and one of the men was smothering the campfire, Rachel could think of no excuse to postpone the inevitable. She groaned as she stood. "That rock needs a cushion."

"I'll give you a massage," he offered with a grin.

"No, thank you."

"Your loss. Come on, I'll walk you to the facilities, since we only have one flashlight."

When they finally headed for their tent, most of the camp had settled in for the night. There were murmurs of voices rising from various tents, but otherwise, the silence of the forest fell around them.

"Look at all the stars," John said, catching her arm before she could duck into the tent. He'd turned off the flashlight, making it easier to look heavenward.

She straightened and looked up, admiring the beauty of the night, and his arms came around her, as they had done while they were seated on the rock. Tensing, she tried to pull away.

"Relax, Rachel. I'm just keeping you warm."

"Much warmer, and I'll go off like a Roman candle," she muttered and then regretted her words.

"You, too?"

"Why do you continue to—to touch me if you know what it's doing to us?" she whispered fiercely.

"I can't help myself," he murmured before turning her around and kissing her.

The white-hot heat of the brightest star seemed mild compared to Rachel's response to his kiss. All evening he had caressed her, cradled her, making her want more and more of his touch. She met his embrace as if they were long-lost lovers.

"You two need to get inside your tent before the teenagers see you and get ideas," Mary's husband suggested with a laugh as he walked past them.

"Right," John responded huskily.

Rachel buried her face in his chest, embarrassed to have been observed in her surrender to John's sexy kiss.

"Come on, sweetheart," he whispered, pulling her after him into the tent.

When he would have continued their embrace once they were inside, she backed away from him.

"No, John. We can't. Everyone else may think our marriage is real, but we both know it's not." She reached the far side of the tent, an entire five feet away, and stopped, holding her breath.

"That marriage license looked pretty real to me," he growled.

"The license may be real, but the marriage isn't. I let my hormones rule my head once. I won't do it again." She hoped she sounded more confident that she felt. Her knees were shaking. If he ignored her protest and took her back into his arms, she'd be lost.

"Get ready for bed," he ordered in clipped tones and turned and left the tent.

After the first shocked moment, Rachel didn't waste any time. She changed from jeans to jogging shorts and a T-shirt. Then she pulled the sleeping bag from the air mattress and took it to the other side of the tent. At least she had her own pillow from home. Her head would probably be the only part of her body that wouldn't ache in the morning.

By the time John returned, she'd settled into her new bed, her back turned to the tent entrance. Even so, she knew at once when John stepped inside.

With the flashlight left sitting on the air mattress so he wouldn't have any trouble locating his things, he also wouldn't have any difficulty understanding what she'd done. Jacey had insisted on toting along a beach towel, in case it was warm enough to swim the next day, and Rachel had spread it out on the air mattress for John.

There was a moment after his entrance when he didn't move, and Rachel tensed, waiting for his reaction. Then he moved to the back of the tent where she'd left the bag. The sound of his zipper being lowered was almost more than she could bear as her imagination ran wild. She heard the denim brush against his flesh with agonizing slowness as he removed his jeans.

Rachel covered her ears beneath the cloth of the sleeping bag, trying to avoid the sounds that aroused her imagination. It was going to be hard enough to sleep on the rocky ground without hearing every breath John took.

Even so, she kept waiting for him to lie down on the air mattress. Suddenly, she was swung up into the air, sleeping bag and all. Her gasp was shushed by John, his face close to hers as he clasped her against his chest.

"You're being stubborn, Rachel Crewes. I told you we were both sleeping on the air mattress."

"Put me down, John," she whispered urgently. Her voice was the only weapon she had, since her arms were inside the sleeping bag.

"I intend to. On the air mattress."

"John, we can't sleep together. It would be too—" She didn't know exactly how to explain what it would be unless she used the word *torturous*. And she didn't want to give away that much about her feelings.

"I'm not going to make love to you until you're willing, Rachel. I promise you that. Tonight, we'll just sleep. But it will be together, on the air mattress, not you huddled up on the rocks and me over here. That's dumb."

Before she could organize any logical reply, he placed her on the soft cushion and started unzipping the sleeping bag.

"Scoot over unless you want me to lie down on top of you."

She scurried to the other side, pulling her pillow with her. His suggestive remark hadn't helped matters.

He plopped his pillow down beside her, slid into the sleeping bag and turned off the flashlight. The immediate response of her body to the comfort of the mattress almost overcame her response to John's body next to hers. She pressed against the zipper on the far side, trying to allow as much space between them as possible, but his heat stole beneath the cover to envelop her.

Just the thought of his long legs next to hers, his broad chest only a heartbeat away, made her breathing speed up. *I'm going to be panting like a dog if I'm not careful.* She concentrated on taking deep breaths, hoping to keep her mind off his nearness.

"Relax, Rachel. We're just going to sleep," he repeated.

Yeah, right. Did he really believe it would be that easy? To distract herself, she thought of several names she'd like to call John Crewes for that calm remark. When a slight snore interrupted her thoughts several minutes later, she turned to stare at him in the darkness.

He was asleep? While she was lying here feeling tortured, he had drifted off to sleep? She fought the urge to slam her elbow into his chest. She hated suffering alone. Especially when the suffering was his fault.

If he hadn't kissed her under the stars, if he weren't so sexy, so loving, she'd be able to resist him.

She shifted in the sleeping bag, and her arm brushed against his chest. Softly moaning, she moved away. Then one foot encountered a strong leg. She ran her toes against the hair on his leg, unable to resist the little tease.

Abruptly, he shifted, looping one leg over hers.

Holding her breath, she waited to see if he'd awaken, but he didn't. She released the tension with a sigh. Relaxing against him felt heavenly. Could she trust him?

He was asleep and seemed to be a deep sleeper. And he'd proved she could trust him when she was awake.

Maybe she should follow John's example and just go to sleep. And dream of running her hands all over his big, strong body, of having him wrap his arms around her, of loving her.

It was so tempting to give in to the desire that filled her. But in a year it would all be over. And her heart would be broken.

No, she couldn't give in. But she could dream...just a little.

A LOUD NOISE BROUGHT Rachel partially awake.

"What's that?" she mumbled.

"Just thunder. I think it's raining," John's voice sounded beside her. "Nothing to worry about. Go back to sleep."

Feeling secure, Rachel obeyed him automatically, her eyes drifting shut. His hand rubbed her stomach, beneath her T-shirt, and she stirred again, sighing with pleasure.

"I'll bet you were beautiful when you were pregnant with Jacey," he muttered.

She half laughed, half moaned as he continued stroking her. His thigh moved atop her leg, an easy feat since they were pressed, spoon-fashion, together. It felt so natural, as if they'd always slept like that, that she only settled against him more. Dimly feeling his arousal, she felt as if she were suspended, waiting for him to bring her fully awake. When he only held her, his hand resting against her stomach, she drifted back to sleep.

"MOMMY SAID WE shouldn't wake them up," Lisbeth whispered to Jacey. When Jacey didn't respond, she tugged on her shirt. "Jacey!" she whispered louder.

Jacey turned around, irritated with her friend. "I'm not going to wake them up," she whispered in return.

"I'm just going to get my bucket and shovel. Mommy let me bring them so I could play in the sand."

Jacey returned to her task of slowly unzipping the tent flap. That wasn't her only purpose, of course, but she couldn't tell Lisbeth that she wanted to see if her plan had worked. She wanted to see if her mommy and daddy were sleeping in the same bed the way Lisbeth's had.

The first thing she'd done when she'd awakened this morning was to look at Lisbeth's parents. Just as Lisbeth had said, they were in the big sleeping bag together. Lisbeth's daddy had his arm over her mommy.

Lisbeth had told her last night, before her parents came to bed, that sometimes she got jealous of her mommy because she got more attention from her new daddy than Lisbeth did. Jacey had thought about it, but she didn't feel that way.

She knew John loved her. She couldn't explain it, but she knew. Just as she knew her mommy loved her.

She also knew mommies and daddies had to love each other if they were to stay married. That's why she had to help her mommy and John love each other. And it seemed to her the best way to do that was for them to do things like Lisbeth's parents.

Her heart beating faster, Jacey lifted the tent flap and fearfully searched the shadowy darkness. Had her plan worked?

Looking at Lisbeth over her shoulder, she motioned for her friend to stay back. Then she tiptoed into the tent, letting the flap fall behind her.

She snuck up to the edge of the air mattress and stared down at Mommy and John. They were even better than Lisbeth's parents, she decided, because they were both snuggling together. Lots closer, too.

In fact, she wondered if maybe Lisbeth had been wrong. 'Cause the way they were sleeping, there was lots of room left over for Jacey. That would be neat, the three of them in bed together. She couldn't hold back a giggle at the thought.

"Jacey?" John whispered, raising his head to look at her.

"Sorry. I came to get my bucket and shovel."

"Okay, sweetheart. I think they're still in the back of the station wagon. It's not locked. Be quiet and don't wake your mommy."

"I won't. Bye-bye."

Jacey emerged from the tent with all the excitement of Christmas morning. It had worked! They were sleeping together, just like a real family.

JOHN LAID HIS HEAD BACK down on the pillow, giving himself a minute to evaluate the situation. He was in the sleeping bag with Rachel, his body plastered to hers, his hands in inappropriate places, and all he wanted to do was wake her up slowly and make unending love to her.

Not exactly what he'd promised.

If Rachel awoke before he extricated himself, she'd never forgive him. Or trust him again.

With a reluctance that was almost overpowering, John slid out of the sleeping bag. Once he was standing, he took off the jogging shorts he'd worn to bed and slipped into jeans and a polo shirt.

Rachel hadn't moved at all. After picking up his tennis shoes and socks, he peered over the bed until he could see her face. She was breathing evenly, her eyes closed, and he remembered with longing the rhythm of her breathing matching his through the night.

With a sigh, he tiptoed from the tent.

RACHEL WAITED A FULL five minutes after John's departure before she moved. She didn't want him to know Jacey had awakened her when she had John. Or that Rachel had realized how closely entwined their bodies had been. Or how heavenly it had felt.

After all her protests of the night before, John must think her a terrible tease. She hadn't stuck to her side of the sleeping bag even before she'd fallen asleep. With guilty pleasure, she remembered touching him, relaxing against him. Then there was a vague memory of a thunderstorm and John comforting her. His comfort had been so stimulating, it was a wonder she hadn't begged him to make love to her.

What was she going to do? Every time the man got near her, her heart raced, her hands itched to touch him. She longed for his kisses.

How was she going to continue to resist her husband?

Chapter Fifteen

First thing Monday morning, John made arrangements to buy Rachel's house in her name. The landlord had been a little reluctant to sell, but John had gone above market value to entice him. Since John wasn't financing his purchase, they agreed to close on it Thursday.

Rachel was going to be angry. But John didn't care. He was enjoying buying things for her. Quite a change from his first marriage.

At least, finding ways to give gifts to Rachel took his mind off sleeping with her. And after Saturday night, that hadn't been an easy task. When he'd crawled into bed last night, he'd missed her warmth next to him. He'd missed more than her warmth. He wanted to make love to her. For the rest of his life.

He spun around in his chair and stared out the office window. "Okay, I admit it," he professed to an invisible audience. "I love her."

He'd promised himself he'd never fall in love again. But he had. And he didn't regret it.

At least this time was different. He'd fallen in love with Jacey first. When he'd seen Rachel, he'd wanted her, but he hadn't loved her. But Rachel's courage, determination and big heart had him falling faster than a bungee jumper.

As for Jacey, she was one child in a million. He'd never realized he wanted children, a family, until the little moppet had looked over his fence.

And even though he bought the house next door for Rachel, he didn't intend for her to move back into it. He wanted her to move, all right, but only across the hall into his bed. Permanently.

"Mr. Wester is on line one," his secretary said through the intercom.

"Thanks. Hi, David," he said cheerfully as he picked up the phone. Today he was ready to take on the world.

"John, I hope I didn't interrupt anything important."

"Nope. Well, I was just thinking about how much I love my wife and daughter, but nothing other than that."

"Glad to hear it. The three of you made a welcome addition to the weekend. And that's what I called about."

"Yes?" John said cautiously.

"I want you, Rachel and Jacey to be on the video I'm going to produce about blended families. What do you say?"

"Don't you use actors for those?" John asked, stalling for time. He didn't think Rachel would agree to David's request.

"Never!" David exclaimed, sounding offended. "We always interview real people. We're not using smoke and mirrors, John. We only tell the truth."

"I appreciate that, David. But I'm not sure Rachel would agree to your request. She's a very private person, you know.'' So private she didn't even want to talk to John, much less the viewers of the video.

''I can understand that, John, but the three of you would be really terrific. Would you ask her and see what she says?''

''Well, of course, David, I'll ask her. Can I give you her answer tomorrow? She teaches, you know, and it's almost impossible to talk to her during the day.''

''Sure. You can have several days to make up your minds. We're doing a bare-bones script, though most of it is impromptu. We won't be ready to make any hard decisions until the end of the week.''

''Thanks. I'll let you know.''

He hung up the phone and thought about his promise. He was pretty sure Rachel would say no, but at least he had something to talk to her about. All of Sunday, Rachel had avoided even discussing the weather with him. As soon as Jacey had been tucked in last night, she'd retreated to her bedroom, claiming papers to grade.

With David's request, he'd at least have her attention for a few minutes. Maybe they could reestablish the friendship that had been growing between them. He had to have that as a beginning.

Because he was determined that one day, when she was ready, Rachel would be his wife in every sense of the word. But first he had to prove to her that she could trust him. Her experience with Jacey's father had left her unable to trust. Especially sexual attraction.

With a groan, he promised himself he'd keep his distance, not touch her, unless she asked him to. He laughed. Yeah, right. That was hardly likely to happen.

He turned back to his work. Time to get busy if he wanted to get out of the office at a decent hour. And dinner with Jacey and Rachel was on the top of his list.

AFTER THE CAMPING TRIP and the success she'd had bringing her mommy and John together, Jacey was happy on Monday morning. She couldn't wait to talk to Lisbeth about the fun they'd had together over the weekend.

"Hi, Lisbeth!" she called out, racing across the room to her best friend.

"Hi." Lisbeth didn't smile or move. She remained slumped across the top of her desk.

"Are you sick?"

"No."

Jacey leaned over to peer into Lisbeth's face. "Then what's wrong?"

"Nothing."

"I mean really, Lisbeth. Did you get in trouble?"

"No."

Jacey rounded the desk and put her arm around her friend. "I had fun this weekend."

"Me, too."

"Then why are you so sad?"

"I can't tell you."

"Why not?"

"Mommy said."

A sudden thought struck Jacey and she turned fearful eyes on her friend. "You're not going to move away, are you?"

"No! It's not that bad."

"Then—"

"At your desks, children. It's time to start class," Mrs. Wilson called out.

"Later," Jacey promised as she moved to take her place.

When recess was announced after reading circles, Jacey returned to her friend's side. "Are you still sad?"

"Yes."

"I won't tell anyone if you tell me what made you sad."

Lisbeth looked around and then turned back to Jacey. "You promise not to tell anyone?"

"I promise."

"Mommy may have another baby."

"Wow!" Jacey exclaimed, her eyes widening in surprise. "That's neat."

"No, it's not. They'll love the new baby and not me. It will be Daddy's real baby."

"Can't they still love you?" Jacey asked, frowning.

Lisbeth shook her head, her bottom lip pushed out. "I don't think so."

"Lots of families have more than one kid."

"Yeah, but they all have the same daddy. Daddy's not really mine." Lisbeth propped her head up and sighed.

"How do mommies have babies?" Jacey asked, as she pondered what Lisbeth had said. Would her mommy have a baby? Would John not love Jacey if Mommy did have a baby?

"I don't know. I guess it's when they get married. It just happens."

Jacey stared across the room, her finger in her mouth, as she thought about what Lisbeth had revealed.

"JACEY, THAT BAG IS too heavy for you, sweetie. You take this one, and I'll carry the big ones." Rachel set a small bag on the tailgate of the station wagon for Jacey. She liked to help her mother, and Rachel encouraged her. She believed Jacey should share in the chores even as young as she was.

"Okay, Mommy."

They reached the door and Rachel balanced a bag on her knee as she leaned against the wall to fish out the key. When she got the door open, Jacey preceded her into the house.

"In the kitchen, sweetie. Just put your bag on the breakfast table." Rachel did the same before going back to the car for another load. "If you'll get my book bag from the back seat, that would be a big help."

"Okay."

Rachel frowned as she watched her daughter go out the door ahead of her. Jacey had been remarkably silent today. Something must be bothering her.

"Jacey?"

Her daughter turned around as she reached the car door. "Yes, Mommy?"

"Is anything wrong?" She watched as Jacey immediately turned away from her.

"No."

Concern filled Rachel. She'd always taught her daughter to be truthful. Lately that rule had gone by the wayside, but she was surprised that Jacey wouldn't tell her what was bothering her. And something obviously was. Rachel postponed her motherly inquisition until they'd finished unloading the groceries. Once they were back in the kitchen, she and Jacey began putting away their purchases.

"Put the cookies and crackers on the third shelf, okay?" Rachel had reorganized John's pantry as soon as she'd moved in. And filled it. A few canned goods and a box of crackers had been all she'd found.

As she gathered up the fresh fruit and vegetables, she said, as offhandedly as possible, "You know, when something is wrong, it helps to talk about it."

Jacey shot her a look out of the corner of her eye before she concentrated on stacking the boxes she carried on the third shelf. "I know," she finally said in a low voice.

"Then why won't you talk to me?" Rachel asked softly.

Jacey trudged back to the grocery sacks as if all the weight of the world was on her shoulders. "Okay. I need to know how you make babies."

Rachel blinked several times, hoping her shock wasn't showing on her face. Without answering, she walked to the refrigerator and opened it to deposit the fruit and vegetables. Then she faced her daughter.

"Why do you want to know?"

"Someone at school today was talking about getting a baby. I just wondered."

"I see. Well, a baby grows in the mommy's stomach until it's big enough to hold, and a doctor takes it out at the hospital."

"How does it get in there in the first place? Do you have one in your stomach?"

"No! No, I don't, sweetie. And babies—babies happen when a mommy and daddy make love... sometimes."

"Oh."

Rachel braced herself for another question, because she could see in Jacey's face that she wasn't satisfied. The sound of the front door opening interrupted them, however.

"Daddy's home!" Jacey exclaimed and ran for the front of the house.

Rachel returned to the task of putting away groceries, trying to organize her thoughts as she worked. She suspected Jacey would ask more questions. Rachel only hoped she saved them for bedtime and didn't ask them in front of John.

John and Jacey entered the kitchen together, her arms around his neck as he carried her.

"Grocery shopping? I didn't realize—I haven't given you any money for groceries, Rachel," John said as he looked at the sacks on the table.

"I had some money."

"But that wasn't our deal."

No, it wasn't. But she didn't like remembering their deal. It made his actions seem cold-blooded, based on money. Idiot! When was she going to wake up? Of course, that was the reason for his behavior.

"I'll open you a checking account tomorrow. And I need to get you some credit cards, too," he said with a frown, as if making a mental list.

"Really, John, it's not necessary."

"Yes, it is."

She couldn't bear another argument. They brought her too close to the edge. She did much better if she stayed in control. "Dinner isn't ready yet. It will be in about half an hour."

"No hurry. Want me and Jacey to put things away while you get started? That way we can keep each other company."

Jacey seemed delighted with the idea and wriggled out of his arms to the floor. "Yeah. Come on. I'll show you how Mommy likes everything."

"Good idea, little one. I could use a few lessons." He sent Rachel that sideways grin of his and she turned her back on the two of them.

Rachel found it unnerving to work with John in the same room. Fortunately her dinner plans were simple. After they stowed away the groceries, John and Jacey settled down at the table to chat with her while she worked.

Jacey finished telling John about Earl's latest escapade at school. Before he could comment, she asked another question.

"John, do you and Mommy make love?"

"Jacey!" Rachel exclaimed, her face bright red.

Jacey frowned at her mother. "What, Mommy? You said that's how babies are made and I just wondered—"

John didn't appear nearly as disturbed as she was, Rachel noted.

"What your mommy means, sweetheart, is that people don't talk about making love. It's very personal, just between two people."

"Like you and Mommy?"

"Like me and Mommy."

"Then how will I know?"

"Know what?"

John's question was perfectly natural, but Rachel knew the answer and wasn't anxious for Jacey to explain.

"Jacey, I don't think—"

"If we're going to have a baby," the child replied, ignoring her mother's protest.

"Ah," John said, as if he understood how little girls thought. "Someone at school must be going to have a baby—I mean, their mommy."

"Maybe," Jacey said.

"I knew school was educational," John said to Rachel, a grin on his face. "But I thought it was from books."

Rachel couldn't hold back a smile in return. "It's called sharing."

"Yeah. Well, little one, if we have a baby, we'll be sure to let you know way in advance."

"But why would you want a baby? You have me." Jacey's little face was anxious as she looked up at John.

Rachel suddenly realized the reason for Jacey's questions. Before she could reassure her, however, John spoke.

"A baby would never replace you, Jacey. We could have a hundred babies, and none of them would be you." He cuddled her closer to him. "Have you ever had a favorite baby doll?"

She nodded, one finger in her mouth.

"Well, what if you got a big stuffed lion that you really loved?"

"I did, John. You got it for me."

"I know, sweetheart. Did that big lion make you love your baby doll any less?"

She shook her head no. He hadn't resolved all her questions, however. "But the baby would be your baby and I'm not."

Rachel moved over to the table and sat down in the chair next to John. They had reached the crux of the problem, she knew. Surprisingly, she trusted John to give the right answer.

"That's not true, Jacey. You see, you and I chose each other. You picked me to be your daddy, and I picked you to be my little girl. If we have a baby, we have to take it no matter what it looks like. It could be as ugly as sin!"

"John!" Rachel protested, but she couldn't subdue her grin.

John grinned back at her, but he talked to Jacey. "It could even be a boy!" he exclaimed in mock horror.

Jacey giggled. "Like Earl!"

"Oh, no! Not like Earl!" he said, hamming it up just like Jacey.

He tickled her tummy and they both laughed. Rachel sighed. She'd known John would make Jacey feel good. Whatever else she thought about him, she knew he loved Jacey and would never hurt her.

Jacey put her arms back around his neck. "I love you, John. I'm glad you chose me."

"I'm glad you chose me, too," he assured her, hugging her to him. Over Jacey's shoulder, he stared at Rachel.

"We mustn't forget Mommy," Jacey said, pulling away from John and scrambling out of his lap to come to her mother. "I love you, too, Mommy."

"Me, too, Mommy," John said, with that teasing glint in his eyes.

Rachel smiled back at him, grateful for the tender care he gave Jacey. And her heart ached with a yearning she tried to resist. But she couldn't. She wanted him to say those words and mean them.

With Jacey still in her arms, John pulled her to her feet and embraced both of them, his lips covering Rachel's in a sweet kiss.

"Help! You're squeezing me," Jacey protested with a giggle.

John pulled back and took Jacey from Rachel's arms. "Okay, okay, we'd better let your mommy cook dinner. I'm starving!"

"Me, too!" Jacey said, curling up in his lap as he sat down.

Rachel turned away from them, hoping they wouldn't notice her trembling. John's tenderness unnerved her.

"You know, I've been thinking," Jacey said after a minute.

"What have you been thinking?" John asked in an absentminded tone.

"I think we *should* have a baby."

Chapter Sixteen

John rapped on Rachel's door. Just like last night, as soon as Jacey had been put to bed, Rachel had retreated to her bedroom to grade papers.

He'd suggested she use the dining room table, or make herself comfortable in the den. She refused both options. He was pretty sure he was the stumbling block, not his house.

The door opened only a couple of inches. Rachel peered through the narrow opening. "Yes?"

"I need to talk to you."

Her eyes widened in alarm. "I'm sorry about Jacey's questions, John. I'll explain to her that—"

"I'm not concerned with Jacey's questions," he told her hurriedly. "I'm glad she feels free to ask them."

Rachel didn't appear to be greatly reassured, but she didn't close the door on him, either.

"May I come in?" he asked. He read the reluctance in her face, but she finally opened the door wider.

"Yes, of course."

He walked in, noting the neatness of the room except for several stacks of paper spread out on the bed. "How's the grading going?"

"Slowly."

She continued to watch him with big eyes. He knew he had to explain his request before she would relax—if she would, even then. "David called today."

"Is something wrong?" she asked anxiously, taking a step closer to him.

In response, he put his hands on her shoulders, rubbing back and forth in an attempt to comfort her. "No, of course not. He said we were terrific on the camping trip." His attempt to reassure her was having an adverse effect on his concentration. Somehow his gaze remained fastened on her full lips, and he fought the urge to kiss her.

"Then why did he call?"

"Because he's going ahead with the new video series—you know, about blended families. And—and he wants us to be in it."

She drew back, horror on her face. "No! John, we couldn't!"

"Well, we could, but I agree it probably wouldn't be a good idea," he admitted, easing her back close to him. "But David thinks we'd be a terrific addition. And I promised I'd ask you."

"The answer is no." Her response was emphatic, with no room for discussion.

"Just so I can explain it to David, why?"

"Why? John, it's bad enough that we're lying to David and his wife and all the other people we've met. But to make a video for nationwide distribution? That would be horrible."

Privately, he agreed with her. But he didn't want to bring their talk to an end. "Is it that hard to pretend to love me?" He kept his question light and added a grin to let her know he wasn't serious.

"You're just looking for compliments, Mr. Crewes," she said and pushed at his chest playfully.

He captured her hand against him, loving the warm tingling her touch brought. "Everyone needs a little encouragement."

"Not you!"

"Yes, me. Surely you can tell me *something* you like about me." When she gave him a stubborn look, he added, "I can name several things I like about you. The way you care for Jacey. And your cooking. I'm going to have to watch my weight or I'll be a blimp by the end of the year."

He looked at her expectantly.

"Okay, okay, you're wonderful with Jacey. No father could be more loving or patient." She stopped but he raised an eyebrow to encourage her. "And—and you're wonderfully generous."

"Thank you. My turn, again." He eased her body against his, fully in his embrace, as he said, "You have beautiful blue eyes, and the softest, sexiest lips I've ever seen."

Her cheeks flushed with color and she tried to pull away. "John, this is getting out of hand."

"You're just trying to stop because you don't like anything about me," he teased, a mock pout on his face.

"No, I— Okay, you have the most expressive eyebrows I've ever seen."

"That's not very sexy," he complained.

She responded to his challenge, her eyes twinkling and her lips smiling. "You would prefer me to tell you that you have magnificent buns?"

"Really? Well, they can't compare to yours." He let his hands slip to that part of her anatomy.

"John! Behave yourself. We're just having a discussion."

"Yeah. An adult version of show-and-tell. And I'd like you to model that piece of underwear you were dangling under my nose the other night. I've had a lot of dreams about you in that black bra."

Her cheeks grew even redder and she unconsciously looked down at her bosom.

He groaned. "You're wearing it now, aren't you?" He had his answer in the guilty, self-conscious look on her face, but she attempted to deny it.

"Of course not! Don't be ridiculous!" She tried to push away from him, but the movement only stimulated his already overheated body.

His arms tightened around her and his lips captured hers as he gave in to the volcanic urges he'd been resisting. The moment he'd realized she was wearing the black bra beneath the sedate print blouse that topped her jeans, he was lost.

If she made any effort to resist him, he didn't notice it. Her arms encircled his neck and she ran her fingers through his hair. He took advantage of her surrender to press her against him from their knees to their shoulders. Her breasts seemed to burrow into his chest as he kissed her, and he brought one hand up to stroke them.

She gasped as his mouth trailed kisses from her throbbing lips to her neck before returning to her lips.

This time, when he urged her to open to him, she didn't hesitate. Their tongues dueled, both winning, as his hands caressed every inch of her. When his fingers settled on the buttons of her blouse, she was too busy kissing him back to notice.

The unbuttoning was a slow process because he grew distracted several times. Rachel slid her hands beneath his knit shirt and caressed his body. He wanted to strip them both naked immediately, but he was too busy tasting the nectar of her lips. He couldn't bear the thought of breaking off the kiss.

Eventually, however, he pulled apart her blouse to reveal the black lace bra in all its glory, her aroused nipples pushing against the delicate lace, begging to escape.

He trailed his lips along the edges of the bra, his tongue dipping into the valley between her breasts. Rachel's panting as she pressed against him, her lips covering his forehead and then moving to his ear, only inspired him to greater liberties. The bra fastened in front and he freed her swollen breasts from their enclosure before covering them with his mouth.

Rachel whimpered and one leg curled around his hips as she sought to be even closer to him. More than willing to grant her wish, he lifted her, his hands encasing her hips, and moved to the bed. Even as her head touched its softness, he was on top of her, his mouth saluting each breast before moving back to the softness of her lips.

Lost in the storm of passion they'd created, he was totally unprepared for Rachel's reaction. Wrenching her lips from his, she began shoving him off her frantically.

"The papers! The papers!" she screamed.

Her urgency slowly penetrated the fog of physical reaction. "What's wrong?" he gasped.

"We're crinkling the papers! My students' papers!" Rachel shoved harder and John slid to his knees beside the bed. Rachel pushed herself up, her concentration on her schoolwork, unconscious of her gaping blouse and full breasts. John, however, couldn't take his eyes from the view. Such enticement led him to touch again, but this time Rachel wasn't receptive.

She slapped at his hands and pulled her blouse together with one hand. "Stop it, John. We have to stop it."

He did stop, but as he stood, he asked her, "Why?"

"Because we're ruining my papers."

"I have a big bed without any papers. Come on." He took her hand and pulled her from the bed.

"No! No, I'm not going to your bed. We're making a mistake, John. This is a temporary marriage, remember? We promised not to—to do this sort of thing."

"I don't remember promising that," he said, his brows lowered.

She pressed her swollen lips together, and John could hardly restrain himself. The memory of their softness crushed against his mouth, their generosity, their caresses against his skin, almost unleashed what little control he had.

"*I* promised. No more, John, please."

He recognized the determination in her voice. But he regretted it. "Whatever you say," he muttered and turned away. He looked behind him once as he closed the door, but she had her back to him.

When he reached his room, he fell on the bed with a groan. He'd seen her in the black lace bra, as he'd wanted. Now the only question he had was, How would he ever sleep again? Visions of Rachel without any bra at all were sure to remain in his head for the rest of his days. As well as the taste and touch of her. He would be miserable without her.

AS SHE HEARD THE DOOR close, Rachel sank back down on the cleared area of the bed. The riot in which her senses were participating was a protest against John's withdrawal. They begged for completion, but she'd refused.

She bit her bottom lip until tears appeared in her eyes and then fell, sliding down her cheeks. What was she to do now? How was she to live in such close quarters with the one man in the world she couldn't resist? Shivers raced up and down her spine as she remembered his touch, his kisses, his desire.

Removing the stack of papers from the bed, she slowly undressed. There was no point in trying to work now. She'd never be able to concentrate on the effect of inflation on the value of the dollar. Or on one student's estimation of the president's policy on individual rights.

Her body was clamoring for its right to be loved. By one sexy, nearby male. That was all she could think about. She slipped on her nightgown and turned off the light. Sliding into her lonely bed, she lay there, aching, wanting. How much self-denial could one person bear?

RACHEL MADE SURE SHE was occupied with the toaster when she heard John's steps on the stairs.

"Mommy, John's here," Jacey sang out.

Reaching for a coffee mug, Rachel filled it and took it to the table, but her gaze never reached his face. "The toast will be ready in a moment."

"Thanks," John said, but still Rachel didn't look at him.

"What's wrong, John? Are you thinking about something again?" Jacey asked. "Like when we visited Lisbeth?"

Out of the corner of her eye, Rachel saw John reach out and rub Jacey's head.

"Yeah, baby, I'm thinking. Have a good day at school," he said and stood.

"But you haven't eaten your breakfast," Rachel protested, looking at him for the first time. She was shocked to see circles under his eyes, a weary look on his face.

"I'm not hungry." He tried to smile, but all he managed was a grimace.

With a muttered goodbye, he left the house.

Rachel automatically buttered the toast that popped up and then filled her mug a second time and sat down at the table beside her daughter.

"Do you think John has a sick tummy?" Jacey asked, concern in her voice.

"What? Sick? Um, no, sweetie, I don't think he's sick. Maybe he worked too late last night." Or, maybe, like her, he hadn't been able to go to sleep until the wee hours of the morning.

After dropping Jacey off at kindergarten, Rachel continued on to her school, but she ran on automatic pilot. What was the matter with her? She'd had other nights when she couldn't sleep.

But it wasn't only the lack of sleep that bothered Rachel. It was her situation. She had agreed to live with a man, her husband, for an entire year. But she'd insisted that it be a marriage in name only. Her logic was faultless. The parting at the end of that year would be much easier without any physical complications.

But the year would be misery.

As last night had been.

All day long she debated her choices. It was during second period that she admitted to herself that she loved John Crewes. A student had stood waiting for an answer to his questions for several minutes, finally prodding her.

She apologized, but she was operating in a fog. Her mind was taken up with John. Loving him didn't make her choices any easier. Fifth period, when a student came in late and she ignored him, one of her favorite pupils raised his hand.

"Are you all right, Ms. Cason?"

"What?"

"Are you all right? Chuck came in late for the second time this week and you just smiled at him."

She sighed and turned to Chuck, who was now glaring at the other boy. "No, I'm not feeling well, so I guess you got lucky, Chuck. Don't try it again."

"No, Ms. Cason. I won't. Uh, Ms. Cason?"

"Yes?"

"We all noticed that ring on your finger. Did you get married?"

Rachel stared at the gold band. All the other days before coming to school she'd carefully secreted the ring in her purse. Today, as distracted as she was, she'd forgotten.

She looked at all the interested faces in her classroom. Finally, she admitted, "Yes, I got married."

A spontaneous cheer arose and she stared at them in surprise. "I didn't know it would please you so much," she said, but she also hadn't known how much it would please *her* to admit her marriage.

"We just think it's neat," Julieann, a cheerleader with a penchant for the romantic, said with a sigh.

"Well, we need to continue with our discussion about the Korean War," Rachel insisted, determination in her voice. As if admitting her marriage to her students had been the answer she was seeking, she sloughed off all the self-questions and got down to work.

Rachel left school as soon as her last class ended. She didn't pack up any more papers to grade. She didn't straighten the odds and ends on her desk as she usually did. Her thoughts were on something, someone else. She had an errand to run before she picked up Jacey. A very private errand.

Once that had been accomplished, she picked up her daughter and then stopped at the grocery store. She was going to fix a special dinner this evening.

"We're going to have strawberry shortcake?" Jacey asked in surprise.

"Yes, we are."

"But it's not my birthday."

"I know, sweetie, but—but I feel like celebrating."

"Why?"

Rachel smiled as she pulled into the driveway. John's driveway. "Because we're happy."

"Yeah!" Jacey agreed, a big grin on her face.

"Come on. We've got a lot to do before John gets home."

Jacey, always willing to do something John might like, hurried to her mother's assistance.

Two hours later, the strawberry shortcake was stored in the refrigerator, the steaks were ready to go on the grill on the patio, where the baked potatoes were already roasting, a freshly made salad awaited its dressing, and hot rolls were just coming out of the oven.

Rachel kept looking at her watch.

"Where's John?" Jacey asked for the thousandth time.

"I don't know."

The ringing of the phone was her answer, and she approached it with dread.

"Rachel, it's John. I'm going to run late this evening. I hope that isn't a problem."

Rachel looked at all their preparations. "No, not at all. I have dinner ready, but I can reheat it when you get here."

"Don't worry about me. I'll probably grab something here. I'm not sure when I'll be in."

Apparently John had made some decisions today, also, and his didn't resemble hers. But she wouldn't go down without a fight.

"Jacey and I made a special dinner. I think you'll like it." She hated to use her child but she did. "Jacey will be very disappointed if you don't eat some of it."

There was a long pause, and she held her breath for his answer. "Are you sure you want me to come home now?"

"Yes, I'm sure."

"I'll be there in twenty minutes."

There was a click as he hung up, but it was Jacey tugging on her sleeve that reminded her to hang up.

"What did he say, Mommy?"

"He's on his way home, sweetie. He didn't want to disappoint you."

Jacey gave her a satisfied smile and said, "He's the best."

"Yes, he certainly is."

True to his word, John pulled into the drive almost to the minute he'd promised. Jacey greeted him at the door and led him to the table. He gave Rachel a weary smile, reminding her of herself before she got her second wind.

He looked better after eating the meal they'd prepared.

"Rachel, that was a terrific dinner. But I hate for you to go to so much trouble after teaching all day." His gaze roamed her body as he spoke, and she felt herself heating up.

"I enjoyed it. And Jacey helped me a lot."

"Just what did you do to help Mommy?" John asked, reaching for Jacey and taking her into his lap.

I washed the potatoes and wrapped them in that shiny stuff," Jacey replied importantly. "And I helped Mommy wash the strawberries."

"Strawberries? I didn't eat any strawberries," John said. Jacey responded with a giggle she tried to hide beneath her hand.

"We made our special dessert, only served on special occasions," Rachel explained.

John groaned and rubbed his stomach, his flat stomach, and Rachel's mouth went dry. "I don't know if I have room for a special dessert."

"It's got whipped cream, too," Jacey added, her eyes glowing in anticipation.

"Well, maybe just a little piece," John said. "And if I can't finish mine, I'm sure you'll help me, right, Jacey?"

Jacey didn't need to help John. They both cleaned their plates. Only Rachel didn't finish her dessert. Her gaze remained fixed on the man across from her, as did her thoughts.

Had she made the right decision? Yes. They couldn't go on as they had. It was too hard on both of them. Her gaze traced his lips, his shoulders, his chest, and strawberry shortcake held little interest for her. She had a better dessert planned for later. Much later.

John entertained Jacey while Rachel cleaned the kitchen, although he offered to help. Rachel refused. She didn't need him near her now. There was no point in suffering needlessly.

She mopped the kitchen floor after the dishes were done. Anything to keep her mind off what was to come. Even with the extra work, she still had time left before Jacey's bedtime. When she suggested a swim, Jacey didn't hesitate.

"Wow! This really is a special night, Mommy. I really can swim in the pool?" she asked, looking at John.

"Sure, if your mommy wants to. Do you have a swimsuit?"

Jacey nodded even as she hit the floor, running.

"You can't go into the pool until I get my suit on," Rachel reminded her as she disappeared.

"I'll go change, too," John said, standing.

"You don't have to. I thought you might like a little time to yourself. Jacey's kept you pretty busy tonight."

Their gazes met and Rachel almost fell into his arms at the longing she saw there.

"No, it's better if I swim. I didn't sleep too well last night."

Although her cheeks reddened, Rachel just nodded and went upstairs to change. The new swimsuit revealed a lot more of her than her old one, but she wasn't worried about that tonight. It seemed to be a consideration for John, however, as he first caught sight of her.

He swallowed several times before saying, "Nice suit, Rachel."

"Ready?" Jacey pleaded, dancing from one foot to the other.

"Yes, we're ready," she assured her child, but her gaze remained on John. Only the splash as Jacey entered the pool distracted her attention.

An hour later, she tucked an exhausted-but-contented Jacey into her bed.

"Mommy, this was the best night. Isn't it great living with John?"

"Just great, sweetie." After her prayers and a good-night kiss, Jacey was asleep almost before Rachel could leave her room.

Half an hour later, after careful preparation, Rachel crossed the hall and knocked on John's door.

"Come in," he called.

As he'd been last week when she'd stormed into his room, John was propped up in his bed, reading a newspaper. His gaze widened as she walked into his room and closed the door behind her.

"Is something wrong?" he asked, sitting up.

"No. But I bought something for you today." She held out a brown paper bag. "I thought you might want to—to use it this evening."

Chapter Seventeen

John stared at Rachel as she stood beside his bed. He'd spent very little time sleeping last night after their aborted lovemaking. Now she was standing there, wearing a sexy ice-blue negligee, her hair falling about her shoulders, smiling at him, holding out a paper sack.

What was she trying to do—kill him? Did she think showing him what he was missing would help him sleep? The woman was crazy.

"Look, thanks, Rachel, but you didn't need to buy me anything. I'm about ready for bed, so why don't we, uh, talk in the morning." He snapped the newspaper and forced his gaze from her sexy presence to the printed word.

"But, John, I made a special trip. Won't you at least look at what I bought you?"

"Rachel, I'm really not in the mood for games. I didn't get much sleep last night, and the swim almost did me in. You're not helping the situation by coming in here dressed like that. I think it's highly unfair of you to do so."

She looked down at the gown she was wearing and then back at him. "It kind of goes with my gift."

"Unless you've got an aphrodisiac in that bag, I think you're mistaken," he growled, his patience fading fast. Was she a tease?

Her full lips formed a pout that almost drove him crazy. "You think you'll need an aphrodisiac?"

As he was about to snap an answer, he came to an abrupt halt. The look in her eyes finally told him he was missing something.

"No," he replied, drawing out his answer, "I wouldn't need an aphrodisiac to want to make love to you, Rachel." He watched her every move, wondering what she was up to. There was a surging hope in him that she might want to take up where they'd left off last night, but she was going to have to make that clear to him. He couldn't stand that much frustration again.

"Good. Take your present, John."

With his gaze never leaving her, he reached over for the sack. "What is it?"

She crossed her arms under her breasts, only drawing his attention to their ripe fullness, and said nothing. For the first time, he noted some signs of nervousness.

"Are you going to answer me?"

"I hope all the answer you need is in the sack. I certainly went to enough trouble and embarrassment to buy it."

Although he was reluctant to look away from her, he unfolded the top of the bag and looked inside. His eyebrows snapped together and he upended the sack, dropping three boxes on the bed.

"I—I didn't know what kind, so I picked three. I hope they're—"

"Rachel!"

"I didn't think we should take any chances. I mean, I know it's only for a year but—"

"Rachel!"

"I don't think we'd survive a year like last night," she finished with a rush.

"I know I wouldn't," he assured her fervently, swinging back the covers and reaching for her at the same time. One of the boxes of condoms fell to the floor, but John ignored it. There were still two more to choose from.

"You're sure?" he asked, already aroused as he pressed her silkily-clad body against him.

"Oh, yes." She sighed as her mouth met his.

John decided he'd been a gentleman and given her a chance to withdraw. Any more discussion could take place later. Much later.

His briefs joined her negligee on the floor and he pulled her down on the bed with him. She met him more than halfway as he resumed their embrace where they'd left it last night.

Finally, he could touch her everywhere, smooth her soft skin with his fingers, kiss her from one end to the other, feel her beneath him. To his delight, Rachel showed no hesitation in touching him in return. Never had he experienced such joy.

When he entered her, making them one, he did so carefully, knowing it had been a long time for her. But Rachel urged him to greater heights as she stroked his back and moaned softly. The sound was like a crooning that pulled him closer.

Rapidly they progressed until John felt Rachel peak just as he could no longer hold back, and they joined in such passion that the world disappeared. Only sensation and love remained.

When their pounding heartbeats eased, he wrapped her in his embrace, afraid to let her go. He'd dreamed of making love to Rachel, but the reality was more than he'd ever imagined. He was afraid that if he turned her loose, he might never hold her again.

"Rachel?"

"Mmm?" she murmured sleepily, her lips moving against his neck.

"You... That was incredible."

Although she said nothing, she pressed even closer to him, her breasts flattening against his chest, stirring him again.

He ran a hand down her back, enjoying touching her soft skin, then placed kisses on her neck.

"I should go back to my room," she whispered.

"No! No, don't go."

"But Jacey—"

"We're married, Rachel. You're my wife, remember? Married couples get to do this all the time." He held his breath, afraid she would refuse to stay.

"I don't see how they have the stamina," she finally said.

"You'll get your second wind," he promised. "After all, you bought three boxes of condoms. You must've had great expectations." He kissed her soft lips before she could answer.

When he raised his head, she reached up to run a finger down the side of his face. "I didn't mean you had to use them all tonight, John. I thought... I mean, we're going to be married a year. I didn't see any point in torturing ourselves as we did last night."

John frowned. That was the second time she'd mentioned the limit to their marriage. But he had a year—a much better year than he'd expected, after last night. He would convince her to stay. He had to.

"You're right. I'll go buy some more condoms for tomorrow night," he told her.

A shiver of pleasure ran through him as she chuckled. "Even you aren't that macho, John Crewes. I doubt we'll need another box for at least two nights."

"I'll do my best, Mrs. Crewes," he assured her, drawing her beneath him again. And he did.

FOR THE SECOND NIGHT in a row, Rachel didn't get much sleep. But passion was the reason this time, rather than frustration. When John wakened her at dawn, it took several minutes of his delicious attention before she responded. Afterward, he held her again in his arms, stroking and soothing, making her feel loved and protected.

"You'd better call in sick, sweetheart," he murmured. "I haven't let you rest much."

"You haven't rested, either," she returned.

He chuckled—a low sexy laugh that, incredibly, made her want him again. If she didn't control herself, John was going to think she was a nymphomaniac.

"I feel great. Call in sick, and then go back to bed. I'll take care of Jacey."

"I can't let you do that, John. It wouldn't be fair," she mumbled, liking the idea more and more as she thought about it.

"Yes, you can. What's the number to get a substitute?"

Rachel told him and he dialed it, then pressed the receiver to her ear. When the recorder came on, she asked for a substitute teacher to take her classes.

"Now," John whispered, dropping a kiss on her forehead, "go back to sleep. I'll see you this afternoon."

The last she remembered was the sound of the shower in the master bath going on.

WHEN RACHEL FINALLY awoke, it was almost noon. Feeling a shade guilty, she hurried to the shower. The hot, steamy water helped ease the stiffness her night of passion had left. She could scarcely consider their nighttime activities objectively. What little experience she'd had in the past didn't compare with the overpowering desire that filled her when her husband touched her.

She hoped she'd done the right thing. It felt right. It felt incredible, if she was honest. But in the shadowy future, the end of their marriage lingered, mocking her happiness. A year. That was all she had.

Shutting off the water, she wrapped a towel around herself and stepped from the shower. Who knew what could happen in a year? John seemed . . . seemed attracted to her. Even as she thought that, she blushed. His attentions the previous night had been more than that, surely.

She harbored hope in her heart that he felt something more than lust for her. He had to. He couldn't make love to her as he had without *some* feeling, could he?

She briskly toweled off, dismissing such disturbing thoughts. Not having had a day to herself in so long, Rachel decided she should avoid such probing questions and make good use of her time. She would move her belongings from the house next door. Then Polly could call her friend.

After several hours of hard work, Rachel made herself a sandwich and sat down at the kitchen table. She was proud of what she'd accomplished. Everything except the furniture was moved in. She'd check with John and see if she should call a mover to handle the larger items.

First, however, she should call her landlord to let him know she was moving out. It wouldn't hurt to tell him about Polly's friend, also. Mr. Lawson had been kind to her when she'd moved in, and she didn't want him to lose any business because of her change of circumstances.

"Mr. Lawson?" she asked when he answered the phone. "This is Rachel Cason, that is, Rachel Crewes. I got married."

"So I heard. Congratulations."

"Thank you. I know this is short notice, but I've moved out of the house. Of course, I'll pay the rent for this next month, but Polly across the street has someone who wants to rent it, so my moving shouldn't be a problem."

The man chuckled. "Not for me. And I guess not for you, either."

Relieved at how easily he took the news, she said, "Thanks for being so nice about it. I know I have a lease, but—"

"Mrs. Crewes, since you're going to own the place now, I think you can let yourself out of the lease if you want, don't you?" He was still chuckling, apparently appreciating his little joke more than Rachel.

"What do you mean?"

"Oops, hope I haven't spoiled a surprise, but your husband called me Monday. He made me an offer I couldn't refuse and we're closing on the house tomorrow. He said he was putting it in your name. *And* he's paying cash. Nothing like landing in honey, is there?" Again he chuckled.

Rachel didn't feel like laughing. With her voice just barely above a whisper, she apologized for disturbing her former landlord and hung up the phone.

She stared across the kitchen table, her sandwich forgotten. He'd bought her a house. For when their year ended, of course. And as payment.

That ugly thought made her gag. She'd hoped last night might have some meaning to John. When he'd caressed her, she'd believed there was more to it than desire.

But then she'd never been any good at understanding men. She'd believed Jacey's father had loved her, too.

At least Dirk hadn't tried to buy her favors, making her feel like a prostitute.

She squeezed her eyes shut, hoping to hold back the tears that filled her eyes. John Crewes was not going to make her cry. He wasn't, she assured herself as her tears splashed on her sandwich.

After an hour of weary debate, Rachel had made her plans. Although her heart was breaking, she knew she couldn't stay with John. She had offered him her heart last night, but he'd only wanted to rent it. For a night, a lot of nights, a year. Then he expected her to move back to the house next door.

That would be convenient for him.

And a disaster for her.

She couldn't do it. Better to leave now, while the pain was fresh, instead of dying a little each day. There was no way she could pretend everything was all right. All three of them would be miserable if she tried that.

Jacey. Tears formed again, but she quickly brushed them away. Jacey would just have to accept that John wasn't going to be a part of their lives. Her little girl would have her first heartbreak at the tender age of five. Rachel hoped it would be her last, but her experience with men didn't make Jacey's future look good.

What a disaster. All because of show-and-tell. She would hate show-and-tell for the rest of her life. Because she'd mourn the loss of her love just as long.

The phone rang. She glared at it as if it were her enemy. The caller probably was her enemy. It could only be John.

"Hello?"

"Hi, sweetheart. Are you awake?"

She'd been right. It was John. The sexy burr in his voice almost brought her to her knees. "Yes."

"Rachel? Is anything wrong?"

"No."

He paused, but when she remained silent, he said, "Maybe you'd better take a nap. Because tonight *I've* got a surprise for *you.*"

"More presents?" she asked tonelessly.

He didn't seem to notice. "Why not? You gave me a pretty special gift last night."

"I didn't ask for anything in return," she snapped.

"You *do* need a nap. And even if you didn't ask for this present, I think you'll like it."

Before she could respond, he had another call. "Gotta go, sweetheart. I'll be home as soon as I can."

Which meant she didn't have all that much time. Spurred on by the ache in her heart, Rachel ran up the stairs and began packing bags for both her and Jacey. She couldn't remove all their belongings before it was time to pick up her daughter, but she could gather enough things for several days. They'd go to a hotel until she could find them an apartment.

At least she wouldn't have to worry about the lease she'd signed on the house next door. All she had to concern herself with was two broken hearts.

When she picked up Jacey at her school, her child's bright smile almost started the tears all over again. She fought them off. She'd already cried enough today. Driving in silence, she listened to Jacey's chatter about her day, scarcely registering her words.

As soon as they got home, she made sandwiches for the two of them. Since she hadn't eaten the soggy one she'd fixed earlier, she forced herself to chew a few bites, but there was no taste; or if there was, she didn't notice it.

"Can I have some strawberry shortcake, too?" Jacey asked as she ate her sandwich. "And why aren't we waiting for John?"

"John's busy. And we're going to have a treat, you and me," Rachel said, hoping to instill some pleasure in her voice but failing miserably.

"A treat?" Jacey asked cautiously, watching her mother.

"Yes, a treat. I'll get you some dessert, now."

Her attempt to distract Jacey with the strawberry shortcake didn't work. "What kind of treat, Mommy?"

"I thought we'd go stay in a hotel for a few days."

"A hotel? You mean Disney World?" Jacey asked eagerly. "I didn't think we'd get to go!"

"Disney World? What are you talking about, Jacey?"

"Lisbeth said her parents were taking her to Disney World, and I said we were going too, but—" She broke off abruptly as she stared at her mother.

"Jacey, that's not true."

The excitement fading from her little face, Jacey frowned and asked, "Then why are we going to a hotel?"

"I thought it would be fun."

"Is John going, too?"

"No! No, John's not going."

"Then I don't want to go."

No, she hadn't thought she would. Neither did Rachel. But they didn't have a choice. She couldn't remain as John's paid companion; and Jacey couldn't stay, either.

"I'm sorry, Jacey, but we have to go."

Again the phone rang.

"Rachel, I'm on my way home. Don't cook dinner."

"No."

"See you in a few minutes."

After hanging up the phone, Rachel picked it up again and dialed a number. "Polly? Could I bring Jacey over for a few minutes? Thanks. I'll be right there."

"Why am I going to Grandma Polly's house?" Jacey asked, a frightened look in her eyes that made Rachel unbearably sad.

"Because I need to talk to John alone."

"We're leaving him, aren't we?" Jacey whispered.

Rachel swallowed back her tears. "Come with me to Polly's, sweetie. I won't be long."

Jacey didn't ask any more questions.

After leaving her daughter with Polly, Rachel put their suitcases in the station wagon. She wasn't going to run away without telling John goodbye. He didn't deserve such shabby treatment. In fact, he hadn't done anything wrong. Except not love her. And he couldn't help that.

So she'd wait until he came home . . . with another present. And she'd tell him goodbye.

Chapter Eighteen

John whistled as he drove.

Life was good. What he and Rachel had shared last night would have made even the worst day a gem, but he'd had a good day. Rachel was going to be surprised when she heard what he'd done.

He patted his chest, just over his inside pocket. Yes, she was going to be surprised.

He wanted to buy her the world, to make every wrong right, to love her forever. And he had a year to convince her. He was starting tonight.

When he'd married the first time, he'd thought he knew what love was. He knew now he'd only known what lust was. Maybe some people got lucky, marrying young, but he hadn't. In a few years, when Jacey came to him and told him she was in love, he would have a long talk with her. Because love was something special, something incredible.

Last night, when Rachel had come to his bed, offering her body, he doubted that he could have turned her down, even if he hadn't loved her. But he did. He loved her more than he'd ever loved anyone. Even more than Jacey. And he'd been pretty surprised by his capacity to love a child.

The night spent holding Rachel, touching her, becoming one with her, had confirmed his feelings. Confirmed? He chuckled. Hell, it had set off rockets. It was a wonder the moon hadn't been blasted out of the sky.

Pulling into the driveway, he tried to wipe the idiotic smile off his face, but the thought of seeing Rachel again sent him out of control. Maybe Jacey could watch television for an hour while they, um, communicated. Then they'd all go to dinner.

He practically raced up the sidewalk, calling Rachel's name as soon as he crossed the threshold. When she appeared at the kitchen doorway, he scooped her up into his arms, his lips covering hers.

After a long kiss that only left him wanting more, he buried his face in her neck and whispered, "I missed you. Where's Jacey?"

"At Polly's."

He drew back, a grin on his face. "Terrific. We must've been thinking the same thing." Even as he turned to pull her toward the stairs and the bedroom above, he realized something. While Rachel hadn't fought his kiss, she hadn't responded like last night. Almost simultaneously, he recognized resistance in her body.

Stopping and turning around, he asked, "What is it? Are you sore? Did I hurt you in some way last night?"

"No." She pulled her hand out of his grasp and her teeth sank into her bottom lip.

"What's wrong? Has something happened to Jacey? Dear God, is Jacey hurt?" Panic filled him as his perfect world, less than twenty-four hours old, began to crack.

"Jacey's fine."

He reached out to grasp her shoulders and she stepped back from his touch. With painful intensity he studied her. "Tell me what's wrong, Rachel."

She ducked her head and then looked up at him. "We're leaving."

Pain was in her eyes, tension in her body. Her words struck him like a bolt of lightning. He couldn't move. But he managed to asked the one thing he had to know. "Why?"

"I can't stay," she whispered.

"What did I do that was so terrible? I thought—last night we— Damn it, Rachel, tell me!" This time he grabbed her shoulders and hauled her up against him, but she shrank back, as if his touch was distasteful.

She kept her head down. "You didn't do anything wrong. It's me."

He squeezed his eyes shut, hoping to hold back the unexpected tears that filled them. How could he lose her now? She'd promised him a year. He'd made such plans for the three of them—his family.

In spite of her reluctance, he pulled her close and wrapped his arms around her. "Rachel, please, don't go. You can't go."

He felt more than heard the sob that broke from her. What was wrong? If she didn't want to go, why was she leaving? Nothing made sense anymore.

"I don't understand," he added, a desperate plea in his voice.

She pushed away from him. "What did you bring me today?"

"What?"

"You said you brought me a surprise." She looked at him now, big tears streaming down her cheeks.

"Rachel, what difference does it make? If you're leaving, what the hell difference does it make?"

She sniffed and stiffened her shoulders. "I just wanted to see how grateful you were. It couldn't be bigger than buying me a house, but since I gave you what you wanted last night, I figured it would be spectacular."

Stunned, he couldn't respond. He stepped back, staring at her.

"You've said you're rich, and you must be. But I'm not sure even you could afford a year's worth of payments like the ones you've made so far. I thought I'd save you from bankruptcy," she said, her voice hardening, anger beginning to fill her face. "And here's a word of advice. For your next mistress, you'd better start off cheaper. Then maybe you can last the course."

As soon as she finished speaking, she moved to step around him. By the time he pulled himself together and turned, she was almost to the door. But he beat her there.

He drew a deep breath, trying to bring himself under control when all he wanted to do was shake her until she forgot her foolish thoughts.

"Please move," Rachel muttered, standing rigidly in front of him.

"Aren't you going to pack a bag? Take your toothbrush?"

"They're in the car."

"Ah. So you've been thinking about this all day. That's why you sounded so mad over the phone." He shoved his hands in his pockets to keep himself from grabbing her.

"Move."

"No. I'm not going to move until you hear what I have to say. Surely it's only fair to let the accused speak up for himself, isn't it, teacher? And you believe in fairness, don't you?"

She was rip-roaring mad now, and shaking so much he feared she'd fall. "Yes! Yes, I believe in fairness. But I don't believe in treating a person like a commodity that can be bought and sold. And—and I don't believe in breaking a little girl's heart." Sobs racked her body as she looked away.

"Jacey knows?"

"She—she guessed."

"Damn! How could you do this?"

"I can't stay!" she shouted. "How can I stay, when—when you don't care?"

For the first time, real hope filled John. Why would she want him to care unless she cared, too? He should have known, he realized, his heart rebounding with ferocity. He should have known Rachel couldn't have made love with him last night unless she cared.

"Oh, Rachel." He sighed. "I never said I didn't care."

"It's too late," she protested, sobbing. "Let me go, John. It will destroy me if you don't."

"And it will destroy me, if I do. I love you, Rachel. You promised me a year. I want my year to prove that I love you and Jacey. We belong together."

His hands came out of his pockets, and he gathered her against him. She didn't have the strength to fight him, shaking as much as she was. "No, no, no," she protested, but she buried her face in his shirt.

"Rachel, as God is my witness, I love you—more than I ever thought I was capable of loving anyone. I love you more than all the money in the world. More than life itself. I even love you more than I love Jacey."

She lifted her head and stared at him, the faintest light of hope in her big blue eyes. "What?"

"I love you."

"But—but you bought the house next door for when our year was over. You didn't plan on our marriage lasting."

"I bought the house next door because you didn't seem to want to give it up. I figured it would be a good investment."

"You put it in my name."

"It's your house."

"That's crazy," she said, hiccuping.

For the first time since he'd realized something was wrong, John smiled. Not a big smile, just a rueful grin. "I'm crazy in love with you."

"John, please, if—if you're just saying these things to protect your company, tell me now. I'll write David a letter and explain that it's my fault. That you are the perfect husband. But don't lie to me."

John looked up at the ceiling as he pressed Rachel against him. "Can you believe this woman, God? She won't even take *You* as a reliable witness. I'll try again, sweetheart. May God strike me dead if I'm lying. I love you with all my heart, and I always will."

Although she remained in his arms, she said nothing and he pushed her chin up so he could see her face. "Well?"

"Just a minute. I don't want to rush God. He could be busy." There was a teary twinkle in her eyes even as her lips trembled.

It was more than enough invitation for John. He tightened their embrace and covered her lips with his. Heaven might be a wonderful place, but John couldn't believe it could be better than Rachel's kiss.

When he lifted his mouth from hers, he hugged her even tighter. "I thought I'd lost you, Rachel. You scared me out of ten years of my life."

She sobbed against his neck. "Me, too. I've been dying all day. I loved you so much, and then I found out about the house, and I thought—"

"You thought all the wrong things. Sweetheart, I can't help buying you things. I was trying to tell you I love you—not offering you a bribe."

"I'm sorry. I just— And when I told Jacey— Oh, no! Jacey!" She pulled out of his embrace and tried to open the door. "I've got to go to Jacey!"

"We'll both go to Jacey," he told her, taking her hand and pulling open the door.

They raced down the steps and headed across the street, where a very sad little girl sat watching them.

"I'M GOING TO SIT on the front porch and wait for my mommy," Jacey told Grandma Polly.

"But, child, she may be a while."

"I don't think so," Jacey said, turning away so Grandma Polly couldn't see the tears running down her face. She didn't think her mommy would take long to tell John goodbye.

She wished she could understand why they had to leave. Had Jacey done something wrong? She'd promise to be very, very good, if they could stay with John.

It had to be her. Her real daddy hadn't wanted to stay, either. Maybe John was tired of being a daddy. She sat down on the porch step, leaning her head against the post that held up the railing.

She wished he still wanted her to be his little girl. He'd been such a good daddy. The best.

Hearing the door open at John's house, she watched as the two most important people in her world tumbled down the steps and rushed toward her. She frowned. They were holding hands.

Hope leaped in her, but as they got closer, she could tell her mommy had been crying. As much as it hurt, she couldn't let John make her mommy cry.

She stood and hurried down the steps to grab her mommy's leg. "It's okay, Mommy. John won't make you cry anymore. I won't let him."

She gave him a fierce glare, although her heart was breaking as he knelt down beside her.

"Good for you, Jacey," he said softly, a grin on his face. "You're a good girl to protect your mommy."

"Why did you have to make her cry?" she asked sadly. "You must've been really mean, 'cause my mommy never cries."

"Jacey, sweetie," her mommy said, kneeling too, her arms around Jacey. "It's my fault. I thought—I thought John didn't love us."

She looked at her mommy with a frown. "A'course he loves us, Mommy. Anybody can see that."

"You know, Jacey, sometimes children can see better than adults. Our eyes get tired and we miss the important things." Her mommy reached out to touch John's face. "You know we said we were just going to be married for a year? Well, John wants us to stay forever. Is that okay with you?"

"Are you sure?" Jacey asked John, turning to face him. "'Cause it would make us both cry a lot if you changed your mind."

"I won't ever change my mind. I'll be your daddy forever, sweetheart, if you'll have me."

She threw her arms around his neck. "Yeah! And maybe we can even get a baby." She giggled with excitement.

"I wouldn't be surprised," John said, scooping her up into his arms.

"John!" her mommy protested, but Jacey didn't think she was mad, 'cause she was smiling real big.

As long as things were going so well, Jacey thought she should ask for one more thing. "And maybe we can go to Disney World with Lisbeth?"

John jerked to a halt, and Jacey screeched and grabbed his shoulders, afraid she'd fall.

"How did you know?" he asked.

"What's she talking about, John?"

"Uh, that's part of my surprise."

"Going to Disney World?" Rachel asked, stunned. "But I have to teach summer school."

He grinned. "That's another part of my surprise."

"John Crewes! What have you done?"

"You folks okay?" Polly asked, stepping out onto the porch.

"We're terrific," John assured her. "Thanks for watching Jacey for us."

"Glad to do it. And glad to see she's happy again."

"Yeah. We're all happy now." John put an arm around her mommy's shoulders. "Come on, you two. We'll finish our discussion later. Right now, it's time to go home."

Jacey beamed. Time to go home. Because now they were a real family.

And they were going to Disney World!

DEBBI RAWLINS

MARRIAGE INCORPORATED

To my critique group:
Brenda, Crystal, Karen, Kathy and Maureen,
who were always there to nudge and encourage me.

And to my husband, Peter,
who always believed I could do it.

Chapter One

Parker James watched the gloved waiter balance each champagne glass strategically on the rim of the next until the pyramid was complete. It cleared the chandelier by only a foot. Parker smiled. The whole thing would probably come crashing down any moment.

With pompous flourish, the waiter stood over his creation and poured the bubbling wine into the top glass. The elegant ballroom quieted but for a few appreciative whispers. The champagne artfully cascaded down the crystal pyramid, filling each goblet with its effervescent promise. A round of refined highbrow applause followed.

Damn. For a moment there, Parker had thought the evening might have possibilities, after all. He cradled his own slim-stemmed glass, wishing it were a beer instead, and surveyed the well-heeled crowd. Where the devil was his attorney? The collar of his tuxedo seemed to be shrinking by the minute, and he still had no idea why he'd let Harvey Winton talk him into coming to this benefit dinner.

"I see you made it." Harvey's voice came from behind him.

Parker turned to face the older man. "Me? I've been here for twenty minutes."

Harvey adjusted the monogrammed cuffs of his custom shirt. "Well, I knew you'd be deliberately late—if you showed up at all—so I hedged my bet."

"Fine. Now, can we leave before I have another attack of visual indigestion?"

"Leave? If your curiosity weren't piqued, you wouldn't be here in the first place."

"Curiosity, hell. You said you may have an answer to..." Parker glanced around, uneasiness tickling the back of his neck. Two of his investors were over by the caviar. He lowered his voice. "We both know why I'm here."

"That we do." The sympathy in the attorney's voice did not equate with the amusement in his cagey brown eyes. For an instant it disturbed Parker. But he was probably just being paranoid. So much was at stake.

"I don't understand why we had to meet here." Parker pushed a frustrated hand through his tawny hair. "Why not at my office?" He looked out the plate-glass windows and trained his eyes on the fading Hawaiian sunset framing Diamond Head—anything to avoid the other man's scrutiny. Harvey was more than his attorney, more than a friend. He was the father that Parker James II had never been. And right now Parker couldn't let Harvey see his self-doubt.

"I have my reasons. Can I get you a fresh drink?" Parker shook his head. The attorney started to turn away, then hesitated, slanting him a wry look. "Have a beer, Parker, you don't have to drink champagne just because you're a James."

Parker swallowed a resigned chuckle. It wasn't even safe to *think* around Harvey. He turned his attention back to the elegantly decorated room, scanning faces and recognizing many of those in attendance as people with whom he did business. But, in general, most of the people here nauseated him. They were more his parents' crowd. Not his.

Parker's gaze swept the room again, stopping to rest on the entrance.

"He's not coming," Harvey said, returning with his drink. "I talked with your mother this afternoon. They had a scheduling conflict."

"Who said I was wondering?"

"Weren't you?"

"No." Damn but Harvey knew him too well. "You're sure we need to be here."

"Quite." The attorney looked around at the prominent guests. "Besides, it's good for your image."

Parker didn't need the reminder. There was a lot of money riding on his project. A lot of ego, too. And as much as Parker would like to disagree with his friend, Harvey was right. His family name and his newly earned reputation as Honolulu's most promising up-and-coming real-estate tycoon would only take him so far. Rebellion had gotten him into a lot of trouble a decade ago. And now, in some ways, he was still paying.

"I've got enough to worry about." Parker dusted imaginary lint from his tuxedo jacket. "Now, when are you going to explain how being here will solve anything?"

"As a matter of fact," Harvey said, nudging his chin toward the door. "I think the solution to your problem just walked in."

Parker followed Harvey's gaze to the young woman coming through the door. She wore a simple black strapless dress. A single strand of pearls fell upon flawless tanned skin. Her glossy black hair might have hung to her waist, but it was wildly out of place as if she had just climbed off a motorcycle. She went from one person to another, smiling and shaking hands, never once apologizing for her appearance.

Parker liked that. A smile formed on his lips. "Who is she?"

"Ashley King."

"My savior, huh? Does she have a small fortune looking for a home?"

"Quite the contrary. Besides, you need a miracle, not money."

"Spit it out, Harvey. What's the angle?" He craned his neck to get a better look at Ashley King. Annoyed as he was, Parker's impatience faded.

The woman was petite. Only about five foot two, if he had to guess. Small and curvy, her hips swayed to a gentle, silent rhythm as she worked her way around the room. He couldn't get a good look at her face though, and he had already resigned himself to the fact that being that small, she'd most likely have a high, squeaky voice.

She finger combed her hair away from her face and tilted her head back, laughing at something a young man had said. Her neck was long and graceful and beckoning. Parker fastened his gaze on that silken expanse of vibrant skin and something flared inside him. He swallowed hard. Quickly he raised his eyes to her face, but it was too late.

Like a black satin veil, her hair fell forward, obscuring her profile. Frustrated, Parker maneuvered himself to within a few feet of her. Then he heard her laugh. Deep, throaty—a Kathleen Turner kind of laugh. Staring in surprise, he watched her turn wide hazel eyes on him.

"Hi. I'm Ashley King," she said and offered him her hand. "Isn't this a lovely party?"

He was still recovering from her voice when she favored him with a wide, enticing smile. Beads of perspiration formed at his hairline. "I'm Parker James."

"I know the name well." A small disapproving frown appeared at her brow but just as quickly fell away. "You must be the third."

"The third what?" There it was again. That seductive laugh.

"Parker James III. You're far too young to be the second."

"Oh, yeah." Parker cringed inwardly. He'd always hated being addressed as "the third" and had subconsciously put it out of his mind. Catching sight of an amused Harvey out of the corner of his eye, he gestured the man forward. "This is Harvey Winton." He paused. "Or do you two know each other?"

"I don't think so." Ashley turned her attention to Harvey. "But you do look familiar."

While Ashley and his friend exchanged greetings, Parker used the time to study her. She wasn't pretty in a classical sense, but she possessed a certain magnetic charm. He'd already sensed that, as she had made her way around the room, people were drawn to her. His gaze lingered on her small oval face, her eyes, warm and golden like maple syrup. How could she possibly help him?

Unless it was to seduce some high-ranking government types. But that wasn't Harvey's style. Besides, the thought repulsed Parker. He was no Boy Scout, and there certainly wasn't much he wouldn't do to get out of this jam, but he felt oddly indignant that she could be involved in anything so sordid.

"And what type of law do you practice, Mr. James?" Ashley's low, soft voice floated through his reverie.

"Me?" Parker tried to keep the stiffness out of his tone, but when her natural assumption finally sunk in, he felt his answer tangle in his mouth. His bow tie seemed to tighten a notch. "I'm not a lawyer."

"Oh . . ." A spark of interest brought out green flecks in her guileless eyes. "I thought the James name was synonymous with law and politics."

"I'm not like the rest of my family." Amazing, there was someone on this island who didn't already know that.

Ashley flashed a puzzled look at Harvey, who was busy studying the olive in his drink. "Well, I'm certainly glad you could attend our benefit. Obviously you think it's a worthy cause," she said, her smile still brilliantly intact. "Wasn't it wonderful of the board to lend us the museum for the evening?" She placed her hand on Parker's arm. Just as quickly she withdrew it.

Startled, Parker had felt the electric current between them. He looked deep into her astonished eyes and found some consolation there. She'd felt the connection, too. He could see it in the small heave of her chest, hear it in the slight quiver of her voice.

"It looks wonderful, doesn't it?" She gestured around the grand room where each flower was fastidiously in place, each glass crafted from the finest crystal and each dress more glamorous than the next.

And although Ashley looked as elegant as any woman there, Parker instinctively knew this wasn't her scene. So what did she have to do with all this? And how was she going to help him?

She had averted her gaze and laughed again at something Harvey said. Even though Parker had no idea what they were talking about, he felt his own lips curve in response. A tiny dimple had formed at the corner of her rose-tinted mouth and a twinkle of gold and green sparkled in her flashing eyes. The sensuality of her throaty laughter vibrated throughout his body.

He wanted her to tilt her head back again. He wanted to feast on all that silken skin dipping into soft cleavage. He wanted to...

Parker shook himself. There was something dangerously infectious about Ashley King. And if they were going to do any kind of business together, he'd better remember to keep it just that—business.

"May I get you a drink?" Parker asked all of a sudden. The air was closing in on him. He needed space.

"No, thanks. I'm fine," Ashley said. "But if you'll excuse me..."

Parker had already begun backing away, a lump blossoming in his throat. Just before he turned toward the bar, he saw the curiosity in Ashley's face, the amusement in Harvey's.

Where was all the Ivy-League confidence his parents had paid for? At the moment, gone. He had downed half his champagne refill when Harvey caught up with him.

"Slow down, man. You're going to be needing a clear head."

"A clear head for what, Harvey? I'm tired of the riddles. I'm tired of this evening. I'm just plain tired. Tell me what the hell is going on. And who the hell is Ashley King to me?" He gulped down the rest of his drink.

"Your fiancée, hopefully."

Parker almost lost his mouthful. Instead, it made a painful jerking descent down his tightened throat. "Are you crazy?" he finally spat out.

"Sometimes more than others, but in this particular instance I'm quite lucid." All traces of indulgence vanished from Harvey's face. "And dead serious."

Parker grabbed the other man's arm and hauled him over to a private corner. Voice lowered, he asked, "What's going on?" He made a cursory sweep of the room, pinpointing the proximity of each of his financial backers.

"I've tried every loophole, called in every favor. That Hawaiian homestead land is like sacred ground." The attorney shook his gray head. "There's a long list of hopeful and eligible applicants. Distributing it is a hot political issue. Not only does that put it out of reach, but if it were common knowledge that you want it to protect your resort, all hell would break loose. We need a backdoor approach."

"Even for one lousy strip of it?" Parker asked in frustration, not really needing an answer. He wasn't keen on ripping off the Hawaiian people, not even for "one lousy strip." But this was a complication he hadn't anticipated, and right now he felt plastered up against a brick wall. If just one investor got wind of this and pulled out, no telling how many others would follow suit. He exhaled deeply. He couldn't begin to fathom the predicament that would put him in. "What does this have to do with Ms. King?"

"It seems..." Harvey sighed and pulled out a cigarette. "The only way you'd be able to gain control is to marry into it. And Ms. King is a very eligible candidate."

"You *are* crazy." Parker stepped back, fumbling with his tie. For a hundred and twenty bucks, it should be able to unknot itself.

"Of course, getting her to agree is another matter. But that shouldn't be too much of a problem."

"Why not?" Parker threw up his hands, shaking his head. "More importantly, why am I even asking? This is absurd."

"Because she needs the money."

"And where is this money supposed to come from? If things don't get ironed out soon, I'll be bankrupt."

"Exactly. So to put it in your own vernacular, this may be the only way to save your butt."

Parker jammed his fisted hands into his pockets. The evening had gone from bad to worse. And as if he didn't have enough of his own problems, now all he could think about was why Ashley King would need money badly enough to marry for it. But he wouldn't give Harvey the satisfaction of asking. Anyway, it was irrelevant. Marriages of convenience, business marriages or whatever the hell they called them, were a thing of the past. Archaic. Out of the question.

"You could do much worse." Harvey took a long, seemingly bored drag off his cigarette, then blew a stream of smoke in Ashley's direction.

"Nasty habit, Harvey. Give it up." Parker pretended not to follow his friend's gaze, but darted a quick glance in time to see her flick that magnificent black mane over her bare, silky shoulder. "Besides, I prefer blondes."

"I don't think your investors much care what you prefer. Do you?"

Parker winced at the reminder. There was more at stake than his reputation and money. "This is just plain crazy." He paced a little, knowing how wild animals felt in a cage. "There's got to be . . ." He stared at his attorney. "You know, Harv, I don't see what the hell you find so funny about this whole situation. Every time I look at you, you've got a damn smirk on your face."

"Amusing," the other man corrected. "Not funny."

"Amusing?"

"It's too bad Ms. King wasn't as susceptible to your charms as the other ladies about town."

Parker glanced over his shoulder at whatever was capturing Harvey's attention. Two women, one blonde and one redhead, were looking his way. He knew them both socially but had never been impressed enough to pursue anything. He gave them the expected wave. They smiled their reply.

"Honolulu's finest," Harvey murmured and raised his glass in salute to the two women.

"Spare me," Parker said. He turned back to face his friend and rolled his eyes.

"You might have been a bit more charming to Ms. King. It wouldn't have hurt to bat those popular baby blues of yours at her."

Parker slammed down his glass and reached for a bottle of beer off the tray of a passing waiter. "Give it a rest, Winton," he ground out through clenched teeth, then headed for the door and away from Harvey's irritating snicker.

Across the room, Ashley kept Parker James in her peripheral vision. It was easy to do, since his tawny head was visible above most others. Something about him interested her. It wasn't physical, she assured herself, ignoring the quickening of her pulse as she recalled the sleepy blue of his eyes, the fullness of his lips.

He wasn't anywhere near her type, not that her social life was hopping these days, especially with her tight volunteer schedule and her daily visits to the hospital. But there was something intriguing about him....

Ashley turned her attention to the impeccably manicured woman who'd cornered her and tried to concentrate on what the wealthy matron was saying. After all, the woman had just donated a king's ransom to Ashley's beloved Hawaiian Immersion Program. With the contributions Ashley and her committee had secured, the program was about to get its start.

She breathed a happy inward sigh, then caught sight of Parker heading for the door. He carried himself with purpose and confidence...the best money could buy. If only some of that James fortune would make its way to one of her pet charities. But that was unlikely—and surely what accounted for the pang of disappointment she felt at watching his broad shoulders disappear through the smoked-glass doors.

Besides, Ashley had a far graver problem to worry about. Her heart heavy, she forced a smile for her chatty companion, ignoring the irony that she and her father were one step away from being a charity case themselves.

IT WAS A PERFECT MAY afternoon and Parker decided to do something he never did...skip out of his office two hours early.

He pulled up beside his sprawling beach house, then stepped out of his cherry red Porsche and walked to the mailbox. God, it was a great day. He squinted up at the bright sun and cloudless sky. Today, nothing would stop him from that swim and game of tennis he'd promised himself. Two of life's little pleasures that he never seemed to have time for anymore.

While sorting through the mail, he meandered back to the house. Bills. A pizzeria advertisement. More bills. Then a small linen envelope caught his eye. He tore the seal.

"A wedding invitation? Oh, Christ." He jammed the contents back into the envelope. His life had been a spinning top ever since Harvey had presented his hare-brained idea, and now reminders of it were popping up when least expected.

At least he had made it clear to Harvey. Absolutely, positively no way would he marry Ashley King, or anyone else, to secure that strip of homestead land.

He thought about the posh resort he'd broken his back to have built during the past three years, and about the overlooked tract of poverty-afflicted homestead land that would threaten wealthy consciences if visible from the resort windows. And only one lousy strip of unclaimed land separated it all.

It was also the only thing separating him from redemption.

Not only were a lot of investors with big money riding on him, there was his father—and his father's long, unforgiving memory.

Maybe Harvey's attempt at creativity hadn't been such a bad thing after all. It certainly had gotten Parker moving. Since Saturday, he had had architects and landscapers working around the clock to camouflage the stretch of unsightly homestead structures. He'd also promised large bonuses to keep it quiet.

The relocation of trees alone was going to cost him a small fortune, but he already had his accountants liquidating some of his assets. Although his latest effort was no guarantee, he would overcome this problem. He'd make a hefty profit, reestablish his name, and he'd do it by himself. Not that the money was particularly important. Parker'd known wealth most of his life. Then he'd had next to nothing during his more rebellious years. And although having money was better, it wasn't essential—no matter what his family seemed to think. For him, money had merely become a by-product of his personal success. And not having it handed to him made it a whole lot sweeter.

Parker shifted the mail to one hand and fumbled with his key ring until he found his house key. He let himself in the entrance of his suite rather than in the front door, hoping he could sneak off to his room without fending twenty questions from his housekeeper.

He slipped out of his jacket and hung it on the valet. He tossed his tie on the chest of drawers.

"Parker?" A tentative voice called out.

"Yes, Mrs. Lee, it's me," he assured the housekeeper and dropped his shirt near the hamper. The woman had always had sharp ears. In his teen years, it had been his cross to bear.

"You're home early. Anything wrong?" She called from the kitchen where she spent most of her time.

"Nothing at all." His socks landed somewhere near his shirt.

"And Parker?"

"Yes, Mrs. Lee."

"Pick up your clothes."

Parker grinned. Only Mrs. Lee and Harvey would think of speaking to him like that. When he had returned from the mainland for good, he'd noticed how much older she looked. She had worked for his parents for as long as he could remember. But the large plantation-style house had become too much for her, and he was pleased it hadn't taken much convincing to get her to work for him. She was a proud woman and would never accept anything resembling charity, but at least this way Parker could make sure she didn't overdo it.

He kicked the clothes into a pile, promising himself he'd get to them before Mrs. Lee. All he could think of right now was diving into that pool and soaking up some sun. He pulled on a pair of battered old trunks and headed outside.

After only five laps, Parker was winded. When had he gotten so out of shape? Harvey had tried to tell him how all-consuming this project had become, and he'd probably been right. As well as his friend knew him though, Parker suspected the attorney didn't fully fathom the importance of making this resort a success.

He hauled himself out of the pool and was about to settle onto a chaise longue when he heard a car pull up along the side drive to the house. The distinct purr of the engine alerted his senses. Only one person he knew had a car that finely tuned. Sweat mingled with the chlorinated water. He toweled off both and waited.

"Good afternoon, Parker. Beautiful day."

He draped the towel around his neck and turned to study his father. Even in his late sixties he was virile and commanding. His shock of white hair was perfectly styled. It wouldn't dare not be.

"Afternoon, Father. What brings you by?"

"I wanted to have a word with you. I stopped by your office but they said you'd already left, so I just took a chance you'd be home."

Why didn't his father just come out and ask him, Parker wondered. Ask him why he saw fit to leave work for a senseless afternoon in the sun.

Parker could feel residual defiance begin to fester. He squelched it fast. He wasn't perfect, no matter how much his father wanted him to be. He'd reconciled himself to that fact long ago, but deep-rooted hurt had a way of sneaking up and stealing pieces of maturity and rationale. "Well, you've found me. Can I get you something to drink? Some iced tea?"

"I won't be that long. But I would like to retire to some shade, if you don't mind. My skin can't take the sun like it used to."

"Of course." Parker gestured to the patio. He watched his father walk ahead of him, shoulders slightly stooped. When had he allowed that small imperfection? Parker wondered. "Playing much golf lately?"

"No. Not much at all. I've been leaving that to the younger men. And you, playing much tennis?"

"I've been too busy." Parker shook his head. For the first time he could remember, his father looked old. "But I'm playing a couple of rounds with Tom Booker today."

"How is Tom?"

"Good. What is it you wanted, Father?"

Parker James II issued a short elegant snort. "A little pleasant conversation, perhaps?" He smiled wryly at his son's cynical expression. "All right, how about some news on the Makena project?"

"You heard everything there is at the last board meeting."

"No problems?"

"Everything is on schedule."

"Well, son, I thought you should know...." His father paused, rare uncertainty shadowing his bright blue eyes that were so much like Parker's. "There are some rumors flying around."

"What sort of rumors?" Parker was glad for the towel around his neck. He didn't want his father to see him sweat.

"Nothing specific that I've been privy to. Just that there might be some problems."

Parker shook his head but was saved from responding by the phone's ringing. He twisted around, stalling, hoping Mrs. Lee would call him. His rescuer appeared.

"Parker, it's Harvey Winton." Mrs. Lee shrugged plump shoulders. "I tried to take a message, but he said it was urgent."

"Excuse me a moment." Parker swallowed a relieved sigh as he stepped past the sliding-glass doors and slid them closed behind him. He picked up the cordless phone and greeted Harvey.

"We've got trouble," the attorney said, his voice unusually tense.

"Go on."

"Rumors. None accurate, but they always cause questions."

"Do you know who's behind it?" Parker automatically glanced out at his father, who was watching him intently through the closed glass door.

"That's hard to tell. Not that it matters. I wanted to advise you right away, because there is one question you will have to answer and I'm not quite sure what to tell them."

"What's that, Harvey?" Parker pulled the towel from around his neck and mopped his sweaty forehead. At that moment Parker James II slid open the door and his gaze fell on the small but elaborate spider tattooed on his son's shoulder. The visible reminder of the day Parker'd had too much booze and too little sense. It was the day he had quit law school. The day he had disgraced his family. A day he would never forget.

"Parker, some of the board members want to know why you're suddenly liquidating assets," Harvey stated after a significant pause.

"Tell them..." Parker's gaze took in the piercing censure of his father, his disapproval almost searing Parker's skin. "Tell them I'll be paying for a wedding."

Chapter Two

"How much longer until she gets here?" Parker asked for the third time.

"She is still due to arrive at eleven-thirty." The ever-patient Harvey looked as if he were ready to bind and gag Parker.

"Are you sure she understands the terms of the contract?" Parker adjusted his tie and glanced at the office clock. Ten more minutes.

"Yes, she understands. Yes, she has enough Hawaiian blood to qualify. And no, I'm not certain she will agree. Now, how many more times would you like this repeated?"

"Until I hear Twilight Zone music, damn it. I hate this, Harvey, I hate this whole stinking thing."

"So you've said."

Parker leaned back in his leather chair, brought steepled fingers to his lips and narrowed his eyes. "If I didn't know better, I'd think you were deriving far too much pleasure from all this."

"I'll let that slide since you're under so much pressure." Even that was said with a slight—and annoying—smirk.

Parker stretched out his legs and the chair settled with a clunk. "It just seems so cold-blooded."

"Your getting married at the tender age of thirty-five or the business about her father?"

"For God's sake, the man's seriously ill. I wouldn't think joking about it would be your style."

"This isn't a joke. Mr. King's medical upkeep is very important to Ashley. That's the only reason you have a prayer at all."

Parker winced. "That's my point."

"That's business."

Parker tried not to think about the means, only the results. He looked at the wall clock again. This had to be the longest morning of his life. The only good thing about it would be seeing Ashley again. The thought of her sweet, serene smile calmed him.

"I think she's here." Harvey pushed back in his chair, straining his ears toward the reception area outside Parker's closed door.

Parker swept half a stale doughnut off his desk and into the wastebasket. He started to brush the leftover crumbs into his hand, but his palms felt gritty enough. He hastily arranged a stack of papers over them instead, then stood while Harvey opened the door.

Ashley King looked smaller, more fragile than she had the previous Friday night. Her wan smile, directed at Parker's secretary, faded as she came through his door.

Parker cleared his throat. "Nice to see you again, Ms. King." For a moment, Parker didn't think she was going to accept his proffered hand. Her eyes didn't sparkle as they had the other night. They were shadowed and dull.

"Let's not pretend this is anything other than what it is, shall we?" She withdrew her hand from his almost as quickly as she'd extended it, then accepted the chair Harvey pulled out for her. "I have a list of questions my attorney has advised me to cover. I'm sorry she couldn't be here. She's in court."

Parker didn't like the idea of anyone else—even an attorney—knowing of the proposal. Harvey had taken care of the confidentiality issue with a separate contract, yet it still made Parker uneasy. But Ashley was right. This was a business deal, no matter how you looked at it, and of course she should have legal counsel. This whole idea really stunk, but did he have a choice? Obviously Ms. King didn't either.

He watched her remove a typed sheet from the briefcase on her lap, then the contract Harvey had drawn up. Her hand trembled. Parker's gut clenched.

"First of all," Ashley began. "There is no indication as to how long this agreement would be in effect." She directed her statement to Harvey, and Parker got the distinct impression she was avoiding his gaze. Several times she flicked at her shoulder as if, by habit, adjusting her hair, only she had pulled it back into a tight knot at her nape. Right now, she looked like the schoolteacher she was.

"We purposely left that open for discussion, Ms. King," the attorney replied. "Obviously we would prefer an extended period of time, to protect our position. However, we understand that since you are only twenty-nine..."

Ashley's chin lifted a few cool degrees. "What else do you know about me?" Her eyes, flashing green with temper, found Parker's, then switched back to Harvey. "I imagine you've done a complete check, haven't you?"

"Well, naturally we needed to—"

"I expect the same consideration, Mr. Winton. At your expense, of course. I choose the investigator, you issue the check. Next point." She bent her head, perusing her list.

Parker felt a streak of indignation straighten his spine, and then he relaxed and smiled. Wouldn't he have done the same thing? He liked her spunk. He liked her. Maybe this wouldn't be such a bad deal after all.

"Mr. James?" He looked back just in time to see her blow absently at a softly curling tendril that had strayed. His gaze fastened on her full pursed lips. Then again, maybe he should run like hell while he still had the chance.

"Mr. James," she repeated.

"Parker," he said automatically. "Call me Parker." If they were going to be married, she should at least call him Parker. The absurdity of the situation sobered him once again. He leaned forward, elbows resting on his desk. "Look, Ms.—uh—Ashley, this original contract," he said, tapping his copy, "is not etched in stone. It's a guide to meet both our needs."

"Fine. And I'm just trying to voice mine."

"Go on."

"With regard to my father," Ashley said hesitantly, and Parker could see the bittersweet emotions play across her face. The light that had entered her eyes only moments earlier vanished. "I want the type of medical expenses you'll cover clearly defined."

"Whatever he needs."

Harvey coughed. "He means whatever is reasonable and customary."

"You sound like an insurance agent, Harv." Parker looked at Ashley. "If it's within my ability, your father will have it." He waited for her eyes to respond, watched for some small reprieve, but she shuttered them from him.

"What is it exactly that you want, Ms. King?" Harvey asked.

"I want my father to be comfortable." Her words were soft. Tension lines appeared where her dimple should have been. And Parker felt like a bigger heel than ever. He tried to concentrate on the paperwork before him and ignore her wounded look. Forget heel. He felt like a snake.

"What else concerns you?" he asked gruffly before he said something utterly stupid.

Ashley raised her eyes level with his, resolve replacing sentiment. "I want a community center."

"A what?" Parker's voice echoed Harvey's by a second.

"I don't have to remind either of you how valuable and important that homestead land is to native Hawaiians. If it weren't available, many of them would be homeless. If only to salve your own conscience, I'd think you'd agree to that."

"Wait a minute." Now she was pushing it. No one was going to beat up on his conscience but him. "This project is also going to create one hell of a lot of jobs. Don't tell me we don't need more of those."

"And are these great jobs going to pay enough to afford housing in this already inflated market?"

"Are you going to lay inflation on me, too?"

"That's the deal, Mr. James." Ashley looked directly at him, her expression impassive.

"You've drawn the mistaken conclusion that I have unlimited resources. Medical treatment is not cheap. Are you willing to compromise that for this community center?"

"Don't you have the James stamp of approval? That should count for quite a bit," she said, disdain in her tone.

"Leave my father out of this." Parker had lowered his voice to a monotone. "No one, absolutely no one, can get wind of this arrangement, or everything is off. And I'll leave both you and your father so high and dry you won't know what happened."

"We're not getting off to a very good start," Harvey interjected. "Maybe you should have your attorney call me, Ms. King."

Silence crackled like heat lightning. Parker leaned back in his chair, staring at the battle preparation on Ashley's face. Slowly he let out his pent-up breath. "You'll get your damn community center. But only after..."

"After what, Mr. James? After my father is dead?"

Parker had been gut-punched plenty in his younger days, but at this moment, nothing he recalled had felt worse than Ashley's accusing stare. "After the resort begins to turn a profit. That's what I was going to say."

Ashley turned her bright eyes away from him. "I'm sorry," she whispered. "That was uncalled for."

Briskly, he shuffled some papers on his desk. "Think about my offer. That's the best I can do. But I will add this, there's no question about the resort's eventual profitability. Take that for what it's worth."

"I don't need to think about it. That seems reasonable enough." She paused. "As long as I have control of the land in the meantime." She blinked, then looked away for a moment, and Parker had the uneasy feeling he was missing something. "And I'd like that in writing," she added.

"Don't trust me?" Parker's eyebrows rose slightly.

Ashley merely smiled. "Do we have a deal?"

"As long as you agree not to build anything in the interim." Parker tipped farther back in his chair. "And I'll have that in writing, thank you. Anything else?"

He glanced at Harvey, who stared at him intently, an odd smile lurking at the corners of his mouth. The attorney wasn't getting any younger, and it was past time for him to retire. He hadn't been acting like himself lately. After this was over, Parker vowed he'd let up on him. It wouldn't be easy. Harvey had always been his most trusted friend.

"Well, there's the courtship..." Ashley finally said.

"Courtship?" Parker's eyes skidded back to her.

"I know it sounds old-fashioned." A faint pink tinged her cheeks. "And I agree, but my father will expect it. You see, Mr. James, it's just as important to me that this union seems real. I don't want my father to know I've compromised myself."

Her words stung. It made him sound like some kind of pervert. "For starters, I think you'd better get used to calling me Parker. Now, how long is this, uh, courtship supposed to last?"

"It depends on how well I can convince him there's been someone in my life."

"Is there?" The thought hadn't occurred to him before. Surely Harvey would have warned him.

"No. That's going to make it more difficult."

"Would he believe in love at first sight?"

"Not..." Ashley uncrossed her legs, then recrossed them in the opposite direction, darting an uncomfortable look at Harvey. "Please don't take this wrong. But not with someone like you."

"Meaning?"

"You're not my type."

"And what is your type, Ms. King?"

"You'd better get used to calling me Ashley."

"Ashley." Parker had never claimed to be a patient man. Now she was definitely pushing it. "What will it take to convince him?"

"Let's see. Have you ever done anything worthwhile...uh...charitable, that is?" Ashley demanded without a trace of apology.

A brief chuckle escaped Harvey before he turned it into a cough and cast an amused gaze at the ceiling. Parker could only hope Harvey had caught the warning look he gave him, even though Harvey already knew Parker's contributions and past involvements were either anonymous or a taboo subject.

"Nothing you'd be interested in. Have any suggestions?" Parker asked in a clipped tone.

"Well, I'm quite involved in the truancy tutoring program. If you were also involved..." she continued, doubt clouding her eyes, "he might believe we'd met there and that we'd hit it off."

"That's fine. Tell him that."

"Great. It might work. What day would you like to begin?"

"What?"

"Tutoring."

"I didn't mean I'd *really* get involved. I meant that you should tell him that."

Ashley shook her head. "That won't work. He'll have questions."

"And you'll have the answers."

"But he'll ask you when you go to the hospital."

"Why would I do that?"

She stared back at him. "As my fiancé, surely you'd want to visit him, ask his blessing."

This was getting far too complicated. Parker looked helplessly at Harvey.

"She's right, you know," his friend said.

"All right," Parker said through clenched teeth and reached for a notepad. "Where and when do I show up?"

Ashley gave him directions. After they'd come to an agreement and settled several other issues, she tapped her papers into a neat pile and put them in her briefcase.

Parker's stomach told him it was well past lunchtime, and he was considering an offer of lunch when Ashley, poised for flight, dropped the final question.

"I realize this doesn't need to be contractual, but what will the sleeping arrangements be?"

All of a sudden, food was the last thing on his mind. "I'm not sure I follow you," Parker said slowly. He really had to change cleaners. They were shrinking his collars.

"What percentage of the time will I be expected at your place? Do you entertain much?"

"I expect you to move in." He put both palms up. "This has to look like a real marriage. Don't you understand that? Harvey?" he pleaded for his friend's assistance.

The older man laid down his pen and abandoned the notes he'd been taking. "Ashley—may I call you that?" She nodded and he continued. "It is imperative that we don't leave ourselves open for speculation. You will have your own room and one that only appears, and I stress *appears*, to be shared with Parker."

"But that's—"

Harvey held up his hand. "Parker has a live-in housekeeper who must also be convinced. I'm sure you two can get around that, however, but not without a joint room."

"Can't you let her go?" Ashley flashed an agonized look at Parker. "I'll do the housework."

"She's been with me a long time," he said, shaking his head. Mrs. Lee had been a major concern. Although she had a heart of gold and would never do anything to intentionally hurt him, she also had a big mouth. One that had been a problem in the past, but something Parker had long ago accepted. He would never turn her out.

"She really should be retired, but Parker has a soft—" the attorney began.

"That's enough, Harvey," Parker warned, then faced Ashley. "Mrs. Lee stays. But don't worry, I'm sure it won't be difficult to stage a quarrel soon after the blessed day. Enough to justify separate rooms for a while." He hoped he didn't sound put off over Ashley's attitude toward him. After all, the only thing he cared about was her signing on the dotted line.

"We're adults." She sniffed. "I'm sure we'll be able to handle it. I'll keep my apartment, though. No one has to know about that."

"I have a big house, Ashley. There's plenty of room."

"I'm keeping it, anyway," she said, a stubborn green glint in her eyes.

"We'll leave that open for discussion." Not that Parker meant it. She could not maintain her own apartment and that was that.

"Sure," Ashley said with raised eyebrows and no conviction. It was obvious that issue was closed for her, too. She stood and smoothed out her slacks. "I'll go over what we discussed with my attorney and get back to you within the week."

"Tomorrow. I need to hear tomorrow."

"That's not enough time."

"Yeah? Well, I hadn't planned on a courtship. We don't have any more time." Parker stood, too. He towered over her by a foot. They couldn't agree on one blasted thing. And he still preferred blondes. What had he gotten himself into?

"I'll be talking to you in the next couple of days." She stuck out her hand. He engulfed it with his. Her palm felt damp. Or maybe it was his.

"I'd like to know before I show up for this tutoring thing," he said, not wanting her to have the final word.

"Of course," she replied with deceptive sweetness. "You wouldn't want to waste your time."

Without saying anything more, Parker watched her shake Harvey's hand, exchange a few words, then leave his office. Lunch forgotten, he lowered himself to his chair and gave a frustrated push away from his desk. "Couldn't you have found someone a little more contrary?"

"Do you blame her?" Harvey asked.

"This isn't exactly what I had planned for the next few years either."

"Nothing is signed. You can still pull out."

"And do what? Sign bankruptcy papers instead?"

"If I were you, I'd just be thankful we found someone eligible and in a tight enough bind to be useful."

The reminder of Ashley's problem humbled Parker. But just a little. "She doesn't look very Hawaiian." Parker looked up from the paper clip he was unbending when Harvey sighed. "I wasn't going to ask again. If you tell me she is, I believe you. I was wondering if there's any sort of relationship to *the* King family, as in mega land holdings."

"One and the same. She's one of the granddaughters."

"Then what the hell would she need money for?" He dropped the paper clip altogether.

"Her father fell out of grace years ago, before Ashley was born. Most of the family lives on Maui. I'll bet she doesn't see them much, if at all."

"But the man's ill, for God's sake."

Harvey shrugged. "Some things can't be forgotten."

Parker knew the truth of that all too well. "What did he do that was so unforgivable?" he asked, toying with a pencil, not sure if he really wanted to know. Tentacles of sympathy wrapped themselves around him. Her wounded look flashed in his mind. He snapped the pencil in half. This was a business deal, he reminded himself.

"He married a mainlander."

"Great." Parker rested his head on the back of his chair and stared at a faint watermark on the ceiling. For many Hawaiians it was almost sacrilegious to mix blood, especially with a Caucasian. "So if Ashley marries me, she'll put the final nail in her coffin."

"You're not a mainlander. Your family's been here for generations."

"We both know it goes beyond that."

"Sometimes," Harvey agreed. "But in this case the woman was a gold digger. She did a good job of spending King's money before she hightailed it back to the mainland."

"And she's Ashley's mother?" Unbidden sympathy once again skittered through him before he shoved it away.

"Yes, but she didn't stick around too long. I'm not sure what Ashley considers her."

"You certainly know a lot about the family," Parker said.

"I've been around a long time, and I'm nosy."

"Think this scheme has a snowball's chance?"

"Without a doubt."

"We're nothing alike, you know."

"Oh, I'm not so sure about that."

"She's a damn bleeding-heart liberal," Parker continued, shaking his head. "I can tell."

"Probably."

"She'll drive me crazy."

"I think you'll do your fair share."

"There's too much friction between us. People won't buy it."

"Friction. Interesting choice of words."

"Spare me the raised eyebrows. We don't see eye-to-eye and you know it."

"Then use it to your advantage."

"How?"

"The passion is already there, change the angle."

"That will *never* happen." Parker rolled his eyes and flicked the pencil halves away. "Think she'll do it, Harv?"

"She loves her father more than anything in the world. I don't see how she can pass it up."

This conversation didn't make Parker feel any better. In fact, it made him feel predatory. He had to keep in mind that she had just as much to gain as he did.

That wasn't quite true. For Parker, this was a tightrope he couldn't share. He had both everything to gain and everything to lose. Right now, he wasn't sure his soul could withstand the loss.

He messed with some papers on his desk before looking up into Harvey's inquiring gaze. "How about some lunch?"

"You go ahead. I have some calls to make."

"Can I bring you something back?"

"Sesame chicken salad or anything light. I've got a full calendar this afternoon."

Parker felt a little guilty. He had a full calendar, too. But he had to get out for a while. Harvey was looking tired these days, but Parker couldn't bring himself to push the idea of retirement too hard. His friend's ego had also suffered the ravages of age. Besides, Harvey had always been there and Parker couldn't imagine not having his reliable counsel.

"I won't be long. Just need to clear the cobwebs from my brain," Parker called over his shoulder as he headed through the reception area.

Harvey returned to his own office, and watching through the glass inset bordering his closed door, he waited until Parker stepped onto the elevator before picking up his phone. He waited a moment for the connection to be made. Hearing the anxious greeting on the other end, he smiled.

"Not to worry," he said, leaning leisurely back into his chair. "We have him right where we want him."

Chapter Three

"I wish you could have been there, Crystal." Ashley slid a hatbox under her bed. "The guy is unbelievable."

"So why are you even considering his proposal?"

"This, coming from you?" Ashley slanted her friend and attorney a wry look. Beneath the slicked-back hair, she knew there was a spiked punk rocker waiting to emerge as soon as the power suit came off. "The queen of adventure herself?"

"That's all right for me, not you. Besides . . ." Crystal tugged at her lapels. "I am trying to clean up my act."

"Right." Ashley suppressed a smile, then frowned as sobering thoughts flooded her overtaxed brain. "There's something you need to take into consideration when you review the contract."

"Such as?"

"Parker James is a shark."

"Oh yeah?" Her friend chuckled and waggled her eyebrows. "I don't recall quite that description after the benefit."

"That was before I knew what a low-down scheme he'd concocted." Ashley stopped, unable to keep from wincing at her self-righteousness. Especially after what she was about to admit to Crystal.

"So, tell him to take a hike."

"I wish I could." Ashley sighed, sat on the edge of her bed and kicked off her sandals. "But that's not an option."

"You could call your grandparents." Crystal said hesitantly, then made a show of touching up her lipstick.

"And start a war? My father would never forgive me, and I can't take the chance of exciting him." No one had to know they had already refused her calls. "That leaves me with the shark."

"But such a good-looking one. Half the women I know—"

"Don't even think it. This will be purely business, and that's why you need to make sure that contract is ironclad."

"No problem." Fingering out spiky bangs, Crystal asked, "Think I should wear my hair up or down?"

Ashley started to say something, then clamped her mouth shut. Crystal was not taking this seriously enough. Ashley stared at her friend's young Amerasian face and thought about the lines of experience and wisdom in Harvey Winton's.

In spite of being nothing alike, she and Crystal had been best friends since grade school. And although they had always championed each other, Crystal was new on the legal track and Harvey Winton had a hard-nosed reputation. So much was riding on this "blissful" agreement, it made Ashley nervous. Right now, she felt as if she were being sucked under by a tidal wave. Guiltily, she wondered if she should retain a more experienced lawyer. She could handle being shark bait, but not at her father's expense.

Ashley's thoughtful silence seemed to go unnoticed by Crystal, who was busy adding two more earrings to each ear.

Without further deliberation, Ashley made her decision. Whatever Crystal lacked in experience, she more than made up for in loyalty. No matter what else happened, Ashley wanted her father taken care of, and she knew she could count on Crystal for that. That left Ashley free to pursue the second part of her plan.

"There's something else," Ashley said nonchalantly, then took a deep breath while Crystal finished fiddling with a silver ear cuff. "I want that land, too."

Crystal's eyes briefly met Ashley's in the mirror before she swung around to face her. "Why?"

Ashley leaned back on the bed, bracing her elbows behind her head. "It's perfect for a shuttle service to Magic Island." A smile spread across her face. "I can see it now, the revolutionary new gambling mecca of the Pacific."

After a brief silence, Crystal laughed. "You had me going there for a minute." She turned back to spiking her hair.

"Think about it." Ashley sat up and spread her hands. "It would be only a fifteen-minute plane ride, forty-minute ferry ride, tops. That wedge of land is ideal for a short private airstrip and it butts up to enough ocean footage for a dock. It's perfect."

Crystal gave her a long, incredulous look. "Aren't you forgetting something rather major? Like Hawaii hasn't legalized gambling yet, much less allotted an island for it."

"It's only a matter of time. We both know that. And when it happens, I want a piece of it."

Crystal put down her hair pick altogether and turned slowly back toward her friend. "This doesn't even sound like you, Ash."

Ashley pulled her bare legs up on the bed and crossed them. Resting her chin in her palms, she sighed. "Do you know how much I have in my savings account? Zero. My teaching pension? Not worth mentioning. I wrote a check to the hospital last week that just about put me in there along with my dad." She shook her head. "It's scary, Crystal. I'm wiped out, and if anything else happens to either my dad or me..."

She threw up her hands. "Besides, I'm tired of living like this. Someone stands to make a bundle and it might as well be me."

"Look." Crystal nudged Ashley aside and sat down next to her. "I know if gambling is legalized you'd like to see it confined to one island."

"Not just one island," Ashley corrected. "Kahoolawe, also known among my more enlightened peers as Magic Island. The navy doesn't need it for target practice anymore. It's useless as is. But with an amusement park, casinos and enough resort development, so much of the tourist traffic will be eliminated from the residential islands."

"You don't have to convince me," Crystal said, holding up a hand. "It's the resort owners here and on the other islands you have to worry about. They don't want to share the market, not with existing hotels and restaurants to fill. That's why they're pushing for the floating casino idea rather than a self-contained island. That way, they'll still have plenty of hungry and tired tourists coming back every evening. And there's a heck of a lot of money behind them to make sure things go their way."

"Don't be such a pessimist." Ashley lifted her chin, but her spirits didn't quite make the same ascent. There was too much truth in what Crystal said. "This is still a democracy and a lot of others believe as I do."

Her friend stared up at the ceiling for several minutes before commenting. "Okay, let's say that this Magic Island theory of yours has a chance. How would you fit in?"

"A service center." Ashley's eyes lit up. "With money exchange, translation assistance, concierge service—and the air and sea shuttles would, of course, be the most profitable. And best of all, it could be manned primarily by the kids I tutor. Most of them need jobs—"

"Hold it. And where, in heaven's name, would the money come from?"

"Parker."

"I knew it. You've gone totally bananas." Crystal started to leave, but Ashley grasped her arm.

"Not just from him. As long as I have the land, the state will have to take my bid for the shuttle service seriously, and once I've accomplished that, investors will start coming out of the woodwork."

"Not Parker's woodwork. His money, his investors' money, his family's money is all heavily tied up in hotels here and on Maui and Kauai. And they sure as hell don't want to see any tourist moola going to other resorts." Crystal widened sympathetic eyes that suggested her friend had gone over the edge. "Parker will flip."

"Parker is not going to know." Ashley swept her hair back with a shaky hand.

"I'm going to be sorry I asked...."

"I sort of skirted around it. I told him I wanted a community center."

"And?"

"And nothing. He didn't ask and I didn't volunteer. If he thinks it's for the kids I work with, then that's his problem."

"You know damn well, Ashley King, that's exactly what he thinks." Crystal's lips curved up in conspiratorial joy.

"Oh, well..." Ashley smiled back. That's exactly what she'd counted on. And having been named volunteer of the year twice in a row hadn't hurt. "It's half true, anyway. Those kids need the jobs and I plan on giving them all a considerable amount of interest in it."

"Don't try and rationalize your conniving little heart now, my formerly altruistic friend." Crystal rubbed her palms together in delight, ignoring Ashley's grimace over the well-placed jab. "It's just getting interesting. But why didn't you apply for the land yourself?"

"Homestead land isn't supposed to be zoned commercially, but apparently Parker and Harvey Winton have friends in high places." Ashley rolled her eyes toward the ceiling. "And truthfully, I'm not at all happy about how they're going about this, but since it's going to be done with or without me, I want in."

"Oh, yeah, for the community." Grinning, Crystal picked up her purse and slung it over her shoulder.

"Believe what you want, but I won't be the only one benefiting from this deal," Ashley sniffed.

"If you pull it off."

"If I pull it off," Ashley agreed, trying not to think about the alternative.

"You know Parker won't give you a cent if he finds out."

"What he'd probably give me is a one-way ticket to the loony farm." He'd give her a heck of a lot more than that, she suspected.

"And you'll be giving him a run for his money. Sounds fair to me." Crystal chuckled, then hesitated at the door. "I was wondering..." she began, her forehead puckered in thought. "Do sharks mate for life?"

LONG AFTER HER FRIEND had left, Ashley sprawled out on her bed, wide-awake, an attack of cold feet well underway. Two glasses of milk hadn't eased the burning in her stomach. And Crystal's teasing words still stung, even though Ashley truly didn't consider herself in the same category as Parker. His reasons were purely self-serving, while her first concern was for her father.

And until now, wanting to turn Kahoolawe into the Disney island of the Pacific had been nothing more than a pipe dream. But with the land, Parker's money and the James name... Ashley could almost smell success.

She rolled over and stared at the ceiling. Dollar signs replaced the zeros in her teacher's pension fund, even as the foreboding thoughts of Parker's reaction fought for her more practical nature. Wanting a secure future didn't make her a bad person, she assured herself. And she wasn't so naive as to think Hawaii didn't need the tourist industry. But that didn't mean there wasn't a better way. And Parker, of course, was certainly getting what he wanted.

But when it came right down to it, even with all the rationalizing she'd done in the past two days, Ashley dreaded the time when she would finally have to face-off with Parker. Because no matter how she twisted the equation, Parker and his investors could stand to lose sizable profits with the development of a Magic Island.

And he'd be far from pleased with her part in Project Teacher's Pension.

Ashley smiled at the impromptu name. It had a nice ring to it. She concentrated on that and tried not to think about the more dreary "what-ifs" that lay ahead. The many hours she'd spent at the hospital were beginning to take their toll. She hadn't cut back on volunteering, and she had another two weeks of teaching Hawaiian social studies before summer vacation.

Besides, time was no longer a viable commodity. She couldn't afford to use it for negative thoughts. That's why she wouldn't stall by investigating Parker. It wasn't necessary. The James family was well-known, but she had been miffed at her meeting with Parker and had felt like being difficult.

She shifted positions and prayed for sleep—sweet, numbing sleep. She had classes to teach today and Magic Island supporters to contact.

She thought about the enormous project she was about to undertake and about the father who'd always been there for her. Keeping perspective on his welfare would ultimately be her biggest asset. If her attention remained centered on that, she'd have her best chance of pulling this off. Life had to go on as usual. It would keep Parker from being suspicious.

Parker. Why did her thoughts keep returning to him? *Marriage.* That thought wasn't any better. Ashley punched her pillow and shook off the warm shiver that coursed up her spine. Maybe she'd squeeze in a Dale Carnegie seminar. What she needed was some basic positive thinking.

She let her mind drift back to Crystal, and the thought of her unconventional friend meeting Parker and Harvey for the first time made her smile. It turned into a yawn, and then she stared at the ceiling for the next two hours.

IF HARVEY TOLD PARKER not to be nervous one more time, he'd forget what a good friend the man was and pop him right in the mouth. Parker wiped invisible smudges from the marble pen holder and adjusted his leather blotter. "Hey, Louise," he yelled out to his secretary. "Turn down the thermostat, will you? It's hotter than hell in here."

The woman in a mustard cotton sweater rolled her eyes at Harvey as she passed Parker's open office door.

"I heard the elevator bell." The attorney straightened exaggeratedly in his chair. "Maybe you'd like to greet her with a lei in the hall?"

"Cut the sarcasm. I'm not in the mood." Parker snuck a glance pass the reception desk. "This is only a formality, right?"

"That's my best guess. We've already agreed to—"

"It's her." Parker cut him off in a lowered voice and rose from his chair. Harvey followed suit.

Her waist-length hair hung free this time, and he caught glimpses of it as it swayed gently like a mantle of black satin. Her hips moved in the same mesmerizing motion, and her dancer's legs were bare and brown.

"I'm sorry I'm dressed so casually." Ashley tugged at the skirt of her yellow floral dress, a soft pink heightening her cheekbones. "I have a tutoring session after this, and I didn't have time to run home and change."

Parker realized he was staring. Except he still couldn't stop himself, as he watched the fabric flutter from her graceful hands. Hula, he thought. She had told many stories with those hands. He wondered about what other kind of pleasure they could bring.

"Oh, no. You look great... I mean fine... you look fine." He yanked unnecessarily at a chair. "Here. Sit."

He looked from one pair of raised eyebrows to the other. "Please have a seat. You, too, Harvey." He swung the door closed, stopping it from slamming at the last moment.

"I understand we're in agreement," Parker said from his own chair, rubbing the familiar, reassuring leather arms.

"I made some minor changes. I believe my attorney had the contract delivered by courier?" Ashley looked to Harvey for confirmation. She didn't smile. Her mouth quivered a bit, and her beautiful hands had balled into small, tight fists.

"Yes, we have it," Parker said before his friend could speak. "Harvey, would you excuse us?"

"But I don't think—" Harvey turned his doubtful expression on Parker.

"Good. Then could you not think outside?" He exhaled a harsh breath, not liking his own curt tone. "The damned thing is already signed. Just give us a few minutes alone."

Shaking his head, Harvey rose to leave, but so did Ashley. "I really need to be going myself. I—I just thought I should stop by in person to confirm everything."

"Wait." She looked as if she were going to bolt for the open door through which Harvey was exiting, so Parker grabbed her wrist. "Don't go yet." He could feel her muscles tense beneath his fingers. Her eyes widened and she swallowed hard. He should have let her go, but he didn't.

"I don't need to be shackled, Mr. James. I'll stay for a few minutes." Slowly she curved back her hand, palm out, to escape his grasp.

He released her then, but let his fingers trail away. "Parker," he reminded her, remaining close.

Ashley took a step back, her progress halted by a wicker chair brushing her hip. Shooting swift glances toward the outer office, she extended her hands as if warding him off.

"I'm sure my entire staff is curious about you," he said in a low tone, not attempting to back off. "But of course no one knows of this arrangement but Harvey."

"What's your point?"

"Don't look so nervous. We're about to be engaged. Let's try to look like it."

"Now? Here?" She tried to back up the stubborn chair.

"Nothing dramatic. I merely don't want you to act so frightened when I get near you."

"Frightened? Of you? That'll be the day."

"Prove it." He edged closer. "For their sake, of course." His eyes held hers, as he nudged his head toward the open door and the gathering lunch crowd trying not to look interested.

"What do you want?"

"A smile would be nice, for starters."

Slowly, a small dimple appeared at the corner of her mouth. He put his hand at her waist and the dimple vanished.

"You're not trying very hard." He felt his own lips curve, unforced. He brought his lips to her ear, intoxicated by the blend of gardenias and sunshine that surrounded her. He felt his eyes drift closed.

"Parker?"

He pulled back. This woman was lethal. "That should do it for now." He glanced out at the few office stragglers oddly eyeing him and forced a smile. "Let's get out of here." He started to reach for her elbow, thought better of it and snatched his jacket instead.

"What are you talking about? I have a tutoring appointment."

"I'm supposed to be getting involved with that, remember?"

"Now?"

"Now." This time he did grab her elbow and headed full speed for the elevator. What the hell was he doing? He should be getting away from her. Not going with her. But they had unfinished business.

After a tense elevator ride and a short argument over who would drive, they left in Ashley's battered Toyota station wagon. Sprawled out as much as the small car would allow, Parker lounged back and said, "First thing we have to do is get you a new car."

"Forget it." The side mirror was missing. Parker watched Ashley roll down her window and stick her head out to clear a left turn.

"I don't think I heard you correctly."

"I said, forget it. This one suits me fine."

"Right."

She darted him a warning look. "There's something we need to talk about. As stipulated in the contract, I'll be where I need to be and I'll say what I need to say, but don't expect to change my life."

"I'm glad you brought up the contract. I can understand your attorney's involvement up until now. But no more. This can't look like a business deal."

"She's my friend."

"Then she is welcome in our home as your friend. No more of this communication-by-courier crap." *Our home.* The words sounded strange. He tugged his tie loose and glanced over at Ashley. He'd expected a scowl or at least a grimace; what he hadn't expected was a smile.

"Actually," she said, turning up the wattage directly at him. "I can't wait for you to meet her—and Harvey, too."

"I'd like that." Parker felt his shoulders relax. "Maybe we can have some sort of get-together with a few of our friends. Let them start getting used to the idea of us as a couple before we spring the news."

"Perfect." Ashley looked inordinately happy, still smiling, humming to herself. Parker felt somewhat uneasy but wasn't about to second-guess her sudden high spirits.

"When do you think we can legitimately pull this off without raising suspicion?" he asked with deceptive indifference.

"I've signed the contract." Her smile receded and her shoulders straightened. "Harvey is taking care of the paperwork to have the land transferred to my name. Using his political connections," she added with sarcastic disapproval. "I don't see what the rush is."

"I don't like loose ends."

"Sorry you consider me a loose end."

"That's not what I meant."

"Look." She slowed the car, veered off to the side of the road and parked. "There had better not be something you two aren't telling me. I don't know how Harvey managed to get this in the works so fast. Or how he was able to get land for multi-family use assigned to me alone. And I don't think I want to know." She was jabbing her finger in the air now. "But you'd better be straight with me."

"Calm down, damn it. I'll just feel more comfortable when everything falls into place. That's all. There's no hidden agenda."

She stared at him for a long time, just on the verge of speaking. She was jumpy, he could tell, and he wondered how much of it had to do with him personally.

"You have my word," Parker added, not at all mollified when misgivings darkened her eyes. It made him want to take her reassuringly into his arms, and he had to blink away the absurd notion.

"Now," he said, looking around for the first time. They weren't in the best of neighborhoods. "Can we get going?"

Ashley issued a short, humorless laugh. "We're already here." She got out of the car and pulled a large canvas bag along with her. "Welcome to the rest of paradise," she said, shutting the door and leaving him dumbfounded in his seat.

It took a few seconds for realization to set in before he got out and caught up to her. She was nearing a rundown garage when he finally managed to regain her attention.

"Is this where you do that tutoring project?" he asked, his peripheral vision taking in boarded-up windows and rusted-out abandoned cars.

"Did you expect a country club?" She turned away from him and headed in the direction of a small weathered church.

"It was only a question," he replied softly, easily matching her angry stride.

"These kids need tutoring because most of them have to work and help the family. When they start missing too much school and fall behind, they drop out altogether." She sighed and slowed her pace. "We have to break the cycle or they'll end up at dead ends just like their parents did."

"I don't doubt that, and I think what you're doing is admirable."

"But...?" She glanced warily at him only to find him smiling at a little girl who had stepped off a porch. Her face was dirty, her clothes torn and her thumb stuck in her mouth.

"Is it safe here?"

"No. She's about to mug us at any minute." Ashley threw up a hand. She cooled her harsh tone and spoke a couple of Hawaiian words to the toddler, making her grin from ear to ear. She patted the tangled mass of black curls, then picked up her pace. "These people are poor, Parker, not criminals. Or maybe you think it is criminal to be poor."

"Now, wait a minute." Firmly, but gently, he grabbed Ashley's arm, forcing her to stop. Her bare arm was warm from the sun. It felt fragile yet vibrant under the pressure of his fingers. Her eyes shot shards of firey green and her mouth parted in indignation. She had more passion bottled up in her than any woman he'd ever come across. He didn't know if he should shake her or kiss her.

"It doesn't look like I have a choice."

"What?" he asked, blinking.

"About waiting." She looked significantly at his hand locked around her arm.

He dropped it. "I'm sorry."

"It's ironic that after all these years of coming here, this is the most violence I've encountered."

"I said I was sorry," he said, wincing. "But did it occur to you that I might care what happens to you?" And amazingly, at this moment, he did.

She turned her incredible eyes on him, and her mouth softened into a wry tilt. "I believe Rhett Butler said it best. Frankly, my dear, I don't give a damn."

Chapter Four

Ashley didn't know what it was about Parker that irked her. Part of it was that everything seemed to come easy for him, but there was something else, too...something she couldn't quite put her finger on.

Anyway, she'd be smart to be a little nicer to him, to not rock the boat. She certainly wasn't in any position to be provoking him. And although all this wonderful rationalization was fine when she was alone, being in such proximity to him sent all her good intentions right out the window.

The fact that the past two hours had been no picnic didn't help. The kids were unusually restless and far too inquisitive about her "new friend." Playing twenty questions and fending off adolescent hostility over the unexpected intrusion had exhausted her. By the time they had packed up, she was itching to be rid of her companion. Her nerves had had enough of Parker James.

"I've got to get to a phone, Ashley," Parker said as they left the church. "Let Louise know how long I'm going to be. She'll have to cancel some of my appointments."

"There's no need for that." She waved to the kids and headed for her car at a fast clip. "I can have you back in twenty minutes."

"That anxious to be rid of me?" he teased, and she felt the blood rush to her face. "And here I've been on my best behavior."

"By following me around?"

"I thought I'd been courting you."

Ashley caught his spreading grin out of the corner of her eye. "Are you trying to make me crazy on purpose?" She waved a hand around. "Or is this some natural talent?"

"I have many natural talents," Parker drawled in a low, sexy voice, and Ashley had to stop herself from glancing back over at him. "But patience with hostile kids is not one of them."

She slowed down near the car and sighed. One of her older pupils had verged on insolence. She was hoping Parker hadn't noticed. "Kimo can be a little trying and I really do appreciate that you didn't take the bait."

"A little trying? The kid looked like he wanted to carve me up for sushi. He obviously doesn't like *haoles.*"

"Especially ones wearing three-hundred-dollar shoes." She slid her gaze from his feet, up his body, to his eyes. "And five-hundred-dollar suits." His silky gaze awaited hers. She stared back a moment too long before looking away. "If you're still interested in helping out, I think you'd be more effective if you dressed for the neighborhood."

"I'm still interested."

Her eyes flew back to his. Something in his tone sent her imagination off like a rocket, and his gaze roaming her face, sent a warm shiver through places that shouldn't be shivering.

Ashley took a quick, deep breath. "Well, I won't snub any help, as long as you're sincere." She walked around to the driver's side and tossed in her bag. "Those kids already have the deck stacked against them."

Parker climbed into the passenger seat as Ashley slid behind the wheel and laid his hand on her arm when she started the ignition. "I won't lie to you. I'm getting involved in this to make our relationship look legit. But I also genuinely admire your dedication, and as long as I'm involved those kids will have my full attention." His eyes were startlingly blue, earnest. And too close.

She shifted her arm a bit, telling him he could let go. He didn't.

"I believe you, Parker, but...even Kimo?" She arched a brow, ignoring the unsettling feeling caused by his warm palm on her flesh.

"Especially Kimo, probably," Parker groaned.

"He'll come around. He's real protective of me, and it didn't help that his girlfriend played up to you."

"So, the little sucker's got the hots for Leilani."

Ashley shot him an amused look and smiled. "I think you may just fit in after all."

He smiled back, allowing a few silent moments to pass, his thumb absently stroking her skin. And then he dropped his hand from her arm as if it were a hot potato. "Where to next, so I know what to tell Louise?" he asked, his tone all business again.

"The hospital," Ashley said, exhaling an uneven breath. "Are you still in?"

Parker hesitated for just an instant, pinching the crease in his pants. "I am."

"We're not far. You can call her from there." Ashley glanced over at his guarded face. "And you can wait in the lobby if you want."

"I'd like to meet your father, unless you think it's too soon."

"I'm not sure." She sucked in her lower lip. "I mentioned you last night so you wouldn't come as a complete surprise. But he's not expecting me today and I don't want anything to look amiss. I just want him to get used to you."

"This is your show," he said with a tight smile.

Something had spooked Parker, so Ashley respected his silence the rest of the way. She had enough of her own problems to worry about, anyway. She had no idea how her father would react, but the sooner he got used to the idea of her and Parker as a couple... Ashley drew in a large gulp of salt-scented air. Heck. The sooner *she* got used to them being a couple, the sooner she would have money for his medical bills and the land she needed to submit her bid to the state.

They arrived at the hospital in record time and were halfway down the long hospital corridor when Ashley broke away from her mental tailspin long enough to look at Parker. "You look horrible," she said. "You're as white as a sheet."

"Don't tell me. He's in the last room." Parker's lips thinned considerably. A light film of moisture shone at his temples and Ashley's eyes widened on him.

"You don't like hospitals, do you?" She pressed a comforting hand to his wrist.

"I hate them." He grabbed her hand in a death grip and pulled her along.

She had to slow him down when they reached her father's room. She knew others who had hospital phobias and felt a moment's pity for him. "We're here." She yanked her hand from his vise. "Maybe by the *next* visit he'll expect us to be holding hands," she said jokingly. Mentioning next time was an error. Deeper lines formed between his brows. "We won't stay long," she assured him and led the way in to the semiprivate room.

Keoki King sat up in his bed, his black eyes wide and alert, his flowered orange-and-yellow shirt a jarring contrast to the stark white sheets. A lunch tray was pushed to the side, a deck of cards and two haphazard stacks of quarters crowded the empty plates. The thinly disguised odor of tobacco lingered in the air.

"Leialoha, I was not expecting you." He opened his arms wide to his daughter.

"Oh, Dad, you haven't been taking money from the nurses again," Ashley scolded softly as she hugged him and kissed his cheek.

"Better than money." He grinned. "I have two more weeks of not having to wear that." He pointed to a wadded-up hospital-issue nightshirt on a chair near the drawn privacy curtain around the other bed, then put his finger to his lips and said in a hushed tone. "I have a new roommate."

Ashley nodded and lowered her voice. "This is the friend I was telling you about." She turned to Parker and grasping his forearm, pulled him closer. "Meet Parker James." The special smile she turned on Parker was for her father's benefit, but the fact that it seemed to have a tension-easing effect on Parker pleased her.

"And Parker, this is my dad, Keoki King."

"Mr. King, it's good to meet you." Parker stepped forward when the older man stuck out a weathered brown hand.

"Everyone calls me Keoki." His dark eyes were frank and measuring. "So, you are the one making my Leialoha so happy these days."

"Dad." Surprise and mortification seeped through Ashley's tone. Why would her father say such a thing? True, her spirits had been up because of the money raised at the benefit. And she had been terribly excited over the possible resurrection of Magic Island. But still, it was an odd conclusion for him to draw.

"I am an old man and time is short," her father said. "I have to say what I think." Winking, a faint smile lighting his face, he added in a stage whisper, "Is it serious? I may still see grandchildren?"

"Oh, Dad. Quit teasing." She chanced a peek at Parker, who had relaxed and was smiling. Was he enjoying this? *The jerk.*

"I'm glad I have you on my side, sir. Ashley's a tough one to catch. I'm flattered she's said so much about me," Parker said so earnestly Ashley could barely keep from gaping. He'd obviously missed his calling.

"I haven't," Ashley assured him.

"She did not have to," Keoki said, nodding his head with untold wisdom. "I could tell. But she spends too much time with her charities. Make sure she pays attention to you."

"I have a feeling that'll be unavoidable," Parker said in a dry enough tone that it took all of Ashley's willpower not to give him a dirty look.

"Tell me about yourself, Parker James," her father continued, blithely unaware of Ashley's agitation.

Parker gave him a skeleton story—the truth sometimes embellished, sometimes distorted, but always in evidence. Ashley waited patiently, trying to gauge her father's reaction, until a nurse motioned that it was time to leave.

Trailing Parker out of the hospital, Ashley acknowledged that today's visit had been better than most. Her father was in unusually high spirits, which made hers soar. It also allowed her to consider her plans for Magic Island with minimal guilt. Everything seemed to be coming together, except Parker's earlier comment came to mind. No more loose ends, he had said. And now Ashley agreed. This marriage had to take place as soon as possible.

"THE COAST IS CLEAR, my friend." Keoki reached down under his mattress and produced a fat, half-smoked cigar. "Where are my matches?"

Pulling back the privacy curtain, a disgruntled Harvey Winton hopped off the adjacent hospital bed and meticulously smoothed his slacks with a nervous hand. "I don't know how you get away with all this," Harvey said, giving up his lighter. "One of these days those nurses are going to quit running interference for you."

Keoki grinned and patted the deck of cards. "They owe me far too much money. Trade is cheaper."

"Don't get too cocky. If they figure out you cheat, they just might let Ashley catch us together."

"Cheat?" Keoki pursed his lips around the unlit cigar, then removed it. "Huh. You are just a poor loser. I am right about this plan. You will see."

Harvey drove a reckless hand through his neatly arranged hair. "Right. I should never have let you talk me into this." He shook his head. "If Parker finds out that there's no homestead land..."

"Parker? What about Ashley? You have not seen my Leialoha's temper. If she finds out it is we who own the land... It is best that we get them married right away." He tapped the side of his head with his index finger. "Before they have too much time to think."

"And before you're released from the hospital," Harvey reminded him. "You know she's doing this for you."

"Yes." Keoki stared out the window. "And I do not think I can keep her from finding out my treatment is nearly complete. We must move quickly."

"I'd say it's out of our hands. And none too soon, I might add."

"Oh, but you are wrong, my friend. We have much to do if I want to see little *keikis* soon."

"Really, Keoki. Grandchildren?" Harvey cocked his head, remembering the earlier conversation he'd overheard. "Wasn't that a bit overdone?"

"So, she can think I am a little senile." He clasped his hands behind his head and lounged back into the pillows.

"Senile? You old coot, you haven't changed in forty years."

"Has it been that long, my friend?" Keoki smiled at his boyhood pal.

"Longer, but who's counting? Like one long poker tournament, we've won some and lost some." A brief silence followed, each friend reflecting on their wins and losses.

"And this is our biggest gamble of all," Keoki said, suddenly very serious. "But I know *here,*" he thumped his chest, "we are doing the right thing. Those two, they were made for each other."

"I truly hope so."

"Parker should have been your son," Keoki said lightly, wishing he could reassure him. Already Keoki saw the uncertainty of their impulsiveness in his friend's eyes...something he knew in his heart of hearts need not exist.

A wistful sadness crossed Harvey's face before he frowned. "Why? So he can disown me when he finds out about this stunt we've pulled?"

"You are doing a fine thing for him. You said yourself he works too hard, he is too driven. And my Leialoha is much too busy with her volunteer work. She will never have her own children if she keeps taking in strays."

"Well..." Harvey looked out the window to the green cloud-shrouded mountaintops. "I certainly hope she keeps this stray."

"She will, my friend, she will." Keoki clapped him on the back. "We will see to it." Then his brown face puckered in a frown and he picked up the battered playing cards. "The next shift starts at midnight," he whispered. "Think we'll need a new deck?"

"I'M TAKING YOU BACK to your office now," Ashley said as she coaxed her sputtering Toyota onto the freeway.

"Then what are you going to do?" Parker asked.

"Go home and grade papers."

"When do you tutor again?"

"Day after tomorrow."

Parker let out a soft whistle. "How often do you go?"

"At least twice a week, three times when I can get enough of the kids together."

"Pretty aggressive schedule."

"Time isn't on their side."

"It's not on ours either," he reminded her. "How about dinner tonight?"

"We've already spent most of the day together." Her tone made it clear she thought that was enough.

Parker sighed. "It's a good thing I have a secure ego. We need to be seen in public. It also wouldn't hurt to get to know each other better."

"I have a feeling that's going to be inevitable."

"Then don't fight it. Have dinner with me."

"But my papers..." He had a point about being seen.

"I'll help you after dinner."

"You?" Ashley looked over at him. He looked so sincere and charmingly boyish. He was still tieless, sleeves rolled up, tawny hair falling across his forehead. She wondered if he realized he'd gone to the hospital looking like that.

"I'll pick you up at seven. Okay?"

"Seven-fifteen," she countered, unwilling to give him the final say, and caught the smirk he was trying to hold back.

"Seven-fifteen it is." This time he out-and-out grinned, pinning her with an amused stare as they pulled up in front of his office building. "I think it's time we got something out of the way."

Ashley gritted her teeth. If he was about to deliver an "I'm the boss" speech, she'd throw up. "Yes?" She turned to him with thinned lips.

Parker twisted in her direction and curved his hand around the nape of her neck. He pulled her toward him. In astonishment, her lips softened and parted slightly. At that exact moment, he brought his warm, moist mouth to hers. A groan of surprise rumbled from her throat. Right away, she knew that to be a mistake. He held her chin in place and increased the pressure of his lips.

She felt the tip of his tongue tease the seam of her lips, felt his breath, warm and beguiling. She didn't pull away. She didn't kiss him back. Totally floored, she did nothing.

It was Parker who finally, in a lingering fashion, broke away. "I'll see you tonight." He grabbed his jacket from the back seat, unfolded his tall body from the confines of his seat, then strode away from the car.

Ashley sat motionless, watching his broad shoulders disappear through the revolving door. She swore she could still feel the heated pressure of his hand at her neck, smell the faint scent of after-shave clinging to her warm cheeks.

A horn blasted from a car behind her, waiting for her to exit the loading zone. "Damn him." She dropped the hand that had somehow made its way to her awestruck mouth and threw the car into gear.

"I'VE RESERVED YOUR favorite table," the waiter said as he ushered Ashley and Parker through the main dining room to an open candlelit balcony overlooking the ocean.

"I appreciate it, Larry, especially on such short notice." Parker tried to slip the man what looked like a twenty-dollar bill, but the waiter pushed it away.

"Please, Mr. James, you've already done so much," the older man said in a hushed tone and hurried away.

Ashley busied herself with settling into her seat and pretended not to notice the interchange, but she couldn't help but be curious about what the other man meant.

"Nice view," she said as she removed the artfully arranged linen napkin from the wineglass with a little too much snap. She had to shake this mood. She hadn't wanted to let Parker get away with that unwelcome kiss and had almost stood him up for dinner. But then she'd decided that would give the kiss too much weight.

She had, however, considered getting even by borrowing one of Crystal's outfits, but then she scratched that. Too obvious. In the end, she picked out her nice white sleeveless silk dress and decided to be an adult about everything...which basically meant she would pretend that brief scintillating kiss had never happened.

"Nice menu," she commented, her eyes glued, unseeing, to the elegantly scripted writing.

"Nice conversation."

"I'm tired." Ashley wasn't in the mood for his teasing.

"Try to look somewhat cheerful, will you? I purposely came to this restaurant because I wanted some quick exposure for us. And I know a lot of people here."

Ashley struggled to turn up the corners of her mouth. The attempt was only half successful.

"Look." Parker waved at an older couple, then leaned across the table and reached for her hand. "If it's about the kiss this afternoon, I'm sorry. It was bound to happen, and I thought we should get it out of the way."

Get it out of the way. Everything was calculated and arranged for him. "I haven't thought twice about it."

"Liar."

She looked over the top of her menu and realized he had his fingers on the speeding pulse at her wrist. She snatched her hand to her side. "We can end this dinner right now."

"Good." He waved at someone else being seated. "Let's get something to go and take it to your place. We can tackle those papers."

"I've already done them," she lied. No way was he going to her apartment.

"All of them?" He eased back in his chair and narrowed his gaze on her. "Your father's right. You work too hard."

"I'll determine that. Shall we go?"

"To your place?"

"No."

"Mine?"

"No." She flicked at her hair, then remembered she'd put it up in a twist.

He laughed. "Might as well stay here then. The lobster is exceptional. I strongly recommend it."

She watched Parker peruse the menu and started to relax. Lobster did sound awfully good. It had been a long time since she'd been able to afford a small luxury such as that. And after the day she'd just had with Mr. Self-assured she deserved it. She closed her menu and Larry promptly appeared.

"Two lobsters," Parker said, handing the waiter his menu. "Extra butter."

Ashley darted Parker an incredulous look and held her tongue for as long as she could... a whole two seconds. "And I'll have the *ahi.*" She flashed the confused Larry a brilliant smile. "Broiled, please."

Parker grinned and nodded to Larry, who frowned and took the menu Ashley extended to him.

"And we'll also have a bottle of your finest champagne," Parker added.

"Very good, sir," Larry said with a nod before heading for the kitchen.

"You must be hungry," Ashley commented sweetly when the waiter was out of earshot.

"I am." Parker agreed, leaning back and patting his flat stomach. "Especially for this particular lobster dish. Did I tell you it's their specialty? They coat two perfect tails with garlic and herbs, and it comes out on a sizzling platter with lots of drawn butter and warm french bread.''

Ashley swallowed, then sipped from her water glass.

''It's a shame you don't want any.'' Parker's lips curved up slowly. ''But if you're real good, I may give you a taste.''

Ashley was about to give him a taste of something, but a couple of his friends stopped by their table. Parker was quick to draw her into the conversation and Ashley had to hand it to him, he sure could play the attentive date.

Once they were alone again, Ashley swept a glance around the dining room and asked, ''Pleased with your audience?''

''Pardon me?''

''For my... coming out.''

''Oh, yeah.'' Either he had missed her sarcasm or was ignoring it. ''Lots of key people, lots of big mouths, too.''

Surprised by his disdainful tone, she studied his sullen profile while he surveyed the crowded restaurant. For an odd moment, Ashley felt like Parker was playing a role. He didn't seem to belong to this social circle.

In fact, she'd sensed that at the benefit the first evening she'd met him. His mere presence had meant a large contribution to the Hawaiian immersion program, and for that she was grateful. But unlike many of the others, she'd gotten the feeling he wasn't there for the sake of being seen. He'd even seemed downright uncomfortable. Just like he looked now.

Ashley turned away from him and looked out over the darkened ocean. A scattering of city lights reflected like sea stars. She squinted into the blackness beyond, wondering if bright lights from Magic Island would some day be visible from Waikiki. Closing her eyes briefly, she sniffed the salty air and listened to the waves crash to swells before they rippled and licked the shore. God, how she loved these islands. How could her mother have left?

"A nickel for your thoughts?" Parker asked. He was his old smiling self, his personal demons momentarily gone. Even though she didn't want to, she wondered about him.

"Inflation," he said, misinterpreting her puzzled look. "A penny doesn't work these days."

She laughed. "Tell me about it." And then the reminder of why she was sitting here in the first place wiped all humor from her face. Even worse than inflation these days was her empty bank account.

Watching her, Parker, too, turned somber. Absently he rubbed his chin.

"Let's get married right away," he finally said out of the blue. "This week. That way the contract can go into effect and we don't have to worry about..."

"Me backing out," Ashley finished for him, leveling him with a steady gaze.

"It's not that." He looked long and hard at her. "I think it'll take off some of the pressure."

"I don't feel pressured."

"Sure. Then why do you look like you're going to bolt for the door at any minute?" Ashley barely got her mouth open to refute him when he leaned forward and tilted up her chin with his long, tanned fingers. "We don't have to be adversaries, Ashley."

"Then what are we?" Ashley sucked in her lower lip, cursing herself for the stupid remark and even more for its throaty delivery. She angled her head out of reach, but he caught her hand and stilled it from its fidgeting.

"We could be friends," he said lightly, while he stroked her inner wrist with his thumb.

Ashley turned her hand over into his, ignoring the hint of surprise in his face. She merely didn't want him anywhere near her pulse.

"Would that be so bad?" he asked, his voice raspy.

"Just friends," she cautioned, hoping the wind and surf disguised the breathless quality in hers. It would be far easier, she acknowledged, if he weren't so attractive.

He squeezed her hand tighter and she gave him a shy smile. The champagne he'd ordered arrived, but Parker didn't let go. And Ashley didn't let go either. Only when the pop of the cork startled them both, did Ashley slip away from his touch. She looked into his smiling blue eyes, caressed by moonlight and the soft glow of candles, and all but sighed.

Parker sent Larry away and assumed the task of pouring the sparkling wine. "Before we make a toast, I have something for you." He topped off both glasses, then reached into his breast pocket and produced a small velvet box.

"I guessed on the fit, but we can have it sized." He looked like a kid at Christmas. Ashley knew the feeling. She'd always been happier giving her father gifts rather than getting them herself. She smiled at his endearing enthusiasm, then peered into the box he'd flipped open.

"What the hell is that?" Her eyes were almost as big as the three-carat monstrosity that stared back at her.

Parker blinked several times. "What do you mean? What does it look like?"

"You can't expect me to wear that."

"No. I thought you'd dangle it from your car mirror."

"Do you know how many people that could feed?"

"Only one and his dental bill would be outrageous." His blue bedroom eyes were narrowed into impatient slits.

"Why, that thing could buy groceries for a family of ten for a year." Or part of an airstrip, Ashley's incensed mind suddenly realized.

"Probably three years. Tough." Heads turned and he had to lower his voice. "You *will* wear it." He glanced around the room, shaking his head. "I told Harvey you were a damn bleeding-heart liberal," he muttered under his breath.

"Mr. James," she hissed back in an even lower tone. Remember Magic Island, the rational side of her brain valiantly tried to whisper. "Would you like me to tell you what you can do with that ring?"

Parker slumped back and sighed. "I can hardly wait."

Chapter Five

Their meals arrived and Parker quickly shoved the ring box back into his pocket to avoid a scene. His appetite was gone and so was his good humor.

He watched Ashley through arms and plates and fresh pepper being ground, and even with all the activity he could see the angry sparks of green brightening her eyes.

Well, he was angry, too. The ring had little to do with status. She'd been so unselfish in this arrangement that he'd been anxious for her to have something personal. But she'd thrown it back at him.

In silence he watched her eat, doing more poking than eating, before he picked up his own fork. Pushing his champagne aside, and sloshing most of it onto his hand, he signaled for Larry and ordered a beer. Ashley still made no attempt at conversation.

In no mood to be civil or socially correct, Parker waved off the chilled glass the waiter brought with his beer and tipped the bottle up to his lips. He chugged a long, hard swallow and put it down with a small thud.

Without skipping a beat, he stabbed a chunk of lobster, dipped it in the melted butter and nearly bit the fork tip off as well. Her silence suited him just fine. He chanced a look at her.

Although he'd never have classified her as pretty in the traditional sense, he'd always considered her attractive. But he had to admit that on her, bullheadedness looked pretty damn good. Thick black lashes cast long shadows on flushed satin skin and her lips formed an unconscious, sensuous pout. A new kind of tension eased into his consciousness.

Parker took another pull of his beer. He resumed his routine of spearing his lobster and splashing butter all over, when he heard a muffled sound and looked up.

She had been watching him but glanced away. The dimple at the corner of her mouth begged to appear. Ashley took a small bite of the fish she'd ordered, taking a long time to chew, then the grin emerged.

"What's so funny?" he growled.

Ashley shook her head and looked down at her plate, pressing her lips together. Parker felt his own mood lighten in response to her ill-fated attempt at composure. But in the space of a heartbeat, her good mood seemed to evaporate.

"Not our wedding, that's for sure." Ashley raised her eyes, resignation clouding them. "Like it or not, I think we need to talk about it."

Parker didn't particularly like it, but the fact that Ashley appeared to like it even less annoyed the hell out of him. When had he become so thin-skinned? This wasn't personal. "Not to mention the ring," he tossed in. Then, pushing aside any unaccountable irritation, he asked, "When do I see your father again?"

"Not for a couple of days," Ashley replied, stubbornly ignoring further discussion of the ring. "I don't want him to think we're rushing things."

"He seemed rather receptive to me."

"Yes," she replied with a trace of sadness. "I don't quite understand that. Of course with all the medication and everything else, he's not exactly himself these days."

Parker's defenses once again shot up, even as reason tried to step in. He was taking it personally again. Ashley's confusion over her father's response was valid, he knew. But emotionally it stung. He swallowed some beer, and along with it any tempting sarcasm.

Parker allowed the conversation to lull, giving them both some reflection time before decisions had to be made. He watched Ashley watch his plate and an undeniable nasty streak snaked its way to his tongue.

"Want some of this lobster before it gets cold?" he asked, forking a healthy piece and dipping it in hot butter. He poised the mouthful in front of her and let it drip temptingly back into the small chafing dish. A satisfied grin threatened him at the longing look she gave it.

"Oh . . . I've got plenty here."

"C'mon. It's good. Best on the island." He drowned the lobster in the butter once more, then put it to her lips.

She hesitated a moment, then plucked the morsel off his fork with that full, luscious mouth. He reveled in the look of ecstasy that crossed her face, her eyes shut, tongue licking remnant traces of butter from her lips.

"Have another bite." His fork was ready for delivery, even as she shook her head.

He wanted to recapture that exquisite expression. She'd look that way in bed, her hair spilling out over the sheets. The sudden thought startled him. He pushed it from his mind. So much for paybacks.

"I've been meaning to ask you something." He took a cool, calming sip of beer and changed the subject, knowing full well that it was the subject of their marriage they should be discussing. "Doesn't Leialoha mean 'welcoming flower'?"

"Yes. It's my middle name."

"I'm surprised it's not your first." Steeped in tradition as Ashley was, like the rest of the King family from what he knew of them, he'd been curious about that.

"My mother wouldn't have it." She shrugged indifference that wasn't quite believable. "She said her family wouldn't understand a foreign name. Not that I ever met any of them."

"Where is she now?"

"Somewhere on the mainland. Idaho or Iowa, someplace like that."

Parker struggled with his conscience for a moment. He was prying and he could tell she was uncomfortable, but he wanted to know about Ashley. "Do you miss her?" he asked quietly.

Ashley looked out over the darkened ocean, the sea breeze blowing escaped tendrils about her face. She rested her arm on the balcony railing and wrapped her graceful fingers around the decorative bamboo. "How can you miss something you never had?" she asked softly.

Good question. Parker followed her gaze out to the water. He should be able to answer that himself. He looked back at her, wanting to tell her he understood. He couldn't, though—not without baring his soul. "When did she leave?"

"When the money ran out. I was five." That shrug again, but this time smaller, less confident. "But that's ancient history." She straightened, leveling her eyes with his. "What about your family? Do they know about me?"

Another pleasant topic, Parker thought wryly. His succulent dinner suddenly looked bland and he pushed his plate aside. He was about to tell her that what his family thought didn't matter, when someone with a mass of white hair caught his attention at the entrance of the restaurant.

"Speak of the devil," Parker murmured, peering over Ashley's head. When she turned to see what he was staring at, he captured her hand and her attention. "My parents just walked in. Do me a favor and follow my lead. Okay?"

"But—"

"I don't have time to argue, Ashley." He hated the edginess in his voice, hated Ashley hearing it. "Would you trust me on this?"

Ashley hesitated for a brief second and he could feel the unspoken questions in her fingers as they flexed in his palm. Her eyes darkened with uncertainty but she slowly nodded her head.

He looked back up to greet his father's surprised expression, quickly forced a smile and stood.

"Oh, Parker." His mother was the first to approach and stood on tiptoes as he kissed both her unlined cheeks. "I was just commenting to your father that you haven't been by in ages. And here you are." She stood back, holding both his hands, looking at him as if he were ten years old again.

"You look great, Mother." Parker freed his hands and slipped an arm around her. It really was good to see her. She looked as young as always, and Parker was pleased that his father's overbearing personality had never daunted her spirit. "You look good, too, Father," Parker added, just as he was expected to, and nodded to his father.

"You're looking quite well yourself." His father's intense gaze descended to Ashley, who sat quietly with wide, curious eyes.

Parker cleared his throat. "Mother, Father, this is Ashley King. Ashley, these are my parents...." Her eyes widened a fraction more on him and he knew he sounded too formal. It abruptly struck him how well she could already read him, how well he thought he could read her. And how much more comfortable than his own family she made him feel. "Parker and Barbara James."

Smiling, Ashley promptly stood and shook each of their hands and before Parker knew it, she had invited his parents to join them.

"We don't want to intrude," Barbara responded and looked longingly at her son, who quickly altered his expression and ceased the warning looks he'd been sending his meddling companion. "Besides, Karen and her husband will be joining us, and your table is only meant for four." She stopped and glanced at Ashley. "Have you met Parker's sister?"

"No. But I'm sure I will." Ashley smiled sweetly at Parker.

"Don got a new car, that's her husband, and he simply won't allow the parking attendants to touch it yet. So he let us off, but they'll be along any minute," his mother rattled on while Parker shifted positions.

His father's tolerance for standing in the middle of a crowded restaurant looked just about spent, and Parker couldn't be more relieved. This wasn't exactly the way he'd planned on having them all meet, especially since he hadn't told either party anything about the other. Ashley wasn't exactly shy about saying what she thought and a little prep time might be in order. He reached up to loosen his tie and felt a protusion at his breast pocket.

He patted the unfamiliar object and was suddenly reminded of Ashley's ring. In that instant, an unexpected idea took hold.

His sister and her husband had come through the door and he waved them over. With damp palms, he pulled two borrowed chairs to their table, ignoring his parents' look of surprise. He made short work of the introductions, ordered another bottle of champagne along with four more glasses and got them all seated before anyone knew what had happened.

"Well," Parker said, taking a deep breath and drumming his fingers on the edge of the table. He looked from one expectant face to the next. "What's new with all of you?"

His sister's eyes narrowed on him for several seconds before she glanced at Ashley. A slow, mischievous smile Parker knew all too well, spread across her face. The fact that maybe this wasn't such a hot idea crossed his mind.

"I think your answer to that question might be more interesting," Karen said and took a long, deliberate sip of the champagne she'd just been poured.

She'd handed him his opening. Parker fenced with a moment of well-warranted doubt and rested his gaze on Ashley's amused face. The hint of smugness that slightly curved her full rose-tinted lips, along with the tiny mocking dimple that flexed at the corner of her mouth, was his undoing.

Slowly he dipped his hand into the inside breast pocket of his jacket. The small velvet box was firm and real under his unsteady fingers. He took a quick breath.

"For one of the few times in your life, Karen, you may be right." Parker gave her a teasing grin that belied the tension knotting his gut. Nonchalantly he withdrew the small box, concealing it from view, his hand wrapped tightly around it. No one seemed to notice. No one except Ashley.

She reached for her glass and dropped her napkin to the floor. He felt a hard pinch at his calf before her head bobbed back up. His eyes begged her panicked ones for understanding. Before he could change his mind, he transferred his gaze to his family.

"Actually, I'm glad you're all here." He fumbled with the box under the tablecloth, silently cursing his clumsiness, as he slipped the size four ring on to the end of his index finger. "Now, maybe Ashley won't say no when I pop the question."

He turned to her and stared into the angry sparks of green cutting him to shreds. Her reaction was far beyond the notice of his family, who all stared slack-jawed at him. He pried the diamond off his fingertip and picked up Ashley's limp hand.

"Well, I'll be damned," Karen murmured into the brief silence.

"Ashley, will you marry me?" Parker asked, slipping the ring on Ashley's finger.

A long, dry swallow traveled Ashley's throat and her mouth quivered into a scant smile. "I'm speechless," she finally croaked out. And Parker pressed his lips to hers to keep her just that way.

"WOULD YOU TRUST ME on this?" Ashley mimicked an hour later as she briskly led the way to the car. "Great beginning, Mr. James."

"Don't call me Mr. James." Parker handed the valet attendant a book of the restaurant matches by mistake. He muttered a single succinct curse that netted him several sidelong glances, then fumbled in his pocket and replaced the matches with a five-dollar bill.

"Maybe I should call you sir, or maybe master would be better." Ashley jerked her seat belt in place. "Except slavery has been outlawed. They actually pay people to work in the pineapple and sugar plantations now, or didn't you know?"

Parker slammed his door. "Look, isn't it better that we got it over with?"

"Better for whom?" Ashley waved her hand around, caught sight of the flashing diamond and made a disgusted sound. "Give me the ring box," she ordered, crossing her arms and tucking her hand out of sight.

Parker simmered while he abruptly fished in his pocket and produced the object of her request. He felt her fingers tremble as she snatched it from his hand.

"We have to tell my father immediately." Ashley sighed and rested her head back against the leather seat. "Before he hears it from anyone else."

For the first time, Parker experienced a flicker of remorse. Being surprised by his family's sudden appearance had done strange things to him and he hadn't stopped to consider Ashley's position. He had taken advantage of the situation for his own benefit and now her defeated look really got to him.

Parker drove the car away from the restaurant's entrance and pulled into a parking stall near the street. He let the car idle and took her cold, reluctant hand in his.

"We can go to the hospital right now. I'll even ask him on bended knee, if you want." Just the thought of going to the hospital again invited a cold sweat, but he couldn't help grinning at the way she suddenly straightened, even though it was too dark to get a good look at her face.

"On *both* knees. That's what I ought to make you do." She tapped a finger against his palm as if seriously considering it, and before Parker realized what he was doing, he brought her hand to his lips and stilled her fidgeting.

He pressed one kiss to the tip of the restless finger, then another to the back of her silky hand. When she didn't resist, he turned it over and buried his mouth in her soft palm. He felt the cool metal of the ring against his cheek and felt a sense of deep satisfaction that she hadn't yet removed it.

"What do you think you're doing?" Ashley asked in a tight, breathless voice.

"Practicing." He kissed his way to her wildly beating pulse and felt his own speed up.

"What for?"

"To convince your father." He trailed up farther with a light touch of his tongue.

Ashley yanked her arm back and landed a hard whack on his lips in the process.

"Ouch." Parker jerked his head up and put a reflexive hand up to his bruised mouth.

"You let me worry about that," Ashley said in a clipped tone. "All you need to practice is writing checks." She pulled the ring off her finger. "Because, Buster, I'm going to cost you plenty."

PRACTICE. Ashley couldn't shake the word from her brain even after a night of fitful sleep. Parker was smooth, charming, a real snake. And Ashley was a damn fool.

Chemistry. Now here was a word. She'd been poor in that particular subject in high school and she was proving to be even poorer at it now. She never could understand it then, and now, when Parker touched her...well, all she understood was that he simply couldn't touch her anymore.

She had barely gotten off the phone with her father when Parker pulled up to her apartment in his showy red Porsche. Out of a perverse sense of revenge, she insisted on driving, well aware of his aversion to her beat-up Toyota.

"Did you talk to him?" Parker asked after they were on their way to the hospital.

"Yes." Ashley sighed. She knew who he was talking about. Her father had been on her mind most of the night. "I dropped more than enough hints. It shouldn't be too much of a surprise when we do tell him."

"How did he take it?"

"Too well."

"Ashley? About last night." Parker adjusted the air-conditioning vents directly at his face. Ashley fidgeted with her hair.

"Forget it, Parker."

He didn't say anything for a long time, and Ashley did all she could to keep her eyes on the road and off him.

"I think I have a happy medium with the ring deal," Parker finally said, glancing at her bare fingers.

Ashley remained quiet with her eyes straight ahead. She had already come to a decision about that herself, but she was curious about his peace offering.

"Wear the ring for the duration of our marr..." The word seemed to stick in Parker's throat. "Wear the damn thing and when our arrangement is over, you can sell it and do whatever you like with it. Feed five families if you want." Ashley had the feeling that hadn't come out as he had planned, and she had to hide a smile when he tried to roll down the window but it stuck halfway. "And get this piece of junk fixed."

Lifting her chin, she took a corner a little too fast. She owed him one for that last crack. If she had felt a tad guilty knowing the ring would pay for part of the airstrip, she didn't now. When he acted like a horse's rear end by ordering her around, it took away some of the sting.

Ashley pulled into the hospital lot and parked the car. The sight of the dismal gray building reminded her that there was more at stake than quibbling over a diamond. Ignoring Parker's curious look, she withdrew the burgundy velvet box from her purse and slipped the ring onto her finger. "It's a deal," she said and got out of the car.

Parker had to move fast to keep up with her. He was having enough trouble keeping up with her fleeting moods, he didn't want to have to physically chase her down. He reached out and grabbed her upper arm to slow her. "Hold it."

She stopped and he saw her body settle on a deep sigh. He'd accomplished his purpose, but he didn't want to let her go. Her hair, black and glossy in the bright sun, was lifted off her shoulder by a tropical breeze. It floated away and then back, long and heavy to her waist.

"Are you ready to tell your father now?" He loosened his fingers, lingering on her sun-heated flesh.

"I think so." She nodded, turning to him, and he immediately sensed that for whatever reason some of her earlier fire had fizzled out. "Oh, Parker, something is very wrong with him." Rare vulnerability clouded her eyes and his heart thudded. "He's seeing things that aren't there."

"Hallucinations?"

"No." She shook her head, her hair billowing like a satin sail. "About us I mean."

"That's good. It'll be easier on him." And us.

"But it isn't like him to be so gullible. It's simply not credible that you'd pop into my life like this. Besides, he knows how stubborn I am."

Parker laughed softly. "If he's having trouble remembering that, I'll vouch for it."

Ashley laughed a little, too. "If he forgot that, I'd really be worried." The humor fell from her face and large, sad eyes met his. "I *am* worried."

It seemed natural for Parker to hug her to him. He wrapped his arms around her, her head nestled under his chin. Closing his eyes, he placed a light, undetectable kiss on top of her head and inhaled the now familiar scent of sunshine and gardenia that spoke her name.

He blinked at the sunlight and stared ahead of them at the gray hospital outlined by green mountains and blue sky. His phobia forgotten, he rested his slightly roughened chin in her soft hair.

"Maybe it's wishful thinking," he said after a while. "Maybe he's so anxious to have you happy and settled, he's convinced himself."

"You think so?" Ashley angled away from him, looking so trusting, wanting to believe.

"People do it all the time. It's a form of survival." She was doing it now, Parker thought, and he brought her in close again. He had done it many times himself.

"You could be right." She moved back, and he had little choice but to let her go.

"The doctors have always been straight with me," she said, a shy smile of gratitude on her lips. "I don't see why they'd hide the truth at this point, although it's strange. I could swear they seem to be avoiding me. Probably just my imagination." She smoothed her hair and the diamond caught the sunlight. It sparkled like a million stars in a black, cloudless sky and bespoke promises of romance and commitment.

And for just an instant, Parker wondered what it would be like to be gifted with the love of someone like Ashley Leialoha King.

"SO, YOU WANT TO marry my daughter." Keoki King expertly shuffled two stacks of quarters with one hand. Not once did he look at what he was doing but kept his eyes directly on Parker as if he could see right through him.

"Yes, sir, I do." Parker shifted from one foot to the other.

Ashley fluffed her father's pillow for the fourth time.

"Don't call me sir, Parker. I have told you before, my friends call me Keoki. And in my experience, people have been either friend or foe." The older man pierced him with an unwavering stare and managed to look quite formidable despite the ludicrously bright blue-and-green aloha shirt he wore.

"Keoki," Parker promptly corrected. He was being tested. Perhaps all fathers were demanding and manipulative. Not just his. But Parker would play the game. For Ashley's sake.

"Do you love her?" Keoki asked bluntly.

Parker heard Ashley's small gasp and he slipped his arm around her waist, pulling her up against him. He gave her a reassuring squeeze, his gaze fastened on Keoki.

"I do," Parker said clearly, without stammering, without hesitation.

A slow, wide smile lit up Keoki's face. "Then you have my blessing." He clasped Parker's hand and held out an arm to Ashley, who immediately fell into his embrace. To anyone watching, it looked like a Norman Rockwell scene, only Parker knew the quiver in Ashley's shoulders was not from joy. And that undeniable fact dealt a strange blow to his gut.

"When is the happy day?" Keoki asked after a fair amount of hugs and sniffles had been exchanged.

"We haven't gotten that far." Ashley swiped back her hair and glanced at Parker.

"I'm free tomorrow," Keoki commented.

Ashley laughed.

Parker laughed.

Keoki didn't. Frowning, he looked from his daughter back to Parker. "You're right. We need time to prepare."

"Prepare?" Parker and Ashley said together and looked apprehensively at each other.

"We weren't planning a big wedding," Parker stated slowly. "Something private, maybe a civil ceremony."

Keoki's frown deepened. "But everyone will want to share your happiness. Your friends, family..."

Just what he needed, Parker thought, a big production made out of this outrageous farce. What they *did* need was for it to be quick, quiet and legal. It would make the ultimate break easier. He darted a solicitous look at Ashley. "Well, actually..." he spouted. "Tomorrow sounds like a great idea."

"I agree." Ashley immediately jumped in. "I don't want a big fuss."

"But, Leialoha..." Keoki shook his head. "I must insist."

Parker watched Ashley's shoulders sag a fraction. Then her eyes turned that warm honey brown that made Parker's insides feel soft and gooey like melted caramel. Her mouth was soft and yielding...and she clearly was unable to say no to her father. And if push came to shove, Parker, without a doubt, would be putty in her hands.

"The truth is, sir, uh, Keoki," Parker said before he surrendered his last shred of control. "I can't wait any longer." He pulled Ashley into his arms and, feigning an intimacy between them, kissed her long and hard.

Reflexively, Ashley put her hands flat on his chest. He braced himself for the inevitable shove. But her warm palms rounded up to his shoulders and her surprised mouth softened against his.

He felt her moist invitation and his heart did a double somersault. He pressed her to him by the small of her back before sliding his hands to the curve of her buttocks. Somewhere in the distant fog, an intrusive sound penetrated his muddled consciousness. It sounded suspicously like a cough. Parker cocked open one eye.

Keoki grinned.

Parker reluctantly but quickly disengaged himself from the man's daughter. He took a large gulp of air and looked at Ashley's flushed face. Her formerly honey brown eyes were shooting a dangerous assortment of green. She was embarrassed. And angry.

And Parker didn't say a damn word.

"I see your point," Keoki said, still grinning. "Shall we say, day after tomorrow?"

KEOKI PULLED OUT THE half-smoked cigar from its hiding place, almost before he saw the last flash of his daughter's pink sundress disappear around the corner. He was so excited he nearly forgot to bring out the can of air freshener along with it. He was on his last warning from the nurses, but he just could not help it. He had a lot of celebrating to do.

He puffed on what was likely to be his last cigar for a long time and thought about his next plan of action. Things were moving along better than expected, but he wasn't out of the woods yet. It would not do at all for Ashley and Parker to have a private wedding. That would make a divorce far too easy.

And Harvey wouldn't be much help, Keoki figured, since he was getting entirely too squeamish about the whole matter. Keoki pondered the problem for another few minutes while he enjoyed his final puffs, then smiled and reached for the phone. He had another trump card, and if he played his hand right he would not have to incriminate himself at all. He coughed into his hand until his voice was suitably raspy and hoarse, then leaned back into his newly fluffed pillows and waited for the connection to be made.

"Crystal?" he queried in his most pathetic voice. "I need your help."

Chapter Six

"We have some fast moving to do," Parker said when they'd reached the hospital lobby. "We need a marriage license, a minister. What else?"

Ashley hurried on, ignoring him. He reached out and grabbed her arm. "I'd like some cooperation in this."

"Oh? Now you want my opinion." She glared at him and tried to shake loose of his hold.

"You weren't exactly helpful back there."

"And you were? You had a lot of nerve acting that way in front of my father."

"We're supposed to be getting married, for Pete's sake." Parker realized he'd raised his voice and sighed. He knew what she meant, and he hadn't intended on getting carried away as he had, but she hadn't had any business looking at him like she had, either. Her eyes all warm and dewy...geez, just thinking about it made him nuts.

Several people stopped to stare, so Parker pulled her toward the more private parking lot. He knew she'd noticed the gawkers, too, so she let him get away with it. When they reached her car he blocked her from opening the door, tilted her face to his, then trapped her with his other hand.

"Look, lady—" Parker began.

"Can't get your way by manipulating a harmless old man, so now you'll try bullying me?" She was so small that even with her chin lifted in indignation, he had to really lower his head to look into her unblinking eyes.

Different as night and day, he thought with a mental shake, in so many ways. In looks, ideology, temperament...well, maybe not temperament. The idea made him smile.

Her tongue darted out to moisten her lips—her pouty, coral-tinted lips. He felt her warm breath, smelled the butterscotch candy her father had given her. And try as he might, he couldn't remember what he'd been about to say. Nor could he drag his gaze away from her mouth.

"Not at all," he whispered before his lips descended upon hers.

She remained rigid at first, but her lips softened a little, and her hands made their way up to rest tentatively against his collarbone. It was weak encouragement, but Parker ran with it. He tangled his hands in her hair, gathering it away from her neck and throat, and wondered how all that black silk would feel against his naked chest.

With eager lips, he traced the delicate skin along her jaw. Her floral scent teased and drew him to the soft flesh of her ear. He lingered—nipping, tasting, feeling the increasing pressure of her fingertips, hearing her soft, unguarded sighs.

Somewhere a car door slammed, followed by another. It could just as well have been a faint echo to him, but apparently it was like a cold shower to Ashley. The sensual clawing of her graceful fingers turned into a hard shove.

"We need to get to my apartment," she said on a deep breath. "Get in."

"Sounds like a helluva good idea to me." His breathing wasn't any better as he struggled to get all his masculine accessories back to a socially acceptable state.

"So you can get your car and go home," Ashley hissed, making him hurry around to the passenger side. If her tone was any indication, she'd probably take off without him.

"I only meant we should probably start preparing for your move," he replied with exaggerated innocence. Too much sexual energy flowed between them. It would only be a matter of time before they both responded. He knew it. And whether she liked it or not, he could tell Ashley knew it.

"I'll take what I need to your house when it's necessary." She threw the car into gear and jerked out of the parking stall.

Parker didn't like the way she said that. It lacked a sense of gravity. "It might be a good idea to do that now," he said warily. "Besides, you need to meet Mrs. Lee."

Ashley glanced over at him and slowed the car. "Your housekeeper."

He nodded. "I've casually mentioned your name to prepare her, but she's certainly not expecting me to bring home a *bride* the day after tomorrow."

Ashley gave him a dirty look that had him regretting his choice of words, but she nodded in tight-lipped agreement and steered the car in the direction of his house.

An hour later Parker peered out the wide glass window that overlooked his pool and the ocean and idly watched his dog chase the outgoing tide. Mrs. Lee had cornered Ashley the moment they had arrived, and now Ashley was the victim of his housekeeper's requisite tour. He loved the older woman, but she was a real busybody. She'd also be a good test for their pretense, he reminded himself as he waited impatiently.

Parker tried to cast an objective eye on the natural wood interior of the split-level living area. Most women he brought to his house were impressed. For that matter, anyone who'd ever seen it had been.

But not Ashley.

Parker took great pride in having designed most of it himself, had even participated in the manual work. It had been a labor of satisfaction for him. A gratifying reminder of all those years he'd spent bumming around the mainland, learning one odd job after another, relying on his wits and two hands and not his grandmother's trust fund or a high-powered attorney's salary.

Ashley, however, saw it differently. He had felt it in her disapproving appraisal, heard it in her censoring silence. And for that, he couldn't really blame her. Most people only saw the silver spoon, they couldn't know that he'd never liked the taste. That's why the arguments with his father had started, culminating with his withdrawal from law school. The first James in generations not to carry on the tradition. What a disgrace. What a crock.

Parker's patience had been all but spent when he heard voices approaching.

"You should have told me sooner, Parker. This is very sudden." Mrs. Lee wagged her customary finger at him. Her eyebrows drew together in suspicion and she cast a pointed look at Ashley's stomach. "You not *hapai,* are you?"

"Mrs. Lee," Parker warned.

"I have a right to know." She sniffed. "If there is going to be a *keiki* around to take care of and diapers to wash, maybe I have to charge you more money."

"Don't worry." Ashley laughed. "No *keikis.*"

"Soon." Smiling, Mrs. Lee patted her ever-present bun.

Ashley and Parker both opened their mouths to deny it, but the ringing of the telephone curtailed the need to vent their indignation. The older woman moved her bulk in the direction of the den and had barely barked out a greeting when they heard the door close.

Parker shrugged. "Well, I guess it's not for me."

"She's quite a character," Ashley commented.

"That she is. Did she give you the third degree?"

Ashley rolled her eyes. "Did she ever."

"Do you think she bought it?"

"It helped that you've been talking about me for the last week and a half." She cocked him a wry look.

Had it only been that long? The realization stopped Parker. Impossible. "Yeah, well...exaggerating is another one of her faults." He rubbed the back of his neck. "She may have overheard me talking to Harvey but I know she doesn't suspect anything or I'd have gotten a lecture."

"I think she may be in shock," Ashley said, smiling.

Parker shook his head. "She probably thinks you're someone I've brought here..." He cut himself short, surprised at his own callousness.

"It's okay, Parker." Ashley's smile faltered. "This isn't love, honor and cherish for real." She stepped up to the window. "That's a great pool."

"What do you think of the house?" he asked, watching her perfunctory assessment of his creation. A small part of him still wanted to dazzle her with the unlikely talent he'd discovered in his own two hands.

"It's fine." She moved away and reached for her purse, which dangled from a dining-room chair. Her gaze snagged on the marriage license he'd left on the table, and the same anxious look crossed her face as when they'd picked it up not more than an hour ago.

"Will you be ready to do this?" He narrowed his gaze on her. If her feet were getting cold, he wanted to know now.

"As much as I'll ever be." She sighed.

"You don't have to like it. But you do need to be enthusiastic." His voice lowered as he slanted a look toward the den.

"For an audience, I will."

"Is it going to be that bad, Ashley?" His ego asked the question, but something else inside him wanted the answer.

"I don't know," she admitted.

"Well, it's not going to be any picnic for me, either." He jammed his hands in his pockets. Three or four years of her stubborn self-righteousness were going to make him certifiable. "Just keep in mind what you have to gain."

Ashley looked straight into his eyes, not really seeing him, and then her solemn gaze drifted toward the ocean. She stared out at the solitary horizon for several seconds and then a slow, confident smile blossomed across her face. And once again Parker had the uneasy feeling he was missing a big piece of the puzzle.

ANYONE WOULD HAVE THOUGHT it was Crystal getting married today and not Ashley. She was as jumpy as a tourist walking barefoot on hot Waikiki sand at noon.

She'd started off by being late and now, every time Ashley turned her back, it seemed Crystal was on the phone. Ashley supposed she should be glad that her friend was being so cavalier about the exchange of vows. After all, it really was no big deal.

"Higher heels," Crystal said, casting a critical eye at Ashley's reflection in the full-length mirror. "And nail polish." She paused, a thoughtful look on her dramatically made-up face. "Although you don't want to compete with the ring." She shoved bracelet after bracelet up her arm. "But definitely higher heels."

"Not with a *holoku,*" Ashley said, gathering her hair in one hand and draping it over her shoulder in front of her. She picked up her hairbrush and glided it through.

"Does Parker know you're wearing that?" Crystal eyed the traditional Hawaiian wedding dress with misgiving. The collar was high, the sleeves long and fitted, the satin skirt floor-length and full.

"It was never a topic of conversation."

"Will he be freaked?"

"I don't know." Ashley hadn't given it a thought. She'd never had wedding-day dreams like many of her friends, but she'd always known that if the time came she'd wear her grandmother's dress. The one her mother had chosen not to.

Crystal took the brush out of Ashley's hand. "Let me do that." The two friends exchanged a familiar smile, filled with shared childhood memories. "Remember when we were eleven and I rolled your hair in bubble gum?"

"How could I forget?" Ashley laughed. "Your mother made you pay for my haircut with your allowance, and you never let me hear the end of it."

"That was brutal," Crystal said, grinning. "But your father paid me back. He let me win at poker."

Ashley gasped. "You never told me that."

"He made me promise." Crystal worried her lower lip. "You know I'd do anything for him, don't you? I mean, I never could refuse your dad a thing."

"I know." Ashley frowned at her friend's sudden fidgeting and took the brush from her hand. "Is anything wrong?"

"No." Crystal widened her eyes under lifted brows. "I just wanted to be sure you understood that. Well..." She twisted each of the four rings on her fingers. "What do you think of Parker's house? Is the pool perfect for skinny-dipping orgies, or what?"

"Oh, please." Ashley chuckled, then narrowed her gaze on Crystal. "How do you know he has a pool?"

"A guess. He probably has everything else, too." Crystal released the bracelets she was twirling up her arm with a clang. "So, any skinny-dips in the near future?"

"Can you see Parker James skinny-dipping?" Ashley laughed. But a tempting picture came to mind, which put an abrupt end to her amusement. She didn't want to imagine the new Parker who was beginning to emerge. The one who smiled at little girls and took the time to reassure an old man he didn't know. The Parker who made her heart beat much too fast.

"Actually, I'd love to." Crystal looked at her and sighed. "Lucky you."

"That isn't part of the deal." Ashley sank onto her bed and tried on a pair of shoes, refusing to engage in destructive fantasies. Any type of personal relationship with Parker would be just that... a fantasy, or maybe fallacy was more appropriate. "How about this pair?"

"Perfect." Crystal nudged her aside and sat next to her. "According to the grapevine, interest in Magic Island is alive and well. I even got roped into some legal work."

Ashley nodded, familiar excitement skipping down her spine. "My phone's been ringing off the hook."

"Better not let Parker get wind of it."

"No kidding." Ashley flipped her hair out of the way. Most of the time he looked as if he needed little excuse to wring her neck, as it was.

"If he dumps you over it, I get first dibs on him." Crystal tried to hide a grin.

"You can have him."

"The hell you say. I know you too well, Ashley King," Crystal said, leaving the bed and wagging her finger. "You are hot to trot with that man, whether you'll admit it or not." She strode past Ashley, ignoring her look of astonishment.

"Do you actually think I want anything to do with that pushy, self-centered, egotistical, social snob?"

"You might've convinced me with three less adjectives. But you gave it away by almost hyperventilating." Her friend, perilously close to being ex, gathered the makings for her newest hair color and threw them into a sack. "Are you sure you're not doing anything special after the ceremony?" she asked breezily.

"For the third time, no." Ashley made a face. "This is business, Crystal, that's all." Only business. Ashley hoarded a deep breath and smoothed out the skirt of her *holoku*. "Why do you keep asking me that?"

Crystal shrugged and turned to give her a long, serious look. "No reason." She took Ashley's hand and squeezed it, her eyes misty. "You just look so... so gorgeous."

On impulse Ashley hugged her friend, pretending for a moment that her life was not about to be turned upside down. "And you're the best." She fought the catch in her throat. "Ready?"

An uncharacteristic blush climbed Crystal's face. "I'll remind you of that in a couple of hours," she muttered as she headed out of the room. "I need to make one last call before I lead us both to the slaughter."

ANYONE WOULD HAVE THOUGHT it was Mrs. Lee getting married today and not Parker. He hadn't gotten a moment's sleep the previous night with all her bustling around, making room for Ashley's things and rearranging the house until he almost didn't recognize it anymore. They had argued over that, and then they'd argued over what he should wear for the exchange of vows. By the time the vanload of flowers had arrived that morning, he'd had it. So he'd picked up his things and bolted for the nearest hotel. Though not before threatening his housekeeper with every bit of blackmail he could, if she told a single living soul before he gave her the go-ahead.

And now, even after a brief nap and a five-mile run, tension still cramped Parker's shoulders. Karen was going to kill him when she found out she'd been excluded. So would his mother. He could have called them—should have, actually. But the thought of his father's unwanted judgment had kept the phone out of his reach. After all, this wasn't his family's business.

He was disappointed, though, that Harvey couldn't be here today. The attorney had declined Parker's request to be his witness, having made a prior commitment. The ceremony was a farce, merely a means to an end, but Parker had wanted Harvey there. Tom Booker, another friend, had accepted. He'd been off the island lately, so he hadn't found the situation odd or asked a lot of questions.

But now, both Tom and Ashley were late. Parker waited outside the hospital, cursing under his breath. He hadn't wanted to have the ceremony at the hospital, even if it was in the open courtyard, but when it came right down to it, he couldn't refuse Ashley. She wouldn't disappoint her father and Parker couldn't disappoint her.

He shifted the long florist box from one arm to the other and shook out his clammy free hand. It was unseasonably cool for mid-May, but he was about to shed his sport coat and roll up his sleeves. His body heat was up at least ten degrees. Even quitting law school hadn't seemed this taxing.

He looked longingly at his fast red Porsche and thought about heading for the airport. San Francisco had to be nice this time of year.

And then he saw her.

The long ivory *holoku* she wore barely cleared the ground as she walked toward him, giving her an ethereal air. A large gardenia, startlingly white against her black flowing hair, was tucked behind her ear. A small and fragile package of pure and earthy beauty, housing determination and a will of steel. An unexpected serenity chased the edginess from his body. A smile came unbidden to his lips.

"You look lovely, Leialoha." Her startled hazel eyes searched his. He'd even surprised himself. Silently, he praised her father's sixth sense for so aptly naming her "welcoming flower" twenty-nine years ago. A self-fulfilled prophecy in Parker's opinion, and without conscious thought the name had fallen from his lips.

"Thank you, Parker," she said in a soft voice, the dimple at the corner of her mouth appearing slowly. "This is my friend and attorney Crystal."

He blinked, not having had the slightest clue of anyone else's presence. He cleared his throat, looked over at the taller woman and tried not to gape. Somehow the label of "attorney" didn't quite compute. "Nice to meet you, Crystal." He transferred his package, then shook her multiringed hand.

"Same here." Crystal ran fuchsia-tipped fingers through her spiked hair. They were unsteady and he could tell her smile was forced. Great. Even she was nervous.

"Is the minister here?" Ashley asked, her voice low.

"He's with your father. I don't know what's keeping my friend Tom." Parker gestured to the air and noticed the florist box. "Here, this is for you." He lifted the top and with great care removed the *maile* lei.

The wariness in Ashley's face stopped him for a moment. "I'm doing this right, aren't I?" He looked from one woman to the other. "Isn't *maile* supposed to be for weddings?"

Ashley nodded, unspeaking, her eyes uncommonly bright.

What the hell was wrong with her? He'd thought she'd be pleased. Did she want a bouquet instead? "Look, you don't have to wear it. I just thought—"

"I want to," she broke in, putting a hand on his when he tried to stuff the lei back into the box. "This is very sweet, Parker." She stroked the *maile* leaves with a feather-light touch, her lashes lowered. "I'm afraid I don't have one for you." Eyes widening, she searched his face. "It's traditional for the groom, too, but I didn't think—"

"That's okay, Ash." He took her hand and brought it to his lips, a smile forming there. "It's okay."

Crystal cleared her throat. "Why don't you two go inside? I'll wait for your friend Tom. I have a feeling I'll be able to spot him."

Ashley glanced heavenward, and Parker flashed a grin. "I wouldn't bet on that." He grinned further at Crystal's inquisitive look, then took the lei from Ashley's fidgety fingers and placed it around her neck. He pressed a firm, warm kiss on her unsuspecting lips before steering her toward the hospital.

"I think I like Crystal," he said after they'd entered the lobby. He stuck close to Ashley, his hand at her back. Inhaling her sweet scent, he was able to ignore the odor of drugs and ether, which for reasons he had yet to comprehend had always managed to permeate the air clear to the lobby.

"You do?" Ashley's eyes grew round and her dimple peeked out at him.

"Yeah, but maybe I'd better reserve judgment." He slid his hand to the curve of her neck and grinned down at her obvious surprise. She didn't shy away from his touch and the steady pulse he found there reassured him. "She may be a bad influence."

Ashley laughed. "I promise I'll never color my hair ravishing raspberry, and blue shadow will not touch these eyelids." She cocked her head to the side and gave him a teasing grin. "But the quadruple ear piercing I'll have to think about."

"Heaven help me." He cast his gaze up briefly before looking back at her. "Actually, what I want to ask her about is some harebrained project called Magic Island. Rumor has it that she's somehow linked to it, and I want to know what those fanatics are up to." He felt the pulse at her neck leap at his fingertips just before she stepped out of reach. "It has to do with the new gambling law up for vote. Nothing you need be concerned with," he assured her. "I doubt your friend's even involved. Those idiots are to the left of left field."

Parker tried to take Ashley's hand but her fingers tightly intertwined with each other and she averted her sweet face, her chin making a defiant ascent. He cursed his stupidity. Magic Island had nothing to do with Ashley, and even if Crystal was somehow involved, she was Ashley's friend. And, of course, Ashley would be defensive.

He pulled his tie a fraction looser and eyed the ugly green walls closing in on him. If the powers that be didn't keep this death trap so hot he wouldn't have been such an insensitive cad, Parker thought with absolute certainty as he glanced down at the trembling hands of his soon-to-be bride.

CRYSTAL AND TOM, in his gray suit and worn sneakers, caught up with them just as they reached the open courtyard. Quick introductions were made at the entrance, where torches has been stationed on either side and twin flames shot up to meet the waning sun. A small gathering of nurses, patients and other strangers huddled around a trio softly singing Hawaiian love songs.

Ashley watched Parker's jaw slacken. His incredulous gaze swept the transformed courtyard. Ashley herself was only mildly surprised. She'd heard the whispers and caught the secret smiles this morning when she'd snuck in for a brief visit with her father.

Now that she stood at the entrance, she realized that in true Hawaiian style the nurses had invited themselves and had staged quite a backdrop for the ceremony.

Flowers were everywhere. Sprays of white and lavender orchids weeped from the arched entryway and fanned the air just above Parker's head. Petals from snowy-white gardenias and pink plumerias carpeted the ground before the minister, their potent and heady fragrance dancing with the breeze.

And under a large corner palm, her father waited, a flower in his hand. He hadn't seen her yet, as he continued teasing a pair of orderlies. He looked good, better than he had in months. And Ashley felt a layer of anxiety vanish.

Parker touched her arm and she turned to look at him. "I thought we agreed on privacy." He shook his head in bewilderment, his gaze skimming the crowd.

"My dad's nurses." She shrugged helplessly. "I think they're responsible." Her attention rested on Parker and the fine lines of tension bracketing his mouth. He looked handsome and tanned in his white dress shirt and taupe blazer, his jaw so strong, his eyes bluer than the sky. His slacks fit his long legs to perfection.

Ashley swallowed around the lump in her throat and let her eyes close briefly. Magic Island notwithstanding, she was out of her ever-loving mind for going through with this arrangement.

Looking back at Parker, she slipped her hand into his and was pleased to see some of the tension immediately disappear from his face. She gently urged him the rest of the way through the entrance.

As soon as they entered the actual courtyard, the crowd quieted and Ashley felt the pressure of Parker's hand increase. Certain all eyes would be on them, she cast a reluctant gaze around at the unwanted fanfare. But her dread proved groundless. All attention was on her father, who strode, straight and proud, toward her and Parker.

A nurse stopped him to drape a yellow plumeria lei around his neck. When several others offered him their hands in congratulations, he beamed with pride and suddenly something became very clear to Ashley. All this pageantry had little to do with Parker and herself. It was for her father.

Ashley raised her eyes back to his contented face and knew in her heart she was doing the right thing.

"Parker, about all these people..." she whispered before her father approached. "I know we didn't—"

"It's okay, Ash." Parker released her hand and put a silencing finger to her lips. His gaze drifted to her father. "He looks happy, doesn't he?"

Ashley drew in her lower lip, a surge of gratitude rendering her speechless for an instant. Then she laid her hand on Parker's arm. "Are you ready to do this?"

He swung his attention back to her and pierced her with a steady gaze. "I am." He recaptured her hand and they met her father midway. She accepted the flower and kiss her father gave her, then stayed close to Parker's side as they moved to stand before the minister.

Ashley felt rather than saw Parker looking at her. She tilted her head back and looked at him, bringing up a hand to shade her eyes. The lines of tension were entirely gone from his face as he moved to shield her from the sun. He took her hand away from her eyes and kissed it. "You look beautiful," he whispered as the preacher opened his Bible.

Ashley smiled, not because she believed him, but because he was playing the game so well. Yet a small part of her wanted him to think she was beautiful, and to her utter embarrassment tears welled up in her eyes.

She bowed her head and blinked them back while the ceremony progressed. She repeated the vows she was instructed to repeat, nodded when it was appropriate. And when the minister told Parker to kiss his bride, Ashley closed her eyes, lifted her chin and waited for him to brush her lips with his.

And waited.

"You may kiss the bride," the minister repeated deliberately.

Ashley slowly opened her eyes.

Parker grinned, slid his hands up her arms and pulled her to him.

She caught her breath and held it as Parker claimed her mouth. His kiss was long and hard and thorough. His hands caressed her back and he held her so close Ashley couldn't have breathed if she'd wanted to.

When the crowd erupted into cheers, she felt Parker's smile against her branded mouth, then he angled his head back and gave her a sleepy-eyed, lopsided grin.

Ashley felt the heat from her middle rise to her face. She exhaled a long, steadying breath and did her best to return his smile. Then she stepped back and clasped her palms together before one of them made sharp contact with his aristocratic face.

"Nice performance," she hissed and smiled at the same time.

"Thank you." The corner of Parker's mouth twitched. "But I think I need more practice."

Ashley stepped back and gave him a warning look before spinning away toward her father's waiting arms.

It wasn't hard to get away after that. The onlookers were satisfied, her father was on cloud nine and most of the patients were being herded back to their rooms.

After waving off Tom and Crystal, Ashley slipped into Parker's Porsche and rested her head back against the soft leather seat. "You can let me off at my apartment," she said once they were on the freeway.

"Is that where we're spending our wedding night?"

"Frankly, I don't care where you spend yours." In spite of herself, Ashley glanced at him. "But you can bet the resort it won't be with me."

Parker laughed. "Be careful. That resort will eventually pay for your community center."

Ashley casually shifted her attention out the window. She didn't need the reminder. What she needed was to get home and warn Crystal that Parker would be asking her about Magic Island.

Crystal was Ashley's best friend and loyal to the hilt. But she was also the worst liar Ashley knew. Forewarned, Crystal would be fine; but if cornered, there was no telling what would pop out of her mouth.

"Besides," Parker continued. "To get Mrs. Lee off my back, I had to promise her we'd go back to my...uh...excuse me, our place."

Ashley didn't answer at first, but she couldn't very well tell him to stuff it, since he'd been so civil about meeting the minister at the hospital. And besides, as long as she was with Parker she had time to get to Crystal.

"Fine. I'll go home after that." Parker's lips thinned and her conscience reminded her of how much that hospital visit had cost him. "Then if you like, we'll have dinner out later."

"Don't you have one romantic bone in your body?" Parker frowned as he shot her a sidelong glance before returning his attention to the road—the road, she noticed, that had long ago headed away from her apartment.

"This isn't supposed to be romantic," she reminded him slowly, almost swallowing the last word when he wickedly cocked one eyebrow up at her.

"Normal newlyweds wouldn't be dining out on their wedding night," Parker commented.

"We aren't normal."

"Speak for yourself." Parker chuckled. "Or I'll pull over and show you how normal I am."

His tone was pure suggestion and Ashley felt herself shrink toward the door, seeking oxygen from the open window.

"Never mind," she muttered, then changed the subject. "Where does Mrs. Lee think we're spending the night, anyway?"

"I don't know," Parker said. "She was driving me so crazy with rearranging the house, the subject never came up. Half the flowers on Oahu must have been delivered this morning. I think she had one of her bags packed, too. She probably thinks we'll be spending it at home."

She watched him sweep back the hair the wind had tumbled across his forehead. His hands were strong and tanned... and looked entirely too capable. And Ashley decided she didn't much care for the idea of spending the night with him. In fact, she'd had enough of him today. Period. Being with him was one thing, but being with him in front of an audience was quite another. It had been one heck of a strain. But she could indulge him and Mrs. Lee for at least the next half hour. Then as soon as Mrs. Lee left, so would Ashley.

They were about three blocks from his house by the time she'd formed a plan of action in her mind. She was about to propose it to him when the car swerved and Ashley looked up to see that they had just missed a parked car.

"What the hell is going on?" Parker sized up the long stretch of cars on either side of the street. "These people can't park on both sides like this."

"Someone must be having a party," Ashley offered and straightened to get a better look.

"Not someone," Parker said in a low, awestruck voice, while slowing down the car. "We are."

Chapter Seven

Parker was half tempted to step on the gas and get the hell out of Dodge. He was three seconds from doing just that when his sister and mother stepped out the front door and waved. Ashley's father was right behind them. Harvey Winton followed behind him.

Parker clenched his teeth as they coasted down the driveway and he noticed that two of the parked cars belonged to investors of his.

"I hope to God you don't know anything about this," he said through gritted teeth while trying to smile for their welcoming committee. He hadn't seen his father yet. Hell, he might not even have come. It would be just like him, Parker thought, to make it clear that once again he disapproved of his only son.

"You've been in the sun too long if you think I had anything to do with this." Ashley blew out a sharp breath, then her gaze riveted on her father. "What in the . . . he's not supposed to be out of the hospital."

"Yeah? Well, he looks fine to me." Parker shot her a suspicious look.

"I swear to you, I don't know what's going on." Ashley reached for the door handle with unsteady fingers.

"Look, Ash." He touched her arm and she swung her gaze back to him, her eyes wide and questioning. "I didn't mean to imply that you're involved with any of this." He waved his hand in a helpless gesture. "Whatever this is. We'll handle it, okay?"

"Okay," she whispered as he ducked in for a quick reassuring kiss. Their audience applauded and converged on the car.

They were hugged and jostled all the way to the front door, and as soon as Parker stepped inside, the events of yesterday and this morning came into sharp focus. Mrs. Lee's short temper, her furniture-rearranging frenzy, the delivery of roses, orchids and gardenias, which were now placed everywhere.

Parker shook his head, wondering who Mrs. Lee's accomplices might be. A large buffet table laden with an assortment of island delicacies extended the length of the glass window overlooking the pool, while waiters circulated with trays of canapés and champagne. His mother and sister were busy escorting in three musicians who had just arrived, but they immediately got them situated and headed for Parker.

"I haven't decided if I've forgiven you yet, but I figured you'd need this." Karen handed Parker a beer, then sipped from her own champagne glass.

"*I* definitely haven't forgiven you," his mother admonished. "I did all I could not to call you last night after Mrs. Lee phoned us. Parker, didn't you think we'd want to attend the ceremony?"

Parker fought with his conscience in silence for a moment. He hadn't wanted them to find out this way. They didn't deserve that. "Where's Father?" he asked and took a long pull of beer.

Karen looked at her mother, who was about to answer, and cut in. "We didn't have much notice, Parker. He already had an engagement. So did Don. But they both wanted to be here," she added hastily.

"Yeah." Probably playing golf together, Parker thought. Don was more than a son-in-law. He was everything Parker wasn't. But Parker had let go of that hurt years ago. "Well, this was last minute for us, too." He smiled an apology. "But I was going to tell you."

"Men," Karen muttered, shaking her head.

"Don't be sexist." Parker laughingly warned as several people approached. He handed her his near-empty bottle and added, "Make yourself useful, will you?"

"I'll get you later." Karen laughed at his favorite childhood taunt, then hugged him before she and her mother stepped aside for the next group of well-wishers.

Everyone was in high spirits, laughing, talking and drinking the free-flowing champagne. Several of his business associates approached to offer congratulations. Parker smiled, accepted the slaps on the back, did some slapping himself.

He couldn't wait to get the hell out of here.

Scanning the crowd, he spotted Ashley with her father in a corner.

"I can't believe they let you out of the hospital," she was saying when Parker installed himself next to her. "Those doctors should be shot for allowing this."

"Now, now, Leialoha." Keoki patted his daughter's hand. "I am fine. Look at me." Smiling, he spread his arms.

"Well...you do look good." Ashley worried her lower lip, then glanced at her new husband. "But it wasn't fair to Parker. He hates hospitals, yet he agreed to have the ceremony there for you." She took one of Parker's hands, her fingers a light caress, before her palm, soft and warm, pressed against his. Her eyes, golden and honeyed with gratitude, lingered on him.

Parker's heart swelled to his throat. Speechless, he gazed down at her. She had stuck up for him. Of her own free will, and not merely for the sake of their pretense, Ashley had chosen to stick up for him. Parker could see it in her eyes, feel it in her touch. And he had never felt so humbled as he did right then.

He wanted to tell her she was wrong, that he hadn't done it for her father. He wanted to tell her that he'd done it for her. But he didn't trust himself to speak.

"Well, if it is any consolation," Keoki said, looking from his daughter to Parker, a satisfied gleam in his eye, "the white coats will be here for me in less than an hour."

"Pop," Ashley scolded. "I didn't mean that. Of course I'm glad you're here." She dropped Parker's hand to hug her father and Parker, in the midst of a hundred people, was struck with the sudden feeling of loneliness.

The feeling was odd, unfamiliar, and he didn't like it one bit. In fact, it frightened the hell out of him.

"Who's idea was this?" Parker asked as safer feelings of anger and irritation reasserted themselves. He ran a finger around the inside of his collar. "We didn't want all this...this..."

"Nonsense." Keoki guffawed. "You only get married once."

Parker and Ashley exchanged quick glances.

"You're right, Dad." Ashley patted his hand. "It's a wonderful surprise."

Several people interrupted to congratulate the newlyweds. And eventually Keoki was spirited away by a few of his old cronies, leaving Parker and Ashley by themselves for a few blessed moments.

"Have you figured out who's behind all this?" she asked behind a forced smile, as she continued to nod to people.

"No. And right now I don't care. I just want out of here," Parker answered in a hushed tone.

"We can't."

"Why not?"

Ashley turned wide eyes on him. "Because all these people are here for us."

"Precisely," Parker commented dryly.

"We can't just leave. It would be rude."

"Not if we were late for our honeymoon." Parker's brain scrambled for an idea.

Ashley's eyebrows drew together. "What honeymoon?"

"Trust me on this, okay?"

"Where have I heard that before?" Ashley sputtered before turning to wave to a friend. "Forget it."

"Look, Ash—"

Crystal popped out from around the corner, a glass of champagne in each hand. "Peace offering." Her grin was sheepish, her face red.

"So, you're the culprit." Ashley planted a hand on her hip. "Crystal—"

"Oh, Ashley...you know how your dad is. What else could I do?" Crystal extended the glasses to them.

Ashley took hers, but Parker only shook his head. "Now I may have two bones to pick with you. What do you know—"

Parker was interrupted by a loud cough from Ashley. He swung around in time to take the champagne glass she pushed on him, while she held her other hand flush to her chest. "Are you all right?" He passed the glass back to Crystal and drew Ashley into his arms.

She nodded, looking up at him, her eyes large and bright. "Too many bubbles," she whispered. Then, to his utter amazement, she stood on her toes, wrapped her arms around his neck and kissed him.

Parker had to catch himself from stumbling back. She'd taken him by surprise and was clinging to him as if her very life depended on it. And as much as he enjoyed her unexpected passion, they were creating quite a scene.

Parker glanced at a gaping Crystal, while gently prying Ashley's fingers apart. He pulled back and smiled at her. Her eyes were glassy, her mouth trembly. And in another minute he would take her straight to bed, wedding guests be damned.

"You were right," she whispered. "Let's get out of here." She flashed a come-hither smile that just about caused the rosebud on his lapel to bloom.

"Say good-night, Ashley," he ordered hoarsely, his gaze locked with hers.

"Good night." Her voice was barely audible, and she didn't even spare her friend a glance.

"Pass on our regrets, will you?" Parker said over his shoulder to a dumbfounded Crystal as he scooped Ashley up in his arms and strode out the front door.

"WHY MOLOKAI? I don't know why we couldn't have just stayed at my apartment." Ashley twisted the gold band around her finger over and over again.

"I thought maybe this might be a special night." Parker hadn't meant to sound so sarcastic, but the woman was making him crazy. They had gotten all of two blocks away from the party when she'd done a total about-face. What the hell ever happened to truth in advertising?

"Look, we didn't have time to argue about it," he continued. "If we'd waited any longer it would have been too dark for a commuter flight, then I'd have had to pull some strings."

"Do you always get what you want, Parker?"

He pulled the rental car out of the Molokai airport. "If I did, you'd have shut up an hour ago."

"That can be arranged." She crossed her arms over her chest, lifted her chin and angled it so she could look out the window at the jagged coastline. Waves foamed white and angry, spraying the aged lava rocks.

Parker had lost it. He raked a hand through his hair. Had totally lost it. He hadn't told anyone to shut up since he was eleven years old. He glimpsed Ashley out of the corner of his eye and his disposition immediately softened. Her crossed arms kept her fidgeting fingers restrained, but her tiny foot was tapping wildly. She was nervous.

That must be the reason for her sudden Mr. Hyde impersonation after that titillating scene back at the party. Armed with this new recognition, Parker relaxed and waited a few minutes for her to cool off.

"It was a stressful day, Ashley," he began after a short time. "I'm sorry for anything negative I contributed. What do you say we make the most of this trip?"

Her foot slowed down, then she brought her face around to give him a slow contrite smile. "I'm sorry, too—"

"Enough said," he cut in before she tried to explain herself. "It's getting too dark for any sightseeing, but what would you like to do tomorrow?"

"I'm not sure." Ashley blinked and stared back thoughtfully. "I've never been to Molokai before."

"I'm surprised. There's more Hawaiian history here than on any other island besides Niihau."

"I know it sounds rather provincial, but I haven't been to all the islands. There's always so much to be done on Oahu." She squirmed a little, an attractive blush tinting her cheeks. "I guess this will be fun."

"There's a lot to see. We'll have to skip Kalaupapa, the old leper colony, and the wildlife preserve at the Molokai Ranch," he said, excited that he'd be the first to show her the island. "I have to be in the office on Monday, but I know exactly where I'm taking you tomorrow."

"Where's that?" she asked, smiling at his enthusiasm. He noticed she fingered the *maile* lei he'd given her. It pleased him that she continued to wear it. For Hawaiians, it was a symbol of luck. For Parker, the fact that she still wore it was a good sign.

"It's a surprise." He lightly touched the tip of her nose and winked. Ashley's tongue darted out to moisten her lips. She swiped at some loose tendrils. Parker settled back, willing his hands away from her. Even the most innocent touch made his senses reel.

He pulled into the hotel's circular drive and quickly surrendered his keys to the valet attendant. It hadn't really occurred to him until this moment that they had no luggage... no clothes. He smiled. That was more than okay with him, though he had a feeling Ashley might have a slight problem with that particular oversight.

They were promptly escorted to the suite that he had arranged for them from the Honolulu airport, and Parker gladly tipped the bellman for *not* bringing the clothes they didn't have.

"This is quite a place," Ashley said once they were alone in the suite. Champagne chilled in a stemmed antique bucket near a cream-and-navy sofa. Heart-shaped petit fours were arranged on a paper lace doily, framed by a gleaming silver platter on the coffee table. The air was richly scented with dozens of roses in varying shades of pink, springing from tall crystal vases throughout the parlor.

"It's the honeymoon suite," Parker commented casually and opened the sheer drapes to let in the panoramic ocean view. Ashley darted him a nervous sidelong glance before peeking out the wide sliding-glass doors. A cascade of purple bougainvillea plunged from the balcony to the sea.

"Want to see the bedroom?" Parker asked, then had to suppress a smile when she swiped at her hair.

"This must have cost a bundle," she said, ignoring him.

"Oh, no. You're not going to give me another lecture on my errant ways, are you?"

"That depends."

"On what?"

"Where and when you're taking me to dinner. I'm starved." She grinned, and Parker was relieved to feel the earlier tension between them dissolve. "And where isn't half as important as *when.*"

"I'll tell you what." Parker stepped forward and put his hands on her shoulders. She looked up at him with confusion in her eyes, and then her gaze lowered to rest on his mouth. She moistened her lips. His thoughts faltered.

"Did I ever tell you how ornery I get when I'm hungry?" she asked, swallowing hard.

"You mean, more than usual?" Parker forced a chuckle. He should get a medal for what he was about to do. Ignoring her unwitting invitation, he gripped her shoulders tighter and steered her toward the bathroom. "I'll give you first dibs on the shower, while I run down to the hotel boutique."

"The hotel boutique?" she questioned over her shoulder, then stopped at the bathroom door and faced him. Her eyes widened. "Oh." She looked down at her wrinkled *holoku* and grimaced. "You don't know my size."

"This time," he said, hurrying to the door with a wicked grin. "You really do have to trust me."

SOMETHING VERY STRANGE was happening, Ashlcy decided, as she took her seat at the table set for two on the short pier. With the help of a nearly full moon, a crystal lantern and the illumination of the hotel looming behind them, she could clearly see Parker's face. Her heart had somehow moved to her throat and who knows where her appetite had gone.

Nothing had gone right yet today, and now conflicting emotions were threatening her very sanity.

Disappointment was the last thing she had any right to feel, Ashley chided herself...well, maybe second to the last thing. The green silk dress Parker had bought for her fit perfectly, was quietly elegant, undoubtedly expensive...and except for the thin straps, quite conservative. It was almost boring.

The trouble was, his demeanor had indicated something far more exciting, daring, tantalizing. And the longer she'd waited in her sinfully sensuous bubble bath, the more she'd wanted to excite him, dare him... tantalize the socks off him.

Except if she sent Parker one more mixed signal after the spectacle she'd made of herself back at the party, he'd surely have her committed. But when he had opened his mouth to ask Crystal about Magic Island, Ashley had acted on her first impulse.

And therein lay the larger problem. Why had that been her first impulse? She could reason that it had been the simplest thing to do, but she knew that would be a lie. For as much as she hated to admit it, Ashley had the sinking feeling she was falling for this... this... She sighed. Even her contrived thoughts allowed her no indignant respite.

"Obviously, making a menu selection from here would be impractical, so I've already ordered for us." Parker must have misinterpreted her sigh as he leaned forward, a questioning look on his face. His skin looked exceptionally tan against his starched white shirt collar. The breeze ruffled his hair, putting it into a state of sexy disarray.

"Fine." She blinked, then reached into the glass-bowl centerpiece and twirled the gardenias floating at the bottom.

"Don't worry. It'll be a lot."

"What?"

"Of food. I wouldn't want to be accused of starving you on our first day of marriage."

Ashley looked blank at first, then laughed after she got past the shocking *M* word. They really were married... if only in name... and land deed. "You know, I really hadn't planned on eating so much that you'd have been too embarrassed to be seen with me in a restaurant."

"I wouldn't take the chance." Parker shook his head.

Ashley flicked a light spray of water off her fingertips at him.

"If it's a water fight you want, I'd be happy to oblige." He grabbed her wrist, his eyes sparkling with challenge.

"Not in your fancy clothes, you wouldn't."

"Wanna bet?"

"No." Ashley laughed and pulled back her hand. "Why did you want to dress up, anyway?" She eyed his tuxedo, knowing it wasn't his preferred attire.

"I thought it an appropriate prelude," he said calmly, and Ashley nearly flipped off the unfamiliar gold band she'd been twisting around her finger.

His expression was serious at first, and Ashley felt a web of apprehension weave through her. Then his eyes began to crinkle at the corners, and he asked with pure innocence, "Does prelude mean before or after an event? I always get that word mixed up."

Ashley thought of at least two answers she'd like to give him, but refrained from either.

Holding back a grin, he lifted his fluted glass. "To a smooth beginning."

"I think it's too late for that," Ashley replied and touched her glass to his, refusing him the satisfaction of any further reaction. "I don't suppose you bought me anything to sleep in."

The corners of Parker's mouth curved up, but his glass, in midair between them, distorted the true shape of his lips and made the smile seemed positively diabolical. "Of course. Otherwise that would be like..." He took a leisurely sip while watching her over the rim. "Forgetting dessert."

Ashley scrambled to think of something clever to say, but her heart competed with the distant pounding surf and her brain put all nerve endings on alert. She sipped the cool champagne instead and wondered if she could ever think of chocolate cake in the same way again.

With equal amounts of disappointment and relief, she noticed two waiters appear on the beach. She watched them approach with trays of silver-domed plates, grateful that she need not respond, ignoring the fact that she already had.

"You weren't kidding," she said when the food was placed before them. "It must've been embarrassing just ordering all this." She peered into papaya halves filled with crab and shrimp. Bowls of lobster bisque and plates of cold poached salmon were uncovered. Her mouth watered, her appetite firmly back intact.

"They'll bring my dinner next." He waved off the amused waiters, instructing them to bring the last course in an hour, then ducked the wadded cocktail napkin she threw at him. "Not enough for you?"

"Keep it up and I won't share." She forked a combination of shrimp and crab.

"Sure you will. Won't you?" The pleading he tried for fell a little short, but he leaned forward and waited.

"Well..." Ashley pursed her lips. "Just a little." Slowly she pushed the bounty toward him.

"Mmm. Superb! What else will you share?" He pierced her with a look that made her think he was talking about more than food.

Suddenly the meal held even more appeal. Ashley ate with relish, talking between mouthfuls, steering away from anything Parker implied. By the time the double chocolate mousse arrived, it didn't even seem tempting. But that didn't stop her.

"For a small thing, you sure can pack it away," Parker said after the dishes had been cleared and they were having their coffee.

"No short jokes or the truce is off."

"How about fat jokes?"

"You like fighting?"

"No. But I don't like considering this a mere truce, either," Parker said.

"How would you regard this?"

"Two people who can enjoy each other's company, while they each achieve their goal."

"We're too different, you know."

"To get along?"

She wasn't going to fall for this. There was no being led down the garden path for her. "We're getting along right now."

"Are we?"

"I enjoyed dinner, the conversation. And I didn't complain once about all this...this extravagance, did I?"

"You just did." Parker laughed. "In your own charming way, of course."

Ashley was glad he could make her blood pressure rise. It helped keep things in perspective.

"Care to walk off some of this dinner?" he asked before she could come up with a smart retort.

"Good idea." She pushed up from the table with a groan. "I don't think I could even get mad over a fat joke tonight."

"Good, because I was wondering how to broach this..." Shadows from the tide flickered across his face, giving him a pensive expression. "Are you one of those women who blimp out once they've snagged a husband?"

She stared at him for a moment, then punched his arm. "You turkey." He laughed, capturing her fist and bringing it to his lips.

"It would serve you right if I did." She lifted her chin and turned toward the ocean, letting the breeze cool her cheeks. He hadn't let go of her hand yet, and she didn't think she wanted him to. Gradually, she let her fingers relax from their balled position. His fingers slipped with ease between hers.

"Better take off your sandals," he suggested. "Unless you'd rather stick to the sidewalk around the hotel."

"Let's walk in the sand." She stooped down to do as he advised, and he removed his shoes as well. She laughed as he hopped on one foot and then the other to remove his socks.

"You could've helped me." The curve of his lips tempered his grumbling.

"I thought you were the floor show." She turned away with a smile and headed toward the shoreline, kicking playfully at the sand. "Besides, it was your profound idea to play dress-up."

In three strides he caught up, hooked her around the waist and hauled her up against him. He planted a swift kiss on her lips before she could do anything but breathe. "Today was special," he whispered. "Why not dress up?"

"Put me down or never complain about my weight again."

He pulled back in mock horror. "Me? Purposefully command your wrath? Surely you know I'm not that stupid."

"I know no such thing," she said and loosely put her arms around his neck. He let her slide with agonizing slowness down the length of him, until her feet sank into the soft, moist sand.

"Know about what?" he asked, his breath a soft caress on her cheek, his arm still firmly around her waist.

"Why do you ask such absurd questions?" The ocean pounded in her ears, and stars twinkled their amusement against the cloudless tropical sky. She was tired of bluffing, tired of trying to remember what they'd been talking about.

His lips started at her temple, then trailed along her jaw, nibbling their way to her mouth. Ashley dropped her head back and felt the pressure of his hand in her hair, entwining it, pulling at it, until her throat and neck—and surely her heart—were fully exposed.

"What about our walk?" she asked, her voice at minimum service level.

"The goal is," he murmured, running his tongue down the column of her throat, "to get the heart rate up." He licked at her collarbone. "This works for me."

"A walk... hmm." She ducked slightly from his nibbling. "Would be more appropriate."

"Ah." He caught her earlobe between his teeth. "But not as much fun." She felt the vibration of his lips, felt the tiny bumps rise from her flesh.

"But safer." In spite of her words, she lingered in his arms, felt her toes curl down into the sand as she stretched up to him.

"For what? Your conscience?" He tried to snag her lower lip with his capable ones.

Ashley jerked her head back. Her feet sank back down hard. "My conscience is fine. Is yours?"

"Mmm. Everything is fine, honey." Parker tried to pull her back against him. His eyes were closed, a satisfied smile on his lips she'd love to erase.

"Try again." Her tone was as shaky as the hand she brought up to tuck her hair back.

"What?" He opened his eyes and gave her a puzzled look, one she did not find endearing.

He had no idea, she thought with amazement, then thought about it for another second and decided it wasn't worth getting into. "I'm tired. Don't bother walking me back." She pivoted in the direction of their abandoned shoes.

"What's the matter?" he called out.

"Nothing." He hadn't figured out that the truth hurt, that the only relationship they had was based on a strip of land and a piece of paper. But she was grateful for the reminder. Without it, no telling what kind of fool she'd have made of herself.

"I'm tired, that's all," she told him more gently and truthfully, realizing with great sadness that for them fighting was the best way to keep their distance.

Chapter Eight

"I'll go back with you." He scooped up their shoes and sandals, and they walked in silence up the torchlit path to the hotel.

It was later than Parker thought. There was no sign of life in the dimly lit hotel lobby set back from the beach. Most of the guest rooms were blacked out, and the restaurant overlooking the ocean appeared nearly empty.

He didn't know what had spooked Ashley on the beach, but it would be a shame to waste such a beautiful and private night. "Want to sit by the pool a while?" he asked, stopping at a plumeria tree and plucking one of the blossoms.

Ashley slanted him a wary look. "Don't you have a full day planned tomorrow?"

"We don't have a timetable." He positioned a lounger for her and gestured to it.

"I think I'll pass." She dusted the sand from her feet and took her sandals from him.

"What? Can't wait to get me up to the room alone, huh?" he teased, clapping the sand from his shoes. And then it occurred to him, that notion could be possible. His gaze jerked up to her indignant one. And then again, maybe not.

Wishful thinking, James. He bit back a resigned grin and stroked a petal of the plumeria, then presented her with the fragrant flower. "I wish it were a gardenia."

"How did you know I like gardenias?" she asked with a slight frown.

"Simple." He shrugged. "Your perfume."

"I don't wear perfume."

He thought she was kidding at first, but he looked into her wide, questioning eyes and knew it was the truth. "I swear I can smell gardenias every time I'm with you." And when I'm not, he acknowledged wryly.

Ashley merely lifted a brow, a strange look on her face. Clearly she thought it was one heck of a line. And with her precarious mood, that wasn't a good sign.

"I mean it," Parker insisted. Good going. He rubbed his jaw. He'd surely get the line-of-the-year award.

"That's sweet, Parker." She put her hand to his cheek. Her lashes lowered for an instant and then her golden gaze bore into him. The angry green sparks were gone, but the warmth he craved wasn't quite there either.

"You don't believe me," he stated.

"Of course I do." She curved her hand to cup his face.

He relaxed, the tension he'd felt only a moment before dissolved. Mistakenly, he'd thought she'd been upset with him.

"Want to sit by the pool or go upstairs?" He captured her hand and pressed a long kiss to her palm.

She laughed, low and throaty, and gazing up at him, pushed her fingers through his hair. "It's so balmy. Let's stay," she said, her voice a sensual purr as she swayed against him, her long black hair flowing into the night.

He'd never been much for dancing, but Ashley's body pressed against his, oscillating with the flower-scented breeze, made his feet anxious to comply.

She let her head drop back, a bewitching smile on her lips, and she looked intensely at him. Exhilaration sparkled from her eyes, made all the more alluring by the shadows from the lighted water. Heat engulfed him. One shoe fell from his free hand, the other remained dangling from his fingers.

"Do you wear contacts?" she asked in a dreamy voice, her gaze unabashed adoration.

A sigh of relief almost escaped him. He was home free. Since he'd been a kid, women had fawned over his "bedroom blue" eyes. He cast silent thanks heavenward before answering in a modest voice. "Why, no."

"Good." She treated him to one more beatific smile, then put both hands on his chest and shoved.

He faltered in the middle of a sway. The one remaining shoe flew from his hand, an earthy curse from his lips. And with a large splash he landed in the kidney-shaped pool.

"That ought to cool you off...you...you arrogant, self-indulgent jerk." Ashley planted her hands on her hips. Parker kicked and sputtered, trying to stay above water.

"Me? Lady, you have one helluva nerve." He treaded water long enough to spit out his opinion before the weight of his anger—and his drenched tuxedo—dragged him down again.

"So have you," Ashley tossed over her shoulder as she headed for the path to the elevators.

Parker didn't know how he'd managed, in all his soggy leadenness, to make it to the edge and hop onto the decking. But he gained on her before she could make it to the building.

Ashley twisted in surprised horror as Parker pulled her against him. "Want to play rough?"

"You're getting me wet," she struggled in his arms. "Silk can't take water."

"And tuxedos can? You called the game, sweetheart."

"This is not a game. It was never a game," she hissed. "You tried to make it one." She gave him a futile push, then stumbled back against him. "Let go of me before someone comes to investigate the commotion."

"I'll tell them we're newlyweds." He shrugged, unconcerned, but she sensed a potent anger simmering below the surface. His lips were a breath away from her ear, his hands molded themselves to her wet, clinging dress. "That'll explain everything."

"What are you doing?" Ashley felt the first rise of panic. Her feet barely touched the ground as he propelled her back toward the pool. "Let's go to the room."

"Not yet. We have unfinished business here."

"Okay, I'm sorry." The tips of her toes skimmed the ground as she tried to put the brakes on. "Where are we going?" she asked, dreading the answer.

"To give you," he informed her in a hoarse whisper, his chest heaving beneath her hands, "a taste of your own medicine."

Ashley hit the water before his last word was out. She sank several feet and struggled against the urge to chop and slap at the water. She wouldn't give him the satisfaction. After several seconds she surfaced, swallowing a fair amount of water and indignation. She extended her arm and sliced through the water, reaching the side in several strokes.

"Nice job," Parker commented and reached a hand out to her, a smug smile on his egotistical face.

For a split second Ashley wondered if she had enough weight to pull him back in, but just as quickly she abandoned the whim. This particular war was over...for her, anyway. Maybe she had reacted too strongly. If only he weren't so...so...

"Staying in all night?" Parker left out his hand.

She looked up at him. Then again, maybe with the water's added weight, she could haul him in. "I'm tempted," she said, ignoring his offer, then placed both palms on the puddled deck and levered herself out.

"Tell me you didn't deserve that." He grinned and shrugged out of his dripping jacket.

"I didn't deserve that." With some remorse she watched him retrieve his ruined shoes, then looked down at her own irreparable clothes.

"I am sorry about the dress." He'd appeared beside her, his voice soft, the outside of his index finger rubbing against her upper arm.

"I'm sorry, too," she answered, hoping it didn't sound breathless. The air was mild, the water warm, his finger steamy. She shivered.

"Cold?" He slipped his arm around her. His face and seductive breath hovered above hers.

"No." She wouldn't look up. It'd be stupid. She pulled the fallen dress strap up her shoulder, then succumbed to temptation and raised her eyes to his. "I—I don't know why I did that. It was pr-probably childish." Her voice faltered under his intense gaze.

"Probably?" He laughed softly, hooking a finger under her dress strap, lightly scraping his knuckle back and forth across her skin. It caused an unbearable friction.

"Well, you irritate me." She made a halfhearted attempt to elude him, but his other arm encircled her.

"You *want* to be irritated," he corrected.

"Why would—?" His mocking expression stopped her. It would be pointless to deny it. She grabbed a handful of her hair, turned away and wrung it out. "It's better than doing anything foolish."

"Like this?" He stilled her hands and brought her head around.

She thought her chin actually tilted up before his fingers made contact with it. "Yes." Her voice was weak.

"Then let's be foolish." He brushed his lips against hers, then licked the moisture from the corner of her mouth.

"We really shouldn't," she murmured. They were both insane to be even thinking about getting involved. The arrangement could only work if they didn't. She had far too much to worry about as it was. This wasn't an option.

She closed her eyes and slid her arms around his neck.

A soft groan vibrated from Parker's throat as he tightened his hold. He lifted her up against his chest. He was tall and strong, and Ashley's feet no longer touched the ground.

She met each of his hard, hungry kisses, her neck arching back from their potency. His mouth left hers to forge a fiery trail down the column of her throat to the damp skin around her collarbone.

She heard his labored breathing, felt his chest heave against hers and understood the control he was fighting to maintain.

Pressing her hips against him, she began a slow rotation. She heard his breath suck in, missed its warm caress of her skin. His fingers bit into her buttocks, making the thin silk a useless barrier.

"No fair doing the hula now," he whispered, his protest a hoarse attempt. He shifted his own hips, then hiked her up higher in his arms. Her dress went up, too, leaving her thighs bare and vulnerable.

"I'm too heavy for you," Ashley murmured to the sky as she lifted her face to the perfumed air. Eyes closed, she could still see a thousand stars.

"Not even close." He nipped at her chin, then with his tongue traced sensuous patterns, dipping and darting to the top of her sagging dress. Her nipples pebbled and strained against the wet silk.

She clasped the sides of his head, fisting the wild half-wet tawny hair. One strap slid down her shoulder. Then the other. The weighty dampness dragged the flimsy material down low on her breasts. His tongue followed.

The ocean breeze glided over her skin, then sailed on through the night, stealing with it the rest of her willpower. His hot, moist mouth strained for her tender nipples. And Ashley offered them with each struggle for air.

A car backfired in the distance. Ashley opened her eyes and blinked. She stiffened. "Put me down, Parker." She took in a lungful of air, glancing from side to side.

"Hmm?" His eyes still closed, he nipped at the swell of her breast.

"We're right out in the open." She pulled up on her dress and adjusted the bodice.

"I can fix that." He lowered her, kissing her hard and wet when she was halfway down. "Come here." He pulled at one of her hands, pivoting toward the pool, while she rearranged a dress strap with her other hand.

"What are you doing?" Ashley planted both feet firmly together at the edge of the pool steps.

"Going where no one will see us." Parker had already placed one tuxedo-clad leg into the water.

"You really are crazy." Eyes wide and disbelieving, she shook her head. "I'm not going back in there. It's . . . it's wet."

"So are you." He gave her the final tug that brought her halfway down the steps. "I'm not giving you time to cool off, either."

She started to voice her irritation at his crass observation then repressed a giggle instead. The determined yet earnest look on his face was priceless. "Oooh." She backed up and shivered. "I think you're too late. The water seems colder this time."

"I'm not surprised." He tugged her forward again and grabbed both her hands. "We did heat things up pretty well." He found the sensitive area behind her ear and ran his tongue to her lobe.

"Someone could still see us," she whispered, hoping he didn't feel the goose bumps that surfaced on her skin.

"No one's around. Even the restaurant lights are out now. Relax, Ashley." He slid the straps back down her shoulders. "It's just you and me." He licked where each of the bands of material had been. "And we have all night."

Just one night, Ashley thought, closing her eyes. We'll steal this one small night. Reasons and regrets seemed far away as Parker reached behind her and pushed his hands up under her dress to her silk panties.

Her hands floated on top of the water until she could stand it no longer. She plucked at one of his shirt buttons until it was free and then loosened the next. He pulled back when he discovered her mission, and although she couldn't quite meet his gaze his mouth was parted in anticipation. The third and fourth buttons were fast and easy.

Drops of water glistened from the dense thatch of hair on his chest. His nipples were distended and dark against the tawny hair. Ashley put her hands on him, shyly at first, but his groan of pleasure gave her confidence.

Stepping farther back, Parker slid the remaining inches of silk down over her breasts. She had no idea when he'd freed the zipper, for the top of her dress fell easily to float over the moonlit water. Only her long hair, tangled and clinging about her, shielded her nakedness from him. With aching tenderness, he peeled away the strands, kissing the sensitive areas they had guarded.

"You're beautiful," he whispered, cupping her breasts.

"Don't blow it now." Her laugh was short and nervous.

"You are. Like a Hawaiian goddess." He brushed the last of the hair away. His gaze rested on her face for a moment and then smoldered its way to her breasts. He circled the rosy tips with his thumbs, his head tilted in solemn fascination.

Ashley's voice stuck in her throat and she experienced an incredible sense of loss when his hands fell away.

"Come here." He reached under her arms and carried her up as if she were a child. "I want to feel you against me." As soon as he had her where he wanted, he locked his arms around her. Her nipples pressed to his hair-roughened chest. Slowly he swayed from side to side, while keeping her still. "You feel so good."

Anticipation bubbled and churned within her. Cool water, Parker's warm, hard body, air scented with a thousand flowers...surely she would drown in sensation.

To steady herself, she wrapped her unanchored legs around him. For a heartbeat, he stopped and looked down at her, his eyes masked by the shadows. She wanted to see them, wanted to be reassured. But when she gripped his shoulders, she felt the tension there and knew the next move would have to be hers. Before sanity could reclaim her, she undulated her hips, encouraging him to resume their sensual water dance.

It was all the inducement he needed. His mouth came down fast, his tongue like velvet against her skin. He changed the pace, made new rules, teased his way around her collarbone, then up to her lips. He lingered at her mouth, and with a sweet aching slowness tasted and probed.

Ashley began to breathe an even pattern when Parker deepened the kiss, his mouth demanding and rough with need. His fingers, woven through her hair, held her helpless. Not that she cared to go anywhere, do anything different. She kissed him back, matching his hunger.

"Oh, Ashley." He dragged his mouth away from hers, his words raspy and halting, his gaze roving her face. "We have to stop now if we're going to stop at all." He looked down at her breasts and watched the water ripple over them, first covering, then exposing them, the cycle repeating itself.

He cupped one breast, then put his mouth on her. She let out a small gasp, reveling in the feel of his warm tongue, the cool water. "No fair stacking the deck," she panted.

"I didn't say I'd be fair," he murmured against her sensitive skin and hesitated, holding her. Even the vibration of his words roused her tender need. But he was giving her a chance... a chance to preserve the relationship they could never again recapture.

Her body wanted to ignore the opportunity, but doubt niggled at her—even as she magnetized to his touch. Another moment, surely another moment wouldn't matter before she allowed reality to square off with emotion.

She tunneled her fingers through his hair and guided him to her other breast.

"Eh-hem. Excuse me, folks." The voice came from behind Ashley, her bare back up for the speaker's view. "I'm hotel security, and the pool is closed for the evening." If it were at all possible, the man's high-pitched voice sounded more embarrassed than Ashley was feeling.

She didn't turn to look at him, as mortification replaced desire. Heat climbed her face. She stared, wide-eyed, at Parker, who brought his arms around her, sheltering her from further discomfort.

"Sorry." Parker quietly cleared his throat. Looking over her head, he grinned at the man, and she was awed by his composure. "If you'll either turn your back or leave for a few minutes, I promise we'll be out of here."

"No problem. I'll continue my rounds." The man's voice was already fading, but Ashley didn't budge.

"He's gone now," Parker said softly. He gave her a quick hug before releasing her and pulling up the front of her dress. "Ash, I'm sorry about this."

She slipped each of her arms under the straps. The dress felt tighter, her breasts tender. She adjusted the fit, keeping her eyes lowered. "It wasn't your fault. I was just as much a participant."

"I can still be sorry." He hooked a finger under her chin and nudged her face up. "I sure know how to romance a girl, huh?" He chuckled. Her face burned. "Next time, I promise to do better."

Ashley, tight-lipped, angled away from his grasp and reached around, trying to zip up the wet clinging silk. Parker buttoned his shirt halfway, then took the zipper from her hands and finished the job.

"Ashley?" He waited patiently until with great reluctance she returned his gaze. The words "next time" echoed in her head, and even as she vowed there wouldn't be one, she quivered with anticipation.

"He didn't see anything," Parker continued. "The man kept staring at his shoes. He was probably more embarrassed than you were."

Quite impossible, but she didn't care to hang around and debate the point. She headed for the pool steps.

"Wait." Parker trudged up behind her just as she emerged from the water. His eyes lingered for a moment on the curves accentuated by the wet fabric. He looked as if he wanted to touch her, but he kept his hands fisted at his sides. "I need to know, Ash. What would have been your answer?"

Chapter Nine

Ashley had gotten very little sleep on her wedding night. Unfortunately, it wasn't for the traditional reason. She was confused. She'd spent part of the night thanking God for the security guard and the rest wondering how she was going to keep her hands off her husband.

She poked around at her breakfast of eggs Benedict and chanced several peeks at Parker. His unanswered question from the previous night hung between them.

After their romp in the pool the previous night, he'd left her an oversize T-shirt in the bathroom, then, without a single word, he had taken the couch. But with the birth of a new day, "tell me what you want" was the clear message in his eyes—his beautiful, compelling eyes. Had they always been that blue?

Ashley sighed out loud. Her gaze darted up to meet Parker's intense one. She looked away and coughed into her linen napkin. "What time did you want to get started?"

"As soon as you're through playing with your food."

She eyed the demolished egg concoction in front of her. His plate was clean. Obviously his appetite remained unaffected. She looked back at him in time to catch the twinkle in his eye.

She put down her fork. "I'm ready when you are."

"So agreeable. I like that in a woman." He grinned, then signed the check presented by the waiter.

He was trying to goad her. Ashley ignored him. "Can I assume this is suitable for what you have planned?" She waved at her new white shorts and lemon-colored halter top.

Parker stared at her a long time, taking in the V-neck top, the gold pendant with her scripted Hawaiian name dangling there against her tanned skin. His lips curved up.

Darn him for making her want to squirm. She was beginning to wonder what exactly he *did* have planned. "I thought we had a tight schedule." She pushed back in her chair and threw her napkin on the table.

"We could cancel and spend the day in the room."

"Forget it." She tossed her hair over her shoulder and headed for the door. "I didn't bring the checkers."

"Strip poker, then?" He strode up beside her, sounding almost comically hopeful.

Ashley bit her lower lip to keep from smiling. "Next you'll tell me you've never played the game in your life."

"Never. Scout's honor."

"You were never a Scout."

"No," he agreed. "Well, I was for a day. But I got caught sneaking into the Brownies' camp."

"Why am I not surprised?"

"Hey, I'm innocent. I thought they meant real brownies." He looked hurt at her skeptical look. "Scout's honor." They both laughed.

Ashley reached the elevator first and punched the button. "Since you ignored my question, I'll assume I'm dressed okay."

"Fine." Parker backed her up to the elevator doors, his hands bracketing her. "May I take the same liberty with my unanswered question?"

She staved him off with her palms against his chest just as the elevator dinged its arrival. He dropped his hands to allow for the opening doors but kept her gaze snagged with his. "I guess you've been saved again, Ashley James."

She took a deep breath and stumbled back into the waiting car. It was suddenly as clear as the brilliant midmorning sun. No matter what Ashley wanted, or what lies she told herself, she knew for certain it was only a matter of time. And deep in his very blue eyes, this undeniable truth was mirrored tenfold.

"PARKER, THIS IS incredible." She turned wide eyes on him, pushed her fingers through her hair, lifted it high, then let it cascade back down to her waist.

He watched the thick, glossy satin settle and wondered how it could be the color of midnight at high noon. Her face was alive with enthusiasm, fresh and glowing, free from unflattering makeup. Suddenly, he felt like the luckiest man on earth. The sparkle in Ashley's eyes had been put there by him. Well, he had a little help from Wailuku Village.

"You like it, huh?" Of course she did, but he wanted to bask in her gratitude a while longer.

"I love it." She grabbed his hand, hers so small and fragile, and pulled him toward one of the grass huts. "You're sure it's authentic?"

"From what I understand, this is an exact replica of a Hawaiian village years before any white men arrived. Our guide should be here any minute."

"This is exciting. Do they make the feather cloaks? How about food? Do they net fish and maintain taro patches?" She stopped for a few seconds, a small crease drawing her eyebrows together. "How about the *alii*? Is that established? That's Hawaiian royalty," she added for his benefit.

"I know what that means." He made a face, annoyed that she thought him so ignorant of the culture. However, his knowledge was limited and the last thing he wanted was a conversation that got him in over his head. He looked at his watch. Where was that guide?

"Hey, that looks like a ceremonial dance over there. My goodness." Ashley shook her head in awe. "Those canoes are hand carved. Look at the craftsmanship."

Parker watched her excitement grow, and contentment filled him. He hoped today would dissolve the new invisible barriers she'd raised after the pool incident.

"Look past the thatch hut near the carved figures," she said, and Parker bent his head to follow the direction of her extended arm.

Drawn to her unique scent, he lowered his face close to hers. She didn't appear to notice, so he ducked in for a quick kiss on her neck. She jumped and brought her face sharply around. Perfect. He kissed her swiftly on the lips.

"Parker," she scolded and shifted a small distance away from him, casting a quick glance in both directions.

"It's okay. We're supposed to be newlyweds. Remember?" She shot him a wry look as he slipped an arm around her waist. "Now, what were you showing me?" he asked before she could give him any grief.

"Over there. They're having some sort of ceremony. I wonder what they're passing around? I'll bet it's not coconut milk." She turned to him, bringing her face inches away. She hesitated and her gaze dropped to his mouth. Unconsciously, her tongue darted out to moisten her lips.

Parker was about to forget the entire plan and haul her back to the room. He glided his hand along her jaw and angled his face to hers.

"The tour starts now, so don't start anything else." They both turned to look at the grinning guide. He was short, brown and ample bellied, covered only by a loincloth. He held a spear in one hand and a clipboard in the other. "You folks must be the Jameses."

So now the idiot shows up, Parker thought. He glared at the man, while Ashley welcomed him with one of her beguiling smiles.

"Have you taken the tour before?" the guide asked. Ashley shook her head. Parker grunted something unintelligible.

"I'll give you some brief history before we start. When Captain Cook discovered the islands, he found that each one had its own monarch. The *alii*..." The man droned on while Ashley nodded, totally engrossed in what he was saying. They strolled through the different areas of the village and it was obvious Ashley knew as much as their guide, if not more.

Parker, on the other hand, couldn't figure out half of what they were talking about, especially when they slipped into too much of the Hawaiian language. Holding his own, he laughed when Ashley did, nodded knowingly when he thought he should. He was curious about some things, but no way was he going to ask. That was out of the question. Why, that would be like... like asking for directions when he got lost.

By the time the two-hour tour was over, he was hot and thirsty and could think of nothing but a tall, cool drink and a steamy shower with Ashley.

"We have a couple of hours before our flight leaves," he told her as he steered the rental car back to the hotel. "Are you hungry?"

"Not at all. I'm too excited."

Great. Parker shifted his gaze to her without turning his head. All the more time for that shower.

Ashley laid her head back on the seat and let it loll in his direction. "That was wonderful." Her lips curved upward. "*You're* wonderful for taking me there."

He returned her smile and reached for her hand. Things were looking up. The tension between them was gone. She looked relaxed, even her hand rested easily in his. And all Parker could think about was how right it felt, being with her, trying to please her.

The realization hit him like a tidal wave. Somewhere along the line, Ashley had become important. Had it only been three weeks? At the moment, he couldn't remember how life had been before her. He gravitated toward the open window and gulped for a breath of ocean air.

This wasn't part of the plan. He clenched his jaw. It wouldn't work between them. She was too idealistic. He wasn't about to spend his life, or his money, building community centers. Especially now, when he was finally making a name for himself without his family's influence or money. He'd waited a long time and had worked hard for it. Ashley didn't understand that. They'd disagree for the rest of their lives. And their children were bound to suffer the consequences.

Oh, jeez. Now, he was thinking about kids. Sweat formed at the back of his neck. He withdrew his hand from hers and rubbed a clammy palm on his jeans before wrapping it around the steering wheel. He glanced over at Ashley. Her honey-colored eyes remained focused on him, a bit curious now but still soft and dreamy.

His breath sputtered in his chest. Was it possible? Could they make it work? If she kept looking at him like that, he'd begin to believe anything.

"You look happy," he said, his hand again finding hers.

"I am." She sighed. "I wish it weren't ending so soon."

He squeezed her hand. "Me, too."

She gave him a lazy, sensuous smile. "I'm impressed you knew so much about the village."

He shrugged and tried to look blasé.

"I'm embarrassed that I hadn't known of the village's existence before now. Maybe I need to widen my blinders," she said.

"Nah. Well, maybe a little." The village was the last thing he was thinking about when she lightly punched his arm and grinned. Somewhere deep down, Ashley had to know something was happening between them. And when she finally acknowledged it...

"We don't have time for much more than lunch, but since you're not hungry..." He briefly turned hopeful eyes her way before returning them to the road. "Ashley?"

"Hmm?" She twirled a long strand of silky hair, her head back, eyes half closed. Wind whipped through the open T-top of the rental car and teased the deep vee of her halter. It rippled against her golden skin and allowed him a glimpse of the piece of heaven he'd tasted the previous night.

"We have unfinished business," he said finally, immediately chastising himself for the use of the word "business." He gripped the wheel a little harder, determined that she not put him off. "Ashley?"

He steered the car around a curve in the road and into the hotel parking lot before glancing at her. She was asleep. Her lashes lay thick and dark against her cheeks, a slight part at the seam of her lips. If she'd gotten as little sleep as he had the night before, it was no wonder.

Her hands were curled together in her lap, her bare legs crossed at the ankle. It would be easy to scoop her up and carry her to their room. But he didn't think he'd make it to the lobby without her waking up and acting like a wildcat.

He turned off the car engine and sat there, watching the shadows of overhead coconut fronds sway across her face. The resort, her father, his father...everything seemed far away and unimportant. It had been a long time since the resort had had any competition for his attention. Harvey had assumed more and more of Parker's responsibilities. And Parker had been spending more and more time with Ashley and her tutoring project. He'd resented it at first, but lately he looked forward to it. He shook his head. Her idealism was contagious.

He watched her still form and the idea struck him. They needed another day off, plain and simple. She had to be exhausted with the grueling schedule she maintained, on top of worrying about her father. Construction on the resort would continue without him. He could rebook tomorrow's meetings. Who could begrudge him a short honeymoon?

More important, it was a good way for Ashley to get some long overdue rest. If they did manage to tangle a few sheets, he certainly wouldn't complain. It would be an added bonus. But at the moment, watching her sleep so peacefully, all he wanted to do was protect her from herself.

He got out and went around to open her door. After unfastening her seat belt, he hunkered down and took her face in his hands. "Ashley? We're here."

Her mouth stretched into a smile before she opened her eyes. From the innocence of sleep, she put a hand to his face and stroked his roughened jaw. He kissed her palm.

"I must have dozed off."

"That's an understatement. You were snoring like a drunken sailor."

"I was *not*." She dropped her hand to his shoulder and gave him a push worthy of a sailor.

"Tired, grumpy and can't take a joke." He grinned and offered to help her out of the car.

"Thank you," she said, taking his hand and levering herself. He grimaced. Those lovely nails of hers digging into his skin were no accident.

"I've got a great idea. Since we're having such a—"

"Oh, Parker." Her eyes were all honeyed with gratitude again. "I truly am." She slid her arms up his chest and hugged him. He knew it had been strictly on impulse, but he accepted it with relish all the same and locked his arms around her waist.

"Let's stay another day." He pressed a kiss to her forehead, then leaned back to look at her.

"How can we? That's not possible."

"Anything is possible."

"For you, maybe. I have classes to teach, a tutoring session." She threw up her hands. "I have to see my father. Then there's the lei-making contest I'm judging—"

"All small obstacles. Think about the cultural-enrichment aspect." Cultural enrichment, hell. She was going to spend tomorrow in bed...sleeping mostly. "All this exposure will make you a better teacher. How's that for justification?"

"Nice try. But I've got responsibilities."

"And I don't?" His hands slackened at her waist. His temper sparked, but he wasn't going to let her rile him, even though she'd conveniently forgotten he had a company to run.

"Oh, Parker, it's been a fantastic day." She cradled his face in her hands. "Let's not fight."

"Believe me, that's the last thing I want to do." He pulled her closer. "I merely thought another day would be nice."

"I'd love to say yes." She gave him a small, sad smile. "But it's simply not possible," Ashley said, then gave him an inquisitive look. "Exactly what did you have in mind?"

"Well..." He had to organize his offense. He cast his baby blues at her and tried to look a little wounded. After all, he was doing it for her own good. "Did you really like my surprise today?"

"Oh, Parker." She was in his arms again, all soft and grateful, smoothing his cheek. "It was one of the nicest things anyone has ever done for me."

Car doors slammed, murmurs echoed, but the fact that they were in the middle of an open parking lot didn't bother him. His hands rested on the curve of her buttocks as she looked up at him, her scent strong and intoxicating. He leaned back against the car, and cradling her between his thighs, brought her with him. Unresisting, she toyed with the buttons of his polo shirt.

"It doesn't have to end, you know." Over and over again, he combed his fingers through her hair. Ashley closed her eyes to the massaging motion.

"And you accuse me of having my head in the clouds." She laughed and tilted her face up to him. The sun caught a myriad of colors in her contented eyes. "You certainly do surprise me sometimes."

He lowered his head and she stretched up to meet him. Their lips touched in a light kiss. And then another. Her hands were still on his chest and he felt her tentative exploration through the shirt fabric.

The sun was hot, but no competition for Ashley's touch as she dipped in and out of his open collar. He caressed the bare skin between her halter and shorts, slipping his fingers up her top and along her delicate spine. She pressed into him and his control faltered.

"I think you do this on purpose," he whispered on a trail of kisses to her temple.

"Mmm, what?" She pushed at her hair, giving him better access.

"Start things in safe places. Or maybe you have a thing for cars and parking lots."

"Aren't you safe?"

"All depends." He nipped at her ear. "Wanna find out?"

"What did you have in mind?" She smiled. And somewhere in his foggy mind, Parker knew he had to have a portrait of her looking exactly as she did now.

"Stay another night and see for yourself."

"You're incorrigible."

"So I've been told a time or two."

"It is tempting, but I can't." Ashley brushed a fallen lock of hair off his forehead and sighed. "Tell me what you had planned, so I have something to look forward to."

Parker squinted at her. "Then it won't be a surprise. Wasn't that part of today's fun?"

"Partly," she agreed. "But you know what's best of all?" She leaned heavily against him and he felt her heart race. Her eyes were sparkling and her dimple flashed deep.

"What?" His own heartbeat picked up speed. It was only the two of them, no resort to worry about, no family problems. Ashley looked genuinely happy, and he knew he was largely responsible. He reveled a few more seconds in her intimate hazel gaze and waited expectantly.

"I can't wait to tell the kids about it."

"The kids?" He frowned.

"You know, the gang I tutor." She stepped away from him and he let her go. "They won't believe it. Maybe if they work real hard, we could take a one-day excursion here. We could have a car wash or something. . . ." She chattered on and on, looking as animated as she had at Wailuku Village.

The hot afternoon sun replaced the warmth of Ashley's body as Parker watched the distance grow between them. She started in the direction of the hotel and had a hundred-and-one plans for the kids by the time they got to the room.

As a rule, it wasn't his style to sulk in silence. But Parker couldn't think of anything to say as they each filled their shared garment bag and small carryon.

He'd been arrogant enough to think her heart had skipped a few beats for him. But it simply wasn't so. It was those damn kids she thought about.

He picked up their bags from the bed and took them to the living room, where she was making a phone call. He plopped them down in no particular order.

Jealous. That's what he was. He raked a hand through windblown hair. He'd never been jealous a day in his life, and now... it was over a bunch of delinquents.

The worst part was, he had no right. He had bought and paid for Ashley's services... a fact that was becoming harder to accept.

He was waiting for Ashley to get off the phone when he noticed that the carryon's zipper was caught. He tried to free it, but it held fast to something inside the bag. He reached in and brought out a handful of Ashley's ruined silk dress. Images of her in the pool flashed in his mind and a smile of satisfaction tugged at his lips.

The previous night she'd been his. She could deny it, but he'd bet the resort she hadn't been thinking about those kids or anyone else.

But he wanted more. He wanted her trust. And from now on, the only thing he was going to buy was time.

ASHLEY HATED REDUCING herself to being a snoop, but she didn't think she could stand it a moment longer. From Parker's bedroom doorway, she glanced over at the garment bag they had yet to unpack since returning home the day before. She slowly meandered toward it.

Actually, it wouldn't be snooping, she told herself, since her clothes *were* packed along with Parker's. If she happened to run across the nightie she was certain he'd bought her, it would be purely accidental. Ashley didn't believe for one minute that the T-shirt he'd ultimately given her had been what he'd had in mind. Or maybe she didn't want to believe it.

Since returning to Honolulu, Parker had barely uttered three sentences to her. He hadn't even complained when she had elected to sleep at her apartment the night before. And since Mrs. Lee was on another island visiting family until tomorrow, Ashley had the same choice to make tonight.

It would be a whole lot simpler if she didn't feel so guilty, she acknowledged, or if she actually *had* classes to teach, students to tutor, a contest to judge. But the fact was, all those reasons had nothing to do with her having refused to stay on Molokai another night. An important meeting concerning Magic Island this morning had everything to do with it.

Ashley swung the garment bag from the luggage rack onto Parker's bed and unzipped the side pouch. She figured she had at least another hour before Parker got home from work. Plenty of time to retreat to her apartment... after she satisfied her curiosity. Although she wasn't sure what that would prove, except...

She wasn't going crazy. Ashley smiled and pulled at the familiar cream-colored boutique sack. It caught on a tangle of clothes, but she could see a sliver of something pink... lacy... she couldn't quite...

"You beat me home." Parker's voice came from behind her. Ashley dropped the sack and clutched her chest.

"You scared the devil out of me." She jammed the package back in and turned to the door, her heart pounding like a war drum.

"Sorry." He grinned. He looked tired.

"I was just unpacking." Ashley realized she was still stuffing things back in and stopped.

"I see." Parker jerked his tie loose. He started to fling his jacket onto the bed, but settled it on the valet instead.

It suddenly occurred to Ashley that she was sitting on Parker's bed, in his bedroom. And he was undressing. She stood. "I can do this later."

"Everything's probably ruined." Parker paused. His eyes seemed to darken and memories of their pool escapade rattled Ashley's last strand of composure. "But we probably ought to at least give the dry cleaners a go at it."

"Good idea." Ashley snatched up the entire garment bag and staggered under its weight. Parker came from behind to circle her with his arms, absorbing the bag's weight and steadying her.

Ashley straightened. She felt shakier now than without his help. "I'll drop it off on the way home," she said, trying to subtly free herself.

"Home?" Parker turned her toward him and took the bag from her arms. "What do you think this is?"

Ashley forced herself to look up. She was prepared for sarcasm, maybe even anger. But the trace of uncertainty he blinked away surprised her.

"I'm not sure, Parker," she replied honestly. Then she left both him and the garment bag and hurried out the room.

"ARE YOU STILL TALKING to me?" Crystal asked as she pulled out a chair opposite the table from Ashley.

"Barely." Ashley looked up and frowned at her friend. "I thought about ignoring your message and standing you up for lunch."

Crystal grinned. "And forgo the chance to tell me about your wild and crazy honeymoon?"

"It wasn't a honeymoon." Ashley felt the heat start at her neck. She quickly picked up her menu, burying her face in it.

"Really?" Crystal laughed. "You were so hot to trot at the reception, I about dropped my nose ring."

Ashley abruptly lowered the menu and peered closely at her friend. "You don't have a nose ring."

"Gotcha." Crystal leaned forward. "Tell me everything."

Ashley sighed. Her father had already admitted guilt regarding his role in initiating the wedding reception. It hadn't stopped Parker from chewing out Mrs. Lee for her complicity, but Ashley knew admonishing Crystal would be useless. Besides, there was a far more important matter to address. "Don't talk to Parker."

"Why? Will he have a better version?" Crystal's dark eyes sparkled with curious delight.

"I'm serious. He thinks you're linked to Magic Island."

"Well, I am, in a way."

"Yeah, well, he wants to know what you know."

"Oh." Crystal settled back in her chair. "If he asks, what should I tell him?"

"Nothing." Ashley shook her head. "Right now he's busy with the resort." Or so Ashley supposed. He certainly hadn't been busy with her in the past three days, since they'd come back to Oahu. "But if he brings it up, tell him that you offered some legal services but no one has contacted you about it."

"Does he know about you?"

"Heavens, no." Ashley's eyes widened, her voice lowered. "And he's not going to find out. The committee met yesterday morning and will meet two more times this week. We're gaining a lot of support, especially now that we have some concrete proposals for the state. And I don't need Parker throwing a wrench into the works."

Crystal said nothing at first. She pressed her lips together and studied Ashley until the waiter came, took their orders and left. Finally Crystal said, "You're still going through with it."

"Going through with it?" she echoed cautiously.

"Your service center for Magic Island." Crystal narrowed her eyes on Ashley. "After the way you left the party, I thought—"

"I had to do that, Crystal." Ashley flipped her hair back. "It was the only way I could keep him from surprising you with a question about Magic Island."

Crystal's eyes widened. "I really thought..."

Ashley shook her head and lowered her gaze. "It was an act. That's all." She looked back up at her friend, who returned her stare with a suspicious frown.

"Okay," Crystal said after a thoughtful silence. "I won't say anything to Parker."

PARKER OPENED THE entry door and sniffed the air. Roast pork and fried rice. He wasn't surprised that Mrs. Lee had cooked his favorite dish. She'd been totally unrepentant this morning when he'd picked her up at the airport, but when it came down to it she knew that the party had not been a great idea. Especially since Parker Senior had elected not to show up. And being the peacemaker that she was, Mrs. Lee was making it up to Parker in her own way.

"What died in here?" Parker called teasingly out to the kitchen.

Mrs. Lee came through the swinging door, snapping her dish towel in the air. "If it weren't for your new bride, I'd take this towel to you like I did when you were a *keiki.*" She stopped and looked around. "Where is she?"

"Ashley?" Parker laid down his briefcase and picked up the newspaper, casually glancing at his watch. "Isn't she home yet?" For the past three days, he'd been patient with Ashley's decision to remain at her apartment, but his equanimity was definitely waning. And if his lovely wife didn't get her sweet fanny home soon, he was going to wring her lovely neck.

"I thought she'd be with you." Mrs. Lee's finger came up wagging. "What kind of lovebirds are you?"

"Cuckoos are more like it," someone mumbled from down the hall—or so it sounded to Parker, and he glanced that way.

Ashley breezed in. "I was right behind you, Parker. But I came in through your...uh...our suite entrance. I had something to drop off." She darted Mrs. Lee a nervous look, then gave them both a bright smile. "What smells so good?"

She started to brush past Parker, but he caught his housekeeper's inquisitive look, hooked an arm around Ashley's waist and hauled her up against him. When she opened her mouth, Parker took full advantage of her beginning protest by slipping his tongue between her lips. He felt her relax against him for a moment, then she jerked her head back and looked directly at Mrs. Lee. Her chin quivered as if she wanted to say something, but she kept her mouth clamped shut and sent Parker a murderous look.

"It's about time." Mrs. Lee chuckled and made an about-face for the kitchen. "Dinner is in half an hour."

Ashley edged a safe distance away from him and as soon as Mrs. Lee was out of earshot, she hissed, "Try that again and I'll bite your tongue."

"Mmm. Sounds kinky." Parker smiled while pulling his tie through his collar. He tossed it onto the back of an overstuffed chair and took a step closer to Ashley.

"Sounds painful to me." She took two steps backward.

"Maybe." He shucked off his jacket and advanced three steps.

"What is this? A striptease?" Ashley laughed nervously and tried for a nonchalant pivot toward the kitchen.

"If you like." Parker shot out a hand and grabbed her wrist.

"I don't like," she said through clenched teeth as he brought her up hard against him. Her gaze sparked angry green as she lifted a defiant chin and looked him right in the eyes. "Do *not* take advantage of the fact that Mrs. Lee is here. Or I warn you—"

"Don't make idle threats..." Parker advised. Ashley narrowed her I-dare-you gaze on him before he could remind her of what she had to lose, and he quickly amended what he was about to say. "Because it turns me on."

Her eyes widened. So did Parker's smile.

"A warthog would turn you on," she whispered fiercely and twisted away from him.

Parker laughed out loud. "Give yourself a little more credit than that."

Ashley gave him a dirty look. "I think I'll help Mrs. Lee," she said pointedly and made it to the kitchen door.

"Wait a minute." Parker crooked his finger, beckoning her to him.

Ashley stared at him with a disbelieving shake of her head. "You're crazy. I ought to just have you committed and be done with it."

Parker lowered his voice even further, his face serious. "I merely want to remind you that this is for real." He paused when the spunk disappeared from her expression, and he mentally cursed himself. But Ashley had made herself so scarce since their return, they hadn't discussed much about Mrs. Lee. And Parker had to admit he had hated to even bring up the nasty business that so crassly described their relationship. "We have to be convincing, Ash," he said gently.

"Don't worry, Parker." Ashley hesitated with her hand flat against the kitchen door, her proud face focused on him. "You'll get your money's worth."

"PASS THE SYRUP, please." Parker watched his new wife fumble with the small pitcher of freshly made pineapple syrup while he restacked his pancakes.

"Thank you," he said once she had placed it in front of him.

Ashley gave him a small nod. "Butter, please."

Parker obliged her with a bland smile and the white ceramic crockery.

The sun was at the horizon, spouting off its usual fireworks of orange and pink and promising the start of a fresh new day, but Napua Lee's heart was heavy. She was dreadfully worried about her two wards.

It just wasn't natural, she lamented to herself, as she watched Parker and Ashley eat their breakfast in silence. Newlyweds should be laughing, touching, smooching, as they had in her day. She strained her memory back to when her Leonard was alive. She smiled. It was so long ago, but she could still remember the carefree days of shared whispers, secret touches.

Her smile faded. But not these two. Normally, they stayed clear of each other, and when they were together and thought she wasn't listening, they fought like cats and dogs. But Napua prided herself on keeping on top of things and little escaped her. Parker liked to call it nosy. She sniffed. But the way he managed things, what did he know?

"Mrs. Lee, do you have a cold?"

Napua met Parker's concerned gaze. "No. Do you two want to go out to dinner alone tonight?"

Parker arched a brow and darted a quick look at Ashley. "I don't think so," he answered slowly.

Ordinarily, Napua would have laughed at the confused look on his face. He obviously thought he'd forgotten some occasion. But she didn't laugh. She was peeved.

"Everything you make is so wonderful, Mrs. Lee," Ashley added politely. "I'd just as soon eat here."

Humph. Napua did not return Ashley's smile. She drummed her plump fingers on the table and covertly regarded Ashley's stiff posture and her shadowed eyes. She was just as bad. Stayed away for hours at a time, that one did. And was as quiet as a church mouse whenever Parker was around. Worst of all, Napua had a keen suspicion that Ashley didn't always sleep in Parker's bed.

"Well." Parker placed his napkin on the table and stood. "Got to get to work."

"Are you going to be late tonight *again?*" Napua asked.

"I don't know." Parker picked up his keys and started for the door. He stopped, as if remembering something he'd forgotten, and brushed his wife's cheek with a hurried kiss. "I'll call."

Ashley gave him a tight smile of acknowledgment and he left.

Napua fidgeted. She counted silently to ten and waited for Ashley to do as she had done every day this week—wait for Parker to pull out of the garage and then leave for the day herself. Generally, Napua would consider their obvious rift none of her business, but she saw the longing looks Ashley gave Parker, saw the melancholy helplessness in Parker's eyes. And it all but broke her maternal heart.

Ashley predictably thanked Napua for breakfast and had headed out the door just as the phone rang.

"Hi, Mrs. Lee." Napua recognized Crystal's voice immediately. For a day and a half before the wedding they'd been thick as thieves, planning the surprise party. And despite Crystal's odd appearance, Napua liked the young woman.

"Is Ashley still home?"

"You just missed her." Napua wondered what Ashley's friend made of all this.

"Do you know if she went to her apartment?"

"Her apartment?" Napua was horrified. "Why would she still have that?"

Silence greeted Napua's ear. "Hello?"

"I'm here, Mrs. Lee. But I've got to run."

"Just a minute, Crystal. I'm worried about the kids."

Crystal chuckled. "I'm sure there's nothing to worry about. The kids are fine."

"I don't like it that Ashley still has an apartment. They don't spend enough time together, as it is."

"Well... I'm sure she'll have it cleaned out and be outta there in no time." Crystal hesitated. "The party may have been a mistake, Mrs. Lee. I think they need to be left alone."

Alone. Apartment. "How big is it?"

"What?"

"The apartment. One or two bedrooms?"

"One, but—"

"That's it. Crystal, you are a very smart girl. My *aloha* to your family." Napua could hear Crystal still calling out to her as she replaced the receiver. But Napua had no time to dally on the phone. Smiling, she patted her bun and pulled out the Yellow Pages.

Chapter Ten

Ashley knew something was wrong as soon as she pulled into the circular drive. The front door was open and she could see Parker gesturing frantically to Mrs. Lee. Reluctantly, Ashley left her faithful Toyota and trudged up the sidewalk.

"*When* did we discuss this?" Parker was asking his housekeeper. His hands had landed on his lean hips and Mrs. Lee's spread fingers were firmly planted at her plump ones. If the woman had been seven inches taller, they'd be nose to nose. "We *never* discussed this."

"You are as stubborn as your father. Do you think I would make this up?"

Whatever had riled Parker to begin with was nothing compared to the look on Parker's face at the mention of his father. "*When,* Mrs. Lee?" he ground out once more.

"A year ago. Maybe two." Mrs. Lee shrugged, looked away, then caught sight of Ashley.

"*Two* years ago?" Parker bellowed.

Mrs. Lee sent him a disgusted frown. "Maybe one." Then she turned back and smiled at Ashley. "Good," she said, stepping forward to pull Ashley into the circle. "Your wife will settle this."

Ashley looked from Parker's angry face to his housekeeper's determined one. Actually, in Ashley's opinion, she didn't think his wife would be settling anything. She tried to step back and then she smelled it.

"Whew! What is that?" Ashley wrinkled her nose, her gaze bouncing back and forth between Parker and Mrs. Lee.

Parker threw up his hands.

"Paint," Mrs. Lee answered, unconcerned.

"Paint?"

"We're remodeling," Mrs. Lee went on patiently. "*Your* husband..." She glanced at Parker and lifted both sets of chins several degrees. "Your husband and I discussed it some time ago. But I never got around to it."

"If we *had* discussed it, which I seriously doubt..." Parker stopped pacing long enough to send her a threatening look down his nose. "You picked one hell of a time to start."

"Oh, Parker. It can't be that bad." Ashley laid a hand on his arm.

"My bed... our bedroom is all torn up."

"Well..." Ashley's mind spun as she tried to calculate exactly how that would affect her.

"The guest rooms are *also* torn up," Parker added meaningfully. "The only damn room that isn't is Mrs. Lee's." He skewered the older woman with another accusing look.

"O-okay..." Ashley offered and lightly squeezed Parker's arm in an effort to calm him.

"What's the big deal? I already made your hotel reservations." Mrs. Lee sniffed.

"Ouch!" Parker pulled back his arm. He lowered his gaze to the red mark Ashley's nail had left.

"Sorry," Ashley mumbled. She pushed the offending hand through her hair to ease its weight off her back. The temperature had suddenly climbed ten degrees. She didn't want to stay in a hotel. Not with Parker, anyway. Staying together in one room was far too close, too intimate. No way. They didn't do at all well in hotels. "How long are we out of commission here?"

"A week." Parker and Mrs. Lee said together.

Ashley scrambled in silence for a suggestion to make, a plan to offer... a way to get the hell out of this.

"I've put out your suitcases." Mrs. Lee headed for the hallway, then stopped and slid them a sly glance. "It's too bad you don't still have your apartment, Ashley. But the honeymoon suite should be nice." The housekeeper patted her bun and continued down the hall.

"Honeymoon suite?" Ashley lifted a brow at Parker.

He jammed his hands into his trouser pockets.

"Apartment," they both said at once.

Ashley quickly picked up Mrs. Lee's trail. Parker followed right behind her. The strong odor of fresh paint assaulted them immediately.

"I'm not happy about this," Ashley whispered over her shoulder.

"Oh, and I am?" Parker was close. She could feel his breath stirring her hair. If she turned now, she could be in his arms, feel the strong wall of his chest, feel the soothing rhythm of his heartbeat. And she could get herself in a whole lot of trouble. How could he so effectively irritate and arouse her at the same time?

"After all," he groused, "I'll be the one stuck in enemy camp."

Enemy camp? Ashley stopped cold.

Parker didn't. His arms came reflexively around her as he tried to ease the collision.

But it wasn't arousal that she felt. It wasn't even irritation.

Enemy camp? Magic Island? A wave of dread stormed her. Ashley had just made a horrible mistake.

"YOU DIDN'T TELL ME you had cats." Parker toed the litter box, an expression of contempt on his face.

"You hadn't told me you had a dog," she shot back.

"I didn't know I had to clear it with you."

"You didn't. Just like I didn't feel I had to clear Kiwi and Cinnamon with you."

"Kiwi and Cinnamon? What kind of names are those?" His good humor had gone the same way of his unattended libido. He'd never known a woman who could confound him so thoroughly.

"Perfect ones." She picked up the fat calico and nuzzled its neck. Lucky bastard, came Parker's unbidden thought. "Because you're both so sweet," she cooed in a nonsensical lilt. The cat squirmed when Ashley stopped to send a skeptical frown at Parker, and she set the bundle of fur down. "What about your dog... Prince? Isn't *that* original? Or maybe it's symbolic?"

"Look," he began through clenched teeth. Ashley was upset about something and was doing her best to annoy him. In fact, she'd been trying to annoy him since they'd gotten back from Molokai. Unfortunately, her success rate was phenomenal. He was about to tell her that they would not be opening a zoo back at the beach house, when a loud squawk from another room halted him. "What was that?"

"A bird." Ashley turned to straighten some books.

"As in, *your* bird?"

"No," she answered sweetly. "*Our* bird."

"This is getting ridiculous." Parker felt his hands making their newly automatic route through his hair. He looked into Ashley's sparkling eyes and knew she was enjoying his irritation. He summoned a long-deserted patience and said, "I can't wait to hear what you call it."

"It's a him."

"What's *his* name?"

"Pilikea." Ashley quickly busied herself with some paperwork she'd left on the table, careful to avoid his eyes.

She was flipping at her hair again—a sure sign of trouble. "What does that mean?" Parker asked with a modicum of dread.

"Trouble," she muttered on her way to the kitchen.

Parker snickered out loud at the irony. "Any symbolism there?"

"You want some coffee?"

"I want to know about your feathered friend out there. I *really* don't like birds." Parker had followed her and now paced the narrow kitchen that was much too small for such an activity. "They're noisy, stubborn and a general pain in the ass." He stopped and leveled her an I-mean-it-this-time look.

"Well..." She angled her head a bit, drawing her eyebrows together, a sly smile tempting her lips. "So are you, but it looks like I'll have to put up with it."

He stared back, his annoyance dissolving. She had the most expressive eyes. Right now they were animated with humor and mischief. She was silently laughing at him, and he wanted to hear that laughter out loud. He loved her laugh. He loved her ability to make him want to laugh—when he didn't want to strangle her, that is.

"I suppose you're right. But it doesn't seem fair that I'll have two of you to contend with," he said, grinning.

"Touché."

Parker affected a pensive look. "Does that mean 'touch' in French?"

Ashley eyed him for a long moment, then produced a can of coffee from the cupboard. "We need to set some ground rules while we're here."

"Oh, let me guess." He briefly closed his eyes and held a hand to his temple. "No touching, right?"

She snapped her fingers in the air. "Give the man a prize."

"Of my choosing?" Parker did all but rub his hands together.

"It's a figure of speech, James." She slanted him a wry look, then popped the lid off the new coffee can. She leaned over to inhale the potent aroma.

Parker angled his head back for a better view of her enticing bottom and gorgeous legs, which this new position afforded him. It was going to be a long week, he decided. It had already *been* a long week. His self-imposed hands-off policy since returning from Molokai was killing him.

"Is there something I can do for you?" Ashley asked in a clipped tone.

He leisurely raised his gaze to her face and grinned.

She rolled her eyes and automatically tugged at the hem of her shorts. "Which brings us to rule number two."

"Nice try, sweetheart, but my thoughts are off-limits."

"Don't call me sweetheart."

"Now you're confusing me. Is that rule two or three?"

Ashley puffed out her cheeks and loudly exhaled. She fussed with the coffeemaker, plugging and unplugging it, then plugging it in again. She whacked the top of it and it gurgled to life.

"Think we can afford a new one?" Parker crossed his arms over his chest and lounged back against the counter.

"That's exactly what I mean." She slammed one cabinet shut, then bumped a drawer closed with her hip. "This is *my* apartment. No changes, no negotiation." She turned to face him and shoved her hair back. "And no answering the phone."

"What?" He straightened. "You're joking, right?"

Ashley shook her head. "I'm serious about this, Parker."

"You know how many calls I can possibly receive a night...calls from the construction site. I can't operate without a phone."

"Use your mobile."

Parker just stared at her.

"I'm not saying you can't call out." She turned to wipe off the counter. There wasn't a crumb on it. "And if I'm home and it's for you, of course I'll answer it and turn it over to you. But when I'm not...well, I'd prefer...I insist you don't answer it."

Parker watched her straighten the small appliances that didn't need straightening, watched her jiggle the coffee carafe. The coffee didn't perk any faster. He studied his shoes for a moment, then looked back up at her. "Why, Ash?"

"Why?" she echoed faintly.

"Why?"

"Because I receive a lot of important calls."

So did Parker, but he elected not to point that out. He didn't think he could do so without heating up the discussion. "I *am* capable of taking a message."

Ashley gave him a look of dismissal that was his undoing. The hell with trying not to show he was angry, because damn it, he was. "Besides, none of this should be a problem. You're always *here*. You certainly haven't been at our house."

Ashley stopped her aimless straightening and plastered him with a haughty look. "I'm surprised you've noticed."

"Yeah, well, I'm surprised you're surprised. Because you haven't been around enough to notice if I've noticed." He'd promised himself he wouldn't raise his voice.

She opened her mouth to speak, then closed it again. A frown puckered her brow. "I think I take exception to that."

Parker stared back angrily at first, then a slow half grin spread across his face. "Which part?"

"I'm not sure." She laughed unevenly. "I think you lost me."

Parker watched her dimple flash, the honey color touch her eyes. No question about it. *He* was lost.

"Parker?" Her voice was soft and imploring.

"Yeah." He took her hand.

"About the phone." Her fingers moved restlessly against his.

"Yeah?"

"I need your promise." She squeezed his hand when he didn't answer right away. "I really would like to keep my affairs private."

Parker stepped back suddenly as if he'd been slapped. *Affair.* The single word had the impact of a full-blown tidal-wave alert. He dropped her hand. It fell to her side and a guarded look darkened her eyes.

Trapped oxygen threatened to explode from his chest. He let out a large breath.

His wife had a friggin' boyfriend!

Parker watched Ashley moisten her lips, watched her graceful hand flutter to her throat and wished to God he didn't still want her.

Shell-shocked, he continued to stare and waited for the numbness to ebb.

"You do understand, don't you?" Ashley asked. "After all, I'm sure I don't know everything about your life. And I don't expect to. I don't even want—"

"You're wrong." His voice was low, almost too low.

Ashley shut up and inclined her head to him.

"What you see is what you get," he said, slowly shaking his head. She simply didn't want what she saw, and that saddened him far more than he would have thought possible. "Who is he, Ash?"

"Who's who?"

The fact that she had the gall to look puzzled irritated the hell out of him. It was a welcome respite. "Oh, please. Let's be adult about this." Parker threw up an exasperated hand. Good advice, he warned himself, and brought his hand back to lean on the counter. "I asked you before if you had a boyfriend. You should have—"

"A boyfriend!" Ashley's expression went blank. Then she actually started laughing just as the telephone rang.

Parker looked from her to the noisy wall instrument, but she just kept laughing and made no attempt to answer it.

After the third ring, Ashley gulped back her last giggle. The phone stopped. A noisy click came from the other room, then Ashley's recorded voice sailed through loud and clear.

All amusement disappeared from her face. Her eyes widened in horror.

The caller's message began.

Ashley dove for the phone.

And to his utter amazement, so did Parker.

"OH, NO. EVERYTHING is fine. But I'll have to call you back." Ashley watched Parker out of the corner of her eye. He'd allowed her not a speck of privacy by stationing himself at the door. His hands were locked at the top of the frame as he leaned in toward her, glaring the entire time.

"Yes, I'll be there." She hid a smile when Parker let out a deliberate and impatient sigh. "And..." She roughed up her voice, going for a breathless quality. "I'm looking forward to it."

She kept her head down while she hung up the phone, furiously willing away any sign of a smirk. Manuel Gomes of the Make Magic Island a Reality committee must be thinking she was a few bricks short of a load, but it was worth it to see Parker's disgusted expression. Ashley wondered how long she ought to let him think she had a boyfriend.

She schooled her expression to pure innocence and looked up at him. "Now, where were we?"

"You were about to tell me who he is."

"Who? Him?" Ashley sent a pointed look at the phone. Parker's expression was thunderous at best and she had to swallow another chuckle. If she didn't know any better, she'd think he was jealous. "He's a student."

"You're seeing one of your students?" Parker dropped his arms to his sides. "I don't believe it." He shook his head in bewilderment.

"Not in the way you obviously think, Buster." Ashley pushed herself away from the counter and gave the stalled coffeemaker a jolt, then faced him. "I hate to pull the role of victim out from under you, but read my lips. I don't have a boyfriend."

And Parker looked as if he was doing just that. His gaze locked on her mouth for a long moment, then he ran it up to her eyes. Ashley held her breath at the strange look he gave her.

"Then why the cloak-and-dagger?" he asked slowly.

She laughed. "A little overstated, wouldn't you say?"

"Not from where I stand. You've looked as though you're about to jump out of your skin ever since we got here. And then this idiotic phone thing."

If he only knew, Ashley thought, he'd probably prefer that she *did* have a boyfriend. "Look, it's just that this apartment is so small." So was a hotel room. "Maybe we should stay with your family."

Parker let out a choice word. "You know better than that."

"Do I? Actually, I don't know a damn thing. All I know is that you have some kind of problem with them—I think that's pretty obvious to everyone—but other than that, you haven't told me diddly-squat."

He issued a long-suffering sigh.

"I believe it's fair to know what I've gotten into." She leaned a hip against the counter and stared at him.

"You married me, not them." Parker added another jostle to the coffeemaker. "All you have to worry about is acting like it once in a while."

Ashley knew by his tone she should let the subject drop. "How often do you see them?"

"How often do you see the Kings?" he shot back.

She felt herself jerk as if she'd been dealt a physical blow. She didn't want to think about her father's estranged family, about the mother she had never known. Unconsciously, she crossed her arms and hugged them to her, watching Parker's blue eyes turn the color of regret.

"Look, Ash, about the bird." He rubbed the back of his neck and glanced away for a moment. "It won't be a problem."

"I've decided to keep him here, along with Kiwi and Cinnamon."

"What about when the house is finished?" Parker asked slowly.

"I'm keeping the apartment, Parker."

"We hadn't agreed to that."

"It wasn't up for discussion." Ashley uncrossed her arms and searched a cabinet for two mugs.

"It is now."

Ashley looked at the childish drawings taped to her refrigerator, the collection of logo magnets Crystal had started. Though the apartment had never truly felt like home, it was familiar. No strings attached, it was hers. She set down one mug and faced him. "I need to keep it, Parker."

He didn't answer right away. He just stood there looking at her, and she could tell he was trying to understand. A small part of her wanted him to.

"Did you and your father live here together?" he finally asked.

"No. We had to sell the house. I moved here after he entered the hospital." She lifted a shoulder and glanced away. "It was a matter of economics."

"And what about all your belongings?"

"You're looking at them." She sent a pointed look at her refrigerator art and started to laugh. Until she caught the hint of condolence in his eyes. An ugly knot coiled in her stomach. She slammed down the other mug. "Don't you dare pity me. I didn't ask for it. And I sure as hell don't need it."

Parker issued a short, humorless laugh. "Furthest thing from my mind." He shook his head and drilled her with such an intense gaze it took the wind out of her temper.

She helplessly returned his stare until another thought crossed her mind. "And I'm not a martyr," she warned, watching him effectively mask any clue to his thoughts. "Make no mistake about that."

Ashley felt the stubborn lift of her chin and cursed her reflexive reaction. She felt open and vulnerable while he stood there silently, looking as if he knew all her secrets. She wanted to blurt out about Magic Island, wanted to see his smug, knowing look turn to shock.

She didn't want his understanding, didn't want his support. All she wanted was the security and financial independence his name and connections could afford her.

Ashley braced herself against the counter and looked into his heart-melting blue eyes. And most of all, she didn't want to feel the way she was feeling right now.

"Keep the apartment, Ash," Parker said finally.

"And the phone situation?"

"It's your phone."

"No further questions asked?"

"None."

"Don't think you're doing me a favor." Ashley took a deep breath. "Because you're right, it's my apartment, my phone."

Parker nodded, his gaze still fastened to her wary one, and Ashley was left without a doubt that he fully understood her need for independence. The bond that stretched between them was as real as the oxygen deserting her lungs.

"You give me far too much credit, Ash," Parker said, unplugging the coffeemaker. "I have a far more basic motive."

"What are you doing? The coffee isn't finished."

"I have a better idea." He moved closer.

"Parker?" She backed up.

His lips curved into a slow, sensual smile. "Let's neck."

Chapter Eleven

"Are you crazy?" she asked with a nervous laugh.

"Just trying to set the mood." He snaked an arm around her waist and pulled her flush against him. "We already have fighting down pat, I figure we need to practice the other part." He'd pressed his lips to her neck and his words came out garbled. She felt his grin punctuate his outrageous excuse.

"You *are* crazy." Her pronouncement came out weak on the tail of a giggle. His chin was stubble-rough and it tickled.

"Maybe," he agreed, and took full advantage of her exposed neck as she arched away from him.

"Stop that." She pushed at his shoulder, but again a small, traitorous giggle weakened her position.

"Isn't this more fun than fighting?" His tongue trailed behind her ear, flicking at her lobe until he pulled it into his mouth and nipped boldly at it.

"No."

"Sure it is." His lips traveled her jaw until he made contact with her mouth. He pressed a long, soft kiss there until she attempted another protest. Then he slipped his tongue between her unsuspecting lips before she could utter a word.

She meant to stop him. Had every intention of getting away. But he held her firmly against him and his hands felt strong and good, his desire blatant. And for a moment Ashley forgot that this was the very last thing she should be doing.

Her tongue danced with his, her breasts pressed to his chest. Her head spun with denial. It wasn't supposed to be like this. She pushed back a little, self-conscious that he could feel how wildly her heart pounded.

Parker broke the kiss and pulled back, too, gazing at her with such intensity she wanted to look away. "Isn't this better?" Using his thumb, he brushed a soft caress across her lips before tracing her jaw. "Say it, Ashley."

"No." Her voice was damnably weak.

"It's not so hard to admit." His whisper was hoarse and close, his breath mingling with hers.

"No." Ashley shook her head, refusing to give up that last shred of protection, that remaining bridge to sanity.

"Okay." He chuckled. "But would you mind sounding this breathless for company. That ought to fool everyone."

"Damn you, Parker James." Ashley spun away from him and seriously considered dumping the half pot of coffee over his arrogant head. Without intending to, she glanced down at his pants. He needed a cold shower, not hot coffee.

"Life's not fair," he said, grinning when he noticed where her attention was directed. "Guys always get caught."

"Go home." She marched out of the kitchen.

"Aren't you forgetting something?"

He followed her, and when she realized she actually had forgotten, she turned and faced him with a groan. "Rule number—"

"I thought I already showed you what I think of your rules." Parker nudged her chin up. "Shall we go over it again?"

Ashley stared into his amused gaze and willed herself not to react. Slowly, calmly, she slid her hands up his chest and around his neck. She got up on her toes and touched her nose briefly to his. She tipped her head back and parted her lips in invitation. Parker's expression of utter surprise was her reward.

He let his hand slip from her chin to curve around her, his lips forming a satisfied smile. Before the chuckle that threatened to erupt could escape her, she slanted her mouth over his, leaving only a breath between them and whispered, "Enjoy the couch."

PARKER RESIGNED HIMSELF to the fact that he was never going to be able to understand women. One in particular was on his mind as he sat on Ashley's uncomfortable couch and flipped on the television with the remote control.

It had been five days since he and Ashley had moved into her apartment. Five even longer nights. And Parker didn't remember ever having watched so much television in his life. But even with all the work he had to do at the office, it was virtually useless to stay late or bring paperwork home. All he could think about was Ashley...and her damn clandestine phone calls.

For the most part, he'd at least convinced himself that there was no boyfriend involved. Ashley was stubborn, argumentative and altogether too maddeningly enticing, but she wasn't a liar. She had said there was no boyfriend, and Parker believed her. He had to.

He'd scanned several channels when he heard the key in the lock.

"Hi. You're home early," Ashley said brightly as she came through the door, a large grocery sack in one arm.

Parker ignored his automatic inclination to get up and help her. If he'd learned one thing in the past five days, it was that Ashley wanted and needed zilch from him. That fact did more than irritate him, it downright ticked him off. He sprawled deeper into the couch and grunted.

Ashley paused for a few seconds, commented on the heat and the blissfulness of married life, then breezed on into the kitchen. Parker skipped through four more channels.

"Want a beer?" Ashley asked when she reappeared. She flicked on a ceiling fan and held out one of two moisture-beaded cans to him. He accepted his with a mumbled thanks.

She pressed hers to her bare neck for a moment and briefly closed her eyes before taking a long sip. Parker watched a drop of moisture slide down her smooth tanned skin and disappear into the scoop of her pink T-shirt. He took a long pull of his beer and jabbed another number on the remote control.

"You really ought to get more exercise than channel surfing," Ashley said and hitched one hip up on the opposite end of the couch back. She wiggled into a more comfortable position and ended up with one bare thigh a scant foot away, eye level with Parker.

He gave her a murderous sidelong glance that didn't quite reach her face. She tugged at her shorts. He tipped the can to his lips.

The phone rang.

"I'll get it," Ashley said, hopping off the couch, while Parker made a face and silently mimicked her exact words along with her.

"No sh—" Parker shook his head and finished his beer. He heard Ashley's delighted laughter float above the television voices and he quickly lowered the volume.

He'd just about had it with being a nice guy. When he'd agreed to play her phone game the previous week, he hadn't anticipated that it was going to be like a veritable switchboard operation around here. The phone rang constantly, and Ashley either spent her time on calls or running out to meetings. And Parker was damn tired of feeling like the only person left out on a joke.

The only thing he did know was that she was working on something...something big...something she'd elected to keep from him.

He picked up his empty can, strolled soundlessly toward the kitchen and stopped within hearing range. From the glimpse he could get of her, Ashley's back was to him, so he waited with his fingers wrapped around the can, on the verge of crushing it, and listened for all he was worth.

"How about lunch tomorrow?" Ashley asked the caller. "We can go to the meeting from there."

She paused for her answer, then lowered her voice. "I haven't heard yet, but I only submitted the bid ten days ago...yes, but..."

Her dark head started to swivel in his direction. Damn. He squashed the can with a loud crunch and smiled at her when she laid her gaze on him, lifting his foot as if he'd never broken stride.

"I really can't talk right now." Ashley's tone was hurried as she gave him her back once more. "Tomorrow, then."

Parker tossed the can in the recycling bin under the sink. Ashley replaced the receiver and immediately opened the refrigerator.

"Any ideas for dinner?" she asked. Her voice was calm, but she made the mistake of swiping at her hair as she made an inordinately thorough inspection of the fridge.

"Maybe we should go out." Parker reached around her for another beer. As always, the scent of gardenias assailed him. He gripped the top of the door and lingered a moment, his face inches above her shiny black hair, his very aware body a tempting proximity to her hula-enhanced hips. He swallowed. A dry, painful swallow.

"Why?" Ashley backed up. "Oh..." Her curvy little bottom met Parker's growing interest.

He reluctantly backed up, too. Ashley flashed him an oh-my look that was almost comical as she ducked under his arm and scooted past him.

"You're right," she said, grabbing her abandoned beer from the counter. "Maybe we should go out for dinner."

Parker chuckled. "That wasn't my reason, but you're probably right." He snatched the beer he had originally been after, closed the refrigerator door and imitated her earlier actions by bringing the cold can to his neck. That wasn't exactly what needed cooling off, but it would have to do.

"Why did you want to go out?" she asked, easing her way toward the door.

"I didn't want us to have to mess with cooking and cleaning up." He followed her. "I've got to go out in a couple of hours..."

Ashley plopped on the couch, tucking one tanned slender leg under her, and looked up expectantly at him.

Why hadn't he thought of it before? If he included Ashley in more of his dealings, maybe she'd be more open with him. Maybe she'd tell him what she was up to.

"Actually, I've got to attend a meeting with some resort reps, investors, city council members..." Parker laughed. "Don't roll your eyes. It's something you might be interested in. It's a real hot topic tonight," he drawled enticingly and sat next to her.

Ashley arched a brow and the corners of her mouth started to lift. "Really?"

"Maybe we could go to that little restaurant in Chinatown you're so fond of...." He shrugged. "Then you can go along with me."

"That might work." Ashley drew up her other leg as well and settled back into the cushions. She gave him a brilliant smile. "What exactly is this hot topic?"

Parker knew he had her now. Her eyes were turning that golden-honey color he'd come to know and crave. She looked relaxed, sinking into the floral pillows, her hair fanned out like a veil of black silk. The former edginess he'd felt began to slip away. It appeared the evening might have possibilities after all.

He put down his beer can and angled his body toward her. "Magic Island," he said. "Know anything about it?"

ASHLEY PACED HER SMALL kitchen and darted several looks out the window. For the second time, she picked up the phone receiver and listened for the dial tone. It was still working. So why didn't it ring? She returned the instrument with a little too much force and quickly picked it up again, listened, then replaced it with as much care as her sorely tried patience would allow.

Manuel simply had to call before Parker returned. It would kill Ashley to have to wait until tomorrow to find out what had gone on at Parker's meeting.

She'd called the Magic Island committee chairman as soon as she'd gotten rid of Parker. No easy task in itself. She couldn't actually remember all of what happened after Parker had dropped the bomb. She'd been too stressed out. But she had managed to send him off to dinner by himself, which had given her enough time to notify Manuel Gomes so that they could send a spy out to the meeting. She did, however, remember enough to know that Parker had left angry.

Ashley glanced at the clock and out of the corner of her eye, caught the sweep of headlights across the grassy area outside the apartment. Damn. She grabbed a diet cola out of the fridge, dove for the couch and struck a nonchalant pose.

The unnecessary jabs at the lock were a dead giveaway as to Parker's mood before he came through the door. She heard his mumbled curses and looked up as he flung his keys onto the rattan side table. She offered a tentative smile.

"Headache any better?" he asked, rubbing the back of his neck.

The blank look she gave him didn't help the skeptical gaze he fastened on her. "Headache. Yes. I mean, no. It's gone." She nodded her head. "Back to normal."

"Great." He couldn't have made the single word sound more sarcastic if he'd practiced an hour.

"How was your meeting?" She sipped her cola.

"A damn three-ring circus."

A flood of the carbonated drink swooshed down Ashley's throat. She grimaced against the burning sensation. "What happened?" she asked warily.

"What didn't?" Parker asked over his shoulder on his way to the kitchen. He came back with a can of guava juice. "Halfway through the meeting, some idiot starts spouting off about how we're ruining the islands by allowing the tourists to 'trample our culture.'"

Ashley cringed. Why would Manuel have sent John Aoki?

"And then the other one starts in on—"

"There were two?" Ashley realized her slip immediately. Her gaze darted to his. He frowned. She lifted a shoulder. "I mean, I didn't realize this was a pro-and-con type meeting," she offered lamely.

"It wasn't." Parker kept his attention focused on her a long time. "And there were four."

She swallowed back her surprise. Obviously nothing had gone as planned. And now Ashley *had* to know what happened, if not from Manuel...she took a quick breath and gave Parker what she hoped was an indifferent shrug. "Was anything resolved?"

"Hell, no." Parker pinched the bridge of his nose. "Those people are insane. The whole lot of them. There isn't a logical bone in their fanatical bodies. They won't listen to a single word anyone who disagrees with them has to say."

"That's quite a generalization," Ashley said with a tight smile.

"Believe me, I know." Parker gave her such a strange look, it made her squirm. He doesn't know a thing, she assured herself, it was her conscience knocking things out of whack.

"Do you know what they want to do?" He gestured to the air, obviously not wanting an answer. "They want to turn Kahoolawe into some sort of Disney-type island with an amusement park, casinos and resorts."

Ashley shifted her weight from one hip to the other and widened her eyes. "So?"

"Don't tell me you think that would be a good idea?"

She put her palms up and gave him a half shrug and a noncommitted smile. She wanted to give him a strategic jab in the solar plexus. It was, in fact, a damn good idea.

"Do you know how long that would take? That island is totally barren. We don't even know if it's safe. The military bombed the hell out of it, using it for target practice for a number of years. The whole thing is probably as stable as a piece of Swiss cheese."

"That's not true." Ashley bit her lip.

He gave her an odd look. "The point is, we don't know. The thought of planning an amusement park, of all things, gives me the creeps. Would you want our kids going there?"

Our kids? A lump blocked Ashley's air passage.

Parker blinked several times. He shifted positions. "I know that's overreacting," he said, "but I think it's foolish to take a chance on that island, when the floating casino idea makes so much more sense."

He was wrong about the risk and definitely wrong about the floating casino being a better idea. She wanted to tell him so, but instead she offered matter-of-factly, "Some civic groups have already begun replanting on Kahoolawe."

Parker narrowed his gaze on her. "What do you know about any of this?"

"Nothing, really." She got up. "Want more juice?"

"Has Crystal been filling your head with this... this Magic Island nonsense?"

Ashley silently counted to ten and headed for the kitchen, trying to put some distance between them. When she turned to answer, she came face-to-face with him. "No," she said slowly and truthfully.

"I knew I should have spoken to her before this." Parker unbuttoned the top of his shirt and pulled the collar away from his neck.

"Crystal does not influence what I think." She sent the empty cola can rattling across the counter. "I even have a mind all my own. Imagine that?"

"I didn't mean it that way." Parker put his hand out and the can came to a halt. He moved in, slipped his hand under her hair and cupped the back of her neck.

"I know I'm touchy on the subject. But the implication that the rest of us don't care about these islands really gets me. That's just not..." He shook his head in such sad earnestness, Ashley had to press her lips together to keep from spilling her guts. "Look, Ash, no matter how I feel personally, this is business and people know how cause oriented you are. I just don't want you to get hurt."

With firm but gentle fingers, he kneaded the tense muscles at her nape. He held her with a steady gaze and a lopsided smile. Ashley quickly lowered her lashes. It was a little hard to be loyal to the cause while he was regarding her with those beautiful blue eyes.

He crooked his finger under her chin and nudged her face back up to his. "Tell me you won't get involved and I'll drop the subject."

"Parker, I appreciate your intentions." She tried to draw back. He wouldn't let her. "But what I am or am not involved in is none of your concern."

"Sorry, sweetheart, but this time it would be. I've got too much on the line, and I don't need my name tied to the likes of Sam Chun or any of those other crackpot zealots."

"Sam Chun?" Ashley echoed faintly.

"Not that I'm accusing you of keeping company with them."

"Was *he* at the meeting?"

"Sam? Yeah, *was*. We took care of that."

Ashley felt her body go boneless and Parker brought his other arm around her. Had Manuel Gomes gone out of his mind? First John Aoki and now Sam Chun, two of the most irrational, hotheaded supporters of Magic Island. Ashley shivered. She didn't even want to know who the other two attendees were.

"Are you feeling okay?" Parker pulled her close. "You aren't cold, are you?"

She shook her head but snuggled against him. She didn't trust the expression on her face.

He smoothed her hair and rested his chin on top of her head. Gingerly, she pushed her hands up his chest. She felt his heartbeat gaining momentum, felt her own racing toward him.

"Whose foolish idea was it to talk business?" Parker angled back a bit and smiled down at her.

Ashley exhaled. "Not mine." Her return smile came easy in the wake of the most truthful thing she'd said all night.

"Well, since I was the one who initiated such an unacceptable discussion," Parker lowered his face several fractions, "I think I'll remedy it."

Ashley arched her head back in time for his lips to brush once, then twice across hers. Her eyes drifted closed, and her mind tumbled beyond rhyme or reason.

With quickened pulse, she waited for the next touch of his lips.

His warm breath transfused her skin as he dipped his head to nuzzle the side of her neck. Her shirt slipped off her shoulder and he ran his tongue along the unguarded path. A sensitive shudder rocketed through her, and Parker stopped long enough to give her a long, blazing look.

Ashley's lips parted. Something had to be said, someone had to stop this.

He circled her waist and hoisted her onto the counter. Her sandal slipped from her foot, and with it the last vestige of denial.

She tunneled her hands through his hair and met his mouth with equal hunger. His tongue plunged after hers and she gladly gave up her last breath to dance the dance with him. He propelled one hand up the gaping cuff of her shorts, stroking her bare thigh, leaning her back, taking what she offered.

Out of the sensual fog, a bell sounded. Parker kissed and kneaded, but it rang again. He slipped a finger under the elastic of her bikini panties and the bell shrilled. What was happening?

He took a ragged breath and reached around her with his other hand.

As if mired in an out-of-body experience, Ashley watched the phone receiver make contact with his ear. She heard his voice but his words didn't register.

Moments of endless silence penetrated the fog.

She looked into Parker's stunned eyes only inches from her own. The sensual blue turned a somber navy.

Parker handed her the phone. "It's the Honolulu county jail," he said quietly, and turned to walk away. "Sam Chun needs bail money."

"MRS. LEE, PLEASE have Ashley pass the syrup." Parker sat rigid in his chair. His hair was in need of a cut, his eyes lacked their normal sparkle.

Ashley pushed the pitcher of coconut syrup a tad short of his reach.

"Thanks." Neither woman missed his sarcasm.

"Mrs. Lee, may I have the butter, please?" Ashley gave Napua a smile, but its usual warmth was as toasty as a Hawaiian snow cone.

Parker handed Mrs. Lee the butter, which was well out of her reach. Napua sighed heavily and nudged it across to Ashley. Things were bad . . . very, very bad.

She watched Ashley nibble on a piece of waffle that wouldn't keep a mynah bird alive. Napua eyed Parker. He was assaulting his waffle as if it were the devil himself.

Napua shook her head. *Disastrous.*

It had been four days since the house had been completed and Parker and Ashley had returned home. Napua had had the rooms filled with fresh flowers, had excitedly cooked a dinner fit for King Kamehameha himself. She'd even arranged to spend the weekend with a friend in order to give the lovebirds their privacy. It had all been in vain. Napua had known it the minute they'd stepped from the car, and if she hadn't, the deliberate slam of each door would have convinced her.

And then things got worse. Ashley stayed at home less and less, and when she was here she and Parker quibbled over everything from how many chocolate chips should go into Napua's cookies to what time the sun would set.

Napua plopped her elbow on the table and rested one plump cheek in her hand. What had gone wrong? And what was she going to do about it? She'd only heard bits and pieces of their various arguments, but it had been enough to know that Parker was unhappy with one of Ashley's charity involvements. And Ashley was unhappy in general.

And although she still thought the apartment idea had been a good one, Napua felt terribly responsible. But now she was at a complete loss about what to do.

Parker pushed back from the table and stood. Napua watched him through narrowed slits. Surely this morning he would at least kiss his wife goodbye.

Ashley continued mashing her waffle without looking up. Parker picked up his briefcase. "Ashley, could I see you a moment?" he asked, darting Napua a quick glance.

The younger woman took an inordinate amount of time dabbing her mouth with her napkin, and Napua could see Parker's patience slipping.

"I'll be in the kitchen," Napua said and rose quickly, taking along her barely touched plate.

Immediately she discarded her breakfast and stationed herself at eavesdropping distance.

"We have to talk at some point," Parker said in a low, controlled voice.

"I think you've done enough of that," Ashley replied sweetly.

"I wish *you* had." Parker's tone was curt.

"I've already told you everything you need to know."

"The hell you—" Parker sighed heavily and lowered his voice. "Nothing, Ashley. You've told me absolutely nothing."

Napua heard Ashley's chair scrape the floor and immediately thought of her poor wood parquet which had been freshly polished. She put a hand to her mouth to keep from being discovered.

"That's because I don't have anything more to say, Parker. I'll see you tonight."

"Don't walk away from me," he warned.

"Then don't push me."

Silence stung Napua's ears. She bit down on her finger, listening to the fading footsteps, waiting to hear a door slam.

None did. Instead, Parker's faint voice questioned Ashley as to what she had expected.

Napua straightened. Expected? Or had he said expecting? She strained her ears, clutching her chest.

The door slammed. Twice.

Napua rounded the corner and stared dumbstruck at it. And then a slow, knowing smile settled on her round, relieved face. If there was going to be a *keiki* around the house, she'd have to act fast. And she knew just the person to help her. She hurried to the telephone and punched out a set of numbers.

"Karen?" She waited for Parker's sister to finish her yawn. "How would you like to be an aunt?"

Chapter Twelve

"You should have checked with me first," Ashley grumbled as she threw some Dramamine into her purse.

"Sorry, Your Highness." Parker stomped past her with some clothes he'd grabbed from the closet. "But you weren't home long enough."

"She's *your* sister," Ashley warned. "If you want to start something before we meet her and Don for the afternoon, that's up to you."

Parker sighed. "No, I don't want to start anything. And you're right. I should have checked with you first."

Ashley kept fiddling with the contents of her purse, but slid him a furtive sidelong glance. That was the most civil he'd sounded in over a week.

Parker pulled off his shirt and stood fumbling with the buttons of another. Curly, dark, tawny hair swirled over his tanned chest and around his flat nipples. His jeans were tight and low, and not yet snapped at the top.

Ashley swallowed. Damn him. She peered back into her purse, trying to remember what she'd been looking for.

"Ash, can you give me a hand with this?" He frowned in concentration at the button tab.

Reluctantly, she dropped her pocketbook onto the bed. And then she heard the tear.

"Oh, great." Parker exhaled. "I think it's beyond help now." He gave her a sheepish smile and held out the shirt. The once too small buttonhole was now large enough to drive a truck through.

"It can be fixed." She took the shirt from him and raised her gaze to his face. His hair was framed by the sunlight that streamed through the open door from the hall skylight. If she didn't know any better, he'd look like an angel. But she did know better. And Parker James was no angel. "But not in time for today."

"I'm sure Mrs. Lee will do it." He reclaimed the torn article, wadded it up and tossed it on the bed.

"You'll pay dearly for that." Ashley arched a brow in the direction of the crumpled-up heap and laughed.

Parker gave her a strange look. "I'll pick it up before she does." He stopped, but kept his eyes narrowed on her. "It's good to hear you laugh again, Ash."

She ran a palm up her bare arm and struggled against the pull of his gaze. She allowed it for an instant, then broke contact.

Mentally, Ashley shook her head. It was either laugh or cry, she thought wryly. This past week had been the week from hell. First, the third degree from Parker, lurking from Mrs. Lee, then silent treatment from Parker, crazy demands from the Magic Island committee, and to top it all off, her father was having delusions about being able to leave the hospital.

And worst of all, Parker believed she was being manipulated into helping with the Magic Island "cause," as he called it. He thought of her as so darn altruistic that the real reason hadn't occurred to him. Money...basic greed, plain and simple. Well, the desire for security wasn't exactly in the same category as greed, Ashley reasoned, but that didn't make her feel any better. Parker might be a shark, but he'd been an honest shark, and right now she merely felt like the rear end of one.

Ashley took a deep breath and chanced another peek at him. His hair was longer than she'd ever seen it and curled in an aimless arrangement at his neck. His lips were pursed in uncertainty, his chin dimpling slightly with the action. Once again, a familiar ache settled in a grudging spot in her southern hemisphere.

She wanted to spill her guts to Parker. She wanted to tell him he was wrong about Magic Island. She wanted to prove to him that the concept could work. She wanted total honesty between them. She wanted to stop their unspoken war.

Instead, what she did was reach in the closet for another shirt. "Are you going to be ready on time?" she asked and tossed it to him.

He rubbed his jaw. "If I don't shave."

Ashley bit back a smile. She wondered what his sister would think of his new beach-bum look.

"But I guess that won't matter," Parker grumbled. "No chance of running into anyone twelve-thousand feet in the air. Have you ever taken one of these aerial tours before?"

"No. And don't use that tone with me. I'm not the one who agreed to this."

"I know. I know." He pulled the shirt over his head. Ashley breathed a sigh of relief and returned to organizing her purse. "But Karen wouldn't take no for an answer. She went on and on about how she and Don haven't gotten to know you. Plus, she did the guilt-trip thing about me not informing her of the wedding in advance. . . .''

''And you fell for it like a two-ton sack of rice.'' Grinning, Ashley turned back to him. His hair was in disarray from pulling on the shirt, and Ashley automatically leaned forward to smooth it out.

One tawny curl had caressed her little finger before she realized what she was doing. She grazed his neck and felt the heat of his skin as she tried to pull back her imprudent hand.

He wrapped his long fingers around hers and held her hand in midair. He gave her a long, searching look, then slowly buried his lips in her palm while holding her gaze.

She froze for an instant, then closed her eyes, tentatively flexing her fingers against his cheek in a stroking motion.

''I've missed you,'' he whispered.

''I've been here,'' she answered in a soft voice.

''Not here.'' He banded his arms around her and pulled her up against him. His mouth descended upon hers with an urgency that should have been frightening. But it wasn't. Parker's taste, his scent, his touch. . . they were all becoming familiar to her. More than familiar, they felt unbearably necessary.

She opened her mouth to him and he pushed his tongue to hers. It was like velvet on satin, satin on velvet. He explored her mouth, while his hands rubbed a path down her back and over her buttocks. The spandex of her biking shorts felt skimpier and skimpier with each pass of his hand as he stroked her over and over.

''I want you, Ashley.'' His breathing was heavy, and she could feel evidence of his arousal.

"I know," she whispered. Why couldn't she admit it? She wanted him, too. *Chemistry,* her brain chanted, it's only chemistry.

"You feel so good." Parker kissed and licked and suckled until Ashley didn't think there would be enough oxygen left in the room. His fingers hesitated at the top of her shorts. He played with the elastic for a few seconds. When she didn't make a move to stop him, he dipped inside. His warm and sure fingers glided over her hipbones, past her bikini panties and down her thighs.

She buried her face in his neck and glanced down to see the shape of his knuckles moving under the clingy material. He'll stretch the fabric, she thought with irrational hysteria, as he neared the place he'd never been.

The elastic of her panties gave way, and his thumb grazed the nest of curls guarding her desire. She was hot and wet, and she wanted to rip the shirt right off his body. But uncertainty slackened her grip on his shoulders. Reflexively, her thighs moved together.

Parker immediately stilled his hand on her thighs. "It isn't right yet, is it?" he asked, stroking her cheekbone with the thumb of his other hand.

"I don't know," she whispered and averted her gaze, knowing she was a liar. She didn't want him to ask. She wanted him to take what she didn't have the guts to give.

"What will it take, Ash?"

She moistened her lips and forced her gaze back to him. "Something more than chemistry."

The twitch was there at his jaw again. She saw the convulsive movement in his throat. "Is that what you really think?"

Ashley slowly nodded. His embrace slackened.

The doorbell chimed.

Parker briefly closed his eyes. "What timing," he said and gave her a weak grin. Slowly, he slid his hand from her shorts and unabashedly adjusted the tightness of his own pants.

"I'm sorry," Ashley said, not even sure what she was sorry about. She turned her cheek to his heart and rubbed it against the exposed vee at his chest.

"Me, too." He sighed and rested his chin atop her head for a moment. Then he pulled back and tilted her gaze his way. "Because, sweetheart, you're dead wrong."

"I THOUGHT THIS TOUR was of Oahu only," Parker said, frowning as the small plane made a wide turn and headed out over the Pacific.

"Oh, didn't I tell you?" Karen waved an unconcerned hand. "We're doing Maui, too."

"What!" Parker's voice thundered above the roar of the laboring engine.

Ashley had been about to protest, too, but from the look on Parker's face, he was about to do enough of that for both of them. So she settled back in her seat and looked from brother to sister.

It felt good not to be in the hot seat for a change, although she didn't believe Karen ever truly had to worry about that. Parker obviously adored his sister. He'd been his most charming self ever since she and Don had arrived at the house to pick them up. No one would ever know that he and Ashley had been fighting all week...or jumping each other's bones just moments before.

Ashley loosened her seat belt a notch and let out a breath. She wasn't sure what Parker had meant about her being wrong, wasn't sure if she wanted to know.

Hopefully, this extended plane ride would provide the necessary distance from their crazy lapse of sanity.

Parker waited a minute until the plane began to level off and the engine quieted a bit. "Look, Karen—"

"You're missing Hanauma Bay." Karen excitedly pointed out the window to the reef-crowded inlet. Hundreds of snorkelers assumed the appearance of ants as the plane continued to ascend into the cloudless sky.

"I'm going to be missing a hell of a lot more than that if you don't have this plane turn around." Parker cupped his hand over his watch, blocking out the sun's glare.

"Don't tell me you have to work today." Karen wagged a finger at him. "For goodness sakes, Ashley, don't let him get away with that. You two should still be on your honeymoon." She gave her husband a sly wink that was not missed by Ashley. Don returned a leave-me-out-of-this look, before feigning a copious interest in the fading Hanauma Bay.

Ashley swiped back her hair and shifted against the seat belt. Karen looked far too pleased with herself. It made Ashley uneasy.

"I have a meeting at three o'clock, Karen," Parker warned. "And I had better be back for it."

His sister waved him off. "You're just like Dad," she said, and Ashley's eyes darted to Parker. His mouth tightened. "You worry too much," Karen continued, grinning. "Haven't I always taken good care of you?"

"Yeah, right." Parker let out a disgusted sound. His gaze drifted to the horizon as he drummed his fingers on the armrest of his seat.

Actually, Ashley had a meeting, too, and she hoped Parker wasn't going to give in to his sister. Ashley had purposely scheduled it for this afternoon because she knew Parker was going to be tied up. And this was one meeting she had to attend.

She had to warn the committee to back off. Too many hotheads were getting involved, and although they all wanted the same thing, Ashley disagreed with the way they were going about it. They, of course, were free to choose their own way, but she didn't appreciate them using her access to the land as a pawn. If they couldn't come to a compromise, she'd have to rethink her involvement.

"And what do you think?" Karen turned her bright smile on Ashley. "Parker shouldn't be going to the office on Saturdays, should he? Surely you don't work on weekends."

"Actually..." Ashley glanced over at Parker. He turned and lifted a brow at her. "I did have something planned for this afternoon," she said, hearing the involuntary defiance in her tone.

"Yes, well, Mrs. Lee thinks—" Karen stopped short as two pairs of eyes snapped to hers. She sent a wide-eyed plea to Don, who did nothing but crane his neck farther toward the window. "She thinks that...that I should have brought our kids. Parker loves children, you know." Her smile was all bright innocence again. "Expecting any soon?"

"What?" Parker choked out the word, then issued a short, humorless laugh. "You practically went from honeymoon to kids in one breath." He shook his head. "Amazing."

Ashley said nothing. A nervous laugh was the best she could produce.

"Stranger things have happened during honeymoons." Karen nodded sagely. "You do realize Lindsey was conceived during ours." She put her hand in her husband's.

Don patted it and cleared his throat. "Been playing any tennis, Parker?" he asked, making only his second attempt to enter the conversation since they'd first taken off nearly two hours ago.

"Not lately. How about you? Playing any golf?" Parker asked, and for the next twenty minutes the conversation took a blessedly neutral turn.

Ashley let the small talk float around her. She chimed in occasionally, but mostly enjoyed lounging back and listening to the friendly banter between Parker and Karen.

Though not once did she feel excluded. All three made her feel comfortable, like part of the family. And the whole trip would have been quite a nice experience, she decided, had she not felt so terribly guilty. Deceiving people was difficult enough, Ashley was quickly finding, but deceiving people you liked was a killer.

After a while, Karen leaned forward to talk with the pilot and Don resumed his post at the window. Ashley snuggled into her seat and watched the occasional cloud sail by, while Parker fidgeted with something in his hand.

Several minutes passed before curiosity got the better of her and Ashley sidled over in her seat to see what had so captured Parker's attention.

Around and around, Parker twisted the simple gold wedding band he wore. He pushed it a fraction up his finger and studied the ring of paler skin it left behind.

As if compelled by her gaze, he lifted his face to hers. "I'm a marked man," he said, grinning at the untanned skin. "After only three weeks and two days."

His gaze returned to hers and his grin softened into a smile.

Ashley felt a flutter catapult from her chest to her belly. Quickly, she did a mental calculation. He was right. Exactly three weeks and two days.

She looked back down at his long lean fingers, tenderly stroking the textured gold, and she swallowed around the lump in her throat.

Parker touched her arm. "Almost an anniversary already. Can you believe it?"

She looked up into his eyes—eyes so earnest and blue they made hers sting. He gazed back for a moment, then lightly dragged the tip of his finger down her arm.

Ashley shivered. Excited bumps surfaced on every inch of her bare skin as he wrapped his strong hand around hers and brought it to his lips. She felt his contented smile rub the top of her hand, felt her heart surge with warmth, and in total awe she wondered when pretense had merged with reality. Dazed, she sank back into her seat.

He leaned forward and touched her lips briefly with his. "Don't start feeling too safe," he whispered. "I might just blow off my meeting."

Ashley sighed.

A soft groan left Parker and he swooped in for a harder kiss. Ashley gasped for breath. "Unless you want to join the mile-high club," he whispered so loudly that Karen and Don straightened in their seats.

Ashley widened her eyes at first, then narrowed them on him—giving him a slow, saucy grin—and said in her best Mae West imitation, "Don't start anything you can't finish."

The plane dipped suddenly.

"What the devil—" Parker swung his gaze to the window. "We're landing." Ashley shot a look to Karen and Don. Don slumped in his seat. Karen reached into the cockpit and pulled out two very familiar-looking overnight bags.

"Surprise!" she yelled. "Happy honeymoon."

Parker looked at Ashley. Ashley looked at Parker. "Honeymoon?" they echoed.

"Don't worry about a thing. Harvey is covering for you, Parker. And Crystal has you taken care of, Ashley," Karen gushed on, her face brimming with excitement as the plane touched ground. "And we'll be back for you in a week."

"A week?" Parker and Ashley repeated together.

Ashley coughed.

Parker laughed and slipped an arm around her sagging shoulders. "Well, sweetheart, what was it you said about finishing what I start?"

PARKER KNEW HE SHOULD be angry, furious even. He was far too busy with the resort to be railroaded like this. But as he watched Ashley unceremoniously jerk clothes out of the bags that had been packed by Mrs. Lee and smuggled to Maui by Karen, he just couldn't seem to find an angry bone in his body. Besides, Ashley was doing well enough in that department for both of them.

"Which side of the bed do you want?" he asked, nodding to the king-size bed and hiding a smile. He knew damn well which side she wanted—both, with him on the parlor couch.

Ashley favored him with an icy green stare and ignored his question. "Why didn't you simply refuse to get off the plane?"

"Why didn't you?"

She ejected a frustrated sigh and tossed a cosmetic bag into the bathroom. "I didn't think of it." She plopped one of the bags on the luggage rack and pinned him with a suspicious glance. "You don't seem too ticked about this."

He shrugged. "What good would it do? Karen assured me that Harvey has already cleared my calendar and is stepping in where necessary. Besides, you don't know my sister. Once she sets her mind on something..." He shook his head. "Look how elaborate this scheme was. I figure we can kick back for the weekend...go our separate ways if you like." He gave her a covert glance. "Then make arrangements to get ourselves back on Monday."

Before Ashley could verbalize her air of eager agreement, he added, "Unless we find something more... interesting to, uh, engage in."

She sent him a look. Parker pressed his lips together and busied himself with unpacking. One more suggestive tone out of him and she'd probably swim back.

"Oh, great." Ashley planted her hands on her hips and inclined her head to the phone's blinking message light. "I don't think your sister's through with us yet." She paused and lifted a suspicious brow. "Unless someone else knows we're here."

Parker ignored her ridiculous implication and reached for the phone. At the same time, a knock sounded at the door. Ashley threw up her hands and headed for it. Parker frowned and jabbed zero.

Moments later, a room-service waiter pushed a cart holding chilled champagne and an enormous basket of tropical fruit just ahead of Ashley. Parker gave the man a tip and finished listening to his voice-mail message. Ashley plucked an elaborately scripted envelope from the basket and opened it.

She scrunched up her nose. "Who's Herman Voss?"

"Son of a—" Parker slowly replaced the receiver. He gave her a blank look. "What?"

She eyed the offending phone and met his narrowed gaze with a concerned one of her own. "Herman Voss. He sent this." She dropped the announcement to the table. "What's going on?"

"Beats the hell out of me." Parker worked at the kink in his neck. "Herman Voss is one of my investors." He motioned toward the phone with a toss of his head. "That message was from Walter Ito. He's another one." He paced to the sliding-glass doors and stared pensively out over the ocean.

Ashley made a soft sound of exasperation. He looked over his shoulder at her. "And he's kindly arranged to entertain us for the week."

"Entertain...for the week?" Ashley threw back a thick swatch of hair. "Parker? How do these people know we're here?"

"I don't know," he said, shaking his head. "I'd blame Karen, but I'm not sure she even knows either of them. Mrs. Lee, Harvey and Crystal are the only other possibilities. And Mrs. Lee is out."

"So is Crystal. Of course, you'd think she and Harvey would have both known better to begin with."

"Well, my money wouldn't be on Harvey either. But I don't suppose we're going to find out any time soon. Walter Ito has quite a week planned for us."

"We don't really have to stay..." Ashley gaped. "You said we could get back on Monday."

"Not now, I'm afraid. I'm not stirring up any speculation."

She sighed heavily. "A whole week," she muttered, as she trudged up beside him and pushed the drapes further aside. "Look at this place." A long stretch of beach curved into a bay, where it met jagged lava cliffs. A green cloud-capped mountain hovered to the left. Not a person was in sight. "It's...it's deserted. What could there possibly be to do?"

Out of the corner of his eye, Parker watched Ashley blow out a puff of air and he bit back a chuckle. He didn't think she'd appreciate his answer to that question, so he kept his mouth shut and enjoyed the view of her delicate profile against the setting sun.

Ashley's forehead puckered in thought for a few seconds, then she flashed him a crooked grin. "Is this the resort they joke about being for newlyweds or nearly deads?"

Parker's attention snagged on the tiny dimple that flexed at the corner of her mouth. He knew he'd stared a moment too long when her tongue darted out to moisten her lips. She started to back up, but he snaked an arm out to capture her waist. "That's us, Ash. Newlyweds."

Her tongue made another swipe at her lips, then her chin lifted a notch. "Take too much Dramamine, Parker?" she asked sweetly, as she stomped on his foot and pulled out of his reach.

Parker glanced down at the scuffs on his deck shoes and chuckled. She was so light, he'd barely felt it. He looked back up into her smug expression, then reached out his hand to draw the drapes. "No," he replied, ambling toward her. "Too much testosterone."

Ashley's amusement fell away. "You're joking." She sidestepped the bed. "Right?"

"Right." He allowed a slow smile to cross his face.

Her eyebrows drew together in a threatening manner and she slanted a glance toward the vanity night-light that had illuminated with the closing of the drapes. She seemed about to make her move for the bathroom door, when Parker lunged forward and gripped both her wrists.

"One scream and security will be here in two seconds." She flexed her hands back but his fingers locked around her.

"Wanna bet?"

"What do you want, Parker?"

He bunched her wrists together and held them tightly with one hand. With his free one he lifted her chin. "You."

Ashley met him with an unblinking gaze. "You already have that." She raised her chin yet another degree. "Bought and paid for."

Parker felt the blow somewhere in the vicinity of his gut, but he wasn't going to let her get away with it. She always started trouble when he got too close to her—and used it to distance herself. But not this time. He swallowed back the dose of useless pride she had so adeptly summoned.

"You have a very sassy mouth," he whispered. "But we already know that, don't we?" He kept hold of her chin and used his thumb to outline the corner of her mouth. "Hard to imagine such tart words come from these soft lips."

"I'll give you something even harder to imagine," Ashley warned.

"Hey." Chuckling, Parker touched her dimple. "That's my line."

Ashley smiled, displaying a disarming flash of white teeth before they clamped down on his unsuspecting thumb. He jerked back and she pushed away from him.

Biting back a curse, he caught her around the waist and toppled them both to the bed. "Very childish, sweetheart," he scolded, grinning, and successfully pinned her beneath him.

Chapter Thirteen

The light from the bathroom streamed across Parker's face. Ashley watched in fascination as his cheeks and jaw worked to suck away the throbbing from his thumb. Desire, raw and primal, spiraled through her.

"You're too heavy for me. Get off." Her voice wasn't quite normal. He chuckled and she knew he recognized that fact, too.

"You wanna be on top?" His shoe made a soft thud when it hit the carpet. His toe trailed a promise up her calf. "Teacher's choice."

"There's a couple of things I'd like to teach you right now." Ashley twisted to the side, but Parker imprisoned her shoulders with his elbows and captured her face between his hands.

She felt his tongue first, teasing her tightly closed lips. His fingers stretched back into her disheveled hair, massaging her scalp, sending little shivers down her spine. She debated a token struggle, but her thoughts tangled with a more primal need and she reached for him instead.

His shirttail was already loose, so it was easy to travel the length of his warm, naked back with her palms. Muscles flexed and relaxed to her touch. Large, ragged breaths expanded his width beneath her fingers. The thrill of power surged through her and she opened her mouth to him.

Parker's tongue dove smoothly between her eager lips. His hands molded her shoulders, her waist, her hips before he rounded her bottom and pressed her to him. Ashley whimpered softly and he broke the kiss for a moment.

"It's time, Ash."

"I know." Her voice was low, almost inaudible. To erase any mistaken uncertainty, she initiated another kiss, sweet at first and then, fueled by love and desire too long denied, her tongue matched his fire, delving between heaven and hell.

"Ashley?" After a moment, Parker was the one to pull slightly away. "No turning back, okay?"

"No." She reached for him again.

"No distractions," he said, maintaining a slight distance, a satisfied smile tugging at the corners of his mouth as she looked at him through glazed eyes. "No excuses. No interruptions."

"No." Her impatient tone brought a full grin to his lips. Any other time she would've liked to smack him, but right now all she wanted was for him to kiss her.

"And, honey?" His face was somber now. A cold shiver tempered Ashley's heat, until he gently framed her face with his hands. "Most important." He stroked her cheek. "No regrets."

"None." A feeling of serenity, of rightness settled over her. She loved him. And that made it right. Even the other "no" he'd neglected to mention could not extinguish her longing at this moment. Expectation and commitment had not been part of their bargain. Ashley had no illusions now. "No regrets," she stated, strong and certain, and pushed up toward him.

"Ah, sweetheart. I've been waiting—" Parker murmured against her lips.

Ashley kissed him into silence, then allowed a couple of breaths between them. "One more no, Parker," she half whispered, half panted, bringing a finger to his lips. She smiled at his quizzical look. "*No talking.*"

The words were barely out when he banded her with his arms and rolled her over on top of him. He smoothed his palms over her shorts until fabric met skin, and then slid his hands up under her bikini panties. He toyed with the elastic, tracing patterns with his fingers over the swell of her buttocks.

His kisses were gentle and teasing, nipping at her lower lip, moistening it with his tongue. His hair carried the scent of sunshine and promise, and with it the memory of his unfailing support. He'd been patient with her unruly students, kind to her father and so unlike the picture she'd painted of him just a few short weeks earlier. Ashley's breasts strained against him, her body anxious for his exploration. She reached between them and undid the last button of his shirt.

Parker slid his hands from her, kissed the exposed shoulder where her T-shirt had slipped, then lay back against the pillows. His arms rested on either side of him, away from her, his eyes dark with challenge and desire.

This was her test, Ashley knew. It was also her final chance to back down. Her hesitation was brief as she was left to straddle him while he watched. She pushed his shirt aside and ran her palms against the taut skin, wondering at the softness of the thick, dark blond chest hair.

She felt a small quiver beneath her hands and smiled to herself.

She made the return trip down, grazing his flat nipples, tracing the dip between them, delighting in the small bumps that appeared on his skin. But her control was short-lived.

"Damn," Parker swore through clenched teeth. "You like making me crazy, huh?" He sat up and pulled her legs more tightly around him. Reaching around, he pulled up the hem of her top and with it the brief camisole. He tossed them aside and shrugged out of his own shirt.

Ashley's hair fell forward but he brushed it away and fisted a handful behind her. "I want to see you." He released it and she felt it glide down her back, reminding her of her nakedness.

"I'm going to turn on the light," he whispered, and with deliberate slowness Parker stretched for the bedside lamp.

Any other time, Ashley would have cringed from the exposure. But when light flooded their half-naked bodies, assurance cocooned her heart. She was exactly where she wanted to be.

She met Parker's smoldering gaze with one of her own, then let it drift to the tempting expanse of flesh and hair that tapered to the waistband of his unbuttoned jeans and below, to his straining fly.

She shifted unnecessarily on his lap. A smile quickly appeared on his lips.

"You little devil." He grasped her about the waist and set her farther back from harm's way. "Careful, or this will be over before you know it."

"C'mon, Parker, don't chicken out on me now," Ashley chided and wiggled forward, grinning.

"If the teacher wants an apple, she'd better behave." He raised himself up to a sitting position and brought her up against him, seeking the tart sweetness of her lips. Her sensitive breasts tingled with the friction of his hair-carpeted chest. They pebbled and pouted awaiting his velvety tongue, which was making its way from her mouth down her neck.

He didn't disappoint. Suckling one breast and then the other, he gently laid Ashley backward until she was fully reclined, her hair spread out about the satin sheets. He slid his hands to the back of her thighs and massaged and kneaded until he'd worked his way up under the leg of her shorts. She reached for his zipper but he ducked away.

She felt his ever-hardening manhood graze her fingers through the rough denim fabric and knew she could easily have it her way. A smug cloud was beginning to shroud her senses when she felt his deft fingers slip inside her panties, finding the wetness there. A surprise jolt brought her shoulders off the bed.

"Relax," Parker whispered, soothing her back down, his fingers stroking a gentle inquiry. "I won't hurt you."

Yes, you will, was Ashley's last feeble thought before his magical fingers erased the reality of the future.

Rainbows. Fireworks. Forked lightning. They all collided under her tightly closed eyelids. It was hot, then cold, just before the tidal wave swept her into a pulsing native dance. She could hear the drums in the distance. Her heart echoed their beat. Her senses begged their encore. And then the waves became swells, dwindling to ripples, nature's prudent restoration of order.

"Shh, baby."

She opened her eyes and Parker was smiling, stroking her cheek. "Everyone will think I'm beating you."

Oh, my. The fog began to lift. She'd been crying out his name. Embarrassed, she tried to turn her face into his shoulder.

But he wouldn't have it.

"Don't do that," he said softly. "You're beautiful." He stretched out beside her, still holding her, caressing her. "And a wonder for my ego," he added, chuckling.

"You don't have to say those things," Ashley said, ignoring his teasing. She wanted things kept straight between them. It was bad enough she'd climaxed so quickly.

"You're right. I don't. I call it like I see it." He rested his hand under her breast, cupping its light fullness, rubbing his thumb over her responsive nipple. "Now, in your own words. No talking." His hand left her breast. She tackled his zipper, and this time he did nothing to discourage her.

A remnant of her pride was restored when she discovered how hard and heavy he was. But it was no match for the renewed desire that commandeered her wits.

They both shook free of their remaining clothes and lay face-to-face, their bodies inches apart. Parker twirled a long strand of her hair around his finger until he came upon her breast. He traced a light finger around her nipple as if memorizing the texture. Ashley felt the heat beginning to pool again, and partly out of shock, partly in self-defense, she fastened her hand around the length of him. She had the satisfaction of hearing him take a quick and unsteady breath.

With tentative strokes, she worked her own brand of magic. He whispered her name, mixed with endearments. His kisses faltered, his chest heaved. He grabbed her hand to stop her.

"I wanted to take it slow." His voice was hoarse and gravelly. "But you'll have it your way." He rolled toward her, pinned her hand under his until she was flat on her back.

Startled by his sudden move, Ashley's immediate response was to bring her thighs together. Gently, Parker parted them. He knelt before her, fully aroused, his tawny hair sexily disarrayed, a slight tremble in the hand that touched her cheek. "Heaven help me, Ash, but something's happening that shouldn't be."

He bowed down and kissed her with renewed tenderness, then filled her with his explosive desire.

Ashley gripped the sheets. His breathing was hard and heavy, hers nonexistent. She moved her hands to his sweat-slickened shoulders and rode the wave that threatened to wash away every principle in her body.

He murmured her name into her hair, kissed the damp tendrils at her neck. And when she thought she could stand no more, the impossible happened and fireworks once again graced her night.

IT WAS DRIZZLING AGAIN. Or maybe it had rained all night and Ashley simply hadn't noticed. She gazed out through slitted eyes at the ill-fated attempt of dawn's hues slanting in through the partially opened drapes.

She knew where she was, but something felt different. She propped herself up on one elbow, glanced down and quickly pulled the sheet up over her bare breasts. With a furtive glance over her shoulder, she eyed the bare spot next to her. Parker was gone.

A loud sigh left her lips as she sank back into the pillows and stared at the ceiling. She didn't know if she should be happy or disappointed. Then she remembered how gentle he'd been while the pulse had raced wildly at his neck and his fingers shook with restraint. He had been a far better lover than she could have imagined...or maybe it was because she was in love with him.

Ashley sighed again. It didn't matter. There were no promises, no guarantees. There'd only be the memory...and one big mess called Magic Island.

Ashley had had every intention of calling Manuel Gomes the night before to explain her absence, and to find out what had transpired at the meeting. Other priorities, however, had prevented the call.

But now, alone, with reality cooling the sheets beside her, Ashley knew she had to make some decisions about her stand with the committee. And it was time to explain her role to Parker.

The thought sent a shiver clear down to her toes.

And then she pictured his understanding blue eyes, replayed the sweet endearments he'd whispered in the dark, and she stretched like a contented cat. The warm feeling of being sheltered in his arms lingered in every unfamiliar ache in her body.

Ashley swung her feet to the thick carpeting and headed for a much-needed warm bath. The previous night had been her choice and she was certainly prepared to live with that. It bothered her, though, remembering his words. Something was happening that shouldn't be. Was he already having regrets? She turned on the water to full power and prayed it would wash away any trace of doubt.

PARKER HEARD THE WATER draining from the tub as he entered the room and set the tray of food on the bed. He plucked the red rose from the vase he'd set on the nightstand, closed his eyes and inhaled its scent.

Funny, he'd never thought roses were especially fragrant before, but this one... well, it was perfect. He replaced it in the vase, careful to face it toward Ashley's pillow, where he hoped to have her lying before long.

What was keeping her? It would be a shame if she were spending any time fixing her hair. He expected it would be for nothing. He smiled at the thought and rubbed his stubbly chin. This would have to go. He'd shave while she ate. He hadn't wanted to wake her, so he'd showered in the parlor bathroom earlier, but he hadn't had the foresight to take a razor. This morning had to be perfect. Ashley deserved it.

"Parker?" Ashley peeked out from a crack in the door. Her face was freshly scrubbed...and glowing. He hoped he had something to do with that.

"There better not be any other strange men in the room," he growled playfully and shot a hand through the door opening, grabbed her wrist and pulled her to him.

She wore a short red silk kimono which she automatically tugged at. Her hazel eyes wary, she settled against his chest, head tilted back. He tightened his arms around her.

He kissed the tip of her nose and then paid a swift tribute to her lips. "Good morning."

"Good morning back." Her smile was shy and endearing. Then she sniffed the air. "Do I smell food?"

"Thrown over for scrambled eggs." Parker cast a woebegone look to the ceiling. Grinning, he cinched the belt to his robe, then gently pushed her toward the bed.

"Where did that come from?" Ashley's eyes widened. Bacon, buttered toast, fluffy yellow eggs, steaming coffee all awaited her.

"The love fairy. He wants to keep your strength up."

"Parker." She laughed. Lashes fluttering, she looked away.

It was amazing that she could still blush after all they'd shared the previous night. His gaze traveled the black silkiness of her long hair to the smooth, tanned skin of her thighs. All that and a heart as big as the moon. He felt a stirring of desire that could very well cancel their breakfast.

"Eat," he ordered, and urged her to the bed, setting the tray across her lap. He sat beside her and helped himself to a strip of bacon. Munching on it, he watched her dip into the eggs. "Do you like your bacon crisp?"

"What?" Ashley laughed.

"Maybe I shouldn't have ordered your toast buttered." He pursed his lips. "It's strange. Sometimes I feel I've known you forever. But I have a lot to learn about you, don't I?"

Ashley picked up her coffee cup and swiped at her hair. He didn't like the caution he saw in her eyes as they tried to avoid his. He reached out and grabbed the small bare foot she'd tucked under her leg. "Like are you ticklish?"

"Knock it off, Parker." Ashley gulped down her coffee and let out a half giggle. "I'm warning you..."

"Or what?" He kept a firm grasp of her ankle and ran a light finger across her instep. Giggling, she discarded her cup and clutched at his arm, but only managed to lose the kimono halfway down her shoulder.

"Ah, good idea." Grinning, he removed the tray and set it on the nightstand.

"What?" Ashley inched to the other side, tugging up her sleeve, anticipation curving her lips.

Parker was quick. He yanked the sash of her kimono. It fell open. His own robe slid to the floor. He stood before her, naked and fully aroused.

Ashley did only a fair job of hiding a large gulp that made his heart smile. There wasn't any wariness or doubt on her face now, and he certainly aimed to keep it that way. He allowed himself a few more seconds of feasting on her beautiful face, then crawled along the bed until he reached her bare thighs.

"Honey, I had every intention of shaving first." He kissed her calf, then dragged his lower lip up past the inside of her knees. His tongue took over the search.

"I truly did," he murmured, and heard her gasp as he reached his satiny destination.

"THAT WAS FANTASTIC." Ashley's chest heaved with exhilaration and she gasped for the breath that had been knocked out of her.

"It's also illegal." Parker pointed to the No-Trespassing sign nailed to a huge mango tree and grinned. "Want to go again?"

Ashley frowned at the sign. "Should we?"

"Sure. They need to cover their butts so we won't sue them. Besides, it's the high school kids they probably worry about most." Parker took her hand and led her back up the jungly mountain path.

"High school kids?"

Parker stopped and looked at her. "Didn't you ever cut class to go fluming?"

"Cut class?" Smiling, she lifted her chin and a brow.

"Oh, I forgot. You were probably too busy saving the world," Parker teased, but when her expression tightened, he grabbed her hand. "Hey, Ash. I wasn't being critical." He slipped his arms around her and hugged her to him. "I admire what you do, your dedication, your plans for the community center. I admire *you.*"

Ashley managed to accept the swift kiss he gave her without cringing. Why did he have to bring up the community center? The secret phone calls to various Magic Island lobbyists she'd had to make over the past five days had been bad enough. She pushed up on tiptoe and returned his kiss. "Tell me about your rebellious fluming days."

"Rainy days were the best. With the surge of water, we really did some flying. Although at times, it could be dangerous."

"I'm surprised you didn't get your fannies thrown in jail."

Parker threw his head back and laughed. "We did. Well, we got arrested a few times anyway. But the plantation owners never pressed charges. And we always managed to sneak back." He shrugged, a broad smile firmly in place. "We figured that since the flumes weren't needed for irrigation anymore, they needed to be put to good use."

"How thoughtful of you." Ashley plucked a nearby wild ginger blossom and tickled his nose with the soft petals.

"Wasn't it?" He made a grab for her, but she managed to dodge him.

"I'll race you to the top."

"Hey, no fair." He swatted at some overgrown ferns and scrambled after her. "The path isn't wide enough."

"Don't be a quitter, Parker." Ashley laughed over her shoulder, then leapt over some fallen bamboo.

She made it up the steep path another six yards before she realized that the only response she'd gotten was the rush of a nearby waterfall. She clutched the fronds of a coconut tree for balance and turned to him.

He hadn't followed her, but stood motionless, a peculiar expression on his face.

Ashley's smile faltered. "Parker? What is it?" She released the frond and stumbled more quickly than she'd intended, back down toward him.

Narrowly escaping bodily injury, Parker caught her in his arms as she came barreling down, the momentum of her speedy descent nearly knocking them both off their feet.

"Hey, lady, I've already fallen for you," Parker joked as he righted them on the path.

She turned in his embrace to face him. The smile he gave her didn't quite reach his eyes. "What's wrong?"

"What's wrong?" He glanced down at her knee. "You just about wiped out the need for birth control."

"You know what I mean." She waited, watching him, knowing that he wanted nothing more than to ignore her probing.

"Nothing, really." He paused, but Ashley remained stubbornly silent. "It was a seventies kind of flashback, you know," he added in his best surfer accent and grinned.

Ashley didn't buy his sudden nonchalance for a minute. Her brain replayed the past few minutes of their conversation, but she'd only teased him about being a...

"Parker? Did this flashback have anything to do with quitting law school?"

Parker's hands fell away from her. One made it to the back of his neck, the other sliced through the air in a helpless gesture. "What do you know about my going to law school?"

"Not much." She shrugged. "Just that you went but didn't like it."

"Didn't like it," he repeated in somewhat amazement. "Who told you that?"

"Mrs. Lee. Was she wrong?"

"No. She wasn't wrong." Parker laughed. It held no humor. "I didn't like it."

"So?"

"My father liked that fact even less."

Ashley moved closer, circled her arms around him and took over the task of massaging the back of his neck. She slipped her fingers under his and found the knots of tension there. "That doesn't make you a quitter, Parker."

He looked down at her and brushed the pad of his thumb across her cheek. His eyes crinkled at the corners. "I know," he whispered.

And Ashley wished she could believe him.

"I WISH THIS WEEK HAD never ended." Ashley zipped up her toiletry bag and stuffed it into her carryon.

"It hasn't yet." Parker snuck up behind her, grabbed her around the waist and tumbled them both to the bed.

"If we don't want to miss the plane, it has." Ashley laughed and pushed his long hair away from his eyes. His face was more tanned than usual from all the outside activities they'd been treated to, which made his eyes seem even bluer.

"What plane?"

"Parker..." Ashley tried to sound admonishing, but the giggle blew it. "You know we have to go back."

He sighed. Ashley did, too. She didn't want to go back any more than he did, but if she didn't she wouldn't be surprised to find the whole Magic Island committee on her hotel-suite doorstep. Talk about the natives getting restless. Only after she'd threatened to pull out altogether had they finally quit phoning her at the hotel. She'd had a couple of near misses as a result. And although that had been handled on her second day here, when the phone rang it still made her jump.

It also made her acutely aware that the time had come to be totally honest with Parker. The mere thought sent the usual shiver down her spine.

"Do you want the air conditioner turned off?" Parker asked.

Ashley blinked. "No. I'm fine." She rolled away from him, rubbing her bare arms. She had to tell him. Today. When they returned to Oahu. The longer she took, the harder it was going to be. Oh, God, it was already hard.

She lined up her bags and reached for her hat.

"If I didn't know any better, I'd think you were anxious to get away from me," Parker commented with a puzzled look on his face.

"I need rest," Ashley joked.

"And you think you'll get it once we get home?"

"I have a feeling I might," she mumbled, and hurried to the phone as it sounded its first ring. It's not that she thought anyone from the committee would be stupid enough to still try her here, but...

As soon as the front-desk clerk identified himself, Ashley's breathing eased. "Your limo will be here in fifteen minutes, Mrs. James. I'll send someone up for your luggage. Is there anything else we can do for you?"

"Nothing. We've had a marvelous time." She looked up at Parker, who was about to answer a knock at the door, and returned his knowing smile. "And I believe the bellman's already here."

"Oh, yeah," the young man rushed on. "Someone left a message for you. They wouldn't leave it over the phone, said you wouldn't want that, but they left an envelope instead."

Ashley bit back the indelicate word that came to mind and immediately focused on Parker. His back was to her as he carried on his muted conversation with their visitor. "I'll be right down for it."

"That's not necessary," the clerk assured her. "I've already sent someone up with it. He should be there—"

Ashley replaced the receiver, unsure as to whether she'd thanked the young man or not. She paced a couple of steps toward Parker and watched his back stiffen as he closed the door.

He pivoted toward her, an envelope in one hand, an unfolded sheet of paper in the other.

He looked up, his jaw twitching.

"Congratulations," he said, blandly. "The state accepted your bid."

Chapter Fourteen

Parker shoved the last of the luggage into their closet and slammed the door in the middle of Ashley's protest that they needed to be unpacked.

"Not this time, Ashley Leialoha." He took several menacing steps in her direction. "We are not skirting the issue. Now tell me what the hell you have to do with those Magic Island idiots."

Ashley took a casual turn around the bed and dropped her watch on the nightstand.

"And Judas Priest, *don't* tell me your approved bid for the airstrip has anything to do with our homestead land."

She swiped at her hair and Parker knew for certain. He knew whatever she had to say, he didn't want to hear.

"Tell me, Ashley. Tell me everything."

She took a huge breath. "Make up your mind," she muttered and tried to sidestep him.

He blocked her exit. "What do you have to do with all this, Ash?"

She looked up at him, her eyes bright with green specks. "Do I know everything there is to know about your resort project?"

"Anything pertinent to you. And, hell, anything you choose to know. I don't keep secrets from you."

Ashley flinched. "Is your implication that I've been lying to you?"

Parker studied her silently for a moment. "I don't even know what to imply. I just want to know what's going on." He let out a chest full of pent-up air and reached for her. "Look, sweetheart, if Crystal has involved you—"

"No. Please." Ashley shook her head and put out a restraining palm. "You're right. I need to tell you everything. And, no, Crystal has nothing to do with this. In fact, she tried to talk me out of it."

She sat at the edge of the bed, twisting her wedding ring. Parker sat beside her and put his hand over hers. "Talk to me. It can't be that bad."

"Wanna bet?" She raised her reluctant gaze to his. "Parker, at this point, I practically *am* Magic Island."

He felt his mouth go dry. "I don't get it."

"If you'll only listen to all the advantages of diverting tourists to a single island—"

"What do you mean you *are* Magic Island?" he demanded in a low, even tone as his gut twisted in anticipation.

"When I came up with the service center and airstrip idea..." She lifted a sagging shoulder. "Everyone got excited about it all over again."

Recognition dawned and Parker slowly nodded his head. "That's why there was a sudden resurgence of the committee." He had wondered why the recently renewed interest. One mystery solved. He narrowed his gaze. "Service center?"

"Yes. To accommodate the airstrip."

"This is like pulling teeth, Ash."

She sighed. "I've proposed to both the committee and the state that I could provide a tourist center for translation services, information, money exchange, you name it. And, of course, the airstrip would be used for shuttling the people over. That strip of homestead land is the perfect location." Her gaze roamed his face as her mouth tensed, waiting for his rebuttal, waiting to deliver her protest.

Parker sat quietly, his expression carefully bland, trying to organize his thoughts, regain his composure. He met her expectant gaze and something in her guileless eyes pierced his cynicism.

Maybe she had no protest, maybe she'd finally realized that it wasn't going to work, maybe she was sorry for having gotten involved in the first place.

He patted her hand and half smiled. "You realize, don't you, that there isn't enough land for a service center, an airstrip and a community center."

Ashley nodded sadly and took a deep breath. She lowered her lashes for a moment before looking him straight in the eyes. "There is no community center."

Parker blinked. "No community center. But you..." He dropped her hand. "You lied to me?"

"I never did that."

"The hell you—"

"Technically, the service center could be considered a community center, because it will be manned—"

"That's a bunch of crap and you know it."

"You didn't let me finish," Ashley pointed out, her eyes gathering storm clouds in its depths.

Parker slowly, painfully rose from the bed and put some distance between them. "Trust me, Ashley," he said through clenched teeth. "You are finished."

CHEERFULLY HUMMING Rock-a-bye Baby, Napua Lee meandered down the hall with a tray of freshly cut pineapple and two mineral waters. Life was good, she decided, on this fine Sunday afternoon. Her two wards had returned and by now, well... She smiled and continued humming.

Napua reached Parker and Ashley's room, balanced the tray on one hand and raised her fist to the door. Before her knuckles made contact with the wood, she froze. The smile fell from her lips. Her eyes grew saucerlike.

Voices rose and fell from the room beyond. They weren't distinct voices, but Napua knew they were angry ones. Her heart heavy, she yanked a linen napkin off the wobbly tray and pressed it to her flushed cheek. "Dear Lord," she whispered. "What are we going to do now?"

"WHAT DO YOU THINK you're doing?" Harvey Winton stood at the entrance of Keoki King's hospital room with a wary look on his face.

"Unpacking." Keoki gave him a disgusted look, then grimaced at the clothes he had only an hour ago deposited in his bag.

"You're supposed to be going home today." Harvey adjusted his shirt cuffs. A nervous habit Keoki knew well. "I'm supposed to be picking you up. Remember?"

"Things have changed." He glanced back up. "Lose the poker face, my friend, we have new plans to make."

"Keoki..." Harvey drawled in warning.

"I know Karen has called you. Do not pretend she has not." Keoki pulled two wadded-up aloha shirts out of the duffel bag. "Crystal has called me. Mrs. Lee has called *everybody.*" He shook his graying head and sank down next to the bag. "What do you think they are fighting about *now*?"

"I don't know. And I don't care. *You* shouldn't care. We did what we set out to do. We got them together. Now, old man, we back off."

Keoki slanted him a menacing look. "Who are you calling old? At least I remember what love is about. I say we up the ante."

"And I say you're out of your mind." Harvey strode over, picked up the discarded shirts and stuffed them back into the duffel. "If you aren't planning on going home like you're supposed to, I'll be happy to drop you off at the psychiatric ward instead."

Keoki absently watched his friend repack his bag. "We'll have to come up with something else. Something that will make them see how far they've come."

"No, Keoki." Harvey snatched the shaving kit from the bathroom sink and threw it in with the shirts.

Pensively, Keoki pulled out a cigar and bit off the end. "Do you think it could be true about the baby?"

"Baby?" Harvey dropped the bag altogether. Obviously this was the first he'd heard of the rumor.

Keoki chuckled. "Karen didn't tell you." Enormously pleased with the dumbstruck look on his friend's face, Keoki lit his cigar.

"They're not having a baby?"

"Maybe this is a good thing. We could revise the contract, make provisions for an heir. That would give them all the more reason to stay together." Keoki lazily blew a smoke ring toward the ceiling, contemplating their best avenue in securing the newlyweds' relationship. He doubted the validity of the baby—Mrs. Lee had been near incoherent when she had called both him and Crystal. Still, it was something to consider.

"I have it." Keoki stubbed out his cigar, his black eyes wildly excited. "We will tell them a mistake has been made, that the land is not homestead land."

"How do you know there's going to be a baby?" Harvey ignored Keoki's blossoming plan and calmly took the nearest chair, staring at him the entire time.

"We will tell them that the land is actually privately owned. And..." Keoki paced to the window, his fingers to his temple. "And that the owner will agree to lease them the land, if they can provide an heir of Hawaiian ancestry. That's it." A slow grin blossomed on Keoki's face as he ignored the other man's gaping disbelief. "Of course the owner will remain anonymous."

"You *aren't* serious." The very proper Harvey pushed his hand through his hair with such force that the gray strands poked comically out of place. "That's the most absurd thing you've come up with yet."

"You have a better idea," Keoki snapped, then put a soothing hand to his belly.

"Yes. Let things be." His friend enunciated each word with purpose, then ran a skeptical gaze over Keoki's pitiful expression and down to his fraudulent middle. "And save your antics for your daughter. It doesn't work with me."

Keoki shrugged and removed his hand. "Crystal still does not need to know anything—"

"You really don't get it, do you?" Harvey shook his head. "We knew they'd eventually find out about our... our plan, but if you think for one minute Parker will believe..."

Keoki had patiently resumed emptying his duffel bag,

waiting, as the inevitable dawned on Harvey. When the look of grudging relief softened his friend's features, Keoki smiled.

It was almost over. Harvey understood that now. Parker and Ashley would never fall for this newest scheme. How they reacted to it, however, would be the biggest gamble of all.

Keoki knew that, too. But he also knew his daughter. And he knew for a fact that she would get to the bottom of this. Even if it meant conspiring with the enemy.

Whistling, Keoki dumped out the last of the bag's contents. "It is a glorious day after all, is it not, my friend?"

ASHLEY DROPPED HER PURSE on a chair in the corner of Harvey's office and motioned through the glass window to Crystal who had just stepped off the elevator. "Do you know what this is all about?" she asked her friend before Crystal could get through the door.

Crystal shook her newly tinted auburn head. "Harvey mentioned something about unexpected revisions to the contract. Doesn't Parker know anything?"

Ashley felt the starch creep up her spine. Her lips thinned. "That insufferable, self-absorbed jerk wouldn't know his butt from a—"

"So, things really are that bad." Crystal pulled a long face, then quickly lowered her head to flip open her briefcase when Ashley gave her a quizzical frown.

"He knows about Magic Island and my role in it," she said, wondering at the rather odd observation Crystal had made. The previous time they'd spoken, she and Parker had been getting along well... very well... too well. Ashley sighed.

"How?" Crystal peered at her over the top of the open briefcase.

"I told him." Ashley passed a hand over her cheek and felt the heat there. "I didn't have much of a choice."

"And he gave you a rough time." Crystal nodded sympathetically. "Is that why you don't look so good?"

"I stayed at my apartment last night. I didn't get much sleep, though," Ashley admitted and let her hand drift down to rest against the butterflies in her stomach. First the horrible scene with Parker and now this secret emergency meeting. "So I haven't been totally with it this morning."

Crystal's wary gaze followed the descent of Ashley's hand. Gradually, her eyes widened as Ashley applied pressure to the havoc being wreaked by her morning coffee. Crystal opened her mouth to speak, but nothing came out.

"They're here," Ashley warned. "I'll fill you in later." She took the seat on the other side of Crystal, as far away from Parker as she could get.

He'd told her he was going to fight her every step of the way on Magic Island. And she believed him. She was prepared to do the same. Unfortunately, it didn't mean her disloyal body would be a willing ally. She clasped her hands together, kept her focus straight ahead and waited for the two men to take their seats.

She was surprised to see that Parker wasn't wearing a suit today. From what she could tell out of the corner of her eye, he had on a rather rumpled sport coat and... jeans?

Casually, she turned her head a few degrees his way. His eyes immediately found hers. They were just as blue, just as compelling as she'd always found them to be. But tired lines fanned out more deeply than usual at their sides. He gave her a sad crooked smile.

"Good morning, Ashley, Crystal." Harvey nodded to them, unlocked his desk and pulled out a folder. "I know you're anxious to find out what this is all about."

"Yes, we are," Parker stated in an impatient tone.

Ashley and Crystal exchanged quick glances. Not even Parker knew what this was about? Ashley scooted back in her chair and leaned forward a bit, listening intently for what Harvey was about to say.

"There seems to have been a misunderstanding." Harvey adjusted first one cuff, then the other. Parker slid Ashley a brief sideways glance. "About the homestead land, we have a slight problem." Harvey cleared his throat twice. "It appears it isn't governed by the homestead act after all."

"Appears?" Parker shouted. "Appears? What exactly *is* the status, Harvey?"

"It's privately owned. Your current contract is void."

Ashley felt the first arrow of realization reach its target and her heart sank like a lead canoe. The land wasn't theirs. She looked over at Parker, who sat in stunned denial, a faint red surging up his neck.

"This isn't like you, Harvey. What the hell went wrong?" Parker finally asked in a controlled voice, and Ashley had to admire his regained composure. If it weren't for the tick at his jaw or the low rumbling of his voice, no one would know how upset he was. And if that same low, rumbling voice didn't remind her of intimate whispers on a moonlit night, maybe she would be more concerned about the future of Magic Island. Instead, the fact that there might no longer be a reason to stay together weighed heavy on her heart.

"I don't want to get into that now," Harvey replied. "I think we need to spend the time reviewing our options. You see, there's still a chance of keeping the land."

Ashley held her breath and darted a look at Parker. He sent her an expressionless one back. Crystal, speechless for one of the few times in her life, threw up her hands.

Harvey took a large gulp from a mug of cold coffee, then stated, "If you will earnestly promise to provide an heir."

Parker let out an irreverent word, and Crystal added a far more colorful one. But for the next two hours Ashley watched, listened and said very little as Harvey outlined the new conditions and fielded questions. Parker also became increasingly quiet, and by the time they all agreed to call it quits for the day, the contract remained unsigned.

Crystal said she had a client to meet and was gone in a flash. Harvey suddenly had to leave for a luncheon meeting. Another meeting was scheduled for the next day.

Ashley folded up the scant notes she'd taken and deposited them in her purse. Parker had risen and stood near the door, watching the lunch crowd head for the elevators, his hands stuffed deep in his pockets. The fit of his jeans was snug enough, and the action caused the worn denim to enticingly caress his taut rear end.

Ashley felt the first surge of residual anger. How dare he have criticized her for such a lamebrained scheme only yesterday and still look so damn good today. She jammed her pen and notebook into her purse.

"I don't buy this," Parker said quietly, continuing to look out the door. "But I can't figure it out either."

Ashley hitched the strap of her pocketbook up on her shoulder and drew her brows together. "Did Harvey seem strange to you?"

"Strange?" He turned and gestured to the air. "That man hasn't been so disconcerted since he had to be potty trained."

Ashley chuckled and Parker gave her a small, tired grin. "What kind of lunatic would come up with a crazy plan like this anyway? No wonder the owner wants to remain anonymous." He shook his head. "Something's amiss, all right. But I'll be damned if I know what."

"You know, Crystal's been acting sort of strange, too." Her purse slid back down her arm. She dropped it to the chair and paced to the window.

"How so?"

"Nothing I can really pinpoint...." She sighed, a long, tired sigh. "And then again, it may be my imagination."

Parker picked up his copy of the contract off Harvey's desk. "Maybe not." He scanned the pages for a moment and asked, "Does Kinwin Corporation sound familiar to you?"

"No. I don't think so." Ashley tapped her finger on the windowsill.

"It does to me." He frowned in concentration. "But it doesn't make sense. The guy wants to remain anonymous, yet allows this company name to appear on the contract...."

Ashley bit her lip. "What do you want to do, Parker?"

He looked up. "Get to the bottom of this."

"And in the meantime?" she asked slowly.

"You're not suggesting we sign the contract?" He dropped his hand to his side. The sheet of paper fell to the floor.

Ashley crossed her arms over her chest. "We both need the land."

Parker ran an insolent gaze over her. "And you're ready to make a baby for it."

"Why, you..." She felt the heat erupt to her face. "No, Parker, that's not what I meant. But you don't want to believe that, do you?"

"Ashley, I'm sorry." He moved forward and put a hand out to her. "I really didn't—"

She stepped back. He hadn't forgiven her for her deception regarding the community center. And he never would. She knew that now. "I'm not apologizing for wanting or needing the security that service center would provide me and my father. I know you can't understand that...."

"You're wrong—"

"Am I, Parker?" Her laugh was humorless. "Your father should be damn proud of you. Karen's right, you're just like him." His expression pinched in aggrieved confusion and she knew she'd be sorry for her hasty words. But he'd hurt her, and Ashley's need to strike back overwhelmed her.

"You pigeonholed me, Parker. You put me up on some damn pedestal." She gestured high in the air. "*Your* pedestal. And when I stepped down, you couldn't take it." She raised her chin, holding back a sniffle. "Sorry I didn't meet your expectations."

Parker took a deep breath. "Ashley, you're—"

She stopped him with a raised hand and reclaimed her purse, along with her copy of the contract. "We need some space, Parker." Sudden tears burned the back of her eyes when she realized the stark truth of that statement, and she hurried to the door. "We'll talk later, try to figure out what this new deal is all about."

Parker watched her go. She didn't bother waiting for the elevator, but took the stairs instead. It was ten flights down. He picked up the legal papers he'd dropped earlier, rolled them up and smacked the inside of his hand with them.

So, they were back to business... back to square one. She'd be willing to talk to him all right, to talk about securing the land.

Well, hell, he didn't care about the land anymore. Had quit caring about it almost a month ago. About the time he had fallen in love with Ashley. About the time that what she'd just accused him of would have been accurate.

But now, today, Ashley had been wrong. That burden was no longer Parker's to carry. For the first time in his life, he knew that he'd truly let it go. Parker no longer needed his father's approval.

Just as Ashley didn't need his.

Parker smiled at the mere thought of Ashley needing anyone's approval. He'd learned a lot from her. He'd even learned that he was worthy of her love.

What she *did* need, however, was a wake-up call.

She didn't need the damn contract, didn't need Magic Island or the land for security. Didn't she realize that? She already had all the money and security she needed, for as long as she wanted it.

Parker leaned his arm up along the window frame and rested his forehead against the back of his hand. Or maybe she did realize it. Maybe she simply didn't want what he had to offer. Or maybe...maybe she didn't want him.

He drew in a large, shaky breath. That wasn't true, he admonished himself, this was his insecurity talking. She was stalwart, proud. She didn't want anything handed to her. He understood that. Like himself, she worked for what she got. He still didn't agree with her manipulation of the community-center situation, but he respected her determination and independence—two of her many qualities he'd grown to love.

He smiled to himself again. Her stubbornness he could probably do without, but it was a small obstacle. Because deep down, he knew she loved him, and he was about to prove it.

Chapter Fifteen

"This better be good, Parker," Ashley said as she opened the door to her apartment. She hadn't seen or spoken to him since that awful day in Harvey's office, and she hoped she didn't look as nervous and wretched as she felt.

"Define the word good." He pushed a large legal folder into her hands and went straight to the kitchen. He had the most unusual smirk on his face when he returned with two beers.

"Help yourself," Ashley murmured, eyeing the cans. She couldn't help that touch of sarcasm even though she was immensely relieved at his easygoing manner—as if nothing had happened, as if she hadn't said those ugly words.

He handed one to her on his way to the living room. "You might want this."

She accepted it and their unspoken truce, and joined him on the couch. She'd barely read halfway down the page when she let it slip from her hand and looked up into Parker's I-told-you-so expression. He gave her a wry smile and took a large gulp of beer.

She took one of her own. "I don't believe it."

"Believe it. I checked and rechecked because I had trouble with it myself."

Ashley picked the paper back up. "Kinwin stands for King/Winton, doesn't it?"

"You got it. Now, what are we going to do about it? That's the question." Parker sprawled back on the couch and Ashley had the irrational urge to smack him. He might not be the guilty party, but he looked so relaxed over it and here she was ready to scream. Of course, she admitted, he'd had time to digest this information. Plenty of time, in fact—it had taken a whole week to hear from him.

She counted silently to ten, then asked, "How did you find this out?"

"That's the damn thing about it. It wasn't that difficult."

"Then why has it been a week?" she blurted out and felt the heat reach clear to her hairline.

Parker grinned and straightened. "Did you miss me?"

"Hardly." She left the couch to prowl the room. "Wait until I get my hands on that conniving old son of a gun...." Ashley suddenly spun on Parker. "And if you make one crack about it running in the family, so help me—"

He held up his hands. "Didn't even cross my mind." He gave her a large grin. "Especially since we're going to be allies again."

She lifted her chin and spent a few seconds relishing the sensation of looking down on him before her curiosity got the better of her. "How so?"

"Well, I'm pretty ticked at Harvey, myself," he said, an odd tilt at the corners of his mouth. "And I figure you may have a score to settle with your father, as well."

"No doubt about that."

"And the way I see it, two heads are better than one."

Ashley brought a finger to her lips. "Maybe," she admitted, mulling over the possibilities.

When the phone rang, she automatically jumped for it. She glanced at Parker. His old guarded expression went into place for an instant, and then they both laughed. It felt good.

Her conversation with Crystal was brief, and when she returned to the living room she was surprised to find Parker with the television on, indifferently flipping through channels. Once again she was struck with the feeling that he wasn't nearly as upset as he might be, as she surely was.

He muted the volume and looked up as she approached. His eyes were clear and blue and filled with something so soft and tender it made her insides go all mushy.

"Well, are you in?" he asked.

"Hmm?" She sank down near him, brought both legs up and rested her chin on her knees. "Do you think anyone else was in on this scheme?"

Parker frowned and glanced heavenward. "I hadn't thought about it." He started to shake his head slowly. "Mrs. Lee may seem culpable, but I know her well enough to know she couldn't keep her mouth shut that long." He blinked. "But she did act rather strangely... Nah, she's just nosy... I think."

"And Karen?"

Parker lifted an uncertain shoulder, a suspicious glint in his eye. "What about Crystal?"

Ashley wrinkled her nose. "She, of all people, should have known better, but she's said some odd things lately—"

"It's a damn conspiracy." Parker slammed his can down and beer sloshed over his hand.

"We don't know that." Ashley watched him lick the liquid from his fingers and unconsciously ran her own tongue over her lips. Parker's gaze snagged on the action.

"Well," he slowly raised his reluctant gaze to her eyes.

"Well," she echoed and put her feet to the floor. "What are we going to do about it?"

"Get even."

"I like your thinking." A lazy smile stretched across her face and she stuck her hand out. "Partner?"

"No kiss?"

She moistened her lips once again and rubbed her palm up her thigh. "Parker...we...I..." She left the couch and put a chair between them. After this was over, there would be no more us, no more we...and she didn't want things to be any more difficult than they already were between them. "Why do you think they did it?"

Parker gave her a long, measuring look. "Maybe," he said, his eyes suddenly looking very tired, "they saw something we didn't."

"I SIMPLY CAN'T FIGURE out what's wrong." Ashley laid a hand on her stomach, put on her best woe-is-me face and peeked out from lowered lashes at her friend. "This is the third day this week I've felt queasy. Have you heard if the flu is going around?"

Crystal visibly swallowed. "Not that I'm aware of." Her glance flittered from Ashley's face to her stomach and back again. "Maybe you should go to the doctor."

"I'm sure it's nothing. Now, where were we?" Ashley leaned over Crystal's desk and did all she could to keep from laughing.

"Are you sure you want to sign this contract?" Crystal asked, her fluorescent orange-tipped finger tapping the sheet between them. "It sounds so... so permanent."

Ashley laughed. A light, tinkling laugh. No easy feat, since she was actually ready to bust something. She couldn't wait to tell Parker. "That's silly. It only requires that we promise to try for an heir. Besides, Parker and I are getting along fabulously."

"Then why aren't you living in the same house?" Crystal squinted at her friend.

Even though it was an obvious and expected question, it stopped Ashley for a moment. "Because I'm trying to sort out my stuff. After the party on Magic Island this weekend, everything will be settled. You'll see."

"Magic Island? A little premature, don't you think? The last I heard, they still call it Kahoolawe."

Ashley shrugged daintily and tried to look glowing.

"And that's another thing. Why are you two having it there, anyway? I know Parker couldn't have given in on that issue yet."

"No," Ashley answered more truthfully than her friend would ever know. "Let's just call it symbolic, but I can't tell you any more or it will spoil the surprise."

Crystal picked up a pencil and drummed it on the desk. "There isn't something you should be telling me, is there?"

Ashley flashed all hazel innocence. "Why, no. Is there something you need to tell me?"

Crystal's response was an impatient sigh, then she busied herself with the contract, making notes in the margins, mumbling to herself.

Ashley leaned back and smiled. This was their second such meeting since Ashley and Parker had devised their plan. Her father had been her target the day before, just as Karen had been Parker's.

"Well," Ashley said a half hour later. "I really feel like a nap." She stretched out her arms and yawned for good measure. "Let's meet one last time before the party on Saturday, shall we?"

Ashley hurried out of the office, leaving Crystal with a puzzled frown and reaching for the phone as soon as Ashley had cleared the corner.

When Ashley pulled up to her apartment complex, she was delighted to see Parker's car already there.

"How'd it go today?" she asked as soon as she came through the door.

Parker had been coming from the hall and stopped dead in his tracks. "You wore that to see Crystal?"

She looked down at the long oversize muumuu and grinned.

He burst out laughing. "I wish I could have seen her face."

Ashley puffed out her flat stomach as far as she could and patted it. "Is that anyway to treat your brainchild?"

Parker continued laughing, hooked his arm around her waist and swung her around.

Laughing along with him, Ashley laid her hands on his chest and fought to catch her breath. She looked up into his smiling blue eyes and nearly lost the battle for oxygen. She pushed at him and slowly he let her slide to the floor.

"How did it go with Mrs. Lee?" She straightened the ridiculously large floral tent around her small frame.

"It was priceless. When I told her that I wanted one of the guest rooms redone in blue and another in pink, I thought she was going to pop her girdle."

"Parker," Ashley admonished but couldn't keep a straight face as she made her way to the kitchen. "What does she think the party is about?"

"She hasn't a clue. I told her the same thing we've told everyone else. Only that we have an announcement to make." He followed her, rubbing his palms together. "The only thing that could possibly go better is if I invite the new decorator to the party." He stroked his chin. "In fact, maybe I will."

"What new decorator?" Ashley ducked her head in the refrigerator and pulled out the makings for a salad. Ironically, during the past week, she and Parker had settled into a comfortable routine of meeting at the end of the day, reviewing the day's strategy and then sharing dinner.

Ashley bumped the refrigerator door closed with her hip. She was going to miss these evenings, she acknowledged, more than she cared to admit. But all that would come to an end after the party Saturday night... the party to announce their pending divorce. Her gaze found Parker's intense one and she swallowed. "The decorator?" she reminded him.

"Oh, yeah. Raquel."

She laughed. "Raquel?"

"Yup. Straight out of the Yellow Pages. Who would have thought she'd be made to order." Parker reached around her and snitched a baby carrot. "Met her for lunch yesterday and today. I'm sure tongues are wagging as we speak."

"Why?" Ashley swept a deceptively casual hand through her hair.

"Tall redhead, legs that won't quit." Parker made a clicking sound with his tongue Ashley had never heard him make before. Then he had the absolute nerve to wink. "Nice touch, don't you think?"

She shot a furtive glance down to her own short legs, wildly camouflaged by the monstrosity of a muumuu. No, as a matter of fact, she didn't think so at all.

"Right," she said and rammed the bag of carrots into his hands. "Glad you had such a great lunch. Dinner is canceled."

ASHLEY WAITED AT THE pier, arms crossed, foot tapping. Her father puffed on his cigar while he talked to Mrs. Lee, Harvey, Karen, Don and Crystal a few yards away. He had been miraculously discharged from the hospital two days earlier. Ashley couldn't wait to hear how that particular feat had come to pass.

But right now she was more interested in why the yacht she and Parker had hired stood waiting, along with everyone else, while her soon to be ex-husband was five minutes late. Picking up Legs, no doubt.

Ashley changed feet and resumed tapping furiously. She was far angrier with herself than Parker, for having reacted as she had the previous night. Her only saving grace had been that it seemed he'd been too preoccupied—or stupid—to realize that she'd been jealous.

Jealous. She had actually been jealous. Renewed mortification sent her foot into a frenzy.

Five minutes later, Parker's cherry red Porsche pulled up. And, sure enough, Legs, the decorator, got out... with Parker's eager help.

The woman had at least seven crummy inches on Ashley. And a gorgeous red mane. Probably out of a bottle, Ashley figured and straightened her spine. She tossed her freshly brushed hair back and tried stoutly for a wide smile. She settled for a smirk.

When several pairs of eyes seemed to settle on her as the couple approached, the corners of her mouth forced themselves up.

"Ashley?" Parker guided Legs forward by the small of her back. "This is Raquel Moore."

Just Ashley? Not "this is my wife, Ashley."

"Nice to meet you." Ashley pushed her hair back and looked up into the woman's flawless face. "I'm glad you could make it."

"I wouldn't have missed it." Raquel gave Parker a cagey wink.

"Everyone ready to get on board?" Parker clasped his hands together, a large grin on his face.

"Have been for the last ten minutes," Ashley called over her shoulder and headed for the yacht.

Their guests were mumbling among themselves as they headed toward the ship's plank, and Ashley could only imagine what they were saying about Parker's companion. Sighing, she slowed her pace. Her actions surely weren't helping matters either.

When Parker caught up to her, she carefully positioned herself on his side opposite Legs. She smiled when the woman eyed her curiously, then whispered in a hushed voice, "We've come this far, don't you dare blow this now."

He surveyed her with faint amusement. "How and why would I do that?"

Ashley darted a meaningful sidelong glance at Legs, then glared at him.

Parker laughed. "You mean Raquel?" he asked with surprised innocence—loud surprised innocence.

Ashley intensified her glare, then marched ahead of them. As soon as her initial irritation wore off, an undertow of sadness swirled tears to the back of her eyes.

This was it, she acknowledged, as she boarded the yacht. This was really it. No more pretending, no more wishing. And no more hoping. Because foolishly, for the past week, Ashley had hoped.

"Are you all right?" Mrs. Lee took her arm, glancing down belly level.

"I'm fine." Ashley's fingers flew to the single drop of moisture that seeped from the corner of her eye. If she weren't so miserable, she'd laugh at the housekeeper's dubious preoccupation with her stomach.

And then the sickening thought wormed its way into her overtaxed brain. Oh God, maybe she really was pregnant! Wouldn't that be the crowning touch? She fought back the hysteria rolling around in her stomach.

"She will be fine." Keoki took Mrs. Lee's free arm and blew a stream of cigar smoke up toward the clear blue sky. "You will see."

"Only if you quit smoking." Ashley plucked the smelly stub out of his fingers and flicked it into the water.

Keoki puffed out his chest, his expression combative at first. Then he grinned. "Parker?" he called out over his daughter's shoulder. "I am glad she is all yours now."

Parker had been watching the exchange. He laughed. "Yup," he said, winking at Ashley. "All mine."

Ashley closed her eyes. She wasn't going to make it. She wasn't going to get through the evening. Scheming and plotting this payback all week had been fun, just being with Parker again had been fun. But now, as he continued to joke, as if he had not a care in the world...and her replacement in the wings...her heart began to crumble piece by piece.

She felt the yacht glide away from its slip and she took her father's arm to steady herself. She opened her eyes and found it was her husband's arm she was clutching for dear life.

"Are you okay?" Parker asked, his beautiful eyes shadowed with concern as he ducked his face close to hers.

"Of course," she whispered back. "It's part of my cover, remember?" She made an attempt to stick out her tummy and laugh. Only her tummy cooperated.

"Okay." Parker breezily accepted her explanation and strode away.

Ashley watched him go. She fumbled with her purse, pulling out a pair of sunglasses and quickly pushing them on. For the rest of the trip, she did her best to mingle with everyone. Either she looked really nauseous or she was doing an exceptional job of playing her part, because she was ready to scream from everyone asking her if she was feeling all right.

As they homed in on their destination, her father found her leaning over the rail, watching the orange sun dip into the horizon.

"Leialoha, I believe we are approaching the wrong side of the island." Keoki squinted at the stretch of forsaken brown landscape. Waves slapped its deserted shores, and even the disappointed birds swooped down for only moments before returning to the more bountiful sea.

A gleeful smile sprang to Ashley's lips, but before she could respond Crystal sidled up to her other side.

"I know you're not into decadence...." Crystal pointedly looked out over the flat, soulless island. "But what gives?"

Mrs. Lee, Harvey and Don gathered around, also interested in the answer.

Parker strolled up along with Karen and Raquel. "I get it." Karen slipped her arm through Parker's, looking rather relieved. "The party is actually on the yacht."

Parker patted her hand. "Wrong." He pulled away and motioned to one of the ship hands to prepare for their arrival. Then he slid Ashley a secret glance and grinned.

Her own lips gladly followed suit. It was easy. Too damned easy. Smiling at Parker, laughing with Parker, sharing his secrets . . . his bed.

Ashley heard the nervous murmurings and turned to see their guests shooting confused glances at each other. The deckhand had tied a rope to the short pier. Unstable looking as it was, it was the only sign of human existence. She felt the giddy return of delicious revenge and looked back over at Parker.

His head was tilted toward Raquel's, his lips inches from her ear, uttering whispers that only a week earlier had been for Ashley.

She pressed her lips together to keep her weak, traitorous chin from quivering. The end of the story had already been written. That was for certain. The only control Ashley now had was focused on how much dignity she could maintain. She took a deep breath and tried to tell herself that it would be worth it to see the smug smile wiped off her father's face.

The whole affair had begun on a lie and now Ashley was even lying to herself. It wasn't going to be okay at all. She indulged in one last private sniffle, then forced the corners of her mouth up and led the group off the yacht.

"What is going on, Leialoha?" Keoki's thick black brows drew together as he patted his pockets in search of a cigar.

"This place is creepy." Crystal ran her hands up her arms, her gaze surveying the craterlike surface of the burned-out island.

Several others nodded and Ashley moistened her lips to hide the smile that was forming. Her attention was drawn to Parker, as if he'd magically compelled it.

His eyes, darkly intense, registered her every movement. He stuffed his hands deep into his pockets and his shoulders hunched forward slightly as if he were cold. It was at least eighty-five degrees.

Ashley swallowed hard and slowly made her way to his side.

"Well..." She gave him a small shrug. "I guess there's no use waiting."

"No," he agreed and pulled his hands from his pockets.

She made an automatic sweep of faces and found Raquel nearby, watching them. Ashley swallowed once more. "I'll, uh..." She let her hand wave through the air. It looked helpless and pathetic, so she straightened and in a stronger voice continued. "I'll get their attention."

"Wait, Ash." Parker put a hand on her arm.

Her gaze flew to his.

"Do you want to announce the divorce, or shall I?"

"I...no. You do it." Ashley swept back her hair, then faced their curious guests with her chin lifted.

And waited. But nothing came from Parker. She looked over at him.

His eyes were dark and stormy as his hand shot out to grasp her arm. He pulled her back far out of earshot, and she would have stumbled if he hadn't anchored both his hands firmly around her upper arms.

"God, Ash. How can you stand there and look so cool about this?" He let go of her and pushed one hand through his hair. She opened her mouth to say something, but he put a finger to her lips.

"I wanted to say something clever, do something earth-shattering. Hell, I don't know." He shook his head. "This isn't going anything like I planned."

He had the strangest look on his face and she put a comforting hand on his forearm.

"Look, Ash, I want you to marry me. Again. Now."

Ashley's eyes widened.

"Don't you dare say it." Parker ran a hand over his face. "You know I love you. And you love me."

She wanted to say something, tried to speak, but only a small, guttural sound came from her throat.

Parker sighed. A large, shaky sigh. "Don't you?"

"What about..." Ashley sent a quick glance at the other woman.

"Raquel? She'll do it."

Either he was going crazy, or Ashley already had. She squeezed the arm she had in her grasp. "Parker?"

"She's a judge, Ash. Raquel's a judge. I brought her here to marry us. But I want this time to be different. I want to hear you say you love me."

Ashley had never seen such sweet vulnerability as she saw on her husband's face at that moment. She touched her hand to his, but his shook so badly that she had trouble entwining their fingers.

"I do, Parker. I do love you." She raised her other hand to his face and stroked his cheek. "And I don't need to repeat the vows, but I will."

Parker let a slow smile spread across his face, then lowered his lips to hers while he picked her up and pressed her close to his heart.

After a long, tender kiss, Ashley pushed to the ground and glanced over at their smiling friends and family. She'd almost forgotten. "What about them?"

Parker smiled again. "I say the rest of the plan stays in effect."

Ashley centered her attention on her father's smug face. He clapped Harvey on the back, stretched his arms to the heavens and then clasped his hands behind his neck. His chest puffed out like a proud peacock. "Me, too," she said, grinning.

Parker followed her gaze and surveyed their audience. "Karen's going to kill me," he whispered, his blue eyes alight with amusement. "Harvey, too." The attorney stood ramrod straight, his eyes ever watchful.

"Mrs. Lee won't make us dessert for a month," she pointed out cheerfully. The housekeeper had wound a white linen handkerchief around one pudgy hand, the other she used to grip Harvey's arm. Happy tears glistened from her eyes.

"She probably won't feed us at all," Parker added.

She would if I were pregnant. The stubborn thought reinsinuated itself and Ashley drew in her lower lip. She couldn't be, could she? Her hand made a reflexive journey to her nervous belly. "Parker?"

He looked down at her, touching her with his beautiful eyes and loving smile. She stared up at him, the question dying on her lips as she found the answer she needed.

But Parker's gaze drifted to her hand, then his eyes searched hers. He covered her hand with his, his long fingers stroking her stomach. "Ashley?" There was a sweet urgency in his voice.

She shook her head and turned her hand over, their palms meeting. "I don't think so." She smiled. "But would you mind if I was?" She felt only slightly guilty for already knowing the answer, yet wanting to hear the words.

"I love you," he whispered, his eyes the soft color of promise. He swallowed, then lowered their clasped hands to their sides. "I say we get out of here."

"I agree."

He angled back in mock surprise. "That may be a first."

Ashley lightly socked his arm and laughed. He brought her fist to his curved lips for a quick kiss, then steered them toward the yacht. They motioned for Raquel to follow.

"Hey. Where are you going?" Crystal was the first to holler. She'd taken a step forward, her ludicrously made-up eyes wide with suspicion. The others stood paralyzed with confusion.

"Giving you time to think," Ashley called out once they were safely aboard. "Don't worry. We'll be back tomorrow." She grinned as she watched the stunned group move toward the departing ship in comical slow motion, disbelief echoing in each leaden step.

Then a small frown settled between her eyebrows, as she brought a thoughtful finger to her lips. "You know, this island is going to work out even better than I thought. I bet there's room for at least five casinos."

"Oh, no. Look, Ash." Parker took a deep breath, his beautiful blue eyes widening with wariness. "About Magic Island..."

Ashley laughed, then kissed him into silence.

mps
MAILING PREFERENCE SERVICE

MILLS & BOON®

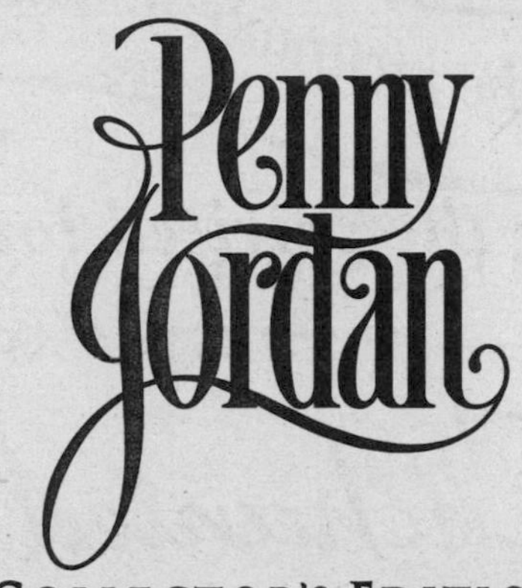

COLLECTOR'S EDITION

If you have missed any of the previously published titles in the Penny Jordan Collector's Edition our Customer Care department will be happy to advise you of titles currently in stock. Alternatively send in a large stamped addressed envelope and we will be pleased to provide you with full details by post.

Please send your SAE to:

Penny Jordan Collector's Edition
Customer Care Department
Eton House
18-24 Paradise Road
Richmond
Surrey TW9 1SR

Customer Care Direct Line - 0181 288 2888